Julie Ellis

A WOMAN FOR
ALL SEASONS

HarperCollins*Publishers*

This novel is entirely a work of fiction. The names, characters and incidents portrayed in it are the work of the author's imagination. Any resemblance to actual persons, living or dead, is entirely coincidental.

HarperCollins*Publishers*
77–85 Fulham Palace Road,
Hammersmith, London W6 8JB

Published by HarperCollins*Publishers* 1998
3 5 7 9 8 6 4 2

A catalogue record for this book
is available from the British Library

ISBN 0 00 225716 5 (HB)
ISBN 0 00 225717 3 (TPB)

Set in Sabon by
Rowland Phototypesetting Ltd,
Bury St Edmunds, Suffolk

Printed and bound in Great Britain by
Caledonian International Book Manufacturing Ltd, Glasgow

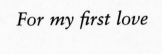

For my first love

Acknowledgements

I would like to express my deep gratitude to the staffers of the Australian Consulate, who supplied me with difficult-to-locate material about Melbourne in the early years of this century. My gratitude also to Jonathan Rosenthal of the Research Services Department of the Museum of Television & Radio, who provided me with radio and television program data.

I would like to thank, also, the staff of the New York Public Library at Fifth Avenue and 42nd Street, the Drama Department of the Lincoln Center Library, and the clerks of the various Periodical Divisions at the Mid-Manhattan Branch – who've been gracious and helpful in filling my myriad requests for microfilm.

My thanks, as always, to my daughter, Susan, for diligent research assistance and word processing services – and to my son, Richard, of Sentinel Copy, Inc. for so imaginatively bringing order to my masses of research material.

Chapter One

London was the focus of the world this late June of 1902, with the Coronation of Edward VII scheduled for the twenty-sixth. Private trains chugged into Victoria Station carrying royalty from all over Europe, the Middle East, and Asia – as far away as Siam and Japan. They arrived with mountains of luggage and such huge entourages that the station forecourt was closed to ordinary traffic to accommodate the new arrivals. Newspapers predicted the Coronation would be the most brilliant such occasion in history.

Then on Tuesday morning, 22 June, the House of Commons received word that the Coronation must be postponed. The King had just undergone an emergency appendectomy. Workmen – not yet aware of the postponement – were still setting up grandstands. Standards, flags, and festive decorations were on display at windows.

But in the elegantly furnished sitting room of Simon Woolf's three-story red-brick house in Lexham Gardens his sixteen-year-old, raven-haired daughter, Elisabeth, had just banished all thoughts of the Coronation from the minds of her mother and grandmother.

'I don't care what Papa says!' Elisabeth's violet eyes – set in a delicately lovely face – blazed in rebellion. She ignored her mother's shock at such filial disrespect. 'Felix is up at Cambridge. Ben will be there in three years. This is the twentieth century – why can't a sister be educated as well as her brothers?'

'It's unladylike for a woman to be highly educated.' Her mother avoided her eyes. 'You've heard Papa say that a hundred times.' Mama agreed with whatever Papa said, Elisabeth thought impatiently. 'You'll continue your piano lessons with Miss Lane now that you've finished at school. You'll –'

'Mama, I'm a "modern girl" – I want to be independent! For that I need a proper education.' Modern girls fought for the vote. They became 'typewriter girls', teachers – some even went on the stage. They learned to drive motor cars.

'What does Miss North at your school say about this?' her grand-mother intervened warily. In moments of anger Simon Woolf was apt to upbraid his mother-in-law for 'encouraging Elisabeth's un-orthodox thoughts'.

'She says she's sure I would be accepted at Cambridge if I stayed at school for two more years and studied hard.' Elisabeth turned accusingly to her mother again. 'I could get a good teaching job or any amount of other interesting work.'

'Nonsense.' Celia Woolf reached to pour herself another cup of tea – her refuge in these periodic confrontations with her daughter. 'You don't need to go out to work. Your father will always provide for you.'

'God wouldn't have given women brains if He didn't expect them to use them!' Elisabeth had no real yearning to teach – but college attendance would be the beginning of her independence.

'This all comes from your listening to those horrible suffragettes,' Celia Woolf moaned.

'It comes from my helping Ben with his geometry and Felix with his Latin. I have a brain – it's sinful not to use it.'

Felix would study to be a doctor. Ben was to be a lawyer. Papa, who was a tailor and now owned a string of shops, was anxious to lift his sons above the stigma of being a tradesman. But a daughter was supposed to sit at home. Didn't Papa know there were women in London who were lawyers and doctors – even accountants? He didn't *want* to know.

'I wonder how His Majesty is feeling after his surgery?' Celia turned to her mother in an effort to derail Elisabeth's conversation. 'How sad that the Coronation must be postponed. Whatever will happen with all the food prepared for the Coronation banquet?'

'I'm sure there're ways of preserving some of it.' Rae Kahn sighed. 'But there must be an enormous amount that can't be saved.' Then her face brightened. 'I suspect it'll be distributed to the London charity organizations that try to provide food for the hungry and the homeless.' Her eyes sparkled in amusement. 'No doubt in Whitechapel for the next day or two the hungry will be dining on sumptuous dishes provided by King Edward's chefs for royalty and heads of state.'

'Mama, don't say that to Simon,' Celia warned her mother. 'You know how he feels about Whitechapel.'

Elisabeth knew that Whitechapel – a predominantly Jewish area – was a place her father preferred to ignore, though he secretly contributed funds for the poor on most Jewish holidays. He liked to forget that he had plucked his wife and mother-in-law from a dismal existence there.

It was hard to imagine Papa wildly in love – as Grandma confided he was at first sight of Mama. Grandma had come to London from Berlin when she had been a young widow with a small child and no family except for impecunious cousins. She'd worked as a maid, eventually saving enough to open a tiny shop in Whitechapel – a shop always on the verge of extinction.

The staff in the Woolf household consisted of a cook, a parlor maid, housemaid, and a coachman. Grandma and Mama were ever conscious of their rise from Whitechapel to Lexham Gardens – and the fact that Papa made this possible.

Each year the three women of the family, along with Ben – Felix, as the older son, remained with his father – went for a week to Berlin to visit their cousins, whose financial situation had improved through the years. And for a week the German cousins visited the Woolf household in London. For Elisabeth these were exotic occasions, though her lack of knowledge of German was frustrating. But she managed some conversation in French, which the cousins also spoke.

Mama – who spoke German – and Grandma were always so happy. Though Papa pretended annoyance at the disturbance to his household routine, Elisabeth suspected he enjoyed seeing Mama so pleased at being with her cousins. When he was kind to Mama and Grandma and the boys, why was he so mean to *her*? But she knew the answer to that. She refused to accept her place as a female. How could Papa be so old-fashioned?

How could Mama be so adoring of Papa when he clearly considered himself her superior? In Papa's eyes all women were inferior to all men. Would there ever be a time when women would truly band together and demand their rights?

'Elisabeth, I'd like to go to the theater tonight.' Her grandmother broke into her introspection with a conspiratorial air. 'Shall we see *The Importance of Being Earnest* again?'

'Papa will be working late tonight,' her mother remembered.

Papa worked late many nights. Sometimes Elisabeth suspected this was good. When at home, Papa ruled. Mama always explained that Papa worked hard to provide the family with a good life. How could it be good, Elisabeth thought, if she couldn't go to university?

'I'll tell Dora to serve supper early,' Mama continued, 'so you won't be late for the performance.'

Elisabeth sighed. Every confrontation about her studying to go to Cambridge ended with a sudden change of subject. Ben didn't want to go to Cambridge – he wanted to run away to Paris to study painting. But he never would, she decided – he'd just dream about it. Ben never went against Papa's wishes. Still, she reminded herself with a meager flurry of triumph, tonight she and Grandma would go – for the third time – to see *The Importance of Being Earnest* and she'd see David Winston again – the handsome young actor she secretly admired.

Mama would instruct Hugo to drive them to the theater in the brougham and to pick them up when the curtain came down. Hugo knew not to say anything about this to Papa. Mama and Papa went to the opera three or four times a year – but Papa said 'respectable families' didn't go to the theater. And Papa yearned to see his family regarded as 'respectable'.

Since Elisabeth was eleven, Grandma had been taking her to the theater. They would sit in the balcony stalls. Grandma – usually so thrifty – had long ago abandoned the dreary task of queuing for hours for the inexpensive gallery seats – though she still talked about the day some years ago when she'd been amongst those waiting for tickets to whom Ellen Terry herself had sent out tea.

While Dora, the parlor maid, served their supper, Elisabeth contributed little to the table conversation – most of which revolved about the Coronation.

'Do you suppose all the foreign royalty will return when the Coronation is rescheduled?' Celia asked her mother.

'I doubt it,' Rae said. 'Only the royalty that remains here – waiting for the event to happen – will be in attendance.'

'Which theater are you going to tonight?' Celia tried to bring Elisabeth into the conversation.

'It's just a small playhouse,' Elisabeth said, 'with a company struggling to continue. No big stars.'

'I understand it's *quite* amusing.' But Celia's approval seemed ambivalent, because of the reputation of the author of the play, Elisabeth interpreted. At the theater Oscar Wilde's name wasn't even mentioned. Papa wouldn't allow him to be discussed in the house. Why couldn't Papa and Mama understand this was a new century? People were driving motor cars, installing electricity in their houses, leading exciting lives that would have shocked Queen Victoria.

'I'll go out to the kitchen and tell Anna to have supper ready in an hour.' Celia rose to her feet. 'You'd better leave early for the theater. The streets will be mobbed with carriages tonight – so many people rushing to get out of the city.'

Elisabeth sat at the edge of her seat in the balcony stalls – her eyes fastened to the slender young man who played a small role with passing skill but much personal appeal.

'The audience is behaving well,' Rae whispered in approval. The gallery audience here usually preferred melodramas or morality plays. It was a tribute to the cast that they were not offered noisy comments or suggestions.

'It's a wonderful play.' At school the girls talked about Oscar Wilde in whispers. Of course, she must not let Grandma even suspect that she understood the dark secret of the scandalous and flamboyant playwright's life. Not even 'modern girls' could be that daring.

Elisabeth sighed with sweet regret when the performance was over. Tonight she would dream about David Winston, she promised herself, reveling in her secret passion.

As they were filing out of the theater Grandma talked about the wonderful plays she had seen as a girl. Grandma looked almost beautiful – even though she was sixty years old, Elisabeth thought with pride – when she talked about her life in Berlin. She'd asked Grandma once why she had not remarried when Mama was little. She must have been so pretty and so charming.

'Elisabeth, it would have been unfair for me to marry again. The baby – your mother – would have always come first. And I'd had one perfect marriage – it would be greedy to expect more.' Her eyes had brightened with laughter. 'And what man would want a wife who insisted on speaking her mind the way I do?'

But for Mama's sake, Elisabeth thought tenderly, Grandma didn't often speak her mind in Papa's presence. Grandma was like a servant.

In Papa's eyes – and she gathered most men were like Papa – women were servants, to be spoiled at a man's will. But this was a new century. When would men wake up and realize that?

At the approach of July the women of the household – along with fifteen-year-old Ben – prepared to leave London for their usual summer holidays at Whitby, over 150 miles north of London. They always rented the same house. Elisabeth adored the large, sprawling red brick residence that sat at the edge of the cliff and looked down upon the sea. The first night or two she was always fearful that she might walk in her sleep and hurl herself into the surging water below. Grandma, too, loved the house. Mama always fretted that Papa couldn't be with them.

Elisabeth accompanied Mama and Grandma on their pre-holiday shopping trip to elegant Harrods, then on to lunch at High Holborn restaurant. Mama knew how Grandma – still clinging to memories of impoverished days in Whitechapel – enjoyed these occasions. Elisabeth felt a sybaritic pleasure at dining in the famous marble-pillared restaurant, with its beautiful table linens, gleaming silverware, abundance of cut flowers, its classical music.

Not even Mama knew that Grandma occasionally took Elisabeth to the old haunts in Whitechapel. Walking through the cluttered streets permeated by the aromas of fried fish, herring in barrels, challah baking, was like visiting a strange country. The sounds, too, were foreign to her ears – the whir of endless sewing machines, the muffled sounds of pressers' irons. Signs on shop windows were in Yiddish, German, Russian, Polish. And once Grandma took her to a Yiddish theater to see the great American actor Jacob Adler.

At supper the night before their departure for Whitby conversation revolved around the Coronation – now to take place in August.

'It would be nice if we could stay at the seashore for another month,' Celia said wistfully. 'And if you could be with us, Simon. We could rent out this house for the month of the Coronation. I read in The Times that –'

'I'm not renting my house,' Simon Woolf interrupted in annoyance. 'I don't want strangers prancing through. Besides, you know I can't get away from the business. Especially now.' His smile was complacent. 'We're working night and day to fill our orders.' Elisabeth knew her father's tailor shops catered to the aristocracy. 'Do you realize what it costs to be present at the Coronation? The official costume, the cloak, the coronet, plus carriages, servants, hospitality. At least a thousand pounds,' he said with respect. 'And not all the peers are blessed with cash. Some of the outfits we're making are upon the weekly payment system.'

As her parents and grandmother talked business – and her brothers appeared bored with any topic that didn't revolve around their schools or cricket – Elisabeth dwelled on the knowledge that she wouldn't be able to go to the theater for a whole month, plus the week that the family would spend in Berlin with the German cousins. Would she ever see David Winston again? Would he become a famous actor one day? Oh, she hoped he would!

At her mother's insistence the family retired early tonight. They would leave for Whitby immediately after breakfast tomorrow.

In the family tradition Simon Woolf – along with Felix – accompanied the other four members of the family to Victoria Station and saw them off with grandiose gestures of affection and solicitude.

Aboard the train Elisabeth focused on her reading, and was immediately caught up in the fascinating characters in *Wuthering Heights*.

Mama seldom opened a book. When she did, it was a novel by Marie Corelli or Ouida – what Ben called 'popular trash'. Mama and Grandma would talk about settling into the house and wonder if the servants provided would be the same as in earlier years. Once he'd finished reading *Punch*, Ben would pretend to be asleep while, Elisabeth guessed, he imagined the paintings he yearned to create, or the fast motor cars he longed one day to drive.

It was terrible to think that she wouldn't be going back to school in the autumn. A 'modern girl' was supposed to be independent. To be independent, a girl needed to be truly educated. Surreptitiously she'd read Mary Wollstonecraft's *Vindication of the Rights of Woman* – loaned to her by her English teacher – and was enthralled by Wollstonecraft's declarations. Mama warned her never to talk about 'feminism' in front of Papa. In the Woolf household, women were expected to stay in their place.

How could she sit at home with Mama and Grandma and do embroidery, continue her piano studies and French, and go out only with her mother? Except for school, she met nobody interesting, and now she'd been removed from school. Papa discouraged Mama from entertaining – though he'd be willing if their guests were Rothschilds or Sassoons or Cassels. Papa was a snob.

What did she have to do to make Papa realize that this was the twentieth century? *She could not just sit at home and vegetate.*

Chapter Two

Elisabeth loved the house at Whitby. Her mother and grandmother seemed to blossom here. They spent much of each day – when the weather allowed this – in tending the garden at the rear of the house. Often moody and silent in London, Ben was relaxed and happy here. Papa wasn't always leaning over his shoulder to remind him how important it was to get top marks at school. But this summer, Elisabeth taunted herself, was not like other years. She wouldn't be going back to school in the autumn. What would she do with her life?

Fortuitously the house lured her into hours when she could suppress her feelings of rebellion. She stood at a window in her upstairs bedroom or in the sitting room and was mesmerized by the grandeur of the sea. Some days she sat at the water's edge with Ben while he sketched.

It was understood in the family that sketching and painting were never to be more than a hobby for Ben – though Elisabeth and their grandmother were awed by his talents. Elisabeth sympathized with his dislike of the profession chosen for him by their father. Papa, she knew, considered artists on a level with actors.

'Artists and actors are the scum of the earth,' Papa derided at regular intervals. 'Nobody has respect for them.'

But that wasn't true, Elisabeth thought defiantly. Famous actors and actresses were welcomed into the smartest set in London society these days. Artists like John Singer Sargent were invited everywhere. *Why* must Ben be a lawyer? Why couldn't *she* go to Cambridge?

Their final week at the house was shadowed by daily downpours that gave way only to dismal, depressing drizzle. Elisabeth was relieved that they were to leave for their annual visit to 'the cousins' in Berlin. Papa had been an only child – like Mama. He'd lost touch with family. But Grandma's cousins were warm and loving – and cherished by both Grandma and Mama.

The cousins hadn't attained the financial security of which Papa was so proud, but they lived comfortably these days. Elisabeth and Ben went with the younger cousins to the Tiergarten and marveled at this wonderful zoo. They strolled along the famous Kurfürstendamm and enjoyed the sights of the city. In the evenings, while Grandma and Mama reminisced with the older cousins, Elisabeth and Ben gathered with the young cousins around the piano in the pleasant, cluttered sitting room and sang. Or they listened to the gramophone.

Then the four visitors returned to London, where most residents were caught up in the slightly diminished Coronation fever. The event – scheduled now for 9 August – was being awaited eagerly by the populace, though foreign royalty were not expected to return.

Elisabeth felt adrift, waiting for something to happen in her own life – without knowing what that could be. Yet when she awoke on the morning of 9 August, she was instantly aware that this was a momentous date. The first Coronation in sixty-four years.

Through the night, workers had prepared the streets with arrays of flags, standards, decorations. Grandstands had been erected outside Westminster Abbey to provide extra seating for those invited to attend.

Elisabeth knew that Papa and the boys had left the house early this morning. The shop that was Papa's headquarters was located on the procession route. Here they would have a fine vantage point.

Mama had said she'd not be watching the Coronation procession. She hated crowds. She and Grandma would remain at home. 'Papa and the boys will tell us all about it later.'

Elisabeth ate breakfast with undue haste this morning. Mama had said she could go out alone to watch the procession but had warned her to watch her purse for pickpockets would be sure to be among the crowds.

By the time Elisabeth left the house, the streets were mobbed with prospective onlookers and festive with decorations. Resplendently uniformed officers on horseback were in evidence along the route. Eager spectators were positioned on roofs, leaned out of every window. Many of those that lined the route had been there since dawn. Elisabeth was conscious of an undercurrent of restlessness among the crowd as they waited.

'They wuz supposed to be leavin' Buckingham Palace ten minutes ago,' a woman complained to her companion. 'Wouldn't you think we'd be hearin' somethin' by now?'

'Aw, shut yer noise,' he retorted and gave her a hefty shove that thrust her with startling impact against Elisabeth.

'Careful!' a masculine voice – oddly familiar – ordered, while strong arms kept Elisabeth from falling.

'Sorry, guv. Didn't mean no harm.' The shover was cowed.

'Are you all right?' her rescuer asked Elisabeth, and gently released her.

'I'm fine,' Elisabeth stammered, and gazed up into his eyes. Her heart began to pound. 'You – you're David Winston!'

'Yes –' He seemed suddenly shy.

'I've seen you three times in *The Importance of Being Earnest*,' she told him. *This was like a fairy tale.* 'You were so good.'

'Thank you.' He seemed almost embarrassed by this tribute.

'It must be exciting to be an actor,' she said impulsively – ignoring Mama's admonition not to talk to strangers. She was standing here with David Winston! 'I mean, for a little while each night, you're somebody else. It – it's like a wonderful game of make-believe.'

'It's something like that.' All at once she was startled by the intensity of his gaze. 'It's a lot better than some of the jobs I've had.' His smile was wry.

It was as though they were suddenly alone here – the crowd fading into the distance. He was just as handsome in person as onstage, Elisabeth thought. Slight of build, chiseled features, expressive gray eyes and sandy hair.

'Are you truly eager to see the procession?' he asked after a silence laden with portent. Each reluctant to end this encounter.

'No,' she whispered.

'There's an ABC tea shop not far from here.' His smile was appealing. 'Would you like to go there for a cup of tea?'

'Yes,' she said instantly. She was a 'modern girl', she defended herself in a corner of her mind. The ABC tea shops were respectable, favored by the new professional and business women. This was unbelievable – to go for tea with the actor she'd seen in *The Importance of Being Earnest*! David Winston, who invaded her dreams night after night.

'My name is Elisabeth Woolf.' It was only polite to introduce herself.

'How do you do, Miss Woolf?' he said with an air of quiet pleasure, and guided her through the crowd.

They pushed their way towards the tea shop. Today they were its sole clients. A waitress who came over to take their order was astonished at their appearance here this morning.

Elisabeth had never been in an ABC tea shop. Mama preferred the more elegant High Holborn restaurant or the one in the Marshall and Snelgrove department store. But Elisabeth was hardly aware of her surroundings – only of the presence of David Winston in the chair across the table from her.

Conversation was labored for the first moments, then Elisabeth – determined to break this awkwardness – coaxed him to tell her about life in the theater.

'Ours is a very modest company,' David reminded. 'But I'm lucky to be with it.'

He told her about his growing up in an orphanage from the age of four. Seven years ago – on his fourteenth birthday – he'd been sent out into the world to provide for himself. He'd worked in a cotton mill, in a shoe factory, then as a minor clerk. Two years ago, quite by chance, he'd met an American who was struggling to keep afloat his new acting company in London. David had begun as a stagehand, but had learned some parts as an understudy. Then, in an emergency he'd been thrown into an acting role.

'I've been acting with Mr Henderson's company ever since,' he explained. 'It's hard to keep a play open without a star, but so far he's managed. It's a lot more fun than spending twelve hours a day at a mill machine.'

Elisabeth was enthralled when David confided that the free lending libraries were his second home.

'Libraries are wonderful,' she said enthusiastically. 'I would die without books to read.'

David listened with endearing compassion to her confession of rage that her father refused to allow her to stay at school and work to get into Cambridge.

'Why shouldn't women go to college?' David agreed with her. 'Why shouldn't they vote?'

Oh, she had found a wonderful friend, Elisabeth thought – not daring to consider David Winston might become more than that. Oblivious of time and place they exchanged confidences, joyful that they shared so many convictions, enjoyed the same plays.

'I love Ibsen,' she said with infinite respect. 'I've read *A Doll's House* a dozen times. Ibsen understands that women need to be free, to be *people*.' She sighed. 'Not like my father.'

'Do you go often to the library?' he asked.

'I'll be there tomorrow,' she said instantly, and identified the library she visited. 'At two o'clock.' Her smile was a dazzling invitation. She wanted to see David again.

'At two o'clock. I'll see you there.'

Both reluctant to separate, they ordered more tea, explored more subjects. Sensing that she was eager to know more about life in the theater, David talked about the side that audiences never saw – the hordes that competed for even the smallest, most insignificant role.

'Once a new play is announced, the producer's waiting room is crowded with people anxious to be working. You have to be decently dressed or you won't stand a chance – and often that means you're behind on your rent or having only toast and tea for every meal. You live in the cheapest lodgings available – usually in Bloomsbury or Soho. There's little glamor in the profession unless you're a star.' Elisabeth absorbed every word. 'The managers often are demanding, the authors – the living ones – anxious, and backstage tempers flare with little reason except for frustration that life isn't better. Still, hope springs eternal, and most hope for a dazzling future.'

'That comes to only a few,' Elisabeth surmised sympathetically.

'You know what really angers us?' David Winston said with fresh frustration. 'Every time someone is picked up by the police as drunk and incapable, he's reported in the *Police News* the next day as being an actor. Or as an actress,' he added with a teasing glint.

'I should be going home.' Surely the procession had passed this way by now. What would she say to Mama and Grandma – 'I was so far back in the crowd I could see very little'?

'May I walk you there?' David signaled to the waitress to bring their bill.

Elisabeth hesitated, instinct warning that this friendship must be secret. 'As far as the corner,' she stipulated, and she knew as their eyes met that he understood. But nobody would stop her from seeing David Winston again. Something precious had entered her life.

*　　*　　*

Each weekday Elisabeth met David at the public library. Soon they were on first-name terms. They walked about London, which he knew far better than she. He was so clever, she thought, listening while he expounded this afternoon on the site they'd chosen for their destination.

'You're only three years older than Felix,' Elisabeth said, her eyes bright with admiration, 'but you know so much. Without going to Cambridge.'

'The library has been my university.' His smile was rueful. 'I was allowed to stay at school until I was fourteen because I worked after school, as a streetsweeper. The money I earned went to the orphanage.'

'I've never done anything useful with my life,' Elisabeth fretted. 'Sometimes I wonder if my brain will just shrink to the size of a pea for not being used.'

'Beth, you're not only beautiful – you're bright.'

'Felix says I'm not very clever,' she confided. *He thought she was beautiful.* 'And Mama says it's unladylike for a girl to appear to be able to think. We're supposed to go through life pretending ignorance so that men will seem clever in comparison. But women *are* going to university these days.'

'The library is your university, too,' he consoled. 'When I was sixteen and seventeen I devoured history books. I was shocked when I first understood how little we learn from history. Each generation makes the same mistakes as those who went before. Wouldn't you think we'd learn?'

'David, you should be somebody in government,' Elisabeth decided impulsively. 'Maybe some day the Prime Minister.'

'I'd like to do something to make the world a happier place,' he said, then chuckled at such pretensions. 'But meanwhile let me entertain the patrons who come to the theater to see our company.'

Some afternoons they visited an ABC tea shop or a Lyons Corner House, though Elisabeth was scrupulous about not allowing this every time they met because she understood that his money was limited. She knew not to offer to share this small expense.

On a dismal autumn afternoon when they paused on the Thames Embankment to gaze into the murky water, David reached to draw her into his arms.

'These last weeks have been the most wonderful time of my life,' he whispered. 'How did I live before I knew you?'

'I thought I'd die when I couldn't go to university – then you came along.' Her face was luminous.

'I've wanted to hold you this way since the moment I saw you standing there watching for the Coronation procession,' he said tenderly. 'Then fate pushed you into my arms.'

'Not fate, my guardian angel,' she corrected, and closed her eyes as his mouth came down to meet hers.

Now their hours together became a search for private moments when David could take her into his arms. She was simultaneously ecstatic and frightened each time they kissed. One day she must tell Mama and Papa about David – but she was fearful of their reaction.

Elisabeth, like David, worried when attendance at the theater consisted mostly of 'deadheads' – people who were given free admission to provide the appearance of a near-full house.

'We're not rehearsing a new play,' he reminded anxiously, on a gray, drizzly day in late September while they took refuge in a crowded tea shop. 'Mr Henderson says we may close in another week or two.'

'Then what?' Her heart began to hammer.

'I don't know. He's talking about getting a company together to go to Australia. He has an offer down there.'

'That's so far away!' How would she survive without David? Her life now centered around spending an hour or two of each day in his company.

'I know.' His eyes met hers – saying what he had not yet dared to voice.

'I don't want you to leave London,' she whispered, and under the table their hands reached out to clasp.

'I don't want to leave you,' he said softly. 'Elisabeth, I love you –' A quiet desperation in his voice because they both knew the obstacles that lay between them. 'I wish we could be married.' But how could he support a wife? That was what he was thinking, Elisabeth understood.

'I love you, too.' But David knew that.

'I won't go to Australia,' he resolved. 'I don't have to work in the theater. There are other jobs.'

'But you're so good,' she insisted. 'You *should* be in theater.' Fleetingly she considered asking Papa to give him a job in one of the shops. Instantly she dismissed this. Papa had only contempt for actors, and if he suspected how David and she felt about each other, he would be furious. Worse, not only was David an actor, he was not of her faith.

'If the play closes, I'll give myself three weeks to find another part. After that I'll have to take whatever comes along.'

'I wish Mama would let me work.' If they both had jobs, she dared to dream for a moment, they could be married. Women worked these days, even society women. Several years ago Lady Duff Gordon had opened her shop, 'Lucile'. Other society ladies had followed her example, and nobody looked down on them. Only on middle-class tradespeople, she thought with a new cynicism.

'I'm staying in London,' he reiterated with determination. 'I promise you that, Beth –' His pet name for her that no one else had ever used.

'I'll ask Grandma to take me to the theater again tomorrow night,' she decided, and David smiled at this small effort to help the acting company.

Could she take Grandma backstage to meet David? Grandma would love him. No, that wouldn't be wise, she rejected. Grandma might just slip and say something to Mama.

How was she to bring David together with her family? There must be a way. *David must for ever be part of her life.*

Chapter Three

Late in October David told Elisabeth – while they lingered over tea and buns at Lyons – that Roger Henderson was closing the play after that evening's performance.

'We all guessed it was coming,' David admitted, 'though nobody here wants to go with him halfway round the world. And it's a year's commitment. Roger's been in contact with several unemployed actors he knows back in New York and he's sending a telegram to line up a company for Australia.' He paused as she winced at his mention of Australia. 'Beth, I've told you – I'm not going with Roger to Melbourne. How could I put such distance between us?'

'You'll start looking straight away for another place in a theater company?' Her eyes searched his. She knew about the shocking conditions in British factories – and the pittance the workers were paid. David's earnings were small in Henderson's struggling company but princely compared to those of factory workers, whose families skipped meals in order to survive.

'I'll look,' he promised, 'but I may not find.'

Elisabeth appeared even more downcast.

'Never mind. I won't starve. I'm young and willing – I'll find something. But let's not think about that now. Remember what you told me your grandmother always says when you fret? "Don't expect life to be perfect – forget the bad things, cherish the good." We're here together. That's the good.'

Today Elisabeth felt a new urgency in leaving David at the corner of her street in Lexham Gardens. After tonight's performance he would be out of work. He could be working soon, she tormented herself, except for her. Mr Henderson wanted him to be an important part of the Australian company. Not only would he act, but he would be Mr Henderson's personal assistant. But David didn't want to leave her.

She approached the entrance to the elegant Woolf house – visualizing the shabby boarding house where David lived in a tiny, one-windowed bedroom. She had never been inside, of course, but at her insistence David had walked her past the drab structure that was his home.

As expected, she found her mother and grandmother having tea in the sitting room, where a fire was burning against the autumn chill.

'Elisabeth, will you never tire of visiting the library?' her mother asked, but her smile was indulgent.

'I meet my friend from school there,' she fabricated. 'The one who couldn't go on to university,' she added with a touch of ever-simmering rebellion. She never brought friends home with her. Papa discouraged that: 'I don't want a flock of strangers running through my house.'

'I was talking with Papa last night about your studying French again,' her mother said with the air of confiding pleasant news. 'He –'

'I don't want to study French anymore,' Elisabeth flared.

'But your young German cousins are so fluent. You could –'

'No!' David was out of work, and Mama talked about her studying French!

'Elisabeth, try one of those cinnamon buns,' her grandmother intervened cajolingly. 'Anna found a recipe that's wonderful.'

Distressed by David's situation – haunted by an inchoate fear that despite his declarations to the contrary, he might take off for Australia – Elisabeth sought refuge in silence. She pretended to enjoy nibbling at a cinnamon bun while her mother and grandmother talked about Felix's progress at Cambridge.

'More tea?' her mother asked Elisabeth.

'No, thank you, Mama.' She retreated into the role Mama expected of her.

Along with her mother and grandmother, Elisabeth was startled by sounds in the hall.

'It's Simon,' Celia said in astonishment, then rose to her feet in anxiety. 'What is he doing home at this early hour?'

'Celia!' Simon's deep voice blended pleasure with imperiousness. 'Wait till you hear what I have to tell you!' He strode down the hall and into the sitting room. 'Ah, you're here, too, Elisabeth,' he said with satisfaction – and managed a faint nod to his mother-in-law. 'That's good.'

'Simon, what's happened?' Celia appeared only slightly mollified by his obvious good humor.

'We're invited – the whole family –' he announced, 'to tea at the Rosensteins' house. Not this coming Sunday but the following Sunday. The Arnold Rosensteins,' he emphasized. 'Not the Rothschilds, perhaps, but a substantial banking family.'

'Why would they invite us to tea?' Celia exchanged a puzzled glance with her mother.

'We don't know the Rosensteins.' Rae was wary. 'I mean, we've seen them at the synagogue on occasion, but –' She gestured her bewilderment. The Rosensteins moved in more rarefied social circles than the Woolfs.

'The youngest son, Eli, is still unmarried.' Simon directed a fatuous smile in Elisabeth's direction. 'He saw Elisabeth at services when we attended three Saturdays ago. He was much taken with her. He asked questions. Even though her father is a tradesman, he wants to court Elisabeth.' Elisabeth stared at her father in disbelief – cold with shock. 'He's a dutiful son. He discussed this first with his father.'

'But Simon, she's so young,' Celia protested.

'The same age as you when we were married,' he reminded. 'The father, naturally, approached me. They wish, of course, to meet the family. I told Mr Rosenstein that his son must court Elisabeth for six months. Then – provided Elisabeth conducts herself properly and marriage is proposed – there will be another six months to prepare for the wedding.'

'I don't want to get married!' Elisabeth blazed. 'Mama, tell him!'

'Elisabeth, don't be hasty,' her mother soothed, an uneasy, warning glint in her eyes. 'The Rosensteins are a fine family. You'd have a wonderful life.'

'I don't want to be courted. I'm not going to tea with the Rosensteins!' Her eyes swung about the room. Her mother's eyes were downcast. Her grandmother seemed desolate. 'I won't marry him,' she defied her father. 'You can't make me!'

Darting from the room she heard her father's burst of rage. But she wouldn't marry Papa's choice of husband for her. She'd never marry anybody but David.

*　　*　　*

Elisabeth locked her bedroom door and threw herself across her bed. Her heart pounding, she lay there, hearing her father's voice soaring from downstairs as he repeated his news. This was 1902 – Papa couldn't force her to marry Eli Rosenstein.

For the next hour she heard her father denouncing her reaction to what he considered a fine future for his only daughter. Then – from exhaustion – she fell asleep. A pounding on her door woke her.

'Elisabeth, come down to supper,' her grandmother coaxed. 'Dora is ready to serve.'

'I'm not hungry. I don't want any supper.'

'Darling, you mustn't make yourself sick over this. Nothing's decided yet. Come down to the table.' Rae's voice was deep with compassion.

'I can't,' Elisabeth insisted. 'I won't marry Eli Rosenstein. Papa can't make me marry him.'

'Elisabeth, perhaps he won't want to marry you,' Rae soothed, a hint of connivance in her voice. 'He may see that you have different ideas from his own. You know how you're always saying, "God wouldn't have given women brains if he didn't expect us to use them"? Use yours, my darling. The Rosensteins are a proud family. Once Eli understands you want no part of him, he'll abandon the courting. You're a clever girl – you'll know how to manage that.'

'I just want to go back to sleep.' She would not play silly games with Eli Rosenstein. 'Please, Grandma – go down to supper.'

At breakfast next morning Elisabeth was conscious of her mother and grandmother's solicitude. Her mind in chaos, she said little. In the course of the morning she helped her mother inventory the contents of the linen closet. This afternoon Mama and Grandma would go to Gamages to buy a fresh supply of linens – all of which must be marked in red cross-stitch with Mama's initials, as was the custom, along with the date of purchase and the number of pieces in the set.

With the morning task completed Elisabeth sat down with her mother and grandmother to a luncheon of cold roast beef, baked potatoes and an apple tart. She was impatient when the other two lingered over their tea. She yearned to be with David, to report her outrage at her father's efforts to rule her life. Grandma was confident that she could thwart Papa's efforts. Her own mind insisted her father could not force her into a marriage she rejected – but her heart was fearful.

When she arrived at the library, she found David waiting for her. He was at once aware of her distress. They made no pretense of searching for books today. His hand at her elbow, David led her from the library – where Elisabeth suspected they were the subject of romantic interest to a pair of librarians.

'You're upset,' David said when they were out in the anonymity of the crowded street. 'What's happened, Beth?'

'It's Papa,' she whispered, and in a shaky voice reported what had occurred.

'We'll be married right away.' He was calm but resolute. 'We can't wait.'

'David, how can we?' David was without a job. She had no skills. 'How will we live?'

'We'll manage somehow,' he insisted. 'It may not be what you're accustomed to,' he conceded, his eyes somber, 'but we'll be together.'

'Can we marry without telling my parents?' Papa would do anything to prevent this.

'We're both over sixteen,' he reminded. 'You are, aren't you?' he joshed gently.

'Of course, I am.' She yearned to believe they could marry, even while she remained alarmed by the technicalities.

'I've looked into the requirements,' he confessed. *He'd been thinking about this.* 'We'll go to the Registry Office today and explain that we wish to be married. We're both of legal age. I have lived in London for at least fifteen days. That's all that's required. By tomorrow we'll have a license and can be married immediately. Beth, you want to do this?'

'Oh David, yes!'

Both caught up in wonder at what was about to happen, they walked to the Registry Office. After a frustrating wait, they were able to apply for their license. Tomorrow they would be married.

Elisabeth refused to consider the explosion that would follow when her father discovered she was David's wife. She was a 'modern girl' – this was her decision to make. Not Papa's.

From the Registry Office they went to a modest jewelry shop. There they bought a simple wedding band – blunt in their insistence on the least expensive circlet the jeweler offered. To Elisabeth it was beautiful. Now David accompanied her to their usual parting place.

Tomorrow would be their wedding day, she told herself as they dawdled in farewell – her face luminous.

'Tomorrow night you'll be my wife,' he whispered, his mind in tandem with hers. 'Nobody can keep us apart.'

'I won't sleep a minute tonight,' she said. 'David, we'll manage. You'll find a part in a new play. I'll work at a tea shop. I can do that,' she decided in a burst of confidence. She mustn't think about Papa and Mama's reaction. Later, she'd face that.

Elisabeth hurried into the house – knowing David would watch until the door closed behind her. Her heart was pounding, but she wasn't afraid. After tonight she'd be with David for the rest of her life.

Elisabeth awoke the next morning after a night of restless sleep with an immediate realization that within a few hours she would be David's wife. Through a gap in the curtains she could see that the morning was chilly and gray with the threat of rain in the air. In a corner of her mind she remembered one of Grandma's cherished myths – 'The girl who marries on a rainy day is blessed.'

She lay beneath the blanket for a few minutes longer, though the temperature in her bedroom was already comfortable. She'd pretended to be asleep when Clara had come in earlier and gone through the laborious act of preparing the grate for another day's fire. Now the coals were tinged with red and gray, sending out a delicious warmth that reached almost to her bed.

She was torn by conflicting emotions – euphoria that within hours she and David would be married, trepidation at the prospect of telling her parents of her marriage. But Papa was one to quote the Bible on momentous occasions – and didn't the Bible say that a wife must cling to her husband? She would still be part of the family. She couldn't conceive of a life that didn't include Mama and Papa, the boys, and Grandma. But would the family accept David? Grandma, yes, she thought tenderly. But the others . . . ?

She mustn't think morbid thoughts, she scolded herself, and tossed aside the bedclothes. With sudden impatience she dressed before the fire. How long the day would be until she left to meet David! These were her last few hours as Elisabeth Woolf. She would soon be Elisabeth Winston.

She wished in a surge of sentiment that she had some exquisite dress to wear today – some creation by Worth of Paris. But that didn't matter. She and David would be living a far more modest life than what she'd always known. But they would be rich in the way that counted – in their love.

By the time she went down to breakfast she was struggling to hide the tumultuous feelings that did battle within her. She felt recurrent guilt at deceiving Mama and Papa – but what else could she do? They would come to love David. They'd understand – even though he was not of their faith – that she and David belonged together for ever.

As she had suspected, the morning dragged. Each minute seemed endless. David would be waiting for her at the corner at half-past one. Together they would go to the Registry Office. She didn't dare think beyond those moments.

Mama talked about a charity committee meeting this afternoon. Would that mean they'd sit down to luncheon early today? Please God, let it be early. She wouldn't feel safe until the words had been said that made her David's wife.

There was no way Papa could have their marriage annulled, she soothed herself – even though he knew important people through his business. David said that couldn't happen. They were of legal age. They could make their own decision to marry.

What could she do if Papa tried to annul their marriage? There *was* a way to stop him. She grasped at this thought with shaky bravado.

As Elisabeth left the house, she was aware of an occasional droplet of rain. She spied David, waiting for her at the corner. She waved, hurried towards him. He reached to pull her close for a moment.

'You're a beautiful bride,' he whispered. 'You're always beautiful.'

Caught up in rapturous urgency they hurried to the Registry Office, presented their license, waited their turn. The civil ceremony was performed, and then she was David's wife. Hand in hand – both radiant – they emerged from the Registry Office into a drizzle that threatened to become a downpour.

'We'll go for tea,' David said gently. 'I wish I could afford to take you to the Savoy.'

'We'll go for tea, and then you'll take me home. To our home,' she emphasized. 'Later I'll go to tell my parents.' But already her heart began to pound as she considered the scene that would follow. Papa would scream – Mama would cry. 'David, I want to be truly your wife before I tell them.' Papa could not undo their marriage then.

Nice girls were not supposed to know what happened between a husband and wife, but modern girls knew, and talked about this among themselves. At first – before Elisabeth had known David – she'd thought, how awful to do that! But then she fell in love with him, and she knew it would be truly wonderful.

They went to an ABC shop for tea – their eyes making passionate love above their teacups while David's knee found hers beneath the table. She wanted to be in David's arms. She ached to feel his body close to hers. She was eager to know the magic of their love.

'I wish I had a fine house for my wife,' he said tenderly when they left the tea shop and headed for his boarding house, 'instead of a tiny bedroom.' Where David must bring her in secret until his landlady learned that he was married.

Her head on his shoulder, hands clinging, they made their way up the flights of dark, narrow stairs to his room. He unlocked the door and drew her inside, closed the door behind them – shutting out the world.

'I love you so much,' he whispered, helping her out of her jacket.

'I love you.' Her smile dazzling, she reached for the buttons at the neck of her frock. She felt no shyness, no fear – only a need to be loved by him. 'You must think me wanton, shameless.' But her eyes told him she reveled in these precious moments.

'You're my wife, whom I adore,' he told her and reached to help her undress in the semi-darkness of the room.

Their clothes in two heaps beside the bed, they reached for each other – glorying in the tumultuous emotions they shared. The room was silent except for the muted sounds of their passion as they touched. She felt the hard mattress beneath her back now and the weight of him above her. A faint, startled cry when he entered her – and then they were moving together with wondrous pleasure that was unlike anything she had ever known.

'Let me go in with you,' he urged when they approached the Woolf house. He was anxious about the reception she would receive.

'Not right away,' she insisted. She was arriving home much later than usual. And Papa must have come for tea, she realized, for Hugo, his driver, waited in front with the brougham. 'I'll tell them – then I'll come out for you.' But she was trembling now with trepidation. When Papa was home for tea, he would be returning to the shop for an evening's work. He would not be in a happy frame of mind. 'Wait at the corner, David.'

With a reassuring smile she left him and hurried to the house. She found Papa with Mama and Grandma in the sitting room. They'd just finished their tea. Mama had summoned Dora to clear away the table.

'You weren't here for tea,' her father scolded, rising to his feet. 'And I shan't be here for supper tonight. A special client is coming in for a fitting. He always expects me to be present on these occasions.' Papa sounded both annoyed and proud. Well, no point in delaying.

'I have something special to tell you,' Elisabeth began, groping for the right words. Forcing a smile. 'On the morning of the Coronation I met a young man – you know how everybody talked to one another that morning. A wonderful young man. We've been meeting each other many afternoons at the library.' She paused at Papa's sudden sharp attention.

'What kind of young man is free to cavort with you in the afternoons?' he demanded. 'Enough of such nonsense. Suppose the Rosensteins heard about this?'

'I won't marry Eli Rosenstein!' she blazed. 'I –'

'You'll do as you're told! I'm your father! I make these decisions!'

'Not in this century,' she defied him. 'I'm married to David.' She paused as he gaped in disbelief. 'We were married at the Registry Office this afternoon.' Her voice was shaky yet convincing. 'I have the papers to prove it.'

'I'll have it annulled!' her father shot back. 'You're a child. You're –'

'I'm sixteen years old. My marriage is legal.' She took a deep breath, gearing herself for what must be said. 'I'm David's wife, Papa. Nothing can change that.' Her eyes were eloquent, her message unmistakable.

She saw his ruddy face go white. He was trembling as he turned to his wife. 'Celia, our daughter is dead. We –'

'Simon, no!' Celia pleaded. Grandma looked on in agony.

'Our daughter is dead,' he repeated. 'The family must recite the Kaddish.' The prayer for the dead. He swung to face Dora, hovering in the doorway in shock. 'Dora, show this person –' he gestured towards Elisabeth without looking at her – 'show her to the door. We must recite the Kaddish for our dead daughter.'

Chapter Four

Trembling, Elisabeth walked past white and shaken Dora – out of the door Dora held wide – and into the approaching dusk. This was a nightmare. She'd awaken in a few moments and find it wasn't real.

She saw David hurrying towards her – his face anxious because her slow, uncertain gait warned him of disaster.

'Are you all right?' He slid an arm about her waist. 'Beth, what happened?' Solicitude turned to anger as she clung to him in anguish.

'Papa turned me out,' she whispered. 'He told Mama the family must recite the Kaddish for me.' She understood his stare of incomprehension. 'The Jewish prayer for the dead,' she explained. 'David, how could he do this?'

'That was his first reaction,' David comforted, leading her away from the house. But she sensed his shock. 'We'll go home now. I'll introduce you to Mrs Robbins, my landlady. And tomorrow morning,' he soothed, 'you'll go to talk with your mother and grandmother. Your father needs time to accept that we're married.'

'I knew he would be furious, but this –' She gestured her disbelief.

'Give him a little time. Talk to your mother and grandmother tomorrow – after he's left for his shop.'

'I knew he would be angry – I didn't think he would behave this way –' Her voice broke.

'You know what we're going to do tonight?' David conjured up a festive air. 'We're going to be wildly extravagant. We're going to a grand restaurant. No boarding-house supper for us on our wedding night.'

'We shouldn't –'

'We should,' he insisted. 'Tomorrow you'll go to your mother. She will have talked with your father. He'll still be upset,' David conceded, 'but he'll have calmed down. He's a rational man – he'll realize how wrong he was.'

'David, it was awful. They're my *family*. But Papa says I'm never to see them again. To Papa I'm dead.'

'Sssh.' He took one of her hands in his. 'He's had a shock. Tomorrow everything will seem different to him.'

David took her to a charming restaurant in Soho, favored by the Bohemian element of London. The place was extravagant for David's straitened circumstances but modest by the Woolf family standards. The atmosphere was convivial, and Elisabeth struggled – futilely – to become part of it. She was relieved when David decided it was time to go to his boarding house and introduce her to his landlady as his bride.

Later, in his tiny, bleak bedroom David made love to her again in a desperate effort to make her forget for tonight her father's catastrophic decree. She lay sleepless in David's arms far into the night. She'd thought she was brave and independent – but she wasn't at all. She waited now for the morning, when she could go to talk with Mama and Grandma.

In the morning David insisted he would go with her to her parents' house.

'Papa leaves the house every morning at quarter to eight,' Elisabeth told him. 'I want to be there at eight o'clock. We won't have time for breakfast.'

'I'll wait here,' David soothed, when they reached Lexham Gardens, 'until you come to me.'

For a few tremulous moments Elisabeth lingered with him at the place they'd labeled 'our corner'.

'I'll wait here for you,' David said. 'You mustn't rush.'

'I'm scared,' she whispered.

'Whatever happens, Beth, remember we'll always have each other.'

'I'll remember.'

She walked to the house with compulsive swiftness, at the door reached for the knocker. Please God, let everything be all right now. Moments later she heard footsteps in the hall. The door opened. Dora stood there. Elisabeth heard the sounds of sobbing somewhere on the upper floor.

'Good morning, Dora,' she began, her heart hammering. 'I –'

'The family can't see nobody,' Dora stammered, her eyes averted, repeating the message as instructed. 'They're mourning their dead daughter.' All at once Dora broke into wrenching sobs, then slammed the door shut.

Elisabeth stood motionless. She was dead. To her family she was dead. Nothing had changed overnight.

David rushed forward when he saw her turn away from the door and walk towards him with faltering steps.

'You're going to be all right, Beth.' He reached to pull her close. 'We'll make a wonderful new life for ourselves. You're going to be all right.'

Her hand in his, David led her to a tea shop where they'd gone so often during these last weeks. She fought against a surge of light-headedness – faintly aware of David's encouraging words. Over tea she forced herself to face the future. Papa – and that meant the whole family – wanted no part of her. But she wasn't alone. She had a husband whom she loved and who loved her.

'David, would Mr Henderson still want you to be with the company if you had a wife?' she asked in sudden decision. London would be torment to her now. Let them go to Melbourne.

David's face lighted. 'You'd be willing to go?'

'I *want* to go.'

'Let's go and talk to Roger.'

Roger Henderson was delighted that David wanted to join the Australian-bound company. He was willing to provide transportation for Elisabeth as well.

'Everything's on schedule,' Roger said with satisfaction. 'I received a telegram just this morning. We'll pick up the other members of the company in New York City. We'll cross the country to San Francisco by train, then take a ship from there to Melbourne. Elisabeth, you'll work with the company, too.' Elisabeth exchanged a glance of happy astonishment with David. 'You'll help with props and wardrobe,' Roger told her. 'You'll like Melbourne. I hear it's a wonderful city.'

Three days later – battling last-minute misgivings – Elisabeth was helped into a railway carriage of the Liverpool express which would carry David and Roger Henderson from London to the port at the amazing speed of sixty miles an hour. There they would board a ship for New York City.

'These stubby little British cars are nothing like American

railroads,' Roger derided good-humoredly. 'Over there the coaches are long, with vestibules. I know,' he conceded as David was about to speak, 'England has its fine palace cars – but they're not for the likes of us.'

Henderson was operating on a tight budget.

Elisabeth was relieved that Roger was in a talkative mood. She didn't want to remember that she was leaving London to travel halfway around the world. Leaving behind her parents, her grandmother, her brothers, perhaps for ever. In all her sixteen years she'd never been separated from her mother, her grandmother, nor her younger brother for more than a day. At unwary moments she felt devastated – despite her determination to believe, as David reiterated, that they were embarking on a marvelous adventure.

'Of course, some ships will make it to New York Harbor in far less time than the ten-day vessel we're taking. But the cost is much less on this. And I guess you two won't mind a honeymoon on board ship,' Roger added in high spirits.

At Liverpool they left the train at the Riverside Station, adjoining the busy dock where the ocean-going steamers waited. Roger Henderson guided them through the bewildering, frenetic routine of leaving the train – with porters bustling importantly among the passengers – and going through the inspection station at the port before boarding their ship.

'We're not sailing on a Cunard or White Star Line,' Roger pointed out good-humoredly, 'not one of the awesome "greyhounds of the sea". But it'll be pleasant, though without the luxury of fancy dining and orchestra music.'

If Mr Henderson was curious that her luggage was so limited, Elisabeth thought, he kept this to himself. She had left home with only the clothes she wore and a few shillings in her purse. David had acquired an advance from Mr Henderson that allowed her to buy a few essentials. She and David were ever conscious that their funds were meager – but they both had jobs in the company, Elisabeth reassured herself, with contracts for a whole year. They would manage.

At last Elisabeth and David were settled in the tiny cabin that was to be their private domain for the next ten days.

'You're not to be afraid,' David told Elisabeth with mock sternness. 'Melbourne is an important city, larger than most European capitals, and with several theaters. This is a great opportunity for all of us.'

For Elisabeth this was a period of timelessness. With David, she took long walks on the deck each day, listened while he talked about the new life that lay ahead in Australia. He explained how their company was a very modest one.

'Roger is working with a very limited budget. The men in the company will handle the stagehand jobs. The women will pitch in as seamstresses when costumes require alterations. There are no understudies – so we all have to stay healthy,' he pointed out with an effort at humor. 'But if we work together as a team we'll be fine.'

Every night they lay together in one small bunk and made love. At unwary intervals Elisabeth's mind darted back to London and the house in Lexham Gardens. What had happened there still seemed unreal, a nightmare from which she would awaken at any moment. Mama's agonized face, Grandma's anguished eyes, were etched on her brain. Ben must miss her too.

How could Papa thrust her out of the family this way? Families were supposed to be for ever. How could Mama let him do this to her? But then Papa's wishes always came first.

She tried desperately in the long days and longer nights aboard ship to hide her anguish, her anger, her feelings that life would never be truly right again. She was relieved that the passenger list was light, that Roger Henderson spent much of his time working on the plays they were to present in Melbourne. Neither she nor David experienced any seasickness, though the dining room was almost deserted as the weather grew rough and their speed diminished.

At last their ship arrived in New York Harbor. Elisabeth and David hovered at the deck's railing and gazed with awe at the Statue of Liberty, the largest statue in the world. Yes, this was a grand adventure, Elisabeth told herself defiantly.

'How long will we stay in New York?'

'Four days,' David told her, 'while Roger signs contracts with the actors, and shops for costumes. We'll have time for a lot of sightseeing.'

Despite the fascination of roaming about New York Elisabeth was inundated at painful interludes by a sense of loss. David was her husband and she adored him – yet wasn't it natural that she missed her family? After much indecision she bought two postcards and addressed one to Mama and one to Grandma, to report on her presence in New York and to tell them she would very soon be crossing America to board a ship to take David and her to Australia. Even if they wanted to reach her, they couldn't until she and David had a permanent address in Melbourne.

'I love you all,' she concluded on each, signed both, and mailed them.

On a cold, gray morning the Henderson Repertory Company – now consisting of eight members – went to Grand Central Station to board the first of the trains that would carry them across the country to San Francisco. On sight Elisabeth liked John and Ethel Cameron, the middle-aged couple who would play major roles. She was somewhat in awe of Dorothy Ames, the thirty-ish leading lady who appeared enamored of Gilbert Williams, the handsome young leading man – all wrapped up in himself, Elisabeth decided. Henry Wilson – their elderly character man, who confided he had once toured America with Sarah Bernhardt – was charming, gallant – in Elisabeth's eyes a perfect surrogate grandfather.

'For any bit parts we'll pick up local talent,' Roger confided.

Elisabeth and David were amazed by the size of the United States. They relished the sights they saw from their train as it sped across the country: impressive cities interspersed by enormous stretches of farmland. Gazing out at twilight at a rural town in the middle of the country, Elisabeth envisioned Ben sitting here beside her longing to paint this awesome view.

Elisabeth was proud of the way David seemed to take charge of the group – and she knew Roger was pleased.

'We'll be on the ship from San Francisco to Melbourne for at least five weeks,' David pointed out while the company gathered together on the observation car of the train as it approached San Francisco. 'We can open our first production a few days after we arrive in Melbourne if we rehearse on the ship, are word-perfect by the time we dock.'

'The theater is ours from the day we arrive,' Roger announced. 'I'll move up the dates of our advertising in the four Melbourne dailies. David, you have the makings of a true entrepreneur.'

The company lingered only a few hours in San Francisco before boarding their ship. Still, Elisabeth managed to send postcards to her mother and grandmother with a few special words for Ben. Once they were settled in Melbourne, she could give them an address. She hoped – despite Papa – that they would write.

Their second morning aboard ship – with Elisabeth beside him for 'good luck' – David approached the captain and asked that the company be allowed to use the dining room between meals for play rehearsals.

'It's a long trip,' he reminded with persuasive charm. 'We'd be happy to present scenes from our play for your guests at intervals. Entertainment will lessen the strain of so many weeks at sea.'

The captain welcomed this suggestion, and Roger was delighted.

Elisabeth was happy to be involved in rehearsals. She was assigned to handle props. She held the book, cued actors when they forgot their lines. Solicitous at Mr Wilson's difficulty in memorizing his brief role, she undertook to help him at odd hours. Yet on many nights she lay sleepless in David's arms – fighting against the knowledge that she was taking herself halfway round the world from her family.

The long sea voyage was taking its toll on company members, as with other passengers. Dorothy Ames and Gilbert Williams had become mortal enemies, conversing only in their roles. David organized evening entertainment to help assuage the boredom. Elisabeth reveled in his ability to take charge in a quiet, efficient manner. Papa was efficient in his business, she remembered, but Papa screamed at everybody in sight except for his clients. David was wonderful. They would build a fine life together – and in time Papa would understand. She wouldn't allow herself to believe otherwise.

Three days before the new year – at the approach of dawn – Elisabeth stood at the ship's railing with David and watched the light of Melbourne Harbor come into view.

'Our first real home,' David said tenderly, dropping an arm about Elisabeth's waist.

All at once Elisabeth felt the protective façade she had erected about herself these past weeks crumble into nothingness. Home was London. Home was with Mama and Papa, Grandma and the boys. Oh yes, she loved David – she wanted to build her life around him – but this must mean her family was lost to her.

'Beth?' As always, he sensed her change of mood.

'Oh David –' Her voice broke. She buried her face against his chest. 'I'm so scared –'

'Where's my brave, independent woman?' he chided gently.
'I lost her somewhere.' Elisabeth made an effort at levity.
'We'll find her,' David promised. 'You'll see.'

Chapter Five

Despite her towering sense of desolation Elisabeth was caught up in the excitement of arriving in Melbourne. The warm summer day in such contrast to what they'd left behind in winter-cold London, New York, and San Francisco. The company was met by the owner of the modest playhouse where they were to appear. Stewart Ainsley was an affable Londoner who'd been living in Melbourne for the past twenty years but played up the role of expatriate.

'This is a great city once you understand it's not London,' he told the group when he'd marshaled them through Customs and escorted them via horsedrawn carriages to the Ainsley Theater. 'Nor New York,' he added for the benefit of the largely American company.

'It's a beautiful city,' Elisabeth said with a burst of admiration. 'Such wide streets, such elegant buildings!'

Ainsley was elated when Roger Henderson told him the company had rehearsed aboard ship, and were almost prepared to go into performance.

'That's wonderful!' He beamed at each in turn. 'Tomorrow you'll devote to rehearsals – so that you can get the feel of the stage. The following night you can open. Melbourne is a city devoted to the theater. The finest performers from London and Paris come here regularly, so there's plenty of competition. You'll have to work to build up an audience, but Roger assures me you'll be able to do that.'

Mr Ainsley's participation consisted of supplying the theater, a person to handle the box office, and a pair of young girls to usher. In addition to Ainsley's monthly rent, David explained to Elisabeth, the impresario would receive a small percentage of the box-office receipts, which accounted for his providing a ticket-seller.

What happened to the last company? Elisabeth worried in a corner of her mind. The theater had been closed for five months. But Roger

– she forced herself to think of him by his first name rather than the more formal 'Mr Henderson', which was more comfortable for her – wouldn't have invested so much money if he wasn't confident the company would bring in audiences. David was sure they'd succeed here.

She'd write a letter to Mama and to Grandma at her first chance, she promised herself – and remembered wistfully that it would be at least twelve weeks before she could receive a reply. They *would* write to her, wouldn't they? In a way, she thought, Grandma knew David. She'd seen him so often onstage.

Now she forced herself to tune in to the conversation around her. The others were questioning Ainsley about their living accommodations, the possibility of something more comfortable than a rooming house since they were assigned to a year's contract.

'For the first week or so you'll be living in quarters I've arranged,' Ainsley explained. 'Melbourne abounds in hotels and boarding houses, but the hotels are mainly for rich tourists.' His smile was indulgent. 'Or of a class avoided by respectable travelers. You'll be staying with two private families who set aside rooms to rent out to professional people. You'll be comfortable there and can remain for as long as you like. But I have a list of furnished two- and three-room bungalows that are available – some with tiny front and back gardens. And the rents are suitable.'

On their first day in Melbourne the company was treated to lunch at a local restaurant – though Mr Ainsley conceded this would not be at one of the fashionable places on Swanston or Collins Streets.

'There are two kinds of restaurants in Melbourne,' Stewart Ainsley confided, 'the high-priced and the low. The food is the same – the high-priced are smarter in appearance.'

Although they were very clearly dining in the less expensive category, the food was tasty and generous in portions, the waitresses eager to please. Again, Elisabeth asked herself what happened to the last company at the Ainsley Theater – the most modest in Melbourne, Ainsley pointed out with a disarming show of candor. Or is he validating our wages? Elisabeth asked herself with new cynicism.

After lunch, the company members were escorted to the two boarding houses where they were to stay. Elisabeth was pleased that John and Ethel Cameron were assigned to the same one as she and David.

'I asked about the last company,' Ethel Cameron whispered to Elisabeth. 'It seems the leading lady and the juvenile both came down with typhoid. But Roger says that's rare these days.' Still she seemed uneasy.

'I'm sure we'll be all right,' Elisabeth comforted. That was a logical explanation. David had guessed they'd become homesick and returned to England or America. 'We're to have our own little bungalows with gardens,' she reminded Ethel. 'We'll have a wonderful year here.' It would be nothing like the house at Lexham Gardens, but she and David didn't need a big house.

Elisabeth and David settled themselves in their small but comfortably furnished bedroom at the boarding house, then set out to see the city. For the remainder of today they were to be tourists. Elisabeth had made extensive notes about what they were to see.

'Beth, you're not going to visit all of Melbourne in one day,' David joshed. 'Let's focus on our particular section.'

'You're always so practical,' Elisabeth sighed with mock dismay.

'Of course, you'll want to go to the library,' David teased.

'I'm not sure I'll trust you there.' Her eyes were luminous with love. 'No assignations with other women.'

'You mean you're keeping me on a leash?'

'A tight one.'

'You keep looking at me like that and there'll be no sightseeing today. I'll have another destination in mind.'

'Not until after supper,' she demurred. 'First show me Melbourne.'

They walked endlessly about the city, impressed by the handsome shops of brick and stone. They saw the Town Hall, the new Parliament House on Spring Street, the stone Treasury with the magnificent flight of steps leading to the entrance. They admired the fine Public Library with its sculpture and picture galleries – and the technical museum attached. They were impressed by the two universities and the Working Man's College, where ambitious and talented artisans studied to improve their skills.

After viewing the two elegant cathedrals, they lingered before the synagogue on Boarke Street. Elisabeth clung to David's hand as her thoughts darted back to the London synagogue she'd attended with her family through the years – though not with the regularity her mother wished.

'You can come here whenever you like,' David said gently.

'It's like a piece of home.' That was what Grandma had said about the tiny synagogue in Whitechapel which the two of them had surreptitiously visited.

All at once Elisabeth was exhausted. 'Let's go back to the boarding house. Tomorrow will be a busy day.'

The rehearsal was scheduled for ten o'clock. Somewhere in the course of the day, Elisabeth decided, they must find time to look at the bungalows Mr Ainsley had talked about. Boarding house fees were high on their wages – and they must never be like those people Papa scoffed at, who had to buy everything on the weekly payment plan.

Later, lying awake in David's arms at a time when she had expected to be sound asleep, she considered the life that lay ahead of them. She wasn't going to think about home. She was going to think about now – with David.

Their life in Melbourne quickly settled into a pattern, for which Elisabeth was grateful. With amazing speed they rented a weather-board two-room bungalow, its tiny front garden offering a pair of rose bushes in dazzling bloom. The drought that the company had heard was causing much havoc in sections of Australia was not afflicting Melbourne. Elisabeth wrote and mailed letters to Mama and Grandma, with a special insert for Ben – and reminded herself that it would be at least twelve weeks before she could receive a reply. Papa wouldn't have to know they were exchanging letters. Not for a while.

Each morning Elisabeth made breakfast for David and herself while he straightened up their bedsitting room. After breakfast they went to the theater for the rehearsals of the second play Roger had scheduled. Elisabeth loved being caught up in that make-believe world. At rehearsals she sat beside Roger, absorbing every tiny detail of play production. At performances she was the prompter, and helped out as dresser. At odd times she cued Henry Wilson, struggling to memorize lines for the new production.

Between rehearsals and performance Elisabeth and David shopped two or three times a week at the fascinating Melbourne food markets, of which there were several. Hand in hand they strolled along the avenues of the corrugated-iron-roofed market, selecting food for their meals. Elisabeth wistfully remembered such shopping expeditions with her grandmother. Her letters wouldn't even have reached London yet, she realized.

Elisabeth and David watched for signs that their audiences were increasing. They knew that they couldn't compete with the long-established theaters such as the elegant Royal, but Roger was anxious to see their audiences enlarge.

'We'll be fine,' David told Elisabeth at the end of their fourth week in Melbourne, relief in his voice. 'This town loves theater. We don't have to worry about the company folding.'

Elisabeth was startled. She'd thought that low attendance meant that Roger was seeing little profit. He'd pointed out early on that he was prepared to survive three or four slow months. And David was certain Roger would never discharge any member of the company. 'Most actors, singers and musicians in Australia leave the country as soon as they can in search of bigger opportunities abroad,' Roger had explained. It was a beautiful country but with only a tiny population to provide audiences. 'Even Nellie Melba spends more time in Europe than at home,' he'd added with a chuckle.

They might be stranded in Australia, but she was with David, Elisabeth consoled herself. David was so clever – he'd always find a way for them to survive. He was even on friendly terms with Dorothy Ames, their leading lady, though she was disliked by every other member of the company.

Elisabeth was grateful to be so busy that she couldn't dwell on her homesickness. Papa would repent, she told herself regularly – he couldn't keep her out of the family for ever. Sometimes she had been conscious of a wary truce between Papa and Grandma. Like herself Grandma resented the attitude in the world that men made all the decisions and women accepted them. But Grandma always expressed deep affection for Papa. 'How can I not love your father?' she'd reproached after one of Elisabeth's rebellious moments. 'Your father and mother gave me my most precious gifts – my granddaughter and my two grandsons.'

By the end of their fifth week in Melbourne, everybody in the company was uneasy about Dorothy's hostility towards Roger. She was unhappy that the advertising didn't provide her with star status. She complained about her costumes. She was bored with playing the same role so long. 'When do we do the new play? Damn it, Roger, we've been rehearsing almost five weeks!'

'She's impossible,' Ethel whispered to Elisabeth while they waited for their prima donna to appear one Monday morning. 'But Roger can't throw her out because without her we'd have to close.' Roger's budget didn't allow for understudies.

'Where the hell is she?' Roger demanded in outrage when Dorothy had not yet appeared by eleven o'clock.

'Let me go over to her boarding house and check,' David said with a calm not reflected in the others. 'Roger, why don't you rehearse the scenes she's not in while I'm gone? Elisabeth can read my part.'

'Yes, go.' Roger agreed. 'All right, everybody, places for Act One, Scene Two.'

Thirty-five minutes later David was striding down the aisle of the theater. Roger held up his hands to stop the rehearsal.

'What's with Dorothy?'

'I talked to her landlady,' David reported. 'She's packed up and left. She told the landlady she was moving in with a friend.' He managed a wry smile. 'The old girl said the "friend" was probably the gentleman who left at the same time. They gave no forwarding address.'

'How could she walk out like that?' Roger railed. 'We have a performance to give tonight!'

'Without Dorothy?' Ethel Cameron was dubious.

'We have to perform.' Henry Wilson was grim. 'We're just beginning to win regular audiences here in Melbourne.'

'We're without a leading lady,' Roger reminded. 'That damn bitch! She knew she was throwing the whole company in jeopardy. God, wait till Ainsley hears about this!'

What would she and David do if the company closed? Elisabeth asked herself in sudden panic. They'd be stranded here on a strange continent.

'We'll go on tonight,' David said quietly. 'We'll lose everything if we don't.' He reached for Elisabeth's hand. 'Elisabeth will replace Dorothy.'

'David!' Elisabeth was white with shock.

'Elisabeth knows every line in this play,' David told the others. 'She can pull it off.'

'Elisabeth?' Roger turned to her. 'You know the part?'

'I know the lines,' Elisabeth stammered. 'But I've never been

40

onstage except for school plays.' Yet all at once she felt a surge of excitement. *Could she do this?*

'We'll start rehearsing with Elisabeth right now,' Roger decided, desperation galvanizing him. 'I'll stay on the book myself,' he promised. Prompting was normally Elisabeth's duty. He consulted his watch. 'We've got time for three full run-throughs. Elisabeth, if you're in trouble during performances one of us will throw you the lines. The cast will push you through the blocking.' His eyes were commanding her to agree.

'I'll try,' she said after a moment, her heart pounding. It was important to David and her, to the whole company. She felt simultaneously exhilarated and terrified. 'But pray for me. All of you,' she ordered. 'I'm scared to death.'

The hours seemed to fly past as the company went through the grueling three run-throughs. In between Ethel Cameron pinned Elisabeth into costumes that must be made smaller for her. 'Don't worry, Elisabeth – I'll baste everything in time. The audience will never guess they weren't made for you.' Ethel promised to help her with her make-up, and to style her hair to add years.

David was beside her every moment – encouraging, approving. She rarely faltered – and when she did, someone contrived to give her the errant line. She knew them, she chastised herself in exasperation. Why was she making mistakes?

'You can do this,' David whispered as he held her close. They heard the audience arrive, settle into their seats with that little flurry of excitement that is part of theater attendance. 'Forget about Elisabeth – you're the character in the play. Move inside her head. *Be* her.'

'Do you suppose Sarah Bernhardt feels this way before performances?' she laughed shakily. 'At our school plays I was too dumb to be scared.'

'You'll be wonderful,' David told her. 'Better than Dorothy ever was.'

'Do you suppose Roger will raise my wages if I pull this off?' She was determinedly flippant. 'And I won't even ask for star billing!'

At least this was Monday, Elisabeth reminded herself – the night of the week when their audiences were smallest. But she had to bring this off. Ainsley would cancel Roger's lease on the theater if they didn't perform. There'd be no money for wages. That mustn't happen.

Elisabeth willed herself to focus on the role she was playing. She whispered a prayer under her breath as the curtain rose. It would be fully five minutes before she made her entrance. She stood in the wings with David's arms about her while she waited – grateful that his presence wasn't required until after her own.

Twelve hours ago she'd been having breakfast in their bungalow, and now – after three hectic run-throughs – she must brush aside her exhaustion and go onstage and be vivacious and confident.

'All right, Beth, watch for your entrance,' David cautioned. 'Do just what you did at the run-throughs. You'll be fine.'

She heard her cue. With a dazzling smile she made her entrance. She wasn't Elisabeth now. She was this delightful character in the play. She was almost unnerved when she heard the first laughter in response to a line of her own. But this was the impetus to push ahead. *She was doing all right.*

Between acts Ethel checked on her costume to make sure the basting stitches were holding.

'You're a natural,' Ethel purred. 'I knew that this afternoon at rehearsals.'

'I'm scared to death,' Elisabeth admitted. How many times had she said that? Yet she felt so good!

At the end of the performance David had to drag her onstage with the rest of the cast for the curtain calls.

'You were wonderful,' David whispered. 'Better than Dorothy.'

Though this was what David called a 'slow night' – with a small audience – the reaction was warm and approving. Elisabeth was dizzy with exhilaration as she took her bow. She was startled to realize that the audience's response to her own appearance was the strongest. Of course they must understand that she was a last-minute replacement – that was why she was so well received.

The curtain came down. The audience began to stream out of the small playhouse. David held her smotheringly close.

'We did it!' Roger strode towards the cast in high spirits. 'Let's go over to my place and break open that magnum of champagne I was saving to celebrate our one hundredth performance. Tonight rates it.'

Out of costume and make-up the company traveled by omnibus to Roger's bungalow – the walls adorned with posters and playbills testifying to his theater background. Ethel dug out glasses while Roger brought out the champagne, struggling amid colorful language to remove the cork. The others shrieked in approval when this was accomplished.

Roger began to pour. 'You understand, of course, Elisabeth,' he said, handing her a glass, 'that we're depending upon you to see us through until I sign on a replacement for Dorothy?'

'Yes,' she whispered.

'I don't know how you did it, but you saved our bacon tonight. It's like a small miracle.' Now some of his ebullience seemed to evaporate. 'And you'll have to keep it up until I find a replacement for Dorothy.'

'That won't be easy,' John Cameron warned. 'This isn't New York – nor London.'

'I've placed ads in two of the dailies. They'll run in tomorrow morning's editions. Meanwhile,' Roger pursued, striving for optimism, 'we'll all work with Elisabeth. We'll put the new play aside for the moment, focus on pulling Elisabeth through this one.'

'The audience liked her,' Henry said quietly. 'She got laughs that Dorothy never did.'

'I don't mind filling in,' Elisabeth told Roger, but a heady realization had taken root in her mind: she didn't want Roger to find a replacement. She wanted to be a permanent part of the company.

'All right, let's drink up, then call it a night,' Roger said. 'Rehearsals tomorrow at noon.'

Elisabeth had expected to fall asleep the moment she was settled in bed for the night. It had been an exhausting – harrowing – day. But not even the unfamiliar glass of champagne had slowed the pace of her mind. Now she knew what she wanted to do with her life. In addition to being David's wife, she wanted to be an actress.

David wouldn't object, she told herself with conviction. Grandma had had to leave the theater when she married – but those were different times. David had been proud of her tonight. His eyes had told her that. But it would be another wedge between Papa and her. To Papa actors and actresses were 'scum'. It meant nothing to him that Queen Victoria had knighted actors she'd admired. For all Papa's respect for Queen Victoria, he closed his mind to this. He was forever closing his mind.

She turned on her side, dropping an arm about David. He was sound asleep, she thought, suffused with love. It had been a long, arduous day for him. But he wouldn't stand in the way of her becoming an actress. He believed in women's freedom to make something special of their lives.

Would she be able to make Roger understand she belonged in the company? That tonight wasn't just a lucky accident? She must repeat tonight's performance tomorrow – and then again and again. She must convince Roger she could be as good as Dorothy before he auditioned and hired somebody else.

She struggled to lie still – not to awaken David. Her mind churned with new ambition, was invaded at truant moments with self-doubts. At last she fell into troubled sleep, awakened to the aromas of fresh coffee bubbling on their tiny stove and cinnamon buns warming in the oven.

'David, you let me sleep so late,' she scolded, sitting up in bed and calling out to him.

'You deserve it.' He appeared at the entrance to their bedsitting room with a cup of coffee. 'We don't have to be at rehearsals until noon.'

'But I need to rehearse with you first.' She reached eagerly for the coffee. 'You must tell me what I did wrong last night.'

'You were a breath of fresh air on that stage. I was astonished.'

'I'm not sure I can do it again.' Again, self-doubts eroded her confidence. 'Oh David, what if I'm terrible tonight?'

'You wouldn't dare to be. For one thing –' he was serious now – 'don't let that egotistical Gil upstage you. He tried to a couple of times last night.'

Elisabeth was puzzled. 'What do you mean – "upstage me"?'

'When you have lines, never give the audience your back. Last night he deliberately moved upstage so you had to turn away from the audience to speak to him. *Never*,' he reiterated, 'give your back to the audience when you have lines. Unless, of course, there's a strong reason for it – like you're trying to present a certain emotion with your shoulders.'

'David, you're having me on. How can I express emotion with my shoulders?'

44

Unexpectedly David chuckled. 'I think I'm a better coach than actor. I'll work with you, Beth. For a little while I sold programs at a theater in London. I watched Bernhardt – and every night was a lesson. Beth, yesterday was a marvelous turning point in our lives. Bless Dorothy for walking out like that.'

Elisabeth and David were the first to arrive for rehearsals. David drew her onto the stage to demonstrate bits he felt would improve her performance, but at the sound of Roger's voice in conversation with Ethel and John, she froze.

'David, I'm so scared,' she whispered. 'Suppose I go on tonight and forget every line?'

'Well, look at the early birds,' Ethel drawled. 'Our heroine is standing by to save our hides again.'

'You were damn good, ' John told her.

But Roger seemed nervous, she thought.

'Elisabeth, let's start with your first entrance,' Roger ordered. 'We don't need Henry or Gil for that.'

'Yes, Roger.' She didn't want him to find somebody to replace Dorothy. She meant to be the replacement herself.

The day passed with dreamlike swiftness. Then Ethel was helping her with her make-up, her hair.

'I know it's supposed to be safer to have electric lighting on stage, but I miss the gaslight. So flattering,' Ethel sighed. 'But at your age it doesn't matter. And I doubt whether you and David will be stuck with little road companies like John and me. Still, there's always the chance that some producer will see us and bring us into an important Broadway production. In the theater you have your dreams until you go to your grave.'

Elisabeth's hands were icy, a peculiar tightness in her throat as she waited for her entrance – but onstage she pushed aside fear, became the vivacious young lady she was portraying. She clung to the make-believe character, making her real. Between acts she focused on what was to come, spoke to nobody, managing only a prayerful smile for David.

At last the performance was over. Suffused with relief she joined the curtain calls. Coming offstage she exchanged an involuntary glance with Roger. She saw a new respect in his eyes. Maybe – just maybe – he'd decide he wouldn't need to audition a replacement for her.

'You surprised Roger,' David whispered to Elisabeth, dropping an arm about her waist as they walked to the tiny dressing rooms. 'He wasn't sure you could repeat last night's performance. I knew you could.'

'He's afraid to gamble on somebody without experience.' She sensed the battle going on in Roger's mind. Yes, she'd handled Dorothy's role well – all right – adequately. Twice. But she'd seen Dorothy play it so many times. She'd just duplicated Dorothy's performance. But how would she cope with a new role – one she would have to create herself?

'Let me talk to Roger,' David began. She'd confessed to him that she longed to replace Dorothy permanently. 'I'll –'

'No,' she interrupted. 'Roger has to make the decision himself. At the moment he's on the fence. You could push him in the wrong direction. I must convince him I can fit in with the company.'

But how? And, with the advertisements for a replacement already published, time was breathing down her neck.

Chapter Six

The rehearsal the following day was scheduled to help Elisabeth with the 'blocking' – the stage movements. Roger called for a rehearsal at one o'clock. Arriving a few minutes early, Elisabeth and David heard him in conversation with someone onstage.

'He doesn't sound happy,' David murmured. 'I hear that strained tone that says he wants to break off the interview.'

Elisabeth felt a tightness in her throat. 'Is that someone replying to his advertisement?'

'Probably. It said to apply between ten and one every day this week. Don't worry, Beth, he won't find anybody who is as good as you. In his heart he knows that.' Still, David's eyes betrayed his own anxiety.

At this afternoon's rehearsal Elisabeth willed herself to concentrate, thrust aside fears. She was startled when, in the middle of the first act, Roger stopped her. Her heart began to pound. She'd thought she was doing well.

'Elisabeth, that business you did there – you know that pixie look, the shrug of your shoulders – can you remember to keep that in? It's good.'

'Sure.' Roger thought she'd just happened to do that, but she'd worked it out this morning – and David liked it. 'I thought it might bring a laugh.'

'Keep it in.'

On the following afternoon Roger astonished the cast by asking for a run-through of the new play. He didn't want them forgetting lines.

'Here's the script, Elisabeth,' Roger said off-handedly. 'You don't mind reading Dorothy's role?'

'No, of course not.' Her smile was sweet and obliging. Her mind charged into action.

In the first act Elisabeth read from the script. The others, except for Henry, were word-perfect, for they'd been rehearsing five weeks without an opening date scheduled. That had been one of Dorothy's complaints. David had speculated that Roger wasn't happy with her performance.

At the end of the first act Roger called a fifteen-minute break.

'I'm going on without the script,' Elisabeth whispered to David. 'I know all the lines from rehearsals.' Her eyes met his, pleading for reassurance.

'You're the fastest learner I've ever known. Yes, forget about reading and play the part. Make Roger wake up.'

Like the others, Elisabeth went on without the script. She was conscious of the sudden tension in the air as the others realized she knew this role. Gilbert Williams – playing leading man to her leading lady – was giving more than he had ever managed with Dorothy. There was a new electricity onstage.

'All right, take ten minutes,' Roger ordered at the end of the scene. He seemed testy. She had shaken him up, Elisabeth guessed. He was nervous about making a fast decision. 'Henry, for God's sake, get up on your lines.' Roger hesitated. 'We have to add this play to our repertoire soon.'

When Henry approached Roger, Elisabeth thought it was to make excuses about his usual difficulty in memorizing, but she clutched at David's arm as the conversation between the two men became audible.

'Roger, wake up! Elisabeth is a natural. I've been in this business for forty years. I know fine talent when I see it. Hang on to her.'

Roger cleared his throat in the nervous gesture they all knew.

'Elisabeth,' he called. 'Come over here.'

Striving to seem casual Elisabeth walked to his side. 'Yes, Roger?'

'How much of this part do you know?'

'All of it.' Demureness blended with confidence in her reply.

'You'll need a hell of a lot of work,' he said with a pretense of gruffness, 'but we'll introduce the new play – with you as leading lady – in two weeks.'

'Yes, Roger. Thank you.' She fought to hide her elation. David glowed.

But at her first opportunity for private contemplation she felt confidence ebbing away. Suppose the audiences didn't like her in the new play? She had learned her first role from watching Dorothy on stage. This time she must create the character herself – with the help of the director, she acknowledged. And David would coach her.

This is what I want to do with my life. Please God, let me bring this off.

Roger abandoned the search for an actress, focusing instead on hiring someone to replace Elisabeth in her backstage roles. He discovered a former stagehand who'd worked for a long time in the London theater, but who had settled in Melbourne a dozen years ago.

'I had to put a lot of distance between my old lady and me,' Amos Swift confided to David and Elisabeth in the course of his first day with the company. 'She got religion a few years after we married – always on my back if I took a nip, yelling at me if my language got a bit salty. I couldn't take a deep breath around her.'

'Do you miss London?' Elisabeth was wistful. Would there ever be a time when *she* didn't miss London? Miss her family?

'Now and then,' Amos admitted. 'But we're still British. Don't the British Navy protect us? We're part of the Empire, even though it's a long haul back to London. We lead a good life here in Melbourne.'

Elisabeth and David's lives revolved around the theater and the company. As David pointed out, they weren't famous actors but they were building an audience. Elisabeth knew she was holding her own with the company the night the new play was introduced into repertoire and she received the warmest applause at the curtain calls.

'You did it, Beth!' David chortled when they were alone. 'Of course, Gil's miffed. He wants the biggest applause for himself.'

Conscious that she waited anxiously for a reply to her letters to her mother and grandmother, David tried to fill their hours away from the theater with diversion. Early every Sunday afternoon they went to the Royal Park to see the animals on display there – various species of monkeys, lions, leopards, pumas, tigers, wolves, water buffaloes, all of which Elisabeth adored. To her this was Melbourne's answer to London's Zoological Gardens in Regent's Park. But at the end of their third month in Melbourne, with no mail from London, Elisabeth fought against surges of depression. Perhaps her letters had gone astray, she thought. Then she'd write again. It was difficult to accept that Mama and Grandma would not respond.

Sitting down to write her letter, she debated uneasily. Should she tell them about her working with the company? Grandma would be amazed but approving. Mama would be terrified that Papa might learn of this new insult to his beliefs. But then, to Papa she was dead. If Ben knew, he would understand.

Next morning she mailed her letter – addressed jointly to Mama and Grandma – with the painful realization if there was no response to this – and again there would be an agonizing twelve-week wait – then she'd know Mama and Grandma were afraid to go against Papa's wishes. *She was dead to the whole family.*

Early in April she was responding with indignation – like David – to the growing movement for what was being called 'a White Australia'.

Amos, too, was upset by this. After a virulent article on the subject appeared in a local newspaper, he invited Elisabeth and David to his bedsitting room to discuss this.

'I know there's been trouble in the United States,' Amos conceded over tea, 'I know about the war fought over there about slavery, but in London who bothers if a man is white or black if he's a decent sort? This "White Australia" feeling – well, it's shit.' He turned to Elisabeth. 'Pardon my language.'

'I don't understand their thinking.' David sighed. 'How do they presume to say that the native Australians are "lower down God's scale of creation than the whites"?'

'They're afraid of their jobs, according to this morning's newspaper,' Elisabeth pointed out. 'They complain that Africans and Asians are willing to work for far less than white Australians.'

'It's wrong to talk about a "White Australia". Thinking people should join together and fight this!' David rose to his feet, began to pace. 'How can Parliament talk about not allowing Kanakas to be brought over into Queensland after next year?' Kanaka, Elisabeth had learnt, was the Australian word for a native of the South Sea Islands.

'Who but Kanakas want to work on the sugar plantations in Queensland?' Amos shuddered eloquently.

'Now they're talking about expatriating all Pacific Islanders from Australia by 1906. And the word is that most members of Parliament agree to this!'

'I heard,' Amos confided, 'they've used a test in some European language to deport immigrants on what they call "educational grounds". That ain't fair.'

Elisabeth listened while David and Amos dissected the subject. But part of her mind grappled with the possibility of David's becoming involved in Australian politics. Hadn't she always said he should be in politics? He was so clever and eloquent – he could do much good. Yet the prospect of putting down roots in Melbourne was disconcerting. She loved the city – but London meant home and family.

Late in April Elisabeth realized she was pregnant. She was engulfed by tumultuous emotion. This was the ultimate recognition of their love – the child given to her by David. Yet how would she continue in the theater? Even before telling David that she was certain she was pregnant, she tried to think through this new situation.

She could continue to play at least through her fifth month, she decided. Costumes would conceal her pregnancy until then. Roger wouldn't be happy, she realized – but he would have three months to replace her.

She fought against a devastating sense of loss at the prospect of withdrawing from the company. But her face grew luminous as she envisioned herself holding their baby in her arms. Later she would return to the theater, she promised herself, but most important now was their child.

She was conscious of an urgent yearning to confide her news to Mama and Grandma. But there'd been no answer to her letters, she taunted herself. Papa still ruled in the Woolf household. Why couldn't Mama and Grandma be strong just this once and defy him?

This was Mama and Papa's first grandchild. Maybe knowing about the baby would knock down the wall between Papa and her, bring her back into the family. She'd write again, tell them about the baby. Fresh hope spiraled in her. Oh, she wanted to feel the comfort of Grandma's arms about her. She wanted to be part of the family again.

When they lay in bed together – discussing the evening's performance as usual – Elisabeth interrupted David to tell him about the baby. She felt his arm about her grow tense. His mouth was ajar in surprise. Was he upset? Angry?

'Beth, you're sure?' His voice was uneven. But in the muted light of the room she saw the incandescent glow that suffused him. David wasn't angry, she told herself.

'I'm sure.'

He drew her close. She felt his heart pounding against her. 'We'll be a family!' She remembered his bleak childhood in the orphanage. To David, too, to have a family was to be blessed.

'We'll have to tell Roger,' she began. 'He'll need –'

'We must find a doctor,' David broke in. 'Amos knows everything about Melbourne. He'll tell us what to do.'

'Unless there's been some miraculous change in the system, there's a long wait ahead,' she said with gentle laughter. 'We've plenty of time for that.'

'The old system is fine. We'll manage to wait.'

'You'll be a wonderful father,' she said exuberantly. Not like Papa.

'We'll start thinking straight away about where our child's to go to school. And even if it's a girl, she'll be properly educated, of course.' He was remembering Elisabeth's own frustration about not being able to study for university entrance. 'And by the time she's grown, women will be voting.'

'Didn't you tell me Parliament is already talking about "universal adult" franchise? That newspapers are predicting it'll pass by the end of the year?' Elisabeth glowed. 'There's no end to what our daughter might do with her life!'

'Don't be disappointed if it's a boy.'

'Either will be wonderful.' She clung to him in joyous relief. He was happy about the baby.

But as Elisabeth had suspected, Roger was shaken at the prospect of having to replace her.

'You've spoiled me,' he reproached her. 'You brought something special to the company. But you'll still belong to us. And later you'll come back. Meanwhile, I'll have to start combing through possibilities here in Melbourne or Sydney.' She sensed his concern though he tried for an air of optimism.

Ethel and John – who'd never had children – immediately designated themselves as grandparents-in-waiting. Roger promised to increase David's wages when the time arrived for Elisabeth to leave the company.

'I have no patience with inept actresses. David will earn the extra money coaching whoever I have to settle for.'

Elisabeth was touched by the way the members of the company – except for Gil – offered such affection and solicitude. Ethel was sewing clothes for the baby with such abandon that David pointed out Elisabeth was not expecting triplets. Roger was grimly auditioning week after week, ever conscious of the way Ethel had to keep adjusting Elisabeth's costumes.

Each day Elisabeth prayed for a letter from home. Surely, she told herself, the prospect of becoming a grandfather would soften Papa's heart. But no letter arrived from London.

When Elisabeth was growing nervous about Roger's delay in finally selecting a replacement – ever mindful that David would be without a job if the company closed – she learned that a young actress from Sydney was coming to Melbourne to audition.

'Thank God,' she told David in relief. 'If this one's as good as she sounds, the company won't close.'

Lila Atkins was tall, with the voluptuous body of an earlier-day Lillian Russell. Her hair was blonde and fashionably arranged. She exuded charm and self-confidence. She might be a horrible actress, David thought as he waited to read with her, but her looks just might override that.

She was nowhere near as good as Elisabeth, David judged in a corner of his mind while the actress auditioned. She wasn't even as good as Dorothy. But she seemed eager – that was a starting point.

'That's enough,' Roger interrupted when they approached the end of the scene. Lila glanced up expectantly. 'You've got a hell of a lot to learn. But I'll take a chance on you – provided you're willing to accept heavy coaching. David's good. You have to do everything he says.'

'Oh, I will,' she promised, her smile electric. 'I'll work very hard.'

But from their very first session, David was uncomfortable with Lila. He had to admit that she went out of her way to be friendly with everybody in the company. At the end of the first week – with Lila rehearsing with the cast during the day and Elisabeth playing at performances – Ethel whispered to Elisabeth in the tiny dressing room they shared that she didn't like Lila.

'Maybe it's because I know she makes John all hot and bothered, but I just don't trust that one. At the first chance she'll walk out on the company with any man who promises to make her a star. I've known a dozen like her.'

'Let's hope Lila's a fast learner. Or somebody's going to have to rewrite this play.' In the last two weeks Elisabeth had begun to pop out all over.

To everyone's relief Lila had the lines down within a week.

'So she's not exactly good,' Henry conceded to Elisabeth and Ethel. 'She's a body onstage. The rest of the cast will have to carry her.'

'With that body – and the way she throws it around –' Ethel said drily, 'she'll probably carry herself.'

Roger behaved with admirable restraint until Lila had gone through five performances. Then he cornered David.

'You've got to show her how to read her lines!' Roger fumed. 'Spend more time with her. I die a little every time she opens her mouth. And I know,' he picked up before David could remind him, 'she's all we've got now.'

'Maybe if I had her listen to Elisabeth,' David began. 'Make her focus on Elisabeth's delivery . . .' He paused because Roger was shaking his head impatiently.

'David, you don't know women. She won't take it from Elisabeth. *You* have to drag a performance out of her. I don't care how you have to do it.' His eyes were unnervingly eloquent. 'This week everybody's free until performance time. Bring Lila into the theater every morning and beat some sense into her. Tell her she looks gorgeous, but you want her to make the audience realize she's a fine actress, too. *Do it, David.*'

The following morning David headed for the theater with soaring misgivings. He didn't anticipate spending time alone with Lila in an empty theater. No man alive could misinterpret the invitation he constantly read in Lila's eyes.

Chapter Seven

David settled himself nervously at the table that he'd pulled into the center of the stage. The house lay in shadows, cold and ominous. A small work light illuminated the area where he sat. He tried to focus on the script that lay before him. Roger's words ricocheted across his brain: 'Last night five people walked out at the end of the second act.'

Every member of the company knew that Lila's performance was responsible for that. She was the sour note onstage. They couldn't afford to lose audiences. The word would circulate that they were giving bad performances. How long could Roger hang on?

He tensed at the sound of footsteps. He'd told Lila he would leave the front door open.

'It's so cold in the theater!' Her sultry voice drifted accusingly towards him.

'It's warmer onstage,' he called back. 'Keep on your coat and you'll be fine.'

He pretended to be searching for a segment of the script on which he'd decided to work. Lila walked up the small flight of stairs at the side of the stage and crossed to the table.

'It's so cold here,' she complained again. 'Why don't we work in one of the dressing rooms? We have little heaters there.'

'All right.' David rose to his feet – self-conscious but determined to appear casual.

Opening her coat and displaying the daringly low neckline of her red wool dress, with tiny gold buttons to the waist, Lila chattered about the theater in Sydney while they walked backstage to a tiny spartan dressing room.

'I think it's so sweet of you to work with me,' she murmured. 'I do so want Roger to be pleased with my work.' She slid out of her coat and hung it away; removed her hat with a languorous gesture, tossed it on the narrow couch at one side of the dressing room.

Averting his eyes from Lila's hour-glass figure, David sat in one of the chairs beside the narrow dressing table. 'We'll start with your first entrance. That's got to be solid. Of course, the audience is drawn to you because you're a beautiful actress.' He forced himself to follow Roger's instructions. 'But to hold the audience you have to play the role well.'

'Oh, I want to do that!' She sat in the other chair – all at once serious.

They rehearsed Lila's entrance a dozen times, with David breaking in with strained patience. Lila would never be anything but a beautiful body onstage, he told himself in frustration.

'That's a little better,' he said at last, grateful for small improvements. 'We'll move on to your next scene.'

'It's warm in here.' Her seductive smile unnerved him.

'Let's go on to the next scene,' he repeated, more terse than he'd intended. Why was she unbuttoning the neck of her dress that way? It wasn't *that* warm.

'Let's walk through the blocking in the first scene of Act Two,' she said with an air of spontaneity. 'I can feel the role better on my feet.'

'All right.' Damn! She was all but falling out of the neckline of her dress.

David walked awkwardly through Gil's role, too late remembering this was the love scene between the leading lady and leading man. Following the stage business, Lila leaned towards him, reached a hand to his arm. Then all at once her arms were about him. She lifted her mouth to his, moved her hips crushingly hard against him. In a startled haze he felt himself reacting.

This was insane, he thought, but reason departed and he allowed Lila to draw him down upon the couch with her, her skirt high above her thighs now, her hands at his waist in her impatience.

A faint groan escaped him as he became the aggressor, his body matching hers in its demand. Forgetting that the door to the theater was open – anyone could wander in from the street. All that mattered at this moment was to satisfy the urgent need that had gone unfilled for weeks.

'Oh God!' He lay limp above her. His mind in chaos.

'I knew you'd be good.' Her smile was smug.

He saw her glow of triumph. He was dizzy with shock. It wasn't passion that pushed her to seduce him, he thought in sudden comprehension, it was the need to show her power.

'Lila, this is never to happen again.' He rose from the couch, rushed to straighten his clothes. *Make her understand.* 'Because if it does, I promise you, Roger will throw you out of the company.' His eyes held hers, daring her to dismiss this statement. Ambition was winning, he decided after a moment of heated confrontation. 'I'll work with you, try to help you improve your performance. But this won't happen again.'

'What time shall I be here tomorrow?' She was on her feet, buttoning the front of her dress. 'Teach me what I need to know.' At this moment she looked young and vulnerable – and scared. This was her big opportunity.

'The same time tomorrow.' He was fighting for calm. 'And tonight, try the first scene the way I told you. Roger expects better from you than you're giving.'

Walking back home on this cold, gray day, David tried to sort out in his mind what had happened. All these weeks lying with Elisabeth in his arms but not making love because of the baby had taken a toll on him. What he had felt with Lila was lust. Lila was no better than those women who prowled about Regent Street by night in search of men to buy their favors. How could he have stooped so low?

He wasn't fit to hold Elisabeth in his arms again, he chastised himself. But he'd made it clear to Lila there would be no repetition. He debated about confessing to Elisabeth, dismissed this. She would be hurt, disappointed. Better that he keep silent.

In the weeks ahead Elisabeth was sympathetic to David's distress that Lila seemed incapable of improving her performance. She knew he worried about the survival of the company – its prospects shaky from the beginning. As Roger's assistant, David was aware that the receipts each week just managed to cover their expenses. One or two bad weeks and they'd be in serious straits.

She realized, too, that her letters home were not altering her father's attitude towards her marriage. Still there was no response. Mama would be afraid to tell Papa about her letters, or to reply. But Elisabeth would continue to write every few weeks. She couldn't believe that Mama and Grandma – and the boys – weren't happy to hear from her.

She encouraged David to attend the Sunday morning meetings of a group in Melbourne that was opposed to those who cried out for a 'White Australia'.

'Come with me to the meeting tomorrow,' David coaxed as she sat down with him for a post-theater supper on a Saturday night in September.

'Looking like a circus tent?' Elisabeth giggled. 'Pregnant ladies are supposed to go into hiding. As though it's shameful to be carrying a baby!'

'I don't have to go to the meeting –'

'Yes, you do,' she insisted. 'I can't believe what I'm reading in the newspapers! "We must preserve Australia for the white man,"' she mimicked. 'All this talk about Australia being the last chance for the white race, and that we must save Australia from becoming "a mongrel nation torn with racial dissension".'

'A lot of people in Queensland don't support this,' David acknowledged. 'They know their sugar plantations would be in jeopardy without African-Australian workers. Other Australians don't want those jobs. I just wish I had more time for the group. But yes, Beth, we have to fight such intolerance.'

Elisabeth paused, her mind darting to another worrisome subject. 'How's the situation with Lila?' She knew David tried to be calm, but that he was troubled by the hostility Lila created in the company.

'Ethel and John just manage to be civil. Henry ignores her except onstage. Gil's too wrapped up in himself to care about anybody.' David shrugged. 'Roger blames her for the way our audiences have been falling off – though he doesn't say that to her in so many words.'

'But if looks could kill, she'd be dead.' Elisabeth reached for Roger's favored cliché.

'So far we're hanging on.' David tried to be cheerful, 'though Roger says Ainsley's on his back about signing up for another year.'

'Will that happen?' She was startled – unnerved – by this possibility. They'd come here with the prospect of staying one year. She cherished a vision of returning to London with David and the baby, writing to Mama that she was there – and being welcomed back into the family. Her heart pounded each time she imagined this.

'Would you be unhappy if we stayed on in Melbourne?'

'No.' She contrived a dazzling smile. 'I love being here.'

The final weeks of Elisabeth's pregnancy seemed endless – as Ethel had warned her: 'My two sisters had seven little ones between them – and those last two months you couldn't talk to them.' But she was pleased at the way David was becoming involved with his group that – like several others – was fighting the 'White Australia' campaign. On several occasions group meetings were held in their tiny bungalow. The others looked up to David as their leader, Elisabeth saw with pride. Hadn't she always told him he would some day be important in government? There was no doubt in her mind that this would happen.

She liked Dr O'Casey, who was to deliver the baby. He was a burly, fifty-ish Irishman who'd been trained in Dublin but had come to Melbourne during his second year of practice and was devoted to the place: 'You're lucky your baby's being born in Melbourne, one of the finest cities in the world.' But the closer she moved to the delivery date the more often Elisabeth lay sleepless far into the night. She was to give birth so far from home and family. Without Mama and Grandma beside her.

The baby was to be named Amy if a girl and Aaron if a boy, she'd decided – with David's approval. 'Aaron for my grandfather on Mama's side. Grandma will be pleased.'

Was Papa seeing to it that her letters were destroyed before Mama and Grandma received them? At unwary moments this fear tormented her, although he left for work before the post arrived. When the baby was born, she would send a photograph to Mama and Grandma. Always she harbored the hope that seeing this first grandchild would dissolve Papa's rage at her.

On a dreary, unseasonably cold evening in early December – while David was still at the theater – Elisabeth felt her first labor pain. She sat motionless, focusing on this indication that the baby would soon enter the world. Dr O'Casey had warned that a first baby could be long in coming, yet her eyes sought out the clock. David would be home in another thirty minutes or so. She wanted him here with her.

She waited until he'd eaten the supper she'd prepared for him to tell him she was in labor.

'I'll go for Dr O'Casey!' His face drained of color, David leaped to his feet.

'He won't be needed for hours, David,' she soothed, then paused as a fresh – stronger – pain knotted her stomach.

'I'll go now!'

'No. Sit down, David.' She smiled as the pain ebbed away. 'Dr O'Casey's got other things to do than to sit here and hold your hand. I won't be needing him until the morning. Let the man get a decent night's sleep.'

'I'm scared.' David reached for her hand.

'A new role for both of us – but we're quick learners.' Her hand tightened on his. 'Maybe you should go over to Ethel's house in a little while and tell her. She wants to be with me.' Elisabeth managed the pixie smile he loved. 'And she'll bring John with her. Somebody has to look after you. But if he comes with cigars, tell him they're not to be lit in this house.'

At 7.12 a.m. – with Dr O'Casey hovering encouragingly above her bed and Ethel wiping perspiration from her face – Elisabeth fought the incredible pain that engulfed her, then with urgent determination thrust her baby into Dr O'Casey's waiting hands.

'It's a girl,' he said, moments later. 'Oh, and has she a pair of lungs!'

Elisabeth was enthralled with tiny Amy. They were a family now. Mother, father, and daughter.

'She looks just like you,' David said with wonder. 'Same eyes, same mouth, same nose –'

'She has your hair,' Elisabeth said. Amy was fair. 'Ethel said she's never seen a newborn baby with so much hair. I've even considered sending you to buy a hair ribbon!'

'I hate to leave you to go to the theater tonight.'

'I'll be all right. Mary Allen insisted she'll stay with me till you're home again.' Mary Allen was their next-door neighbor, with a brood of four teenagers and a latecomer aged three. 'You're not to worry about us, David.'

'Her hands are so tiny.' With awe David reached for one. 'I was afraid to hold her at first,' he confessed. 'But Dr O'Casey said she wasn't made of china, and dumped her into my arms.'

'She'll bring us good luck.' Elisabeth dropped a kiss atop the mass of feathery soft hair. 'You'll see.'

But later, with David at the theater and Mary Allen in the kitchen making her a pot of tea, Elisabeth felt a tidal wave of sadness. Mama and Papa, Grandma and the boys should be here – admiring Amy, predicting a wonderful future for her. Especially she yearned for Grandma. But Amy was bereft of grandmother and grandfather, great-grandmother and uncles.

She brushed aside the tears that filled her eyes, spilling over.

'Now, now, none of that,' Mary Allen scolded, coming into the room with the tea tray. 'It's always like this after the baby comes,' she comforted. 'Each time with my own I remember that –'

I will not brood, Elisabeth silently ordered herself. For David and Amy I mustn't pine for what is not to be. I'll wake up each morning and think about the good things in my life. I'll thank God for David and Amy.

But she knew she would never be able to banish the hope that one day she and David and Amy would be welcome in the house in Lexham Gardens.

Chapter Eight

Life seemed to be passing in a euphoric haze for Elisabeth – except for those treacherous moments when her mind crossed oceans to dwell on her family in Lexham Gardens. She fretted that Amy – so sweet and beautiful – was denied love that should be hers. Still, David was so loving, so tender with Amy, that their daughter must know she was precious to her parents. She wouldn't miss other family. Yet visions of Grandma holding Amy in her arms haunted Elisabeth. Mama, too – but especially Grandma. She imagined Ben at his sketch pad, offering endless sketches, then paintings of Amy. But each time she exhorted herself to remember Grandma's favorite saying: 'I wake up each morning and think about all the good things in my life.'

At intervals she brought Amy to rehearsals. Ethel and John, Henry, Roger, Amos – they were Amy's family, she told herself. And Mary Allen next door kept telling her if she wanted to go with David to the beach at St Kilda on a Sunday afternoon, Amy could stay with her own brood.

Elisabeth was proud, too, of the way David was giving so much of his free time to his small group fighting the 'White Australia' movement – though now he felt guilty at taking time away from Amy and herself.

'You're doing it for Amy and me,' she told him whenever he apologized for this. Fiercely proud of his efforts, she added, 'You're fighting for what we both believe in.'

It seemed depressingly clear that Parliament would enact a 'White Australia' policy to exclude Asians and Africans from residence in the country. This policy had widespread support. The only subject of dispute was the way to handle it. Sometimes Elisabeth worried that David's group – and others like it – would become the object of violence. Amos scoffed at this.

'My dear, they're such small groups they barely get their voices heard,' he soothed. 'Not that I don't agree with David,' he added conscientiously, 'but groups like his can't put down the fears of working-class people that they're going to lose their jobs to Asians and Africans. The others that are so uppity, well, it's not the time yet to change their thinking. My mother had a favorite saying – I think it's from the Bible: "To everything there is a season, and a time for every purpose under the heaven."'

'I like that.' The quotation was a soothing balm to Elisabeth. A time would come when she could go home again – with David and Amy.

'This is not yet the moment for people to learn to be tolerant of others,' Amos brought her back to the present, 'but that *will* come – because of those like David. One day Amy will be very proud of her father.'

After consultation with the company Roger had signed a lease on the theater for another year. Though Lila created much tension among the cast – and even with Roger – the company was building a steady following. Yet Elisabeth felt discomforted at being committed to another year so far from home.

Every Saturday morning Ethel came for 'my visit with my adopted granddaughter', always with some small gift for Amy. The two women sat for long moments in companionable, loving silence as they watched Amy kick up tiny feet while she played with the latest toy.

'Such a happy little girl,' Ethel crooned one sun-drenched Saturday morning.

'On Monday she'll be three months old.' Elisabeth dropped a kiss atop Amy's head. 'But it seems as though she's always been part of our lives.'

'We must have a birthday party!' Ethel effervesced.

'Ethel, for three months?'

'This is a very special little girl.' Ethel reached for one doll-like hand. 'Didn't you just tell me you suspect she has a first tooth coming through?' Now Ethel leaned forward to probe the tiny mouth. 'Yes! It's there! How many babies have their first tooth coming through at three months?'

'She was so fretful last night,' Elisabeth worried. 'She's usually so happy.'

'Poor little angel. So young and already to learn pain. But she'll have her birthday party,' Ethel decreed. 'I'll bake a cake. We won't bother inviting Gil or Lila – they wouldn't come anyway – but I'll tell the others.'

Early Monday afternoon – as prearranged – the invited guests assembled in Elisabeth and David's bedsitting room for cake and ice cream. Henry brought a bottle of wine.

'You know, I'm forty-seven years old,' Amos complained, 'and I've never had a birthday party.'

Amy murmured unintelligible but clearly delighted sounds as she was passed from one pair of affectionate arms to another.

'Where the hell is Roger?' Amos asked and broke off in apology. 'Amy, you didn't hear your Uncle Amos cursing.'

Ethel gazed out a front window. 'There he is, coming up the path now.

Roger strode into the room with an air of agitation.

'We decided we'd have to start without you,' John chided.

'We have a major problem.' But for a moment Roger abandoned his grim mood to hoist Amy into the air in the position that always elicited crows of delight.

'What's the problem, Roger?' David reached to take Amy into his arms.

'Lila,' Elisabeth surmised before Roger could reply. 'She's the usual problem.'

He nodded. 'This is worse than normal. She shoved a letter under my door about an hour ago. She thinks she's being real generous,' he drawled. 'She'll play three more performances before she sails for London.'

'Did someone die and leave her a million pounds?' Amos quipped, but he was as stunned as the others.

'I gather she pushed her folks into giving her money to "embark on a real career",' Roger mocked. Admittedly, job opportunities for women in Melbourne were limited. They could go into domestic service, be seamstresses or teachers. Only rare openings in the arts were available. 'She and Nellie Melba.'

Elisabeth remembered Amos's story of Melba's first concert in Australia since she'd become famous. Back in September 1902. 'She came home to sing for her own after years of entertaining all over Europe and England. Hours before she was to sing people were standing outside Town Hall – where she'd first sung, as an amateur at some fancy charity affair. The police came out to keep the traffic moving. And when Melba walked out on that stage, the audience went wild. At the end of her performance they kept demanding encores – and then she sat down at the piano and played and sang, "Home, Sweet Home". There wasn't a dry eye in the hall when she finished singing.'

All at once Elisabeth was conscious that troubled eyes were focused on her. How could they expect her to return to the cast when Amy was only three months old? Her heart pounded in anticipation of such a move, but her mind was realistic.

'I can't,' Elisabeth stammered. 'There's Amy –'

'Bring her with you to the theater,' Ethel said calmly. 'One of us can always be with her when you can't. She won't be the first to be raised in a backstage dressing room.'

'Mary Allen,' David suggested, 'she'll be pleased to earn extra money. When you're at the theater, Amy can be with Mary. I'm sure she'll agree. You know she adores Amy.'

'David, Amy's so tiny.' Elisabeth's mind was in chaos.

'She'll be fine with Mary,' David encouraged. 'How many times have you run next door to her for advice? She's had four of her own – she's warm and loving. You won't be depriving Amy of anything by being away from her for a few hours each day.'

Elisabeth was ambivalent. The company was in crisis. And she yearned to return to the theater. Was she being selfish? But without a quick replacement for Lila, the company would close. Everybody would be out of work, stranded here . . .

'I'll try it for two weeks,' Elisabeth stipulated and sensed the relief of the others. 'We'll have to see how Amy takes to being with Mary and her family. And I'll need lots of line rehearsals in the next three days.'

'You know all of Lila's roles,' David derided gently. 'And yes, you'll have plenty of line rehearsals. You'll be fine, Beth.'

But what about Amy? Would Amy be fine? Could she walk away from her precious baby for all those hours each day? If only Grandma were here!

Life fell into a new pattern, more comfortable with each passing day. Bless Mary, Elisabeth told herself each night. Mary was warm, loving

– and Amy accepted her own absence. Still, Elisabeth was attacked by recurrent bouts of guilt: was she a bad mother?

There were nights when she and David took turns pacing the floor with wailing Amy, as first teeth fought their way through aching gums. And over and over again, Elisabeth asked herself if it was wrong not to be there for Amy at every hour of the day and night.

Then the teething pains relented for a while. Elisabeth and David reveled as Amy learned – with crows of triumph – to sit upright in her pram. In the coming months Amy crawled joyously about their cottage, stood upright and took her first steps.

With the arrival of Amy's first birthday Elisabeth pondered with David over an unforeseen development that had arisen in their lives. A member of David's political group had come up with an enthusiastic and wealthy backer who was willing to finance a small office plus a modest salary for someone to work full time for the group.

'He's willing to put up funds to carry us for the next two years,' David explained, simultaneously elated and apprehensive. 'But only if *I* agree to take on the one salaried job.' David tried for humor. 'Can you imagine? He's got this weird idea that I'm the only one who can handle the job. But how can I walk out on Roger?'

'Give Roger three months to replace you,' Elisabeth advised. 'The backer will agree to that.' She was enthralled with the first indication of a political future for David. The day would come, she dreamed, when David would run for the Melbourne City Council. In ten years he'd be in the House of Representatives. 'Three months should be long enough for Roger to find someone,' she persuaded him. Yet she, too, shared David's sense of disloyalty.

'He can bring over an actor in that time,' David conceded. 'But what about someone who can handle the business side?' This was an important aspect of David's duties.

'Teach me.' Elisabeth reached out to this challenge, exhilarated by it. 'You do the box-office receipts and the budget. I was always good at mathematics. And if I run into problems, you'll be here to help me. David, we can do this!' Nothing must stand in David's way.

From unexpected quarters a replacement was found for David. Ethel's nephew in New York – who had completed a year on the road with a modest company – was anxious about finding another job. Months of sitting in producers' reception rooms had provided nothing.

'Cable Ralph,' Ethel urged. 'I know he'll be glad of the job. He's young and good-looking and he takes direction. Come on, Roger, give him a chance.'

'This nephew of Ethel's has to be fairly good,' David reasoned, in conference later with Roger and Elisabeth. 'The company kept him on for a full year. And if he needs coaching, I'll find time to help him.'

Cables were exchanged between Roger and Ethel's nephew, Ralph Wallace. In seven weeks he would arrive in Melbourne. David, Elisabeth thought tenderly, would straddle two worlds in those weeks. Already he was conferring with the political group's benefactor about their course of action for the coming months.

Elisabeth was proud that Australia had given women the right to vote, though frustrated that she had not yet reached the voting age. Grandma would be so pleased to know that women could vote here, she thought – remembering how her grandmother had followed the efforts of London suffragettes like Mrs Pankhurst and her daughters.

She'd abandoned her monthly letters soon after Amy was born. She would write twice each year – on Amy's birthday and on Rosh Hashanah, the Jewish New Year. Always, wistful hope lingered that she would receive a reply.

She relished her new duties with Roger. Now she felt herself truly a part of the theater, yet she felt that she shared David's world, too. She loathed the hostility towards Asians and Africans. With David she regularly visited the fine Chinese market, which always exuded a pleasing calm rather than the noisy clamor of some of the other ethnic groups' trading. They admired the good humor of the Chinese market gardeners, with their charming children. She recoiled from the oft-repeated complaints that Asian workers were 'too thrifty, too hardworking, and too provident'.

With the Parliamentary exclusion of Kanakas being brought into Queensland – where the sugar planters had been vociferously opposed to such a ruling – the price of sugar rose. Planters discovered white workers demanded far higher wages to labor in the arduous, tropical conditions of the sugar plantations. Now African-Australian seamen were being denied employment on coastal ships.

She and David were relieved that Ethel's nephew Ralph was working out fairly well.

'He'll never be a star.' David was honest. 'But he's competent.'

At intervals through the past years, Elisabeth understood, famous performers such as Tyrone Power of the United States and Sarah Bernhardt from France had extended their world tours to include Melbourne. Roger's company was at the bottom rung of the established Melbourne theaters, but their audiences were growing – due, David proudly pointed out, to Elisabeth's presence in the company.

Despite Elisabeth's appearing with the company, Amy was thriving. Except for irregular bouts of homesickness for the family back in London, Elisabeth considered her life perfect. Both she and David were intensely involved in work that they loved. Amy was a bright, happy toddler.

Though Amy had not yet reached her second birthday – and Mary warned Elisabeth two would mean a trying time for a young mother – Amos talked about the fine school system in Melbourne.

'The schools here are just like those in London,' Amos boasted. 'They teach the same subjects. The children salute the Union Jack. They sing, "God Save the King".'

'Amy won't be going to school for a long time,' Elisabeth reminded with gentle laughter.

Would they still be here in Melbourne when Amy reached school age? David looked on the city as home now. Why else would he be spending so many hours working for what he thought was right for Melbourne? Here he had a chance to rise up in the world. It was a beautiful city. The people were friendly.

Put London out of my mind. Life is perfect now.

For Amy's second birthday – in early December 1905 – Elisabeth and David decided to take her to one of the 'luncheon rooms', a favorite among affluent tourists and locals intent on entertaining in the grand manner.

'Because,' Elisabeth explained to David in a sentimental mood, 'my earliest and fondest memories are of having lunch with my mother and grandmother in a fancy restaurant in London.'

'At the age of two?' David lifted an eyebrow in skepticism.

'Amy's precocious. And after all, she's the daughter of a man who may someday become Prime Minister of Australia.' With a start she realized she had given voice to a subconscious belief that Melbourne was, indeed, to be home.

'Don't set your hopes too high,' David warned humorously. 'I could be deported as an undesirable immigrant.'

'You can't be – you're British,' she pointed out and paused. 'Is there trouble brewing at the office?' Lately one of the local newspapers had been running editorials about 'the troublemakers who're fighting against a true White Australia'.

'Nothing special.' He shrugged, dismissing the editorials. 'We've had some hate mail in the last week. But we expect that.'

All at once Elisabeth felt herself encased in ice. 'What did the letters say?'

'The same mad things I gather the suffragettes in England still receive: you know, desist or else.'

'They could be dangerous.' How could David be so calm about this?

'A handful of insane people. What can they do?'

'I'm scared,' she whispered.

'That's ridiculous. In a way, this reaction is even encouraging,' he analyzed. 'It shows we're making some headway. They're worried about us.'

'So am I. David, I'd die if something awful happened to you.'

'No, you wouldn't,' he objected, reaching to pull Amy away from a precarious pyramid of building blocks. 'You'd have Amy to raise.'

'David, how can you talk like that?' Her voice was shrill.

'Darling, I was teasing. What happened to your sense of humor?'

'It got derailed by your hate mail.'

'Then put it back on track. We have a birthday luncheon to attend. Amy, you're about to visit your first restaurant. And remember to mind your manners.'

'David, she's only two. If she drops a fork, we'll forgive her.' Elisabeth sought to sound festive, but in a corner of her mind she tried to deal with a new anxiety.

The 'luncheon room' David had chosen was elegant and charming. For a painful moment Elisabeth's mind darted back to luncheons with her mother and grandmother at the High Holborn in London. Amy gazed avidly about the room, plied her parents with questions. A couple across the room gazed at their table and smiled.

'They're admiring Amy,' Elisabeth whispered fondly.

A moment later the woman left her table to cross to theirs.

'I know it's rude of me to intrude,' she apologized, 'but I just had to tell you how much I enjoy your performances at the Ainsley

Theater. My husband and I are always there each time you appear in a new play.'

'Thank you –' Elisabeth managed a startled smile. 'It's so very nice of you to tell me.'

David beamed. 'Your public, madam,' he teased when the woman returned to her own table. 'You're gaining recognition in this city.'

'It was sweet to hear.'

Grandma would be so excited if she knew. Grandma, too, had loved being part of the theater. Papa was wrong when he condemned actors and actresses. They provided pleasure for so many people. Elisabeth felt this across the footlights – but hearing someone say it lifted her into euphoria for a moment. People came to the theater and for a little while forgot their own troubles, their personal griefs. Along with the rest of the company she was making a contribution to the world.

By the time they were aboard the tram that would take them home, Amy was yawning. Minutes later her eyelids drooped.

'It's time for her nap.' David lifted her into his arms. With a contented sigh she rested her head against his chest while his arms held her close.

'She loved the restaurant,' Elisabeth said with satisfaction. 'And she was so good.'

Amy slept soundly, stirring as they arrived at the house.

'Roses,' she said, pointing to the riotous array of pink roses on the bush on the tiny front lawn – the air fragrant with their scent.

'I'll cut one and put it in water,' David promised. But already Amy was asleep again.

While Elisabeth removed Amy's shoes and put her down for her usual afternoon nap, David went outside with garden shears. This had been such a perfect day, Elisabeth told herself, her face luminous with love for her small daughter and her husband.

She was startled by the sound of a shot. Who would be hunting in this neighborhood? she thought with reproach. Children played in the streets. Then she stiffened in shock at the sound of screams outdoors. She identified Mary's voice, and raced to the door.

'The bastard got away on his bicycle!' a man yelled in rage.

Elisabeth darted out to see a small cluster of people gathered about the patch of grass before the house. And then she saw David lying on the ground – a single rose just beyond his outstretched hand. His head in a pool of blood.

'Oh my God!' She stumbled towards him, dropped to her knees beside him.

'He's gone, my poor baby,' Mary told her. 'I saw a man on a bicycle shoot him. It was murder!'

'No!' Dizzy with shock, Elisabeth refused to believe he was dead. How could that be? 'David! David, talk to me. Talk to me!'

Chapter Nine

Elisabeth moved about in a haze of unreality while those close to her herded her through the agonizing hours ahead. Mary took Amy to her own house, with Elisabeth darting next door to see her precious baby at reassuring intervals. Ethel and John remained at her side. Roger and Henry took charge of funeral arrangements.

How could this have happened? Elisabeth demanded, distraught and angry. How could God let this happen to someone so good? Papa would say: 'It's God's punishment for marrying out of your faith.' But she didn't believe that!

For a precious chunk of time she and David had had a perfect marriage. Too perfect to go on for ever. They had what few people on this earth ever experienced – three perfect years. For Amy's sake she must be strong. She must raise their child with love and security – as David would wish.

She remembered what she'd said to David when he'd admitted receiving hate mail: '*David, I'd die if something awful happened to you.*' And he'd said, '*No, you wouldn't. You'd have Amy to raise.*'

Roger told her that he would close the theater for one week in respect for David – and she knew this was a financial sacrifice.

'But after that you must pick up your life again,' Roger advised. 'You need to work. It's what David would expect of you.'

Roger didn't say it, but he understood there was little money in the bank account she'd nurtured with such pride. She'd been so touched that he – along with others in the company and David's political group – had helped her pay for David's burial. They were her new family. She realized, too, that she must manage on one salary now, learn to budget.

Ethel was confident she could do this. 'You have an old head in a young body. You'll be all right.'

Elisabeth dreaded the arrival of the new year. It seemed a tortuous reminder that she must go on with her life without David. At intervals Amy asked plaintively for 'Papa'. Struggling to keep her voice steady, Elisabeth told Amy, 'Papa had to go away to help some people.'

She remembered how Grandma had come to London with Mama after the death of her husband. Grandma raised Mama on her own. She would do the same for Amy.

Elisabeth ordered herself to face one day at a time. Roger was optimistic about the company's future in Melbourne. She alternately loved and loathed the city. It had been good to them, she reminded herself. David had adopted this as their home. They'd shared three beautiful years together here.

She wasn't prepared for the morning late in January when Ethel – pale and shaken – came to her with devastating news.

'Roger wants us to come to his house this afternoon,' she reported. 'Elisabeth, how can I tell you?' Ethel closed her eyes in anguish.

'Ethel, what's happened?' Elisabeth's heart began to pound.

'Just before dawn this morning –' Ethel paused for a moment, as though struggling to comprehend this new disaster – 'a fire broke out in the theater. There was a lot of damage. Roger wants to explain what lies ahead for us.'

They wouldn't be working. Elisabeth was cold with shock. How would she and Amy survive? How would the others survive? More than anyone else in the company she was familiar with Roger's limited finances. He couldn't pay salaries unless there were nightly box-office receipts.

'What time does he want to see us?' Elisabeth asked.

'Two o'clock. You'll come with John and me.'

'I'll ask Mary if I can leave Amy with her –' Elisabeth's mind was in chaos. What would happen to them now?

At a few minutes past two the whole company gathered in the sitting room of Roger's tiny cottage. He was pale, bleary-eyed.

'I had three hours' sleep last night,' he told them. 'At dawn some-one came to tell me the theater was burning.'

'Is it bad?' Henry asked, his voice unsteady.

'The damage is heavy,' Roger conceded.

'What about insurance?' Elisabeth probed.

'Ainsley says he's insured – but he's convinced it'll be at least four months before we can reopen.' His troubled eyes moved from one to the other. 'I'm on thin ice – I can't pay full salaries for all that time.

73

I'll sit down and figure out how much I can handle.' He managed a wry smile. 'Elisabeth, you're the company mathematician. You'll help me work out figures.'

'What about our touring around the country?' Elisabeth suggested. 'Sydney, perhaps.'

'I'll look into that right away,' Roger promised. 'I want us to stay together. We've got something good going here.'

'We can keep the plays in rehearsal.' Ralph was determined to be optimistic. 'Even start learning the new one.'

'I'll look immediately for engagements for us out of the city,' Roger said. 'At least, we know Ainsley will start renovations right away. He can't expect me to pay rent until we can play again.'

Roger made a frenzied effort to find outside bookings for the company, but first one week, then another passed with no results. Elisabeth worried that Roger's bank account would be empty before they could resume performances.

In a desperation he shared only with Elisabeth, Roger cabled a theatrical agent in San Francisco.

'I did some booking with him several years ago,' Roger confided. 'Let's see if he can come up with something to tide us over.'

'It'll take us five weeks just to get there.' Elisabeth was fearful.

'I'm asking for a four- to six-week engagement. That would fit in great with our schedule.'

A day later a cable arrived in response to Roger's. A company scheduled to come into San Francisco on 20 April had closed on the road. The agent needed a replacement. For the next two days cables flew back and forth.

'It's a deal,' Roger announced in triumph. 'They'll arrange for our transportation both ways. We'll sail for San Francisco the day after tomorrow. It'll be tight, but we'll make it on schedule.'

Elisabeth knew it would be painful to sail to San Francisco without David at her side. She would remember how sweet, how tender he was with her during the long weeks aboard the ship that took them from San Francisco to Melbourne. She'd remember how terrified she'd been as their ship sailed into Melbourne Harbor, and how David comforted her.

It was her fault David was dead. It was she who had urged that they sign up with Roger to go to Melbourne. If they'd stayed in London David would be alive.

As David had arranged on their trip to Melbourne over three years ago, the cast was provided on board ship with rehearsal space in return for entertainment for passengers at regular intervals.

Aside from the daily hours of rehearsal Elisabeth devoted herself to keeping Amy happy despite the confining situation of shipboard life. Every moment of every waking hour she was conscious of David's absence from her side. At sight of a spectacular sunset over the Pacific, her first instinct was to turn to him to share this with her.

During the last week on board rough seas slowed their progress. Elisabeth knew Roger was fearful that they'd arrive too late for their scheduled opening. She prayed this wouldn't happen.

Most passengers remained in their cabins these final days of the journey. The dining salon was all but deserted at meal times. Desperate to divert Amy, Elisabeth spent hours strolling about the deck with her small daughter – both miraculously escaping the seasickness that afflicted many passengers.

Then at last – at mid-morning of 17 April – the ship approached San Francisco Bay, shrouded in fog. Clutching Amy in her arms, Elisabeth stood at the deck. Her mind darted back to those moments when she had stood with David on the deck of the ship that was taking them away from San Francisco. Her fault that David was dead, she tormented herself again. Why hadn't they stayed in London?

At the dock the company was met by the agent who had arranged their engagement here in San Francisco. He was ebullient, relieved that their ship had arrived. The company would open its engagement tomorrow night.

'I have rooms reserved for you,' he reported. 'Not quite Palace Hotel style, but you'll find the rents are very low.' In recognition of the company's modest funds, Elisabeth approved, exchanging a pleased glance with Ethel.

'You've made sure the performances have been advertised?' Roger probed. 'And we'll have rehearsal time at the theater?'

The agent nodded. 'Ads are appearing in the *Examiner* and the *Call*. And you'll be able to hold rehearsals this evening and tomorrow morning.' He glanced about at the members of the company with an affable smile. 'You might want to hook it and see one of the plays in town or the opera. Caruso is singing at the Grand Opera House and –'

'We won't have time for that,' Roger interrupted. 'We need to rehearse, get the feel of the stage. First show us to our rooming house so we can leave our luggage.'

The agent was all at once uneasy. 'I wasn't able to book all of you in one rooming house. Not at the rents you suggested,' he told Roger defensively. 'But two of the houses are on the same block and the rooms for others – for the single men of the company – are across town in one house. They're all easily accessible to the theater. And I've arranged for transportation to the rooming houses by automobile. We have quite a few in the city now,' he added with pride.

'At least, we're traveling in style,' Ethel confided to Elisabeth as the two women and Amy were handed into a waiting automobile by John – he, too, impressed by this conveyance.

'It's a stylish city.' Elisabeth tried for a moment of humor.

'Mama, I'm hungry,' Amy complained, clinging to Elisabeth.

'We'll go out to lunch soon,' Ethel intervened before Elisabeth could reply. 'John and I will pick you up as soon as we drop off our luggage,' she told Elisabeth. Their first destination was Ethel and John's rooming house. The one where Elisabeth and Amy would stay was three doors away.

Now the four passengers in the car – which seemed at moments to be dubious about its ability to navigate the terrain – focused on the passing scenery. Soon they were driving into an area of warehouses, factories, seedy hotels and small rooming houses – all of clapboard.

'This isn't the San Francisco the tourists come to see,' Elisabeth frowned in distaste.

'Don't worry, love,' Ethel soothed. 'We'll only sleep here.'

Ten minutes later Elisabeth and Amy were ushered into the small, shabby bedroom that was to be their home for the next six weeks.

'I don't like it here,' Amy whispered, though they were alone now. 'When can we go home?'

'Soon, darling,' Elisabeth promised, lifting their suitcase to the bed. She, too, recoiled from their drab surroundings. 'Let me wash your face and hands so we'll be ready when Aunt Ethel and Uncle John come for us.' The bathroom was down the hall and shared by other roomers.

Shortly – with relief – Elisabeth heard Ethel and John in lively conversation on the stairs. She reached to open the door.

'I'm glad you're on the second floor,' Ethel greeted her. 'We practically climbed up to the sky to our room – on four narrow, dark, creaking flights of stairs.'

'Stop complaining, woman,' John scolded. 'Let's go out and get some lunch and see this fabulous city.' He hoisted Amy into his arms.

'I hope you're wearing comfortable shoes, Elisabeth.' Ethel glanced down at her own. 'We'll be doing a lot of walking in this town.'

After a satisfying lunch that restored Amy's usual high spirits, they sought out the theater.

'I saw in a local newspaper somebody left in our room that *The Dictator* was playing here.' John pointed to a theater. 'It closed a few days ago.'

'That's the company that's going to be in Melbourne in a few weeks,' Elisabeth recalled.

'Yes.' Ethel nodded. 'They've been touring all across this country. John Barrymore is with them.' She uttered a blissful sigh. 'He's so handsome.'

They arrived at the more modest theater where they were to appear to find posters in place advertising their opening performance. Inside they greeted the other members of the company with candid relief at rejoining their own. As pre-arranged, the stage setting was ready for their performances with only minor adjustments. Amy seated beside Roger, they began rehearsal.

Once on stage Elisabeth forced herself to thrust aside all anxieties, to concentrate on the character she was playing. Sometimes she felt guilt that she could separate herself this way from the grief that otherwise never quite left her. But David would expect this of her.

After rehearsal the group sought out a cheap restaurant for supper. They were all impressed by the splendor of San Francisco. Pausing before the Grand Opera House where Caruso was singing in *Carmen* tonight, Elisabeth found her thoughts hurtling back through the years to the awesome night when Papa and Mama had taken her and the boys, along with Grandma, to hear Caruso at Covent Garden.

When Amy's eyes began to droop, Elisabeth reluctantly decided it was time to return to their rooming house.

'I wish we were in the same place,' she admitted to Ethel and John when they lingered over good nights at the door.

'Do you want me to stay over with you this first night?' Ethel was solicitous. 'John won't mind.'

77

'Thanks for the thought.' Elisabeth managed a wisp of a smile. 'But Amy and I will be fine. We'll see you in the morning.'

In the bleak darkness of the night, Elisabeth lay on the limp mattress of the bed and tried to will herself to sleep, the only sound in the room the ticking of the clock she'd placed on the table beside the bed. Still, her efforts were futile. She mustn't stir, she cautioned herself, lest she awaken Amy. Exhausted and stiff from lack of motion, she at last drifted off into brief, troubled slumber.

She awoke, conscious of gray dawn that crept into the room through the shade. Amy lay sprawled on her stomach, fair hair spilled across her face. Elisabeth reached down to draw the washed-thin blanket about Amy's small, sleeping form. She squinted at the clock in the semi-darkness of the room. It was 5.12. Somewhere outside she heard the harsh panicky shrieks of a horse – probably a milkman making his rounds, she thought. Why was the horse carrying on like that?

Then an ominous rumble – a low, unearthly moaning – splintered the morning silence. An instant later some eerie force thrust her from bed to floor, Amy tumbling atop her. Terrified, dazed, she clutched at Amy, the room, the floor beneath them in some wild dance.

'Mama?' A thin terrified wail.

The shaking stopped but only for brief seconds. Again, the insane movement of space, the sound of masonry and glass crashing outside. Church bells began to ring. Elisabeth staggered to her feet, pulling Amy into her arms as a chunk of wall split wide – showing empty space where earlier a house had stood.

'Amy, we have to get out of here,' she gasped. Instinct told her the floors above them had been sheared off by this terrifying earthquake, and now lay somewhere below. 'Amy, hold on to me!'

With trembling hands – flinching at the wrenching sounds that filled the air – she dressed, dressed Amy. They must get out of here before the roof came tumbling down on them.

With Amy in her arms she staggered out of the room. Daylight poured into what had once been a dark, narrow hall and stairs. Down below two men were hurrying out the door.

'It's going to be all right,' Elisabeth whispered through colorless lips as she made her way down the stairs, Amy dazed and silent now.

Beneath a strangely green sky – with a sliver of moon on display – Elisabeth stared at the street, littered with debris, dark with people on the move, still too stricken to speak. Women in nightgowns, men in drawers. A man with shaving lather on his face. Children clinging to parents. A man beside Elisabeth and Amy pushed a wheelbarrow piled high with bedclothes, topped by a toddler tied down for security.

Fearful, Elisabeth walked on unsteady feet towards the house where Ethel and John were staying. She moaned at what met her eyes. All five floors lay in a heap of wood, plaster, glass and metal. Already a team of men were digging for survivors.

'No use looking here,' one man said quietly. 'Let's go where we can do some good.'

Elisabeth stood motionless before what only a few minutes ago had been a rooming house occupied by people. She remembered those few minutes last night before she'd said good night to Ethel and John. 'Do you want me to stay over with you this first night?' Ethel had asked, and she had said, 'Amy and I will be fine.' If Ethel had stayed with Amy and her, she'd be alive.

Was she cursed, Elisabeth asked herself in silent agony. Were all who loved her doomed to die?

Chapter Ten

Her mind numbed by the devastation on every side, Elisabeth walked without any real destination – Amy in her arms. Like those around her, she was dazed and disbelieving. Chunks of sidewalk rose into miniature walls, a hazard for the unwary. The ceaseless clanging of church bells became a kind of mockery. Clouds of dust arose from collapsed buildings, piles of plaster and brick and timber mute evidence of a city in devastation.

A man clutched a huge painting – all he was able to save, Elisabeth thought in a corner of her mind, and remembered she'd left the lodging house with nothing. A woman pushed a pram loaded with pots and pans.

Were the others in the company all right? How could she find them in this madness? They were in a lodging house across town somewhere. Had the whole city been hit this way?

Black smoke spiraled into the sky, flames shooting upward. In the distance fire sirens wailed. Elisabeth saw a man working to remove an injured woman from a pile of rubble, and her instinct was to rush to help, but someone else was already there. Her task, she told herself, was to find a safe place for her precious daughter, now mercifully asleep in her arms.

'They'll be setting up a camp at Union Square!' a man called out, and the stunned silence of the survivors gave way to loud, incredulous talk. How – *why* – had this happened to their beautiful city?

She must go to Union Square, Elisabeth decided. Now rescue teams were everywhere, so she felt less guilty at not helping. Amy was heavy in her arms. Her feet ached.

On Market Street – along with hundreds of others – Elizabeth was startled to see that almost every window in the landmark Palace Hotel had been shattered, though the structure still stood, seven stories high and three hundred feet square.

'La fanta mi salva
L'immondo ritrova –'

For a startled moment a magnificent male voice that could belong to only one tenor galvanized the attention of the crowd below.

At a window in the Palace Hotel stood Enrico Caruso, arms outstretched. Elisabeth remembered that last night he had appeared at the Opera House. How strange, she thought dizzily, to be standing before the Palace Hotel and listening to Caruso sing.

As unexpectedly as the singing had begun it ended. Somewhere in the crowd a woman sobbed. A man gave his jacket to an elderly woman clothed only in a flimsy nightgown. Most of those heading towards the square cast recurrent glances at the funnels of black smoke that rose into the sky. Could the fires be controlled?

Hordes came from every direction, in varying stages of undress. People spoke little, only in low, stunned tones. Elisabeth's eyes swept with desperate hope from face to face, praying that by some miracle she would discover that the others in the company were alive.

She paused in front of the St Francis Hotel. Who was that strangely familiar, handsome young man, dressed in full evening dress? Of course – John Barrymore. She recognized him from theater posters. He was talking with amazing calm to a portly woman – also calm – who sat atop a trunk and sipped from a wine glass.

Barrymore's eyes strayed, settled on Elisabeth. His smile was dazzling. 'You're an actress,' he intoned. 'With that beautiful face you must be.'

'Yes.' She managed an answering smile. 'From Melbourne.'

'I'm going there – if I can reach my ship.'

'I know. I was sorry not to be there to see you in *The Dictator.*'

'Jack!' his companion said imperiously. 'More wine, please.'

'Oh, yes –' He turned away to retrieve a bottle from beside the trunk, and Elisabeth moved on.

Amy in her arms, she crossed to Union Square. Exhausted, she sat on the grass along with hundreds of others. She heard someone remark that – despite what had happened – the restaurant in the St Francis Hotel was now serving breakfast. For a moment her instinct was to leave the square and go to the restaurant. The building must be safe if they were serving breakfast. But she had no money, she realized in shock. She'd left their lodging house without her

81

purse. All her worldly possessions remained in that room – by now undoubtedly consumed by the fires that had swept the area, and moved beyond.

'Mama –' Amy awoke. Her voice plaintive. 'I want my breakfast.'

'Darling, that'll have to wait,' Elisabeth soothed. Someone in the crowd about her had just said that rescue wagons with food would surely be arriving soon: 'The city won't let us starve.'

'I don't want to wait!' Amy's voice was simultaneously imperious and hurt. 'I'm hungry now.'

'Would she like a Hershey chocolate bar?' a melodious male voice – its accent unfamiliar – asked. Elisabeth turned to face a young man with unruly dark hair and probing eyes. 'I have a niece about her size, and she just loves the new Hershey bars.'

'Yes!' All at once Amy glowed. 'Give me!'

'Amy, say please,' Elisabeth scolded and turned to the friendly young man who radiated such warmth. 'And thank you –'

'Please, thank you.' Amy extended one hand. Her smile cherubic.

'It's very kind of you.' Elisabeth managed a wisp of a smile.

'My sister says the government ought to give Mr Hershey some kind of medal for making his chocolate bar.' He chuckled at Amy's delight as she ripped away the wrapping and munched eagerly. Elisabeth felt a sting of tears. She remembered Grandma surreptitiously supplying the boys and her with much-loved Fry's Chocolate Cream bars. Mama and Papa limited these to very special occasions. Papa insisted the children mustn't be spoiled.

'The fires seem to be merging.' Elisabeth was apprehensive. 'Before they were scattered about – a lot of small ones.'

'The Fire Department is out in full force. It'll take time, but they'll control it.'

'From your mouth to God's ear,' she said softly.

'This isn't the first time San Francisco has been hit by an earthquake, though none ever as awful as this. But the city knows how to cope. I'm Jerry Schiff,' he introduced himself. 'I've been here for only a week. I was debating about whether to head for Alaska or for Los Angeles. I know the gold strikes are far behind us, but Alaska sounds like a real adventure. But then down in Los Angeles there's this man who opened a moving picture theater. He calls it the Electric Theater.'

'What's a moving picture theater?'

'It shows moving pictures – like in life – on a screen. Thomas Edison – you know, the same man who invented the electric light and the phonograph – has patented a camera that can photograph *moving* pictures.' He nodded admiringly. 'Smart.'

'Oh, I'm Elisabeth Winston.' How rude of her to have asked questions instead of being polite. 'My daughter is Amy.'

'*Good* candy,' Amy approved, her smile edged in chocolate.

'Our timing was bad. We arrived yesterday morning.' It wasn't wrong to be talking this way with a stranger, Elisabeth thought defensively. All around them strangers were exchanging personal confidences as though each had known the other for years. 'From Melbourne,' she added. 'Australia.'

Jerry lifted one eyebrow. 'You're a long way from home. Tourists?'

'No. I came here with an acting troupe,' she explained. *Where were the others? Were they all right?* 'We were scheduled to open tonight –'

'You're an actress!' He seemed entranced by this discovery.

'My husband was an actor. He brought me into the company.' She paused. 'He was murdered last December because of his political beliefs.'

'How awful for you.' His eyes expressed his compassion. 'And for Amy. But you'll carry on,' he said with conviction.

'I must.' Her hand tightened at Amy's waist. But what would happen to them now?

'I spent the last year in New York.' Jerry's smile was tentative. 'I probably should have stayed there. I've got this habit of making impulsive moves. I wasn't quite sure how – but I wanted to be involved in theater.' An unexpected shyness seemed to invade him now. 'Not as an actor. I had some wild ideas about becoming a producer. I like bringing things together. But nobody was interested in a twenty-one-year-old with a head full of ideas but no real experience – just putting together amateur shows down in Glendale, Georgia.'

'Where is Georgia?' She was puzzled. 'I was born and raised in London – I don't know much about the United States.'

She listened while he talked about his home town, about his parents and sisters. He missed his family, she thought, observing his tenderness towards Amy. Yet he churned with a need for adventure.

'Here comes a wagon.' He rose to his feet, peering into the

distance. 'They're bringing coffee and rolls.' He repeated the news that was spreading through the square. 'I never thought I'd be so eager for a cup of coffee.'

He lifted Amy into his arms and helped Elisabeth to her feet. Together they joined the line that was forming. She didn't feel so desperately alone, Elisabeth realized, grateful for Jerry's presence. Somehow – though gas lines had been broken throughout the city – bakers had managed to provide rolls. Coffee had been prepared.

With coffee and rolls in hand, Jerry chose a spot for them to settle on the grass, pretending for Amy's benefit that they were having a picnic. He enthralled Amy with his fanciful story about Mr Hershey, who was going to build a whole town dedicated to making chocolates, and he talked about his niece in Glendale, Georgia, who would go nowhere without her blanket.

Slowly the morning passed. Rumors ricocheted through the square. Mayor Schmitz had issued a proclamation: saloons and liquor stores – those left standing – had been ordered closed. No liquor was to be consumed. Federal troops, pressed into rescue operations along with the police, had been issued authority to kill anybody caught looting. All gas and electricity had been cut off. And a curfew had been declared: there was to be no movement about the city after dark.

New arrivals in the square brought tales of amazing heroism on the part of the Fire Department members and the Federal troops. The hotels around Union Square were long emptied of guests. Explosions rent the air as firefighters dynamited buildings in the hope of controlling the fires. In the afternoon supper was cooked and served to the homeless – now numbering thousands. At the approach of dusk army tents were brought in and set up. Fortunate to receive one, Elisabeth and Amy prepared to spend the night in the tent allotted them. Jerry would sleep on the grass just outside their tent – providing them with a sense of protection.

In the middle of the night a tiny outcry told them that a pregnant woman they had noticed earlier, now in a tent a hundred yards away and tended by a young intern, had given birth. The night was unusually warm, Elisabeth decided – and shuddered when she realized the heat came from the ominously encroaching fires.

She slept with Amy in her arms, waking at frequent intervals with instant recall of their devastating situation. How fortunate that they had met Jerry Schiff this way. It was like finding a big brother. Amy adored him on sight, Elisabeth thought gratefully, though she conceded part of that derived from his gift of the chocolate bar.

By dawn Elisabeth abandoned efforts to sleep, but lay still lest she awaken Amy. By six o'clock most of those in the square were awake. Coffee was being prepared. Water was brought in via sprinkler wagons from outlying areas. All cooking was to be done outdoors. Emergency regulations had been issued for bakers to make bread to sell at no more than ten cents, and only five loaves to each customer. Many had fled their homes without funds.

Jerry reported he'd heard that those in Union Square were to be moved to Golden Gate Park and parts of the Presidio because the dozens of small fires of last night had joined together into a menacing inferno moving in their direction, as they could see.

'I didn't sleep much last night,' Jerry admitted. 'I kept trying to figure what our best move would be. Market Street is still open, a policeman just said. It's an escape route to the ferry. I don't know what kind of a wait we'll find there, but the ferry will get us over to Oakland and away from the fires.' Already – without waiting for the emergency food wagons to offer a modest breakfast – a few people were beginning to leave Union Square.

'I ran with Amy from our building without even my purse. Will the ferry take us without money?'

'I'm sure they will,' Jerry said gently. 'But you don't need to worry about that. I have money. I think we ought to get moving.'

Elisabeth and Jerry – with Amy riding on his shoulders – joined the stragglers heading for Market Street. Amy didn't understand what was happening, but Jerry was making this seem an adventure. They turned onto Market Street, the fires raging on either side intensifying their anxiety to reach the ferry.

It soon became clear that the word that Market Street was still open had circulated. Throngs coming down from the Mission Hills were joining what had been a meager exodus. There was little talk, the marchers focusing on reaching the ferry. Old women struggled to carry what little they had been able to salvage. Younger women clung to children, fretful from exhaustion. A middle-aged couple dragged an antique chest between them. People were determined to save objects that seemed dispensable in the circumstances. At intervals a wagon rolled along, imperiously ignoring the walkers.

'Jerry –' Elisabeth tugged at his sleeve, pointed to an elegantly dressed older woman leaning against a cluster of steamer trunks and sobbing in racking gasps.

Jerry walked to her side and leaned over solicitously. 'Can we help you?'

The woman made an effort to control her sobs. 'My maid went off and left me here. She said she'd be right back – but I should have known better. I saw her boyfriend just ahead – she went with him and left me here. She said she was taking me to the Ferry Building –'

'You can go there with us.' Elisabeth hesitated. 'But you won't be able to take your luggage.'

'I don't care about my luggage.' It was a plaintive wail. 'I don't care about Odette. We were supposed to take the train to New York today – that's why Odette had packed for me. But I didn't want to go to New York. I let Odette persuade me that I needed a change of scenery –' Now she gazed down at Amy, who was gazing raptly at her necklace. 'Such a pretty little girl. I never had children –' A break in her voice now.

'Pretty necklace.' Amy returned the smile.

'Then it's yours,' she said and reached to take it from her neck.

'Oh, you mustn't!' Elisabeth was distressed. She suspected it was valuable.

'Let her have it. It'll give me a moment of pleasure.' The woman dropped the necklace about Amy's neck. 'We're all going to die, aren't we?'

'No, we're not,' Jerry insisted, though the drama of their situation was obvious. 'We're going to walk to the ferry and head for Oakland.'

'My sister lives in Oakland –' She closed her eyes for a moment. 'We haven't spoken in years. I don't know what we fought about . . .'

'Then go to your sister's,' Elisabeth told her. 'She's probably worried sick about you – knowing what's happened here.'

'Do you think so?' She gazed from Elisabeth to Jerry, as though pleading for reassurance.

'Of course.' Elisabeth reached to take one jeweled hand in hers. 'She'll be so glad to see you.'

'How will I get there?' Terror gripped the woman again.

'You'll go with us to the Ferry Building. We'll cross to Oakland with you and help you reach your sister's.' Elisabeth looked up at Jerry for confirmation.

'I'm so tired –' The stranger was doubtful. 'And my luggage –'

'Take the small valise with you and leave the rest,' Jerry ordered. 'I'll carry it for you.'

'You remind me of my husband,' she told Jerry as he reached for the valise. 'He was forceful like you. He's been gone eleven years now.'

'Let's start walking.' Elisabeth strived for calm. 'Lean on me,' she encouraged. 'When you're too tired, we'll rest.' But she was inwardly alarmed by the fires that moved ever closer. When they'd left Union Square there had been a few stragglers. Now the exodus was huge.

Elisabeth breathed a sigh of relief when at last they arrived at the massive Ferry Building. It was standing – the waterfront had not been entirely destroyed. Here was their escape. But she was appalled when she saw the many thousands waiting to be taken across to safety.

They stood together at the edge of the traumatized mob, the roar of the burning city ever present, drowning out voices, an aura of panic simmering beneath the surface.

'Stay here,' Jerry ordered, his eyes searching the crowded pier. He transferred Amy to Elisabeth's arms. 'I'll be right back.'

'Where is he going?' The woman they'd befriended was anxious.

'To see if he can make a deal with a private boat,' Elisabeth surmised. Like Jerry, she saw boats other than the ferry were making the trip across the bay. 'With all these people waiting, it could be days before the public ferry can take us over.'

'We could starve!' The woman's voice was shrill.

'We won't starve,' Elisabeth soothed, her eyes following Jerry. Even while she prayed that Jerry would find an accommodating boatman, she felt guilt that they might be more fortunate than others. But wasn't life always like that? Jerry had funds and a sharp mind.

At the water's edge, she saw Jerry in conversation with a man whose boat had just come ashore. Then Jerry was making his way back to them.

'Some of the boatmen are vultures,' he said, his face taut with contempt. 'They're making crazy deals. This man I was talking with is willing to take us over, but he wants a fortune.'

'I have money.' Their companion thrust her purse at Jerry. 'Take whatever you need to get us to Oakland. I have over a thousand dollars in large bills.'

'We won't need that much.' He held a hand aloft in a signal to the waiting boatman.

At her insistence Jerry took the funds that would give them all immediate passage to Oakland. He handed back the purse, picked up the older lady's valise while Elisabeth reached for Amy again.

'Let's go,' Jerry ordered.

The only other passengers aboard the launch were a family of five affluent Chinese. The owner didn't wait to take on others – which disconcerted Elisabeth. The Chinese woman sobbed in the course of the journey across the bay while her children talked in low shocked tones – about the devastation of Chinatown. Her husband appeared to be in silent prayer.

With remarkable speed they arrived in Oakland, to find refugees wandering aimlessly about the streets. Elisabeth saw that relief teams were already in action.

'Where does your sister live?' Jerry asked their companion.

Haltingly the woman told him. 'You saved my life,' she whispered and reached to open her purse.

'No.' Jerry forestalled any financial offer. 'You've paid for our transportation.'

'Then take my two tickets to New York City and redeem them,' she insisted. 'I don't even want to see them!' She shuddered in recall. 'I was insane to let Odette persuade me to go there.' She thrust the tickets into Jerry's hands and reached for her small valise. 'Elisabeth, you take this. It's a change of clothing. A bit large for you,' she said apologetically, 'but it may be useful.'

'Thank you.' All at once Elisabeth was conscious of her grass-stained dress, her rumpled jacket. All she had in this world.

'Now, if you can help me get to my sister's house, I'll be fine.'

With one decisive gesture Jerry commandeered a car that bore a sign indicating it was serving as a cab. In the midst of disaster, Elisabeth thought, many were profiteering.

'Bless you all.' The older woman kissed Elisabeth, then Amy. 'God sent you to me.' She reached up to embrace Jerry, then allowed him to help her into the cab.

The other three watched while the car proceeded towards its destination.

But where are Amy and I to go? Elisabeth asked herself. Thank God, they were safe from the fires – but what lay ahead for them?

'These are tickets for passage on the most luxurious railroad line crossing the continent!' Jerry said in amazement. 'Beth –' she started at the sound of David's pet name for her – 'let's use the tickets to take us to New York. You're an actress. I'll be your personal manager. Together we'll storm Broadway.' His voice was electric. 'I'm bringing to New York the young and beautiful toast of Australia,' he plotted.

'But I wasn't "the toast of Australia",' she pointed out. Wherever had he acquired such an idea? 'I was creating a following in Melbourne – in a very modest company.' Was she the sole survivor of that company? Would she ever know?

'So we'll lie a little. We're both young and ambitious. You're beautiful and talented. Together we're an unbeatable partnership. The earthquake was the miracle that brought us together. It was fate.'

Elisabeth was mesmerized, visualizing him spinning magical words to famous Broadway producers. Then reality smacked her across the face. They were two nobodies – how could they carry out what Jerry plotted?

'I don't know –' How could she chase across America with Amy? Her mind was in turmoil.

'We have round-trip tickets. If you don't like New York, you can come back here.'

'Jerry, you have such gradiose ideas,' she stammered. 'You've never seen me on stage. How do you know you can find roles for me in New York theater?'

'Because I look at you and I see something very special. I know that you light up a stage. That's a gift – it's not something that can be taught.'

'I want to believe you,' she whispered, 'but I'm frightened –'

'Do you want to go back to Melbourne?'

'No.' What was there in Melbourne for her now?

'Then we're going to New York.' Jerry's face was luminous. 'I'll make you the toast of Broadway!' He inspected the tickets, pulled out his pocket watch. 'We've got exactly one hour and twelve minutes to make the train.' His eyes dared her to reject this challenge.

For Amy she must rebuild her life, her mind ordered. Jerry could help her do that.

'Then let's ask directions to the station!' Her voice was electric. 'We mustn't miss our train!'

Chapter Eleven

Elisabeth was awed by the splendor of the luxury train that was to carry them eastward. Elegant wood panelling was polished to mirror sheen. Upholstery echoed that offered in the finest houses. She gazed about the drawing room she was to share with Amy with a sense of disbelief. They'd traveled from the devastation of San Francisco into accommodations that were almost royal in opulence.

'It's like a fairy tale.' Jerry chuckled as Amy bounced with delight on the brocade-upholstered sofa that by night would become a bed. 'Even Odette would have been traveling in style.' They'd paused briefly in his compartment, then walked down the aisle to Elisabeth and Amy's drawing room, which by night would provide two spacious beds – each with a reading lamp.

'My father always insisted we travel first class at home,' Elisabeth admitted, 'but something like this would have been reserved for the royal family.'

'Mama,' Amy said, all at once shy.

'What, darling?'

Amy stood up on the sofa, reached to whisper into her mother's ear. 'I have to make a pee-pee.'

'Jerry, excuse us for a moment.' She lifted Amy into her arms and pulled open the door that led to their personal facilities.

'No bathtub,' Amy pointed out as Elisabeth decorously closed the door.

'If you want a bath,' Jerry called after them, 'there's a full bathroom on board. Along with a barbershop – which I need badly.' He massaged an unshaven jaw. 'Plus there's a smoking room, a library car, and an observation car. And there's a maid and a valet on board,' he continued as Elisabeth and Amy emerged, 'to help with any small emergencies like a button that needs to be sewn on. And a shorthand writer and a typist for businessmen.'

'How do you know all this?' In a rare light moment Elisabeth lifted an eyebrow.

'I read it on a leaflet left in my compartment. And of course,' he said with a bow to Amy, 'there's a dining car where we'll have supper later.'

'I think it's time Amy had a nap.' Jerry was right, Elisabeth thought. For now – aboard this masterpiece of a train – they were living in a fairy tale.

'We could all use a nap.' Jerry's smile was compassionate. 'I'll come and wake you in time for supper.'

In moments Amy was asleep on one sofa. Elisabeth lay on the other, but sleep was elusive. The trip from New York to San Francisco with David infiltrated her mind. He'd been so sweet and solicitous, knowing how devastated she was at Papa's pronouncement. There had been moments after his death when she'd wished that God would take her, too – but she knew this was wrong. For Amy she must be strong, build a new life. That's what David would expect of her.

Tears – still quick to spring into being – filled her eyes as she recalled the moments when she'd held Amy in her arms for the first time. Again, she heard David's words: 'This is the most beautiful event of our lives – more beautiful than anything that can ever happen to us. We've created a daughter.'

Restless, she sat up and reached for the valise that lay at her feet, conscious that her clothes were hardly suitable for dining in such luxurious surroundings. But people aboard must know about the earthquake and the fires. The whole world must know.

She opened the valise and discovered a lilac silk dress – cut in the new Empire style, with the high waist flattering to the young and willowy – packed so carefully by Odette that hardly a wrinkle showed as she lifted it from its resting place. She held the dress against her body. If she could take in the sides, it would fit her. The maid Jerry talked about, her mind pinpointed. She would ring for the maid and ask for a needle and thread.

But first feminine curiosity demanded she check further the contents of the valise. She brought out a grey silk, pleated shirtwaist, then a flared skirt and matching jacket. The skirt was too short, she noted with regret – but perhaps in New York she could add a ruffle at the bottom. She admired the exquisite silk petticoat and a delicate cotton nightgown that lay together. At the bottom of the valise was a beaver jacket. Oh yes, their benefactor had been a woman of much means.

Her hands trembling, she reached for the bell that would summon the maid. In minutes a smiling middle-aged woman arrived. Haltingly Elisabeth explained their situation, and the maid radiated sympathy.

'I'll bring a needle and thread. The dress is only a little too big,' she decided. 'I can do the seams in twenty minutes. You'll be able to wear it to the dining car.'

'The skirt is too short.' Elisabeth held it against herself and sighed.

'Oh, madam, no,' the maid contradicted. 'It's the fashion this year. I read about it in the newspapers. The idea is to show off pretty shoes.' Now her appraising eyes settled on Amy, still asleep. 'And there's curtain material that I can use to make a dress for the little one,' she said tenderly. 'Such a terrible experience you've been through! But it's all behind you now.'

Over supper in the dining car – the tables beautifully set, ferns on display – Jerry confided that he was impressed by the passengers aboard. They themselves were the only refugees from the San Francisco earthquake.

'I met a few passengers in the smoking room, which looks like a lounge in a fancy men's club. All wealthy important businessmen.' He reflected a moment. 'I've been invited to join a poker game tonight.' Elisabeth's eyes widened in alarm. 'I won't gamble away our nest egg,' he soothed. 'I want you to hold money for me – and don't give it to me if I come knocking at your drawing room later. Remind me I told you to hang on to it.'

'All right . . .' But she was uneasy.

'You'll be holding on to enough to see us through our first month in New York City. We won't be staying at the Waldorf – that'll come later. I know I'll have you booked in a play within a month. Maybe not as a star – but you'll be on the way.'

'Jerry, you've never even seen me act,' she said with recurrent doubts.

'You told me you did well in Melbourne, and you're beautiful. That's a great asset in the theater. You won't be a showgirl. You're not a candidate for the Floradora Sextette.'

'What's that?'

'The Floradora Sextette – and at regular intervals, I understand, they're replaced – are six of the most gorgeous showgirls in New York, who're in *Floradora*. That's a popular musical. They don't *do* much,' he conceded, 'but the audience go wild the minute they come onstage. No,' he said firmly, 'you won't be a Floradora Sextette replacement. You'll be competition for the likes of Ethel Barrymore. She's exquisite *and* she can act.'

'I saw her in London in *Peter the Great*, with Sir Henry Irving.' For a moment home seemed so close.

'I saw her back in New York in *A Doll's House*,' Jerry recalled.

'I played Nora in Melbourne.' Elisabeth's face brightened. 'I love Ibsen. But ours was such a modest company. We played in a tiny theater.' And now the company – except for her – was gone.

'Melbourne's twelve thousand miles away. Who'll know it wasn't one of the major companies? We'll take a tip from Barnum, the greatest showman of all time: "After much persuasion I persuaded the toast of Australia to come to New York." I'll –'

'Mama,' Amy interrupted plaintively, 'you said I could have ice cream if I was a good girl.'

At anguished moments – as the train sped through wide expanses of open Western land – Elisabeth remembered the amazement she had shared with David at the vastness of America. She'd shared every thought, every question with him since the day they were married. But she must learn to face the world alone. As Grandma did when she was widowed. And every day Elisabeth thanked God for Jerry's presence in her life – a warm, solicitous brother to replace Ben and Felix.

Often she thought about her family back in London. She had not written to Mama and Grandma about David's death – as though this would deny the truth – but she had explained that the company was going to San Francisco, in California, to play an engagement. As though, she mocked herself, they might, after all this time, be writing her.

The train arrived in Chicago. They changed to the new Twentieth Century Limited, which would carry them to New York City – only eighteen hours distant. The prospect was simultaneously exciting and intimidating. Jerry kept telling her they would 'take New York by storm'. During the three days and nights of the San Francisco–Chicago stage of their trip, he'd spent each day with Elisabeth and

Amy in their drawing room. But evenings, he went to the smoking room to play poker with several male passengers, seeking to push away the monotonous hours of travel.

Not until they were aboard the Twentieth Century Limited did Jerry confide that his winnings from these games were high.

'You hold this with what I gave you before,' he ordered Elisabeth, and presented her with an impressive roll of bills. 'And don't you let me have any of it if I find a game aboard. That's our stake for New York.'

'I won't let you have one cent,' she promised, a hint of laughter lighting her face. 'And wouldn't you be out of luck, Mr Schiff, if Amy and I decided to run off and leave you?'

'You're not the type,' he drawled. 'I'm not scared.'

'Oh, you make me sound so dull!'

'Don't you ever believe that,' he said with an intensity that startled her. 'I picked up some of the Chicago papers in the station.' His mood was ebullient again. 'Wow, is the earthquake getting heavy coverage! It'll be written up in history.'

He handed Elisabeth one newspaper, and both settled down to read. Amy was already half asleep.

'They're still dynamiting in San Francisco,' he said, grimacing. 'The fires are out, but badly damaged buildings have to come down.'

'The Southern Pacific is moving people away without charge,' Elisabeth noted in relief. She was still haunted by guilt that she, Amy and Jerry had been able to escape when so many thousands were left waiting at the pier. 'The paper says, "Every boat, every ocean-going steamer, every train and even wagons are moving people from the disaster area."' But what about the others in the company? she wondered. Had they escaped?

'That's behind us,' Jerry was firm. 'We don't look back – we look ahead. This is a new century.'

'As I kept telling my mother when she insisted I wasn't to go to university.'

'I dropped out of college at the end of my first year.' All at once Jerry was somber. 'My folks weren't happy about that. I'm the youngest – and the only boy. But my two sisters got their degrees.'

Elisabeth was astonished. 'Jerry, why didn't you go on with your education?'

'I stayed that first year – restless all the time. I knew it wasn't for me. I crave excitement. Adventure. I wasn't going to find that in a small college town in Georgia.'

'I was desperate for a proper education, but my father wouldn't hear of it. Because I was a girl.' The old rage surfaced for a moment. 'My brother Felix will be a doctor and Ben a lawyer – but I could be nothing.'

'To me college was a prison. I wanted to soar. Of course,' he mocked himself, 'I haven't done much soaring. My oldest sister said, "If you want to soar, go up in a balloon." None of them understood what I was trying to say.'

'You've had adventures.' A wry tone in her voice now. 'I think the earthquake would qualify as that.'

'I've had this weird feeling ever since I saw my first nickelodeon five months ago that I was watching the birth of a fascinating new industry. That I wanted to be part of it –'

Elisabeth was puzzled. 'Nickelodeon?'

'I guess it hasn't reached Melbourne yet.' Jerry grinned. 'For five cents – a nickel – in some cities in this country people go into a store, sit in an uncomfortable chair, and for twenty minutes watch the "flickers" and listen to piano music.' He chuckled at her raised eyebrow. 'Motion pictures,' he explained. 'They're called "flickers", I suppose, because in the beginning the images on the screen flickered so that some people got headaches from watching. But now they're better. The first one I saw was called *The Great Train Robbery*. I'll take any bet that one day they'll be even bigger than stage plays. But that's a long way off. I'm interested in *now*.'

'I've never seen a nickelodeon.'

'You'll see one in New York,' he soothed. 'More companies are starting up every day to make motion pictures because people love them. Where else can you – for five cents – sit back and forget your troubles for twenty minutes or maybe even longer?'

Doubts tugged at Elisabeth. 'You just see figures moving on a screen?' she asked skeptically. 'How do you know what's happening, what they're saying?'

'It's written out below. Hey, movies may do more than anything else to make people learn to read.'

In these final hours of their journey across the continent Jerry talked non-stop about the New York theater.

'God, it's exciting, Beth! There you have the finest talents in the world. When I left, less than two weeks ago, Maude Adams was starring in *Peter Pan* at the Empire. Sarah Bernhardt – admittedly getting on in years but still wonderful – was appearing in *Camille*. Alla Nazimova – she's Russian, you know – was playing in *Hedda Gabler*. In English.'

'Did you see them?' Elisabeth was starry-eyed.

'Only Bernhardt,' he admitted, 'so I could write home and tell my sisters I'd seen her. But I did see Langdon Mitchell's *The New York Idea* with Mrs Minnie Maddern Fiske. It's about an off-again, on-again couple and the divorce court. That's the kind of play I'd love to produce. Very modern.'

Jerry admitted he'd tried for jobs as stage manager, prop man – anything that would give entrée into a theater – without success. He talked about the famous theatrical producers – Charles Frohman, David Belasco, Florenz Ziegfeld. 'Ziegfeld brought Anna Held over from Paris and London and –'

'Who are Ziegfeld and Anna Held?' She knew about Frohman and Belasco.

'Florenz Ziegfeld is this young producer – well, not that young,' he conceded, 'he's about fifteen years older than me, but everybody in theater considers that young for a producer. Anna Held was the toast of Paris music halls. You remind me of her – small, slender, exquisite features. He brought her over here – and ditto.' He paused. 'They've been married for several years.'

'But she's a music-hall performer,' Elisabeth pointed out. 'I can't sing a note.'

'But we'll use the same kind of advertising. It'll work just as well for a dramatic actress.' Jerry exuded enthusiasm. 'Ziegfeld spread the story that Held took a bath every day in a tub filled with milk. The public was fascinated. There's always some wild story about her now.' He squinted in thought. 'I gave up too fast on theater. I wanted to become the boy wonder of theater – but I knew I needed something besides my big ideas. Sitting there in Union Square Park I looked at you and saw my passport to Broadway. Ziegfeld has his Anna Held. I have Beth Winston.' He chuckled at her startled reaction. 'Beth is shorter – better for lights on a Broadway theater. Start thinking of yourself as Beth Winston,' he commanded. 'The rising new star from Australia.'

'I'll work on it.' She managed a shaky smile. Why not Beth Winston? It would be a kind of memorial for David, using his pet name for her, endowed with such love.

It amazed Elisabeth that Jerry knew little about the fine earlier playwrights. She had spent delicious hours at the Melbourne Library, devouring playwrights David had urged her to read.

'Oh, I know Ibsen and Shaw,' he said defensively. 'God, there are half a dozen plays by Shaw on Broadway this season.' He grinned, sheepish now. 'I saw *Mlle Modiste* and *Forty-Five Minutes from Broadway*. And *The Lion and the Mouse* by Charles Klein. Everybody says it was about John D. Rockefeller Sr, though, of course, it had to be disguised.' He sighed in good-humored self-mockery. 'I guess my tastes are not exactly lofty.'

'Jerry, you should know fine theater as well as what's popular,' she chided with such earnestness he laughed.

'What's popular today might be tomorrow's classics,' he teased. 'But I promise you, we'll go to the theater one of these days real soon. We won't be sitting in the boxes – we'll be climbing heavenward to the cheap seats, at least, that is, until producers begin to recognize my star,' he said with a flourish.

Would it be that way? If not, then perhaps she could be a waitress at a tea shop – or an assistant in a department store. But what about Amy? Here she'd have no Mary Allen to look after Amy while she worked.

But Jerry made it clear they were a partnership. While she rehearsed or was in performance, he'd take care of Amy – until the day came they could afford the best of nursemaids.

The last hours of the journey sped past. Elisabeth's heart was pounding when the Twentieth Century Limited arrived at Grand Central Station. She harbored poignant memories of boarding a train here with David at her side. They'd traveled to Melbourne with such hopes in their hearts. But what they'd had was too beautiful to last, she told herself yet again.

She was astonished by the ceremony that accompanied the arrival of the train in New York City. A special red carpet was unrolled along the platform. This had happened in Chicago when they came aboard, but she and Jerry had supposed it was in honor of some famous personage.

'They're paying homage to the pocketbooks of the passengers,' Jerry whispered.

'Do you suppose we ought to walk *alongside* the carpeting?' For a few moments she shared his amusement.

Unlike the other passengers, they left the train with only the one valise that held Elisabeth's meager new wardrobe. Elisabeth wore the elegant gray suit – faintly self-conscious at the brevity of the skirt. A sympathetic valet had pressed Jerry's suit and polished his shoes. Amy was charmed by the dress and cape the maid had made for her in record time.

Porters gathered together clusters of expensive steamer trunks and fine leather valises. A festive aura permeated the atmosphere. Elisabeth reached for one of Amy's hands and Jerry took the other as they walked up the platform to the main section of the huge railroad station.

'We'll go straight ahead and out on 42nd Street,' Jerry said. 'With any luck at all we'll be able to find rooms at my old rooming house on West 26th Street. As I warned you, it won't be the Waldorf-Astoria – but it'll be cheap and convenient.'

They walked out of Grand Central Station onto bustling East 42nd Street, delightfully warm this late April day. Subconsciously Elisabeth tightened her hold on Amy's tiny hand. People walked past with such haste, she thought in distaste – oblivious to others. This wasn't Melbourne, which seemed to welcome every stranger. Her eyes soared upward to inspect the intimidating skyscrapers.

'One day people will stop and stare at Beth Winston,' Jerry predicted extravagantly. 'The way they did when Lily Langtry appeared in public in New York. We're young and ambitious,' he exulted. 'Nothing can stop us!'

But Elisabeth understood now that Jerry's pronouncements were meant to bolster his own confidence. New York was a frightening place. Was he right? Was she good enough to win a place in the heady reaches of the New York theater?

She had a child to raise. She couldn't afford to fail.

Chapter Twelve

A blinding fog closed in about London's Lexham Gardens, seeming to isolate each house within the area from all others. Mindful of her daughter's exhortation not to go out for her customary walk under such conditions, Rae Kahn wandered restlessly about the house. She opened the front door with a meager hope that in the last few moments the fog had lifted, only to gaze out into an opaque wall, close the door.

Heading upstairs again she paused before the console table in the hall where the morning's *Times* lay neatly folded. Normally it would lay untouched until Simon Woolf arrived home – either for afternoon tea or dinner. But her eyes strayed to the headline of the newspaper. She froze in shock as she read it. A catastrophe earthquake, followed by devastating fires, had leveled much of San Francisco with '*MUCH LOSS OF LIVES*'.

Elisabeth had said in her last letter that she was sailing for San Francisco! When was it dated? Rae struggled to deal with the logistics of time. Were Elisabeth and Amy in San Francisco when the earthquake struck? Or were they still aboard ship?

Ignoring the unspoken rule that the *Times* remained on the console table until the master of the house removed it to read, Rae reached with trembling fingers for the newspaper, hurried upstairs to the privacy of her bedroom, her heart pounding in alarm. The final sentence in Elisabeth's letter charged across her mind. 'We'll be leaving for San Francisco tomorrow. It's a long trip – almost five weeks.'

Had Elisabeth and Amy arrived in San Francisco by the time of the earthquake? Were they alive? Unhurt? Cold and trembling she rose from her chair. London *Times* in tow, she left her bedroom to seek out her daughter.

Celia Woolf was in the sitting room – engrossed in one of the risqué novels by Lady Duff Gordon's sister, Elinor Glyn, that she read surreptitiously and with delight.

'Celia, we must talk.' Rae tried to conceal her agitation.

'About what, Mama?' Celia discarded the Glyn novel and reached for the Liberty's silks catalogue that lay beside her on the sofa. 'Why are you so upset?'

'Read this –' Rae extended the morning's edition of the *Times*. 'How can we find out if Elisabeth was there?'

'Mama, you shouldn't disturb Simon's newspaper,' Celia scolded, but her face was drained of color as she read. 'Oh, dear God –' Her voice a tortured whisper. 'No, she was still en route,' she added with sudden strength. 'And take Simon's *Times* back to the table. He'll be upset if he comes home and it's not there.'

'Celia, we're talking about your child!' It was a strident admonition. Celia's eyes darted to the door in alarm lest the servants overhear. 'My grandchild and great-grandchild!'

'We can do nothing.' Celia struggled for calm. 'Simon must never know we read the letters Elisabeth sends. The servants mustn't know.'

'What kind of a man did you marry?' Rae exuded contempt. 'How can he keep up this farce?'

'To Simon our daughter is dead.' Celia was erecting a wall between herself and her mother. Rae fumed in silence. 'I have to accept his will.' She flinched before her mother's grunt of rage. 'Mama, if Simon discovered that we didn't destroy her letters unread – that we went against his wishes – he would throw us out of this house. I can't go back to fighting for survival in Whitechapel! I can't gamble on losing my sons!'

Rae felt herself drained of strength. 'I'll put the *Times* back on the table.'

Later – after Simon had read the newspaper – she would retrieve the back page before it was discarded with the rubbish. She would cut out the article about the San Francisco earthquake and paste it into the secret scrapbook that held the letters received from Elisabeth from time to time. And she would pray there would be another letter, that she would know that Elisabeth and Amy – the precious great-grandchild she'd never seen, never held in her arms – were alive and well.

Chapter Thirteen

Elisabeth and Jerry – with Amy in his arms – climbed the high stoop of the dilapidated brownstone that had been his home for a year. Smiling reassuringly at Elisabeth he rang the doorbell. Moments later they stood in the hallway of the rooming house on West 26th Street while he exchanged warm greetings with Maura O'Brien, his former landlady. He explained about having been caught in San Francisco at the time of the earthquake.

'Oh, bless the Lord you came out all right. It was a sign,' she said solemnly, 'that you should come back here instead of gallivanting around the world.' She gazed with friendly curiosity at Elisabeth and Amy, waiting for an introduction.

'Mrs O'Brien, this is my recently widowed sister and my niece,' he fabricated, and they saw the long-widowed landlady's instant sympathy. 'Beth and Amy Winston. They were with me in San Francisco.'

'Oh, the three of you were caught in that awful thing,' she clucked. 'And was the little one terrified out of her wits?'

'She was brave,' Elisabeth said. 'Thank goodness, my brother was with us.'

Mrs O'Brien seemed puzzled. 'Your brother has this sweet way of talking – like people from down South – but you talk different.'

'Beth's late husband was English – she went with him to live in London after their wedding. She picked up the British way of speaking.'

'It's lovely,' Mrs O'Brien approved.

'We need a room for Beth and Amy and one for me,' Jerry said. 'Can you put us up?' He managed his most charming smile.

Mrs O'Brien had two-tier rentals, he'd long ago discovered. While the poker games aboard the train had been a bonanza, he was familiar with the high cost of living in New York and anxious not to run up huge bills.

'I have a nice room for your sister and your niece – but there's only the hall bedroom that would be available for you.' Her eyes were apologetic. 'Somebody just moved out of that this morning.'

'Both rooms will be fine,' he said ebulliently, and reached for his wallet.

'I have a granddaughter just a little older than Amy,' Mrs O'Brien said gently to Elisabeth. 'I know she's a real comfort to you.'

'Oh yes –' Elisabeth reached for one of Amy's hands.

'I was wondering,' Jerry began, his mind rushing ahead to future needs, 'do you suppose – just in an emergency situation where Beth and I need to be away – that you could look after Amy for an hour or two? For a stipend, of course.'

'It'll be my pleasure,' Mrs O'Brien said. 'I do this at times for my roomers.'

After explaining to Beth about the kitchen privileges allowed to certain roomers – 'and I know I won't have to tell you I expect them to clean up after using the kitchen –' Mrs O'Brien showed them first to Beth and Amy's room.

'There's the double bed for the two of you,' she pointed out. 'And the bathroom is just down the hall. If somebody's being a hog, you just knock on the door and tell them to move along.'

Twenty minutes later – with dusk approaching – the three of them left the house and walked northward to find a place to eat. After a few blocks Jerry reached to pick up Amy.

'It's a haul for little legs.'

'Where exactly are we going?' Elisabeth was enthralled by the city.

'To a Childs to eat,' he explained. 'Every tourist has to eat at a Childs – of which there are several in the city – at least once. Later,' he promised, 'we'll dine at Martin's and Rector's. When we're rolling in hundred-dollar bills.'

Before walking into the nearest Childs – white-tiled floors and walls, tabletops of white marble, waitresses in white uniforms – they stood out on the sidewalk and watched at a window while a white-dressed chef flipped flapjacks with amazing agility.

'I'm hungry,' Amy announced, dismissing the show, and they went inside to dine on the restaurant's most famous item.

By the time they emerged from Childs night was approaching.

'I want to show you the Rialto,' Jerry said with an aura of anticipation. 'The first time you see it must be at night.' He laughed at her bewildered gaze. 'The Rialto is the theater district – the Great White Way.'

'Why at night?' Elisabeth demanded.

'You'll understand soon enough.' He was wallowing in the pleasure of being here again. 'There –' He paused at 28th Street and Broadway to point at a sign. 'That's the Fifth Avenue Theater. And West 28th Street between Broadway and Sixth Avenue is called Tin Pan Alley – that's the hang-out for the songwriters and music publishers.'

Then all at once – almost in unison – the marquees of the string of theaters in their northward trek burst into magical brilliance. Elisabeth was entranced by the names emblazoned there: Maude Adams, Minnie Maddern Fiske, James O'Neill, Margaret Anglin, Henry Miller. Even Amy seemed dazzled by this electronic display. Jerry kept up a running commentary about the theaters in their path.

Ahead lay the dramatic new Times Tower, which gave a new name to Longacre Square. It was now known as Times Square. At 39th Street they stood before the impressive Casino Theater, which usually offered light opera, and Jerry pointed out the Metropolitan Opera House across the Street.

'It's exciting,' Elisabeth admitted, simultaneously intrigued and fearful. This was the world Jerry vowed they would conquer.

On their first morning in the rooming house, after the light breakfast Elisabeth prepared for the three of them, Jerry called for a 'strategy session'.

'I have to work out my approach to producers,' he explained, sitting in the one chair provided in Elisabeth and Amy's bedroom, his presence here acceptable under his assumed brother/sister relationship with Elisabeth. 'I don't want us to go the route of the theatrical agents – that's like playing Russian roulette. I go straight to the producer. I'll say we lost a lot of your publicity material in the earthquake, but I need something to prove you were a success in Australia. We'll work up a scrapbook that –'

'Jerry, I wasn't a big success,' she broke in uneasily. Their major concern – hers and David's – had been to keep the company rolling, to earn enough to be fairly comfortable. She loved acting, taking a role and making it come to life. She had never thought about being what Jerry called 'a personality'. 'I did well in a very small company.'

'Beth, you have to make everything seem big in theater.' He reached for the notebook he'd dropped at the foot of the bed, where Amy sprawled, making drawings on the pages he'd pulled out for her. 'Tell me some of the roles you've played, and I'll write some reviews to go with them.'

'Jerry, that's dishonest!'

'It's being smart. I'll make up this little scrapbook that we "just managed to save in the earthquake". Then I'll have a printer set up and make copies. We'll need photographs. I'll find somebody who works in the field – he'll know what we need –'

'Suppose they write back to Melbourne?' She was cold with alarm. 'Roger ran ads in some of the newspapers, but they were small. Occasionally somebody wrote up a current production, but –'

'No buts,' Jerry said breezily. 'No producer's going to bother writing all the way to Melbourne. I'll show him big ads and publicity about how wonderful Beth Winston was in *A Doll's House* and so on. Sugar, this will work.'

'Jerry, maybe I'm not good enough.'

'You'll be great,' he predicted. 'I have an instinct about these things.'

Elisabeth struggled to share Jerry's confidence. For three days he labored over reports about 'Melbourne's brilliant young star', revised endlessly. Then – ignoring Elisabeth's protests – he prepared to search for a printer to reproduce pages supposedly from the Melbourne dailies.

'Jerry, nobody is going to believe this!'

'They'll believe,' he insisted. 'This is New York. It's the age of advertising. The age of "the personality".'

'You could be in for an awful shock. I'm an actress, not a "personality".' In Melbourne – in London – people came to the theater to see acting, to see a fine play. 'I can't be a walking advertisement, play-acting offstage as well as on.' Jerry had regaled her with stories of the antics of Lillian Russell, Evelyn Nesbit, and Frankie Bailey – and, of course, Anna Held. She recoiled from being part of such exploitation.

'I'll create a personality. You've got a special aura about you – I'll work from that, circulate exciting stories about you. You were a heroine in San Francisco,' he improvised. 'You –'

'Jerry, you sound more like Barnum than Ziegfeld.'

'Haven't you heard about what Barnum did for Jenny Lind?' He paused, snapped his fingers. 'Tomorrow we go for photographs. This man thinks he's Leonardo da Vinci, but I've seen his work and he'll be worth every cent.'

'How many cents?' And how long before she was earning money?

'We're all right,' Jerry soothed. '*You know.*' Meaning, she understood, that their savings were in her hands. But how long would it last? Everything in New York was so expensive.

Jerry accompanied her and Amy to Madison Square Park, where she would sit with Amy on one of the benches and enjoy the morning sunlight. Shoots of young grass pushed their way through the spring-warmed earth. Trees displayed endless buds. Already a group of women – some clearly nannies, others young mothers – were scattered about benches, each accompanied by baby carriage or small children. All at once overcome by shyness, Elisabeth settled herself on an unoccupied bench somewhat removed from the other women, yet at a comfortable distance from the collection of derelicts that had laid claim to one area.

'Tell me a story,' Amy ordered after her overtures of friendship had been ignored by two little girls who played on the grass under a nanny's watchful eye. This wasn't like Melbourne, Elisabeth warned herself, where everyone was so friendly.

'Come sit here beside me.' Elisabeth reached to hoist Amy onto the bench. They couldn't have gone back to Melbourne, she reasoned yet again. Their theater company no longer existed. And in truth, she needed to leave Melbourne behind her. Memories were so painful.

Jerry was sure they'd be successful together. Sometimes his towering aspirations frightened her. It would be enough for her to know that she could raise her precious child in comfort. Jerry craved fame and high living.

And now, she told herself, she must write to Grandma about David. She must write to Mary, back in Melbourne. Mary must be so worried and maybe she would have some news of the others in the company.

Life settled into a pattern. Each morning Elisabeth took Amy to Madison Square Park. One little girl – an elf in lovely clothes from the city's most expensive shops – was drawn to play with Amy. Knowing that they had lost everything in the earthquake, Mrs O'Brien had offered to supply Amy with dresses outgrown by her own small granddaughter. But these immaculate, neat hand-me-downs only taunted Elisabeth with her own uncertain financial situation.

After lunch each noon she put Amy down for her afternoon nap. She had discovered the Muhlenberg branch of the public library system on West 23rd Street, where books could be taken out even by newcomers to the city. While Amy slept, she read. Jerry was making what he called 'rounds' of producers' offices with the improvised scrapbook he had devised.

Jerry allowed himself one cocktail each afternoon at the Metropolis, on the southwest corner of 42nd Street. It was a business investment, he'd explained to Elisabeth – allowing him to sit around in a place where theater people gathered to exchange gossip.

'I hear John Barrymore made the ship that was to take him to Australia,' he reported one evening to Elisabeth. They both smiled in bittersweet remembrance of the handsome young actor formally dressed in the first hours after the earthquake. '"Diamond" Jim Brady was at the bar today – holding court. I heard him talk about running into Barrymore in San Francisco the morning of the earthquake. "Only Jack Barrymore would dress for an earthquake,"' he mimicked Brady.

As Jerry had warned, Elisabeth had been horrified by the fee demanded by the photographer who supplied her photo for the supposed scrapbook. But she had to admit it was superb. But if – *when* – she walked into a producer's office for a reading, would he be disappointed that the photograph was so flattering?

Jerry was right, she upbraided herself. She must stop thinking of herself as Elisabeth Winston. From now on she was Beth Winston. She closed her eyes and heard David's voice murmuring his pet name for her. Part of David would always be with her. Even now, there were many nights when she cried silently for him.

Suspecting there would be no reply despite the trauma of her news, she wrote yet another letter to her mother and grandmother. She told them about the earthquake, that there was no going back to Melbourne – for a fleeting moment hopeful that Mama would write, 'Come home with Amy. Papa forgives.' She explained that she was in New York now and searching for work in the theater.

Mailing the letter, she was conscious that with the new fast ships London was barely six days away. The thought was comforting.

'I don't know what the hell's wrong with these damn producers,' Jerry complained while they shared supper in her drab bedroom on a late May evening. 'It's like they never heard of Australia – except for Nellie Melba and the Aborigines.'

What she had feared.

'Tomorrow,' he said with sudden resolve, 'I'm going up to talk with this press agent everybody brags about. We need some action.'

'Jerry, our savings are going down.' Her heart was pounding. What happened when they ran out of money?

'If it's too wild, I won't make a deal.' He squinted in thought. 'I'm messing up somewhere. I just have to figure out where. But let's splurge a little tonight. We'll ask Mrs O'Brien to sit with Amy and go to the theater.'

'Should we?' She hesitated, fearful yet eager. Thus far, they'd been to the theater only once – climbing up to the gallery to see Richard Mansfield in *The Scarlet Letter*.

'We should.' He grinned. 'Provided, of course, that Mrs O'Brien is available.'

Mrs O'Brien agreed to come and stay with Amy. Elisabeth and Jerry hurried out into the balmy evening and strode northward to the Empire Theater, where Maude Adams was appearing in *Peter Pan*. The brilliant lights of the marquees, the air of conviviality that filled the atmosphere, was intoxicating. She needed to be playing again, Elisabeth thought, and not just because of the money. When she was in a play, she had a center to her life – and a cherished escape into another world.

Sitting in the gallery Elisabeth was caught up in the mesmerizing performance of Maude Adams. She and Jerry joined in the clamorous applause that elicited endless curtain calls. Walking out of the theater into the night, she was euphoric. Here was theater at its very best.

'I heard a woman behind us say she'd seen the play forty-seven times,' Jerry confided in high spirits. 'But why are there so few American playwrights? Barrie is British. Shaw – with six of his plays on the boards – is Irish. We're seeing – or rather,' he conceded humorously, 'those who can afford it are seeing – Pinero, Ibsen, the French plays in Sarah Bernhardt's repertory. Where are the American playwrights?'

'What about Clyde Fitch?' she challenged. 'Even in Melbourne we knew about him.'

'But *The Climbers* – a classic now – was turned down by producers up and down Broadway,' Jerry scoffed. '"Who'd want to see a play that begins with a funeral and ends with a suicide?"' he quoted. 'The producers are only interested in appealing to the lowest mentalities.'

'With the summer so close fewer plays will be offered.' All at once the magic of the evening disappeared in reality.

'There're the roof garden theaters.' Jerry was defensive. 'George M. Cohan's *The Governor's Son* will be opening at the New Amsterdam Aerial Roof Garden, and a new musical at the roof theater at Madison Square Garden.' Jerry sighed. Both companies were already in rehearsal, of course. 'You know what we have to do? We must have you seen in places like Rector's – where producers are always appearing. I know –' he anticipated her retort – 'they're damned expensive. But you have to be seen. Did I tell you the story about Alla Nazimova?'

'The wonderful Russian actress?'

'So now she's playing in *Hedda Gabler* on Broadway. But the way I hear it, when she opened last year at the Herald Square Theater, few people came. Down on the Lower East Side Emma Goldman and some friends raised enough money to bring the company down to the Third Avenue Theater. Then the critics and Broadway stars began to come down to see her. Now she's playing – in English – on Broadway.'

'Jerry, I don't have a language problem.' Laughter lit her eyes.

'You need to be seen by important people. For the next four weeks,' he decreed, 'we'll have supper at Rector's once every week. You'll go out and buy a gorgeous dress. You can't wear the same lilac silk each time we go out.'

'We can't afford that,' she objected.

Jerry grinned. 'I'll have some money after tomorrow night. I'm escorting a rich widow to the opera. For this service I'll be well paid, plus she's taking me to Brooks Brothers to buy me evening clothes. You'll buy a gorgeous dress.'

A rich widow paid him to escort her to the opera? What strange ways people had here in New York City!

Elisabeth was shocked at the cost of the elegant, Empire-style lilac silk gown Jerry insisted on buying for her.

'You'll always appear in lilac,' he said. 'And none of the sequins and bead embroideries that are being worn today. You'll stand out at Rector's! Everyone will look and ask themselves, "Who is that beautiful girl?" And no fancy jewelry.'

'That won't be a problem.' Her only jewelry was a chain with a locket containing David's picture, and she would not borrow the necklace the rich stranger had given Amy in San Francisco. But what would David think of all this craziness?

Jerry decided they would arrive at Rector's shortly before midnight. By that time the place would be crowded – she'd have maximum exposure.

'The classic deal is to have cocktails at the Hoffman House bar, dine at Martin's or at the Café des Beaux Arts, go to the theater, then head for Rector's for supper,' he explained as they walked uptown, Broadway mobbed with hansom cabs, broughams, here and there an Oldsmobile or Cadillac or a Maxwell. 'If you're still vertical after that, you go to Jack's for breakfast. But for now we'll settle for a couple of hours at Rector's. It's an investment.'

Elisabeth struggled with self-consciousness. Why was the way she looked so terribly important? She would never be a showgirl or a chorus girl. She was an actress. She loved *theater* – not this crazy world of off-stage pretense.

'Rector's is just ahead,' Jerry interrupted her introspection, 'that long, low yellow building.' He pointed to the east side of the street to a two-story, brilliantly electrified Greco-Roman structure.

Elisabeth's heart pounded as they walked into the crowded restaurant, mirrored from wall to ceiling, the décor green and gold, with dramatic crystal chandeliers providing lighting.

'We'll be sent upstairs,' Jerry whispered. 'You have to be somebody important to sit down here on the main floor. But don't worry – there's a spillover of producers who land upstairs because the main floor tables are taken.'

While they were being escorted upstairs, Jerry pointed out the table where a much bejeweled Lillian Russell sat, surrounded by adoring men.

'She's getting on in years and spreading out, but she's still magic. And there's Evelyn Nesbit with her husband, Harry Thaw. She used to be Stanford White's girl. Everybody said she and John Barrymore were wild about each other at one time, but "Stanny" broke that up.'

Elisabeth didn't really care about the Broadway gossip. She didn't belong in this world. What could Jerry accomplish by taking her to these places? Yet when they were seated at their table, she was startled to note that several pairs of male eyes beamed in her direction. The realization was unnerving.

'We'll come here again next week,' Jerry whispered complacently. 'Maybe Charles Frohman and Florenz Ziegfeld aren't sitting up here in the back country, but the man across from us who can't keep his eyes off you is a fairly well-known producer. I'll find out tomorrow if he's scheduling a new play. I tell you, Beth, this is the way to open doors for you!'

Chapter Fourteen

New York was in the midst of an early hot spell. Last night Jerry took Elisabeth and Amy for a trolley ride on one of the 'open cars' in service during the spring and summer, a favorite Manhattan escape in sweltering weather.

'By asking for transfers from one line to another we can ride all the way from the Battery to far up in Washington Heights for the same nickel,' Jerry had explained.

This afternoon the small bedroom Elisabeth shared with Amy was uncomfortable after the mild summers in Melbourne. Washing Amy's face with a cool damp cloth, Elisabeth remembered the pleasant summers by the sea at Whitby with Mama, Grandma, and the boys, and felt a surge of guilt that she couldn't provide this for Amy. She'd read about the new electric fans that were being used to cool the mansions of the wealthy. Old buildings like this weren't electrified yet.

Jerry was sure wonderful times were ahead for them. She yearned to share his enthusiasm, but so much that was awful had happened to her and Amy in such a short time, this eluded her. Grandma would say, 'We have to accept what God metes out for us. We can't ask questions.' Of course, she conceded, they'd been in the city only a few weeks.

Jerry was trying so hard to make what he called 'the right contacts'. He'd checked out the producer they'd seen at Rector's, but the man had no backing for his new play, Jerry discovered from the theatrical crowd at the Metropole.

Again tonight, they 'invested' in a supper at Rector's. It was a fascinating experience, Elisabeth admitted, the atmosphere festive, the patrons colorful – and the food exotic. But the men who leered in her direction were either actors, politicians, or gangsters.

'One more night,' Jerry decreed when they emerged from their second supper at Rector's. 'Then we'll find another hunting ground.'

The steamy weather continued. Elisabeth spent more time each day at Madison Square Park, where there was some minor surcease from their sweatbox of a bedroom. Most of the nannies and their charges were absent now – off, Jerry explained, to Southampton or an Adirondack cottage. On a Monday that showed little sign of a break in the heat wave, Elisabeth remained in the park until Amy was listless and sleepy, then settling herself beside one of the small windows in their room, she tried to focus on the new Edith Wharton novel she'd borrowed from the library.

Moments later she was startled by a knock on the door. Jerry never came home this early. She hurried to respond lest a second knock awaken Amy. Jerry strode into the room with an air of jubilation.

'We're escaping the heat tonight. I've got reservations for us at the Madison Square Roof. We're seeing the opening night of *Mamselle Champagne*!'

'How did you manage that?' Opening nights – even this time of the year – were booked far in advance.

'I met this drunk at the Metropole. He'd had a wild battle with his girlfriend – so we're going in their place! The Roof will be loaded with important people!'

Elisabeth, too, glowed in anticipation of this unexpected diversion. 'But first let me see if Mrs O'Brien can stay with Amy.'

'She'll stay,' Jerry predicted. 'The old girl likes the extra loot.'

Mrs O'Brien arrived at the last moment – when Elisabeth was becoming apprehensive.

'Oh, we never had heat like this when I was growing up in our little town near Dublin.' Lugging a pitcher of lemonade, she fanned herself vigorously.

'Nor in London.' Elisabeth's smile was wistful.

'Of course, we grew up with this heat down in Georgia.' Jerry cast a warning glance at Elisabeth. If Mrs O'Brien knew they were not brother and sister, visiting privileges would be forbidden. 'Hot as Hades.'

Arriving at the magnificent Madison Square Garden, Elisabeth and Jerry paused to admire the yellow and terracotta structure.

'It's enormous,' Elisabeth pronounced in awe, noting the arcade of fashionable shops at ground level, and envisioning the huge amphitheater inside that played host to horse shows and prize fights among other events.

'It's Stanford White's masterpiece,' Jerry said with infinite respect. 'Look up at that central tower. The bronze figure atop is of Diana.' Jerry paused to chuckle. 'When the figure first went up about fifteen years ago, it was considered scandalous.' Elisabeth lifted an eyebrow questioningly. 'It was the first nude figure ever exhibited in this country.'

'I think this is a very prudish place,' Elisabeth decided. 'Do American museums dress up classic nude figures?'

'Of anybody over age three.' Jerry guided her towards the entrance.

Emerging from the elevator and walking into the roof garden, they felt a most welcome breeze. Arches of vines were intertwined with colored light bulbs. The fronds of the potted palms moved gently in the air. Their table, they were pleased to discover, was near the stage.

Almost every table was already occupied, the women elaborately gowned, the men all in evening attire. In soft whispers Jerry pointed out famous 'personalities'.

'You see the very tall man sitting over there?' Jerry pointed to a red-haired, red-moustached man alone at a choice table. 'That's Stanford White, the architect. I told you, he designed this building.'

Elisabeth told herself it was impolite to stare, but the impulse was strong. She saw a young couple arrive – the girl oddly familiar. She'd seen photographs of her somewhere.

'Jerry,' she whispered, 'who's that beautiful girl in the white dinner dress and black picture hat?'

Jerry whistled under his breath. 'That's Evelyn Nesbit with her husband Harry Thaw. They'll keep their distance from White,' he surmised.

'Why?' Elisabeth asked.

'Before Thaw married her, Evelyn Nesbit was Stanford White's girl. When she started an affair with John Barrymore – about half his age – White shipped Evelyn off to a convent for a while. Then she upped and married Thaw, whose family is so-o-o rich.'

Now the conductor lifted his baton. The performance began. Elisabeth focused on the stage. She forced an air of avid interest, though in, truth, *Mamselle Champagne* lacked sparkle. After an especially dull number a few people made a stealthy departure. But she and

Jerry would stay, she resolved. This was their first opening night.

Jerry poked her foot under the table. She looked up in enquiry. His face wore a luminous glow.

'Somebody finds you more interesting than what's on stage,' he whispered.

'Considering what is on stage that wouldn't be difficult.' But she managed a show of interest out of compassion for the cast.

'He's supposed to be casting a new play.' Jerry was like a lion-hunter moving in for the kill, Elisabeth thought. 'I'll be at his office first thing tomorrow morning.'

But the producer that had attracted Jerry's attention was bored with the musical. He rose to his feet, murmured something to his companion and walked to Elisabeth and Jerry's table. He leaned forward and handed Elisabeth a card.

'If you're an actress or interested in becoming one, come to my office in the next day or two. I'm in the process of casting my new production.'

Before Elisabeth could manage a reply, he strode away.

Elisabeth handed the card to Jerry. 'That's Colin Bradford. We're in business,' Jerry said, reaching over to squeeze her hand. 'I'll go over to talk with him tomorrow morning.'

'He's not producing a musical, is he?' Elisabeth was wary. 'I can't sing a note.'

'The way I hear it, he's signed up a new American playwright. You know how rare that is in this country. That should bring the production a rash of publicity.'

She tried to focus on what was happening on stage, but the effort was futile. Was Jerry right? Was this their big chance?

The handsome young leading man was just beginning a song when a gunshot, at close range, rent the air. Along with the rest of the audience Elisabeth stiffened in shock. An instant later two more shots rang out. A woman screamed. Others joined in. Panic erupted.

'Harry Thaw's shot Stanford White!' Jerry said amidst the clamor. The man Jerry had identified as Thaw was striding towards the exit, the pistol held aloft in one hand as though to tell the audience the shooting was over.

A white-faced man emerged from backstage, climbed atop a table to order the orchestra to resume playing. 'Go on with the show!'

The orchestra made a weak attempt to resume, but those on the stage were too stricken to continue the performance. Others poured forth from the backstage area. White slid from his chair, knocking over his table as he fell to the floor. The man from backstage now pleaded with the audience to move out quietly. Another man pushed his way towards White.

'I'm a doctor! Let me through!'

Elisabeth sat frozen in her seat, her eyes fastened to the blood-spattered body on the floor. She was seeing David's body, sprawled on the patch of grass in front of their bungalow, his head in a pool of blood.

'Beth, let's go.' Jerry drew her to her feet. Tables and chairs were being overturned in the audience's rush to the exit. 'You're all right.' With an arm about her waist, he guided her through the frenzied mob to the elevators.

She clung to him, cold and trembling, in the packed elevator. The image of David – lying on the grass, the single pink rose just beyond his outstretched hand – was as fresh as yesterday.

They walked in silence in the balmy night, Jerry sensing she was too shaken to talk just yet.

'When – when I saw him lying on the floor like that, I remembered David,' she whispered as they approached their rooming house. 'Why did it have to happen that way to us? Life was perfect.'

'It'll be good again,' he soothed. 'You have to look ahead. That's what he'd want you to do. And that man who gave you his card, Colin Bradford, I'll go to his office first thing tomorrow morning, introduce myself as your personal manager, talk up your success in Melbourne.' He paused in thought. 'We'll let him believe I was your manager down there –'

'Why did he give me his card?' She felt a sudden rebellion. 'Because he liked the way I look? That doesn't mean I can act.'

'How many times have I told you?' Jerry scolded. 'The first thing a New York producer wants to know is that his leading lady – or any young actress in the company – looks beautiful on stage. That is, unless the script specifically calls for a homely actress.'

'What kind of plays does he do? Something like we saw tonight?'

'Hey, that's the wrong attitude.' He shook his head in mock reproach. 'So he's not Charles Frohman or David Belasco. He's got the backing and a play. He's our quarry.'

*　　*　　*

At exactly ten o'clock the following morning Jerry walked into Colin Bradford's reception room. The girl at the desk was in deep conversation with an arrogant blonde. Jerry took a chair, striving to appear nonchalant. Thank God, Mattie had taken him to Brooks Brothers and bought him three nifty suits plus an evening outfit. But that woman never stopped talking – not even in bed . . .

The door to Bradford's office opened. The florid-faced, corpulent producer sauntered out. Immediately the arrogant blonde became wistfully charming. Jerry saw Bradford's eyes linger on the low neckline of her dress. She had a pair that would make any man's mouth water, Jerry conceded.

'Come inside, Rita. We'll talk,' Bradford said briskly.

He'd sit here on his ass for an hour, Jerry surmised. Bradford had a reputation for being a woman-chaser. But Beth would know how to handle him, wouldn't she? He felt a flicker of apprehension. Hell, she'd been married. She wasn't some wide-eyed little innocent.

He'd had to remind himself a lot of times in these past weeks that what he and Beth forged for themselves was a business relationship. She was beautiful, bright, and appealing – but it wouldn't be smart for him to try for something more than what they shared at this moment. Anyhow, it was too early. She still mourned her late husband.

Now the office was filling up with the usual show-business types – all anxious for a role in Colin Bradford's new production. But the girl behind the desk knew he was next. He'd held up the card Bradford had given Beth last night, and she'd nodded in recognition.

Earlier than he'd anticipated, the blonde emerged – but from her secretive smile Jerry suspected Colin Bradford would be seeing more of her. He rose to his feet and approached the producer.

'Good morning, sir.' He used the deferential tone that Bradford would expect. 'I'm Jerome Schiff, personal manager of Beth Winston, the young lady to whom you gave your card last night.'

'God, what a night!' Bradford winced. 'Thaw's crazy, of course. And that's what his lawyers will claim. The trial will fill the newspapers for months to come. Not that Thaw will ever see the inside of a jail. That's what everybody's saying.'

'With his money, the kind of legal help he can afford, he'll come off looking good,' Jerry surmised, and Bradford nodded in agreement.

'But enough of Thaw. Come inside and tell me about Beth Winston.' He was cagey now, Jerry thought – and faintly testy.

This morning Elisabeth brought Amy home from the park earlier than usual. She was anxious to hear about Jerry's meeting with Colin Bradford. She felt increasingly uncomfortable that she and Amy were living on the money provided by Jerry. He called her 'Madam Banker' because he entrusted their funds to her. When she'd suggested that perhaps he ought to open a savings account, he brushed this aside: 'Sugar, it's better under your mattress. If it's in the bank and I hear about a poker game, I might pull out a stake.'

Jerry kept telling her they were partners. When she worked, he would take a chunk of her earnings. Later, she'd pay him back for what he provided now. Together, he repeated at regular intervals, nothing could stop them. They were the perfect team.

'Mama, it's hot.' Amy was wistful. 'Is it always hot in New York?'

'No, darling. It'll be cool again. Let's go down to the kitchen, and I'll make us lunch.' The other roomers were out at work during the day, so only she and Mrs O'Brien used the kitchen for midday meals.

'Frances says she's going to the country soon. To a place with a swimming pool.'

'We'll go out to Coney Island one day,' Elisabeth soothed. 'You can wade in the sea there. You'll like that.' Why wasn't Jerry back by now?

Amy was full of questions while they sat down to their lunch. Everything these days was, 'Why, Mama?' Elisabeth struggled not to be impatient with her enquiring daughter. Mrs O'Brien said a curious child was a smart one.

'Amy, you're sleepy,' she said lovingly, watching while Amy dawdled over lunch. 'Let me wash the dishes and clean up here – then you can have a nap.'

The moment she was on the bed Amy fell asleep. Elisabeth reached for the new book by Upton Sinclair and settled in a chair at the window. She started at the sharp knock on the door, hurried to respond.

'You have an appointment with Colin Bradford next Tuesday morning,' Jerry announced triumphantly. 'I gave him the whole song and dance about how popular you were in Melbourne and how you were heading up a six-week tour in San Francisco when the earthquake hit.' He grinned at her reproachful wince. 'This isn't a big role but it's Broadway. You'll be seen by all the critics. Sugar, this is what we've been waiting for!'

'I haven't got the part yet.' But she felt a rush of excitement at the prospect of reading for a Broadway producer. Was she good enough?

'We'll go out to Coney Island tomorrow,' Jerry decided exuberantly. 'Give ourselves a day away from the city.'

'Did Mr Bradford give you any hint about the play?'

'It's a comedy, from what I hear. He's lining up a star now, but he won't give out clues about who it'll be. The rumor was that he had hoped for Ethel Barrymore – but she's up for another play. With a little luck you might be able to understudy.'

'It's too hot to wear my suit.' Elisabeth squinted in thought. 'The lilac silk is too fussy. Maybe I can –'

'You take yourself over to B. Altman's and buy something that'll knock his eyes out. And don't tell me we can't afford it. This is business.'

As Elisabeth had feared, the days dragged until her meeting with Colin Bradford. On a blessedly comfortable Friday morning she went to the elegant B. Altman's. Shocked at the prices but mindful of Jerry's exhortation to buy something spectacular, she chose a flattering lilac-gray silk.

At the appointed time on Tuesday morning – fighting for composure – Elisabeth accompanied Jerry to the Bradford office. She gaped in shock at the crowd that sat or stood about the small reception room. She remembered David's stories of the bitter competition among London actors and actresses vying for parts in a new production, all with high hopes of stardom.

She waited while Jerry confidently approached the girl at the desk – sensing the irritation of the others that it was apparent he had an appointment. Moments later Elisabeth and Jerry were ushered inside.

'Your manager tells me you've had quite a success in Australia.' Bradford greeted Elisabeth with a fatuous smile as he gestured her to a chair beside his desk. Jerry drew up another chair for himself.

'Audiences were very kind.' She felt as though his eyes were stripping away every garment she wore. 'We were so pleased when we were asked to play in San Francisco.' Jerry had drilled her on what to say.

They talked briefly about the San Francisco disaster, then Bradford briefed her on the role for which she was being considered. She suspected he was annoyed that Jerry was with her. Was he afraid that – as her personal manager – Jerry would make excessive demands? They'd be thrilled with any salary he offered!

'You'll read the role of Caroline.' He was drawing two scripts from a desk drawer. 'Her first entrance is in Act Two. I'll read with you.'

Elisabeth wished that he had been more explicit about the character, but began to read. Quickly she caught the substance of the role, and read with a sureness she sensed he hadn't expected.

'That'll be enough for now.' He stopped her after three pages. His eyes told her he was pleased. 'I'll be reading a few more girls for the part, of course. But yes, you are a strong candidate.' He turned to a schedule on his desk. 'Come in again next Tuesday at this same time. Oh, and there's no need for you to come with her,' he told Jerry indulgently. 'We'll talk business if she's chosen for the part.'

Again, time moved with the painful slowness of a prison sentence. On Thursday evening Jerry told Elisabeth that he had a weekend job for the summer. He was to be social secretary for his 'rich widow'.

'Actually she wants an escort for the weekend parties out at Southampton. I'm to go out every Friday evening and return to New York on Sunday night. She's paying me twenty-five dollars for each weekend.' Elisabeth's eyes widened in amazement. That was a fantastic amount.

Again, she battled frustration. Even if she was cast for the Bradford play, she wouldn't be in rehearsal until September. 'I wish there was something I could do.'

'You're doing,' Jerry insisted. 'Tuesday you read again for Bradford. But remember, you don't talk business with him. That's my job.'

Late Friday afternoon Jerry left for Southampton. Elisabeth was conscious of a disconcerting loneliness. In such a little while she'd become so dependent on him. It was as though she and Amy and Jerry were a family. He didn't speak often of his family, but she knew he missed them. He'd gone home only once in the year that he'd been in New York. He was her stand-in brother and she his stand-in sister.

On Tuesday morning Jerry came to stay with Amy while Elisabeth left for her appointment with Colin Bradford. The heat of the day was relieved by a breeze, the sky a picture-book blue. A good omen, she told herself. She was pleased that Jerry had been so approving of her new dress – refusing to be perturbed by the expensive price tag. 'You've got an eye for style,' he'd said. 'That's a real asset.'

Arriving early at Bradford's building, she decided to walk around the block so as not to appear over-anxious about the interview. At exactly ten o'clock she opened the door and walked into the crowded reception room. But she had an appointment, she reminded herself. The girl at the desk glanced up with a smile, recognized her and walked into Bradford's private office.

'Send her in,' Elisabeth heard him say. 'And don't disturb us.'

Bradford was at his desk, flipping through the pages of a script.

'Good morning, Beth.' He seemed in high spirits. That was good.

'Good morning, Mr Bradford.'

'I want you to read the same scene as last time again,' he told her, handing her a script. 'Don't be afraid to play it big. I want Caroline to come over strong.'

'Yes, sir.' She took the script, found Caroline's entrance, and glanced up expectantly.

'I'll give you the cues.' He left his chair to sit at the corner of his desk. 'Take it from the top.'

She focused on the lines, trying not to be aware of the way he was moving in on her. His knees brushed hers now. He didn't realize that, she told herself self-consciously – he was so involved in the lines.

'Take it from the top again,' he ordered, his breathing heavy now, his knee pressing against hers.

She began to read again – contriving to shift her leg from his. But he dropped a hand on her shoulder, moved in towards her breast. Her eyes left the script to meet his.

'You're doing fine.' His voice was thick, his color high. 'You might be just the one to play Caroline.' His hand slid inside the modest neckline of her dress.

'Stop that!' she blazed.

'I thought you wanted this part,' he drawled, slowly withdrawing his hand. But his eyes were eloquent. 'You be good to old Colin, and Colin will be good to you.'

'No!' Awkwardly she pushed him away, rose to her feet. How

dare he treat her as though she were a woman of the street! 'I don't want to be in your play!'

'Your loss.' He was furious at rejection. 'Actresses like you are a dime a dozen in this town!'

Her face aflame, she rushed from his office, across the reception room and into the hall. Her heart pounding, tears of rage spilling over. She waited at the elevator for a few moments, then turned to find the stairs, walked down the five flights and out into the summer air. His words echoed in her mind: '*Actresses like you are a dime a dozen in this town.*'

Chapter Fifteen

Back at home, in faltering tones Elisabeth reported on what had happened with Colin Bradford.

'Beth, you know how men play those games.' Jerry shrugged. 'You're not a little girl. So Bradford thought maybe he could mange a hug or a kiss –'

'That wasn't what he was after.' Color suffused her face. Jerry was upset. He'd been so sure this was their first step up the ladder. But Colin Bradford had been intolerable. 'Jerry, I couldn't –'

'Of course not,' he said quickly. 'But not every producer in the theater is like that.'

Jerry was upset, she tormented herself. Should she have played along? She didn't know how to handle situations like that. And she *wouldn't* – It would be defiling David's memory.

'I know what people say about actresses.' To Papa all actresses were immoral. 'But we're not all like that.'

'Something else will come along.' But Jerry's usual air of confidence was tainted. 'Meanwhile, we're managing. Oh, I was talking to somebody at the Metropole yesterday afternoon. I just might be able to pick up some work for you with this man who's making moving pictures up in the Bronx. Not much money,' he admitted, 'but it could be a good experience for you.'

'Jerry, the moving pictures we've seen at nickelodeons were awful. I know, people are rushing like crazy to see them, but why, when they're so bad?' A few minutes of crude action was ludicrous – while somebody played music at a piano in need of tuning.

'It's going to be the entertainment medium of the future.' Jerry's face wore a messianic glow. 'Sure, the first ones were crude – just scenes of foreign places or prizefights or vaudeville acts. But people demanded more. They wanted real stories – and they're getting them. The technique is improving. One day,' he predicted, 'moving pictures will be bigger than theater. They'll be seen by millions of people in every city and town in the country.'

'They've got a long way to go.' What she'd seen so far had nothing to do with acting.

'If I can track down work for you with that company up in the Bronx, would you do it?' He seemed casual but she knew he was serious.

'I'd try. But I can't imagine acting for a camera. It's cold, an inanimate object. There's a feeling you get from an audience in a theater –' It was a kind of love, she thought. A make-believe family. She took a deep breath. 'If they're willing to pay, I'll work.'

In the days ahead Elisabeth knew Jerry was trying to come up with the names of the men who were making the 'one reelers', as he called them. He searched through the pages of the *Clipper* – the show-business magazine where usually ads were run to tell exhibitors about new films. He religiously read the new show-business weekly called *Variety*, but without success.

'I think they're afraid to advertise since Edison is threatening to sue them for infringing on his patents.'

The summer dragged along on leaden feet. The weekends were drab and lonely for Elisabeth because Jerry left each Friday evening for Southampton and didn't return until Sunday night.

He talked lyrically about the beauty of Southampton, the mansions built along the water's edge, the lifestyle of the summer residents.

'God, Beth, they must be so damn rich! Mattie's got a whole staff of servants. Until she bought her Cadillac two years ago she had four footmen! Now she makes do with a chauffeur. And she's only there for the summer.'

On the last Friday morning of August Jerry confided that this would probably be the end of his job as 'social secretary'.

'Mattie wants to spend the autumn in Paris. I have to tell her I won't go with her.'

Elisabeth's heart began to pound. What would she do if Jerry did go?

'That was just a fill-in job to see us through the summer,' he reminded her. 'In another week or two Broadway will be bustling with new plays being cast. In three months, sugar, you'll be in rehearsals.'

*　　*　　*

Jerry boarded the train for Southampton with dread. He knew Mattie would throw an ugly scene. He envisioned her short, fat body, her hennaed hair, with distaste. Paris gowns and expensive jewelry couldn't transform her into the Floradora girl – forty-five years her junior – that she yearned to be.

The old bitch thought she owned him now. But he had no intention of going to Paris with her for the autumn. New York was where the action was. *Broadway.* In another week or two producers would start casting – he had to be in their offices to promote Beth.

He dozed most of the way, awakening a few minutes before the train pulled into the small, picturesque railroad station. The Cadillac was waiting to drive him to the ocean-front house that Mattie had bought just four years ago. 'I loathed Bar Harbor. There wasn't a man under seventy to be seen.' Only a hundred miles from New York, Southampton was accessible to males from Manhattan. At close to seventy herself, Mattie preferred the very young.

The train chugged to a stop. Disembarking with the expensive leather valise Mattie had provided, Jerry catalogued the weekend activities. In addition to the usual boring dinner, they were to go to some art exhibit at the Parrish Art Museum and then to the Shinne-cock Hills golf club to watch the players tee off. Mattie was more interested in the small Shinnecock Indian boys who were trained as caddies than the golf.

The weekend moved along in its usual leisurely pace. Then at the Meadow Club – where Mattie boasted that there was one ladies' maid for each lady visitor – Jerry's mind bolted into action. He spied Douglas Graham, the Broadway producer, across the room. Did Mattie know him? Of course she did – everybody out here knew everybody else.

'Mattie, you know Douglas Graham, don't you?' he whispered in one bejeweled ear.

'Of course. His mother has a house right down the road from my sister's in Bar Harbor.'

'I'd like to meet him,' he said softly.

'Then you shall,' she gushed.

Moments later Jerry was in lively conversation with Douglas Graham, a slender, elegant man in his fifties. Graham relished gossiping about the stars.

'Of course, Ethel Barrymore is a magnificent young actress.

Winston Churchill – Jennie's son – was mad about her when she was over there, but Ethel's all wrapped up in her career.'

'I'm managing a very young actress who was the toast of Melbourne,' Jerry said with plotted casualness. 'She was to star in *A Doll's House* in San Francisco, but the earthquake took care of that. We decided to give New York a whirl. Beth was eager to familiarize herself with the New York theater scene – you know, see a few current productions – before I present her. She –'

'She doesn't by chance have a British accent?' Graham interrupted. 'Not Australian,' he stressed. 'There's a difference, you know.'

'Beth was born and raised in London. Went to the best schools,' Jerry pursued.

'I'll be out here for the next two weeks, but bring her in to see me when I return to the city. This isn't the leading role,' he cautioned. 'It's small but in the hands of a strong actress, it'll be spectacular. Call my office and tell Jennifer to set up an appointment for you to bring her in –' He lifted an eyebrow in enquiry.

'Beth Winston,' Jerry supplied. 'I'll be delighted to do that, sir.'

Two hours later in Mattie's bedroom she and Jerry erupted in a furious battle.

'What do you mean, you won't go with me to Paris? Haven't I been generous to you? I've groomed you for the Paris trip! Your beautiful suits, the silk shirts!'

'I'll return them,' he said grimly. 'I can't leave New York.'

'Keep the clothes,' she said with a supercilious smile. 'But I want you out of my house first thing tomorrow morning!'

Elisabeth strived to emulate Jerry's optimism about her coming appointment with Douglas Graham, who would be directing as well as producing. Would this be a repetition of her reading for Colin Bradford? She was troubled by the passage of time without her earning money.

Now Jerry seemed obsessed by moving pictures. He talked endlessly about Thomas Edison's Vitascope and Siegmund Lubin's Cineograph – both projectors used to show the films they made.

'Lubin's a real pirate,' he explained. 'There're a lot of them out there. What I mean is,' he said in response to Elisabeth's blank stare, 'that copies are made of hundreds of original films and distributed all over by what's become known as motion picture exhibitors.'

'But they're all so bad,' Elisabeth reiterated.

'This is the pioneer period, Beth. You see these chains of theaters popping up everywhere – that'll be the impetus to working out improvements. Hell, Edison is predicting there'll be a time when we'll see "talking pictures".'

'But for now I'll take theater.' She managed a wry smile. 'The question is, will theater take me?'

'Sugar, you're going to win over the old boy. You're just what he needs. A young, beautiful, talented actress with a genuine British accent.' He chuckled reminiscently. 'He was telling me how the great Edwin Booth was laughed off stage when he played *Hamlet* in London, because of his American accent. He doesn't want an American audience to laugh off an American actress trying for a British accent. He wants the real thing – and that's you.'

On a humid Tuesday afternoon in September Elisabeth and Jerry approached Douglas Graham's office. The *Clipper* carried reports of his casting efforts: 'A pivotal role – demanding an authentic British accent – remains to be cast. Graham plans to go into rehearsal in three weeks.'

Elisabeth was relieved that the reception room was empty. Nobody else – at least at this hour – was reading for the role of the young British girl. She sat in one of the chairs, rows of which encircled two walls of the reception room, while Jerry approached the stern-faced woman who sat at the desk.

'This is the actress you talked about with Mr Graham?' she asked briskly and turned her gaze on Elisabeth. 'And what is your name, my dear?'

'Beth Winston.' The woman at the desk, she understood, was checking out her accent. 'We understand Mr Graham requires a British actress for his production.'

'That's right. Please sit down,' the receptionist told Jerry, and disappeared into an inner office.

Elisabeth liked Douglas Graham on sight. She quickly saw that he was articulate, soft-spoken, and had a genuine love for the theater. She listened earnestly while he gave her a brief yet comprehensive breakdown of the character of the British girl in the play.

'I don't expect a finished performance.' His smile was gentle. 'Mr Schiff, would you please read with her?'

Elisabeth reached for the script, willing herself not to be nervous.

David was here watching over her. He had trained her well. *She could do this part.*

She and Jerry completed the scene. Her heart pounding, she looked up expectantly.

'You have a feel for the role,' Douglas Graham conceded, but his eyes were noncommittal. 'I'd like you to read with Mabel Caldwell tomorrow morning at ten.' He glanced from Elisabeth to Jerry.

'We'll be here,' Jerry said, and Elisabeth sensed his elation.

Ingrained from early childhood by Grandma on the importance of punctuality, Elisabeth made sure she and Jerry were at Graham's office at ten o'clock sharp. Mabel Caldwell was late. To while away the time Graham reminisced about visits to London. He'd seen Ellen Terry, Bernhardt, Eleonora Duse.

'I saw Ellen Terry in *The Second Mrs Tanqueray* in 1893,' he mused and Elisabeth glowed. Grandma had talked about Ellen Terry with such admiration. 'And Mrs Patrick Campbell as Juliet.' He paused to chuckle. 'Of course, she was far past the age – she's forty if she's a day. But one thing I noticed on my last trip abroad: theater in London has changed since Queen Victoria's time. Today few plays become successful without a bedroom scene by the second act. The hero must be in bed with his wife or his mistress – and there's all that business of his climbing into his trousers and she into her dress after showing off her figure in drawers and stockings. And –' He abandoned his monologue at a crisp knock on the door.

'Come in,' he ordered.

The door opened. Mabel Caldwell – tall, imperious, attractive – strode into the room.

'Doug, darling, I'm sorry to be late,' she cooed, yet Elisabeth sensed she was annoyed that her presence was required here.

'I'd like you to read with Beth Winston here.' He nodded towards her. 'And this is her manager, Mr Schiff.'

Mabel Caldwell smiled first at Jerry, then at Elisabeth. 'Of course, whatever you say, Doug.'

Graham pulled a chair up beside Elisabeth for Mabel and provided each with a manuscript. Only another woman would see Mabel Caldwell's hostility towards her, Elisabeth thought uneasily. The two women began to read. She wasn't giving her best, Elisabeth scolded herself in silence. Why was she allowing Mabel Caldwell to upset her?

Still, when she and Mabel finished reading the scene, Elisabeth felt that Graham was pleased. Mabel was inspecting the tiny watch that hung from a gold chain about her neck.

'Mr Schiff, drop by my office tomorrow afternoon. We'll discuss terms. Remember, this is a small role,' Graham emphasized, 'but a fine introduction for a new actress to American audiences.'

'I'll be here,' Jerry agreed, his smile deferential.

'We should be in rehearsal in about two weeks. There're no conflicts?' he asked Jerry.

'No, sir. We've made no commitments for Beth. This is her first reading,' he lied. 'As I explained, she felt she needed to familiarize herself with the American ways before I approached a producer.'

'Tomorrow then.' All at once Graham seemed anxious to be done with this conversation.

'She's a charming little one,' Mabel murmured, but the aura of condescension was not lost on Elisabeth. Nor on Douglas Graham, she surmised. That was why he was suddenly almost curt.

Elisabeth and Jerry said brief farewells and left the room – but not without hearing Mabel Caldwell's mocking drawl.

'Honestly, Doug, you're not serious about using her in the play? I mean, just because her British accent sounds almost credible –'

Elisabeth and Jerry walked in grim silence to the elevator.

'That one is a bitch,' Jerry said. 'But Graham will know how to handle her.'

'I didn't read well,' Elisabeth sighed. 'I kind of fell apart inside.'

'Graham's smart enough to realize you were intimidated,' Jerry soothed. 'He wouldn't be signing you if he didn't believe you were good. This is a part written for you,' he said with satisfaction. 'The critics will love you.'

Now Jerry focused on practicalities. He would take care of Amy during the weeks of rehearsal. If for any reason he needed to be somewhere – 'you know, to keep up my contacts' – they'd arrange for Mrs O'Brien to be with Amy.

'Jerry, I don't have the part yet,' Elisabeth protested.

'It's yours,' he insisted. 'I saw it in my crystal ball.'

The following afternoon Jerry prepared to leave for his appointment with Graham. The morning sunlight had given way to showers. Grandma always said rainy days were lucky days for making business arrangements. That was what she always told Papa, who loathed such superstitions. But today, seeing Jerry off in the rain, Elisabeth clung sentimentally to Grandma's cherished superstition.

'Jerry, don't hold out for a lot of money,' she cautioned. 'Just let him hire me!'

She was almost glad for the rain because this was not an afternoon to take Amy to the park. She wanted to be here when Jerry returned. Please God, don't let anything happen to change Douglas Graham's mind. Jerry had insisted Graham wouldn't let Mabel Caldwell interfere with his casting, though Jerry admitted she was becoming an important star.

Elisabeth fretted impatiently at the wait – all the while trying to keep Amy entertained despite her confinement in their small room. Why was it taking Jerry so long? Had Douglas Graham changed his mind and Jerry was nervous about coming home to tell her?

She leaped to her feet at the sound of a light knock on the door. Jerry would realize Amy was probably napping by now. She pulled the door open. Jerry hovered there with a triumphant smile.

'The old buzzard drove a hard bargain, but you start rehearsals in two weeks. For triple what you were paid in Melbourne. Of course, for Broadway that's small potatoes.'

'Oh, Jerry!' She flung her arms about him in relief. 'I was so scared.'

'This is it, sugar. Your big chance!' He held her in comfort. For a moment she saw something in his eyes that was disconcerting. But she was being absurd, she scolded herself. Jerry was like a brother to her. She'd misinterpreted what she had seen. 'But watch out for Mabel,' Jerry exhorted. 'You're too young and talented to please her.'

'What can I do?' Elisabeth faltered.

'Be your own sweet self. Don't get into shouting matches with her. If she plays nasty, pretend to be forgiving. This is a great role for you.'

Elisabeth was grateful that Jerry had acquired a manuscript for her to study prior to rehearsals. She worked long hours – not just to be letter-perfect but to build a character in all the little ways David had taught her and which were now instinctive. Oh, she wished Grandma could be here to see her on opening night! Grandma would be so proud.

Jerry was to work for two days as a stage manager for a company filming in the Bronx.

'The money is peanuts,' he said in disgust, yet Elisabeth felt his excitement at being part of a film crew. 'But I don't have to worry about being seen by anybody important. After all,' he drawled, 'I'm manager of Beth Winston, a soon-to-be Broadway star. I can't afford to be seen slumming.'

'Where is this Bronx? How do you get there?'

'It's just north of the city. I'll take the El up.'

'I'm glad that in London we have the more civilized underground,' Elisabeth said. 'I'd be terrified to ride on one of those things, hanging up in the air that way.'

'I don't think anything would terrify you,' Jerry said with unexpected tenderness. 'Remember, I was with you in the San Francisco earthquake. You'll have to go on the El one day. You'll be impressed. Not quite the Twentieth Century Limited,' he conceded, 'but the cars are done up with mahogany paneling and velvet upholstery and lots of brass fittings.'

'And this will take you up to where people are making those awful films?'

'They're awful now. But the day will come when the whole world will rush to see the latest "flickers". These are the pioneers. Glory days are coming.'

'Thank God for the theater,' she said softly. 'And please God, let the critics like me.'

Jerry left early in the morning for the Bronx. He warned Elisabeth that he might not be back until very late.

'Stay with the playscript,' he ordered. 'I want to see Doug Graham's face when you walk in letter-perfect.'

Elisabeth was disturbed that Jerry was racing off to work for two days for a piddling amount – though she realized they needed every extra dollar they could muster. All these months she'd contributed nothing. But she'd be earning soon, she comforted herself. Though she was impressed by what she was to be paid, she knew that Jerry felt she should receive more. 'The old bastard is taking advantage of you – he knows we're anxious for you to be seen in New York.'

She was impatient for the first day of rehearsal. Jerry had cued her over and over again. She knew every line of her part – and most of the lines of the other actors in her scenes – yet it troubled her that Mabel Caldwell objected to her being in the cast. Like Jerry had advised, she'd avoid any conflict with Mabel. Mabel Caldwell was a Broadway star. She was playing a very small role.

She'd arranged with Mrs O'Brien – awed that a tenant was to appear in a Broadway play – to care for Amy during rehearsal hours. But the night before rehearsals were to commence, Mrs O'Brien was called away to a sister's bedside. He would take care of Amy, Jerry soothed. Amy would be delighted – she adored Jerry. Since Jerry had come into their lives, she'd at last stopped asking, 'When's Papa coming home?'

Except for Mabel Caldwell, Elisabeth liked every member of the cast. It felt wonderful, she thought this first day, to be in rehearsal again. Only now did she truly realize how much she missed working in theater. And once they'd gone through the first reading, she relaxed. She was exhilarated by the conviction that the play – translated from a recent French success – would be well received.

At Graham's orders a boy was dispatched to a nearby cafeteria – a new institution in New York – to bring back sandwiches and coffee. Probably, Elisabeth surmised, because less time would be lost than if they went out for lunch.

'All right, let's get back to the play,' Graham said crisply when lunch had been consumed. 'I want us to open on schedule.' Now Elisabeth remembered that Jerry said Mabel Caldwell had a reputation for being slow with lines: 'Too many nights at Rector's or Martin's.'

The cast settled themselves again in the semicircle of chairs onstage. Unconsciously Elisabeth abandoned the script, saying her lines from memory, slowly building the character, as David had taught her to do. Then she realized that the rest of the cast had discovered she knew her lines. Mabel Caldwell read through clenched teeth now. The others were curious, seemed all at once wary – as though new demands were being placed on them.

She'd made her first major mistake, she rebuked herself. She reached for the script again, pretended that she'd known only part of her lines. This cast wasn't 'the family' she had known in Melbourne.

At the end of the first week of rehearsal, she confessed to Jerry that Mabel made constant snide remarks about her performance.

'But Mr Graham seems pleased with me,' she said with a touch of defiance. 'And next week we start with the blocking. What will you bet that Mabel tries her best to upstage me at every chance she gets?'

'You know how to handle that.' But Jerry was somber.

'I won't let her ruin my scenes – neither one of them,' she said with a wry smile. It was a small role – but if she handled herself well, it would be a scene stealer.

As she anticipated, Elisabeth had to struggle not to be upstaged. *Why didn't Mr Graham reproach Mabel?* But she knew the answer to that: he didn't want to antagonize his star. Mabel Caldwell brought people to the box office. All right – let Mabel upstage her at rehearsals. That wouldn't happen in performance. She knew how to position herself onstage so that she could say her lines without giving the audience the back of her head.

She was ecstatic when the company's character woman and the leading man both congratulated her on her performance at the end of the second week of rehearsal.

'Of course, you're not making Lady Mabel happy,' the character woman told her.

On the first day of their third week of rehearsal Mabel arrived with an odd air of triumph. On time. She cooed sweetly to Graham about admiring the costumes being designed for her.

'Darling, there are just a couple of changes – but we've worked that all out.'

'All right, places everybody,' Graham said briskly. 'Take it from the top.'

Moments after Elisabeth's entrance Mabel stopped dead.

'Doug, really,' she scolded. 'Why don't you explain to Beth that she's reading that speech terribly? It'll reflect on all of us at opening night.'

'Mabel, let me direct.' Graham refused to be ruffled. But Elisabeth saw the wariness that crept over him. 'We're still in rehearsal.'

Five minutes later – at Elisabeth's most poignant speech – Mabel interrupted again.

'No! You're throwing away this whole scene!'

Elisabeth felt tension suddenly fill the air. The silence was deadly.

'Doug, this is supposed to be a professional company! I can't allow myself to appear with an amateur!' Mabel stalked off the stage.

Elisabeth's heart began to pound as Doug Graham followed his temperamental star into the wings. A coldness crept over her. She felt the alarm of the others. They could hear Mabel's threats, her insistence that she would leave the play unless Elisabeth was replaced.

'I can't jeopardize my position!' Mabel shrieked. 'Either she goes or I go!'

Now the voices in the wings were muted, only occasional words audible. Moments later Doug appeared on stage.

'We'll take off until three this afternoon. Everybody back by then.' Cold and trembling Elisabeth – along with the other cast members – prepared to leave. 'Elisabeth, I'd like to talk to you.'

She knew even before he told her that she was to be replaced.

'The woman's a bitch,' he whispered, though they were sure Mabel had left the theater. 'But there's nothing I can do. I can't replace her at the last minute. It'll be rough to replace you.' For a moment compassion sneaked through. 'But you're an excellent young actress. You'll find something else.'

Chapter Sixteen

Elisabeth walked out into the crisp late morning air in an aura of disbelief. She had known that Mabel Caldwell resented her. Why was she so shaken to find herself out of the play? It was wrong. There should be a trade union in the theater.

She walked swiftly, fighting tears. Jerry would be so upset. He'd warned her about Mabel Caldwell. But what else could she have done? Would Jerry give up being her manager after this? The prospect was frightening. How would she survive in New York then? But she shouldn't be so dependent on Jerry. She should be able to handle her life on her own.

Perhaps she could get a job in a department store like B. Altman, or Lord & Taylor, or Macy's. But who would care for Amy when she was at work? In their rooming house there was a woman who worked at Macy's. She took her two girls to her mother's house on her way to work each morning, picked them up at the end of the day. Mrs O'Brien might be available most of the time – but how could she afford to pay her out of a sales assistant's wages?

David always said that there were hundreds trying for every acting job that was available. '*It takes more than talent and hard work to make a living in theater. It takes a solid chunk of luck.*' Ethel and John had been hard-working. They'd had some degree of talent. But they'd never advanced beyond the shoddiest of touring companies.

Jerry said they shouldn't try for a road company for her. 'That's a real dead end.' And how could she go on tour with Amy? Oh, she knew some women raised their children in backstage dressing rooms – but that wasn't what she wanted for Amy.

She was exhausted by the time she arrived at the rooming house – more from tension than the walk. Jerry would have brought Amy home from the park by now, she surmised. He'd be giving her a sandwich and a glass of milk. Oh, he would be upset when she told him she was out of the play!

Aware of the shock, the comprehension, in his eyes when she walked into their room, she explained what had happened.

'The damn bitch!' He mouthed rather than voiced the words because of Amy's presence. 'But in a way that's a huge compliment. A big star like Mabel Caldwell is afraid of you. Of course, the word around town is that she got where she is on her back. She's managed to go far on very little talent.'

'Maybe I should try for a job in a department store.' But she loved the theater. 'For a little while.'

'No, Beth!' His voice was so harsh Amy glanced up in momentary alarm. 'We've only been in New York for a few months, sugar. It takes time to make a splash on Broadway. We'll be all right. I'll pick up more work with that film company.' He hesitated. 'I might be able to fix up something there for you –' His eyes were questioning.

'I'll do whatever you say.'

'Meanwhile I'll make the rounds of producers' offices. Better than you making the rounds of the theatrical agents.' He grinned. 'After all, the toast of Melbourne theater can't be making rounds like the common folk.'

This was the heart of the casting season – and Jerry was a zealous personal manager. During the following two months he arranged for three auditions for her. The result each time was depressing. She read well, but her British accent didn't fit in with the company.

Jerry took her to see the Graham production, which had garnered good reviews. Still – sitting up in cheap second balcony seats – she knew she could have made the role she'd rehearsed into something truly spectacular. The actress who had replaced her was adequate, no more – as the critics had said. But that was what Mabel Caldwell had wished.

As December approached Elisabeth was beset by painful recall. She was facing the first anniversary of David's death. Always, she thought in anguish, Amy's birthday would be tainted because this was the day her father was murdered. And the police had never caught his murderer. The man on the bicycle who had shot David roamed Melbourne a free man.

So many nights, half asleep, she reached out an arm and came fully awake in the realization that David would never be there for her again. How strange that she could feel passion when David lay buried in the earth. But Amy must have a third birthday party, she resolved. Jerry would stand in for Amy's father.

Grieving inside, she bought a tiny cake for Amy's birthday. Mrs O'Brien was invited to join them. Amy jubilantly made a wish, blew out the three candles. How sad, Elisabeth thought, that Amy had so little time with her father.

Ten days after Amy's birthday party Jerry came to their room to tell her that his sisters had sent him a round-trip train ticket to Glendale.

'My father's all right now, but he had a heart attack. They want me to come home for the eight days of Hanukkah. It'll be two days on the train each way,' he calculated. 'I have to go,' he said apologetically.

'I know.' How she wished she could go home to her family – even for just a day. 'Amy and I will be all right,' she insisted, knowing he was concerned for them. 'And you said just yesterday that every-thing will be slow in the theater around this time.'

Lest Amy should be upset at Jerry's departure, they made a festive ceremony of the occasion. Elisabeth and Amy accompanied him to the West 23rd Street ferry, which would carry him to the Exchange Place terminal in Jersey City. Here he would board the Southern Railway's *The Great Limited*.

They arrived twenty minutes before the ferry was to depart. Jerry clucked in good-humored reproach.

'I'll bet you were even born early.'

'As a matter of fact, I was.' Elisabeth's eyes were bright with amused self-mockery. 'And I've been running ever since.'

'You'll make it to the top,' he promised. 'I've read it in the cards.'

'What happened to your crystal ball?'

'I'm partial to the cards this week.' He lifted Amy into his arms so that she might have a better view of the sun-drenched water of the Hudson. 'Amy, you take good care of your mama until I get back.'

'We'll be fine.' Elisabeth's smile was confident, belying her dis-comforting sense of abandonment.

'Remember what I told you. If there's work for you with the film company, Fred will phone and leave a message with Sarah at the candy store.' Elisabeth understood the candy store kept a phone available for the convenience of their regular customers. 'Stop by a couple of times a day. And keep safe the directions I wrote down for getting out there on the Ninth Avenue El.'

'I have them. And don't worry about me – I can get along on the El without an escort.' So she'd hate working in films – but as Jerry pointed out, the pay was better than working in a department store or what he referred to as 'slinging hash'.

The ferry arrived. Jerry prepared to board it. He swung Amy into the air, gave her a playful kiss, then turned to Elisabeth.

'I'll miss you two,' he said, and leaned forward to bestow a brotherly kiss on Elisabeth's cheek, but there was a warmth in his embrace that startled Elisabeth.

At the Exchange Terminal in Jersey City Jerry boarded the Southern Railway's *The Great Limited*, which traveled all the way down to New Orleans by way of Atlanta. At Atlanta he'd change for a train to Glendale. Leave it to 'the girls' to buy him Pullman tickets, he thought in satisfaction as he settled himself in his seat – pleased that no passenger had surfaced thus far to share the area with him.

Mollie and Hannah – both in their thirties – were still 'the girls' to his parents and himself. Mollie had been married for years. Hannah, unabashed at being an old maid at thirty-one, lived at home. She'd be the one who'd got Mollie to share in buying him the round-trip ticket. Of course, she didn't know that Mollie had also sent him a ten-dollar bill for incidentals. Both slipped him money from time to time. He was their precious baby brother.

Sure, he missed the family. But what was there for him in Glendale? Work with Papa in the pharmacy? He'd hate that. Mollie kept hoping he'd go back to school, become an accountant or a lawyer. Go back to school at twenty-two? She was out of her mind. Hannah truly liked teaching school. Mollie was busy with her kids. They all expected him to be something special.

Maybe he should have stayed in California instead of returning to New York from San Francisco. Fred, at the film company, kept talking about Los Angeles as being the perfect spot to make pictures: 'The weather's always warm. Land is cheap. People work cheap. I hear somebody's planning on going out to film *The Count of Monte Cristo*. I'll bet you it'll be a sensation.'

Los Angeles was three thousand miles away from Thomas Edison and all his injunctions against anybody who made and sold moving picture equipment and films. Edison figured his patents gave him exclusive rights. He kept filing court injunctions against everybody who was trying to move into the field. The last time he worked for Fred, Jerry had been shocked that Edison's spies were right on their tails. They had to move across rooftops to lose them.

By the time the train pulled out of Philadelphia Jerry was restless, dreading the long trip ahead. Crossing the country from San Francisco had been different. That was traveling in luxury – and Beth had been with him. But there was no room for anything but business between him and Beth. She was the gold mine that would make him Somebody. But his body was a traitor. God, he wanted to make love to her!

He'd kill some time in the dining car, he comforted himself. No poker games on this trip. Unless a few Congressmen came aboard when they stopped in Washington tonight. Maybe there'd be a late night game in one of the drawing rooms ahead. Congressmen wouldn't be traveling in the regular Pullman accommodations. Fighting boredom he reached into the pocket of his overcoat for the current issue of the *Clipper*. He'd read until it was time to go in for supper.

Passengers were sparse this time of year. A bit too early for the homegoing Christmas crowds, he surmised.

He consulted the timetable. By four o'clock tomorrow afternoon they ought to be pulling into Atlanta. Another hour from there and he'd be in Glendale. In time for supper.

Mama would have been cooking all day, he thought with a surge of tenderness. But don't let her start in again about him 'settling down here at home and raising a family'. That wasn't his *schtick*. He was born for bigger things.

On the way to the park this third morning of Jerry's absence Elisabeth stopped at the candy store.

'You got a message,' Sarah told her with a cheerful grin. 'Call Fred at this number. He said it's important.'

Her hands trembling – unaccustomed to using a telephone – Elisabeth called the number left for her. This was another candy store phone. The man who responded gave her a message from Fred. She was to report for work at 8.30 the following morning.

'Yes, I'll be there,' she said, fighting panic. Jerry had given her explicit directions, she reminded herself. She knew which El would take her to her destination. She wouldn't get lost in the wilds of the Bronx. 'Please tell Fred I'll be there.' And please, God, let Mrs O'Brien be available to look after Amy. Why wasn't there some nice place where working mothers could leave their little ones during the day?

Elisabeth curtailed their park stay this morning. The area was deserted, the temperature on a downward spiral, the sky ominous, hinting at snow.

'Where's Frances?' Amy was troubled that her favorite playmate wasn't here today.

'The weather is so cold Miss Jamison probably decided to keep her at home,' Elisabeth told her cajolingly. When snow had threatened last week, Miss Jamison had come to the park to invite Elisabeth to bring Amy to the impressive townhouse where Frances lived.

'Couldn't they come to our house?' Amy's eyes – the same lovely violet as her mother's – were accusing.

'We just have the one room, darling.' How could she ask Miss Jamison to come there with Frances? 'But you'll see Frances soon.'

At the rooming house she went directly to Mrs O'Brien to ask if she'd be available to keep Amy with her tomorrow.

'I have an offer to work on a moving picture being shot up in the Bronx,' she explained, and saw Mrs O'Brien's eyes brighten with respect.

'Oh, I love the nickelodeons,' she gushed. 'My daughter says I'm addicted. You must promise to tell me all about it when you come home.'

Mrs O'Brien was more impressed with her small-paying job in moving pictures than she had been with the theater role, Elisabeth thought in astonishment. Mrs O'Brien went often to the nickelodeon. Moving pictures might be looked down on by the upper classes, but they were being embraced by the working classes. Was Jerry right? In time would far more people see moving pictures than would see stage plays?

Now Elisabeth tried to gear herself for tomorrow's venture. No lines to learn, Jerry had pointed out – though Fred insisted on actors saying words that fit the action – 'It makes it more real.' What would she wear? Her coat, bought at a secondhand shop on the Lower East

Side, was lovely. Jerry was impressed by its Lord & Taylor label. She'd wear her gray suit underneath – she'd be warm enough.

In a flurry of alarm that they were lost, she sought out the directions to the 'studio' where she was to go, found them. In a way, she told herself, this was an adventure. That was how Grandma would consider it. And she'd be earning money – and that was urgent.

Nostalgic tears filled her eyes as she thought of Grandma, who'd worked as a maid and saved up enough to open her tiny shop in Whitechapel that was always days from extinction. But Grandma did what was necessary to raise Mama. If she had to work in moving pictures to survive and raise Amy, so be it.

Snow began to fall in early evening. By morning the city was a winter wonderland. Aware that the weather might delay her arrival at the studio, Elisabeth left the rooming house – with only a cup of tea and a roll for breakfast – at 6.30 and headed for the El. Clearly other passengers harbored her fears of delays. The El cars were already crowded.

Elisabeth steeled herself to be calm on this first ride on the El – which traveled at a height for the most part of second-story levels but soared even higher at one area. As she'd feared, snow on the tracks caused frustrating delays. The cars were emptying out as they traveled northward. Approaching her station she noted that only she and a young man engrossed in a book remained. A clock at the station gave the time as 8.20. Jerry said the studio was only a five-minute walk from the station.

She emerged from the car the moment it stopped. The other passenger passed her as she walked down the light iron stairway, enclosed at the side and roofed.

At the foot of the stairs she gazed about uncertainly, checked with Jerry's written directions. Yes, turn to the right here. The area was sparsely settled, but Jerry had warned her about that. She soon realized she was following in the footsteps – literally – of the young man who'd been on the El. He, too, she suspected was headed for the studio, a barn-like, one-storied wooden structure that must once have been used for storage.

A dozen people milled about inside the building. A man whom Elisabeth guessed – from Jerry's description – was Fred was in tense conversation with a man holding what appeared to be a cumbersome camera. She approached Fred with a hesitant smile.

'You're Jerry's Australian actress,' he said before she could introduce herself. 'We can't shoot the outdoor picture we'd planned in this weather, but don't worry,' he soothed, 'we'll use you anyway. You'll play an oriental girl who's been kidnapped and put into a harem. Paul!' he called loudly. The young man Elisabeth had seen on the El came to his side. 'Paul, this is – uh –' He waved a hand in doubt.

'Beth Winston,' she said. An oriental girl in a harem?

'Beth, this is Paul Coleman. He's my stage manager and make-up and wardrobe man. Paul, we're doing *The Jewel of Ali's Harem* since we have to shoot indoors.' He gestured towards an area closed off by a series of screens. 'Chuck's setting up now. Take care of Beth.'

'Don't look so stricken,' Paul said gently, leading her into a small room off the main studio area. 'Fred knows no amount of make-up is going to transform you into the jewel of Ali's Harem. I mean, you're beautiful,' he said hastily, 'but oriental? No.'

'This is my first job in pictures,' she stammered. 'I've only worked in the Australian theater.'

'You're a long way from home.' He chuckled, propelling her to a chair at a makeshift dressing table where two other women – considerably Elisabeth's senior – were applying their own make-up.

'Actually, I'm from London,' she said while he began to try to transform her features into an oriental cast. 'I went to Australia four years ago and joined an acting company there.'

'What kind of parts did you play?' He seemed genuinely interested.

'Mostly Ibsen and Shaw and Pinero.' She gazed into the mirror with amazement as Paul applied eyeliner with a heavy hand – almost achieving the appropriate tilt to her eyes.

'When will this country see playwrights like that?' Paul's face was worshipful. 'It's so hard for an American playwright to get a production in this country.' He hesitated. 'That's what I really want to do – write plays.'

'But I thought theater in New York was so active. Not that I've seen any plays by Americans,' she conceded.

'There's Clyde Fitch and David Belasco.' His smile was wry. 'Not exactly competition for Ibsen or Shaw.'

'Paul!' Fred's booming voice interrupted their conversation. 'Brief the girl and get out to check the set. We've got a picture to shoot!'

'We don't work with individual scripts,' Paul told Elisabeth apologetically. 'Fred talks the cast through the action, but he wants you to speak. Just improvise – it doesn't have to match the dialogue that runs in print below the film.' Now he pointed to a carton at one side of the room. 'Pick out a costume that'll fit and put it on. Then come on out into the studio. Sarah –' he turned to the woman who remained at the dressing table, 'show Beth where to dress.'

Elisabeth was unnerved by the sheerness of the harem costumes. But this was part of the job, she told herself. Though it had never happened thus far, she could be required to wear such a costume in the theater. If she was to be a girl in a harem, the audience would expect her to look the part. She changed with haste and joined the others on the set.

The day seemed interminably long. She obeyed the instructions rattled off by Fred in blunt language. Haste seemed to be the key word. The storyline was crude melodrama, but this appeared to be what audiences liked.

In a corner of her mind she assured herself that Mrs O'Brien would give Amy her supper and put her to bed. From what the others in the cast were saying among themselves, she surmised they would be working tomorrow, also. Finally, she was earning money.

It was past eight o'clock when Fred called a halt with an air of satisfaction and ordered them all to report again the following morning. Exhausted – recoiling from her day's performance – Elisabeth dressed quickly and hurried from the studio. Moments later Paul fell into step beside her.

'At least the snow is over,' he consoled. 'The El won't be held up tomorrow morning. We can grab an extra hour of sleep.'

'I hope Fred was satisfied with my work.' This wasn't acting. So what was it? 'I mean, there's no rehearsal time . . .' She gestured her bewilderment.

'If Fred didn't like you, he wouldn't have told you to come back tomorrow.' Paul was matter-of-fact, but his eyes were compassionate. 'I know – it's a long way from playing Ibsen and Shaw. But it's work – and Fred pays on time.'

Together they walked to the station, took refuge from the sharp night cold in the small comfortable waiting room on the platform. They heard the voices of others approaching the station now. They would be a lively group heading south.

Now Paul began to talk about the problems of young American playwrights.

'American producers think they'll have a success only with a play that's been popular in Paris or London or Rome. They're interested only in how much money they can make. They figure they're not gambling when they buy American rights to a British or European play. But for now,' he said with an effort at lightness, 'we're working in a new art form. Moving pictures. Of course, there's not much art in them at this point – but that'll change.'

Was there no future for her in the American theater? Elisabeth pondered with new cynicism. Was she doomed to languish in moving pictures, cranked out for the nickelodeons that were soaring in numbers? American theater closed to her because of her British accent? Because she didn't know how to play the game? The prospect was disheartening.

Chapter Seventeen

Elisabeth was pleased to realize she'd have Paul Coleman's company on the long El ride. He shared a tiny apartment near Union Square with his older brother, who was studying law at New York University.

'My parents live on the Lower East Side.' That was the Jewish section, wasn't it? 'They could have moved into something better years ago, but they were saving to see Jason and me through school.' He chuckled, his face reflecting his love for his family. 'Or course, they think I'm out of my mind to want to write plays, but they figure when that peters out I'll go after a teaching job. A noble profession,' he derided gently. But it was obvious he had great respect for education.

'My older brother is studying to be a doctor and the younger to be a lawyer – though he truly wants to be an artist,' Elisabeth said. Did they miss her, the way she missed them? 'I haven't seen them in a long time.'

'That's rough.' She felt his unspoken curiosity.

Haltingly – in a few simple words – Elisabeth explained her situation. She felt his shock at her father's actions, his compassion when she spoke about David's death and how she hoped to find a place in the theater so that she could support Amy and herself.

'I know moving pictures are crude today, but I'm convinced they'll improve beyond our wildest imagination.' Paul exuded enthusiasm. 'I suspect there'll be a lot of money to be made. But, of course,' he conceded with a wry smile, 'my heart will always belong to the theater.'

'Do you suppose we'll finish filming tomorrow – or will there be more work?'

'We'll finish this one tomorrow without a doubt. How much time do you need to spend on one-reelers? But Fred keeps rolling. He's aware of the big demand for moving pictures that tell stories. Audiences are tired of vaudeville acts and animal acts and prizefights. And Fred pays us every night – we don't have to worry about his running out on us.'

Elisabeth was startled. She hadn't considered such a possibility. 'It's easier than carrying trays or standing up in a shop for twelve hours a day.' She hesitated, her mind chasing onto another track. 'Tell me about the Lower East Side. Is it like Whitechapel in London?'

The next day Elisabeth was happy to learn that she would be working for an additional two days – with promises of work the following week. Still, she was tense in the realization that her being able to accept employment depended upon Mrs O'Brien's availability to care for Amy.

On her first so-called idle day she asked Mrs O'Brien to look after Amy for three hours in the early afternoon. She'd bought the *Clipper*, read about the casting calls for new plays. Jerry insisted he should approach producers as her personal manager rather than her going around to the theatrical agents. 'No class,' he dismissed this. 'I've got "the star of Melbourne theater" to offer.' But so far nobody was buying 'the star of the Melbourne theater'. This afternoon she would follow the leads in the *Clipper*.

Fighting trepidation she approached the first destination she'd scheduled for herself. The producer was casting a play by Shaw. Perhaps here a British accent would be an asset. Contriving a confident smile she opened the door that led to the Fiske Theatrical Agency. Signs indicated she was to walk up two flights of dreary, dusty stairs. She arrived at the third floor landing, geared herself to open the door that bore the agency's name.

The small, windowless anteroom was jammed with people, some seated in the shabby chairs placed against paint-hungry walls, others standing. Synthetic smiles pasted on faces to hide quiet desperation. A woman sat at the reception desk and pecked away at a typewriter – ignoring the waiting people. Following the routine, Elisabeth walked to the desk, gave her name to the woman there, but was dismissed with a wave of her hand.

'Mr Lewison will be interviewing in a little while.'

She took her place in the only tiny space as yet unoccupied and waited.

Two hours later – after only a handful were interviewed – the receptionist dismissed the others.

'Mr Lewison will be seeing ingénues and character men tomorrow. Nobody else,' she warned.

Every muscle in her body tense, Elisabeth joined the disgruntled parade out of the office and down the stairs into the street. She remembered Ethel talking about the endless days of waiting around in the offices of theatrical agencies. *'You sat there – or stood – day after day in those offices. Your eyes glazed, this silly smile on your face. Always hoping for that wonderful part that would change your life.'* To Ethel, working for Roger in Melbourne might not have been appearing on Broadway, but it was not daily rejection. She and John had been happy there, Elisabeth thought with fresh grief. Roger had been what Grandma called a *mensch*.

Jerry uttered a sigh of relief when he settled himself in his Pullman car in Atlanta. He was always happy to see the family, but they wore him down. As expected, Mama had been tearful, Papa reproachful that he wouldn't remain in Glendale and work with him at the pharmacy. He'd regaled them with his expectations. He doubted that Mama or Papa believed one word he said about his great opportunity as a personal manager. To them theater was a world of decadent, not truly respectable people.

The girls believed. Hannah in her dull job of teaching third-graders, Mollie in her dull marriage with little hope of rising above their current status. Each had secretly tucked a bill into his pocket in his final moments in the house. They knew it took time to build a career in theater. Hell, he was only twenty-two. Rome wasn't built in a day.

He reached for his copy of the *Atlanta Constitution* as the train chugged out of the handsome new Union Depot. But his mind was too active to focus on the newspaper. A bunch of plays were being cast for Broadway. There had to be a part for Beth in one of them. He wasn't wrong – she was special. He'd known that the day they met in all that craziness. Anna Held was doing great with her French accent. Why was a British accent such a handicap to Beth?

He was amused by Mama's delight in the new moving picture that told a story – being exploited by a producer named D. W. Griffith. Atlanta laws required that a chief operator plus an assistant be employed by every theater to guarantee safe operation. The girls pretended to be uninterested, but Mama said they were steady attendees. Would they see any of Fred's pictures? See Elisabeth?

Restless, dreading the long trip ahead, he went in to the pleasantly laid-out dining car as soon as it was open. He smiled, recalling Elisabeth's astonishment at the potted plants in the dining car of the luxury trains that carried them from Oakland to New York. In minutes the elegantly set tables in the car were occupied, the atmosphere lively. He studied the menu, grateful that he'd persuaded Mama not to pack sandwiches for him. Tonight he'd dine in style.

'Sir, would you be willing to share your table?' a white-jacketed waiter asked in apologetic Southern tones. 'We's running short tonight.'

'Of course.' Jerry smiled up at the waiter, then at the small, rotund man in an expensive suit who hovered nearby. 'Please sit down.'

His dinner companion was in a garrulous mood. He explained that twice a year he made this trip to Atlanta to visit his elderly parents.

'It's a long haul, but they expect it.' He consulted the menu, discussed the various items with Jerry. 'It's a sad world when the most pleasure we can find in life is in a good meal.' He paused to inspect Jerry. 'You heading back north to college?'

'I finished with that a year and a half ago.' Instinct told him that the other man had never seen the inside of any college. 'It didn't make my folks happy – my two sisters have college degrees – but I was looking for something more exciting.'

'Did you find it?' the older man asked indulgently.

'In a way,' Jerry said. 'I'm personal manager to this beautiful young Australian actress who's being considered for several Broadway plays.'

'A singer? Or like one of those Floradora Girls?' He winked in approval. 'Getting your share of *schtupping*?'

'This is a business deal,' Jerry said, smiling. 'Beth Winston was a star in Melbourne – she'll knock Broadway on its can once she appears in a play. But I can't complain about the girls in my life. Theater's the place to meet gorgeous broads – and ones that like to have a good time.' All at once signals were popping up in his head. Here was a possible backer for a Broadway production. He could handle that. With enough money you just hired the best people –

and you were off to the races. Why keep knocking his brains out trying to sell a producer on hiring Beth? *Be* a producer.

'In my business who do I meet?' The older man shrugged. 'A typewriter girl who's passable. A seamstress with nice tits. I'm fifty years old. I need something more enticing to get me going.'

'Ever think about taking a fling in the theater?' Jerry managed to sound casual. 'Being a backer gives you a ticket to the best shows in town – and I'm not talking about the ones onstage.' His eyes – his smile – were blatantly eloquent. 'If you know what I mean.'

'It's a big gamble, the way I hear it –' But it was clear his companion was eager to hear more.

'Not if you've got a play that's been a success in Europe. That's the real insurance,' Jerry pinpointed. 'And a star that's beautiful and can really act. Plus a producer who can bring the important ingredients together.'

'You know somebody like that?' His tone was mocking, but Jerry knew he was avid to be sold.

'Me.' The Jerry Schiff charm was turned on full wattage. 'I've got the star. I know how to acquire the play. And the theater,' he emphasized. 'So I'm young. That's great publicity. You know, "the new boy wonder of Broadway". Everybody rushes to see what I can do.'

'You're the type that could sell the Brooklyn Bridge.' But the scoffing was good-humored. 'What kind of money are we talking about?'

Jerry cursed in silence as the waiter slid plates onto their table. Now was not the time to test a figure. Later, he promised himself. Maybe it was just as well. Whet the old boy's appetite some more first.

'I'm Jake Pulanski,' the other man introduced himself. 'I'm in the clothing business in Manhattan.'

It soon became clear that Jake relished talking about his business success – though all at once he appeared uneasy at his candor, and shifted to discussion of the fine food provided by the dining-car chef.

'I don't mind paying for quality stuff. Life's short. I like to enjoy it. My wife died eight years ago, my daughters are wrapped up in their own lives. To them I'm just a money machine. Why shouldn't I treat myself well?'

'The smart approach,' Jerry agreed, showing the proper respect.

'Beth and I were caught in the earthquake in San Francisco. Not much fun there. She was to open in a major production of *A Doll's House*. The theater was a chunk of rubble. I persuaded her that we should do some traveling, see America. You know, to calm her after that awful experience. She wanted to go and conquer London. I persuaded her to come to New York, take a long look at Broadway – which we're doing.'

They lingered long over diner – Jake Pulanski frank about wishing to avoid the boredom of his compartment. Yet Jerry found no opening to bring up the financial aspect of producing a Broadway play. He sensed Pulanski was feeling him out, trying to decide if he was throwing a load of horseshit. Instinct warned him not to push too hard.

'It's late,' Jake said at last. 'Time to hit the hay. Let's talk over breakfast in the morning.'

Jerry returned to his car. A porter was making up his berth. He wasn't in the mood to sleep. He'd go into the parlor car and read for a while. God, could he pull off this deal with Jake Pulanski? Maybe convince him to bring in a crony or two to invest with him? Wouldn't that be something? *Jerry Schiff, Broadway producer.*

He slept in fits and starts, impatient to be sitting across the breakfast table and selling Pulanski on the 'fun' he'd find in being the backer of a Broadway play. Could he sell Jake Pulanski on following up on this once they were back in New York? All he had was a few hours.

In the morning he checked out the dining car twice before the moment was right to enter. On the third try he saw Pulanski settling down at a table. With a confident smile Jerry strode in and joined Pulanski at his table. He was startled when Pulanski himself broached the subject close to his own heart.

'I was thinking about what you said last night – I mean, how a man can have himself a good time in theater. I never did it with a chorus girl or an actress.' His eyes glistened as he considered this. 'How much money goes into producing a play?'

Jerry zeroed in with the figures he'd read in the *Clipper*, saw Pulanski wince. 'Of course, most plays have several backers. You know, you come in with part of the financing, bring in friends for the rest.'

'That makes you a producer?' Pulanski pressed.

'On the books you're the backers, but you're like partners with the producer, in on all the action. You're there at the parties, have choice seats on opening night.'

'We meet the girls?' Pulanski pinpointed. 'I mean, lots of girls?'

'With the kind of financing I mentioned, we wouldn't be producing a musical.' Jerry faked a chuckle. The old boy saw himself surrounded by chorus girls, showgirls – all panting to sleep with him. 'But once you're in the field, you meet them. Theater is like one big family.'

Pulanski reached into his vest pocket, pulled out a card. 'I'll be busy as hell for the first three or four days back in the shop, but next week sometime, call me. We'll go out for supper somewhere and talk.'

'Fine,' Jerry agreed enthusiastically. 'Let me take you to Rector's.' That impressed him. He'd never been there – but he'd heard about the place.

'Me and a friend of mine,' Jake stipulated. 'We're in the same business. He's bored with his life. He complains all the time. They moved to this big apartment on West End Avenue – his wife insisted on her own bedroom. The fancy twin beds, the fancy furniture people keep shoving at them – that wasn't good enough. She gave him four children – enough already, she said.'

'I'll take both of you to Rector's,' Jerry assured him. 'My pleasure.'

Elisabeth listened in astonishment while Jerry described the train trip from Atlanta to Manhattan in colorful detail.

'Jerry, you've never produced a play!' She was simultaneously enthralled and alarmed.

'With the money in hand I'll hire the right people. Everybody has a first time. To succeed in this world you need *chutzpah*.'

'That you've got. How did you convince him?' Yet doubts lingered in her mind.

'He's not sold yet,' Jerry conceded. 'But I showed him a world he's dying to taste. With any luck at all, he'll come up with two or three buddies to share the bankroll. He can afford this, Beth. He runs a big wholesale dress company. He'll probably want to meet you. Be charming and sweet.'

'That's all I'll be,' she warned, remembering Colin Bradford.

'Sugar, how could you think I'd expect anything else?' No, Beth was *his* baby. 'But I'll steer him in the right direction. He'll have his fun. And we'll have our own production company – starring Beth Winston.'

'For now, Fred says he'll be using me a lot. He's hoping for some clear weather so he can shoot outdoors.'

Jerry nodded. 'All of them like to shoot in sunlight. The pictures come out better. That's why some producers are talking about moving out to California. Not San Francisco,' he added as Elisabeth grimaced in painful recall. 'Southern California, like around Los Angeles. The weather down there is almost always warm and sunny.'

'This – what's his name? – Jake Pulanski – could forget the whole thing once he's back at his business.' Elisabeth ordered herself to be realistic.

'I don't think so. I walked into his life at a time when he's hungry for new excitement – and at a time when he can afford it. I'll call him next week. I'll take him and his friend out to supper at Rector's. We'll –'

'Jerry, that's so expensive!'

'The girls each slipped me a few bills. We'll manage. Oh, and I'll have to rent a cheap office. I have to look professional. Now don't get panicky,' he soothed. 'I picked up a *New York Times* at Penn Station. I saw an ad for a small office available for seven dollars – in an elevator building on West 34th Street. Prime territory. I'll be there first thing tomorrow morning.'

Jerry rented the office, hunted down a cheap desk, two chairs, and a file cabinet. He hung copies of the improvised Melbourne publicity and photographs of Elisabeth about the walls. He showed it off to Elisabeth with pride.

'Tonight you take them to Rector's. What'll that cost?' Elisabeth was uneasy. She wasn't working today. She hadn't worked yesterday, and though she was due at the studio tomorrow, she was starkly conscious of the absence of earnings.

'We don't touch the bankroll.' He avoided being specific. Knowing she'd be alarmed, Elisabeth understood. 'I still have enough from the girls' contribution to handle Rector's. Hey, by tomorrow we may be going to open up a bank account for Schiff-Winston Productions!'

Elisabeth shared Jerry's enthusiasm and ambition, but instinct warned her there were hurdles ahead. Jerry envisioned himself another Flo Ziegfeld, who was making extravagant plans – according to reports in the *Clipper* – for a revue starring Anna Held and a bevy of gorgeous girls in brief costumes. Not that Jerry contemplated offering a musical. 'A hit play from the Paris or London stage. A small cast to keep the budget low. But a spectacular set and you in gowns by Doucet.'

Though she would have to be out of bed by six o'clock tomorrow to make the trek to the Bronx, Elisabeth was determined to remain awake until Jerry returned from his supper with Jake Pulanski. Amy had long ago fallen asleep. Elisabeth's gaze moved with compulsive regularity to the small form of her daughter. She was creating a semblance of a family for Amy, she comforted herself. Jerry was 'Uncle Jerry' now. Mrs O'Brien was 'Aunt Maura'. But she yearned for Amy to be surrounded by great-grandmother, grandmother, uncles – and grandfather, she added guiltily. *Papa was wrong in what he had done.*

She tried to focus on *Savrola*, the novel by a young British officer named Winston Churchill, which she and Grandma had read when it was serialized in *Macmillan's Magazine* and which had been published as a novel several years ago. It had been like touching home to find a copy in a small secondhand bookstore last week. But her efforts to read were futile.

Write to Grandma – it was time for another letter to make its way to Lexham Gardens. The letters were always addressed to Mama and Grandma, though she suspected Mama was not happy to read about her efforts as an actress. Borrowing phrases from Paul, she tried to lend an exciting touch to the making of moving pictures. She loved talking theater with Paul. He was so knowledgeable about theater all over the world – and pessimistic about what so often passed for acting in the New York theater.

'*Actors and actresses should be concerned about their craft – not about becoming sensational personalities. What does it matter what they do away from the stage? They should concentrate on being artists.*'

But Jerry insisted it was acting offstage as well as on that made a star today. A star brought people to the box office – at a time when producing was so expensive.

Elisabeth was on the point of dozing off when a light knock thrust her awake. She tiptoed to the door.

'God, am I stuffed,' Jerry whispered. 'I kept eating and Jake kept gaping at everything.'

'Is he interested?' Her heart was pounding.

'In our becoming producers or in jumping into bed with a prospective Floradora girl?' Jerry closed the door softly behind him.

'Jerry, you know what I mean!'

'I think he's interested. I *know* he's interested. He almost popped out of his skin when he saw Lillian Russell sitting three tables away – though he admitted she was too *zovtig* for his taste. And probably twenty years too old.'

'Jerry, where do we stand?' she demanded impatiently.

'At this point, on the fence. His friend couldn't make it tonight. We're getting together again right after New Year.' Elisabeth groaned, contemplating more expenses. 'He's treating,' Jerry added, grinning. 'But I suspect he won't do anything unless his friend comes along. We just have to wait, sugar. And don't look so disappointed. A big deal like this takes time. I've got a feeling in my gut that we'll pull this off.'

'I've got a feeling I'd better get to sleep. I'm working tomorrow.' She stifled a yawn. 'Oh, Mrs O'Brien said she'd be pleased if you could take care of Amy in the morning. She has some shopping she'd like to do.'

'Sure, old Uncle Jerry will take Amy to the park.' He reached to give her a quick hug. 'And don't look so downcast. You know what I always tell you – Rome wasn't built in a day.'

Chapter Eighteen

The last days of 1906 dragged by with the pain of a nagging tooth-ache. Elisabeth was grateful to be called for work at the film studio with astonishing regularity. Still, their financial situation remained precarious. Her first real battle with Jerry occurred early on New Year's Eve, when he wanted to go in search of a poker game. Afterwards he admitted she was right.

'I'll call Jake on Wednesday. Give him a day to recover from the holiday. And don't look so depressed. I told you – I have a gut feeling we're going to pull this off.'

'And you believe in the tooth fairy.' But at least, she had derailed him from a poker game.

On Wednesday morning as scheduled, Elisabeth headed for the El. Around ten o'clock Jerry would call Jake Pulanski. This visit to Rector's would be at Pulanski's expense. It scared her, the way everything in New York cost so much. Sometimes Jerry acted as though they had a money tree growing in the backyard.

She tugged at her coat collar, shivering in the steady cold blasts of wind on this second day of January 1907. She felt a recurrent guilt at being away from Amy for so many hours on the days she worked at the studio. But Amy seemed all right, and she loved Jerry and Mrs O'Brien.

Paul said Fred was nervous at the growing number of complaints about the nickelodeons. 'The priests and pastors are upset that they're open on Sundays. The saloons are afraid it's costing them business. The Society for the Prevention of Crime is demanding that when licenses are renewed they include a clause that no picture be shown that "degrades the morals of the community".' Paul was concerned that the four hundred or so nickelodeons in New York City would be closed.

Much as she disliked performing for the camera, Elisabeth looked forward to spending time with Paul. He was the one sane voice in all that craziness. She enjoyed riding home with him on the El at the end of the work day. He didn't think that because she was a woman she didn't have a brain in her head. They could talk about anything.

Paul was as amazed as she by the obsessive interest of people in the Thaw murder trial. He said they'd be fighting for seats when the trial began on 22 January.

'It'll be a show,' Paul had said distastefully. 'The prosecutor – District Attorney William Jerome – is extremely well regarded. But the Thaw family money has bought six wily lawyers fighting to save his hide. And what do you want to bet they'll succeed?'

But today each minute seemed an hour, and even with Paul's company, Elisabeth was impatient to be home, to be talking with Jerry. Had he got through to Pulanski? Had a meeting been set up?

She tried not to allow her hopes to run wild when Jerry reported he was meeting Jake and a friend the following Monday. Jake was taking them to Rector's. Now Jerry plotted his course of action.

'I've got to go to that meeting and convince them I *can* produce. Not only do I have our star, I have a lead to a new play. One that's been a success in London or Paris or Berlin or Rome.'

'Shaw hasn't written a play since *Major Barbara*. Ibsen died last year, and –'

'Beth, be realistic,' Jerry urged, and she frowned in good-humored reproach. *She* was the realistic member of this partnership. 'Our chance of nabbing American rights for a new Shaw play is nil. Like I said, we have to latch on to a play that's a big success outside of this country – but for which American rights are still open. Probably a first play.'

'You can't spend the money to go abroad. Can you buy foreign newspapers here in this country? Read the theater news from London,' she pinpointed before he could reply, 'and from major cities in Europe. I know enough to translate the French newspapers.'

'And we'll translate the German and the Italian with the help of dictionaries.' Jerry charged ahead enthusiastically. 'Then we'll go after the playwright who's still new enough not to have attracted the major producers.'

'You can't make any commitments,' Elisabeth warned. 'Not until there's money up for the production.'

'It's going to happen, sugar!'

'I know. You saw it in your crystal ball,' Elisabeth flipped. But she, too, felt a surge of exhilaration.

The following Monday Jerry met with Pulanski and his friend. Now it was his friend on the fence, wanting to think about it. Pulanski was eager to be involved. More waiting time, Jerry reported, yet he continued to be optimistic.

'We start reading the foreign newspapers right now,' Jerry decreed. 'We have to have a play. Then I start worrying about a theater.'

Mrs O'Brien announced the time she could dedicate to caring for Amy would be limited: 'I'll be needing more free time for myself.' Jerry increased the money he gave her, and accepted her stipulation that she would be available only three days a week, 'not on weekends'. Jerry would look after Amy the other two days if Elisabeth was working, they decided.

Elisabeth's pay was raised to three dollars a day. Jerry was impressed.

'Fred knows you're an asset. But this is only until we get a play on Broadway,' he emphasized. 'That new play that just opened in London that the critics loved – I'm contacting the playwright to talk about a New York production. I'll –'

'Jerry, you can't,' she broke in. 'Not yet.'

'It'll be weeks before we start talking money. By then we'll have a deal.'

In her bedroom in the Woolf house in Lexham Gardens Rae Kahn looked at the clock on the mantelpiece. Time to go downstairs, wait in the hall for the arrival of the mail. Religiously – since the arrival of the first letter from Elisabeth – she plotted to be the first to see the post. Months went by with no word, but it was important that the others in the household did not realize that from time to time Elisabeth wrote to her mother and grandmother.

Celia was a nervous wreck each time her mother confided that a letter had come. Celia said that in Simon's eyes it was like treason on their part to accept the letters: 'Mama, they should be sent back unopened.' Celia didn't read the letters – Rae told Celia what Elisabeth had written. This was her daughter! How could she be this way?

Rae left her room and headed downstairs. Each morning at this time she felt a wistful hope that this would be one of those times when a letter arrived from Elisabeth. Celia would be so angry if she knew every letter from Elisabeth was tucked away in a scrapbook hidden in her dressing table, to be read again and again. How could she bring herself to destroy them? To destroy the precious photographs of her only great-grandchild?

'It's real cold this morning,' Dora called from the family sitting room. 'I'll light the fire in here now.'

'Thank you, Dora. I'll be there in a few minutes.' Sometimes she suspected Dora knew about the letters from Elisabeth. But Dora would never let on that she did. Dora loved Elisabeth. 'I just want to stand at the door for a few minutes for some fresh air.'

Reluctantly she closed the front door when Dora called to say the fire had caught on nicely.

'Thank you, Dora. I'll sit there and read a while.' Celia had gone to Dickins and Jones to shop for linens. They were having one of their white sales.

The mail arrived. Her heart pounding – as it did each morning – Rae rushed to be the one to retrieve it, searching to see if a letter had arrived from Elisabeth. Joy lighted her face when she saw the familiar large, sprawling handwriting. Hastily she placed the rest of the mail in a neat pile on the console table, then hurried up the stairs to the privacy of her room.

Today Elisabeth wrote about acting in films.

My heart will always be in theater, but at least I'm working. And more and more people are going to see the moving pictures. Not just immigrants and children. And people from the theater are acting in them. I heard someone say that in another year, they'll be doing whole plays – even Shakespeare.

Dear God, how she longed to write to Elisabeth! But Celia had made her swear she'd never do this. When Simon pushed Elisabeth away from the family, Rae felt as though part of herself had died. She never went to the theater anymore. How could she go without Elisabeth at her side? But now, she thought with a touch of defiance, she would go to see these moving pictures that people talked about. Dora was addicted to them. She said they were coming in from all over Europe and America. Perhaps she might even see Elisabeth!

*   *   *

On a windswept night in late January Elisabeth waited impatiently for Jerry to return from a supper meeting with Jake and his friend. As the hours advanced, she struggled to remain awake. Most mornings now she was on the El by 7.30. Fred was using her in roles that she knew she was unsuited to play, yet she welcomed the money. Paul said Fred was plotting to form a stock company that would provide steady employment, a disconcerting prospect for one like herself obsessed by theater – yet the prospect of steady income was comforting.

A faint knock at the door – designed not to awaken Amy – snapped her to attention. She hurried to admit Jerry.

'We're not there yet,' he replied to the unspoken question in her eyes, 'but we are moving ahead.'

'Will we get there before the twenty-first century?'

'These two old boys are cagey. They're as interested as hell but cautious. They've got a third backer on the line. But first they want to meet my star. Beth, don't look so scared,' he scolded. 'They're coming to the office next week to see your publicity. I'll have the photographer do some more shots of you – supposedly in roles you played in Melbourne.'

'That'll need wardrobe.'

'We'll make a trip to the Lower East Side.' He dismissed this with a flourish. 'Then I suspect they'll want to meet you. And don't worry, sugar – you'll carry that off fine.' He chuckled. 'They're the type to be impressed by the British accent.'

Elisabeth awoke to a blustery morning. She shivered at the thought of waiting on the El platform for her train, but today they'd be shooting inside. Aware that the weather might delay the morning trains, she hurried to the station ten minutes ahead of normal schedule.

The train arrived. Elisabeth rushed into the nearest car.

'Beth!' Paul called to her. 'Over here!'

She rushed to the seat Paul was holding for her, delighted to have his company all the way up to the Bronx. She felt guilty that she had said nothing to him about Jerry's efforts to become a producer, but it was all so uncertain. And it wasn't as though she could persuade Jerry to read Paul's play. Jerry was determined to arrange for American rights to a big foreign success – even though that would mean the need for a translation.

'Foreign plays needing a translator are the ones less likely to be grabbed by the likes of Frohman,' Jerry insisted at regular intervals.

'You look as sleepy as me,' Paul joshed now as Elisabeth covered a yawn. 'My brother thinks I'm off my nut, but if I don't get up by 4.30 I have no time to write.'

She listened avidly while Paul talked about his new play in progress. He wanted to do plays that focused on world problems.

'It's funny,' he paused. 'We think of moving pictures as being about as low as possible in the amusement field. In truth, a lot of immigrants are learning to read because of the captions.'

As Paul talked about the moving picture business Elisabeth began to understand the inner workings of the field.

'There are over eight thousand nickelodeons now. To handle the distribution, film exchanges have been set up. They ship movies from the producer to the exhibitor. There are about a hundred of them and it's becoming big business.'

'I wonder when movie producers will start giving the cast scripts, and then printing the dialogue instead of just captions. Wouldn't that make moving pictures more interesting?'

'I talked to Fred about that.' Paul shook his head in frustration. 'He just brushed it aside. But you and I think alike about so many things.' The ardor in his eyes unsettled her. But yes, he was right: they did think alike. If it were not for Paul's presence, she would dread each day she worked for Fred.

What was happening to her? How could she feel this way little more than a year after she'd lost David? But with David, she realized with fresh wisdom, she'd been a little girl playing house – living in a romantic dream. She was a woman now.

She mustn't think this way. Her life must be dedicated to raising Amy. Yet too often of late she awakened in the night and felt an aching need. She reached out – but David wasn't there. She sensed that Paul was waiting for some sign from her that she accepted David's death and was ready to pick up the threads of her life.

No! It was too soon.

In late February Jerry told Elisabeth that they were close to a deal with their prospective backers.

'Now they want to meet you. And one of them has a niece,' Jerry's eyes were eloquent, 'that he wants to see in the play. Just a bit part. Even if we have to write in two lines.'

'When will we meet with them?' She was both terrified and ecstatic. This could be the beginning of a whole new world for Amy and her.

'They're working out a night that'll be clear for the three of them. They want a detailed breakdown of exactly how much money we'll need and where it goes. I'm going to cable that British playwright we've been talking about. He's new – nobody breaking down doors to get to him yet. We won't need a translator – and the lead is a great role for you.'

'Jerry, you haven't read the script!'

'I don't need to.' He exuded conviction. 'The British critics loved it. The plot sounds great – and the lead is perfect for you. I'll cable and make an offer. Asking, of course, for a copy of the play.'

'We don't have the money yet.'

'We'll have it. We'll go to the meeting. You'll be warm and charming. Not too warm,' he added teasingly. 'I'll get a message across that you're spoken for. Sugar, nothing can stop us now. The whole thing is coming together. It's like I promised you. You'd be on Broadway within a year.'

Elisabeth went through the next few weeks in a euphoric haze. The three backers seemed almost in awe of her. It was the British accent, Jerry joshed. It was almost as though she were royalty.

'What kind of a story did you give them?' she accused after she'd met with them and the 'niece' of one. 'I had the feeling they expected me to be wearing a tiara.'

'Well, I hinted that your mother had an affair with the then Prince of Wales.' His apologetic grin was tainted with triumph.

'Jerry!'

'He had a string of affairs. Somebody's going to prove I was lying?'

Without a cent of cash handed over – because the three backers were waiting for a surge in the stock market before selling off assets – Jerry strived to make connections without definite commitments as yet. Elisabeth continued to work for Fred, now openly talking about his proposed stock company. At intervals Elisabeth was attacked by guilt that she was silent about her future plans. She longed to confide in Paul, yet understood this mustn't happen.

Then on a balmy late April day she was suddenly made to understand the illegality of Fred's operation. Because the weather was warm and sunny he'd decreed they'd be shooting on the rooftop of a nearby building. In the middle of the shoot bedlam suddenly erupted.

'Get the fucking camera out of here!' Fred yelled, and the cameraman sprang into action. 'Take cover before Edison's damn spies can nail us!'

'This way!' Paul was suddenly at Elisabeth's side, propelling her across the roof to the side stairs that would take them down to the ground. Elisabeth's heart was pounding. *What was happening?* Others were already scrambling down in obvious alarm. Jerry had told her about battles on the part of Thomas Edison – who owned the patent for the movie cameras – to stop the pirating of films. But they'd been shooting their own picture, not copying!

'They're breaking into the studio,' the cameraman called to Fred. 'They don't know yet that we're up here.'

'Keep your voice down,' Fred ordered. 'Everybody, head out into the woods until they're gone!'

At ground level members of the company scattered. An arm about her waist, Paul guided Elisabeth towards a cluster of golden forsythia that rose a dozen feet in height.

'We'll sit it out behind these bushes,' Paul said. 'They'll leave soon. Are you warm enough? Would you like my jacket?'

'I'm fine.' She *wasn't* fine – she was terrified.

They sat on the sun-warmed grass. Elisabeth felt a coldness that was not derived from the temperature.

'Paul, what's this all about? Why did we have to run?'

'A raid could land us in jail.' His smile was rueful. 'Edison claims his patents prohibit the manufacture and sale of moving pictures and the equipment to do this except by himself. He's filed a bunch of court injunctions to stop anybody who hasn't signed a deal with him – and Fred hasn't.'

'We could go to jail?' Elisabeth was pale with shock. 'I – I didn't know . . .'

'Beth, it's all right,' he soothed, pulling her close. 'Fred's been through a dozen raids in the last year. He never gets caught.'

'But we could go to jail if we were caught?'

'We weren't caught,' he soothed tenderly. 'We'll just stay here until –' All at once his mouth reached for hers.

They clung together, swept up in emotions kept in abeyance until this moment.'

'Paul, no.' She drew away – reluctantly but determined not to pursue this. 'I think you're wonderful,' she whispered. 'But not yet. Please, not yet . . .'

'Not yet,' he agreed.

But the ardor she saw in his eyes was reflected in herself. She'd never thought she could feel this way about any man again.

Chapter Nineteen

Now Elisabeth was fearful of working with Fred's company. What would happen if they were caught in a raid? She'd die if she were sent to jail. Who would take care of Amy? How long could she expect Jerry to look after her?

Word came through that Fred would hold up shooting for three or four days, scout for a new locale. Edison's spies were getting too close.

'Sugar, stop worrying,' Jerry urged. 'The way everything's going, Schiff-Winston Productions will be in operation any day now. Jake says they're getting ready to sell the stocks they've earmarked for us.'

Three days later Fred contacted Elisabeth by the usual method. He was ready to shoot again – in another part of the Bronx. In making the contact for Elisabeth, Jerry arranged work for himself as well on days Mrs O'Brien would be willing to take care of Amy.

'You won't be so scared,' he soothed Elisabeth. 'I'll be working right there with you.'

'But Fred has a stage manager.' All at once she realized she'd never talked about Paul to Jerry. That had been a separate little world.

Jerry grinned. 'Meet Jerry Schiff, actor. Look, how hard is it to act in what Fred does? He needs another live body – male. He told me to come out, too.'

Elisabeth was grateful that she and Jerry didn't meet Paul on the El this morning. Jerry kept their relationship on a brotherly business level, but she remembered the occasional moments when she thought she'd seen something stronger in his eyes. She was conscious of unease at the prospect of the two men meeting.

When she and Jerry arrived at the new locale, Elisabeth was relieved to see Paul involved in setting up in their new location. He managed a wave of greeting to her. There was no time for verbal exchange. Everyone was nervous about their last scrape with Edison's spies. In minutes they were involved in filming. Fred gave the cast the story line. Paul picked up to direct the action so that Fred could work out details on the second one-reeler they hoped to do today.

'Beth, be sure to look into the camera. We want them to see that beautiful face. Ted, move in slowly with the gun. The audience has to be terrified you'll kill her.'

At moments when he wasn't focusing on doing what was required of him, Jerry was uneasy. He sensed an unnerving closeness between Beth and the stage manager. What the hell was going on here?

Hell, Beth had never once mentioned him! But he intercepted tender glances between them, was enraged when he saw Paul drop a hand about Beth's shoulder as he explained a piece of action.

Beth and *he* belonged together – in every way. He'd known that since San Francisco. Nobody was going to come between them. He'd made an offer for that London play – the playwright and his agent were just waiting for him to submit the contracts. At the first of the week Jake and the other two were selling stock, handing over the production money. He'd make Beth a star. She'd forget about that creep.

The day dragged on, seeming endless. He had to make Beth under-stand how he felt about her. She wasn't just his potential star, she was the woman he wanted to share his life with for ever.

'OK,' Fred called out, later than usual. 'Everybody back to-morrow, same time, same place.'

'Come on, sugar –' Jerry reached for Elisabeth's arm, his mind in high gear. Let that creep Paul know he was out of the running with Beth. 'Let's get home before Mrs O'Brien has a fit about our being so late.'

He saw her eyes widen in dismay. The stage manager gaped in shock.

'I'll get my coat,' Elisabeth whispered. Her eyes clung to Paul. But he swung away, strode off to talk with Fred about the next day's shooting.

Jerry was whistling under his breath as he and Elisabeth followed the others out into the night.

Elisabeth fought to conceal her anguish on the long ride home on the El. Jerry evidently didn't realize how the others had taken his words. '*Come on, sugar – let's get home –*' Not that the others would condemn them, but now they'd have a false idea of the relationship between Jerry and her. Paul didn't understand. He had seemed so stricken. He'd want no part of her after tonight.

'Fred knows I can't work tomorrow.' It was his day to take care of Amy. 'I told him when I said I'd come out today. You're not still upset about that near-raid?' His tone was solicitous.

'I'll be all right tomorrow.' She managed a shaky smile.

'Another few days and you're out of there.' He reached for her hand. 'Once the production money is up we'll be on salary.'

Elisabeth dreaded going to work the next day. Exhausted as she was from the long hours of filming, she had difficulty in falling asleep. After three hours of troubled slumber she rose from bed and prepared for the day. It was wonderful that Amy accepted her long absences. Amy made everything worthwhile.

This wasn't one of those mornings when she encountered Paul on the El. At their first encounter today she was conscious of the wall he'd erected between them. She'd lost someone who could have been important in her life, someone achingly special.

Tonight Paul made no effort to walk with her to the El. He pretended to be engrossed in conversation with Fred. She paused a moment in wistful hope, then left along with the others. Thank God, she'd be finished with this drudgery in a matter of days.

The moment she walked into her dimly lit room and saw Jerry's face she knew something unpleasant had happened.

'Jerry, what's wrong?' Her eyes swung to Amy, sprawled in slumber, undisturbed by the low illumination of the lamp. 'Is Amy all right?' Alarm lent harshness to her voice.

'Amy's fine.' He drew a deep breath. 'You didn't read today's *Times*, I gather –' An effort at sardonic humor in his voice.

'No.'

'Big trouble on the New York Stock Exchange,' he said after a pregnant pause. 'Stocks are dropping like crazy. A major bank has closed. The *Times* expects more closings will follow.'

'Have you talked to Jake?' He'd hardly sell stock in a falling market.

'He's upset. He's carrying on about how depressions run a twenty-year cycle. This shouldn't be happening until 1913. And the bank closing has the other two in a panic – they could lose heavily.'

'What can we do?' *They'd been so close.*

'Sit it out. Hope stocks make a rebound. Pray there are no runs on other banks.' He sighed. 'Damn, what rotten timing for us!'

At the end of the shooting the following day – one in which Paul again avoided conversation with Elisabeth – Fred announced that he was suspending filming for a week or two.

'You heard about the closing at the Marine Bank.' His effort at light humor was belied by the alarm in his eyes. 'I've got to come up with fresh financing. But I'll be back,' he insisted. 'I've got a bunch of movies I want to shoot.'

Elisabeth tried to hide her fears about the future. Jerry clung to the hope that Wall Street would experience quick recovery. 'Stocks go up, we're back in,' he recurrently told her. 'And meanwhile we'll find other film work.'

A week later two more banks closed. Jerry blamed it on the very bitter presidential campaigns. Business was in a bad state. Despite his efforts, Jerry could locate no other film work for Elisabeth or himself.

In the midst of an early heat wave Jerry decided they needed a day's holiday. They'd go to Coney Island.

'We'll take the boat out, spend a few hours on the beach, come back in better spirits. This is midweek – it won't be mobbed.'

'Jerry, we can't afford it.' But Amy would love a day at the beach.

'It's cheap. We need to resuscitate our spirits, sugar. Consider it a business investment.' His usual excuse for what Elisabeth regarded as unwarranted extravagance.

By nine o'clock the following morning the three of them were sailing down the harbor to Coney Island. At the rail of the boat Amy clung to her mother and Jerry in delight. A woman passenger seemed enthralled by Amy, spent much of the brief trip talking with her. As the passengers were about to embark, she kissed Amy goodbye, turned fleetingly – first to Elisabeth, then Jerry – and said, 'You make such a pretty family picture, the three of you all so nice-looking.'

Those parting words filtered in and out of Elisabeth's mind as Jerry led them to the boardwalk, then to a lightly populated stretch of beach. In a way she was providing family for Amy.

'Amy, let's see what kind of a sandcastle you can build,' Jerry coaxed while he spread a blanket across a patch of sand for Elisabeth and himself. 'Get to it, sugar.'

They watched in comfortable silence while Amy concentrated on her project. For a little while forgetting the problems that hung over them.

'Beth –' Jerry seemed deep in thought.

'Yes?'

'That woman on the boat thought we were a family,' he said softly. 'More than anything in the world I'd like us to be that.' He reached to cover her hand with one of his. 'I want to take care of you and Amy. I'd told myself I shouldn't tell you how I felt until we were past the rough periods – but I have to tell you now. I've been in love with you since that first day in San Francisco.'

'Jerry, I didn't know –' Or did she, but refused to recognize it?

'Let's get married and go out to California. I've been talking to some of the movie people. They all are convinced that's where every-thing is going to happen. Living out there is cheap – the weather is warm and sunny 355 days of the year. And it's beyond the reach of Edison and his lawsuits and his spies. We could have a wonderful life out there, sugar. No more icy winters. God, I hate them.'

'Jerry, I don't know –' But she couldn't imagine a life without Jerry. He *was* her family now, hers and Amy's. Back in London she'd dreamed about being 'an independent woman' – but now she had responsibilities. She had Amy to raise.

'Maybe not right away, but faster than you think,' Jerry's voice brought her back to the moment, 'movie producers will be thriving out there. Making a mint. You photograph like a dream, Beth – you're what they'll want. I know,' he pushed before she could protest, 'you love theater. But it's tough to break into, and if luck is not on your side, forget it. Movies are going to be bigger than you can imagine. Bigger than theater ever was. Reaching millions of people. In another year most of the producers will be out there. We'll be in on the ground floor.'

'But how can we go out to California? We have so little money.' She shuddered, remembering their shrinking funds. 'What would we do?'

'The girls will loan us money. It'll be our wedding present. Sure, they'll be upset that we're not going home for the wedding, but we'll do that later. I talked with Bert Feldstein – the one who's been shooting one-reelers out in New Jersey. Not regularly,' Jerry con-ceded. 'He's a furrier. But out of season he's getting his feet wet in moving pictures. He says this is his last season as a furrier. He's heading out to Los Angeles to concentrate on making pictures, turning his business over to a brother.'

'It's scary . . .' Her mind was in chaos.

'Not to you.' He laughed, a sound of victory in his voice. 'Remember you came through the San Francisco earthquake.'

Two weeks later Elisabeth and Jerry were married in City Hall with Fred and Mrs O'Brien as witnesses. Mrs O'Brien had been shocked to discover they weren't sister and brother but romantic enough to be pleased. In a corner of her mind Elisabeth dealt with anguish in the realization that Fred would tell Paul she had married Jerry. He would hate her for telling what he'd consider lies: '*I think you're wonderful. But not yet. Please, not yet –*'

Amy clung to her mother's hand during the very brief ceremony. At intervals her eyes moved happily to Jerry. She was enthralled that he would now be her father.

'Papa,' Amy whispered at intervals. 'My new Papa.'

David would want it this way, Elisabeth told herself. He knew the importance of family. He'd be glad that Amy had a fine, compassionate father to stand in for himself.

Jerry had promised his sisters they would go down to Georgia for a religious ceremony as soon as he got his business off the ground. She understood he'd given them some wild tale about a chance to 'hook up with a man who's going to revolutionize motion pictures'.

That same night they boarded a westbound train at Grand Central Station. Not the elegant, expensive Twentieth Century Limited that had brought them to New York. A drab day coach. Their wedding night postponed. Jerry had arranged this, Elisabeth thought tenderly. He was so warm and sweet. He'd been so good to her and Amy. And she remembered those brief startled moments when she'd felt passion for him.

Put Paul out of her mind. That was never meant to be. Jerry was her husband, and that was right. They'd been so close, shared so much for over a year. This would be a good marriage – a family to endure through the years.

Few passengers occupied seats in their car. They'd pick up more passengers at future stops, Elisabeth surmised. Jerry was fussing with their luggage now. Her clothes and Amy's fit comfortably in the somewhat battered valise that had been Mrs O'Brien's wedding present: 'I'll never use it again. I only traveled when my husband was alive – may he rest in peace.'

'Jerry, you collected a lot in the time we were in New York.' She viewed with amusement his valise plus the two large cartons he's managed to bring aboard.

His face grew luminous as he focused on these.

'Sugar, we're going to make a fortune with what's in those boxes.'

'What are you talking about?' She was simultaneously unnerved and intrigued.

'You know the money the girls sent me?' He paused melodramatically.

'I know you were pleased with the amount.' She was wary now. This time Jerry had not given the money to her to hold as in the past.

'I made a deal with Fred.' His smile was triumphant. 'For a quarter of what they're worth I bought his camera and his projector.'

'Why? And why was he willing to sell?' Suspicions darted across her mind.

'They're both in good working condition,' he soothed. 'I made sure of that. Fred was getting panicky about the way the raids were increasing. He said he didn't want to have a heart attack from worry.'

'He didn't consider moving out to California –' How much of their money had Jerry spent on that equipment?

'His wife wouldn't hear of it. They're a big family, all of them living in Brooklyn. Fred would love to pull up stakes and move out there.'

'But it's illegal to use the cameras without a license from Edison,' Elisabeth reminded.

'In California who's to know? Edison only operates in the east. Let him go after the likes of Lubin. Did I tell you, Lubin not only makes pictures? He's got a chain of almost a hundred theaters – in New York, Philadelphia, Baltimore. In Baltimore he has a triple theater.' He chuckled in high good humor. 'You pay your money and choose between three pictures. It's –'

'Jerry, how much do you know about making movies?' Elisabeth interrupted. He hadn't known much about producing plays, but for a little while he'd convinced backers that he could do that.

'Look, you have to organize,' Jerry said softly. 'I know how to use the camera – I've watched Fred's cameraman. I can direct – what's hard about that? And you remember Chuck Rosen?'

'The one who made up Fred's story lines.' A quiet man, about thirty, Elisabeth recalled, who came up with story lines overnight.

'He left for California last week. His wife has chronic bronchitis in New York. The doctor said she needed a warm climate, plenty of sunshine. Her folks have an orange grove near Los Angeles. He'll work with us. We don't need to worry about renting space – out there the weather's always warm and sunny –'

'Except for ten days a year.'

'Ten days a year we can handle,' he said with a pleased grin.

He thought he'd won her over, Elisabeth interpreted. There was always a kernel of logic in his grandiose moments.

'And people work for almost nothing out there. Fred told me how to get in touch with exhibitors. They're handling as many pictures as they can get. The demand is growing like wildfire. Sugar, you and I are going to be movie producers!'

Chapter Twenty

Elisabeth was assailed by doubts as the train approached their destination. She gazed out the window without seeing. Her heart pounded as she considered their situation. Had they been too hasty in leaving New York for a strange city neither she nor Jerry knew? She loved *theater*. She felt ashamed of making movies. But Jerry kept insisting they could earn a lot of money in moving pictures – and money was security. For Amy's sake she must be practical.

Was Jerry reaching too high? He was always such a dreamer. Yet except for the Wall Street panic and the bank closings, they'd be in rehearsal for a Broadway play. He'd have brought this about had not fate intervened. *Believe Jerry.*

Paul, too, saw an exciting future for movies – though he wanted to write for the theater. 'Maybe one day – when movies have become a true art form, I may want to switch.'

With something akin to awe Paul had talked about the momentous potential of movies. 'Beth, in time they'll be seen by millions – no, billions – of people all over the world. Movies will have the power to mold thoughts, to accomplish great things – the way fine books do.' Then apprehension had crept into his voice. 'But will the people who make movies respect that responsibility?'

Don't think about Paul. Not ever. She was Jerry's wife. She and Jerry and Amy were a family.

'Jerry, do you suppose Los Angeles will be like San Francisco?' Before that awful morning, San Francisco had been such a beautiful place.

'Not exactly, from what I hear,' he said after a moment. 'But because the weather is marvelous, tourists are pouring out from every state in the country. Los Angeles has over 100,000 people now.' Less than seventy years ago it had exactly forty Americans. He hesitated. 'We won't be staying right in Los Angeles. At least, not at first.'

'Where then?' Warning signals popped up in her head.

'In a small town right near there, that a lot of people say will become part of it real soon.' His smile was cajoling. 'It's called Hollywood. That's where Chuck's in-laws have their orange grove. It's a young town – just twenty years old, and founded as a temperance colony.' He chuckled at her raised eyebrows. 'Chuck says his father secretly makes Passover wine in their barn. He says the living there is easy. Nobody rushes like back in New York. Everybody's friendly. Amy will love it.' He reached to pull the child into his lap. 'Oh, Chuck's meeting us. He has a place for us to stay – a rooming house near where he lives.' She felt no anxiety about that. She trusted Jerry to handle such problems. But why hadn't he told her they wouldn't be living in Los Angeles? 'He'll help us find a bungalow. With low rent.'

'Now you tell me we won't be living in Los Angeles.' Her eyes appraised him warily. 'What else haven't you told me?'

'That you're gorgeous when you're angry.' His eyes sent an amorous message. 'At least, I haven't told you today.'

'I'm *not* angry.' She was, she thought guiltily. Jerry had a way of telling her important things as though they were afterthoughts. But he was so good to her and Amy. How could she be angry at him? 'I just like to know what's ahead.'

'Ahead is a great life. We'll have to work our butts off for a while – but it's out there for us to grab.'

'I know.' She tried for a flippant air. 'You see it in your crystal ball.'

Then the train was pulling into the red-brick depot. Would it be the way Jerry envisioned? A great life?

Stepping down from the train they spied Chuck. Elisabeth was conscious of a surge of relief. Chuck guided them out of the depot to his father-in-law's Stanley Steamer.

'You're traveling out to the house in style,' he said with a proud grin. 'A Stanley Steamer holds the world speed record.'

'Don't try to be a copycat,' Elisabeth ordered. 'We want to arrive in one piece.' In a corner of her mind she remembered that Ben was always fascinated by speed. She felt a recurrent sense of loss. How was he getting on up at Cambridge? Was he still painting?

'Ellie and I are living with her family for now.' Chuck's voice brought Elisabeth back to the moment. 'They're expecting you for supper tonight.' He chuckled. 'I think Ellie's father is dying to talk to people fresh from New York. Except for his family everybody in Hollywood seems to have settled here from the Midwest.'

In the course of the evening Elisabeth reveled in the warmth shown by Chuck's wife, Ellie, and his in-laws, Bella and Peter Sanchez. They were one of a handful of Jews who'd settled in Hollywood. Their two sons lived in Los Angeles.

'They want nothing to do with orange and lemon groves,' Peter Sanchez sighed. 'Young people have no respect for their elders these days.' But his eyes said he loved his sons deeply.

'We get into Los Angeles every three or four weeks,' Bella picked up. 'And the boys and their wives come out here for supper every other Friday night.'

'We're got electric railways connecting us to Los Angeles,' Ellie explained.

'The boys are both in real estate. You wouldn't believe the way they're building in Los Angeles. Bungalows are being sold on the installment plan. You can buy for as low as ten dollars a month. So it'll take ten years to pay off.' Peter Sanchez shrugged.

'Hey, Jerry, you'd probably make a killing in real estate,' Chuck joshed.

'Not me,' Jerry rejected. 'I see gold in moving pictures.'

Elisabeth intercepted a troubled glance between Bella and Peter Sanchez. They weren't happy with Chuck's involvement with picture making. For now Chuck was working in the orange groves but impatient to write for the movies. And like herself he hoped for higher quality. Jerry kept saying that right now you made what people wanted to see. And that wasn't plays by Ibsen or Shaw or by some new, high-minded writer.

After supper Chuck drove them over to their boarding house. The Stanley Steamer attracted passing eyes. It was one of only three in Hollywood, Chuck told them. It was obvious, Elisabeth thought, that raising oranges and lemons in this 'frostless belt' paid off well for Chuck's in-laws.

Three days later Jerry moved his small family into a furnished bungalow. Jerry and Chuck planned their first venture – to star Elisabeth, though no credits were ever given to the performers. A fact that both Jerry and Chuck deplored. Elisabeth listened impatiently to the plots they discussed. Her own suggestions brushed aside as impractical.

'Remember the audiences,' Jerry scolded. 'We have to give them what they want.'

'Provide better and the audiences will enlarge,' Elisabeth said defiantly.

Chuck began to work on what he grandly called their movie scripts – basically a two- or three-page synopsis. He'd persuaded his wife and mother to be part of their cast. Two of the workers in the orange grove had tentatively agreed, out of avid curiosity, to appear, also.

'No salaries to pay,' Jerry gloated.

When Jerry at last announced they were ready to start shooting, Chuck – who was to double as cameraman – discovered the camera wasn't working.

'That Fred is a rotten bastard!' Jerry railed. 'He convinced me it was fine!'

Combing Los Angeles for someone to repair the camera – still an oddity to most mechanics – Jerry finally found a man who professed an ability to make the repairs, even to add some small improvements. Jerry was stunned when confronted with the fee. With a little urging from Chuck he began to work at the orange grove.

'It's just for a few weeks,' he told Elisabeth. 'So I can pay that pirate to fix the camera.'

Jerry heard about the cowboy pictures being made on Beachwood Drive in Los Angeles by two men from New Jersey, and he was intrigued by what he learned about the filming of several scenes for *The Count of Monte Cristo* at Laguna Beach.

'They came here to do the outdoor scenes – they needed Southern California weather. Not Chicago's.'

'How could anybody expect to film *The Count of Monte Cristo* in one reel?' Elisabeth was shocked.

'They're doing it, and it'll make money,' Jerry predicted.

'Why don't they try for at least two or three reels?' More than that, she thought. Maybe even ten reels to tell an engrossing story. With a flurry of interest she thought about their filming a movie version of *Jane Eyre* or *Wuthering Heights*.

'People aren't ready for two or three reelers.' This was Jerry's usual response when Elisabeth suggested innovations.

Late in August Jerry went back to the mechanic's shop in Los Angeles and arranged for repairs on the camera. Chuck had worked up scripts for a dozen one-reelers by now. Both men were in high spirits, impatient to start filming.

Early in September Jerry began directing their first one-reeler. Chuck acquired a second-hand typewriter, and Elisabeth collaborated with Jerry on a high-voltage sales letter, which she then laboriously typed up and mailed out to the exchanges. Quickly she realized Jerry had been right. This was a booming business. They would be able to sell as many one-reelers as they could turn out.

Elisabeth was happy that Amy could be with her much of the time when they were shooting. Amy thrived on all the attention bestowed on her. It was as though she'd acquired more 'family', Elisabeth thought gratefully.

Ellie and Mrs Sanchez – regular members of the company now – helped watch over Amy. Elisabeth was appalled when Jerry suggested that Chuck work in a small part for Amy in the next two one-reelers they were about to shoot.

'She'll love it,' Jerry coaxed. 'Hell, it's in the blood. Didn't you tell me your grandmother was an actress?'

'For a little while.' How would Grandma feel about movies?

'Mama, let me! Let me! Please –' Amy's face glowed at the prospect of being part of this grown-up game.

'All right,' Elisabeth capitulated. 'But only as long as she enjoys it,' she warned Jerry.

In the months ahead other would-be producers arrived in Hollywood. Strong sunlight was perfect for filming – and Edison was on the rampage back east. Elisabeth remained impatient that, even as the industry grew, nobody was doing anything other than Westerns and cops-and-robbers films.

'It's not the time,' Jerry reiterated. 'We have to give the audiences what they want.'

At regular intervals Elisabeth and Jerry – with Amy in tow – explored Los Angeles. They were amazed at the huge area covered by the city – seemingly endless. They admired the fourteen-story skyscraper at Spring and Fourth Streets – the first building over seven stories in the city. They inspected the windows of the fine shops, strolled through the attractive department stores, saw the University of California. Perhaps one day Amy would study there, Elisabeth dreamed. And they were awed by the expansion of residential areas in every direction.

Chuck's father-in-law had told them with pride about the large Jewish community in Los Angeles, and recommended they see the impressive B'nai B'rith synagogue.

'It's considered the finest religious structure in the city. And when it was dedicated in September 1896,' he continued with relish, 'there was a capacity audience that included Christians as well as Jews. Bella and I were proud to be there.'

'We'll be sure to see it,' Jerry promised.

Tears stung Elisabeth's eyes. It seemed a century ago that she had attended services with the family at the Great Synagogue at Duke's Place in London. And on occasion – like Purim – Grandma had secretly taken her to the celebration at a *chevras* in Whitechapel, where they'd sat behind a trellis in the women's section.

'My folks would be impressed that non-Jews attended the dedication of the synagogue,' Jerry mused as they headed towards the electric train that would carry them to Los Angeles. 'I can't imagine that happening in Glenwood, Georgia.'

In the autumn of 1908 Jerry moved his small family to a larger, unfurnished bungalow, which they were able to furnish by frugal shopping. Jerry fretted that they couldn't afford to expand their studio too – the barn he'd rented months ago. 'Damn, with some capital we could triple our output. We need a backer.'

Amy was in kindergarten now. Elisabeth sent Grandma a picture of her on her first day of school, told Grandma how smart Amy was.

Jerry's parents and sisters were pleading with him to come home for a visit, but he explained he couldn't afford to stop working.

'Maybe next year,' he wrote to them.

In late December word reached the fledgling West Coast movie companies that Edison had made a deal with a group in the business on the East Coast. Edison, Lubin, Biograph, Vitagraph, Kleine, Selig, Essany, Méliès, and Pathé had signed a formal treaty. These were the major companies. They'd formed the Motion Picture Patents Company. Only these members were authorized to use the Edison patents. They set up rules for the entire burgeoning industry.

All theaters were to be assessed a rental for film service, were to pay two dollars a week licensing fee for fifty-two weeks a year. They were to use only film and projection equipment made by members of the Trust, who meant to control Edison's patents and new ones they would obtain in the future – and they meant to control film distribution and exhibition.

'They're crazy!' Jerry yelled when the news reached him. 'They can't control the world!'

'They're not,' Elisabeth pointed out with wry humor. 'Just this country. Didn't you tell me Edison didn't want to spend the money patenting his inventions in Europe? They're making pictures over there with no problems. I read about it in the *Theater Magazine*. As long as five to ten reels,' she reminded accusingly.

'They have a different audience over there –' Jerry's theme song. 'They play to people who're accustomed to going to the theater. Their audiences pay the same admission prices as when they go to a variety house or music hall. We have millions of people over here who don't know theater – but they love movies. This is what their mentality can handle.'

'Somebody should give them a chance to see something better!' Elisabeth shot back.

'It would cost too much. Ten cents is the most they'll be willing to pay.'

'They pay a lot more in Europe!' Elisabeth raged. 'Give them a chance.'

What happened to Jerry's adventurous soul? Once so innovative, now he was following the herd.

Reading the *Theater Magazine* in October, Elisabeth had been enthralled to learn that the more affluent, better-established movie companies back in New York were, indeed, trying to advance the standard of the field. *Romeo and Juliet* and *Rip Van Winkle* had been filmed. The Edison Company, Vitagraph, and Pathé Frères in Paris had set up their own stock companies. In a way, Elisabeth considered, Jerry had a stock company – none of whom was paid a salary.

But the independent movie producers in the Los Angeles area – their numbers growing – soon realized that life for them would be even more difficult now that the Motion Picture Patents Company had been formed. The Trust, as it was called, meant to dominate the business. Join them or get out of the field. If an independent producer's cameras broke down, he couldn't buy replacements. Theaters began to balk at buying from non-members of the Trust. And Trust detectives began to invade the Los Angeles area.

While no one could prove the perpetrators, the independent producers understood the 'accidents' happening in their studios were Trust-inspired. Elisabeth was unnerved by the stories of fires destroying film, of fist fights, even an incident of shooting. Still, the small independents persisted.

Biograph in New York, a member of the Trust, was thriving. Jerry pointed to them to back up his theory that one-reelers were in huge demand.

'This director they have, D. W. Griffith, is grinding them out like crazy. The exhibitors are crying for more all the time.'

'Why are his films so popular?' Elisabeth's mind leaped into action. Sales for their one-reelers were falling off, as were those of other independents – which they all blamed on the Trust. But could it be in part that the market was changing?

'The way I hear it, last year Griffith did something called *Adventures of Dollie*, and audiences loved it. But this new one – according to *Variety* – called *For Love of Gold*, uses a new technique. Instead of the usual one scene, one shot deal, he works with cameras in a whole different way.'

'Then let's see what he's doing.'

Jerry was consumed with curiosity when he learned that D. W. Griffith had been seen around town.

'Biograph means to open up out here,' Jerry pounced. 'What do you want to bet?'

'I don't bet,' Elisabeth reminded.

'This is going to be the center of movie making,' Jerry was convinced. 'Goodbye New York, hello Southern California.'

On a rare overcast day Jerry borrowed Peter Sanchez's Stanley Steamer and drove Elisabeth and Amy to the site of the Keystone Studio, where the recently arrived Mack Sennett was beginning to film.

'Sennett isn't small-time,' Jerry said with respect. 'He's got a big operation going on.' He chuckled. 'Big in comparison to us. So far,' he amended. Jerry lived with the conviction that they would emerge as major movie producers, Elisabeth understood.

They drove out to Edendale – a suburb of Los Angeles. The site of the Keystone Studio had once been a farm. The neighborhood was a mixture of junk yards, rundown small farms, and a pair of small wooden structures that were stores. But Jerry was impressed by what he surmised was the space where they actually shot their films.

'They've got almost an acre there, not counting the outbuildings. Office, storage, dressing rooms,' he guessed. 'That's the kind of operation we need! Damn, why can't Chuck persuade his in-laws to invest?'

But they both knew that would never happen. Ellie was pregnant now, and Chuck was debating about a full-time job with his father-in-law. The movie business seemed less intriguing to him with each passing day. If he left they'd need not only a scriptwriter but a cameraman – Chuck filled both slots.

Late in 1910, only three days after Chuck said this would be his last month in the movie business, the barn that was their studio – where they stored their equipment and where Jerry and Chuck had spent endless time building sets – was burned to the ground.

Jerry, Elisabeth and stricken members of their small company stared in disbelief at the water-sodden ruins of what had been the Schiff Motion Picture Company. The fire had taken place in the middle of the night. Fireman arrived too late to do more than stop the blaze from spreading.

'It wasn't an accident!' Elisabeth raged, remembering other such incidents. 'Jerry, can't we do something?'

'Nothing,' he said bitterly. 'They've burned down our dream.'

Chapter Twenty-one

For almost three weeks Jerry prowled about their bungalow in a deep depression that frightened Elisabeth. What could she do to pull him out of this? Only in the night, in the darkness of their bedroom, did Jerry come alive. He was her husband and it was her duty to respond to him, she ordered herself. He was a fine, sweet man and so good to her and Amy. They were a family.

But traitorously, while Jerry made passionate love to her, her mind darted back to those brief precious moments when Paul had dominated her thoughts. She would learn to love Jerry in that way, too, she promised herself.

Then, in a sudden reversal, Jerry was bursting with fresh optimism. Elisabeth was right – movies *should* move on to a better quality product. He was excited by rumors that Vitagraph was about to open a branch in nearby Santa Monica. Keystone Studio was becoming a major company.

'It's time to focus on quality,' he reiterated. 'Look at what D. W. Griffith is doing. I tell you, Beth, the man's a genius. But the whole system of distribution is wrong. The Trust says film must be bought at ten cents a foot *regardless of quality*. That's wrong! We won't repeat the old mistakes.' This was the old messianic Jerry.

'Jerry, where will we be able to buy equipment? We're low on money –'

'We won't worry about buying equipment.' He brushed this aside. 'There're at least fifteen companies operating out here. They need people like us, with experience. I'm a director. You're an actress. We've made a hundred one-reelers that have sold well.'

'Nobody knows me,' Beth said worriedly. Actresses still received no credits. 'I'll be just another extra.'

'No,' he rejected gently. 'Leave it to me to sell you. It's the old routine – I'll promote you as the toast of Melbourne. They have respect for stage people.'

'Mr Griffith has respect for stage people,' she pinpointed, 'but acting for films is different. It means that –'

'Don't worry about it. You can handle it. In the years ahead the theater won't have one-hundredth the impact of movies. I'll take any bet that in ten years this will be the movie capital of the country. The Trust will be broken. Back in New York Carl Laemmle and William Fox are pushing ahead, fighting the Trust.' He paused, a triumphant smile brightening his face. 'And our working for other producers will be temporary, sugar. I'll be looking for backing from this minute on. And I'll find it. Schiff Production Company will rise from the ashes and be far bigger than it ever was. The Trust won't kill us off.'

Jerry threw his energies into finding work for himself and Elisabeth. He was hired as a director by one of the small companies – operating on what was becoming known as Poverty Row – and brought Elisabeth along with him. She did what was required of her but churned for more demanding parts. Jerry pushed now for two-reelers, saved the company the cost of a scriptwriter by improvising himself as he filmed. But by the middle of 1911 he was battling with their bosses, impatient with their reluctance to gamble on new ideas.

'Beth, we need to move out on our own! This shitty company will be left by the wayside. Audiences are looking for more than they're getting. Yeah, you were right. They're tired of the old crap. They're yelling for better.'

Now at every opportunity Jerry spent time at the Alexandria bar in Los Angeles. The Alexandria Hotel at Main and Fifth was the grandest hotel in town, designed in rococo style with marble columns and crystal chandeliers in the lobby. At its bar members of the growing movie community were apt to socialize, along with wealthy tourists staying at the hotel. Jerry was on the hunt for a backer – and this was his hunting ground.

Charming and gregarious, Jerry collected friends. On this day he came home from the Alexandria Bar – they had not been working because of a heavy rainstorm – to report in exuberant spirits that he and Elisabeth had been invited to a party that night.

'There'll be important people there – maybe Mabel Normand and

Mack Sennett,' he gloated. 'Maybe a bunch of people from Biograph.'

'But I can't leave Amy –'

'I phoned Ellie from the hotel. She said to bring Amy to her – let Amy sleep over. Amy'll love it. She adores Ira.' Ellie and Chuck's son was almost a month old now.

The party was in a smoke-filled suite at the Hollywood Hotel. A phonograph blared out. Their hostess – hennaed, heavily corseted Janie Merrick – was a very wealthy, fifty-ish widow, whose husband had owned a chain of movie houses. She loved everyone involved in movie making. She'd arranged for an impressive buffet to be set up in her suite, along with what appeared to be an endless supply of champagne.

She rushed to greet Jerry and Elisabeth.

'You're that handsome young leading man over at Biograph,' she gushed. 'And who is this beautiful girl?'

'I direct,' Jerry said. 'This is my wife, Beth. Professionally she's Beth Winston. She's done theater in London and Melbourne, Australia.'

'How delightful.' Her smile was perfunctory. She found Jerry far more interesting. 'Now tell me, what have you been directing lately?'

Elisabeth tried not to appear self-conscious. She understood Jerry's excitement at being invited tonight – he saw Janie Merrick as a potential backer. But Elisabeth knew not a soul here. Jerry shot her an apologetic glance as their hostess prodded him towards the buffet. She was relieved that almost immediately a young actor whom she recognized from movies she and Jerry had seen involved her in conversation with a small group of bit players.

Everyone made such a pretense of having a wonderful time, she thought, when most of them, like Jerry, were here in hopes of furthering their careers.

'I hear that Mabel Normand is insisting on directing now,' a statuesque character woman whispered. 'Now isn't that ridiculous?'

'Why?' Elisabeth asked with faint defiance. 'Why shouldn't a woman direct?' *She'd* like that.

'I mean, Mabel's so young.' The character woman retreated. 'She can't have much experience.'

At intervals, Elisabeth noted, groups of twos or threes slipped off into another room of the suite, returned with an air of euphoria.

'Janie's so sophisticated,' a foppish director murmured. 'She's got a cache of "joy powder" on hand for those in the mood.' Elisabeth looked blank. 'Coke, dope, cocaine.'

Elisabeth clung to one glass of champagne throughout the evening. She loathed the cigarette smoke that gave a leaden quality to the air. She was uncomfortable with the almost hysterical gaiety that ricocheted about the suite. She was relieved when Jerry at last decided it was time for them to leave.

'Crazy party, huh?' He was in high spirits as they rode down the elevator to the hotel lobby.

'You could call it that.'

'Sugar, it's good business. I'm meeting Janie for lunch tomorrow. She wants to hear my ideas about setting up our own company.'

'She's playing games,' Elisabeth warned, 'having herself a ball with hungry would-be producers who're young and good-looking.' She remembered Jerry's rich widow Mattie back in New York and was disconcerted.

'Ah, so you think I'm good-looking!'

'To some women,' she conceded, following his mood. 'But don't expect Janie Merrick to put up money for us,' she warned, serious now.

Three weeks later Jerry admitted he couldn't pin Janie down to a business deal.

'I'm going over to talk to the people at Keystone – maybe Mack Sennett himself if I can get through to him – about using you on a steady basis. But I'm not giving up on having our own studio, that'll come later. I'll show him the scrapbook and –'

'Jerry, this isn't Broadway. They're not interested in building stars,' Elisabeth said patiently.

'It's coming. This is Broadway in a new dress, reaching out to every small town in the country. So instead of watching actors and actresses perform on a stage, they're staring at a screen. You're good, Beth, and the camera loves you. I have to move about Poverty Row. Enough of this penny-ante shit.'

Elisabeth was startled when Jerry sold Sennett on hiring her for a series of films.

'The money is shitty – not much more than you've been getting on Poverty Row, but Keystone sells to better movie houses. OK, so you won't have major roles at first, you'll build a following.'

Elisabeth was at first intimidated when she began to work at

Keystone. This was a major studio – several movies were being filmed simultaneously. It was like a factory, she told Jerry at the end of her first day there: stagehands, carpenters, a wardrobe department; a whole camera crew – not just one cameraman grinding away. And she was pleased in the days ahead to learn that here a scene could run for seventy-five feet of film, when the average comedy scene ran ten. But she admitted to some frustration at playing only slapstick comedy.

'Consider this a learning experience,' Jerry cajoled. She knew that between his own on-and-off directing jobs along Poverty Row he was still chasing after investors.

'I'm learning,' she agreed.

At regular intervals Jerry was off to parties. He understood she wasn't comfortable with the movie world's hectic partying, the heavy drinking, the drugs, the couples that wandered off into bedrooms. Nor could she stay up until five a.m. and be at the studio three hours later.

Sometimes she worried that Jerry made the rounds of so many parties. But he didn't drink much – 'How the hell could I talk business if I got all tanked up?' – and she knew he wasn't into drugs. That was a scene that unnerved both of them.

Months rolled past. Jerry was increasingly frustrated at his lack of progress. Every train seemed to bring in more people eager for movie gold. In August the government had filed suit against the Trust under the Sherman Anti-Trust Act. It threatened to be a long trial, but the death of the Trust was in sight.

Elisabeth was beginning to be recognized in the business. Exhibitors were asking for her pictures. By early 1912 her salary had tripled, but she was impatient to move beyond the Keystone comedies.

'We work without writers – we do sight gags. I want to do movies with real stories!'

Mack Sennett films were selling well – but so were movies made by other companies that offered versions of Shakespeare, Dickens, Poe. Griffith even dared adapt poems by Tennyson and Browning.

'Our time will come,' Jerry reiterated. 'I feel it breathing down my neck.'

Rae Kahn left the Woolf house in Lexham Gardens and hurried towards the movie house that had become her second home. She never went to the theater these days. That belonged to another part of her life – when she and Elisabeth escaped regularly to see plays by Oscar Wilde and Ibsen and Shaw.

Out in California Elisabeth was acting in movies. She wrote that they were not as fine as the four-reel *Queen Elizabeth* with Sarah Bernhardt, which was electrifying audiences in America as well as in England. She hoped one day to play roles like Nora in *A Doll's House* in a cinema.

Rae approached the music hall, which now showed films, with warm anticipation. Celia provided her with money to go to the cinema every week, pretending not to understand that this made her feel closer to Elisabeth. Celia had never seen a film. Simon considered them the entertainment of the lower classes.

Films were not new to London, many films were being made right here, and, she'd heard, shipped to the United States. But until Elisabeth was banished from the house, she had ignored the cinema offerings.

Inside the former music hall, Rae took her seat and waited for the performance to begin. At this time of day the audience consisted mostly of women. She heard the rattle of toffee wrappers. Then the lights dimmed. To her astonishment today's offering had been filmed in America. She felt a flicker of excitement at seeing a film that had been made all the way out in California – where Elisabeth lived.

Unconsciously she leaned forward, joining in the light laughter of the audience. Then all at once she froze in disbelief. Her heart was pounding. *That was Elisabeth up there.* Her precious baby. Encased in wonder she left her seat to seek one closer to the screen. *That was Elisabeth – whom she hadn't seen in almost ten years!*

Tears filled her eyes, were impatiently brushed away. How beautiful Elisabeth was. She seemed hardly older than on that horrible day when she walked out of the house at her father's command. How could Simon have behaved that way? How could Celia have allowed it? But she knew the answer to that – even while she railed against it once again.

Too soon the film was over. Now she was impatient to return to the house, to tell Celia about the miracle that had happened today. Celia must come back with her tomorrow! Together they would see Elisabeth.

When she arrived home, she fretted to discover that Celia was not there. She paced about the house, at intervals going to the front door as though to will Celia to appear.

Celia pushed the door open, and walked into the hall. Rae rushed forward to draw her close.

'Celia, you won't believe it!' Her voice was hushed, her eyes bright with joy. 'I saw Elisabeth!'

Celia's face drained of color. 'She's here – in London?'

'In the film I saw. She wrote us about being in films –'

'Sssh.' Celia glanced about nervously. 'Let's go up to my – to your room.' As though, Rae thought with a touch of bitterness, to talk about Elisabeth in the room Celia shared with Simon would be blasphemous.

In silence – like small children with a guilty secret – they hurried with unfamiliar haste up the stairs and to Rae's room. Celia closed the door behind them, turned enquiringly to her mother.

'She looks so beautiful,' Rae said tenderly. 'Still like a young girl. Amy is almost nine.'

'Nobody we know will see her.' Celia was fighting for poise. 'Our friends don't go to the cinema. Simon won't hear about it – he'd be so humiliated.'

'It's not shameful to appear in films.' Rae stared at her daughter in distaste. Why must Simon color her every thought? 'Tomorrow you'll go with me to see Elisabeth. It's a small miracle!'

'No!' The word was wrenched from Celia's mouth. 'I can't do that.'

But the following day, hurrying to the cinema for another brief visit to see Elisabeth, Rae stopped short, took refuge in a shop entrance. Furtively Celia was reaching into her purse for money. She was going to see her daughter on the cinema screen.

Jerry reached for his jacket, turned to Elisabeth.

'Don't wait up for me,' he said as usual. 'Tonight I might just get a chance to do some serious talking with Lester Owens.' Elisabeth knew Owens was the retired oil tycoon who had been appearing at the movie crowd parties for the last month. She didn't know Owens's overheated daughter, Daisy, was making it clear she wanted to know Jerry better.

'If you're not too late, I'll be awake. I want to finish reading *Pride and Prejudice* tonight.'

187

'Make sure you finish your homework,' he said to Amy with mock sternness, and reached to kiss her goodnight.

He walked in the faint chill of the night to the streetcar that would take him to his destination. Since Owens sold his interest in his oil company, he was restless. That meant he was ripe for a new investment. Hell, he could afford to set up half a dozen movie companies.

Jerry analyzed the situation. Daisy was Owens's only child. He'd take any odds she could be very persuasive with Papa if she was so inclined. Owens and his wife were long divorced – he bragged about bringing up Daisy on his own.

For the past five months Daisy had been engaged to a dental student, whom Papa would set up in practice once he'd graduated and had become his son-in-law. Papa didn't know his little girl had been sleeping with half a dozen aspiring actors and directors.

If he had to be added to her stable, so be it, Jerry told himself with only a tinge of guilt. What Elisabeth didn't know couldn't hurt her – and he'd be doing it for *them*. Elisabeth knew he was crazy about her. She was his baby – let nobody think otherwise. He knew other men looked at her with lust, but Elisabeth wouldn't let another man near her.

Tonight's party was at the Hollywood Hotel. Crossing the wide wooden veranda of the three-story stucco hotel he could hear the blaring of the phonograph in the suite occupied by their host. He was greeted with flattering warmth on his arrival, a glass of champagne thrust into his hand. Sure, a lot of the guests were new in town, struggling for a foothold in the movie scene, but he saw enough faces of those high up on the ladder to please him. He wasn't a newcomer anymore, he congratulated himself. He was directing almost continuously these days. Some of these sweet young things were ready to throw themselves into his bed in the hopes he'd further their careers.

But what he wanted – what he'd always wanted since his first look at a movie set back in the Bronx – was to have his own film company. His eyes swept the scene while he lifted a hand in greeting to familiar faces. Owens wasn't here. But Daisy was pushing her way towards him.

'You're late,' she scolded. 'I thought you might not be coming.' Her eyes a brazen invitation.

'We worked late,' he explained. He wasn't mistaking her message, was he?

'I want to dance.' She thrust herself against him, held up her arms.

'If we can find the space –' Three couples were contriving to do the bunny hug at one corner of the room.

'Where's your father?' he asked, prodding her towards the tiny area where the others danced.

'He had to entertain visiting cousins.' She shrugged. 'That's his problem.'

'You came alone?' He lifted an eyebrow in surprise. Not that the dental student ever appeared.

'I did.' Her demure smile was belied by her eyes. He wasn't misreading her. 'My old man won't be home for hours. My buggy's parked outside.' Meaning her fancy sports car, Jerry interpreted. 'Why don't we leave and have a party of our own? I told you, the house is all ours.'

'Why not?' he agreed after a moment. She knew he was married. He knew she was engaged. He'd talk to her about his big plans for a movie studio of his own – which dear Papa could easily afford to finance. This wouldn't be a long-time affair, he told himself defensively. Daisy would soon move on to somebody else – but he and Beth would have their company again. Only on a much larger scale.

They drove to the luxurious Spanish-style house that Lester Owens had rented from a family spending a year in London. Jerry followed Daisy inside, and through to the huge kitchen. There she plucked a bottle of vintage champagne from the icebox. With champagne in tow Daisy led him through the sprawling house to her bedroom, drew a pair of champagne glasses from a cabinet.

'Pour us drinks,' she ordered and disappeared into the adjoining dressing room.

Moments later – while he poured – she sauntered back into the room, barefoot and in only a black lace teddy, a sultry scent about her that hadn't been there earlier.

'You're overdressed,' she clucked, and reached to undo his tie, her hips moving against his own, her high, full breasts on inviting display.

'Let me do that.' All at once he was aroused, eager to throw Daisy across the bed and thrust himself into the voluptuous body. Later they'd talk.

'Don't rush.' She pouted provocatively. 'The servants are off for the night. Papa won't be back until way past midnight. Show me how good you are,' she challenged. 'And I'll show you how good I can be to you.'

She was bright, he thought in a corner of his mind – she knew he had business to talk with her father. But that was all right – if she was happy, she'd see that Papa would pay.

With deliberate slowness he stripped. His heart pounding as she slid the straps of the teddy from her shoulders, slid it down the length of her to the floor. Enough of this play-acting, he thought, and reached for her. Her mouth eager for his, her hands moving everywhere, emulating his own.

God, this one was hot as a pistol!

Chapter Twenty-two

The exodus of movie companies from east to west continued. D. W. Griffith – who had been commuting between New York and California – left Biograph to set up independently in the Los Angeles area. Carl Laemmle was talking about expanding his West Coast operation. Jesse Lasky and Samuel Goldfish rented a farm at Selma and Vine in Hollywood and were preparing to make films, with Broadway producer Cecil B. de Mille – whose most recent show had been a disaster – as their director. Except for Edison every major film company was working at least part time in California.

Elisabeth chafed at the monotony of working for Keystone. Tonight, with Amy asleep in her own room, Elisabeth gave vent to her frustration.

'Jerry, they don't see me as an actress. I'm just a girl in a bathing suit, playing with slapstick comics. I'm twenty-seven years old –'

'You look like seventeen,' he said. At his orders she admitted to nineteen to studio people. Amy was her baby sister, whom she was raising.

'Let's be realistic –'

'Sugar, you're always realistic.'

Elisabeth grunted impatiently. 'How much longer can I go on playing dumb teenagers in bathing suits?' As an actress she still had a future.

'I'll talk to Sennett,' he soothed. 'He's doing some fine stuff now, too. Look at this new comedian, Charlie Chaplin –'

'Don't tell me about Chaplin and Mabel Normand!' she said passionately. 'Sennett sees me in one role: a fairly pretty girl in a bathing suit.'

'A beautiful girl with fine talent,' he corrected.

'I'd never liked movies until we saw what D. W. Griffith was doing. Now I can see an expanding world for movies, but I'm not part of that. I'd sell my soul to work with Griffith.' Her eyes were luminous as she considered this. 'I never thought I could feel that way about films.'

'Soon we'll be doing our own movies again,' Jerry consoled. 'It'll be different. I promise.'

Like herself Jerry studied every inch of each Griffith film they saw, determined to learn his technique. They'd seen how Griffith dared to use close-ups when everybody else rejected them. He was the first director to split a scene into bits that came together as a whole, and he knew how to shorten a scene to build up suspense.

'Griffith's a genius.' Jerry radiated admiration.

'He lets audiences see into the actors' hearts and minds. Someday I want to direct, too.' Defiance in Elisabeth's voice because she anticipated Jerry's reply. They'd gone through this many times – ever since she'd learned that Mabel Normand directed.

'Directing is a man's job.'

'Why?'

'It just is.' He turned away impatiently for a moment. 'But stop worrying about staying at Keystone. I'm sure Lester will come through with money.'

'I know. You see it in your crystal ball.'

It was always the same. Women could do only certain things in life. Still, she was practical about her work at Keystone. Only now and then she *had* to speak her mind. But until Jerry was able to support the family on his own, she must remain with Keystone. Her earnings – much larger than his – accommodated their improving lifestyle. She relished the knowledge that they didn't worry about next month's rent, that there was money to put food on the table, that she could provide small luxuries for Amy. And just last month Jerry insisted they had to have a car. But shouldn't life offer more?

'I know it's been rough for you.' Jerry brought her back to the moment. 'But I can see Lester moving in our direction. He sold his oil wells, and he's bored. It'll be a new plaything for him. Another couple of weeks, Beth, and I'll have him nailed.'

Two or three nights each week he spent in Lester's company, another two nights a week he made the round of parties where movie people gathered. She was recurrently unnerved by rumors she heard about those parties. A lot of drinking there, she gathered, along with the use of cocaine and heroin. Still, she knew Jerry would avoid both alcohol and drugs. He always said they didn't mix with business.

Stories were whispered about the sexual habits of seemingly sweet young actresses and handsome young leading men. Directors could have their pick of women. She wouldn't worry about the wild parties, Elisabeth ordered herself. *She knew Jerry.*

Jerry awoke to the sound of rain pounding on the roof of their bungalow. No work today, he realized. He'd been scheduled to direct a shitty one-reel Western. Elisabeth would be working, though – Keystone was a big-time operation, not deterred by the elements. He'd hang around the house until close to five, then head for the Hollywood Hotel bar. You never knew when a hot contact would surface. Still, he felt optimistic about Lester. It was just a matter of time.

In a few minutes Elisabeth was awake, hurried across the hall to Amy.

'I'll drive Amy to school,' he called after Elisabeth. The few times during the year that it rained he could do that. 'And you go to the studio.'

'She'll love it,' Elisabeth called back.

On schedule the three of them piled into the second-hand Model T Ford. Jerry drove Amy and Elisabeth to their destinations, returned to the bungalow. When the hell was Lester going to make up his mind? Daisy insisted she was pushing him.

He didn't want to think about keeping up the scene with Daisy. She was a wild one, unpredictable. Sure, in bed with her he forgot everything else. But he didn't doubt that soon – thank God – she'd move on to somebody new.

Back home he settled down with a notebook to work out a new budget to show Lester. The old bastard could be tight as hell about how money would be spent, trying to shave here and there. Yet Beth was right: if Lester came through, they should bring in something spectacular.

He was startled at a sharp knock on the door. He rose to his feet, glancing out the window as he strode to the door. Daisy's fancy sports car sat outside. What the hell was she doing here? He pulled the door wide, gazed down at Daisy's saucy smile.

'Well, aren't you glad to see me?' Her eyes were reproachful. 'I knew with all this rain you wouldn't be working. But it wouldn't keep your wife home.'

'What the hell are you doing here?' He tried to sound playful, but he was annoyed. Suppose Beth had been home?

'Ask me in, and I'll tell you.'

'Come in –' He drew her inside with what appeared to be an amorous gesture.

'You're having dinner at the house with the old man and me tonight. He'll put you through another third degree, but he's going into the deal with you.'

'Hey, baby! That's terrific!'

'I told you I'd handle him, didn't I?' She reached a hand to his belt. 'Now show me how you handle me.'

'Here?' He was startled.

'We can't go to my house.' She moved in closer.

'Let me pull down the shades –' Damn, he didn't like this, not here in the bungalow. But already he was aroused. That little bitch knew what she was doing to him. But it didn't mean anything – just to put across the deal with Lester. With what he had at home, why screw around with other women?

Right on schedule Nadine – the teenager who stayed with Amy from school dismissal until either Jerry or Beth came home – arrived at the bungalow. He left a note with her for Beth – explaining he was seeing Lester for dinner: 'Sugar, I think this is the big moment!'

Two hours later – after letting him stew all through a lavish dinner – Lester prodded Jerry into his ballroom-sized living room and announced he was talking to his lawyer about drawing up papers for their corporation. Daisy sat beside her father with a demure smile, her eyes triumphant.

'I'll just be a silent partner – holding fifty-one percent of the stock,' Lester emphasized, 'but to make me feel good I'll be president of the corporation.'

'No problem.' Still, Jerry was uneasy. What other items would the old boy demand 'to make him feel good'?

'And I've been thinking about the name. Let's use something more classy, like Celestial Films. How do you like that?'

'Great.' Lester had a point. Celestial Films would look good in print.

'All right. Meet me at my lawyer's office tomorrow morning at ten –'

'I'll be shooting a film tomorrow.' Until the papers were signed, let him not lose his producer. 'Can we make it the following morning?'

'I'll set it up. Oh, you'll bring along Beth Winston, won't you? I mean, she's not all tied up with Keystone?' A crafty glint in Lester's eyes now.

'My wife will be with me, of course.' What was he leading up to?

'I saw a picture she was in last night. She's got some special quality that reaches out to audiences. I don't mind telling you,' he said expansively, 'she's one reason I'm going along with this. I see her being a big asset to Celestial Films.'

'Beth's wonderful. She'll be as big as Mary Pickford and Dorothy Gish when she's given real roles to play. And we'll do that, Lester.' Jerry exuded enthusiasm.

Within a week he and Lester were scouting for space to rent.

'Not too big,' Lester cautioned. 'Let's keep our expenses low. That's good business.'

They found a barn for rent at $150 a month. Lester bargained with the owner, brought it down to $120. Jerry searched for cameras, projector – less difficult to locate now that the government was battling the Trust. Lester left with Daisy for a trip to Florida, and Elisabeth and Jerry were relieved to be on their own. Now they could choose their first vehicle without any contributions from Lester.

'We need something prestigious,' Elisabeth pinpointed. 'And with a strong role for me.'

'You bet.'

'Why don't we do something by the Brontës?' She made it sound spontaneous, though she'd been thinking about this since Lester Owens had signed the corporation papers. '*Jane Eyre*. Women are big movie attendees – and they love the novel.'

'In two reels?' Jerry was skeptical.

'In four reels.' Her heart was pounding at the prospect.

'Lester will balk.' He himself seemed doubtful. 'He figures on one-reelers. A top budget of a thousand dollars for each. That's how Keystone budgets.'

'Lester keeps saying he won't poke his nose into the business. And he'll be in Florida for a month.'

'The distributor might turn it down.' Yet already Elisabeth saw a glint in his eyes that told her he was tempted.

'Make him understand that this can earn tons of money,' Elisabeth pressed. 'Look how well *Queen Elisabeth* did. In four reels.'

'Yes, but they had Sarah Bernhardt.'

'Then there was *Quo Vadis, Les Misérables. Dante's Inferno* in *five* reels.'

'Those were all European films.'

'Why can't we do the same here? Isn't it time that we caught up with them?'

'Those movies were all shown in legitimate theaters, not movie houses.'

'Why can't we do that? Small companies like ours will fall by the wayside if we don't come up with something special.'

'Our distributor would sell it in four parts –' Jerry shook his head in rejection. 'Or two parts if we're lucky.'

'*Les Misérables* was shown in some houses as a serial. In others it was shown complete. And don't tell me people won't pay more for longer pictures. Jerry, let's do it!'

Elisabeth invited Chuck and Ellie over for dinner. At regular intervals she did this – and often her small family went to the Sanchez house, where Amy reveled in the attention of the grown-ups. It was like family, Elisabeth told herself – ever conscious that Amy was deprived of her family in London. And Amy would visit with Chuck and Ellie's toddler, Ira, before he was taken off to bed.

After dinner, she plotted, they'd talk to Chuck about doing a scenario for them.

'The days of five-dollar scripts are gone,' she reminded Jerry. 'Offer him fifty to do this one.'

'He's putting in long hours at the grove.'

'Chuck loves movies. He'll find time to do this.'

Elisabeth and Jerry – in tacit agreement – waited until after dinner to bring up the subject of Chuck's writing for Celestial Films. Amy had been prodded to her room to do homework.

'I know you're working your butt off at the grove, but if you find time to squeeze this in, it could lead to some real money in a year or two.' Jerry turned on the charm that was usually persuasive.

'Fifty bucks is inviting,' Chuck admitted with a sidewise glance at Ellie.

'You said four reels?' Ellie glanced from Jerry to Elisabeth. 'That's four times as long as what Chuck used to do.'

'It's kind of revolutionary,' Chuck said, 'but I can deal with it.'

'European producers have been doing multiple reels for four years,' Elisabeth reminded. Hardly revolutionary. 'Why do we have to lag behind?'

'What kind of idea do you want me to come up with?' Chuck turned from Elisabeth to Jerry.

'It's an adaptation from a novel,' Jerry told him.

'*Jane Eyre*.' Elisabeth glowed. 'No royalties to worry about. The copyright has expired. We can do it with no problems.'

'In four reels?' Ellie was skeptical.

'Chuck will know how to cut,' Jerry said confidently.

'You're moving into a whole new dimension.' But Chuck seemed exhilarated rather than anxious.

'I think it would be an enormous asset if we could print dialogue under the film instead of working just with subtitles.' Elisabeth gazed from Jerry to Chuck. Jerry had brushed this aside on several occasions.

'It's a gamble.' Chuck was ambivalent. 'I mean, a good percentage of people who go to the movies can't read well. They'd be hostile.'

'It's not the time for that.' Jerry was firm. 'Are you with us, Chuck?'

'I'm with you,' he agreed.

Their next step was to choose a cast. Elisabeth and Chuck sat in with Jerry. Too much was riding on this first film for them to rush, Elisabeth reiterated when Jerry expressed impatience at their delay in settling on a cast. This had to be right.

Chuck was working on the script – harder than he'd ever worked, he admitted. The three of them focused on building the sets. Ellie's father – with a talent for creating fine furniture – was drawn into helping them.

'I'm out of my mind,' he grumbled, but he, too, was caught up in the venture.

Jerry hired a cameraman, fired him two days later when he was scornful of Jerry's instructions about how the first reel was to be shot. He hired another, sat down with him to plot out angles. This one was familiar with – and in awe of – Griffith's camera techniques.

Then Chuck confronted Jerry and Elisabeth with a problem they'd not expected to emerge.

'Look, there's no way I can do this in four reels without killing the story. I've tried – it doesn't work.'

'How long?' Jerry was grim.

'Let's count on five reels.' Chuck turned from Jerry to Elisabeth. 'I *need* that extra reel – and that'll be tight.'

'Let's go with it,' Elisabeth urged. 'This is a major production – and it'll do great if it's done with care.'

On the first day of filming Daisy appeared at the studio. She'd returned from Florida. Her father would follow in another ten days, she reported. Elisabeth was unnerved by her amorous glances at Jerry. Had Lester Owens been persuaded by his daughter to come in with them? Had something happened between Jerry and Daisy Owens that she didn't know about?

Moments later she upbraided herself for such suspicions. Daisy was all but throwing herself into the arms of their leading man. And he seemed most receptive. How could she think even for a minute that Jerry would do anything to endanger their marriage?

At the end of the day, simultaneously fearful and elated, Elisabeth joined Jerry and Chuck in their tiny projection room.

'We'll go back to the beginning,' Jerry told her when she slipped into the chair to his left.

'It looks terrific.' Chuck radiated confidence.

By the end of the third day of shooting – and they sensed the schedule would run to an unanticipated ten or even twelve days – Chuck admitted his scenario would require close to six reels.

'Lester will blow his stack!' Jerry shook his head in dismay. 'Chuck, make some cuts!'

'It'll look like a runaway train.' Chuck turned to Elisabeth for support. 'We have a chance at making a major feature!'

'We've come this far, we can't fall apart now.' Elisabeth managed a façade of calm determination.

'Pray Lester doesn't get back in town before we're finished. We're spending what was supposed to cover six one-reelers or three two-reelers. You know how he squeezed our budget down to the last nickel.' Jerry was apprehensive.

'This is a major production,' Elisabeth said passionately. 'We can't cheat. If it needs six reels, then so be it.'

They were allowing an unprecedented time for filming – ever conscious that there would be a battle when Lester returned. Yet Elisabeth knew that Jerry and Chuck shared her exultation on the night when the last foot of film was in the can.

'It's a winner!' Jerry chortled when they sat in the projection room and viewed the full six reels. 'The best investment Lester ever made!'

Two mornings later – when Jerry was in his office plotting with Elisabeth to develop a one-reeler that would bring in fast money – Lester arrived at the studio. They led him immediately to the projection room.

'Lester, we're putting ourselves on the map with this first picture.' Jerry exuded confidence. 'I'm waiting now to hear from our distributor.'

'What did it cost to make?' Lester sensed something unexpected was in the offing, Elisabeth realized.

'It could be a serial, but we're sure the distributor will want to sell it as a feature.' Jerry used the new word for multi-reel films. 'It's revolutionary. A landmark in the field.' He clung to his air of confidence.

'I don't want to be revolutionary.' Lester's face was flushed. 'How much did this masterpiece cost?'

'Just under six thousand dollars,' Jerry said.

'Are you a lunatic?' Lester stared at him in shock. 'How much time did you take for this – this possible serial?'

'We spent eleven days on it,' Elisabeth picked up because Jerry seemed incapable of speech. 'We –'

'Charlie Chaplin did a movie in one afternoon!'

'A one-reeler – and that was a rare deal,' Elisabeth shot back. 'We –'

'You sold Jerry on this so you'd have a chance at being a star!' Lester shrieked. 'You're the one that was behind this!'

'I'm talking to the distributor about showing it in a legitimate theater at twenty-five cents a head.' Jerry found his voice. 'Lester, we can make a fortune!'

'When your distributor says he's booking this, call me! You did this behind my back. It's fraud. I never should have allowed you to sign checks. I have to talk to my lawyer!'

Chapter Twenty-three

Elisabeth and Jerry lived in constant apprehension that Lester would descend on them with a cadre of lawyers. At the same time they were struggling to convince their distributor that their film of *Jane Eyre* would be a huge success. He groaned at the length, doubted he could set up theater showings at what he viewed as exorbitant prices.

'I'll have to do some research. We may have to offer it as a serial.'

Though neither Elisabeth nor Jerry would voice their suspicions, both suspected the distributor was stalling.

'Lester's waiting for us to report on the distribution,' Jerry surmised glumly while he sat in their makeshift office with Elisabeth and Chuck. 'Then he'll pounce.'

Elisabeth struggled for calm. They mustn't panic. 'We have to focus on our next production.'

'Using what for money?' Jerry barked. 'You've found a printing press that'll spit out hundred-dollar bills?'

'Once *Jane Eyre* is shown there'll be money rolling in.' Elisabeth's eyes defied rebuttal. 'I think we ought to consider something by Jane Austen. Maybe *Sense and Sensibility*.' She'd thrown this out before in conversation with Jerry, had provided Chuck with a copy of the novel.

'*Sense and Sensibility* won't work.' Chuck was emphatic. 'If movies ever talk, then we can do it. It's too delicate, with too little action, to do now.' Thomas Edison's recent highly touted Kinetophone, described as 'Talking Pictures', had failed outside of the laboratory.

In the stark emptiness of the barn that was their studio, the ringing of the phone was a raucous intrusion.

'I'll get it.' Elisabeth reached for the phone. 'Hello.'

'Elisabeth?' She recognized the voice of their distributor.

'Yes, Seth.' Her eyes telegraphed hope to the other two.

'I've been thinking,' Seth said with a casualness that was suspect. 'I might take a gamble on *Jane Eyre*. But I'll need better terms since I'm taking chances. I figure that –'

'Seth, write out what you want, and we'll go over it with our lawyer.' She was conscious of an electric air in the room as the other two became instantly alert. 'We've got a lot of money tied up in this picture.'

'I'll get it right out to you,' Seth promised. Elisabeth sensed an effort to conceal his excitement. 'I'll do the best I can.'

'What's up?' Jerry demanded as she put down the phone.

'I've got a weird feeling that something important triggered that call,' Elisabeth said softly.

'This one's suspicious of everybody,' Jerry joshed to Chuck. 'But let's get a copy of the new *Moving Picture World*.'

Later that day the three closeted themselves with a copy of the industry weekly. Carl Laemmle's *Traffic in Souls* – in six reels – had opened a week ago at Joe Weber's Theater in New York. Audiences lined up to pay twenty-five cents a head to see it.

'Look at those figures!' Jerry chortled. 'Almost thirty thousand people saw it in the first week!'

'It has seven hundred scenes, eight hundred players.' Chuck was awed. 'God, it must have cost a fortune to make!'

'It's based on the Rockefeller White Slavery report and a Vice Trust investigation. It's a sensational subject.' Elisabeth's initial excitement was receding. *Jane Eyre* wasn't sensational.

'They're selling sex,' Jerry pinpointed. 'That's drawing like crazy. But it's six reels, and the audience is paying twenty-five cents' admission. That proves we're on the right track.'

'Seth must think so – or he wouldn't be taking this on.' Amusement lit Elisabeth's eyes. 'He saw that the Shuberts are handling the deal and figured if the Shuberts see six-reel films as the next big attraction, so will he.'

'Let me call Lester.' Jerry was jubilant. 'This is what he's been waiting to hear.'

'Don't make a move until my lawyer sees what Seth's offering,' Lester ordered, when Jerry got through to him. 'This could be big.'

Elisabeth and Jerry tried to be circumspect about their own six-reeler. *Jane Eyre* wasn't *Traffic in Souls*.

'Laemmle's selling sex,' Jerry pointed out again. 'But he's paved the way for more six-reelers. We'll have to sit back and see how to make out with a clean but powerful story.'

Traffic in Souls was proving itself a landmark movie. It was soon being shown in twenty-eight theaters in New York City. Then word seeped through in the first days of the new year that Cecil B. de Mille of the Jesse Lasky Company was also in the throes of making a six-reel picture.

'He's doing an old Broadway hit called *The Squaw Man*,' Jerry reported to Elisabeth. 'It'll be the first Broadway play that's ever been filmed.'

Elisabeth was uneasy. Could they compete with the likes of *Traffic in Souls* and *The Squaw Man*? 'We worked on such a small budget. Of course, to hear Lester, you'd think it was a fortune.' She hesitated. 'Did you get any idea of how much is going into *The Squaw Man*?'

'Probably three times what we spent. I wish to hell Seth would get back to us on what he's setting up.'

'You always point out that girls and women make up a large part of movie audiences.' Elisabeth was intent on raising her own spirits as well as Jerry's. 'And *Jane Eyre* will appeal with them.'

'Lester's excited about it right now. It's a new toy for him. But once we have definite bookings, we'll have to spend on advertising. What do you want to bet he'll balk?'

All at once Seth began to acquire bookings.

'Word of mouth,' he said with satisfaction. 'They love the story, and they love Beth.'

Lester was euphoric, holding court at the Alexandria bar for all who would listen to his reports on 'the finest picture that's seen the light of day'. But when Seth pleaded for real exploitation for *Jane Eyre*, Lester retreated.

'That's part of the distributor's expenditure.' Lester was affronted by the suggestion that Celestial Films pay for this. 'He takes care of ads. He buys posters.' They all knew that *Traffic in Souls* was advertised heavily. Huge posters enticed patrons into the theaters.

'Lester's penny-ante,' Jerry yelled in private sessions with Elisabeth and Chuck. 'We've got a picture that can make a fortune – but people have to know it's out there!'

'It'll draw audiences by word of mouth.' Elisabeth repeated Seth's earlier assessment. 'We won't make the kind of money that *Traffic* is bringing in, but we'll do well.'

To their relief money began to roll in. Fan letters came for Elisabeth. Women patrons loved her. Clearly *Jane* was finding an appreciative audience – even at twenty-five cents' admission and with virtually no advertising. Still, Jerry mourned that they couldn't soar higher.

'Our wings are clipped. The old bastard could put this across with a bang if he'd just open up!'

'We're doing fine. Better than any of us expected.' She was amazed at the size of their audience. How many years would she have to play onstage to be seen by that many people? 'Enjoy this, Jerry.'

They chose another novel by a Brontë sister – *Wuthering Heights* – for their next venture. Chuck was pushing ahead on the scenario. They began to interview for the cast. The money would be there, Elisabeth thought with satisfaction. And she was acquiring a devoted following – a prospective audience for *Wuthering Heights*. At long last she was winning a place for herself up there at the top of the heap. Jerry gloried in the future he saw for them.

'Sure, we're operating in a small way, but we've got a big-time star. Mary Pickford and Lillian Gish, move over for Beth Winston!'

Before they could settle on a cast, they ran into a startling hurdle. Lester's lawyer informed them Lester wished to hold up production until he could see the budget – which Jerry had not presented to him. Also, he had arranged with the bank that all checks had to be cosigned by himself.

'How can he do that?' Jerry stared at the lawyer in disbelief. 'Why?'

'Mr Owens owns controlling interest.' The lawyer avoided eye contact. 'And he feels that you tend to be extravagant.'

'The picture's earning back its investment many times over!' Elisabeth blazed.

The lawyer ignored Elisabeth. The way his client ignored her, she thought in frustration. In Lester Owens's thinking, women belonged in the home.

'Once each week you will submit checks to be cosigned.' He was anxious to be done with this discussion. 'If Mr Owens feels the payments are within reason, he'll cosign. If he's out of town, I have authority to act for him.'

Elisabeth and Jerry sat in grim silence until they were sure the lawyer was out of hearing.

'The lousy bastard!' Jerry rose to his feet, began to pace. 'Lester's cutting our throats.'

'We knew when he demanded fifty-one percent that could happen,' Elisabeth reminded, 'but we had to go along with him.' You had to take chances to get ahead, the way she and David had gambled on chasing halfway around the world to Melbourne. 'We've made a movie that's lifted us out of the Poverty Row image. We've earned respect, Jerry.'

'Respect won't pay our bills,' Jerry said bluntly, lowering himself into a chair. 'Only Lester Owens can do that now. But damn, forty-nine percent of the profits belong to us! Maybe we ought to take that and run. Open up on our own.'

'We can't touch that money.' Elisabeth took a deep breath. 'It goes into the corporate account, and we can't take one cent out without Lester's signature on the check.'

'This movie is making you important, sugar – don't you forget that. Lester admitted you were a major reason for his putting up money for us. The canny old creep knows you're going to be big. You'll be big without him!'

'We have to consider an alternate course.' Elisabeth tensed in thought. How could they trade on what they'd gained thus far? 'You might leak word around town that I'm not happy with Celestial Films. That I might consider moving to another company.' There was a lot of that these days.

'Not yet,' Jerry hedged. 'We're not handing over Celestial Films to Lester. Do you realize we can't even begin to shoot a new picture without showing him a budget – and sticking to it? We can't hire a cast and crew without knowing we'll have their wage checks at the end of the week. He's got us over a barrel.'

'So we'll sit down and work out a budget. Make it a little higher than necessary so Lester can show us how to cut down,' she said drily.

'This is nuts! We've got money in the account to cover a major six-reel film with no sweat. Money for heavy promotion. We've proven we have a market for six-reelers. Why do we have to go through this shit?'

'We'll sit down and set up a budget,' she repeated. 'You go with it to Lester. And take along the latest figures from Seth. They're impressive.'

The following morning Jerry left to meet with Lester, not at the studio as was customary but, at Lester's request, at his house. That was to avoid her being present at the meeting, Elisabeth interpreted. Lester conceded her value to the company as an actress, but he was determined to cut her out of the making of business decisions.

Jerry was perspiring despite the balmy weather when he sat down with Lester in what the former oil magnate grandly called his library – where the leather-bound volumes had been bought by the yard rather than by their contents, Jerry suspected.

'I have a lot of faith in Celestial Films,' Lester soothed, 'but let's not jump off the deep end. You hit it lucky with *Jane Eyre*. Beginner's luck,' he entoned, and Jerry flinched. Lester knew he and Beth had been working in films for years. 'Let's play it safe, the way we talked about when we went into this together. One-reelers, my boy. That's where the action is.'

'Lester, we've established ourselves with a six-reeler – and it's earning terrific money. Exhibitors will be expecting more of them from us.' Fleetingly he considered appealing for help from Daisy, but he knew that avenue was dead. Daisy was off in Mexico with her latest man. 'Seth's distributing us to theaters, not to low-paying movie houses.'

'Making six-reelers is like going to the racetrack. The odds are against you.' Lester launched into a long, boastful monologue about his expertise in business. Jerry listened, his mind in tumult.

'I'll think about another six-reeler,' Lester wound up. 'I need a little time.'

The schedule for *Wuthering Heights* was put on hold. At loose ends – vacillating between a confrontation with Lester and capitulation – Elisabeth and Jerry waited to hear from him. Already bookings for *Jane Eyre* were leveling off. Seth complained this was because there was no advertising.

'How can I keep the movie alive without advertising? You won't even split the cost of posters with me! Even shitty movies supply posters these days.'

A week later Lester called a meeting at the studio – a deserted arena now.

'You'll be there with me,' Jerry told Elisabeth. 'I don't feel good about this.'

Lester arrived forty minutes late.

'I had a session with my lawyer,' he began portentously. 'Look, you and I will never see eye to eye on where Celestial Films should go.' As usual he ignored Elisabeth. 'My lawyer advises me to pull out. You take over my fifty-one percent of the corporation. It'll be all yours.' He made this sound a magnanimous gesture. 'He's worked up some figures.' Lester fumbled in his jacket pocket, pulled out a sheet of paper. 'Here's the way it stands.' He handed the paper to Jerry. Elisabeth and Jerry scanned the pay-out prepared by Lester's attorney.

'You're asking to take over almost everything in the corporate account!' Jerry's voice soared in a blend of astonishment and rage. 'You're leaving us nothing!'

'I'm giving you my fifty-one percent of the corporation. *Jane Eyre* is all yours.'

'We're bringing in our lawyer,' Elisabeth intervened, her heart pounding. Chuck's father would help them find a good lawyer. 'I doubt that he'll allow us to go along with this.'

'You'd be wasting time and money,' Lester said smugly. 'But talk to your lawyer. It's in the contract – I can do this.'

Elisabeth suspected that Lester was right. In an emergency meeting at the Sanchez house that same night a lawyer friend of Peter Sanchez confirmed it.

'How the hell did you sign a contract like this?' he demanded.

'We had no choice,' Elisabeth told him.

'Contracts like this one are why Lester Owens is a rich man and we're in a hole.' Jerry's voice was harsh. 'With all his millions he made us dance to his music.'

Back at home, Elisabeth and Jerry sat until almost dawn in painful conversation.

'Let's try to get some sleep,' Elisabeth said at last. 'We'll need clear heads tomorrow.'

'Lester wiped us out!' Jerry exploded once again, and Elisabeth shushed him lest he awaken Amy. 'We'll see some piddling money come in from *Jane Eyre*. Seth made it clear to us – we come up with another solid six-reeler or he can't promise much. He says the one- and two-reel films are on the way out. This is the year of revolution in pictures.'

'Seth knows we made a major breakthrough as a company with *Jane*. We –'

'Beth, it won't mean a thing if we don't follow up with another winner,' Jerry interrupted. 'Fast.'

Elisabeth took a deep breath, exhaled. 'How do we do that?'

'Damn it, we can't lose what we've built up! You've become an important actress, but we don't know what another company will do for you. We have to move ahead on our own. We'll do *Wuthering Heights*. I'll go to a bank. We'll get a loan. We've got some status now as a company – let's ride on that. Sugar, in four weeks we'll be shooting *Wuthering Heights*. I'll swing a bank loan.'

Elisabeth and Jerry quickly realized that movie producers were not considered good risks at the banks.

'They're dumb!' Jerry railed. 'I read that *Traffic in Souls* cost $5,700 to make and earned close to $450,000! We could have made close to that with *Jane Eyre* if Lester had let us advertise.'

'Jerry, go back into your manager's role,' Elisabeth said gently.

'There's this bank down in Santa Monica that I haven't tried yet. I'll be there in the morning. Maybe they'll see us as a good risk.'

Feeling herself in a ghost town, Elisabeth went to the studio after she saw Amy off to school. Jerry was driving to Santa Monica to talk to yet another bank. She sat at the desk in their makeshift office and studied their bank balance. How much longer could they hold on to the studio? Even the rent seemed monumental in their current state. Where did they go from here?

Three hours later Jerry arrived. Without asking she knew his mission had been successful.

'Sugar, we're in business again!' He lifted her off her feet, swung her around in an exuberant circle. 'I've got a bit enough loan to make *Wuthering Heights*! Once it's in the can – and they see how terrific you are – I'll get another loan for promotion. That old bastard Lester can't stop us!'

Chuck had completed the scenario. They rushed into casting. Jerry spent long hours with their cameraman, intent on making this new movie spectacular.

'We'll do what de Mille is doing with *The Squaw Man*,' Jerry decided, glorying in this new device. 'What they do in theater. We'll give credit on the screen to the cast. It'll be "Beth Winston in *Wuthering Heights*, with blah-blah-blah". And screen credit for Chuck. Sugar, you'll be as big as Mary Pickford and Mabel Normand!'

As with *Jane Eyre* Jerry listened to Elisabeth's suggestions from the directing standpoint, accepted most. He was a fine director, she acknowledged, but sometimes a woman's viewpoint was helpful. More than ever on this latest effort Jerry allowed her to participate in the directing.

At last they prepared to film. 'We'll allow two full weeks to shoot,' Jerry decreed euphorically, 'maybe even three if we need it. This will be our masterpiece.'

Jerry was demanding of the cast. If he wasn't happy with what he saw in their projection room at night, they would reshoot the following day. The atmosphere on the set was electric. Every member of the cast sensed this would be something special.

'Three more days and we wrap it up,' Jerry said with satisfaction when he and Elisabeth and Chuck had seen the day's rushes. 'It's great! It'll make a fortune!'

They went home exhausted but jubilant. Elisabeth and Jerry talked in bed for hours until he reached for her in the dark. Making love would relax him, Elisabeth told herself. They'd worked so hard these last two weeks. Thank God, they were nearly finished. With the long shooting schedule, the bank balance was perilously low.

Elisabeth awoke to the raucous sound of the alarm clock. Reluctantly she pulled herself into a semi-sitting position. She was so tired, so sleepy. But the picture was almost finished – she'd sleep later in the morning next week.

'Jerry –' She leaned forward to awaken him, 'ten more minutes –' her usual admonition when she left their bed to go to Amy.

The morning routine accomplished, they drove Amy to school, then headed for the studio. As usual they arrived forty minutes ahead of cast and crew, both drained of energy but in high spirits.

'Jerry –' Inside the studio Elisabeth stopped dead. 'The window's broken open!' She pointed to the shattered windowpane that had allowed a trespasser to push the window wide.

'Oh God! Not again!' Jerry rushed to the projection room, Elisabeth following.

'Jerry, what's happened?' For a moment she didn't comprehend what had taken place.

'It's the Trust! It can't be anybody else. We were getting too big. They're after us again.'

They stared in shock, in dizzying disbelief, at the slashed reels of film that littered the floor. All their work, the bank loan, had been reduced to rubble.

Was God sending them a message? Elisabeth asked herself. Was this a sign they should move on to something else? *To what?*

Chapter Twenty-four

Slowly – almost methodically – Jerry picked up the six thousand feet of slashed celluloid, deposited them in bags stocked to hold garbage. Elisabeth watched in stunned silence. She remembered the old platitude of her father's: 'Lightning never strikes twice.' But for Jerry and herself it *had* struck twice.

'We'd better call the police.' Elisabeth sat down at the desk and reached for the phone.

'No!'

'Jerry, we have to call them.' She gazed at him in bewilderment.

'We don't want the bank to get wind of this.'

Elisabeth fought against panic. How could they pay off the loan when the film was destroyed? All of their assets were tied up in it.

'I'll board up the broken windowpane.' Jerry looked around for a piece of cardboard.

'Everybody will be showing up soon.'

'Make our checks.' Jerry was brusque. 'We'll pay them today.'

Elisabeth settled herself at the desk with the payroll book. Pale and shaken, she focused on this routine task. Finishing up the checks, she heard the cast and crew arriving. She heard Jerry's strained voice announcing what had happened. For a moment there was silence, then a cacophony of denunciation of the Trust.

'De Mille ran into the same thing a few weeks ago,' their stage manager said as Elisabeth joined them on what had been the set for *Wuthering Heights*. 'But he printed two negatives for every scene and took one set home.' A veiled reproach in his voice.

'I never thought of that –' Elisabeth lipread rather than heard Jerry's four-letter epithet. 'I should have!'

Benumbed by what had happened, though they'd all heard ugly rumors through the years, the others left the studio with checks in hand. From the first day of shooting Jerry had elicited excitement in them about what *Wuthering Heights* could do for each. This was a grim letdown.

'I knew what the Trust was pulling off,' Jerry railed. 'Hell, we were burned out by them. Why didn't *I* think to make a second negative?'

'You were working so hard – you were exhausted. Nobody's ever made spare negatives,' she said defensively.

'De Mille did.' He emitted a long, defeat-laden sigh. 'No point of our hanging around here. Let's go home.'

Elisabeth and Jerry drove in near silence, both trying to cope with this new disaster. At the house Elisabeth went to the kitchen to make coffee, their crutch in times of stress. Jerry slumped in a chair in the living room. It seemed so wrong not to notify the police, Elisabeth thought. They were victims of a criminal action. Yet she understood Jerry's objection.

For an instant she was attacked by a strange dizziness, steadied herself at the stove. At least now she'd be able to catch up on sleep. They hadn't taken one day off since they'd started filming. Jerry had been convinced that this picture would make their fortune. He'd talked about sending her out on tour.

'This picture will make you a star, sugar,' he'd declared exuberantly. 'We'll do what Biograph and Laemmle do – send our star on tour. We'll take ads in the *Moving Picture World*, plant a story about you in *Photoplay*.'

But now there was no picture. Just a frightening bank loan – and little money in their checking account. But she was a saleable actress now. *Jane Eyre* was proving that. She had fan mail from all over the country. Jerry would act as her personal manager, negotiate a wonderful contract for her. They'd meet the loan payments.

She was fearful Jerry would fall into the same depression that attacked him after the fire. She knew not to try to talk to him about their situation just now. But they had to talk. How were they to deal with the bank? Would the bank take the car, their furniture? Most of their savings had gone into the picture because costs had outrun their expectations. With Jerry it was always that way, she thought impatiently – and felt instant guilt. Jerry wanted to do something fine, to provide real security for the three of them.

Should she pick up Amy rather than let her go straight to Ellie, the way she did on school days? No. Amy was so bright, she'd understand right away that something awful had happened. And all at once she realized Chuck didn't know about the break-in. He was so pleased that he was to receive screen credit for the picture: 'Hey, me and Emily Brontë! That's nice billing.' By day Chuck worked in his father-in-law's orange grove. He wrote by night, every free moment he could muster.

Jerry accepted a cup of coffee in silence, sitting in his chair in an aura of defeat. Elisabeth sought futilely for words of comfort.

Amy came home, effervescent as always. Moments later he yelled at her for some casual question. She gaped at him, tears filling her eyes. Elisabeth saw the shock that came over his face – mirroring her own. He was always so sweet with Amy.

'Baby, I'm sorry.' He was on his feet, reaching out to comfort Amy. 'I didn't mean to scream at you. It's just that I've got a real rough problem to solve.'

'Like when Betty's sister is trying to do her algebra homework and Betty comes into her room.' Amy offered instant sympathy. 'It's all right, Papa.'

Unexpected tears welled in Elisabeth's eyes. Jerry was such a good father. Amy and she were so lucky to have him. And then all at once a startling suspicion zigzagged across her mind. That dizziness – she'd blamed it on her lack of sleep. But she was late, she realized. She'd been too wrapped up in the picture to realize it until this moment. Was she pregnant?

She felt suffused with joy. With a tiny sister or brother for Amy their family would be complete. Grandma was always wistful that she'd had only one child. Grandma would be so pleased for her. Wait a few days to be sure, then tell Jerry. But in her heart she was sure.

Even pregnant she could work for another ten weeks, she comforted herself. Nobody would know until then. Jerry would find work for her. Like he said, *Jane* had brought her new stature as an actress.

Not until Amy had gone to bed did she sit down for a serious talk with Jerry.

'Jerry, we have to be realistic,' she began gently. 'We –'

'Realistic is ugly!' he broke in. Why did he look so scared? She'd never seen Jerry like this, not even in the devastation of the San Francisco earthquake and fire. 'You have to know, Elisabeth. I can't lie any more. I didn't get the loan from a bank. I was turned down everywhere.'

She went cold with fear. 'Where did you get it?'

'There are groups of men who'll loan money to people who are poor risks,' he said slowly. 'At insane – illegal – interest rates. I had no choice, Beth. On Monday I make the first interest payment – and they wait on the principal.'

'Loan sharks?'

'I can stall them for another month. As long as they don't know that we have no picture to distribute.'

'Find work for me,' she said urgently. 'Right away. Before . . .'

His air of despair gave way to alarm. 'Before what?'

'I think I'm pregnant,' she whispered. Movie actresses were supposed to be very young and unmarried – *never pregnant*. Much of Hollywood knew about Mary Pickford's abortion, but to moviegoers she was a virginal thirteen-year-old. 'I'm not sure –' She hesitated. 'Oh yes, Jerry. I am sure.'

'We're having a baby?' He seemed awe-stricken. Joyous. Everything else washed from his mind. 'Oh Beth, I can't believe it.' His voice was hushed.

'You'd better believe it,' she derided tenderly. 'We'll have to deal with it.'

'Oh sugar, it's wonderful.' He rose from his chair with fresh vitality and pulled her into his arms.

'Nobody will know for a few weeks. I can do several one-reelers in that time. Maybe even a six-reeler. A lot of producers are excited about doing feature pictures now. That's what audiences want.'

'I'll go after a directing job,' he said, his mind ignited. 'We'll be a team – the director and the star of *Jane Eyre*. We'll handle this, sugar. We've been through rough times before.'

They moved in a dream world over the weekend, caught up in the wonder of Elisabeth's pregnancy, both determined to give themselves a respite from reality. Until Monday.

Each night after Amy was asleep, Jerry made passionate love to Elisabeth in the darkness of their bedroom, each time seeking assurance from her that it was all right. Both erasing from their mind the grim reality of what lay ahead.

On Monday morning Jerry drove to Santa Monica to make the payment of the first month's exorbitant interest. The moment he walked into the spartan offices of the moneylending group, he sensed the hostility of the unsmiling 'collector'. They knew about the destruction of the film. How did they know?

'I detoured here before going to the studio,' he said with an air of bravado. Damn, there was no secrecy in the movie business.

'We hear you had visitors Friday night. We hear you got no more picture.'

'It's rough – we have to shoot all six reels over again.'

'Who's payin' for it?' The collector stretched so that his holstered gun was in full view.

'My uncle back in New York is coming through.' Jerry's throat was dry. 'He's going to become my partner.'

'That's good. Because we're calling in your note. You pay up in full within one week.'

'Why?' Jerry tried for an air of amazement.

'We don't need to tell you why. It's in the small print. Be here next Monday morning with payment in full. In cash,' he emphasized. 'We wouldn't wanna be pushed into takin' rough action. Your wife wouldn't be so gorgeous with her face all messed up. She couldn't make no more pictures.'

'You'll have it.' Cold and trembling, Jerry swung around and hurried from the office. This was unreal.

He drove home, his mind in chaos. He knew these were rough creeps, but he'd been so sure Celestial Films would have the money to pay up, even with the crazy interest rates. They'd be watching him every minute now. How could he raise that kind of money in one week?

He saw Elisabeth waiting at the door as he emerged from the car. She looked scared. Hell, so was he! He'd been in some tight spots in the past – but nothing like this. He couldn't ask the girls for that kind of money.

Inspecting his colorless face, Elisabeth was unnerved. She'd heard Peter Sanchez talk with contempt about 'private moneylenders'. It was a world unknown to her. But she and Jerry were part of that unsavory world now.

'Jerry?' Her eyes searched his.

'It's not good,' he said tersely, and led her back into the living room, closed the door behind him.

'Jerry, what happened?'

'We have to leave Hollywood – without their knowing.' He didn't need to elaborate, his fear told her there was a threat of violence. Their lives were in danger. *This was like a bad movie.* 'We'll go back to New York. No,' he reversed himself, 'we'll go home.' She gazed at him in bewilderment. Where was home? 'Down to Georgia – just for a while. My folks will be thrilled to death to have us there.' His face softened. 'Our baby will be the second generation born in that house. My parents will be thrilled.'

Would they? But this thought was usurped by one more urgent. They must leave Hollywood quickly – and in secret.

'We have to plan this well.' Elisabeth's mind charged into high gear. 'I'll go to the bank and close our account. You stay here at the house, pack for us. We –'

'Hold it, sugar –' Jerry was startled by her rush into action.

'They're bad people,' she reminded him. 'We have to move fast. Pack just two big valises. I'll talk to Ellie, explain what's happening. She'll drive over and pick them up. They won't expect us to act so fast. This evening we'll drive over to the Sanchez house, as though we were just going there for supper – like we often do.'

'Chuck doesn't even know about the picture.' Jerry grimaced in pain. 'Maybe I ought to –'

'You stay here,' she ordered. 'I'll explain to Ellie – she'll tell Chuck.' How would she explain this craziness to Amy? Her precious baby, who'd been through so much.

'Chuck will drive us to Santa Monica – we'll get the train there.' Jerry was dragging himself out of the fog that had imprisoned him. 'The Ford stays in front of the Sanchez house. If we're being followed, they'll see the car and figure we're still there. We'll go out the rear of the house – into the Stanley Steamer without being seen. Oh God, Beth, I didn't mean to land you and Amy in this kind of mess!'

'We'll get out of it.' She had to be calm – strong – for the three of them. 'We just have to move fast.'

Each hour seemed nightmarishly long. Elisabeth spoke with Ellie – upset but determined to help. She went to the bank and closed their account, shuddering at the small balance there. Jerry was sure Chuck would want to buy the car. That would be two or three hundred more. They wouldn't travel to Georgia in a compartment – it would be day coach all the way.

By the time she arrived home Jerry had packed for the three of them.

'I hope I didn't forget anything important.' Jerry gazed about the bedroom, where the valises waited across their bed. The shades down.

'What's important is us. Oh, we have to tell the landlord we're giving up the studio. Chuck can mail our letter in a couple of days.' When they were beyond reach. 'And the bungalow.' No time to try to sell the furniture, not with those sharks at their heels.

'I'd like to take the cameras and projectors with us.' They'd come from New York with earlier versions.

'No, tell Chuck to go and take them for himself,' Elisabeth said. 'Before *they* try to.' These men were thugs – they deserved nothing from Jerry and her.

'They'd be too bulky,' Jerry conceded. He was still fighting panic, Elisabeth sensed. With reason.

Amy was going to be upset, being pulled out of her school, which she loved, away from her little friends. When would life go smoothly for them again? Elisabeth wouldn't think about how it would be in Glendale, Georgia. Not even to Jerry would she voice her fears that his family would not welcome her and Amy. Jerry wouldn't allow himself to think that way, but in the years she and Jerry had been married neither his parents nor his sisters had ever addressed a letter to both of them, never asked about her or Amy in writing to him. It was as though they didn't exist.

'We'll make the trip seem a grand adventure to Amy,' he promised, reading her mind. The Jerry she'd known in San Francisco was making a shaky comeback.

When Amy came home, Elisabeth sat her down to explain that something momentous would be happening in their lives.

'Darling, you know about the film being destroyed at the studio?' Amy nodded solemnly. 'If that hadn't happened, we'd be doing fine. But we've lost the picture, and we have to pay back the money we borrowed to make it. We couldn't get a loan at the bank – so Papa had to go to some bad men. If it wasn't for the film being destroyed, this wouldn't be happening.' She paused, took a deep breath. 'They made ugly threats. We have to leave Hollywood.'

'Where are we going?' Amy was wide-eyed with shock.

'Down to Papa's family in Georgia. But we have to do it secretly.' She explained their plan, Amy absorbing every word with a maturity she had not expected. 'It'll be a kind of adventure.' She repeated Jerry's pronouncement, striving for lightness.

'Can I take my books with me?' To Amy her books were precious. Mr and Mrs Sanchez gave her books at every holiday.

'As many as you can carry,' Elisabeth stipulated.

Elisabeth moved through the rest of the day and evening in an aura of unreality, knowing she must be strong – for the three of them.

As planned – with the phonograph playing Caruso records at high volume, so that anyone lurking outside would believe this was a convivial gathering – Chuck led Elisabeth, Amy and Jerry to the waiting Stanley Steamer behind the house. They arrived at Santa Monica just in time to buy tickets for passage on the outgoing night train, bound for Texas.

Elisabeth stared into the night as the train chugged out of the Santa Monica station. They were together – a family. They would be all right.

Chapter Twenty-five

While the train carried them out into the night, Jerry told Amy – with an air of imparting a fascinating fact – that the trip would take five days.

'You'll see the whole country, sugar.'

'I saw it before. Twice. I'm glad I brought my books.' Amy was making an effort to accept this tumultuous turn of events.

'We change trains in Texas,' Jerry continued. 'I'll send a telegram to the family from there. They'll meet us at the depot.'

'Amy, lie down on the seat across from us and sleep,' Elisabeth ordered, relieved that the train was lightly populated. Earlier a porter had distributed pillows.

'We'll all sleep,' Jerry said. 'Everybody's tired.'

The movement of the train soon lulled Amy and Jerry into slumber. Elisabeth remained awake – a flood of questions taunting her. In her brief life Amy had endured such trauma. How would she handle this latest shock? Elisabeth had been startled when Amy said she remembered crossing the country before. Amy had never talked about it. You think you *know* your children, but does anyone ever know the inner workings of another mind?

The trip across country seemed endless to Elisabeth. She remembered her first transcontinental trip – with David. That seemed in another age. They'd been little more than children. Then San Francisco and the earthquake – and Jerry entered their lives, became their protector. Now she suspected that she must take control for the three of them. Jerry seemed almost rudderless.

On a dreary afternoon their train pulled into the Glendale depot. Elisabeth braced herself for the meeting with Jerry's family. Jerry was at the window, scanning faces.

'There's Mama and the girls!' His smile was brilliant.

Holding Amy's hand in hers Elisabeth gazed out the window. Jerry was on his feet, juggling their suitcases. Now she remembered that Jerry was the baby of the family: 'Spoiled rotten. I admit it.' His sister Hannah – the school teacher – was nine years older than he. His married sister Mollie was eleven years older.

The train drew to a stop. Jerry herded Elisabeth and Amy to the exit.

'Jerry, let me take one of the suitcases,' she tried again. He brushed her aside when she'd offered this a few moments ago.

'Sugar, you're in the Deep South. Ladies don't carry suitcases.'

Moments later a genial porter was reaching to take the luggage from Jerry. He rushed forward to a small rotund woman who appeared older than her fifty-eight years: Jerry's mother. Elisabeth knew the taller of the three women – bone-thin and with prematurely greying hair – was Hannah. Mollie was pretty and well-padded, though an air of petulance detracted from what could be real beauty.

Elisabeth held Amy's hand firmly in hers. Never shy, today Amy seemed intimidated by the presence of strangers. Poor baby, they were dumping so much on her young shoulders. Then Jerry was drawing them forward to introduce them to his mother and sisters. On the surface the three women exuded Southern charm – but Elisabeth sensed an undercurrent of hostility. This was the prodigal son and brother coming home at last – and on the surface they would accept his wife and stepdaughter. And their coming grandchild and niece or nephew, Elisabeth thought with a flicker of humor. She'd noted the covert glances toward her midsection, barely revealing her pregnancy.

'Papa couldn't come, of course,' his mother was saying in the liquid music of Southern speech, which Jerry still retained. 'He couldn't leave the pharmacy. He'd never trust a clerk alone. Last week Zeke quit. Can you believe it, Jerry?'

'Zeke worked for Papa since I was a little boy,' Jerry told Elisabeth. He turned to his mother while they walked towards the family car. 'Why did he leave?'

'He said he was getting on in years, and he wanted to enjoy what life remained for him. All because his old aunt died and left him a little house.'

Elisabeth was conscious of sudden tension in Jerry. He saw himself being pushed into the pharmacy, she suspected. But he knew he'd have to do something here in Glendale. They couldn't just sit back and live off his parents.

She remembered the words of his telegram: 'SURPRISE STOP COMING HOME FOR A WHILE STOP JOYOUS NEWS STOP GRANDCHILD ON THE WAY.' Were they pleased? Despite their almost girlish display of welcome, she was skeptical.

In comfortable walking distance of the pharmacy on Main Street, the Schiff house – a white, two-story clapboard set on a neat plot on a row of similar houses – was not as grand as Jerry had described it.

'You'll have your room, Jerry,' his mother told him. 'You and Elisabeth. And Amy –' She stumbled over the name, but Amy didn't notice. Amy was enthralled with the family cat, a one-eyed gray Persian courting her obvious interest. 'Amy will have my sewing room, which used to be Mollie's bedroom.'

At supper time Elisabeth and Amy met Jerry's father. Fred Schiff was a quiet, gentle man. It was clear to Elisabeth he'd long been dominated by the three women in his life. She suspected the pharmacy was his refuge.

There were six at the table. Mollie had left before meal time. Supper was served by an ingratiating, very young colored girl named Hallie. They're Jerry's family, Elisabeth reminded herself. Their baby's grandparents and aunt. Yet the warmth she had felt at the Sanchez supper table was lacking here.

Elisabeth listened with downcast eyes while her mother-in-law plotted their lives. Jerry would replace Zeke in the pharmacy. But in his telegram Jerry said they'd be here 'for a while'.

'It's almost like fate,' his mother babbled. 'Zeke leaving and you coming home just at this time.' No questions yet about their precipitous departure from Hollywood, but Elisabeth was sure they'd be coming in torrents. 'And there's a grammar school just four blocks away.'

'The school I went to,' Jerry told Amy with an encouraging smile.

After supper they left the dining room for the parlor. Amy sprawled on the floor with Pirate – renamed by neighborhood children after he lost an eye night-courting. Mrs Schiff and Hannah exchanged local gossip while Elisabeth listened to Jerry and his father discuss the powder keg situation in Europe.

'The Kaiser is determined to build an empire more powerful than that of Great Britain. He boasts about building a railroad from Berlin to Baghdad that will take Germany into the Mideast oil fields. The smell of war is everywhere.'

'The British don't want to fight,' Elisabeth broke in. What a fearful prospect! She recoiled from the vision of Ben and Felix fighting a war.

'It may not be up to the British,' Fred Schiff said gently. 'But let's pray it never happens.'

It was arranged that Jerry would start at the pharmacy the very next morning. Elisabeth would take Amy to be enrolled in the grammar school. Jerry's mother made an appointment for Elisabeth with Dr Edwards.

'Dr Edwards delivered me,' Jerry told her. 'You'll like him.'

'A special discount for a second generation?'

It soon became clear that Leona Schiff left the care of the house in Hallie's very young hands. Her own sole household responsibility was to prepare the evening meal. Hallie left each night after cleaning up the kitchen and serving supper. Hannah – with an air of martyrdom, Elisabeth noted – cleared the supper table and washed and dried the dishes. After the second night Elisabeth offered to take on this obligation, which Hannah received as due her.

Though Jerry had explained to her about segregation in the south, Elisabeth was disturbed by this. David had died fighting segregation in Australia. Here she encountered it at every turn. It was something she'd never had to face in London. She rebelled in silence. Their presence here in Glendale was transient, she told herself. But where did they go from here? She knew she mustn't try to discuss this with Jerry. Not just yet.

Elisabeth fretted at her inactivity. It was immediately obvious that pregnant Southern ladies went into near-retirement until after delivery. Leona Schiff made some self-conscious suggestions about a welcome party for Elisabeth, which Hannah quashed.

'Mama, it would just look like we were after baby gifts,' she scolded.

Elisabeth's offer to help at the pharmacy was also rejected by the women in the family.

'Southern ladies of good families don't work,' Jerry explained wryly. 'Except as school teachers.'

Because of her pregnancy the family felt justified in not including her in their social lives. Elisabeth learned to knit and taught Amy. She joined the local library and delighted in Willa Cather's new novel, *O Pioneers!*

She and Jerry – and on non-school nights Amy – made frequent trips to the local movie houses, of which there were two. Jerry dissected every film for new techniques, talked with shaky optimism about the time 'we get back to the business' – yet offered no clues as to how or when this was to happen.

Elisabeth wrote a long letter to Grandma, explaining the new events in their lives. She told her about the prospective new great-grandchild and wondered if Ben and Felix were married. Were there other great-grandchildren? Had Ben or Felix made *her* an aunt? Their children would be Amy's cousins, the new baby's cousins.

With Jerry in the pharmacy his father began to cut his day short at four o'clock: 'If anybody needs a prescription filled, Jerry can phone me.' He enjoyed sitting in one of the four rockers on the front porch and chatting with Elisabeth. No serious conversation ever occurred between him and his wife or his daughters, Elisabeth realized sympathetically.

'It's good to see Jerry in the business,' he confided over an ice-laden glass of tea on a humid afternoon. The streets were deserted. Leona and Hannah napped in their shade-drawn bedrooms while fans whined from dresser tops. 'That's why a father puts in long hours in the store – to build something substantial for his son.' But she read the troubled question in his eyes.

Papa was asking her: *Will Jerry stay home now?* How could she tell him Jerry hated every moment they must remain in Glendale? But like Grandma always said, live one day at a time.

The oppressive Georgia summer arrived almost overnight – like an enervating plague. With time on her hands Elisabeth sewed loose cotton frocks that accommodated her advancing pregnancy. Her compassionate father-in-law brought a fan home for her and Jerry's bedroom, another for Amy's small room. Sometimes, she thought it seemed that her mother-in-law and Hannah were unaware of her presence in the house. She saw Mollie and her small family only when they came for supper – and she seemed nonexistent to this other sister-in-law, too.

Elisabeth was relieved that Amy had adjusted to the new school. Now in vacation time she played with favorite school friends. She was invited to an endless stream of birthday parties. But she arrived home from the latest with somber reflections.

'Mama, I don't think Donna's mother likes me.' Donna was Amy's best friend.

'Why would you think that?' Elisabeth drew her small daughter close.

'Donna's mother was at the party. You know, helping out. And I heard her say, "Amy's mother used to be an actress. Not only that, she's Jewish. You know, the Schiff pharmacy family."'

'I was an actress, and I am Jewish.' Elisabeth managed a smile, but she was unnerved. She remembered her father-in-law saying with a wry smile that in Glendale, 'Jews are assimilated between nine a.m. and six p.m.'

'It was the way she said it, Mama!' Amy's eyes were defiant. 'I don't like her.'

'You don't have to like her.' Elisabeth was casual. 'It's Donna who's your friend.' But now she understood why Donna had been unable to accept her invitation to take both girls to the County Fair the coming week. When she'd phoned, Donna's mother had rejected the invitation: 'We have family visiting Glendale all that week.'

Three days later the world was shocked by the assassination of Archduke Franz Ferdinand – heir to the throne of Austria-Hungary – along with his wife, in Sarajevo, the ancient capital of Bosnia. The assassin was a nineteen-year-old student, a member of a terrorist organization fighting to free Bosnia from Austrian rule and to see it united with Serbia.

'It doesn't bode well for the future,' Fred Schiff said ominously when he'd read the headline of the *Glendale Enquirer*.

But most people here in this country didn't expect an assassination in Sarajevo to affect their lives, Elisabeth considered. Yet listening to her father-in-law, she was troubled. He talked about an alliance that would pit Great Britain against Germany.

If it came to war – and she prayed it wouldn't – Ben and Felix might have to fight their own cousins in Germany. *Grandma* was German. With poignant nostalgia she remembered the visits each year to Berlin. Family fighting against family? How could that happen?

One month after the assassination Austria-Hungary – prodded by Germany – declared war on Serbia. Now there was a rush to take sides. On 1 August Germany declared war on Russia. Two days later Germany declared itself at war with France. On 4 August Great Britain warned the German government it would go to war to defend Belgium unless German troops withdrew from that country. The ultimatum was ignored; Great Britain was at war on the side of France and Russia.

American newspapers reported on the activities in war-torn Europe, yet the war didn't seem to be of major interest, Elisabeth thought in recurrent reproach. Most Americans seemed to feel that their country should not become involved. In the Schiff household Elisabeth and her father-in-law spoke nightly of the conflict, with Jerry becoming occasionally involved in their conversation.

She worried about Jerry's air of depression. His boundless energy, his soaring ambition, had gone into eclipse. She tried with little response to bring him out of his long bouts of morbid silence. Only in bed – making love to her with a strange desperation – did the old Jerry emerge. Once the baby was born, they'd make plans. Jerry would revert to his old self.

And constantly Elisabeth worried about the family in London. She wrote more often now, expressing her alarm for them – for the cousins in Germany. Aching for a response. Assurance that all was well with the family. At a terrible time such as this, why couldn't Mama or Grandma write? Often she remembered British Foreign Secretary Sir Edward Grey's pronouncement when King George V signed the declaration of war: 'The lamps are going out all over Europe; we shall not see them lit again in our lifetime.' Still, most Americans expected the war to be over in six months.

Along with her father-in-law Elisabeth followed the fighting in Europe in the newspapers. Thank God, she thought, England itself was not being attacked, though there were grim reminders of the strengthening German Navy. She read the *Literary Digest* with religious regularity because here was news of what was happening in England, though the reports were not always optimistic. British soldiers were fighting – and dying – in brutal battles in Belgium and in Turkey. Elisabeth prayed that Ben and Felix were all right.

In late October Elisabeth gave birth to a second daughter, to be named Kate for her grandmother's sister who had died in her teens. Jerry and his father gazed at tiny Kate, she thought lovingly, as though a miracle had come into their lives.

'She's beautiful,' Fred Schiff extolled. 'Just like her mother and sister.'

She'd reminded both men not to let Kate dominate the scene. Amy must not feel slighted.

The three Schiff women murmured the admiring phrases demanded by the occasion – knowing their baby brother would be hurt if they didn't. Sometimes their efforts at Southern charm evoked rage in Elisabeth. They loathed her, tolerated Amy. When would she and Jerry escape from this façade of family?

Kate was not lacking for love, Elisabeth comforted herself. Father and grandfather picked her up at the slightest need. Amy and Hallie were her adoring slaves. It mattered not at all that her grandmother and aunts on her father's side never once took her in their arms.

Elisabeth's euphoria at this new addition to her tiny family was punctured with the news that on 29 December three German Zeppelins attacked the northeast coast of England. Still, Americans – except those with family in England – considered the war apart from their own lives.

Elisabeth tried to focus all of her attention on caring for tiny Kate and Amy. With his father as a willing baby-sitter Jerry took Elisabeth off to see every new movie that appeared in Glendale. He was fascinated by the work of Griffith and de Mille, insisted they see some films three or four times so that he might dissect every new technique.

'Movies are coming of age,' he chortled with satisfaction when they'd seen the latest film by D. W. Griffith. 'And look at the movie palaces that are springing up in New York.'

Yet each time Elisabeth tried to discuss their future, he aborted this. She realized he was impatient to return to Hollywood – though they both knew this was impossible. But movies were still being made in New York. Why couldn't they talk about that?

In April – with Glendale erupting into glorious spring – Elisabeth was shaken by the news that London had been bombarded by German Zeppelins. Had Lexham Gardens been hit? Was her family all right?

On 7 May the world was shocked to learn that a German submarine – without warning – had sunk the British steamship, the *Lusitania*, off the coast of Ireland. Of the 1,198 people who died, there were 114 Americans. Despite American rage, the public made a new song, 'I Didn't Raise my Son to be a Soldier', an instant hit.

Americans learned now that night lighting restrictions went into effect throughout England. More men were being called up. Defense of the country against attacks was accelerated – and a fortunate decision because the Zeppelins were being replaced by much more effective airplanes. The raids – along with the sighting of U-boats – were causing huge outcries. Jerry was fascinated by reports of British 'Aces' – hastily trained for the job – bringing down German planes over France and Belgium with commendable regularity.

'God, it must be the most exciting adventure on earth to fly a plane! To be up there in the clouds, above the world!'

'Unless you're in a plane being attacked by a German flyer.' Elisabeth flinched – visualizing German planes zooming in over London.

'In peacetime,' Jerry predicted, 'people will be flying the way they take trains now. Hey, you'll love it!'

In July Elisabeth heard how thirty thousand women had marched down Whitehall with banners proclaiming, 'We demand to serve.' Women were entering government departments, taking over clerical jobs in private offices, working in the engineering shops. And many were leaving domestic service. Women workers called for 'equal pay'.

Glendale was in the grip of a seemingly endless hot spell. The temperature soared. Hallie sympathetically helped Elisabeth sponge-bathe tiny Katie – going through the rigors of heavy teething along with the heat – three or four times a day. Under Elisabeth's watchful eyes Amy waded in a nearby pond along with her school friends. Jerry was increasingly morose – and Elisabeth suspected this was due only in part to the heat.

On a steamy Friday afternoon – while her mother-in-law and Hannah napped in their bedrooms – Elisabeth sat on the porch with her father-in-law and talked in somber tones about the war. Amy and Katie were asleep in their bedroom. Hallie was on the back porch, churning ice cream as a special treat for Amy, who'd never tasted this concoction.

The sound of the phone ringing inside the house was raucous intrusion.

'I'll get it.' Elisabeth rose to her feet and hurried into the house. She reached to pick up the receiver. 'Good afternoon, Schiff residence.'

'Where is Fred?' a querulous male voice demanded. 'Since when does he think he can close the store before five o'clock?'

'The pharmacy is open,' Elisabeth stammered. 'Jerry Schiff is there with the clerk.'

'The hell they are!' the caller bellowed. 'Put Fred on the line!'

'Just a moment.' What did he mean – Jerry and the clerk weren't there? She almost tripped in her rush to the door. 'Papa, some man wants to talk to you. He said the pharmacy is closed.'

'It isn't five o'clock yet.' Fred Schiff grunted in annoyance. 'The heat is getting through to somebody.' He picked up the phone. 'Hello –'

'Fred, this is Jim Barlow. I stopped by the pharmacy to pick up a refill on my wife's prescription, and the damn place is closed. Before five o'clock!'

'Calm down, Jim. Call me at the pharmacy in about ten minutes and give me the prescription number. I'll fill it and drop by your house with it. We'll clear this up –'

'I'll go with you.' Elisabeth's heart pounding. What had happened at the pharmacy? 'I'll tell Hallie to keep an ear out for the children.'

'Now there's no need to be upset,' Fred soothed, but Elisabeth saw the tic in his eye that betrayed his own distress. 'I'm sure there's some logical explanation. Jim probably found the door stuck in all this heat and didn't bother to knock for attention. It's too hot to walk – we'll drive over.'

In minutes Fred was parking at the curb before the pharmacy. Elisabeth flung open the door and rushed to the entrance. Her father-in-law trailed her.

'The door's locked. There's nobody here.' Her voice was strident with alarm.

'I'll get my key.' Fumbling in his haste, he found the store key, unlocked the door.

'Jerry?' Elisabeth fought against frightening thoughts. 'Jerry?'

'Nobody's here –' Fred darted towards the rear, where the cash register stood. 'There's two envelopes.' He pulled them from their nesting place. His voice deepened in shock. 'One for me, one for you.'

Her hands trembling, she tore open the envelope handed over to her.

Elisabeth, please don't be angry. I have to do this. I'm on a train bound for Canada. Don't try to stop me. Don't allow

Papa to stop me. I'm enlisting in the Canadian Air Force. Let me do something right for once in my life. Kiss the kids for me. I'll write as soon as I can. Love, Jerry.

Chapter Twenty-six

While a ribbon of moonlight crept between the drapes, Elisabeth sat beside Amy's bed – Katie asleep in her nearby crib – and tried to explain to his loving stepdaughter why Jerry felt he had to go to fight in the war.

'He went off without saying goodbye, because that would have been too painful,' she fabricated in conclusion. 'He'll write as soon as he can.' With a twist of fate he might meet Ben or Felix. She remembered Ben's fascination with speed. Like Jerry, Ben would want to fly. She prayed that by some miracle they would meet, that at last she might have some word of her family.

Both Elisabeth and Amy were conscious of the shrill wails from Leona Schiff that penetrated the night quiet at intervals: 'I'm a good mother! How could he do this to me?' – the same complaint repeated endlessly. Amy was polite and respectful, Elisabeth acknowledged – but she detested Jerry's cold and arrogant mother and sisters. Jerry had pretended not to see the way his mother and sisters pointedly ignored warm, outgoing Amy. It was as though they didn't see her. They showed only perfunctory interest in darling Katie – their own flesh and blood.

'Mama, can I sleep with you tonight?' Amy asked wistfully.

'We'll sleep here in your bed.' She brushed a tendril of fair hair from Amy's forehead. Let the three of them be together tonight. She and her daughters.

Tomorrow morning she'd insist on helping out at the pharmacy in Jerry's place, she vowed. She couldn't bear the prospect of the two children and herself being dependent on the Schiffs. Bless him, Papa would think nothing of this – but her own pride dictated otherwise.

Leona Schiff took to her bed for four days. Hannah came home from school each day to go directly to her mother's room – not to emerge until supper. Mollie visited her mother daily. Elisabeth was unnerved by the accusatory glances she received from Jerry's sisters. How was *she* responsible for Jerry's running off that way? He hated his life in Glendale – he was running away from that. As he had run before.

Elisabeth prepared supper for the family on those nights when Leona remained closeted in her room. Amy's birthday arrived and passed with scant recognition. Fred tried valiantly to create a pleasant mood when he sat down to meals with Elisabeth and Amy. Hannah took trays to her mother's room for the two of them. He was so sweet to Amy, Elisabeth thought. As loving a grandfather to Amy as to Katie.

As though emerging from a period of mourning, Leona rejoined the family. Imperiously she silenced any talk of war in her presence. For a few days she expressed a wistful hope that Jerry would be rejected, that he would appear at the door with charming remorse at having inflicted pain on her. After a few days she abandoned this stance. Soon she was complaining that no letter had arrived yet from Jerry – assuming that she would be the recipient.

'Leona, give the boy time,' Fred scolded gently. 'He'll write as soon as he can.'

Elisabeth was relieved to be spending much of each day at the pharmacy now. Her mother-in-law and Hannah made no comment about this. Her father-in-law told friends and neighbors she was standing in for Jerry, who, they knew, was training to be a pilot for the Canadian Air Force. In a secret conspiracy with her father-in-law and Hallie Elisabeth was able to handle this arrangement. She saw Amy off to school, watched over Katie until shortly before eleven o'clock, when Hallie – having stormed through her morning household chores – took over. She went in to the pharmacy and remained there until four o'clock. With Jerry away his father remained to close up each night.

Bless Hallie for her devotion to the children, Elisabeth told herself repeatedly. She knew that Katie would be in loving hands, that Hallie would be there when Amy came home from school.

But in these past few weeks she'd started to worry about Hallie. First there was the black eye, then a week later the badly bruised arm. Hallie lowered her eyes and mumbled excuses: 'I wasn't lookin' – I fell down some steps'; 'I was helpin' Mama with the washin' and walked into a tree.' It enraged her that sixteen-year-old Hallie – so sweet and hard-working – must be the object of abuse at home. And *she* could do nothing to stop this.

Three weeks after he'd taken off, two letters arrived from Jerry, one for his parents and one for Elisabeth – brief letters that talked enthusiastically about the training period: 'They're rushing us through like crazy. In another three or four weeks we'll be heading for England.' He reported on their training, the good spirits of his companions.

If he was stationed in England, Elisabeth thought again in soaring hope, he might be able to contact Grandma. At least, he could write and tell her if the house appeared undamaged by German planes. Was Grandma receiving her letters? Not one had ever been returned. She accepted that Grandma was afraid to respond. But it would mean so much to her to know that Grandma read her letters.

Again, weeks went by without mail from Jerry. Then there was a short one, just to say he was all right and on the move. Elisabeth heard her mother-in-law on the phone with friends, boasting about her son, the war hero. Yet Elisabeth continued to suspect that Jerry's mother and sisters blamed her for his enlistment.

At regular intervals she heard from Ellie and Chuck. The orange business was thriving, demanding much of Chuck's time. Young Ira was thriving, Ellie wrote. 'But you know Chuck, he's got this writing bug, and he spends every moment he can find on scenarios. And fees keep going up. Even Papa's impressed with what he's getting for the new one. Another feature, thank God. The first since *Wuthering Heights*.'

With the arrival of fall – and Jerry stationed somewhere in northern England – Elisabeth allowed her father-in-law to persuade her to join a newly forming little theater group.

'They'll be so glad to have you,' he predicted. 'And it'll be good for you. You don't have to worry about Amy and Katie. You can trust me to keep an eye on them while you're rehearsing.'

With an anticipation that amazed her, Elisabeth went to the first meeting. Everyone was charming in the effervescent Southern manner. They knew vaguely that Jerry Schiff had married in New York, that his wife had never been involved in local socializing up till now. Before this first meeting the founding members of the group had chosen Ibsen's *A Doll's House* as their first production. A good omen, Elisabeth told herself, yet one that brought back painful memories.

She said nothing about having played Nora in Melbourne. Oh, it would be wonderful to play Ibsen again – even in a small town amateur production. But she could never walk out on her children – as Nora did. Unwarily she remembered a long subway ride from the Bronx, when Paul told her that one day he meant to write an updated 'Nora'. 'And you'll play it to perfection on Broadway.'

The following Thursday evening she joined the others at the high school auditorium for auditions. Of the nine women present, seven expressed a wish to try out for the role of Nora – even three matrons far past the age. The director was warmly approving as the first two women read, he himself reading the role of Helmer, Nora's husband.

'Though I'm the director,' he reminded archly. 'Later we'll read for the male lead.'

Elisabeth struggled not to wince at the readings – bad even by amateur standards. Then she was called to the stage. It was like coming home, she thought in a surge of pleasure. She accepted the playscript, though she still remembered every line.

As she read, she was conscious of an electric atmosphere in the small auditorium. Did the others realize she'd been a professional? Would that turn them against her? But she forced herself to focus on the play. The years seemed to evaporate. She was on the stage in their small theater in Melbourne. She was playing for an audience that loved her.

Unexpectedly there was a light sprinkling of applause when she finished. She felt giddy with recall of other performances of A Doll's House. She'd been so young then; David so young.

'Very nice,' the director approved and beckoned on yet another would-be Nora to join him on the stage.

The others dawdled in conversation after the auditions for the two major roles. There was talk of going to someone's house for coffee. At the next meeting the director would announce his choices for leading roles. Elisabeth hurried from the auditorium, her mind a kaleidoscope of earlier years.

Melbourne was another lifetime. She and David had been so in love. They'd been little more than children, living a brief fairy-tale romance. What she'd shared with Jerry was more mature. She was ever grateful to him for providing sanctuary when she was lost, hope and security these past years.

How ironic, she thought with a candor she rarely allowed herself, that the great love of her life had lasted a scant few weeks. Even now it hurt to remember the astonishment and pain in Paul's face when he heard the careless words that implied she was living with Jerry. Why hadn't she made him understand that it wasn't like that at all?

On another steamy night when Hannah and her mother had gone off to play bridge, Elisabeth sat on the porch with her father-in-law and talked about the war in Europe – a subject that must not be discussed when his wife was present. Occasional letters from Jerry indicated he relished his share in the war. Elisabeth was ever anxious about her brothers who were likely involved in fighting for Great Britain – and about her German cousins, no doubt fighting on the opposite side. How awful for Grandma, she thought with recurrent anguish.

Elisabeth was startled to see the director of the new little theater group approaching the house.

'He's awed by having a professional actress at his disposal,' Fred whispered with pride. 'He's coming to talk to you about playing Nora.' He was Elisabeth's confidant, knew every small detail about the audition.

'I'll go get us glasses of lemonade.' Elisabeth rose to her feet and hurried into the house.

When she returned with a tray of ice-laden glasses of lemonade, she found the director in lively conversation with Fred about the town's approval of his effort to bring culture into its midst.

'My, yes, we think it's high time we did something to offset this deplorable race to the movie theaters,' he was saying enthusiastically, and Elisabeth and her father-in-law avoided eye contact lest they erupt into laughter.

Moments later the director – after an appreciative swig of lemonade – turned to Elisabeth with a fatuous smile. 'We do hope you'll join the cast of *A Doll's House*.' He paused for an instant. 'We'd like you to play the part of Helene.' The maid.

Elisabeth froze in shock. 'I'm afraid I won't be able to accept it,' she said sweetly. 'With two children I find I won't have the time.'

The director departed quickly, seeming relieved that he was avoiding an ugly scene. Elisabeth and Fred watched him walk down the path to the sidewalk and hurry away into the distance.

'The son-of-a-bitch,' Fred said softly. 'Forgive my language, Elisabeth.'

'My sentiment exactly.' They hadn't wanted an outsider, she understood. She didn't belong to their select, small circle.

'Now if Caroline Goldfarb had auditioned for the play,' Fred drawled, 'she could have had any role her little heart desired. Her father's net worth is about a hundred times mine. She could be their token Jew,' he wound up with a bitterness she had never seen him display. 'In towns like this money has a loud voice.'

Elisabeth was disappointed at not being part of the little theater group formed in Glendale, yet her rejection forced her to recognize that with her work in *Jane Eyre* and *Wuthering Heights* she had found immense satisfaction. Still, her heart belonged to theater.

Now she fought a new restlessness to be back at work in pictures. She, Jerry and the children couldn't return to Hollywood – but a lot of movies were still being shot in New York. For six months out of the year Famous Players and the Lasky company filmed in New York – even Biograph, and a dozen small companies.

When this awful war was over – and people were predicting it couldn't be long now – she and Jerry and the children would go back to New York. *Wuthering Heights* was lost, but *Jane Eyre* had brought her flattering recognition. She wasn't an unknown. She'd work.

In late October Elisabeth and Hallie baked a beautiful birthday cake for Katie's first birthday. Hannah and her mother made a point of rushing off to a bridge game before the cake was served. But it was a lovely party, Elisabeth told herself afterwards. Adorable in a bright red pinafore, Katie managed – with her grandfather's loving guidance – to cut the first piece of cake. Amy coaxed her to blow out the one candle. Hallie stayed late to share in the festivities. How sad, Elisabeth thought nostalgically, that Jerry couldn't be here for Katie's first birthday.

Twice now Jerry had sent her money with a stipulation to 'sock it away for later'. He was thinking of their moving away from Glendale, she realized with relief. They'd go to New York, where he wouldn't have to worry about Hollywood loan sharks. Then a letter arrived from Chuck and Ellie with clippings from Los Angeles newspapers. The loan shark clique had become involved in a local murder. Three had been indicted and were being tried.

Chuck says there's no doubt but they'll spend a long time in prison, Ellie wrote. Once Jerry comes home, you'll have no reason not to return to Hollywood. It's incredible what's happened in the year and a half that you've been gone. Chuck says there are almost 15,000 people working in the industry. Of course sixty percent of pictures are being made in Hollywood these days. Europe's lost its edge. Paramount alone is turning out three or four features a week. Can you believe there are over 50,000 movie houses just crying for pictures?

In December Elisabeth and Hallie were plotting a twelfth birthday party for Amy – to include the presence of five friends. Jerry's mother objected to 'all these celebrations when my son is fighting in the war', but Fred Schiff brushed aside Leona's outrage. Amy would have her birthday party.

Two days before Amy's birthday Elisabeth picked up the phone in the pharmacy, expecting an order for renewal of a prescription.

'Tell my father to come home immediately!' Hannah's voice was strident. 'Something terrible has happened!'

'What is it?' Elisabeth was cold with alarm. 'Hannah?' But the line was dead.

'A problem?' Her father-in-law was anxious.

'Hannah said you're to come home immediately. Something's happened.'

'Come with me.' His voice was brusque. 'Leonard, watch the store till we get back.'

Because the day was unusually cold, Fred had driven to the pharmacy this morning. He prodded Elisabeth to the car in white-faced silence, drove with a speed that unnerved her, eliciting stares from pedestrians and honks from the few drivers on the road.

'Tell me exactly what Hannah said,' Fred ordered as they approached the house.

With the sense of being part of a nightmare, Elisabeth repeated Hannah's words. 'She said, "Tell my father to come home immediately. Something terrible has happened."' Instinct told her Amy and Katie were all right; Hannah had said, 'Tell my father –'

Fred pulled to a jagged stop before the house. He and Elisabeth rushed from the car to the front door. The shades were drawn in the parlor, Elisabeth noticed. They could hear Leona's hysterical crying.

'Where's Amy?' Alarm tied a rope about Elisabeth's throat. Then she spied Amy, standing tense and frightened at the top of the stairs.

'He's gone,' Hannah wailed. 'My precious brother is dead.' She pointed to a sheet of paper that lay on the floor.

With trembling hand Elisabeth reached to pick it up: a cablegram from the British War Department. Jerome Schiff had been killed in action. In a corner of her mind she noted the cable had been addressed to her, as Jerry's wife. Still, she could understand her mother-in-law's need to open it immediately – knowing even before she read the words that something had happened to Jerry.

'Not "missing in action",' Leona sobbed. 'Killed in action!' All at once she stopped crying. She focused her gaze on Elisabeth with a devastating rage. 'It's your fault he's dead! If you'd been a real wife, he wouldn't have gone chasing off to war! He ran to get away from you! You and your two brats!'

Chapter Twenty-seven

Elisabeth sat in the children's bedroom and held Amy in her arms. Earlier shock had frozen her tears. Now they fell unheeded while she tried to comfort her small daughter.

'Mama, why? Why? Why did it have to happen?'

'Darling, we don't have the answers to that. Your great-grandmother would say, "God has his reasons."'

'I don't like God!' Amy stormed.

'Sssh.' Elisabeth rocked Amy in her arms. 'Never say that, my darling. Never believe that.'

Katie stirred restlessly in her crib – as though, Elisabeth thought, she knew the grief that filled this house. She'd have no memory of her father. Amy had little memory of her father. Again – as when David died – she asked herself if this was some terrible payment extorted for her actions against her father.

Leona remained in her room, outraged that her husband was observing only two days to mourn their son. She was determined to observe *shivah*, the seven-day mourning period decreed by Jewish law. Her two daughters would sit with her each day.

'I tried to talk to her,' Fred told Elisabeth as they sat over breakfast on the third morning, an unnatural stillness pervading the house. Hallie seemed to feel she must go about her morning cleaning in silence. 'A pharmacist has an obligation to his customers. I don't mourn less by fulfilling my duties.'

'Jerry would understand,' she said softly. It still seemed unreal that Jerry was dead. She hesitated. 'He wanted so much to please you and his mother.'

'We tried to fit him into our dreams, Beth –' It was the first time he'd used the diminutive.

'He loved you very much.'

'I'd better get to the store.' Pale and drawn from lack of sleep, he rose to his feet. 'You'll be in at eleven?'

'Of course.' She knew this was important to him. Jerry would approve.

'Amy's going to school?'

'She's worried about getting behind.' Again she told herself, Jerry would approve.

With Amy off to school, Elisabeth went upstairs to the children's room. Katie would be waking up at any moment now. Her poor, darling baby – bereft of father so young.

'Mama!' Katie chortled, her face rosy from sleep, arms extended imperiously.

'My precious baby.' Elisabeth scooped her up, lifted her from her crib. 'I didn't think you were awake yet –'

'Elisabeth, we have to talk.' She whirled around at the sound of Hannah's voice.

'Yes?' Her heart pounding without reason.

'My mother wants to see you in her room. Take the baby down to Hallie and come to her.'

'All right.' Why this sudden summons?

She hurried downstairs to leave Katie with Hallie, then returned to the upper floor, gearing herself to face her mother-in-law. The door was wide. She hesitated a moment, then walked into the room.

'Hannah said you wanted to talk to me.' Her eyes moved from her mother-in-law to Hannah, sitting side by side on the window seat.

'I want you out of this house.' Leona's voice was harsh with rage. 'You killed my son. If you'd been a proper wife, he wouldn't have run to fight another country's war. Hannah will buy tickets for you to New York. She'll give you twenty dollars. I want the three of you out of here by tomorrow night.'

Elisabeth gaped in disbelief. What would she do in New York? She hadn't thought into the future. Her mind was still muddled with grief.

'Tomorrow night,' Hannah repeated.

Elisabeth struggled with panic, willed herself to cope. Where could she go with her children?

'Not New York,' she rejected. All she knew was acting. California was the place for her. 'Los Angeles,' she stipulated. Chuck and Ellie

238

were there – she wouldn't be totally alone. 'I won't budge from this house,' she said with fresh strength, 'without tickets to Los Angeles.' Her eyes defied them to argue with her. Jerry's father couldn't know about this – but what could he do? His wife and daughters ruled in this house.

Hannah exchanged a long glance with her mother.

'I'll buy tickets for you and your children to Los Angeles.' *One of those children was her niece. Her brother's child.* 'I'll give them to you at the train. You'll leave Glendale tomorrow. I'll tell you the departure time later. And don't go to the pharmacy this morning.'

Her head high, vowing not to allow the two women to suspect the harrowing impact of their words, Elisabeth spun around and left the room. The timing was horrible but the decision was right, she told herself. How could she remain in this house?

With a sudden need to hold Katie in her arms, she headed for the stairs, too shaken to cry, her mind in chaos. For the children she must be strong. Now she became aware that Hallie stood at the foot of the stairs – her face etched with distress. Hallie had heard.

'Miz Elisabeth, you leavin' with the children?' she whispered as Elisabeth reached the bottom step.

'Tomorrow.' Elisabeth bent to pick up Katie, playing on the floor at Hallie's feet.

'Take me with you.' It was an anguished plea.

'Hallie, I can't do that.' Her voice was gentle. 'How can you leave your family?'

'My mama, she be glad.' Hallie's young-wise eyes glittered with contempt. 'She don't want me in her house.' Of six children Hallie was the youngest, the only one at home.

'Hallie, does your mother beat you?' Involuntarily the question was wrung from her.

'Yes'um.' Hallie lowered her eyes. 'She don't like it 'cause her new husband – that man who come to live with us last year,' she corrected herself defiantly, 'he don't leave me alone. She don't want her man touchin' me. And I don't want it.'

'Oh, Hallie . . .' This sweet little girl living in such horror.

'Take me with you. I'll take care of your house and the children. I'll do whatever you wants me to do!'

'You'll come with us.' Elisabeth's mind charged into action now. How could she not take Hallie with her? 'As soon as I know what train we're taking tomorrow, I'll buy a ticket for you. You'll go with us to California. But you must tell your mother.'

'Yes'um!' Hallie's smile was electric. 'I'll tell her. She'll be real pleased.'

In mid-afternoon Hannah left the house without a word, returned forty minutes later. She paused in the foyer to address Elisabeth, in the parlor with Katie.

'Your train leaves at 3.40 p.m. I'll meet you there fifteen minutes ahead of time to give you the tickets.' And to make sure they boarded the train, Elisabeth interpreted. 'My mother and I will have supper in her room tonight. Have Hallie bring us a tray before she leaves.'

'Yes.' Meaning, Elisabeth was to prepare supper tonight.

Without another word – without a glance at Katie, smiling beguilingly at her aunt – Hannah strode away. In a few minutes Amy would arrive from school. How would Amy take this new upheaval in her young, so troubled life?

Stammering in her anxiety, Elisabeth told Amy that they would be returning to Hollywood on the following day.

'What time?' Amy asked after a startled pause.

'On the 3.40 p.m. train.' Elisabeth was puzzled.

'Can I go to school in the morning?'

'Yes, darling. I'll go with you to explain to the principal.'

'I can tell my friends that we're going back to Hollywood?' Gleeful anticipation blended with ambivalent regret in her voice.

'Of course, you can tell them.' Their stealthy exit had been etched on her mind, Elisabeth thought painfully.

'They didn't believe me when I said I'd been in some movies when I was littler.' Amy's smile was complacent, accepting of this new move. 'I told them I was going to be an actress again some day.'

Elisabeth was startled by this declaration. 'When you finish school – including college.'

Amy wasn't ashamed that her mother was a movie actress. Times were changing. It wasn't something degrading these days.

Elisabeth was in the kitchen in the midst of supper preparations when her father-in-law arrived home. He came out to the kitchen, his face reflecting his distress at the situation.

'Elisabeth, I know I should put my foot down and tell Leona and Hannah that I won't tolerate what they've done, but –'

'It had to be this way,' Elisabeth interrupted. 'It would have been intolerable if I stayed.'

'I'll miss you and the children. The three of you brought something precious into my life.' He reached into his jacket pocket, pulled out an envelope. 'I want you to have this.'

'Jerry sent me money twice. We'll be all right.'

'Take this.' He reached for her hand, closed it over the envelope. 'Consider it birthday presents for Amy and Katie for the next fifteen years. And if you're having problems out there, you let me know.' He cleared his throat. 'I'll be here with the car to drive you to the depot and help you with the luggage. You'll write to me?'

'I'll write.'

Over supper the three at the table tried to pretend this was just another evening meal. Only Hallie's show of cheerfulness as she served seemed sincere. Just before leaving – with a blend of diffidence and defensiveness – she made her announcement.

'Mist' Schiff, I won't be back to work after tonight.'

'Hallie's going with us,' Elisabeth explained. 'Her mother approves.'

'I'm glad,' he said after a startled moment. 'You'll need help with the children – and Hallie's a fine person.'

The following afternoon Elisabeth waited on the front porch with Amy and Katie and their luggage long before they were scheduled to leave. She was conscious of an obsessive need to be out of the house, to put this segment of their lives behind them. Earlier Hannah had left the house, tersely reminding them she'd be at the depot, knowing, Elisabeth suspected, that her father would be arriving soon with the car. Hannah would walk, she thought with a flicker of amusement. They would drive. Hallie would meet them at the depot.

At the depot – while her father and Hallie stood by with the luggage – Hannah gave the train tickets and the promised twenty dollars to Elisabeth without a word, and walked away. The train pulled into the station. Fred reached to enfold first Amy, then Katie into his arms, then he embraced Elisabeth.

'Take care of yourself, Beth. You're a very special lady.'

Fighting tears, Elisabeth focused on getting her brood settled in the rather grimy day coach that would take them on their first lap westward. She was embarking on a long journey where she alone must guide the course. Thirteen years ago today she and David had boarded a train in Grand Central Station in New York that carried them westward. At twenty-nine she'd lost two husbands, crisscrossed the country four times, was embarking on the fifth.

But she wasn't alone, she reminded herself. She had her two precious children – and Hallie. She remembered Ben's favourite poem – W. E. Henley's 'Invictus':

> It matters not how strait the 'gate',
> How charged with punishments the scroll,
> I am the master of my fate:
> I am the captain of my soul.

She would hold her small family together. She would raise her daughters well.

Elisabeth was grateful for Hallie's presence as they traveled across the continent. Hallie had never been further than fourteen miles from Glendale. She was intrigued by every sight, and infected Amy and Katie with her own sense of adventure. In the tedious five days of their trip Elisabeth plotted their course of action. She knew of an inexpensive hotel in Los Angeles. They would settle themselves for the night, at least. She would phone Ellie. Ellie and Chuck would help them find a place to live. And all at once the realization that Ellie and Chuck didn't know about Jerry assaulted her. They – along with Ellie's wonderful parents – would mourn for him.

Chuck knew a lot of people in the movie business. He'd help her get back on track. She had lost a year and a half – but she'd forged a place for herself in moving pictures. That didn't disappear overnight. She would work again – at a good salary.

These last months she'd devoured *Variety*, the *Moving Picture World*, the *Motion Picture News* – which her father-in-law bought for her on his frequent business trips to Atlanta. She even read the fan magazines – *Photoplay, Motion Picture Story Magazine*. Hallie once confided that Hannah hid copies of *Photoplay* under her mattress – Hannah, who made it clear she considered movie actresses immoral, loose women.

Elisabeth uttered a long sigh of relief when she realized they were at last approaching their destination. Amy glowed with anticipation. She'd never realized how Amy missed Hollywood. Now Amy's words tumbled over one another as she tried to describe that earlier life to Hallie.

Then they were caught up in their arrival, the business of seeking out the hotel where they were to stay for the moment. Her heart pounding, Elisabeth telephoned the Sanchez house – praying someone was home. Ellie answered. There was the warm welcome Elisabeth had anticipated, Ellie's shock and grief at learning of Jerry's death, an instant offer of support.

Elisabeth explained that Katie had been put to bed for the night, told Ellie that their entourage now included Hallie. 'I'll drive over in the morning and bring you all back here,' Ellie said ebulliently. 'Yeah, Chuck finally agreed that a woman should be allowed to drive.' They'd fought over this for years. 'You'll stay with us until we can find a bungalow for you. Beth, you were right to come home.'

It had been Elisabeth's plan to enroll Amy in school the next day – even before they had a permanent place to live – but when Ellie met them in the hotel lobby in the morning, she suggested this be postponed a day.

'I'll take you all to the house,' Ellie said. 'Mom and Pop are dying to see you. Then Chuck says I'm to bring you over to the studio where he's working. He wants to introduce you to his boss.' Chuck was now back in movies full time since the industry had really taken off.

'Can I go to the studio, too?' Amy pleaded. 'Please, please, Mama?'

'All right. You can come with us.' This would be only a casual meeting with Chuck's boss. They'd be in and out of the studio in twenty minutes. Then they'd go bungalow hunting. Amy would enjoy that.

At the Sanchez house Elisabeth and the children – and Hallie – were greeted with the beautiful warmth Elisabeth cherished.

'It's wonderful to see you again, Beth.' Peter Sanchez hugged her enthusiastically, turned to embrace Amy, hoisted Katie into the air. 'Now I've got to go off and make a buck.'

Bella Sanchez took immediate charge of Katie – quite happy with this arrangement – while Hallie undertook to unpack for them. Ellie marshaled Elisabeth and Amy out to the car.

'You won't recognize the town,' Ellie warned. 'It's amazing how it's developed. The studios are all working like crazy. You shouldn't have any problem lining up work.'

'Do you think producers remember *Jane Eyre*?' Elisabeth yearned for reassurance.

'It was a while ago,' Ellie conceded after a moment, 'but a lot of people saw it and loved it. Loved *you*.'

At the studio – a massive low structure where several movies were being filmed at the same time – Ellie sought out Chuck.

'Chuck's editing as well as writing now,' Ellie explained. 'He's fascinated by all the new developments.'

They located Chuck in a tiny office at the far end of the building. He hurried forward to kiss Elisabeth and Amy.

'We missed you,' he said quietly.

'We missed you, too.' Elisabeth's face was luminous. For over a year and a half they'd existed in a wasteland. This was home.

'Oh Frank!' Chuck called out, and beckoned to a man in his mid-forties who was striding down the hall outside the tiny office. 'There's somebody here I'd like you to meet.'

The man Chuck called Frank walked into the office, accepted introductions. He was Frank Osborne, whom Elisabeth recognized as a new but important director. He inspected Amy with lively interest. 'And to whom does this little lady belong?'

'My daughter,' Elisabeth said with pride, too late remembering she was supposed to be twenty and unmarried. 'This is Amy.'

'She has an interesting quality.' But Elizabeth had seen his wary frown. He'd recognized her, but he'd also absorbed the fact that she couldn't be twenty with a daughter Amy's age – and there had probably been a husband somewhere along the line. She was aware of the frantic efforts of producers to conceal the fact that Mary Pickford was twenty-two, married and had had at least one affair with an actor other than her husband. They preferred moviegoers to believe Pickford was twelve or thirteen. This was a town that cherished youth and virginity – because that was what the moviegoing public had been led to expect. Producers considered it dangerous to spoil that illusion.

'Frank, Elisabeth is available for –'

Frank ignored Chuck. 'I think we might use Amy. I'm sure she'll photograph beautifully. A cross between Pickford and Gish. Lillian,' he specified.

'She's only twelve,' Elisabeth stammered. 'She has to go to school.'

'Mama!' Amy was avid to pursue this prospect of an acting career.

'She can go to school,' Frank said with a broad smile. 'When she's doing a picture, we'll have a tutor for her on the set. She'll be able to keep up with her classes.' He seemed impatient to make a deal.

'She's a little girl,' Elisabeth protested. She knew about the twelve- and thirteen-hour days on a movie set.

'Mama, I want to do it!' Amy's eyes clung to her mother.

'I'm prepared to offer her a contract for one year.' Frank paused dramatically. 'I'll pay her two hundred dollars a week.'

'Mama!' Amy's eyes beseeched her.

Elisabeth knew she couldn't reject this offer. It would mean security not only for the term of the contract but for years ahead. But she would be a watchdog, she vowed. Amy would *not* work the long hours that she had worked. Amy's schooling would not be neglected.

'There'll be stipulations because of her age –' Elisabeth launched into a bargaining session, knowing Frank Osborne would accept her terms.

She was shaken to recognize that at twenty-nine she was considered too old to be a movie star. In gossip-saturated Hollywood the word would circulate fast that Beth Winston had a twelve-year-old daughter. No matter that she had turned in good performances, that in *Jane Eyre* she had exhibited the ability to draw large audiences.

A year and a half ago she was on the upward track, success at her fingertips. But she'd run from Hollywood – and everything was lost. So quickly she had become a has-been . . .

Chapter Twenty-eight

Elisabeth was grateful for Hallie's presence in their lives. Sweet, loving Hallie took charge of the bungalow and of Katie during the hours her mother was at the studio with Amy. Elisabeth had established rules for Amy's work schedule. Six days a week they would arrive at the studio by eight a.m. Amy would spend an hour in the morning and two hours in the afternoon with the tutor. Amy must leave the studio no later than six p.m. On the days when Amy was not working she would attend school in Hollywood.

After some pangs of guilt, Elisabeth decided to change Katie's name legally from Kate Schiff to Kate Winston. They would all use the Winston name. Peter Sanchez would help her arrange this.

The very first week at the studio Elisabeth had a confrontation with Frank. He ordered Amy to remain until they reshot a final scene for the day. Unnerved but determined, Elisabeth insisted on his abiding by the rules. One accepted infraction and Amy would be subject to Frank's whims.

'Mama,' Amy whispered, 'I'm not tired. Honest.' She was terrified Frank would dismiss her, Elisabeth understood.

'Amy is twelve years old.' Elisabeth managed a calm exterior, but the prospect of Amy's salary being cut off tied a knot in her stomach. 'You agreed to the rules. I insist she have time for a leisurely supper with her family, for homework, and a suitable night's sleep.' He wanted another Mary Pickford or Lillian Gish. *He needed Amy.*

'You're tough,' he scolded, but Elisabeth knew she'd won. At least, for now.

Elisabeth made it clear to Amy – awed by the salary she was to be paid – that they would lead a modest existence. This was a one-year contract. Nobody knew what would happen after this year. Let them have money ahead. She was uncomfortable in the knowledge that Amy had become the family breadwinner. She'd heard much about how Mary Pickford had for years supported her whole family. That mustn't happen to Amy.

Elisabeth quickly recognized that there was no way she could try to search for roles for herself – as Ellie prodded her to do. Her job was to be on the set with Amy, to make sure Frank followed the agreed schedule. *This* was her job for now, she told herself – and allotted a modest salary for herself out of Amy's weekly paycheck.

It was fair, she self-consciously told herself, for Amy to contribute a small amount to the house each week – her share of board and room. The balance of each check was to be banked for Amy's future use. She allowed herself one extravagance: she bought a second-hand car to carry Amy and herself to and from the studio.

The months rushed past. For Amy acting was a game she relished – and Frank was ecstatic about her work. Each afternoon at quitting time Elisabeth consulted with Frank about the following day's shooting so that she could help Amy with her performance. Amy was so talented, she thought tenderly – and eager to accept the advice her mother offered. The way David had helped her all those years ago, she could help their daughter now.

Always she worried about the war, about how London was faring. How was the family? Were the boys in service? In April 1916 the German air raids intensified. Each time she picked up a newspaper or magazine – and she was an avid reader of these – she dreaded what she would learn. London was bombed five times in the course of this month. Most of the casualties were civilians. Were those at the house in Lexham Gardens safe? She read about the quiet heroism of London civilians – who fought fires, rescued the wounded, helped restore damaged houses and shops. Yet it seemed to Elisabeth that life here went on as if no war existed. Didn't Americans understand that millions of men lived tortuous lives in mud and filth – that thousands were dying?

Often she came awake from restless sleep after nightmares about Jerry's death somewhere over France. She guessed that Ben – so gentle, a dreamer, yet fascinated by speed – would be flying. Felix? He spoke two languages other than English – perhaps he was an interpreter.

Few Americans seemed to believe the United States would become involved in the war. She prayed that wouldn't happen. She recoiled from the thought of Paul in the fighting. Everybody said that if the

United States was dragged into the war, married men with children wouldn't be drafted. Was Paul married? Did he have children?

She was startled at her feeling of pain that he might be married. What was the matter with her? That was a tiny episode in her life. Yet she knew there would always be a special corner in her heart that belonged to Paul Coleman.

Amy was happy, Elisabeth told herself at regular intervals. From her part-time attendance at school she'd acquired a best friend. She liked her tutor and her teacher at school, yet Elisabeth worried Amy was being robbed of her childhood.

Frank kept her busy at the studio, with only a few days between pictures, and despite Elisabeth's firmness, Amy's school attendance was on the decline. Still – at Elisabeth's insistence – Amy took the tests that were given in school. She was doing well. Hallie prepared special party suppers each time Amy came through with high grades on a test.

Aware of the raunchy gossip that ricocheted about the almost incestuous movie colony, Elisabeth made a point of never leaving Amy alone while they were at the studio. Just a few days ago a garrulous wardrobe woman had talked about rumors of D. W. Griffith's interest in very young actresses.

'Just about everybody knows about Mr Griffith's obsession for thirteen- and fourteen-year-old girls. Not just on the screen,' the woman emphasized. 'And can you believe what some people are saying – Lillian Gish is her sister Dorothy's lover?'

Everybody knew about Mack Sennett's 'casting couch'. And he wasn't alone. She would make sure that Amy remained clear of the shady side of film-making, Elisabeth vowed. Nothing of the ugliness would be allowed to touch her precious daughter. But film-making wasn't all seedy, she reminded herself. Cecil B. de Mille recognized the importance of dealing with social problems. In time others would, too. Movies could provide an important public service. That was what Paul used to say.

Elisabeth wrote her mother and grandmother at regular intervals – always worried that the letters were not getting through with German submarines so active in the waters surrounding England. Why didn't they write? In these harrowing times they must know how anxious she was. She wrote her father-in-law in Glendale, Georgia, sent him pictures of Amy and Katie. Unlike Grandma and Mama, he replied.

On Amy's thirteenth birthday a party was held on the set at the studio. At home Hallie had spent two days shopping and cooking for a party at the bungalow. Her precious 'older baby' was growing up. Mr and Mrs Sanchez, Chuck, Ellie and Ira were the birthday party guests. Elisabeth and Ellie and Hallie served. Along with steaming bowls of creamy carrot soup they brought platters of food to the table: roast chicken, yams, lima beans – which Hallie called 'butter beans' in the Southern tradition – plus a fish brought by Mrs Sanchez. Later there would be the magnificent birthday cake – all chocolate, as decreed by Amy – that Hallie had made this morning.

'All right, everything's on the table,' Elisabeth said with quiet satisfaction. 'Let's all sit down. You, too, Hallie,' she ordered when Hallie seemed ambivalent. Hallie sat with Elisabeth and the girls at meal time, but this was a party. 'Hallie, we're all family,' Elisabeth said lovingly. 'Sit.'

As always after the first few minutes table conversation settled into business talk. Chuck collected stories – censored because of the three children present – about rising stars.

'Ellie and I went to see Theda Bara in *A Fool There Was* the other night,' he said with a glint in his eyes.

'She's come up fast.' Elisabeth's smile was wry. 'I hear a year ago she was an extra. Now she's being touted as an exotic French-Arab born beneath the Sphinx.'

Chuck grinned. 'And before that she was Theodosia Goodman, the daughter of a Jewish tailor from Chillicothe, Ohio.'

'It bothers me,' Peter Sanchez said, all at once somber, 'that Douglas Fairbanks – who, by the way, is half-Jewish –' he conceded with momentary pride, 'would appear in a movie that uses cocaine as a subject of amusement. This sends a terrible message to our young people.'

'And the not so young,' Elisabeth added.

Chuck turned to Elisabeth. 'Beth, do you remember Paul Coleman? We knew him back in New York. He –'

'I remember him.' All at once Elisabeth's heart was pounding.

'He's out here now. He had a play optioned for Broadway. When that fell through, he was offered a contract over at Triangle. The gossip is that the deal was set by D. W. Griffith. You know how he respects anybody involved in theater. He probably figured a playwright who almost made it to Broadway would lend class to his movies.'

'Paul always said movies would be powerful one day.' Elisabeth struggled to sound casual. Nobody knew the closeness that had developed between Paul and herself in a brief few weeks. Even now, she trembled in recall. 'But he used to be so sure his future lay in the theater.'

'With the money Griffith set up for him, he changed his mind. It's a real financial coup.' But Chuck's voice was coated with compassion.

Elisabeth was relieved when Ellie brought up the latest rumors about Mary Pickford. It was absurd for her to feel this way because Paul was out here, working for Triangle. They might pass each other on the street one day. But Paul hated her, she tormented herself. He'd thought she and Jerry were having an affair – when it hadn't been like that at all. He might not even remember her. Anyhow, her life was set. No room for anything except raising Amy and Katie.

'Can you believe it?' Ellie's voice brought her back to the moment. 'Mary Pickford earns more than President Wilson!'

'Mama, when will Hallie bring out my birthday cake?' a faint impatience in Amy's voice now. 'Katie's almost falling asleep.'

Elisabeth was haunted by the knowledge that Paul was in Hollywood – living and working here. Setting down roots. She yearned to see him even as she dreaded a possible encounter. *Don't think about Paul.*

She must concentrate on the likelihood of Frank's offering a new contract for Amy. In the last three months fan mail had been arriving for her. Audiences loved her. Of course, after *Jane Eyre* she, too, had received a startling amount of fan mail – and just a year and a half later she couldn't find a job. But logic reminded her that she had disappeared from the scene for too long. And *Jane Eyre* never received the distribution of the movies in which Amy was appearing. It was important to be seen regularly. In the last ten months Amy had made eight movies. *She'd* made one feature film.

Unexpectedly it was Amy herself who brought up the subject of another contract.

'Mama, did Mr Osborne say anything to you about me keeping on with the studio?' Wistfulness blended with excitement in her voice.

'I suspect he'll want you for another year.' Elisabeth strived for casualness. The possibility was reassuring, yet once again she asked herself if Amy were being robbed of her childhood.

'I hope so. I mean, if I'm working then we're sure to stay in one place. We won't go rushing off to New York, or somewhere . . .' Amy's voice trailed off with an undercurrent of anxiety that sent waves of shock through Elisabeth.

'Darling, it's not your responsibility to keep working for the family!' Why hadn't she realized that Amy was worried about their survival? She'd convinced herself that Amy adapted to the upheavals in their lives, that the young were resilient. *She* was the mother – it was her duty to care for her children. 'But yes –' she fought to sound reassuring – 'I'm fairly certain Frank will want to keep you under contract.'

Elisabeth focused on what a new contract should provide. Instinct told her she should wait for Frank to bring this up; she mustn't appear anxious. She'd drop little hints that now that Amy was in her teens, perhaps it was time to focus on education. Still, a second contract – at more money – would mean funds to put aside for Amy to go to college. Amy wouldn't be cheated of that – as she had been. Not that money had been a deterrent in her case. It was Papa's backward ideas.

Elisabeth, along with Chuck and Ellie, had thought that two hundred dollars a week was a phenomenal salary for Amy. But Amy had built a following. Her fan mail showed that. She was an asset to the studio. Exhibitors were forced to buy a studio's entire output – and with six or more of Amy Winston's pictures in the block, the studio could be sure exhibitors would buy. So Amy was money in the bank for the studio.

Elisabeth knew the next few weeks would be stressful as she waited for Frank to approach her about a new contract. But she mustn't make the first move. Stars like Pickford and Chaplin and Mabel Normand were paid unbelievable salaries. Nobody knew, of course, when the axe would fall and the fabulous money deals would disappear.

Elisabeth felt a surge of confidence when Frank told her that *Photoplay* was doing a story on Amy in its February issue. How much money could she push Frank into paying Amy? How much money were the pictures Amy made earning for the studio?

She remembered that Chuck had a sister back in New York.

'I know Amy's pictures are doing well,' she told him, 'the real question is how are they doing in a big city like New York?'

'You want to have Dorothy look around at places like the Strand?' he interpreted immediately. 'Let us know what she can see – like are there box-office lines at Amy's movies?'

'That's right.' Everybody in the business realized that Amy was the main attraction in any picture she made now. 'Do you think Dorothy will do it?'

Chuck laughed heartily. 'She'll love it. Anything to do with this business fascinates her.'

'I don't suppose you can find out how much the exhibitors are paying for Amy's films – and for others they buy from the studio?'

'I'll try,' Chuck grinned. 'You're a sharp negotiator, Beth.'

A few days later Chuck had acquired some figures on film rental fees. Those with Amy brought roughly fifteen percent higher prices than others the studio distributed. All right, she had considerable leverage here. Amy's new contract must pay $500 a week. If the bargaining got rough, then she'd drop to $400.

Dangerously close to the expiration date of Amy's contract Frank mentioned the possibility of extending it.

'A *new* contract would be more appropriate, Frank.' An extension would mean the same salary. 'Though I'm not sure I ought to allow her to work any longer. Her schooling should take precedence over everything else.'

They settled down to the cat-and-mouse bargain Elisabeth had anticipated. Elisabeth was matter-of-fact, point by point explaining why she was convinced Amy deserved a substantial raise. To her masked astonishment Frank himself set $500 as her new salary.

'That's it, Beth – not a dime more,' he said at last.

For another thirteen months they'd be doing very well. Elisabeth was simultaneously triumphant and uneasy. *She* should be supporting their household – not her thirteen-year-old daughter. But they managed on what was her allotted salary and what was taken from Amy's check as room and board, she reminded herself. They lived on a modest scale – none of the high style that people in Amy's bracket considered normal. They couldn't know how long this would last.

Shortly before Hanukkah – while Amy was in her afternoon session with her tutor – Elisabeth left the studio to shop for gifts for the girls and young Ira. She roamed about the first floor of Bullock's, debated about what each would like. She turned a corner of an aisle – and came face to face with Paul.

She gazed up at him in a glorious blend of joy, astonishment and confusion. How long was it? Ten years? Now it seemed yesterday. He'd changed little. He appeared tired, unfamiliarly sad.

'Beth . . .' His eyes clung to hers. 'How are you? What are you doing out here?'

'My daughter Amy has been working in pictures for the last year,' she stammered, caught up in tumultuous emotions. 'Remember Amy?' She'd talked about Amy endless times.

'I still think of her as a very little girl –'

'She's thirteen –' *He hadn't forgotten her*. 'I have another little girl now. Katie is two.'

He smiled in sudden comprehension. 'Amy Winston is your daughter! I should have realized that. She's the image of you.'

'You remember Jerry Schiff?' Why was her heart pounding this way? 'He worked for Fred, too.'

'Yes, I remember him –'

'Amy and I met him in San Francisco during the earthquake.' Paul knew she and Amy had been there. She hadn't mentioned Jerry's presence. 'He was like a big brother to us when we were so lost. He appointed himself my personal manager, tried so hard to get me into a Broadway play. It didn't work out. Then we got married and came out here.' Why was she rattling on this way? 'He joined the Canadian Air Force early in the war. He was killed in action a year ago.'

'That was rough for you,' he said gently, and hesitated. 'I've thought about you often. Wondered where you were, how you were. When Fred resumed filming, he tried to get in touch with you. He said he left messages for you at the candy store, but you never replied.'

'We were on our way to California.' It was as though she and Paul had shot back in time. 'And you? Chuck said something about an option on a play?'

'One of those crazy deals. You know.' He shrugged this away. 'One day it seemed we were about ready to start casting, then the backers decided to invest in something else.'

'You said your heart would always be in theater,' she remembered.

'But you expected movies to be much bigger than the theater ever was.'

'My heart's still in theater – but my head told me to stop playing games and face reality. Writing for the theater is like playing Russian roulette. I was offered a contract out here that I couldn't refuse.'

'Chuck told me you were working with Griffith. He's the best – and he respects theater.'

'My – my wife was eager to come out to California.' He was married. She struggled to hide her shock. Why should she have thought differently? What did it matter? Her life was set. No room for Paul. 'She hates the New York winters. We were broke – and then this studio contract came up. And a four-year-old boy wears out shoes awfully fast.' He strived for humor, but his eyes made other statements. Paul still loved her. She clung to this – even though there was no room in their lives for each other. *He was married. He had a child.*

'Do you have pictures of your son?' She didn't want to see them. She wanted to turn back the clock ten years.

'I have a couple of snapshots with me.' His face alight with love, Paul was digging into his pocket. 'Tommy's wonderful. Bright and sweet and affectionate. He thinks he's fourteen.'

Elisabeth accepted the two snapshots Paul extended, inspected them with a tremulous smile.

'You must have looked just like this at four.' How did you appear casual when your heart was breaking?

This was insane. Their timing was all wrong. What was that poem about two ships passing in the night? But she knew – as long as she lived, she would love Paul. And he would love her.

Chapter Twenty-nine

Elisabeth told herself the encounter with Paul in Bullock's meant nothing in her life. She didn't make the rounds of Hollywood parties – she'd probably never run into him again. Yet at unwary moments – on the street, in a shop, at a gas station – she involuntarily glanced about in a subconscious hope of seeing him.

What was his wife like? He'd given no hint, hadn't even mentioned her name. His little boy – Tommy – radiated that same appealing warmth that she had always felt in Paul. They'd parted so awkwardly, as though each was fearful of saying something terribly wrong. There was no room in her life for Paul. No room in his for her.

At the studio filming stopped early on New Year's Eve. Champagne was served. Elisabeth allowed Amy one sip. A festive atmosphere permeated the studio despite the fact that most Americans were terrified that the United States would be sucked into the war. Nobody wanted to conjecture what the coming year would bring. In anticipation of the small party at the end of the working day some of the cast and crew had arranged for family to come to the studio.

Chuck reported that he and Ellie were thinking about buying a new Ford.

'We can buy a Model T for $360 now,' Ellie bubbled. 'Seven years ago they were $850. This way Chuck and I can each have a car. Of course, Mom and Pop think it's wildly extravagant for us to have two cars.'

'You're doing well. Why not?' It didn't bother Chuck any longer that Ellie drove. Why shouldn't women drive? Why shouldn't they direct movies? But when Elisabeth had made a tentative suggestion to Frank Osborne about her directing, he'd considered it a huge joke.

'We're not having a party or anything, but why don't you all come over to the house for supper tonight?' Ellie urged. 'It was Mom's suggestion,' she added before Elisabeth could protest this last-minute invitation. 'Just as I was leaving the house she told me to ask you. And that means Hallie, too. If Katie gets sleepy there's the spare cot in Ira's room.'

'Sounds wonderful,' Elisabeth accepted. At holidays she felt especially vulnerable to unhappy memories. Thank God for friends like Ellie and Chuck and Ellie's parents.

'I hear there's a big pow-wow over at Paul Coleman's house. A kind of open-house deal, one of the cameramen told me. Probably his wife is trying to enlarge his contacts,' Chuck drawled.

'Don't expect your wife to do the same.' Ellie reached a hand out to Amy. 'How did you do on that geography test yesterday?'

Paul's wife was ambitious for him, Elisabeth recognized. Yet she couldn't envision Paul enjoying the Hollywood party circuit. She couldn't believe he wished to be part of the movie colony – so fast becoming a new kind of royalty. But then he might have changed in the intervening years. A few out here were earning fabulous salaries that made them the envy of millions. Perhaps Paul, too, was eager to join that élite group.

More than ever Elisabeth was conscious of the need to protect Amy from the madness that invaded the movie colony. She mustn't become old beyond her years, aware of the drinking and drugs that were part of the movie scene.

Elisabeth launched her first real battle with Frank when he proposed to send Amy on tour.

'No,' she said flatly. 'Her life is disrupted enough. I won't let her be exposed to touring.'

'The public should see that Amy is truly a little girl! Not a make-believe little girl like Pickford. Just a few cities on the West Coast,' he wheedled. 'Then maybe Dallas and Galveston.'

'No!' Her eyes blazed in defiance. 'Her contract makes no such demands.'

'Beth, you know the importance of promotion.'

'No, Frank. No tour. I won't have it.'

He sighed. 'All right, be a difficult mother. But let Amy appear as a guest at the benefit early in March for the orphanage in Los Angeles. They've been after me for weeks. Every major studio is providing a star. I'm to supply somebody to make a personal plea for donations. They figure Amy would be great.'

'Amy can do that.' She felt a flicker of amusement at Frank's startled reaction. He'd expected another battle. David grew up in an orphanage. How could she refuse to help raise funds for this one? 'I'll see to it that Amy memorizes a speech – a short one,' she stipulated. 'I'll discuss it with the orphanage people. And Amy will sign autographs if they think that will be helpful.'

Any had so little recall of her father. She had loved Jerry as her 'new Papa' and lost him too. But let Amy realize she was more fortunate than those children in the orphanage. She had a mother and a sister who loved her very much. She had Hallie who adored her.

In the weeks ahead Elisabeth was amazed at the publicity the studio managed to extract from Amy's coming appearance at the orphanage benefit. The studio wardrobe designer provided an exquisite dress. A beautician was to come to the house to arrange her hair in a way that would photograph to best advantage, since the press was sure to be present.

Elisabeth chafed at all the attention being bestowed on Amy. This wasn't normal for a thirteen-year-old. For perhaps the thousandth time, she asked herself if she was allowing Amy to be robbed of her childhood. Yet Amy seemed happy.

Attendance at the benefit was expected to be heavy. Chuck and Ellie – along with her parents – would be there. Seven popular movie personalities were scheduled to appear. There would be songs, dance, 'live' recitations. And at the close of the program Amy would appear on stage and make a poignant plea for funds.

'You won't be nervous,' Elisabeth soothed Amy. 'It's like being on the stage.' Amy was accustomed to the camera. She'd never appeared before a live audience. 'You know about how I played on the stage in Melbourne when you were very little.'

'I won't be afraid, Mama.' Amy smiled serenely. 'Not as long as you're sitting there in the front row.'

The benefit was held in a large local auditorium. Almost every seat was filled by the time Elisabeth and Amy approached one of the pairs of doors that led inside. The scent of flowers – Cherokee roses, lilacs – was almost overpowering. Lively chatter ricocheted about the large area, stopped suddenly when the audience recognized Amy. All at once a spontaneous burst of applause filled the air.

'Wave to the people,' Elisabeth whispered. 'They recognize you from your pictures.'

Since Amy was not to appear until the close of the program, she was to sit in the front row and be escorted to the stage by the head of the orphanage. Their late arrival had been carefully orchestrated, Elisabeth understood, to bring forth this welcome.

As planned, Ellie and Chuck sat in the front row, next to the pair of reserved seats for Amy and Elisabeth.

'This is the social event of the season,' Ellie murmured. 'Gloria Swanson is here – and Charlie Chaplin and Douglas Fairbanks.'

'I saw Paul Coleman and his wife arrive just after Ellie and me,' Chuck told Elisabeth. 'They're sitting about a dozen rows back.'

Involuntarily she swerved around to inspect the sea of faces behind them. Her heart began to pound when she saw Paul. He was talking earnestly with a man on his left. The woman on his right would be his wife. She was an attractive blonde – tall, smartly dressed. Her smile seemed almost professional, Elisabeth thought, as though she was ever courting admiration.

Sitting there, waiting for the lights to dim and the performance to begin, Elisabeth felt herself spiraling back through time. Remembering those few precious weeks with Paul. His stern avoidance of her after Jerry had made his fateful remark. What would have happened to them if Jerry hadn't given him the wrong impression? Would she and Paul have been married in time?

When they met that day in Bullock's, he didn't seem angry anymore. For a few moments their long-buried feelings for each other had soared into being again. She wasn't wrong about that.

The benefit was a glittering success. Amy made her endearing plea for donations. Volunteers roamed the aisles to distribute commitment forms. Amy was besieged by fans eager for autographs. Elisabeth stayed at her side along with Ellie. She saw Chuck pushing his way to where Paul stood. His wife talked vivaciously with acquaintances in the audience.

Elisabeth forced herself to make small talk with the crowd that surrounded them. She was conscious that Paul's eyes were focused on her. He mustn't gaze at her that way, she silently rebuked him. The world must never guess how they felt about each other. It was too late for them.

Now Chuck was talking with Paul and his wife. The crowd was thinning out. Paul and his wife remained. They walked up the aisle to join Amy, Ellie and Elisabeth. Awkwardly Paul introduced his wife. Her name was Doris. She exuded charm. In a corner of her mind Elisabeth remembered Chuck's describing her as a party-giver, implying she was ambitious for Paul.

'Paul tells me he worked with you back in New York,' Doris bubbled, 'when this crazy movie business was just beginning.'

'It's come a long way.' Elisabeth avoided meeting Paul's eyes.

'Why don't you all join us at the house for a drink?' Doris invited. 'And hot chocolate for this little cherub.' She smiled ingratiatingly at Amy.

'It's way past Amy's bedtime,' Elisabeth demurred. 'But thank you –'

'Of course. How thoughtless of me,' Doris clucked in apology. 'We're having a few people over Sunday evening – why don't you join us then? Nothing formal. Paul, write down our address for them.'

'We'll try to make it,' Chuck said. 'All except Amy. She has a date with school books.'

Elisabeth told herself it would be ridiculous for her to go with Ellie and Chuck to the small gathering at Paul and Doris's house. Yet once Ellie pressed for this, she capitulated. It was as though she had no will, she thought. Just this urgent need to be in the same room with Paul for a parcel of time. Just that. Nothing more.

Loud music drifted through the windows of the elegant Spanish-style house as Chuck pulled to a stop at the curb. Several cars lined the driveway already. Paul lived in this small masterpiece? It shrieked of a monied household. But then movie people rented houses at exorbitant prices in the face of huge salaries. Then contracts ended, and new tenants took over.

Inside the smartly furnished, sprawling living room were several people Elisabeth knew only by sight: a new director from France, who was receiving much space in the trade papers; a rising young female star; a producer of an about-to-be-released film that its publicist declared would introduce dramatic new techniques.

'I'm glad you came.' Paul appeared at her side. Ellie and Chuck were in conversation with the French director, who was candid about the impossibility of filming in war-torn France.

'I'm not sure I should have,' she said unsteadily. For a poignant few moments it was as though they were alone on a desert isle.

'I couldn't sleep last night, thinking about you. Beth, don't disappear from my life again.'

'I suppose it would be all right if we see each other this way – at gatherings.' How could she pretend she didn't reciprocate his feelings? 'Tell me about your work out here.' Swiftly she contrived an impersonal façade. Doris was walking towards them.

'Darling, I'm so glad you came.' Doris radiated high spirits. 'But don't let Paul monopolize you. I have people here you should meet. Paul said you were a fine actress yourself.' A glint of curiosity in Doris's eyes. 'Don't you miss it?'

'Handling Amy's career is a full-time job. And I'm at a bad age,' she said with candor. 'The studios want the very young for leads. I'm not old enough for character roles.'

'I wish I had talent,' Doris said fiercely. 'I'd let nothing stand in my way. But I have Paul.' Was that a warning to her? Did Doris feel threatened? 'His career is mine. He almost had a Broadway production last year. But you know Broadway . . . if you don't have the right contacts, you're lost.'

Elisabeth allowed herself to be introduced to the others. The usual almost hysterical gaiety colored the atmosphere. But, thank God, this wasn't one of those parties where drugs and alcohol ruled.

Much of the conversation revolved around the news about Fatty Arbuckle's new contract with Paramount.

'Would you believe it? Four years ago he was working for Mack Sennett for three dollars a day. Now he's just signed with Paramount for five thousand dollars a week!' A cameraman from Paramount was frankly envious.

'At Paramount they hung a sign at the gate: "PARAMOUNT WELCOMES THE PRINCE OF WHALES",' Chuck said drily.

'That's not the kind of story that'll help Hollywood's image.' Paul's smile was wry.

Tense with the need to mask her feelings, Elisabeth was relieved when Ellie suggested they leave.

'Tomorrow's a work day,' she apologized to Doris. 'But it's a lovely party – thanks for having us.'

Settled in the car Ellie teased Chuck because the rising young female star, after more champagne than she could handle, had made an obvious play for him despite Ellie's presence.

'That Doris is too much,' Ellie continued in distaste. 'She doesn't give a damn about Paul. She just wants to have a star of her own. Somebody mentioned that she inherited a chunk of money from her grandmother, and she's blowing it on the big front in the hopes that it'll help Paul become an Important Writer.'

'She's got him on the hook and won't let him off,' Chuck said.

'How do you know?' Ellie was avid for gossip.

'It's around town. They don't even sleep together. Haven't for two years. Yeah, I know, more Hollywood talk – but this came from a woman who's supposed to be her best friend.'

'If that's her best friend, I'd hate to meet her enemies.' Elisabeth tried to sound flippant.

Doris and Paul were married, and Doris meant to keep it that way, even in a town where divorce was becoming a common event. Maybe none of this was true. People made up stories. But even if Paul were free, there was no room in her life for anybody but Amy and Katie. No one must come between her children and herself. After all these years she still remembered the wall her mother had put up between herself and her children. That mustn't happen to Amy and Katie.

In the days ahead Elisabeth struggled desperately to erase thoughts of Paul from her mind. Her sleep was invaded by tormenting dreams about him. Now – restless, guilty, striving for peace of mind – she left the studio each day for the two hours in the afternoon when Amy was in her improvised classroom or attending classes at school. Her tutor was a highly disciplined and demanding woman – she would brook no interference when it came to Amy's study time.

She had discovered the solace of walking along a strip of deserted beach – found calm in the gentle caress of waves on sun-kissed sand. Today she drove to the sea with a sense of urgency. Sleep last night had been disturbed by reports of the war in Europe. The situation for the Allies was not good.

At the end of January Germany had resumed unrestricted submarine warfare. The peace efforts of Pope Benedict XV had failed. The prospect of the United States entering the war hovered over Americans. Yesterday – 12 March – news came through of revolution in Russia. Czar Nicholas II had been forced to abdicate.

She was nearing her favorite spot. She slowed down, preparing to park, the sound of the ocean sweet music to her ears.

'Beth!' Paul's voice was electric.

For an instant she froze. Now her eyes swept the landscape. Her heart pounding. There he was. She reached for the door, swung it wide. Paul hurried to the car.

'At first I thought it was a mirage. But it *is* you.' Astonishment blended with pleasure in his voice.

'I come here to walk on the beach while Amy's with her tutor.' She stepped from the car, breathless at this unexpected encounter. She hadn't seen Paul since the evening at his house. Ellie said Doris probably expected a return invitation, but neither of them was on the party circuit.

'I come here to check on a friend's beach house – and do some writing. He's in New York, rehearsing in a new play. I knew him back there.' He hesitated, his eyes searching hers. 'The front deck faces the ocean. It's a glorious view. Why don't we have coffee there and watch the waves for a while? Black,' he warned, then chuckled. 'But you drink your coffee black.' All these years later he remembered. 'Fate brought you here –' He was striving for a light mood, sensing her ambivalence. 'We can't thwart fate.'

'I mustn't stay long. I have to get back to the studio.' I should jump in the car and drive away.

'They try to make me work at the studio. I tell them I can't write cooped up in a closet they call an office.' Paul reached into his pocket for the key to the house.

This isn't real, Elisabeth thought.

'I spend about half my time writing at the studio, the other half here. It was a break for me when Hank asked me to watch over the house for him.'

'No more plays?' Had he given up on that dream?

'Not for now.' He was silent while he unlocked the front door to the modest Spanish bungalow, flung it wide. 'Doris inherited a bundle when her grandmother died. She had this weird idea about subsidizing my writing career. I was going to be a terrific Broadway success.' His smile was ironic. 'It hasn't quite worked out that way.'

'I read somewhere that Shaw didn't sell a play until he was forty.'

'My last play was optioned twice, totally rewritten twice. Our money – Doris's inheritance – was getting low. When I was offered a fantastic deal to come out here and write for a year, we came. If you're asking if I'm happy writing for movies, the answer is no.'

'You'll go back to the theater.' Don't let the dream slip away.

'I don't know –' He led her to the kitchen, reached for the coffee pot, opened a canister of coffee. 'What's the old platitude? "Man proposes, and God disposes."'

'We're all sidetracked at intervals.' Would she ever get back to theater? Or doing movies that earned her respect?

'I was out of my mind when you disappeared,' Paul said with sudden intensity. 'I wanted you to be part of my life for ever.'

'Jerry made that awful remark that sounded as though we were living together. And you turned away from me.' Reproach lurked in her eyes. 'I – I hurt so badly, Paul.'

'I'd felt like such a fool –' The coffee was forgotten now. 'I'd laid my heart at your feet, but yours belonged to somebody else.'

'I wanted to explain,' she whispered, conscious of his closeness. 'You seemed furious at me.'

'I was devastated. I'd thought it was just a matter of time before you'd be ready to talk about the years ahead of us.'

'It wasn't mean to be.' But she felt his arms reach out to pull her close. No will in her to stop him. 'Paul, we shouldn't –'

'This is right. Everything else is wrong. I have no marriage, Beth. I've never loved anyone but you.'

His mouth came down on hers. Her hands clutched at his shoulders. *Oh yes, this was right.*

'I'll lock the door –' With reluctance he released her mouth, crossed to lock the door.

She stood motionless, eyes closed, warning herself that this was wrong – Paul was married. Yet knowing there was no way she could abort what lay ahead. Heart outranked the mind. She heard the click of the key in the lock. She opened her eyes, her smile tremulous. In an exquisite silence they walked into the bedroom, the drapes shut tight against the golden sunlight.

'I've waited so long for you, Beth . . .'

His mouth found hers again. One hand slid within the low neckline of her dress, caressed the lush spill of her breasts. The other hand at her back, pulling her close. She waited, impatient to be free of clothes, to abandon herself to the passion that soared within them. A faint sound escaped her when he guided her onto the bed.

'You're beautiful . . .' His mouth at her throat, trailing now to imprison a nipple. The weight of him on her while his legs manipulated hers.

A whimper of pleasure welled in her throat as they met and began the tumultuous fusion into one.

'Oh Beth! Beth . . .'

So good. Let them stay this way for ever.

Afterwards she lay in the curve of his arm, reluctant to abandon this glorious encounter.

'Two years ago I asked Doris for a divorce. It was ridiculous for us to keep up our charade of a marriage. She said she had an investment in me – and she meant it to pay off. I told her the odds were rotten – as a playwright I was riding against the tide. Still, her answer was "no". She has this obsession to be the wife of somebody famous.' He paused, took a deep breath. 'She said if I ever tried to divorce her, she'd see to it that I never saw Tommy again.' His eyes betrayed his anguish. 'I can't let that happen.'

Chapter Thirty

At truant intervals Elisabeth faced guilt that she could feel such happiness in the midst of a monstrous war – a war that now affected the United States. American merchant ships were being sunk by German submarines. The British had intercepted a German message to Mexico that proposed an alliance in the event they were at war with the United States. Germany promised to help Mexico recover territory it had ceded to the United States after the Mexican War.

On 6 April President Wilson declared war against the Central Powers. 'The world must be made safe for democracy.'

Elisabeth felt a towering sense of relief that the United States was joining the Allies. How much longer could the war go on now? When the Selective Service Act was passed on 18 May, she was grateful that Paul would not be subject to conscription. He was slightly beyond the age bracket of 21 to 30. And he was married and had a child – that also put him in the safety zone.

She was fearful sometimes that her joy at this reunion with Paul would shine through and betray them to the world. It was as though a door to a glorious new room in her life had been unlocked. No one – not even Ellie or Hallie – knew about the stolen hours with Paul. Neither would begrudge her this. No one was being cheated. She wasn't neglecting Amy or Katie. Paul had no marriage with Doris. But for those hours when Amy was with the tutor – or attending classes at school – she could be with Paul.

She talked with him about her fears for her family in London. Germany fought ferociously to starve the British by sinking supply ships. Always she worried about Ben and Felix – without a doubt in military service. She worried about Grandma and Mama – and yes, Papa, too, she acknowledged to Paul.

Early in June over nine million men registered for the draft. Life in the United States acquired a feverish pace. The country was not prepared for war, so six major wartime agencies were formed to mobilize the country. Factories raced to build ships. The Food Administration pleaded with the public to save food and 'meatless days' were established. In Hollywood movie stars were caught up in the wave of patriotism that swept the country, spearheading Liberty Loan drives.

On 27 June the first American troops landed in France.

General Pershing refused to send American troops into battle until their training was complete, though the British and French were impatient for their aid. In late October German Gothas dropped the first incendiary bombs of the war. London's anti-aircraft guns drove off the raiders. At this same time American troops saw their first action.

'After this insane war is over, I'll go to London,' Elisabeth confided to Paul on a sun-kissed late November afternoon as they lounged on the deck of the beach house. There would be money for this. While she'd allowed their lifestyle to improve along with Amy's earnings, she made sure that a substantial amount was banked each week for Amy's future. 'I have to know what's happened to my family.'

'With any luck at all,' he said with extravagant optimism, 'I'll manage to go over at the same time. To do research for an important script,' he improvised. 'Doris is terrified of water – she'd never set foot on a ship.' He stopped as Elisabeth tensed. They made a point of not mentioning Doris's name since he'd first told her Doris would never agree to a divorce. 'You'll show me the house where you grew up, the school you attended –'

'Oh Paul, I have no right to be so happy,' she whispered.

The one sad note in her life was that Jerry's father had died of a massive heart attack. The clerk in the pharmacy had written – at his dying request – to tell her of this. 'He said to tell you he loved you and the girls very much.'

Paul frowned when he saw Doris approaching the breakfast room with a cup of coffee. Usually she slept late. When she didn't, she was in a foul mood.

'I'm working at the studio today.' He eyed her warily. 'I have to leave in a few minutes.'

'Haven't they said anything to you yet about renewing your con-

266

tract?' The tension in her voice told him she'd been seething over this lack of action.

'Nothing so far.' He was uneasy. It was a subject he'd been avoiding. He loathed writing the kind of scenarios demanded of him. Yet he longed to remain in Hollywood – to be near Beth. And what future could he see for himself back in New York? Of course, some films were still being made back there . . .

Doris grunted in annoyance. 'Are they waiting for the day it expires?'

'I don't know what they're waiting for.' But he knew. They were impatient for him to come up with a de Mille or Griffith type of spectacle. That wasn't his kind of writing. He wanted to write movies that looked into the hearts and souls of ordinary people, that had social significance. 'I don't know why they hired me in the first place.'

'Somebody in the New York office must have read – and liked your play.'

'That play gave no inkling that I could write another *Birth of a Nation*.'

'Come right out and ask them! Hint you have another offer,' she prodded.

'I'll drop some hints,' he said evasively. He didn't want to leave Hollywood.

On his arrival at the studio he discovered a note on his desk. He was to report immediately to the main office. Something to do with the scenario he was revising? Damn these endless revisions.

He knew from the way his producer avoided eye contact that this encounter would not be to his advantage.

'We're cutting back, Paul. Costs are escalating like crazy. And we're rethinking what we'll produce in the future. We don't feel that what we need is your cup of tea. Sorry, old man.'

Just like that he was washed up. He went to his office, gathered together his personal belongings. They were dumping the scenario he'd been working on these past three weeks: 'We'll be doing a big-canvas movie about Napoleon and Josephine,' the producer had said. 'A lot of battle scenes, court intrigue – that sort of thing. Audiences love it.'

Driving home in the Pierce-Arrow Doris's father had bought for them, he berated himself for being inflexible. He should have tried to give them what they wanted. He wasn't Shakespeare – this was commercial writing! The word would spread around fast enough that the studio was dropping him. If he could pick up anything at all, it would be at a pittance. He flinched, envisioning Doris's tantrum when she learned his contract wasn't being renewed. She'd consider it a personal failure.

Maybe he could come up with something for Amy, he thought with a flicker of hope. He could write the kind of material her studio liked for her. Small in scope, poignant, tender. Already his mind began to focus in that vein. Beth would introduce him to the right people over there. As Doris was always proclaiming, contacts were terribly important in Hollywood.

He pulled into the driveway, his mind fabricating words to make the scene with Doris less traumatic. There *was* a place for him in Hollywood. It was a matter of tying in with a studio that did the kind of material he could write. He'd call Beth tonight, something he'd heretofore made a point of avoiding. They were always super-cautious. He'd work up an outline to whet the appetites of the bigwigs at Amy's studio.

As he walked into the house, Doris strode into the foyer. She'd heard the car, he interpreted.

'You rotten bastard!' she shrieked. 'Having an affair behind my back, after all I've done for you!'

He felt the color drain from his face. 'What are you talking about?' *Beth mustn't be involved.*

'My best friend told me this morning. Who is this little tramp?'

'There's no affair,' he denied. Bluff it, the way Doris would do in a similar situation.

'You were seen coming out of whatshisname's beach house with a woman! It's probably all over town by now!'

'Hank's cleaning woman,' he said tiredly. There *was* a cleaning woman who came in once a month. 'You know about her.' He forced his eyes to challenge Doris. Who had seen him with Beth? They'd been so careful. But no name had been mentioned, he pinpointed gratefully. 'But on a more realistic note, my contract's not being renewed. I don't write de Mille or Griffith scenarios.'

'Just like that?' Doris stared at him in disbelief. The earlier outrage replaced with another. 'No warning? No suggestion you try a different approach?'

'They don't have to give a warning. They told me to forget about

268

revisions on the latest – they're dumping it.' He paused. 'I'll check around at the other studios, come in with a –'

'We won't stay here!' Doris was white with indignation. 'I won't have people calling you a failure. And maybe it was the cleaning woman with you, but people will talk, anyway. You know how they are out here.' Her voice exuded contempt. 'I won't be made to appear a wife whose husband cheats on her. I hate this stupid town!'

'I'll line up work at another studio. I'll –'

'I won't stay,' she broke in. 'I won't be made to look ridiculous. I don't want to hear how your contract was dropped. I don't want to hear ugly gossip about this cleaning woman. We'll leave right away, Paul.'

'Let's don't jump the gun. I can –'

'You never truly liked writing for films. You've always said you wanted to work in theater. We'll make it to Broadway.' Her eyes glittered. 'We don't need this rotten town.'

'Hold on, Doris. There're other studios making pictures here. I'll –'

'I'm leaving. And I'm taking Tommy with me, of course. And if I find out you *have* been having an affair,' she said with a devious smile, 'I'll track down the woman and drag her into the ugliest divorce suit you can imagine. And you'll never see Tommy again.'

This was the peaceful time of evening when Elisabeth relaxed. The children and Hallie were in bed for the night. A beautiful quiet reigned in the house. Earlier there had been a minor battle between Amy and Katie – which Hallie insisted was normal between sisters, even when there was a difference of eleven years between them: 'Miz Beth, it ain't normal when sisters don't fight.' Sometimes Elisabeth was concerned that Katie would resent her absence for so many hours each day, that the little one would feel slighted that she was away with Amy. It was important to be a good mother to both her children.

She settled in her favorite lounge chair, reached for the book that lay waiting on the table beside her. This was her special time – when she could spend an hour with the favored novel of the moment. Although the critics had not liked the new Sinclair Lewis novel – *The Job: An American Novel* – she was eager to read it because it was said to deal realistically with the subject of women in business.

The sound of the phone ringing was a raucous intrusion in the still of the night. Elisabeth reached to pick up, expecting to hear Ellie's voice at the other end. Ellie and she were addicted to late-night phone conversation.

'Hello?'

'Beth, can you talk?' Paul's voice – low-pitched, strained.

Immediately alarm spiraled in her. 'Yes, Paul.'

'Doris took a sleeping pill. She's fast asleep.' He paused. Elisabeth's hand tightened on the phone. 'She knows about our meeting at the beach house.'

'How?' What they'd promised themselves would never happen *had* happened.

'Someone saw us leaving. Whoever it was didn't identify you. I told Doris it was the cleaning woman.' He took a deep breath. 'I don't know that she believes me. She's terribly upset about what I learned today. My contract isn't being renewed.'

'Oh, Paul . . .' Would he be able to find another deal out here? Her mind sought an answer. 'What if I talked to Frank Osborne for you?'

'Doris insists on going back to New York. She's convinced herself I'll make it to Broadway. Beth, I have to go back to New York with her. I can't take a chance on losing Tommy.' Again, he paused. 'She threatened an ugly divorce if she finds out I'm seeing someone else. She vowed I'd lose Tommy. I can't take a chance on that. We – we mustn't see each other again. At least, for now.'

'I'm glad for all these months we've had together.' They'd known a moment might arrive when they'd lose this paradise they'd found together. That moment was now.

'I love you, Beth. I've never loved anyone else.'

'I love you, too.' She fought to keep her voice even.

'Whenever I'm free, I'll come to you. Wherever you are, I'll find you.'

'I'll be waiting. However long it takes.' *Would it ever happen?* 'There'll never be anybody but you.'

'Whatever happens, know I'll be thinking of you.'

'Goodbye, my love.' Her voice was an anguished whisper.

She sat – shaken, desolate – trying to absorb what had happened. For long months she'd lived in euphoria – except for the wary moments when she feared discovery. But life wasn't meant to be a constant Eden. She'd treasure the memories. Life would go on.

*   *   *

Four days later Elisabeth heard that Paul and his family had left for New York. She struggled to adjust to his absence. She knew it would be difficult to go back to a life without him. She hadn't realized how difficult.

Again, she walked alone on empty stretches of beach in those hours when she was away from the studio or when Amy was in school. Again – looking for something to fill the emptiness in her life – she tried to convince the studio bigwigs that she would be a capable director. Watching filming, she envisioned small bits that could add much to the production. Occasionally she dared to make suggestions – and was pleased when they were adopted. But a woman director? *Ridiculous.*

On New Year's Eve 1917, Elisabeth took her small brood to the Sanchez house for a quiet celebration. Bella and Hallie had been cooking and baking for two days. The house radiated a festive atmosphere as the women brought platters of food to the extended dining table. Amy had undertaken to involve Katie and Ira in play until it was time to sit down to the later-than-normal dinner – though early enough so the two youngest could participate.

While they dined sumptuously Peter Sanchez reminisced about the past year.

'It's been a painful year,' he conceded, 'the war going so badly for the Allies, but Pershing will come through, American troops will make the difference. Remember, the Allies have cut shipping losses in half already. That's a huge step forward. We'll celebrate New Year's Eve 1918 in a world at peace.'

In a February issue of *Variety* Elisabeth read that a play by Paul was about to be produced by a new theater company called the Provincetown Players in a tiny playhouse on MacDougal Street in Greenwich Village. The brevity of the item told her this was a fledgling group, yet Paul's play would be seen. It could be important to his career. She yearned to learn more, watched for successive issues. Then – at last – a minuscule review appeared that referred to Paul as a 'promising talent'. Oh, that was good!

In the spring, with the Allied lines being crumbled by a fierce German offensive, President Wilson agreed to the appointment of French Marshal Foch as supreme commander of the Allied forces. General Pershing placed four divisions at Foch's disposal, and in July 85,000 Americans fought with other Allied troops at the Marne.

Opposing armies were often scarcely a hundred yards apart, facing enemy artillery, poison gases, hand grenades, tanks – even bayonets. It was the most vicious war in history.

In Hollywood war movies were being filmed constantly. Last year D. W. Griffith had taken a company that included Lillian Gish to film in war-racked London and Paris. Chuck warned that once the war was over, war movies would be shunned.

Amy was fretting at the roles she was being assigned.

'Mama, I'm tired of playing eleven-year-olds,' she wailed, a familiar cry. 'I'm almost fifteen. Why can't I play grown-ups?'

'Darling, you have more growing up to do,' Elisabeth soothed. 'The studio won't hear of it.'

'I think they're mean. Gloria at school says I look seventeen,' she said defiantly. 'I hate the dresses they make me wear!'

'Another year and I'll talk to Frank about casting you in something older,' Elisabeth promised. 'Right now, the audiences adore you as the wistful little girl caught up in the war.'

'Mama –' all at once Amy was pensive – 'what do you think is happening to our family in London?'

'I wish I knew.' A knot tightened in Elisabeth's throat. Pain blended with rage in her. In these awful circumstances couldn't Grandma and Mama write? Yet, of course, it was unlikely that mail would get through. She had not written since the day President Wilson declared war on the Central Powers. 'But I promise you this, Amy. Once this bloody war is over, we're going to London. If we're not welcome, so be it. But I have to know how they've fared.'

On 26 August the Germans were forced to retreat to the Hindenburg line. In September American soldiers helped to break through the heavy fortifications. Over 1,200,000 of them fought here – 120,000 killed or wounded. On 29 September Bulgaria was the first of the Central Powers to sign an armistice; on 31 October Turkey signed, followed just four days later by the Austrian Emperor Karl. Only Germany remained at war. But on 11 November, the German delegates at last surrendered. The world was at peace – but the cost had been fearful.

In recognition that the war was over, the studio planned a New Year's Eve party at the end of the day's shooting. Champagne bottles were uncorked. Food platters were delivered from the Alexandria Hotel. The atmosphere was convivial.

Elisabeth broke off a conversation with an overly amorous cameraman – emboldened by champagne – and went in search of Amy. Where was she? On a set not used for the past month she spied Amy – gazing rapturously up into the eyes of the thirty-ish stage actor recently brought out to Hollywood under contract. His arms were moving about Amy's back while he murmured words too soft for Elisabeth to hear.

'Take your hands off Amy!' Her voice was shrill with shock. 'She's fifteen years old!'

His arms fell away. 'I'm sorry,' he mumbled. 'I thought she was eighteen.' He swerved around and charged off the set.

'Mama!' Amy was simultaneously disconcerted and defiant. 'He was just talking to me. And he's so good-looking –'

'Talking means at least a foot between you.' Her baby was growing up. 'The way he was moving in, there wasn't an inch. Not that I expect you to walk around with a tape measure.' She struggled for a humorous touch. 'But you're far too young to be getting romantic ideas about a man that old.' She had been just sixteen when she married David, an inner voice taunted Elisabeth.

'I was play-acting.' Amy giggled. 'Gloria says that's just natural.'

'It's time for us to go home.' Elisabeth's mind was in chaos. She would be at the studio every minute from now on. Amy must not become involved in the wild Hollywood scene of booze, drugs and sex. They'd leave this town before she allowed that to happen.

Chapter Thirty-one

As customary Elisabeth and her brood celebrated New Year's Eve at the Sanchez house. At a moment when the others – in a mellow mood as midnight approached – were singing 'Auld Lang Syne' along with a phonograph record, Elisabeth talked with Ellie in the privacy of Bella Sanchez's sewing room.

'I was so upset,' Elisabeth confessed, reporting on the tableau she had interrupted earlier in the day. 'I watch over her so carefully!'

'It didn't mean anything to Amy – she said so herself,' Ellie soothed.

'I know what goes on in this town. I thought I was protecting her. I refuse even to let her appear in any movie that has salacious scenes. She's still a little girl!'

'Be realistic, Beth. Ever since the war began we've seen these crazy changes. There's a moratorium on morals. You know: "Let's live it up, tomorrow we may die."'

Elisabeth grimaced. 'I detest all the drinking and drugs and promiscuous sex in this town!'

'It's not just in Hollywood. It's everywhere. You're so wrapped up in Amy and Katie and pictures, you're not seeing what goes on these days. The young are on a roller coaster. And the not so young, too,' Ellie added grimly. 'It's a phase, Pop keeps insisting. It'll go away in time.'

Elisabeth sighed. 'Let's go back to the others. We're not solving any problems tonight.'

Early in the New Year the movie world was fascinated by the announcement that Mary Pickford, Douglas Fairbanks, Charlie Chaplin and D. W. Griffith were setting up their own producing and distribution company, to be called United Artists. It was discussed with relish at a Friday evening dinner at the Sanchez house.

'They're smart.' Peter Sanchez nodded with approval. 'This way they can control their pictures. They don't have to answer to the front office. And they keep the profits their pictures make.'

'What's happening with Amy's contract?' Chuck was curious. 'Isn't it up for renewal?'

'We're quibbling over money,' Elisabeth explained. 'I know how much Amy's movies bring in. When I bring this up, they show me very creative accounting. To listen to them, they're always losing money.'

'Mama, why don't you talk to the people at United Artists about me working for them?' Amy's eyes glowed. 'I'll bet they'll let me play older roles. I'm ten years old in the one we're shooting now.'

'Your mother played teenagers when she was ten years older than you are,' Ellie recalled.

And hated it, Elisabeth admitted in silence.

'That was a long time ago,' Amy said impatiently. 'Everything's different now.'

'I remember my grandmother saying that each succeeding generation feels itself so superior to the one that came before,' Elisabeth mused. 'Amy, you make me feel old!'

'Each generation considers itself older a decade later than the one before.' Mrs Sanchez chuckled. 'You're young, Beth – and Amy's a baby.'

'Oh, the latest news. I hear that Griffith is planning to do a takeoff of *David Copperfield*,' Chuck reported. 'Their version will revolve around a young girl. I'll bet Amy could play her beautifully.'

'How do you know all these things?' Bella was always amused by Chuck's supply of Hollywood gossip.

Chuck grinned. 'I've got a friend in their script department.'

'Mama, let's not sign again with the studio,' Amy pleaded wistfully. 'Talk to United Artists about me playing in their *David Copperfield* takeoff. I hate what I'm doing!'

'I'll stall on the contract.' How could she push Amy into work she loathed? Yet she doubted that the studio would allow Amy to assume older roles. Not the way audiences flocked to see her as a little girl.

'You'll talk to United Artists?' Amy pushed.

'I'll talk to them,' Elisabeth promised.

*   *   *

Elisabeth hedged on signing a new contract for Amy. She knew that the studio was pleased to continue Amy at her old salary during these negotiations. Chuck managed to acquire a copy of the *David Copperfield* scenario.

Elisabeth read it that same night. Oh, yes! Amy could play Susie. It might have been written for her. The next day she went to talk with Mr Griffith at the new United Artists studio. But the role Amy coveted had already been assigned.

'Lillian Gish will be playing Susie,' Mr Griffith said gently. She should have realized that. 'But if Amy's free and we have a script with a role for a little girl, we'd be happy to consider her. She has a delightful quality.'

Amy cried when she heard that Mr Griffith had rejected her for this movie that seemed so right for her.

'I won't do any more little girls!' she stormed. 'I'm sick of them!'

'I'm going to search for a novel or a play that has a wonderful teenage role.' Elisabeth reached for Amy's hand. 'I'll take it to Frank and make him understand this is what you want to do. You won't play any more ten-year-olds, I promise you, darling.' They weren't destitute. They could live comfortably for years on what was stashed away in their bank account.

'I could have played Susie,' Amy said defiantly. 'I know I could.'

'Of course, you could. But there are other parts, too. We'll find one for you.'

'And you won't sign the new contract until they let me play my own age? Or maybe even a little older?' A bravura smile now.

'I won't sign it.'

At every free moment Elisabeth searched among the library shelves for a book with an early teenage heroine – one that could be adapted for the films. The studio bigwigs were leaning on her to sign a new contract, but they were adamant: no older roles. They had three new scripts lined up for Amy – all in the ten-to-twelve-year age bracket.

Elisabeth was becoming an insomniac – haunted by Amy's unhappiness, frustrated that she couldn't find an answer to this situation. Still staring at the ceiling at past two a.m., she left her bed, searched for something to read. A magazine, she told herself – something light, non-demanding. Relaxing. She settled on a magazine, began to read what she soon realized was the second instalment of a 'two-parter'. Charming! The plot would hold audiences!

Her mind charged into action. Tomorrow she'd take this to Frank, make him understand its tremendous potential. He was bright – he was sure to see it. She was impatient for morning to arrive so she could approach him.

At the studio she cornered Frank, her words tumbling over one another in her excitement.

'Frank, it'll be a marvelous movie. Perfect for Amy. Audiences will love her.'

'I'll read it soon,' Frank promised. 'I have to get on the set now.'

'Ready it today. Before somebody else reads it and signs up the rights. This is a gem, Frank!'

'All right. I'll read it on our lunch break.' She sensed her excitement had reached through to him.

As usual at the end of the day Amy settled down to study while Elisabeth went in to see the day's rushes, sometimes to insist a scene be reshot because of some detail the others had missed. She knew she had a reputation for being a difficult mother – but even Frank usually conceded to her demands. Because she was right.

'I like the story,' Frank told her while they waited in the projection room. 'I'll have somebody in the rights department check on our buying it. Provided the price makes sense.'

'Great.' Elisabeth felt a rush of exhilaration.

Three days later Frank told her they'd made fast contact. They'd acquired the first installment and liked that, too. They were waiting for a contract to be drawn up. They were buying the story.

'You're right – it's a gem. Good work, Beth.'

'It's perfect for Amy.'

'Not for Amy,' he chided good-humouredly. 'She's much too young.'

'Frank, Amy will be sixteen in December. And she's mature for her age. Let her stop playing children.'

'She's a goldmine playing ten-year-olds. We'd be crazy to cast her in an older role.'

'She's terribly unhappy playing those parts. She wants to –'

'What's a kid that age know?' He chuckled indulgently. 'But thanks for the tip. We appreciate it. OK, Ralph – roll it.'

Elisabeth tensed in silent rage. If she were a man, he wouldn't have brushed her off this way. With a man he'd have worked out a deal.

Weeks were racing past. Still Elisabeth stalled on signing. She sensed that Frank was growing edgy. The studio kept escalating Amy's salary under a new contract: a thousand a week, fifty-two weeks a year – whether or not she was working. The contract to run two years. Under those terms Amy would be for ever secure, she thought. In two years she could walk out of the business and go to college. After college she could resume a movie career – *if she wished.* The decision would be hers.

Yet Elisabeth hesitated to accept what seemed a fabulous deal. Amy was so unhappy at the studio. How could she push her into something she hated? This should be a wonderful period in Amy's life. At least, she wasn't totally cut off from those of her own age. Bless the high school for allowing Amy to divide her time between tutoring and regular classes.

Tonight, Elisabeth recalled, Gloria would be 'sleeping over'. On the drive home from the studio Amy talked at her customary break-neck speed about Gloria's new dresses.

'Mama, you won't believe how short they are!' Elisabeth knew this was a gentle reproach because *she* refused to have Amy's dresses shortened.

As usual Katie clamored for all of her attention when she and Amy arrived home. Amy understood this time belonged to Katie. In minutes Gloria arrived. The two teenagers disappeared into Amy's room. The door closed behind them as they shared giggling confidences.

Dinner – it was no longer referred to as supper, at Amy's insistence – was a lively time. Hallie adored having people for dinner, even if it was only Gloria. Because she and Amy had to be at the studio tomorrow – Saturday was a workday at movie studios – Elisabeth ordered everybody to bed shortly before ten.

Tomorrow, for the first time, Gloria would be a visitor on the set. An avid reader of movie magazines, Gloria would be disillusioned when she saw the bedlam in the studio, Elisabeth mused. Still, Gloria was enthralled at the prospect of watching Amy at work. She vowed she'd be quiet, though in the noise that went on Gloria's chatter would hardly be noticed.

After dinner Amy and Gloria retreated behind closed doors again. Elisabeth felt a surge of tenderness as she heard their muted giggling. At least, Amy had some life away from the studio. She wasn't entirely denied a normal life.

Again, Elisabeth was assaulted by insomnia. Well past midnight she was still awake. She tossed aside the light blanket the night required, moved on noiseless feet from her bedroom into the hall. She paused before Amy's door and frowned in silent reproach. Amy and Gloria were still awake.

'Tell me,' Amy pleaded, 'how many boys have you kissed?'

'Maybe a dozen,' Gloria said nonchalantly. 'I lost count.' Elisabeth froze in shock. 'Last week I let Ted touch me here – right on the nipple.'

'You didn't!' Amy sounded awed by this confidence.

Shaken, Elisabeth walked down the hall and into the kitchen, the conversation between Gloria and Amy ricocheting in her mind. She knew what she would do. No more movies. No more Hollywood. They were going to London, away from the insanity that gripped this town. Or if Ellie was right, this country. For a year.

Amy and Katie would go to school in London. All at once excitement soared in her. *She* would go to Lexham Gardens and try for a reconciliation with the family. Wasn't it time this insanity was washed away?

At dinner the following evening Elisabeth announced her decision to the girls and Hallie. For a moment a stunned silence greeted her.

'Mama, what about the money?' Elisabeth sensed a blend of exhilaration, alarm, and ambiguity in Amy. 'Can we take a whole year off?'

'Darling, we can afford it.' Amy shouldn't be worrying about this. 'There's no way I can convince Frank to let you play older roles. We'll come back a year later, and it'll be a different scene.'

'You mean we'll be goin' across the ocean?' Hallie stared at Elisabeth. 'I'm scared to death of ships! Even a canoe.'

'You won't be scared of an ocean liner,' Elisabeth comforted. 'It's big and safe. It'll be like a vacation. No cooking, no cleaning. Just fun.'

'When?' Amy still seemed doubtful.

'Some time in June. After school closes. By then the ships will be done with bringing troops home. They'll be renovated for passengers. We'll go first class.' Her mind darted back through the years to the Atlantic crossing on a decrepit ship with David. The trip had taken ten days. But that was another world.

'Back home folks I know wouldn't believe I'm goin' to London! Their eyes would jus' pop out!' All at once Hallie exuberantly embraced this new development in their lives.

'Mama, can I take Elijah with me?' Katie demanded. Elijah was the teddy bear that Bella and Peter Sanchez had given her for Hanukkah and was her dearest treasure.

'You can take Elijah.'

'Mr Osborne will be awful mad.' Yet Amy's initial concern evaporated quickly. 'He can't make me stay, can he?' Defiance in her voice now.

'We're free to do what we want. Your contract with the studio expired months ago.'

This was a good decision. In London she might find film or stage work for herself. It was time the mother of the household supported the family.

A torrent of emotions surged through Elisabeth in the weeks ahead. *She was going home*. She mustn't allow anything to stand in the way of a reconciliation with the family. Let Amy and Katie know they were not adrift in the world with only their mother and Hallie. At unwary intervals she worried about how Grandma, the boys, Mama and Papa had survived the year.

She arranged for a one-year rental of the house. She consulted with the shipping offices, plotted their departure. She had always been so cautious about spending money – but on this trip she would be extravagant. They would have a first-class suite on the *Aquitania*, sailing from New York on 28 July. She reserved a suite at Claridge's, which Grandma had declared the most elegant hotel in the world.

The day of their departure began with a rare thunderstorm. In a corner of her mind Elisabeth remembered Jerry's saying all those years ago that it only rained in Los Angeles ten days a year. Was she making a mistake in taking the children to London for a year? Would they be homesick? Would they find it hard to fit into a strange country?

At the appointed time Ellie and her mother arrived to drive them to the railroad station. In four days they would be in New York. As before they would change trains in Chicago, leaving the California Limited for the famous Twentieth Century Limited, highly favored by movie folk.

The trip would evoke memories of others, Elisabeth warned herself. It was hazardous to look backwards. She was thirty-three years old, much of her life lay ahead. There were beautiful times awaiting – she would not allow herself to think otherwise – yet it was difficult to forget that she had married twice, was widowed twice, the great love of her life beyond her reach.

'Mama, where do we sleep?' She heard new trepidation in Katie's voice.

'These seats open up into beds,' Elisabeth explained. 'Four of them. One for each of us.'

'Will Elijah like it?' A bellicose glint in Katie's eyes now.

'Elijah will love it.' Elisabeth reached to pull Katie into her lap.

Would Amy and Katie be happy in London? Was she making a terrible mistake in dragging them into a strange new environment? All she wanted in life was to see them happy.

In a private crevice of her mind she thought about Paul. Would there ever be a time when he would be free to come to her? She remembered one of Grandma's favorite sayings: 'Where there's breath, there's hope.'

Chapter Thirty-two

Elisabeth knew the trip across country would be traumatic for her, haunted by ghosts of earlier such trips. Although reduced now to a four-day span, it would be frustratingly long for Katie and even for Amy. She and Hallie focused on making the long hours of inactivity less frustrating for the two girls. Meal times in the luxurious dining car were elongated. Elisabeth asked Amy to read to Katie each day. And always she pulled from memory stories about passing sections of the country.

'Mama, you sound like a geography teacher,' Amy scolded at one point.

'How many girls your age have the advantage of seeing the country first hand?' Elisabeth challenged.

Amy – even Katie – took such things for granted. It was unnerving to realize that they were being raised in a rarefied world of the wealthy or near-wealthy. Nor were they leading normal lives that included father, grandparents, aunts and uncles and cousins. That was a gift she couldn't provide.

In Chicago they changed to the glamorous Twentieth Century Limited. In the dining car excited whisper conveyed the message that Charlie Chaplin was aboard.

'You mean he might have eaten from this same plate?' Hallie demanded in awe. 'Maybe we'll even seen him!' Hallie adored Chaplin. She'd moved about the house in an aura of incredulous happiness after learning he'd been at a Los Angeles benefit where Amy had also appeared.

'He'll have his meals in his drawing room,' Elisabeth warned. 'But, you might just run into him on the observation car.'

'Mama, don't tease Hallie,' Amy scolded and sighed. 'Hallie won't believe I'm a movie star, too.'

'How can a little girl whose bottom I spanked be a movie star?'

But the pride and love in Hallie's eyes were unmistakable. 'And stop braggin', you hear?'

At last the train backed into Grand Central Station, with Katie – whose curiosity was boundless – avidly demanding why the train didn't move engine first into the huge cavernous station.

'The observation car always leads the way into Grand Central Station,' Elisabeth explained. 'They have their reasons, I'm sure.'

Amy and Katie were astonished by the royal welcome provided for the celebrity-favored Twentieth Century Limited. A red carpet was unrolled down the ramp.

'Do they do this all the time?' Hallie whispered while porters came forward to take their luggage.

'All the time,' Elisabeth told her.

'It makes me feel like a movie star,' Hallie's smile was dazzling, 'for a few minutes . . .'

Up above press photographers were waiting, for the emergence of Charlie Chaplin, they all understood.

'Isn't that Amy Winston?' A young woman's voice reached them.

'Naw, she's too old,' a photographer dismissed this. 'But she sure looks a lot like her.'

Glowing in triumph, Amy reached for her mother's arm.

They took a taxi to the French Renaissance Plaza Hotel where they were to spend two nights. Leaving the girls and Hallie admiring their suite overlooking Central Park, Elisabeth went downstairs to seek out a newsstand. In the course of their train trip she'd missed the current issue of *Variety*. Religiously she read this in the wistful hope of learning about Paul's activities.

She found a nearby newsstand, bought the latest edition of the trade journal, and returned to the Plaza. She sat in a lounge chair in the lobby and scanned the pages. She spied Paul's name. His new play had just been signed for a Broadway production. It would go into rehearsal in early September. Let it be a huge success! She found solace in knowing he was moving ahead in the profession he loved.

Elisabeth was tour guide for their waking hours. Amy harbored faint recall of her earlier years in Manhattan. Katie was enthralled by the Automats, impatient that her mother rejected her wish to eat every meal in these exotic establishments. On their second night in the city Elisabeth took the girls and Hallie for a stroll along Broadway and to the streets to its right and left that were home to the legitimate theaters.

Tears stung her eyes as she remembered her first sight of Broadway with Jerry. But Jerry had died in glory – as he would have wished. His father had written that he had received a posthumous medal from the Canadian government.

'Look!' Hallie screeched in delight and pointed to the brilliantly lighted marquee of the Capital Theater. 'Amy, that's you!'

'Mama, it's my last picture.' Amy stared ecstatically at the marquee. 'They put my name up there!'

Until tonight Elisabeth had contrived to conceal such adulation from Amy, lest it turn her head.

'They do that with every movie. I mean, choose a player's name to appear on the marquee.' Elisabeth struggled to sound casual. It was rare, indeed, for Amy to be out in Hollywood or Los Angeles at night, and on such occasions she'd made sure Amy's name was not emblazoned in lights at a movie palace. 'It's part of the advertising campaign.' Amy knew, of course, about the ads that appeared in local newspapers, but that was modest in comparison to this. 'Now let's find a taxi to take us up to the hotel.'

The girls and Hallie were enthralled at boarding the ship that was to carry them to England. Cunard's queen of the Atlantic, the *Aquitania* had been launched in 1914. It had been transformed into a floating hospital during the war but, with peace, had been restored to much of its earlier glory. In conversation with the captain, Elisabeth learned that the awesome Adam Drawing Room had been host in the course of the war to a phalanx of white iron bedsteads, where wounded soldiers could lie back and admire the marble statuary, the excellent copy of a Cipriani masterpiece that hung above them.

For Elisabeth the days on shipboard were traumatic. She was grateful that Hallie contrived shipboard diversions that occupied much of Amy and Katie's waking hours. What would London be like after four years of war? How were Grandma, Ben and Felix, her parents?

At Southampton – as arranged with Claridge's – their party was met by liveried footmen who took charge of their luggage and escorted them to the boat train. Again at Waterloo Station in London, they were met by more liveried footmen and escorted to a waiting limousine to carry them to the hotel.

Elisabeth had geared herself to see a much changed London. To her astonishment there was little sign – only a few months after the Armistice – that London had been ravaged by war. They drove through familiar streets, where she was conscious of unfamiliar shops and restaurants, tall buildings where once had been low ones. Then the limousine was pulling to a stop before an unpretentious red brick building – its entrance flush with the sidewalk. A tiny canopy identified it as Claridge's.

'This is it?' With memories of a birthday dinner at the Alexandria in Los Angeles clear in her mind, Amy was disappointed.

'Don't be put off by the entrance,' Elisabeth whispered. 'This is one of the finest hotels in the world.'

They were escorted past a uniformed, top-hatted doorman, through a marble foyer to an elegant, columned lobby. With effortless speed they were deposited in their suite – fresh flowers scenting the sitting room. Elisabeth subdued an urge to rush from the hotel and to the Woolf house in Lexham Gardens. But first they must find a furnished flat to lease for the year. Claridge's was shockingly expensive.

Later in the day – her heart pounding in anticipation – Elisabeth prodded herself to phone the Woolf house, just to hear a familiar voice long absent from her life – with luck Grandma's voice. But normally, of course, Dora would respond. Was Dora still there, all these years later, or had she gone off during the war to a more lucrative job, as many domestics were said to have done? Unsure of the number now she asked the operator to check it for her.

'I'm sorry, madam.' The operator returned to her after a few moments. 'There's no phone listed for a Simon Woolf.'

'Thank you.' Elisabeth's hand trembled as she replaced the phone. *Where were they?*

Try the shop, she ordered herself. But again, there was no listing for such an establishment, the operator reported. Her mind was in chaos. Why would the family leave London? Or had they moved early in the war years to a safer haven?

In the morning she instructed Hallie to take the girls down to the restaurant for breakfast while she headed off to visit an office advertising furnished apartments in Mayfair.

'Will they let me in that fine place without you?' Hallie was dubious. She was ever surprised when she seemed to be welcome in august surroundings.

'Hallie, you're not in backward Georgia,' Elisabeth scolded for the hundredth time. 'You'll take Amy and Katie down for breakfast and sign our suite number on the bill – the check. We are guests in this hotel.'

'Why don't you have breakfast with us? Are you tryin' to be skin and bones – like those flappers?' Disdain in Hallie's voice for the new breed of young women now emerging.

Elisabeth laughed. 'I'm too old to be a flapper. A suffragette, maybe.' She was still frustrated that, while a few states had granted women's suffrage, no constitutional amendment had yet been passed to guarantee women the right to vote. 'I'll stop in a tea shop for tea and a scone,' she promised.

She fought down an impulse to rush to Lexham Gardens, ordered herself to focus on acquiring a furnished flat. She spent most of the morning discussing prospective places. On the point of being discouraged she was shown one that would be comfortable and within the budget she'd set for herself. Thank God, the exchange from dollars to pounds was favorable. She was determined that this would be a memorable year for Amy and Katie, yet was ever conscious of the need to save for their uncertain future.

They were to take possession of the flat in twenty-four hours. Elisabeth was relieved that this was settled, yet anxiety tugged at her. Why was there no phone at the family house at Lexham Gardens? It could only mean that they were no longer living there. No phone at the shop. This afternoon she would go to the house, ask the current residents for information about the family.

She returned to Claridge's to hear excited reports from Amy and Katie of their sightseeing with Hallie in the immediate vicinity of the hotel. Now she told them about the flat she had leased for a year.

'A flat?' Katie tilted her head in doubt.

'That's an apartment,' Amy explained with an air of superiority and turned to her mother. 'How many bedrooms?' Amy was fearful of having to share with Katie.

'A bedroom for each of us,' Elisabeth reassured Amy. 'And it's lovely. Almost like a house. We move in tomorrow.'

She sat down with Hallie and outlined an afternoon tour that they could follow with no difficulty. She knew her own destination. She was going to the house in Lexham Gardens that had been home for the first sixteen years of her life.

Approaching the house she was conscious that it was somewhat less well-maintained than she remembered. That could be the result of the war – and a decreased domestic staff. Struggling for composure, she approached the front door. Her breathing labored, her hands cold and clammy, she reached to touch the bell. Let it be Dora who came to the door. Let the telephone incident be some stupid mistake.

The door swung wide. A strange, uniformed maid stood there.

'I'm sorry,' Elisabeth said, 'but I haven't been in London for several years. Does the Woolf family still live here?'

'No, ma'am.' The maid seemed annoyed by this intrusion. 'Not for the past year, at least.'

'I wonder – would the current residents be able to tell me where the Woolf family moved?'

'My employers are at their country house. They won't be back for several weeks. But they won't know. The house had been empty for over a year when they bought it.' The woman was clearly annoyed at this intrusion. 'You'll have to excuse me, ma'am. I have work to do.'

For a few moments – encased in shock – Elisabeth walked without direction. Go to Papa's main store on Oxford Street. She headed there in haste. Her throat tight with apprehension, she searched for the shop. It wasn't there. What had been Woolf's Menswear was now a restaurant.

Battling panic, Elisabeth returned to Claridge's. Hallie and the girls were not in their suite. She mustn't think about the encounter at the house. Focus on what must be dealt with now. The day after tomorrow they would take possession of the flat. She must choose schools for Amy and Katie. But tomorrow morning, she suddenly decided, she would go to Whitechapel. Someone there might have some knowledge of Grandma's whereabouts. No doubt in her mind that Grandma had continued her secret excursions to Whitechapel through the years.

Amy and Hallie knew, of course, of her anxiety to locate the family. Katie was too young to understand. She saw the eager questions in Amy's and Hallie's eyes when they walked into the sitting room of the suite.

'The family's not living in Lexham Gardens anymore,' Elisabeth said quietly.

'Where then?' Amy was startled.

'I don't know. But we'll look for them. I've been away a long time.' She searched for words that would mask her alarm. 'People move to other towns. Perhaps Papa retired, and the family moved to the country. Perhaps they wanted to get away from all the bombing in London.'

The following morning, after transferring their luggage to the flat, she saw the other three off on more sightseeing. They were like starry-eyed tourists, she thought tenderly. They were enjoying themselves. It was right to have come here. Let Amy and Katie know their heritage.

Approaching Whitechapel, Elisabeth felt herself hurtling back through time. She'd adored the secret forays with Grandma into the Jewish section of London – so like the Lower East Side of New York, which Jerry had showed her on occasion. Here were the crowded streets she'd walked with Grandma; the cacophany of voices in a multitude of tongues, though Yiddish predominated; the exotic attire of the ultra-orthodox clashing with that of a pair of high-spirited flappers. Remembered aromas drifted to her: herring, pickles, bread baking in ovens.

Few changes in seventeen years, she marveled, inspecting tiny shops on either side of the narrow street that bore a strong resemblance to those she recalled. This had been Grandma's real home, though she cherished and respected the comforts supplied by her son-in-law in the house in Lexham Gardens. Surely someone here would know where Grandma would be. *Ask questions.*

'Excuse me,' she asked ingratiatingly, 'would you know of the whereabouts of my grandmother, Rae Kahn? She used to live in Lexham Gardens, but she came here often.'

Over and over she asked the same question, met with a negative head shake. Why had she expected to find answers? So many people passed through these streets. But there were shops that Grandma visited regularly, if not to shop, to exchange small talk.

She paused before a tiny bakery that sent forth tantalizing aromas of cinnamon and apples. Her heart began to pound. Grandma used to buy her hamantashen here – and rugelach. Trembling, she walked inside. She recognized the round face of the woman behind the counter: Grandma's friend, now older, the grey streaked hair now white.

She pretended to be inspecting the contents of a tray until the woman had finished with her customer.

'Excuse me,' she began, her voice uneven. 'I thought you might be able to help me find my grandmother. She used to come here regularly. Her name is Rae Kahn.'

The elderly woman behind the counter squinted at her, mouth ajar for a moment before she spoke. 'You're the granddaughter who used to come with her!'

'Yes.' Elisabeth's voice was a shaky whisper. 'Do you know where she lives now?'

'Didn't the family write you?' the woman asked accusingly, and Elisabeth realized that Grandma would not have revealed the chasm that existed between them. 'Rae died two years ago. Dora, the maid, came to tell me. When she was dying, Rae asked her to do this.'

'The family has been estranged,' Elisabeth stammered, dizzy with shock. 'Nobody told me. Thank you –' She turned and fled.

Too late she'd come home. Too late to see Grandma again.

Chapter Thirty-three

Dizzy from shock Elisabeth walked through the crowded streets without a destination, remembering the cherished visits with Grandma to her beloved Whitechapel. Always through the years she'd cherished a conviction that a time would come when she would be with Grandma again. Now, amidst the sights and sounds and aromas that had seemed home to her grandmother, she felt a sudden compulsion to kneel before Grandma's grave, to tell her she still loved her, had never stopped loving her. Grandma would be buried in the Hebrew Cemetery in Whitechapel. She would go there now.

She walked into a small shop that sold religious artifacts and asked directions to the cemetery, then hurried there. After a frenzied search she discovered the small headstone that bore her grandmother's name. The grave site was well-tended. Mama would see to that, Elisabeth forced herself to acknowledge. She crouched before the headstone, touched it lovingly. Grandma would always be in her heart. Tears filled her eyes, spilling over unheeded. Had Grandma received her letters – or were they intercepted and thrown away? She would never know.

Exhausted from the trauma of the day Elisabeth left the cemetery. An effort to track down the family through the cemetery files produced nothing. But her search for Mama and Papa and the boys would continue, she vowed. Though not just yet. For a little while let her grieve for Grandma.

Back at the flat she told Amy and Katie that their great-grandmother was dead. She saw tears well in Amy's eyes. Katie climbed into her lap and held her tight. They shared her sense of loss.

A few days later Elisabeth focused on the girls' schooling for the coming year. They would go to state schools, she told them – and laughed at their startled stares. Where else would they go? They had been made to understand that state schools were an American birthright. This question had arisen when the studio had suggested that the posh Hollywood High School for Girls might accept Amy even though she would be absent much of the time and working with a tutor. Elisabeth had been proud that the local 'public' school had been able to handle Amy's needs.

'In London,' she explained, 'public schools are what Americans call private schools.'

'Will I like it?' Katie demanded.

'Maybe not the first day or two, but after that you'll love it,' Elisabeth predicted. Ever ebullient Katie would make friends anywhere.

With the war behind them Londoners were dashing off in droves for seaside summer holidays – the first in five years – while wealthy American tourists were arriving in London.

Each day until school began Elisabeth took Amy and Katie – along with wide-eyed Hallie – to sites beloved of the American tourists. The girls and Hallie were fascinated by the British Underground – though wary of the trams, which Hallie complained never came to a full stop. 'Folks just jump on!'

They visited the Tower of London and Elisabeth showed them where Anne Boleyn lost her head. They saw the room in the Bloody Tower where the two little princes were murdered, viewed through a window the magnificent jeweled crowns worn on state occasions by the King and Queen and the Prince of Wales. They watched the Changing of the Guard at Buckingham Palace and visited imposing Westminster Abbey. Each day another cherished site. All were thrilled at catching a glimpse of Queen Mary – much loved by the British public for her exemplary behavior during the war years.

'Even the Queen observed the rationing laws,' Elisabeth told the others.

'We had ration laws back home,' Hallie reminded. 'We never bought on the black market.'

Elisabeth promised herself that once Amy and Katie were attending school, she'd concentrate on tracking down her parents and brothers. She studied the ads in the various newspapers, clipped out items dealing with private investigators. It would be horribly expensive, she warned herself, but they had sufficient funds.

Wary of charlatans, she interviewed four investigators before making a choice.

'There's no guarantee I'll come up with anything,' he warned, his eyes serious.

'I understand.'

They agreed to a fee and a time limit. She could only sit back and wait, she told herself, yet was restless in unfamiliar idleness. Now she considered searching for work – either in the British cinema or on the London stage – though the prospect was intimidating. From the newspapers she gathered that the theater was in something of a slump. The motion picture companies – dormant during the war years – were contemplating a comeback. The British – not only the working classes but those more inclined to attend the theater – had become avid cinema fans.

A waitress in the Lyons Corner House she favored told her that four years ago Charlie Chaplin had been introduced to British cinema fans.

'At first the newspapers condemned him for not "doing his bit" in the war. But then the troops began to see him at the "camp cinemas" and loved him. He's the one that started us going to the cinema twice a week. Him and Mary Pickford.'

Elisabeth conceded that the quality of American films being shown was not high. But the public rushed to see them none the less, and especially enjoyed the performance of Clara Kimball Young and William Farnum in addition to Chaplin and Pickford. Had any of *her* pictures ever made it to London? The only one of which she was proud was *Jane Eyre*. *Wuthering Heights*, of course, never made it out of the studio.

On an evening when Elisabeth decreed they would have their dinner out at a restaurant, she pointed out the queues forming in front of 'picture palaces' as early as six p.m., though here in London most performances began at eight, as in the theater. All right, she told herself – go out and try for work. It was time.

It was soon apparent that British film companies were hopeful of a coming fight between British and Americans for supremacy in the field. Yet Elisabeth sensed that financing would be difficult for most. Saying nothing at the flat about this venture, she made the rounds of those supposedly casting for films. She was disappointed that nothing was coming of this, though she realized a few days of such activity meant nothing. She would go out five days a week, she told herself grimly. Every week. She had been away from the cameras for five years – but she hadn't lost her ability to perform.

All the while she fretted at not hearing from the private investigator she had hired. He'd warned it would not be easy to track down her family at a time when so many lives had been disrupted by the war. Three weeks after their meeting she received a call from his office. That same afternoon she met with him.

Her heart pounding, she searched his face for some indication of what he had to report.

'I'm sorry, Miss Winston.' His eyes were grave. 'Your father died late in 1917. I was able to locate his death certificate.'

Elisabeth sat motionless, feeling herself encased in ice. So she and Papa were never to be reconciled.

'What about my mother and my brothers?' she asked, her voice unsteady.

'I could come up with nothing. I'm sorry.'

On the Underground en route to their flat in Mayfair, Elisabeth struggled for composure. How could Mama and the boys disappear that way? An agonizing wave of defeat enveloped her. Was she never to find them? She'd say nothing to Amy and Katie about this. They'd both cried when they learned about Grandma. Don't burden them with this latest news.

In a depressed mood, Elisabeth decided to abandon the search for film work. Concentrate instead on theater. There seemed to be some activity now in the West End producing offices. Each day – equipped with reports of casting of plays – she made the rounds of theatrical offices. Her lack of recent stage experience brought polite rejections. Why wouldn't they give her a chance to read?

At the end of her third week of making rounds, she geared herself to lie and update her years on the Melbourne stage. She wouldn't mention the years of film making. Theatrical producers considered movies crude, a low form of entertainment. She spent time coaching herself on her stage background in Melbourne. Who would know?

At the usual hour she presented herself at the office of the next producer on her list. Already, most chairs were filled with hopefuls: self-conscious flappers making last-minute repairs with powder and lipstick, character actors and actresses with the contrived air of self-confidence.

She managed a charming smile, approached the girl behind the desk.

'Sit down, miss, and wait till you're called,' the receptionist said automatically. 'You're number eleven.'

'Thank you.'

Elisabeth took one of the unoccupied chairs, conscious of furtive inspection by the others. The three women who were hoping to read for the same part as she, Elisabeth assumed, exuded an air of competition. In truth, she was too young, but the other female role being cast was twenty. Even the two younger women eyed her warily.

A major British actress was signed for the production. Highly respected Clive Mendoza was to direct. It was the second play of a boy wonder of the British theater. What was *she* doing here? She fought an instinct to flee.

It soon became clear that Clive Mendoza was spending little time on interviews. Each was out in five or six minutes. Perhaps these were just preliminary interviews. Readings would come later, Elisabeth surmised. The tension in the reception room was eroding the self-confidence of those who remained.

Now only three were ahead of her, Elisabeth noted. The door to the inner office opened. A distinguished-looking character actor emerged with a young man who seemed intent on mollifying injured feelings.

'Mr Mendoza will call you to set up a reading,' he insisted. 'His schedule today is too tight for that. But you *will* hear from him.'

The young man gazed about at the others with a cajoling smile. Clive Mendoza's assistant, Elisabeth gathered. He understood that this was a traumatic experience – one that was endured over and over again. His eyes settled on Elisabeth. She was startled by their intensity. Probably she resembled somebody he knew. She managed a shaky smile. *He* reminded her of Paul, but a dozen years younger.

He disappeared into the inner office, opened the door a moment later to summon the receptionist.

'That's Mendoza's son,' the older woman next to Elisabeth murmured. 'Isn't he the handsomest thing? Even with that slight limp the girls must chase after him like mad.'

Moments later the receptionist returned to her desk.

'Mr Mendoza would like to see Beth Winston next,' she announced, eyes apologetic because the three with lower numbers were affronted.

Startled, Elisabeth rose to her feet. How did they know her name?

'Thank you.' Aware of the stony stares of the other three, she walked into Mendoza's private office.

Clive Mendoza sat behind a huge antique desk. Elisabeth recognized him from magazine photographs.

'Please sit down, Miss Winston. My son, Neil, is a fan of yours.'

Fan?

'I saw you in *Jane Eyre*. I was in a convalescent hospital after a war injury,' Neil Mendoza explained. 'They fed us every film they could lay their hands on. Yours was one of the few memorable ones.'

'Thank you.' She'd never realized *Jane Eyre* had hit the export market. A fact their distributor had forgot to report – or to list on rental statements.

'Of course, there's much difference in acting for the theater than for films.' A faint condescension in Clive Mendoza's voice now.

'Before I worked in films, I spent several years onstage in Melbourne. Mostly in leading roles,' she forced herself to point out.

'You're rather young for Elaine,' Mendoza said regretfully. 'Quite a bit too young –'

'Not Elaine,' his son broke in. 'Let her read for Diane. She has the right quality. It came across in the film.'

'But Diane is twenty,' Mendoza protested.

'Onstage she'll be twenty.' Neil radiated enthusiasm. 'Let her read for Diane.'

'Tomorrow morning at ten,' Clive Mendoza capitulated. 'We'll expect you then, Miss Winston.'

At home Elisabeth said nothing of the scheduled reading. It was unreal, she marveled, that a young man in a convalescent hospital in England had seen *Jane Eyre* – and remembered her. And it was beyond reason that she could play a twenty-year-old. Yet her mind mocked this reticence. Five years ago she'd played seventeen, on camera, with close-ups. Was it such a stretch to play twenty with the advantage of the distance provided by a stage?

Arriving at the casting office the following morning, she was intimidated on discovering the playwright was in the inner office with Clive Mendoza. Oh, this was a wild dream! He'd reject her for sure. After a wait – with each minute seeming an hour – she was ushered inside. Immediately she was aware of a certain hostility in the playwright's eyes. He thought she was too old.

After introducing her to the playwright, Clive Mendoza handed Elisabeth the playscript. 'Ian, explain the role to Miss Winston.'

She listened absorbedly to his elaborate description of young Diane, her mind fleshing in the character he outlined for her.

'It's a small part. Very small,' Clive Mendoza emphasized. 'But in the right hands it could be spectacular.'

'Yes,' Elisabeth agreed with deceptive sweetness. *She could play Diane*. This time she would stay in the role.

'Neil, read with her,' his father ordered.

Elisabeth focused on the characterization – caught up in the beautiful nuances the playwright had provided. She had expected to read only the one scene, but without waiting for word from the other two men Neil gave her the page number of the second scene involving Diane.

She read on. Neil was not a finished actor, but he gave so much to the part. At last they reached the final speech, and she paused – breathless, caught up in the character. Immediately she felt the electric excitement in the air. Neil was beaming.

Clive Mendoza cleared his throat. 'That was quite good. But we'll want you to read with our leading lady before we make a decision.'

But Elisabeth knew the part was hers. Finally – after all these years – she would play in the London theater. She listened with deferential attention while Mendoza put through a call to their leading lady, arranged a reading for the following afternoon.

Again, at home Elisabeth cautioned herself to say nothing. Her own conviction – and Neil's – that she would play Diane could be overturned. Say nothing until the contract was signed.

When Elisabeth returned to the flat late the following afternoon, she was enveloped in an aura of wonderment. She would play Diane when the company went into rehearsal in four weeks. Neil, his father's assistant and stage manager, was euphoric. Because he'd proven to his father that he was right, Elisabeth told herself. But she knew that Neil Mendoza was deeply attracted to her. Amazing, his resemblance to Paul. Not just the quiet good looks – that inner intensity she loved in Paul. He'd fought in the war – he'd been wounded. All that, and he couldn't be more than twenty-three.

Elisabeth sat in a corner of the sitting room and made a pretense of reading *The Times*. She waited impatiently for Amy to arrive home. She'd said nothing to Hallie – who had gone to bring Katie home. She wanted to tell the three of them together. Thank God, the girls were settling into their schools. That had been a major worry. Amy had complained the first week or two about 'all the silly rules'. Elisabeth had made a point of choosing schools with 'rules'. In this upside-down world they were living in rules were necessary. It unnerved her the way young girls – almost as young as Amy – were going to cocktail parties, 'necking' with boys, doing the crazy new dances.

She discarded the newspaper at the sound of Amy and Katie's voices in verbal battle.

'Now you be quiet, both of you,' Hallie ordered, but the girls charged into the sitting room to demand that Elisabeth settle their dispute.

'Mama, Katie's terrible,' Amy seethed. 'She talks to just everybody in the street. It's so embarrassing.'

'You're not responsible for Katie's actions.' How many times had she said this? 'And it's nice that your sister's friendly.'

'It's uncouth.' Amy dumped her books on the sofa and headed for the kitchen.

'Wait, Amy. I have some news.' Elisabeth took a deep breath. 'I'm going to be working in four weeks. I have a part in a new play.'

'Now ain't that wonderful!' Hallie beamed.

Amy gaped in astonishment. 'You haven't acted since I was a baby!'

'I did *Jane Eyre* five years ago.' But Elisabeth's smile had lost some of its dazzle.

'That was a movie, Mama!' Why was Amy looking at her as though she'd lost her mind?

'Can we see you in the play?' Katie radiated approval.

'You'll see me,' Elisabeth promised, and turned defensively to Amy. 'I read for the director and the playwright. They liked me.'

'Is it a big part?' Still, Amy was ambivalent.

'Very small – but terrific.' Elisabeth felt a fresh surge of excitement.

'Tell us about the play,' Katie ordered, settling herself cross-legged on the sofa. 'Are you somebody's mama?'

Elisabeth hesitated, all at once self-conscious.

'No. Diane's not married. She's twenty years old and –'

'You're playing a twenty-year-old girl?' Amy was outraged. 'That's the kind of part I could play!'

Elisabeth's heart began to pound. To Amy she was suddenly competition. She hadn't meant that to happen.

'It's just a small part, darling. And on the stage an actress can play much younger ages than her own. There's all the distance between actors and audiences.' Why was she babbling this way? 'It doesn't pay anything like what the studio paid you. But I'll have fun.' She forced a smile. 'Now who votes that we go out for dinner tonight?'

'Me, me!' Katie bubbled. 'Can I have ice cream and cake for dessert?'

'In England,' Hallie said firmly, 'you-all can have one or the other. So make up your mind, Katie. Will it be ice cream or will it be cake?'

Chapter Thirty-four

Elisabeth arrived at the theater for the first day of rehearsals with trepidation. Had she been away from live theater too long? Could she repeat the success she'd earned in Melbourne? The bare stage – with a cluster of chairs about a table – was intimidating. She remembered other such occasions, the familiar atmosphere that blended the bravado, unease, strained self-confidence of various members of the cast.

Neil, now stage manager, smiled encouragingly when she took her place at the table. She had memorized her lines, had developed the character using the method David had taught her all those years ago. The way she, in turn, had taught Amy. Still, she felt pangs of uncertainty at intervals during the day's rehearsal.

Neil came to her side when the cast was dismissed for the day. 'I knew you'd be wonderful as Diane.'

'I was nervous.' She managed a tentative smile. 'It's been a long time since I've worked in theater.'

'It's a talent you don't lose.' He fell in step beside her. 'My father's pleased. I always know when he's happy about something.' Neil chuckled. 'He does a series of tiny nods. I learned that when I was about seven.'

Elisabeth cherished his encouragement. But until the play opened and the critics made their pronouncements, she knew she'd be anxious. She was oddly disturbed that Amy – in the days ahead – asked no questions about the progress of rehearsals, though Katie clamored to be there on opening night: 'I'll take a long nap in the afternoon. I won't fall asleep.' And Hallie was enthralled at the prospect of seeing Elisabeth onstage.

She was conscious of the wise smiles she intercepted at times. The whole cast seemed aware that Neil was infatuated with her. His father was too engrossed in directing to notice, she told herself in relief.

She was flattered by Neil's attentions, drawn to him by his charming warmth and by his striking resemblance to Paul. After the first week of rehearsals, he offered to drive her home: 'I go that way, anyhow. Why should you have to chase after a bus?'

It was pleasant to be driven to her door each day after rehearsals. Neil made a point of lingering in conversation before – with prewar gallantry – running around to open the car door for her.

After the usual hectic dress rehearsal, when the nerves of everyone were raw, he insisted on taking her out to dinner. Guiltily she called home and fabricated a story about being held up for more rehearsal.

'Tell Amy and Katie I'll be home in a couple of hours,' she told Hallie. 'There's always such chaos at dress rehearsals.' She managed a shaky laugh. 'I'm a nervous wreck, of course.'

'You'll be fine,' Hallie insisted. 'I'm just bustin' with pride!'

Elisabeth was the first of the cast to arrive at the theater on opening night. Let me be good, she prayed. Please God, let me be good. Neil made a point of coming over at intervals to offer encouragement. Long before her first entrance she hovered in the wings. Amy and Katie were in choice seats with Hallie. She had to be good for them.

The moment she was onstage she brushed aside anxieties. It was like Melbourne. Exhilarated by the realization that she had been well-received in her first scene, she stood by for the second. When the curtain came down on the third act and the cast took their curtain calls, the entire company was convinced the play would be a success.

After the performance, Hallie and the girls swept past the stage doorman to find her amidst the customary backstage excitement of opening night.

'Mama, you were beautiful!' Katie declared, holding her face up for a kiss.

'I loved the dresses you wore,' Amy said with a dutiful smile. 'You looked very pretty.'

'Beth, you're coming with us to the party?' Neil appeared at her side.

'I think not.' Elisabeth was apologetic. 'It's been quite a night already for Katie.' She'd told Neil much about Amy and Katie. 'But let me introduce my family. This is Amy and Katie. And Hallie – who takes care of all of us.'

She glowed as the others exchanged pleasantries. Amy liked Neil, she thought. And Katie was chatting away as though she'd known him all her life.

'I'll drive you all home,' Neil said. 'And don't you dare say no,' he ordered Elisabeth. 'Hallie, you make sure she sleeps till all hours tomorrow.'

The critics liked the play, offered special praise for the leading lady and for Elisabeth. Elisabeth was ecstatic. Ever since the first day of rehearsal, she'd envisioned her mother reading about the play in the newspapers and rushing to the theater with the boys.

Except on matinée days, Elisabeth made a point of being at home when Amy and Katie returned from school. It amazed her that Amy seemed uninterested in her being in the play. Amy was all wrapped up in her school friends, was indignant that she wasn't allowed to bob her hair – when 'four of my friends at school have bobbed theirs!'

Each night after the performance Neil drove her home from the theater. Knowing the girls were both asleep by now, she made no objection when Neil contrived to linger with her in the car. He was charming and bright and sweet – but he could be so cynical, Elisabeth mourned.

Tonight they sat in the car while a full moon bathed them in a soft light. Elisabeth had just chastised him for the cynicism that erupted from him at intervals.

'We have to live for today, Beth,' he said with an intensity that reminded her of Paul. 'What kind of a world have we grown up in that could let millions of people die in a stupid war? I remember the months in the hospitals after my plane was shot down.' He paused, his eyes darkening in recall. 'I was one of the lucky ones – I managed to get down in one piece. But I looked at those in beds around me – without arms or legs. Or blind, having to spend the rest of their lives in darkness. It made me so sick. Why? Why did the world let this happen?'

'I have no answers.' Elisabeth was somber. 'Since the beginning of time we've seen wars. But surely this will be the last.'

'Beth, you're a hopeless optimist.'

'I wonder sometimes about my family. My mother and my brothers.' It was the first time she had allowed herself to discuss this with Neil. 'It's scary not to know where they are.'

'I don't understand –'

Quietly she told Neil about her father's banishing her from the family home in Lexham Gardens, felt his shock that a father could behave this way. Not Clive Mendoza, she thought. Such a warm, loving father.

'I've learned that my grandmother and father both died. But I can find no trace of my mother or brothers. I'm sure Ben and Felix must have served in the war. I suspect Ben would have been involved in flying. He was always reading up on cars. I can imagine him in a plane.'

'Beth –' Neil seemed involved in some inner turmoil. 'What was your name before your married?'

'Woolf.' Why was Neil looking so strange?

'There's something I must tell you.' His eyes were agonized. 'Ben Woolf was in my squadron.' Her eyes clung to him – her heart racing. 'His plane was shot down the same night as mine. I'm sorry. Ben died in the crash.'

Elisabeth was motionless, ice cold. 'Maybe it was another Ben Woolf –'

'Ben's brother was named Felix. He chose the Air Force because Felix had been a flyer.' He paused. 'Felix was killed in action some months earlier.'

'Oh my God . . .' She was too stunned to cry. 'Ben and Felix?'

'Both were awarded medals,' he said gently. 'Ben was determined to match Felix's bravery.'

'All those years I lost . . .' She closed her eyes in anguish. 'I kept telling myself that one day I'd be with them again. That was one of the reasons I came back to London.'

'I don't think there's a family in England that hasn't suffered a loss.' He reached to pull her close in comfort. 'I know this isn't the time to tell you – but, Beth, I love you so much.'

In a corner of her mind she'd heard Neil's words, but there was room in her heart only for grief. 'I can't believe it. Both of them – Ben and Felix – gone.'

'I'll explain to my father what happened. The understudy can go on for you tomorrow night.'

'No,' she rejected. 'I'll play tomorrow night. That's what Ben and Felix would want me to do.'

*   *   *

Elisabeth debated about telling Amy and Katie that their uncles had died fighting for their country, told herself that she must not burden them with this knowledge. Not yet. And where was Mama? Alone. Devastated. How did she go about searching for Mama?

She was touched by Neil's solicitude in the days ahead, his tenderness towards her. It was Neil who persuaded her to run an entry in the personal columns in London newspapers, asking for information about her mother's whereabouts. She clung to the hope that someone would respond, but trip after trip to the newspaper office yielded nothing. Still, she stubbornly continued to run the entry, ever conscious that she was not alone in searching for family in this postwar year.

New Year's Eve 1919 arrived. Elisabeth felt a tidal wave of homesickness as she remembered other New Year's Eves spent at the Sanchez house. Amy had received an invitation to a party at a friend's house somewhere in Mayfair, but the invitation had been issued by the friend herself and Amy admitted under pressure that the party would be unchaperoned.

'The other girls are going!' Amy stormed.

'Most of your schoolfriends are seventeen,' Elisabeth reminded. 'With all the tutoring, you moved ahead of your age group.' But even then, she thought privately, chaperones should be present.

'You're so old-fashioned!'

How many times a week did she hear that same condemnation? Were parents abandoning all sense of responsibility for their children? There must be rules, guidelines. She was terrified of the drinking and drugs that she'd thought were only a Hollywood problem. Not so.

On New Year's Eve – when there was no performance – Neil appeared at the flat with a bottle of champagne, a basket of goodies and an array of colorful balloons. All at once the house reverberated with gaiety. Amy and Katie adored him, Elisabeth thought, grateful for his presence. And Hallie strived to spoil him endlessly.

At the stroke of midnight Neil punctured one balloon. Amidst startled laughter, he kissed each of the other four. Elisabeth was unnerved by the intensity of his mouth on hers, though she was sure the others were unaware. Ten minutes later he carried Katie – asleep despite her vow to remain awake – to her room.

'I'm glad you came,' Elisabeth told him. 'The girls were feeling homesick, though they'd never admit to that.'

'I wouldn't have missed it for the world.'

He hadn't once told her again, since that horrendous moment when she'd learned about Ben and Felix's deaths, that he loved her, and she was grateful for this. Yet his eyes constantly reiterated this confession. Her mind told her she ought to stop seeing him away from the theater, yet she couldn't bring herself to do this. He sustained her in this awful period of her life, when the homecoming she'd so yearned for was tarnished by grief.

Early in March, with the play continuing its successful run, Elisabeth received a letter from a woman who said she'd known Celia Woolf as a member of her Red Cross group. She suggested they meet at a Lyons Corner House near her home: 'Phone me at the number below, and we can arrange a time.'

Almost inarticulate in her excitement Elisabeth called and arranged an appointment for the following afternoon. Then she called Neil to tell him what had happened.

'Would you like me to go with you?' he asked.

'I don't think that would be right, but thanks for the thought, Neil.'

She waited impatiently for the scheduled meeting. She said nothing to the girls or Hallie. But please God, let this lead to her finding Mama. A full half-hour before the appointed time she was at the Lyons. The woman she was to meet would be wearing a grey wool coat with a bright yellow scarf at her throat.

Elisabeth began to tremble when a woman in a grey coat arrived, also early. The woman's eyes skimmed the others at the tables about the room, saw Elisabeth's tentative smile, noted her own yellow background scarf, and hurried to join her.

'I don't have a lot to tell you,' the other woman told Elisabeth apologetically. 'Your mother and I met in the same Red Cross group from the first year of the war. She grieved deeply for her mother, her husband and sons.' She hesitated. 'You knew about them?'

'Yes . . .' Elisabeth managed a strangled whisper.

'Celia sold the house and the business. After the Armistice she said there was nothing left to hold her here. She didn't say where she was going, but I suspected to cousins in Germany. You know how many of us felt about Germany at the end of the war.' The woman's face hardened. 'With good reason.'

They talked briefly about wartime London. Elisabeth gathered her mother had been reticent about discussing family, though she'd agonized on the possible fate of the German cousins. All at once the woman seemed anxious to break away.

'I'm sorry I couldn't be more helpful. My husband teases me about reading the personal columns.'

'I'm so happy you did. Thank you for coming here.'

Mama was in Berlin, Elisabeth was convinced. Where in Berlin had the cousins lived? She searched her brain without coming up with an answer. It was so long ago that she and Ben had gone with Mama and Grandma to visit them. Was there some way to place entries in the personal columns of the Berlin newspapers? That country was a shambles; civilian deaths had been heavy. Newspapers reported that starvation was rampant. How was she to find Mama under those conditions?

For the rest of the day she was engulfed in hopelessness – though for the girls and Hallie she managed to conceal the desperation that inundated her. Talk to Neil, she told herself when she arrived at the theater. If anyone could help her, he could.

Not until after the performance when they were in his car and en route to her flat did Elisabeth tell Neil about her traumatic meeting at the Lyons Corner House.

'Is there some way I can run an ad in a Berlin newspaper?' Her voice was uneven. 'Neil, how do I find my mother? She's somewhere in Berlin – I know that. But I don't remember where our cousins lived. Why can't I remember?'

'I'll find a way for you to run the ad,' he promised, reaching for her hand. 'Beth, you're so cold . . .'

'I'm scared. I tell myself I have to be strong – but I'm terrified for my mother. The others are gone. She's alone.'

'We'll work this out. Right now you need a drink,' he said firmly. 'Or a pot of tea.'

She winced. 'I don't want to see people. Come up to the flat with me and . . .' She paused, shook her head. 'They'll all be asleep, I wouldn't want to wake them.' In many ways Hallie spoiled the girls, but she was firm about their bedtimes on school nights. They were always in bed and asleep by the time Elisabeth came from the theater.

'Come up to my flat,' he said gently. 'I'll make some tea and we can talk.'

'All right.' Thank God for Neil. He understood her fears for Mama. All the stories coming out of Germany about the terrible state of the country, about people dying of starvation, were unnerving.

She'd known Neil's flat was somewhere in Mayfair. She hadn't realized it was just a few streets from her own.

'I furnished the place with discarded pieces from my parents' house,' he said wryly as he unlocked the door. 'They still can't understand why I insisted on having my own place.' He chuckled. 'Their generation's got a lot to learn.'

'It looks very comfortable.' But she understood his parents' thinking. He'd fought in a war, he'd been seriously wounded – they must yearn to have him home again.

'Come out to the kitchen with me while I put on the kettle.'

While he waited for the water to boil, he talked about some of the movies he'd seen while he was convalescing. Hoping to distract her from troubling thoughts, she understood.

'Some of them were so awful, but I made them run your *Jane Eyre* over and over again. The others used to tease me about having a crush on you. I couldn't believe my eyes when I walked in the reception room at the office and there you were.'

'Lucky for me.' Her eyes brightened in gratitude.

'Lucky for me. I knew the minute I saw you that I wanted to spend the rest of my life with you.'

'Neil, you're so young.' But all at once the atmosphere in the kitchen was electric.

'I went into the Royal Flying Corps young – I came out old.' He reached to pull her close. 'Beth, don't keep pushing me away.'

'This is wrong,' she said unsteadily, but already she was lifting her mouth to meet his.

'Shut up, Beth,' he said tenderly and reached to turn off the light under the kettle.

It seemed so right, she thought in a cavern in her mind, to walk hand in hand with Neil into his bedroom. She closed her eyes and submitted with towering joy to his lovemaking, abandoning submission to become an eager partner. How could something so beautiful be wrong?

They tried to keep this new relationship secret, yet Elisabeth sensed that the others in the company were aware of something new between

306

them. At times she suspected that Neil's father knew about those secret hours at Neil's flat and was uneasy. She wouldn't think about the future, she told herself. She'd be like all the young people who wanted to live only for the day. With Neil she found exquisite relief from the anxiety that tugged at her. Who but Neil would have arranged for the entry in the personal columns that just might bring Mama and her together?

Late in March Clive Mendoza alerted the company to the possibility of ending the London run to tour the provinces. She couldn't go on tour, Beth confided to Neil. How could she leave the girls for months? Hallie was wonderful – but their mother must be there for them, too.

On the drive home after the performance that night Neil talked about leaving the company, too.

'I can be easily replaced,' he said humorously. 'You'll be the serious problem.'

'But you love what you're doing,' she protested. Already she felt a void in her life at the prospect of being apart from Neil.

'I love being with you. Anyhow, the closing date hasn't been set. We'll work this out later.'

They lingered briefly in the car before he walked her to the entrance to her building. They'd had a marvelous lunch at Simpsons in the Strand earlier in the day and then an exhilarating hour in his flat. They were both insatiable, she chided herself, yet felt only indulgence. Being with Neil was almost like being with Paul.

Emerging from the car she glanced up at the front windows of their flat. In the spill of moonlight she spied Amy at an open window. Why wasn't she asleep? Tomorrow was a school day.

With a sense of urgency she kissed Neil goodnight in the shadows of the entrance, then hurried up to the flat. As always the hall was lighted in anticipation of her late evening return from the theater. She locked the door behind her and turned around to face Amy, now emerging down the shadowy hall that led to the bedrooms.

'Amy, what are you doing up so late?' But she reached out her arms in a spontaneous hug. Amy was growing up so fast!

'I couldn't sleep.' Amy dismissed this casually.

'I'll make you some cocoa. That'll –'

'Mama, I'm not a baby!'

'Darling, I know that.'

Amy seemed to ponder for a moment. 'Are you sleeping with Neil?'

'No!' Color leaped into her face. She remembered Ellie's complaint in her last letter: 'These kids today are growing up too fast! They're so casual about sex. They say things we'd never dare to say.'

'He's wild about you.'

There was a tinge of envy in her voice that Elisabeth found unnerving. What had she said once to Neil about Amy and himself? 'You're nearer Amy's age than mine.'

'If you're not sleeping with him, you're being silly. What have you got to lose? He's a real sheik.'

'Is this what you're learning at school?' But instinct told her to conceal her shock. 'I doubt that's part of the curriculum.' She contrived an air of amusement, but her mind was in chaos.

'I'm so sick of school,' Amy began, then lowered her voice at a gesture from her mother. Katie and Hallie were asleep. 'I can't wait for summer. Elaine is going to have her mother invite me to their country house.' Elaine was her best friend. 'There'll be lots of parties. They even have a swimming pool.'

'When school closes, we're going back to Hollywood.' Enough of this craziness. She'd been out of her mind to try to adopt the credo of the young – *Live for today. How do we know what tomorrow will bring?* 'You won't be here to go to Elaine's country house.' To wild, unchaperoned parties.

'Mama!' Amy wailed after a startled moment, then tensed at her mother's pantomimed reproach. 'Why do we have to go back to Hollywood?' she whispered defiantly.

'Because that's our home.' Finally let them have roots. She paused at the entrance to her room. 'You'll finish your last year of high school there.' She must put Neil out of her life. She had two daughters to raise. 'And we'll start thinking about college.'

'I'm not going to college! I'm sick of school!'

'You'll change your mind when you see all your friends going.'

She'd been living in a dream world these last months. Come down to earth. Face reality.

'They won't be going, either. School's not fun when you're grown up already.' Amy hesitated. 'Did you mean it? About our going back home?' Ambivalence crept into her voice. 'Can I write and tell Gloria?'

'You can tell Gloria.'

But, oh, how was she going to tell Neil?

Chapter Thirty-five

All through the following dreary, overcast day Elisabeth worried. How was she to tell Neil that she would return to Hollywood once the school year was over? She'd never pretended to be in love with him. She'd never once said, 'Neil, I love you.' But she'd clung to him, made passionate love with him. Never a word about the future – that wasn't the way of this young generation. *Live for today – tomorrow may never come.*

At the theater she forced herself to focus only on performance. Nothing must distract from that. Yet at intervals she sensed that Neil realized something disturbed her and he was anxious. Not until they were in his car – with torrential rain pounding on the roof – did she tell him she wouldn't be going on tour with the play. Tonight Clive Mendoza had made the official announcement of the London closing.

'Beth, we talked about this before. I told you then. I won't be going, either.'

'My original plan was for the girls and me to stay in London for a year.' She tried to keep her voice even. 'Now it's time for us to go home.'

'Why?' He was startled, baffled. 'You're doing so well here!'

'London's full of ghosts for me.'

'You'll put them to rest. My father's scouting like mad for a new play with a leading role for you. You have a wonderful career ahead in London theater.'

'Neil, I'm thirty-four years old.' He was twenty-four. 'Plays for me will be hard to come by in this crazy age.' The Jazz Age glorified the very young.

'You'll be playing twenty-three for the next ten years. On stage you'll be eternally young. Beth, what's truly upsetting you?'

For a moment she hesitated. 'Last night Amy asked if I was sleeping with you.'

'You're worried about that?' He sounded relieved. 'We'll get married straight away.'

'I can't do that, Neil. The girls will always come first with me. I –'

'I can accept that,' he broke in. 'They'll be our kids.'

'These months have been wonderful,' she conceded. But she'd never meant them to happen. 'I don't know how I could have survived them without you. But it won't work. Please, believe me . . .'

'What can I do to convince you?' he asked after a leaden pause.

'It wasn't meant to be,' she whispered. Knowing there would be a void in her life for a while. 'But I'm grateful for the months we had together. You were so good to me.'

'You make me sound like a Boy Scout.' His effort at humor was bleak.

'These past months were a precious interlude. But the time has come for me to move ahead. You're special, Neil. You'll find someone else – and she'll be so lucky.'

On the trip across the Atlantic aboard the *Mauretania*, then across country on the Twentieth Century Limited, Elisabeth talked enthusiastically about their homecoming. Katie and Hallie were pleased. Amy alternated between bemoaning not being able to spend the summer with her friend Elaine, and looking forward to seeing Gloria again. Amy remained rebellious at the prospect of another year of high school – and scoffed at the prospect of attending college. Her daughter, Elisabeth feared, preferred to embark on a career as party-going flapper. She boasted about having read F. Scott Fitzgerald's *This Side of Paradise* six times.

The tenants in Elisabeth's house would not be vacating for another week, Ellie had written. They'd spend that time at the Hollywood Hotel. Elisabeth had written nothing to Ellie about her determination to resume her career as a film actress – nor had she discussed this with the girls. She hoped her excellent reviews in the London play would help in this. Amy's conversation these days concerned the latest dances, songs, clothes styles. No producer in his right mind would consider casting Amy as a ten-year-old now, Elisabeth conceded. Nor did she seem interested in film work. Now was the time for Amy to be a normal sixteen-year-old – to finish high school and go on to college. When the time arrived, Gloria would go to college. Amy would stop rebelling and join her.

Ellie and Bella Sanchez met them at the station.

'Ellie, you look so young!' Elisabeth marveled. 'We've been away one year and you've dropped ten!'

'It's the bob, the short dresses – and I've dropped fifteen pounds.' Ellie shrugged, but she was pleased.

Both women were astonished at Amy's transformation.

'She went away a little girl,' Bella effervesced. 'Now she's a gorgeous young woman!'

Ellie drove them to the Hollywood Hotel in Chuck's new Pierce-Arrow, which Amy pronounced 'the cat's meow', a newly coined phrase meaning wonderful, Elisabeth interpreted.

'It wasn't his movie work that paid for it.' Ellie's smile was dry. 'It was the time he puts in with his father at the orange grove.'

Later that evening, after dinner at the Sanchez house, Ellie spirited Elisabeth away for a private talk in the kitchen. They'd shared much news in letters, but Elisabeth was impatient to hear about happenings in Hollywood.

'Beth, you won't believe the drinking that goes on!' Ellie grimaced. 'And don't look so surprised – the Eighteenth Amendment means nothing. People – particularly the young – are drinking like there's no tomorrow.' Her face lit with laughter now. 'You know how Pop likes his glass of wine with dinner? So now he's hiding himself away in the pantry and making bootleg wine for the family.'

'I gather most of the movie companies are operating out here now – or at least filming out here.' Still, Ellie's remark about Chuck's making most of his money in the orange groves pricked at her mind. 'What's the story?'

'The business is in a postwar slump. All the studios are hurting.' Ellie was serious now. 'And the cry is for gorgeous, *very* young actresses. It's Mack Sennett all over again – only more so. The way Amy's grown up in this last year she's prime material. That's one sexy girl!'

'I'm insisting Amy concentrate on this last year of high school. Then she'll go on to college.' Never mind Amy's current rebellion. 'Ellie, I want work. London was wonderful! I know,' she pushed on when Ellie seemed about to reply, 'movies are different from stage.

312

But I'm hoping somebody remembers *Jane Eyre*. I told you, it was shown all over Europe. Of course, Jerry and I never saw a cent of that money, and it's too long ago to fight for it.'

'Bob your hair,' Ellie advised. 'And dress young. That's the *schtick*.'

'I can't look like sixteen! Maybe I can get away with twenty-six or seven with some effort.' She paused. 'I'd still love to direct. I hear Lillian Gish is directing now.'

'Gish can get away with it. But women directors in general?' Ellie shook her head.

'Financially we're all right for quite a while. But I'm looking ahead.'

'Why don't you talk to Frank Osborne?' Ellie suggested. 'He's moved way up at the studio. They're turning out films like spaghetti even in this slump. But they're using the slump to cut salaries. Chuck bitches about it regularly.'

'I'll talk to Frank. Where should I go for a bob?'

Elisabeth was relieved when they were able to move back into their house. Then with Ellie along for moral support she went to one of the new beauty parlors and had her hair bobbed. Astonished to realize she liked the result. Bella Sanchez shortened all her skirts. She'd always been slim – Bella was forever scolding, 'You're so thin, a good wind will knock you over.' She experimented with make-up. The reflection in the mirror was youthful, she acknowledged, but not the ingénue that Hollywood favored. But she would talk to Frank about considering her for some parts. She'd been successful on the London stage, she bolstered her shaky self-confidence. That should mean something.

The day before Elisabeth meant to approach Frank, Amy came home in a euphoric glow, along with Gloria – now allowed to borrow the family car. With simmering unease, Elisabeth remembered the overheard conversation between Amy and Gloria that had triggered the trip to Europe. 'Tell me,' Amy pleaded. 'How many boys have you kissed?'

'Maybe a dozen. I lost count.'

'May Gloria stay for dinner?' Amy bubbled, knowing the answer would be yes.

'You two look very pleased with yourselves,' Elisabeth joshed after extending a warm welcome to Gloria. Her bobbed hair, bright lipstick, short jumper that skimmed a pencil-thin body identified her as the quintessential flapper.

'Mama, you won't believe what happened.' Amy exchanged an eloquent glance with Gloria.

'I'll believe,' Elisabeth promised. These days Amy was so dramatic. 'What happened?'

'Well, Gloria had the car today, so we were driving around. And I decided we should go over to the studio.' Elisabeth tensed. 'You know, to say hello to Mr Osborne. At first he didn't recognize me! He said I'd grown up. And then he said, yes, I was ready for grown-up parts. He wants to talk to you about a contract for me!'

'Amy, you have a year of high school to finish.' Elisabeth's heart began to pound.

'We'll have a tutor for me when I'm at the studio. Like before. I'll graduate with my class at the high school. With Gloria.'

'It's important for you to go on to college!' Elisabeth was shaken.

'I'll finish high school, with tutoring,' Amy promised, 'but I won't go to college. That was your dream, Mama – not mine.' Amy took a deep breath. 'He said I was exactly what they were looking for – I mean, for an important part in a major new picture.' Her eyes were triumphant.

'You're sure you want to do this?' Was she trying to mold Amy's life to fit her dream? She could lose Amy if she pushed too hard. Young people today thought they knew all the answers. Amy was a baby, but she was convinced she was a woman.

'I'll be so bored just going to school. I want to be a grown-up movie star.' Amy's eyes glowed. 'He said this new part is great. They'll promote me like crazy!'

A sixteen-year-old shouldn't be thinking this way.

'Mama, you go to the studio tomorrow and talk to Frank.' Up till now he'd always been 'Mr Osborne'. Now he was 'Frank'.

Frank greeted Elisabeth with warmth, yet she sensed a wariness because he knew he would have to deal with *her*. Amy was still a minor. And through the years she'd been dubbed a difficult mother because she'd made demands she felt important for Amy's wellbeing.

'Amy took my breath away when she walked into the studio. Gorgeous, sexy, and exquisitely young! Perfect for the new picture I'm casting. It's going to be a sensation.' He led her through the turmoil of the studio to his office. 'A twelve-week shooting schedule.' He waited for an astonished reaction.

'It's about time.' Elisabeth was cool. She had little respect for the customary short shooting schedules of the independents. De Mille had the right idea. He was directing far fewer films each year – and they were the best. 'The public is getting educated – it wants something better than quickies.' Frank was avid to sign Amy. All right, let him pay high.

Frank showed her into a chair that flanked his large desk – its size attesting to his growing clout at the studio.

'Of course, times have changed out here.' His smile was meant to be benevolent. 'The town's flooded with delicious young beauties, willing to work for nothing. They all want to be movie stars.'

'Frank, I'm not enthralled with the prospect of Amy resuming a movie career.' Her eyes dared him to think otherwise. 'I'd like her to have a normal senior year of high school, then go on to college.'

'She'll have a tutor, of course,' Frank pounced. 'Only because she's Amy Winston. But things have changed in the years you and Amy have been away –'

'*One* year,' Elisabeth pinpointed, annoyed now by the game Frank was playing.

'We'll spend a fortune on this film, promote it like mad. It'll make Amy a star. Not just a child star.' He paused to allow Elisabeth to digest the impact of what he offered. 'But these days money isn't what it used to be.' Elisabeth's eyes – a lifted eyebrow – told him she knew about the twenty thousand dollars a week major stars were earning. 'We pick up new girls on two- or three-year contracts at fifty dollars a week, build them up, the full treatment. Then they move into the big money. Of course, we'll do better than that for Amy,' he rushed to reassure her because she radiated contempt.

'A thousand a week,' Elisabeth said sweetly. The studio's last offer. 'I'd prefer her to stay in school –'

'Beth, you don't understand how the situation has changed! The cost of making a movie has escalated like crazy. We can't pay that kind of money for an unproven actress. I mean, as a child star she brought in the audiences, but this is a whole new ballgame.'

'It's been nice to see you again, Frank . . .' Elisabeth rose to her feet.

'You're holding me up!' His voice held an edge of desperation. He needed Amy.

'Amy has a following. People who saw her as a child star will rush to see her as a gorgeous sixteen-year-old. I can visualize the spreads in the movie magazines. A thousand a week – for two years. After that we'll talk again.'

'Wall Street lost a winner when you didn't go into the business world.' Frank was grim, but she knew the contract was as good as signed. 'A thousand a week for two years.'

Suddenly Elisabeth and Amy were swept up once more in the madness of filming. Amy was given a script. Elisabeth concentrated on working with her. Amy was determined to prove her ability as an adult actress. She knew that much of her success as a child star had been due to the personal charm she'd radiated. She listened intently while Elisabeth dissected the script line by line, reminded her that every tiny gesture, every movement of eyes or mouth or body must convey an emotion. In her early movies Amy had learned the necessity of knowing where the titles would be and to delay reactions. Now she extended her technique under her mother's tutoring.

'In pictures you have no voice,' Elisabeth reminded. 'It's not like acting in the theater. Someday,' she said with a touch of whimsy, 'we'll probably see movies with voices. But not yet.'

She brushed aside her eagerness to continue her own acting career, her success on the London stage pushed into the background. The kind of money that Hollywood offered could provide a lifetime of security for Amy and Katie. If anything happened to her, they'd be alone in the world. Money could be a safe haven for her daughters.

Frank was laying the groundwork to publicize both his film and his new young star. Amy's picture, with lush descriptions of her, appeared in *Photoplay, Shadowland, Motion Pictures*. Elisabeth knew Frank fought constantly with the studio heads for additional money to keep the ball rolling. She made it clear that there was to be no sensationalism involved.

In the last weeks of the filming Hollywood was rocked by a major scandal. Beautiful, bubbly twenty-year-old Olive Thomas – married to Mary Pickford's brother Jack and a rising star – was found a suicide in her lavish hotel suite at the Crillon in Paris. Newspaper headlines shocked the public with the revelation that Olive Thomas was a dope fiend.

'I can't believe it!' Ellie was stunned. 'I remember when she was a model for *Vogue*. I loved her in *The Tomboy*.'

'She was a Ziegfeld showgirl. She was only sixteen then,' Elisabeth recalled. Her instinct was to pack up and run from Hollywood with Amy and Katie. Drugs and bootleg liquor were everywhere, according to lurid newspaper reports. Rumors were rampant about who would be the next Hollywood victim. The story running around the movie colony was that Olive had been chasing around Montmartre in search of a supply of heroin for her addict husband. When this failed, in a drug haze she killed herself.

In this new film Amy played a fascinating young flapper, but Elisabeth laid down the rules. Amy didn't smoke, drink, or take drugs. No scene showing Amy in such a situation could be filmed. No sexy romance was to be conjured up by the writers at the movie magazines.

'I'm thirty-four but I feel like a hundred,' Elisabeth confided to Ellie. 'Amy's generation's ruling the world – we're just bystanders. Amy's playing a flapper, and I grit my teeth and say nothing when Frank has her dancing atop a table – shimmying as though this was the road to heaven. But it's crazy.'

'I look at Ira, and I shudder. What kind of a world are he and Katie going to face? Will all this madness disappear?'

Agents approached Elisabeth, were dismissed. As long as Amy appeared in films, *she* would be her agent, personal manager, chaperone. Every male at the studio knew that he wasn't to take liberties with Amy Winston.

Frank was blunt. 'She's jail-bait. No hanky-panky with Amy.'

The twelve weeks of filming expanded into thirteen – amidst loud groans from the men at the top. Still, Frank seemed undisturbed.

'It's going to be a terrific success,' he predicted while they watched a full run-through in the projection room. Elisabeth realized he was staking his position at the studio on this. He meant Amy to be his 'big find'. He was already demanding high-priced writers for her next film. 'Amy's going to be big in her first grown-up movie. We have to handle her just right.'

Reluctantly Amy returned to routine classes at her high school – waiting for the premiere of her movie in New York and for the studio to choose a second film. 'But even if I'm not working I'm on salary,' Amy gloated. Meanwhile, she was campaigning for a car of her own. She'd be seventeen in December, she kept reminding her mother.

'Gloria got her own car on her seventeenth birthday,' Amy reiterated at steady intervals, 'and she's not even working.'

'Gloria has a father who owns three orange groves,' Elisabeth pointed out. But it wasn't so much the money she feared, as the freedom owning a car would provide Amy. She was terrified, too, that Amy shared Gloria's love for speed – so like Ben's fascination for fast cars.

Both Elisabeth and Amy fretted at the delay in releasing the picture, but Elisabeth understood that Frank was determined to build Amy into a major flapper star. They were to attend the premiere in New York. All the movie magazines would send reporters and photographers to cover it. Elisabeth knew that despite Amy's show of confidence, she was terrified of what the trade magazines – as opposed to the movie magazines – would say about her performance.

Katie remained with Hallie in Hollywood while Elisabeth and Amy, along with a studio entourage, headed for New York for the early November premiere. Elisabeth was ever conscious that Paul's second Broadway play, which had opened to fine reviews, was still running. She secretly planned to attend the matinée the afternoon before they were to return to Hollywood. But the major deal, she reminded herself, was to guide Amy through this first big premiere at a Broadway movie palace.

The studio put them all up at the posh Ritz-Carlton. Amy was interviewed by reporters from the movie magazines. Vivacious, self-confident on the surface, she was, Elisabeth knew, scared to death inside.

'Can't you just hear what the kids at school will say if nobody likes the picture?'

'It's going to do well.' In some ways, Elisabeth thought tenderly, Amy was still a little girl.

Aware of the public's reaction to the Olive Thomas suicide and the revelation that both Thomas and her husband were drug addicts, the studio provided Amy – in these frenetic four days in New York – with the constant presence of mother and director. The flapper might be idealized, but a certain Victorianism lingered with the American public. A fine line must be observed.

Each night Elisabeth called home to talk with Katie and Hallie. After the premiere – where audience reception was gratifying – she phoned to report on this.

'Are you bringing me a present from New York?' Katie demanded. 'But I'll love you even if you don't,' she effervesced before her mother could confirm this.

On the morning after the premiere Frank rushed to their suite with the morning newspapers. The movie critics loved Amy.

'We've got to follow up fast with something sensational.' Frank was euphoric.

'Wrong word,' Elisabeth corrected. 'Great.'

On Saturday afternoon Amy was to be interviewed by a reporter from *Ladies Home Journal*. Elisabeth plotted for Frank to sit in on this so that she could attend a Broadway matinée.

'I can't bear coming to New York and not seeing at least one play,' she told him indulgently.

'Go,' he ordered. 'I'll be there with Amy.'

An hour before curtain up Elisabeth was at the box office. Instinct told her that even though the play was a success, she'd be able to buy a single ticket somewhere in the house. She was joyous at obtaining a seventh row orchestra seat.

She left the box office to roam on the side streets of Broadway, where the theaters were located. *The Jest*, with John and Lionel Barrymore, was a huge success. *Sally* was the big musical of the year. She gazed raptly at the Morosco Theater where Eugene O'Neill's first long play, *Beyond the Horizon*, was playing. She and Paul had loved his short plays. She thought wistfully of the months she'd appeared on the London stage. Would she ever act in theater again?

Elisabeth forced her mind back to reality. Amy was embarked on a new career in a field she loved. In time, she plotted, they might be able to afford to produce themselves. That was where the fabulous money was. Pickford, Chaplin, Fairbanks had proved that. *And she would direct.*

New York, too, she thought, was full of ghosts. She remembered the beautiful weeks with Paul back in those early movie days – when they'd worked at the fly-by-night studio in the Bronx. She remembered the cheap rooming house where she and Amy had lived, with Jerry in a room right down the hall. She'd crammed so much living in the eighteen years since she'd fled from London with David.

But Bella Sanchez's voice drifted across her mind now. Ever romantic Bella, who was forever trying to introduce her to some unattached man: 'Beth, the best years of your life lie ahead of you. Don't shut them out.'

She remembered those last moments with Paul at the beach house. 'Whenever I'm free, I'll come to you. Wherever you are, I'll find you.' And she'd said to him, 'I'll be waiting. However long it takes.' She hadn't waited, she rebuked herself. But Neil had come into her life at a vulnerable moment – and he so reminded her of Paul.

It was sweet to know about his success on Broadway, that in less than an hour she'd be watching his play in performance, though not the kind of a play he yearned to write. This was commercial theater – light comedy – designed to provide Doris with the lifestyle she demanded – and to assure his access to his son. But she was sure he would be following Amy's career, because that provided him with knowledge of *her* whereabouts.

Stop this, she ordered herself. Be realistic. She was thinking more romantically than Bella, pining for what was not to be. She had two daughters she adored, wonderful Hallie, a comfortable life. Stop being greedy!

But part of her heart would always be with Paul.

Chapter Thirty-six

Elisabeth shared Amy's elation when *Variety* wrote, 'Amy Winston's performance was superb. She portrayed every nuance of Laura's character with verve.' A natural instinct for creating a character was emerging in Amy, Elisabeth observed with towering pleasure. And she was like a sponge – she absorbed every bit of coaching. Never quite trusting her instincts, dependent on her mother's approval.

Now the studio was making a frenzied effort to line up new scripts for her. Elisabeth knew the studio heads had decided to make Amy a star. That was the way it happened. Yet she worried that in their haste they might settle for mediocre material.

'They want to keep her working,' Chuck said drily. 'They have to pay her every week.'

Elisabeth tried to persuade them to bring in Chuck to work on screenplays for Amy. They brushed this aside.

'Chuck's all right for the quickies,' Frank told her. 'We need somebody like Elinor Glyn or Frances Marion to write for Amy. A big name screenwriter.'

Elisabeth was concerned when the studio abandoned the long shooting schedule provided for her first film. Amy was going from one movie to another without a break between. By the end of the year, she'd completed three additional pictures. Fan mail was beginning to pour in.

Elisabeth felt guilty relief that Amy's working schedule – limited by contract to a maximum of ten hours a day, six days a week, when fourteen and sixteen hours were common in the movie world – limited her social life. Elisabeth was unnerved by the stories she heard of other very young actresses who managed to drink too much, to flit from man to man, and in shocking numbers to become involved in the burgeoning drug scene. Each day Amy came home to a quiet dinner and homework.

Still, Amy managed long, earnest telephone conversations with Gloria. For brief intervals she attended classes at the high school. She wasn't entirely cut off from teenagers who lived normal lives, Elisabeth comforted herself. And this was the life Amy had chosen.

At the first of the New Year Elisabeth threatened to confront the studio heads about pushing Amy too hard, but Amy sided with them.

'Mama, I want to work!'

'You need a rest,' Elisabeth insisted. 'This is insane! And these four-week shooting schedules are cutting down the quality of your pictures. The fine directors like de Mille have cut back to doing no more than three pictures a year. I'm tired of their ignoring my complaints at the studio. Either they allow more time per picture in the future, or I'll go to court to break your contract.'

'Mama, you wouldn't do that to me,' Amy wailed. But Elisabeth saw ambivalence taking root in her. 'I'm not as good as I was in the first one?'

'How could you be, the way they're rushing through?'

'All right. You talk to them.' Amy was shaken at the thought that she might be appearing at less than her best.

To Elisabeth's astonishment – and Amy's – the studio bigwigs latched on to the publicity value of Elisabeth's taking them to court. 'God, the newspapers – the sob sisters – will eat this up.' Frank glowed as he and Elisabeth emerged from a top-level meeting. 'And you'll win. The studio will treat Amy's films with more respect in the future.'

Elisabeth was uncomfortable in the subterfuge of a plotted law suit, all expenses paid by the studio. The studio heads were triumphant. The publicity was stupendous. Elisabeth worried that Amy was acquiring a bad sense of values. But Amy's shooting schedules became longer.

In June Amy graduated from high school. Afterwards the studio gave a dinner party for her in the dining room at the prestigious Alexandria Hotel. At Elisabeth's insistence Ellie and Chuck, along with Gloria, were invited.

'Chuck says he never saw any actress move up as fast as Amy,' Ellie whispered to Elisabeth as they sat at their table in the Alexandria dining room and nibbled at Beluga caviar. The three tables that accommodated the guests were beautifully laid, the crystal and china exquisite. An orchestra played soft background music.

'She seems happy.' Yet anxiety tugged at Elisabeth. 'I worry, though, that she's so committed to acting. These are years when she should be having fun. Not working.' Their conversation was masked by the lively chatter about the table.

'To Amy receiving all those fan letters every week is like receiving love,' Ellie said gently. 'She wants to keep them coming. And don't tell me I sound like I've been reading too much Freud. Amy lost her own father, then Jerry. Those were tough upsets for a little kid. Now she's getting all this love from her audiences, and she's sopping it up.'

'I've wanted her to have a normal childhood,' Elisabeth gazed down the table at Amy and Gloria, both euphoric at being here, 'to enjoy the high school years and college –'

'Amy will never go to college.' Ellie's smile was sympathetic. 'But hey, that's not the end of the world. Katie will go to college.'

'I'm forever worrying. If not about one, then the other. I spend so many hours at the studio with Amy, I'm afraid I'm cheating Katie.'

'Katie loves life as it is. Stop worrying.'

'I can't help it. Sometimes I tell myself I shouldn't have allowed Amy to move back into the business.'

'Honey, you were acting at her age, and you loved it.'

'I was so much older at seventeen than Amy is. Of course, I loved the audience reaction – every performer does. But even more I found a wonderful pleasure in working to bring a character to life. But for Amy it's like you said: she's seeking love. That means somewhere along the line she's been cheated. I let her down.'

'Fate let her down. You weren't responsible for David's being murdered, for Jerry's rushing off to fight in the war and dying.'

'I think Amy and Katie know how much I love them.' A hint of bitterness tainted Elisabeth's smile. 'I wasn't always sure about *my* mother. Thank God for Grandma.'

'Amy and Katie know you love them.'

'I just want them to be healthy and happy. Ellie, how do you know what you're doing is right?'

'You cross your fingers and pray. Like Chuck always says –' she turned to Chuck for an instant, but he was involved in conversation with the studio's new make-up artist – 'life's a series of hurdles. If you're a good jumper, you make it.'

Elisabeth was an absorbed observer of happenings in the movie field. She knew that, while Amy was earning what seemed a fabulous salary, the huge profits came to those stars who produced their own pictures. Like Mary Pickford, Douglas Fairbanks, and Charlie Chaplin. Now a daring project took root in her mind. In another year, perhaps two, she would produce Amy's movies herself. There was no aspect of the business that she hadn't learned. Why not?

Amy's weekly paycheck was divided into three parts: the percentage Elisabeth allotted to herself as Amy's personal manager, the money deposited in the bank in Amy's name, and the part Peter Sanchez invested for Amy in stocks. All solid stocks, he always assured her – and no buying on margin, despite all the fortunes being made these days by ordinary people who knew nothing about the stock market.

She could produce and direct, Elisabeth plotted. Rent cheap space on Poverty Row. She'd have the initial financing – Amy's money. With that much seed money plus a star – Amy – additional financing would be easy to raise. She'd search for a novel in the public domain, that would require no royalties. Have Chuck do a scenario. He did a beautiful job on *Jane Eyre* and *Wuthering Heights* – though producers pigeonholed him for 'quickies'. She'd rent sets from a major studio – that happened all the time; rent equipment, arrange terms with a film lab. She'd been through this when she and Jerry produced *Jane Eyre* and *Wuthering Heights*. She knew all the angles.

This couldn't happen until Amy's contract was over – but she'd start looking now for a novel that could be adapted. Be ready when the right moment arrived. All at once she felt fully alive. She hadn't felt this way since London.

On one of those rare days when Amy was between films, she and Gloria spent the morning on the Santa Monica beach.

'Amy, those two fellas playing ball are trying to pick us up,' Gloria whispered. 'I'll bet they recognized you.'

'Let's leave,' Amy said instantly. She didn't want to be chased by boys because she was a movie star. Well, almost a star, as Hallie kept saying.

'It might be fun,' Gloria scolded. But she was rising to her feet.

'Let's go to the house and have lunch.' It would be nice to go out with a boy who didn't know she was Amy Winston. But there was never time just to play. Anyhow, she felt all tense and flustered with boys. Why couldn't she be like Gloria?

'I have something to tell you,' Gloria began importantly when they were in the car. 'I just made up my mind last night.' She kept her eyes on the road as she drove. 'Of course, my mother thinks she made the decision. I filled out the forms just to shut her up. I didn't mean to go through with it.'

'What are you talking about?' Amy was puzzled.

'I'm going off to college in September.'

'You said you'd never!' Amy gaped in disbelief.

'I know. But Ralph is going up to Berkeley – and if I'm up there, too, it'll be the berries. And I'll be getting away from home.' She exuded a blissful sigh.

'But they have all kinds of rules on campus. That's what you told me!'

'If you're smart, you know how to get around them.' Her eyes left the road for a moment to rest speculatively on Amy. 'I know it's late, but you could probably get in. Your grades were better than mine. Come on, Amy,' she coaxed. 'Ralph knows some real sheiks.'

'I'm doing too well with pictures,' Amy hedged. In front of a camera she felt good, confident. Not even Gloria realized how scared she was of meeting boys. She was going on eighteen, and she'd never had a real date. Mama wouldn't even allow the studio publicity department to give out stories about 'Amy Winston's new young romance'. Though after Olive Thomas's suicide the studio had issued a warning to all their young actresses about 'being involved romantically'.

'I know.' Gloria sighed. 'You can't give up all that fun.'

'I'll miss you.' Amy was wistful. 'Now I'm going to insist that Mama let me buy a car for my eighteenth birthday.'

Elisabeth was concerned that Amy would be deprived of Gloria's presence in her life except for an occasional weekend when Gloria would drive home. With high school graduation Amy lost touch with all other young people her own age. Elisabeth tried to provide direction for Amy in these first days of Gloria's absence. She arranged for movies to be shown right in their living room, took Amy to Bullock's on a shopping spree. Yet Elisabeth was also uneasy about Amy's closeness with Gloria. She sensed an unnerving rebellion in

Gloria, was aware of a lack of parental responsibility in the family. Gloria's parents – wartime profiteers – were constantly dashing off on trips that left her alone at home with a housekeeper.

Elisabeth worried, too, about the wild party scene in Hollywood. 'It's an awful time to be raising daughters,' she said to Ellie. 'And I know – this craziness is not just in Hollywood.' She forestalled Ellie's frequent comment. 'It's everywhere.'

'Chuck says the studio bigwigs are tearing their hair out because young actresses show up on the set too bleary-eyed to be photographed well. For a lot of them the studio's become a revolving door. They're signed up with the belief they have a lot of promise – and six months later, out.'

'Amy's restless. I can feel it. And she and Katie – despite the age difference – are at each other's throats half the time.'

'I know. My sister-in-law with the two girls says she feels more referee than mother. Sometimes I'm glad Ira's an only child.'

On Amy's eighteenth birthday in early December Elisabeth allowed her to buy a Pierce-Arrow runabout. Earlier Amy had taken a series of driving lessons. This didn't mean *she* wouldn't be at the studio every day, Elisabeth told herself. In truth, Amy wanted her there. At the end of every scene Amy turned to her for approval. Amy knew she would allow no short cuts that might be detrimental to her performance. And no man in the studio dared to lay a hand on Amy when her mother was always present.

At Christmas time Gloria was to arrive home for what she called their 'winter break'. Amy was joyous that she would have a whole week between films just at that period.

'Can Gloria stay with us for a few days?' Amy asked, expecting approval. 'Her parents are leaving right after Christmas for a week at Acapulco.'

'Of course Gloria can stay with us.' Elisabeth loved having the girls' friends stay over – a reaction, she realized, to her own parents' rejection of what they'd called 'an invasion of strangers'. With Gloria home how could her parents go dashing off to Acapulco? At intervals, she recalled, Ellie made snide remarks about Gloria's parents trying to be as young as their daughter. 'When Gloria's older sister made them grandparents, they were horrified. All of a sudden they were "the older generation".'

During Gloria's first four days home she and Amy were limited to long night-time phone conversations. Then Gloria's parents took off, and Gloria arrived with her luggage, her latest jazz records, and her car. Elisabeth relished Amy's obvious pleasure at having Gloria in the house – even while she worried that Gloria was 'fast'.

The two girls slept late the next morning, dawdled over strawberry pancakes and coffee Hallie lovingly served them, then took off. Now Elisabeth went into Katie's room to coax her into wakefulness. This would be a day devoted to Katie.

Always the one in their friendship to make concessions, Amy agreed that they would take Gloria's car. Gloria adored driving. She was still somewhat intimidated.

'Gloria, slow down,' she ordered when the speedometer rose perilously. She knew Gloria was tense, but she didn't probe. When Gloria was ready, she'd spill whatever bothered her.

'I've got a problem,' Gloria admitted now. 'You've got to help me.'

'What's the problem?'

'I'm pregnant. About two months.'

'Oh, Gloria!' She gaped in a mixture of astonishment and alarm. 'How did that happen?'

'The usual way, silly!'

'But you told me you carried a condom in your vanity. You said that kept you from being caught.' Sometimes she felt as though she and Gloria lived in separate worlds. Gloria *did* things. She pretended to do them in movies.

'Yeah, I know. I *do*. It works when the condom is on the fella – not in the girl's vanity. I guess we both got hot and bothered on the back seat and forgot. And we'd both had hooch before . . .'

'Then you'll get married.' Amy strived to be practical. 'It happens all the time.'

'Ralph and I are too young!' Gloria's voice was strident. 'Besides, he doesn't want to get married. His folks would kill him. We talked about it a lot.' She was striving for calm now. 'I have to have an abortion. Of course, we can't let my folks or his folks know. Amy, you have to help me.'

'How can I help?' Amy was bewildered. 'Oh, you mean you'll need money. Sure . . .' She'd manage that, somehow.

'Not that.' Gloria was impatient. 'Ralph told me how the movie studios always have names on hand. For actresses who get pregnant or actors and actresses who get – you *know*, one of those diseases.'

'You mean, you want me to get the name of a doctor from somebody at the studio?' Amy was shaken. How could she do that?

'Ask. Tell them it's for somebody very close to you. If they pretend not to know, throw a tantrum.' A wry glint in her eyes. 'They may think it's for you, but they'll give you a name.'

'I'll talk to Frank,' Amy decided after a moment. Would they believe *she* was pregnant? She felt hot color flood her face. She'd never even kissed a boy except for the cameras – and that was always faked.

'Today,' Gloria insisted. 'It has to be done before I go back to school. Let's drive over to the studio now.'

Amy managed to talk with Frank in his office. Her voice unsteady, she announced her mission. She saw Frank's face pale.

'It's not for me,' she said quickly. 'My best friend's home from college. She's desperate. It's not for me,' she insisted, her eyes holding Frank's.

'I know that,' he said gently after a moment. 'I'll set up an appointment.'

'Right away, Frank –'

'Quickly,' he promised and smiled. 'You might say the studio's a regular customer. Stay right here.'

The following morning Amy went with Gloria to the small, posh private sanitarium in Beverly Hills that catered to movie celebrities. She saw the glint of astonishment when the nurse realized it was Gloria and not she who was here for an abortion.

'Go out and have an early lunch,' a nurse encouraged. 'By the time you're back, you can drive her home.'

Weeks after Gloria had returned to college, Amy was still haunted by what had occurred. Was something wrong with her that she couldn't imagine ever doing *that* with a boy? But she wasn't like one of those women she heard the crews whispering about sometimes. They said that Alla Nazimova – whom Mama said was a great actress – made love with women. She was a lesbian. Though she'd never let on to it to anybody but Gloria, she made sure to see every picture in which Douglas Fairbanks appeared. He was gorgeous. She just wasn't ready to do *that* with anybody.

Early in February of the new year Amy was cast in a movie with an actor new to the studio.

'You'll like Keith Lindsay,' Frank assured her on the first morning of shooting. 'The big boys plan on building him into a major star.' But he seemed apprehensive when he turned to her mother. 'They'd like Keith to escort Amy to the Hollywood premiere. Now don't get upset, Beth. It won't be publicized as a "big romance". Just dinner at the Alexandria, then the premiere. It's his first role other than a couple of bit parts. It'll be good for both Keith and Amy,' he said with a show of enthusiasm.

'It sound like fun.' Amy was exuberant. 'I want to do it, Mama.' There was a new defiance in her eyes. She was eighteen years old. When would Mama admit she was grown-up?

Elisabeth conceded that Keith Lindsay seemed charming and bright. But she suspected his talents were limited. The first week of shooting confirmed this. For a while he would survive on astonishing good looks and an ingratiating manner. It was evident that he was the fair-haired boy of the studio. Other producers sought to build another Rudolph Valentino. This studio meant to create a new Douglas Fairbanks.

On the second Saturday of their filming schedule Amy, unfamiliarly starry-eyed, told Elisabeth that she was going to dinner with Keith the next evening and afterwards to a party at Frank's house.

'I'm old enough to go out with a boy,' Amy said pointedly. 'And Frank and his wife have a party almost every month. They didn't invite us because you always said no.' Amy was straining to be casual. *She didn't go to Frank's parties – or any others – because she didn't want Amy to be part of the movie colony social life.* 'But he invited Keith and a date. And that's me.'

'I'm sure you'll have a good time.' Elisabeth realized it would be a bad move to try to stop this. She must let go. 'And I know Frank won't let the party become wild.' True, she comforted herself.

Most clear-thinking members of the movie colony were disturbed by the notoriety being thrust upon the industry. Church groups were denouncing the movie world. In Chicago Cardinal Mundelein had published a tract, *The Danger of Hollywood: A Warning to Young Girls*. 'Fatty' Arbuckle was soon to face his third trial for murder and Paramount was forced to destroy his unreleased films, thereby losing over a million dollars.

Now the industry was trying to deal with the murder of popular director William Desmond Taylor on the night of 1 February.

Newspapers blared the news that on the night of the murder two major movie stars – Mary Miles Minter and Mabel Normand – had visited his apartment. Police investigation revealed that Taylor had carried on affairs with Mabel Normand, Mary Miles Minter, and Minter's mother at the same time. Hollywood gossips said that neither of the two actresses would ever work in films again. Movie magnates were terrified of retaliation at the box office.

Word ricocheted about the movie colony that the major producers and distributors had formed an organization to police the industry and that a man named Will Hayes had been hired to head it. A press conference had been scheduled to announce this to the nation.

Chuck was cynical. 'It'll last a year – this crusade to clean up movie morals. Then everything will go back to what it was. Except that most of it will be hidden with greater care.'

The studio was enthralled at a hint of romance between Amy and Keith. Each weekend they had a decorous date – in clear view of an admiring audience. While Amy played young flappers, her roles portrayed her as a 'good' girl at heart – not 'fast'. Keith appeared a clean-cut young Douglas Fairbanks. This was a perfect couple for the current mood of movie audiences.

But Elisabeth was anxious. In an era of super-sophistication among the young, Amy was amazingly innocent. And she harbored an uneasy suspicion that Keith Lindsay was an opportunist, using Amy to improve his own image. She never voiced her suspicion. She knew that even Ellie would dismiss this as absurd. Everybody liked Keith.

Was she being overly solicitous? Were her suspicions what Chuck would call 'an anxious mother thing'?

Chapter Thirty-seven

Amy heard the alarm go off in her mother's bedroom. In fifteen minutes Mama would come in to make sure she was awake. She used to hate getting out of bed so early in the morning. Now she couldn't wait to get to the studio. Because Keith would be there. She lay back against her pillows and thought about all the sweet things he'd said to her on their last date. Every young actress in Hollywood – and some not so young – was after him. He didn't say so in words, but he made it clear he was crazy about her.

Was he afraid of Mama? That she'd be angry and make things rough for him at the studios? Frank said Keith would be in her, Amy's, next two pictures. She'd die if Mama spoiled that for him. But she was a grown woman now. It was time Mama stopped treating her like a little girl.

With any luck at all they'd be finishing up the picture today. It had to be edited and all, but the premiere was already scheduled for three weeks from now. Oh, she had a fitting today, probably at their lunch break, for the dress she was to wear. The studio designer was fitting it herself. She was to attend the premiere with Keith. That was great publicity for the picture.

Gloria said she was absolutely dying of jealousy because *she* was working with Keith. Only Gloria knew he kissed her goodnight now. In the car. Gloria couldn't understand why they weren't necking madly: '*Honey, how do you expect to hang on to him, with all those girls just panting to drag him onto the back seat?*'

Sometimes she wanted to do those things that Gloria said every flapper did these days. Sometimes – when he held her in his arms before the camera – she almost forgot they were playing parts. Today they had what Gloria would call a 'hot' scene. Of course, Frank would expect them to fake the 'big kiss'. She hoped Keith wouldn't fake it.

The morning was spent in rehearsing. Then she went to the wardrobe room for her fitting, managed – at her mother's insistence – to eat a sandwich and drink a cup of tea before returning to the set.

'OK, kids, you know what I expect of you,' Frank told them as he prepared to direct them through the final scenes of the film. 'Say the lines that fit the action, and say them as though you mean them, even though the audience can't hear. The camera *can*.' He gestured to the string quartet to begin playing the mood music.

They used the improvised dialogue that had carried them through the lengthy morning rehearsal.

'You're so beautiful,' Keith said. 'When I'm with you, I only want to hold you in my arms.'

But Amy was conscious of something more intense in Keith's voice now. He drew her into his arms, so close her heart began to pound. She felt *that* pressed against her. She managed a response. But this wasn't play-acting. Keith was making love to *her* – Amy. His eyes told her this.

'I'll die if you go all the way to London,' she whispered. 'How will I survive?' It was dialogue that would run beneath the film, but their thoughts were quite different.

His mouth came down on hers. This wasn't his usual goodnight kiss. Sweet and tender. This was what Gloria called 'Wow!'

'All right,' Frank directed, 'break now – come up for air. But slowly. You're both shaken . . .'

Amy didn't hear Frank or the background music or the voices that drifted in from an adjoining stage. All she heard was the pounding of her heart.

Elisabeth knew that everyone at the studio was enthralled by the romance blossoming before their eyes. Amy Winston and Keith Lindsay were the perfect young lovers – on-screen and off. They went immediately into a second film and were together off-screen as much as possible. At home Amy's conversation was peppered with references to Keith. The studio was ecstatic. The movie magazines were lyrical in their description of the two rising young stars.

Keith was amazingly handsome, Elisabeth conceded – but she still felt that his talent was meager.

'He'll get by for a while on those looks,' Chuck surmised. 'But you're right – he won't be around for the long haul.'

She tried to dig up background on Keith but ran into the fanciful reports of the publicity department.

'You don't like Keith,' Amy accused after a brief encounter between him and her mother. 'Everybody else *does*.'

'Of course, I like him,' Elisabeth lied. 'I'm just baffled by the way he avoids talking about his family. Whenever I ask him anything, he changes the subject.'

'He hasn't asked me to marry him.' Amy was almost defiant. 'I think you scare him.'

'Amy, you're so young.' She tried to be casual. Amy wanted to marry him.

'You were sixteen when you married my father,' Amy reminded. 'I'll be nineteen in December. Keith's twenty-three.' She paused. 'Anyhow, his father died when he was four. His mother remarried eight years ago. Keith hated his stepfather – he left home. You can't blame him for that.'

In July Amy's contract came up for renewal. The two studio heads screamed when Elisabeth presented her new salary demands.

'Beth, you're out of your mind! You know we're in a postwar depression. Plus all this insanity in the press about boycotts from church groups, women's clubs, anti-vice committees,' the more melo-dramatic of the two chiefs lashed out at her.

'That won't affect Amy's pictures.' Elisabeth remained unim-pressed. 'Audiences love her.'

'You're crucifying us,' his partner wailed. 'We've been good to Amy. Another year at the same salary – then we'll be in a better position to up the figures.'

'Six months,' Elisabeth compromised. 'I'll approve a six-month extension. Then we'll talk again.'

Late in August, after a Sunday evening with Keith, Amy floated into the house in an aura of bliss.

'I'm marrying Keith,' she told Elisabeth, her face luminous. 'The first Sunday in December. But, Mama, don't let the studio insist on a big wedding. I told Keith I want us to be married here at home, with just family and the Sanchezes. And I want it to be a religious ceremony.'

'Of course, darling.' Elisabeth's mind was in chaos. Maybe Ellie was right. She wouldn't like any boy that Amy wished to marry at this time.

'Keith says he's willing to convert.' Another surprise for Elisabeth. 'Uncle Peter will tell us how this can be arranged.' Peter and Bella Sanchez had been given the status of uncle and aunt. 'And the studio is *not* to send photographers and reporters to the wedding. It'll be a very private occasion.'

'I'll make sure everybody understands.' How could she be talking so calmly about this? And she was astonished – but touched and pleased – that Amy wanted a religious ceremony. That was Peter and Bella's influence, bless them: the Hanukkah parties every year, the Seders at Passover, the observance of Sukkoth – the harvest celebration. Amy and Katie's attendance at the synagogue with her and the Sanchezes on the High Holidays.

Often in the days ahead Elisabeth's thoughts strayed to her own first secret wedding at the Registry Office in London. Would David have liked Keith? And her thoughts focused often on Paul. She knew he had another play coming up on Broadway next autumn. From *Variety* she gathered it was another light comedy, not the kind of play that Paul yearned to write. But Doris was demanding.

Despite the very small, private wedding she'd planned, Amy decided to wear a formal wedding gown. The studio designer created a masterpiece in white satin and lace, with a small veil.

'I know it's silly,' she confided endearingly to Elisabeth, 'but I want to always remember this day.'

'Darling, it's not silly at all.'

'It's silly for me to be a flower girl.' Katie grimaced in disdain. 'I'm too old for that.' But Amy and her mother knew she was delighted with her role.

Keith bought a showplace house for himself and Amy in Beverly Hills. Amy confided that the studio had advanced him the money for the down payment. Elisabeth winced when she heard the size of the mortgage. She conceded a housekeeper was necessary, considering studio working hours, but she was unnerved when she learned Keith had also hired a maid and a gardener.

'Is it a furnished house?' Elisabeth remembered that on occasion houses were sold furnished.

'No. I was thinking – couldn't I take money out of the bank to buy our furniture?'

'Of course. It's your bank account.'

'Mama . . .' Amy seemed to be searching for words. 'Nothing's going to change with us because I'm marrying Keith. I mean, you'll keep on managing my career? Managing the money? You'll be at the studio with me every day?'

'Amy, yes.' She pushed down an instinct to reach out and pull Amy into her arms. She seemed so vulnerable, so unsure of herself.

'I'm not leaving the family – Keith's becoming part of it.'

'Amy, I'll always be here for you, don't ever forget that.'

'Keith says you're awesome.' Amy glowed now. 'I mean, the way you battle the studio for me.'

'Ma!' Katie's effervescent voice came to them from the foyer. She'd just returned from school. 'The kids are saying Amy's marrying Keith.' She charged into the living room with her usual breakneck speed. 'I thought nobody was supposed to know.'

Elisabeth sighed. 'Somebody always leaks the word at the studio. But the wedding will be private.' She turned to Amy. 'I promise you, darling.'

To throw avid fans and movie magazine reporters off the scent, Elisabeth sent out via Hallie a false report about the wedding's taking place a week later. Despite this Elisabeth was furious to realize photographers and news people were staked out in front of the house even as Amy – with Katie and Hallie in attendance – pulled the exquisite wedding gown about her slim yet curvaceous figure.

Peeking from behind the drapes, Elisabeth saw Keith arrive in his brand-new Duesenberg, an extravagance that shocked Elisabeth. She was startled to intercept a private signal between him and a pair of reporters. Keith had alerted the press. He knew Amy didn't want this, she railed in silence as she walked to the door to admit him.

With the few guests seated in a semicircle, Katie – adorable in pale pink silk – scattered rose petals along the path to the *chuppah*. With Chuck as his best man, Keith waited for Amy to be escorted to the *chuppah* by her mother. The scent of roses, banked about the living room, was achingly sweet. Sentimental tears streamed down Hallie's face while the rabbi performed the marriage service. Even Katie and Ira seemed impressed by the occasion. But Elisabeth could not erase from her mind the conviction that Keith had deliberately violated Amy's wish for the absence of press on this very special day.

With the studio's blessing Amy and Keith took off for a week's honeymoon in San Francisco – a 450-mile drive from Hollywood.

Elisabeth worried about their speeding up the coast in Keith's new Duesenberg. Please God, let him drive carefully. She longed to say to Amy, 'Call me when you arrive,' but she knew she mustn't.

The following Sunday – while Elisabeth spent most of the day waiting to hear – Amy called from their new house. She sounded rapturous, Elisabeth thought in relief. Maybe she was all wrong about Keith. Maybe he hadn't alerted the press to the actual date of the wedding. It was so easy to jump to conclusions.

On Monday morning Elisabeth was at the set as usual. Life seemed hardly changed. Frank was gloating, Elisabeth thought, because there was something electric between Amy and Keith that the camera was sure to pick up. Amy was so happy. How could she begrudge her precious daughter that? This marriage would work out, she promised herself, despite all her earlier misgivings.

The current picture was finished, and received fine reviews. Again, with only a two-day break, Amy and Keith embarked on another film. Without discussing this yet with Amy, Elisabeth had chosen the novel that she meant to have adapted for the screen as Amy's first movie for Amy Winston Productions. Amy would play the title character in Jane Austen's *Emma*. She locked out of her mind the realization that there was no role that Keith could play in this.

Elisabeth was shaken when Amy approached her in spring of the new year with a request to be given the bank book and stock certificates that her mother held for her.

'Now that I'm a grown woman – a married woman – I should be able to handle the money myself.' Yet Amy seemed uncomfortable about this.

'No problem, Amy.' Why did she suddenly feel uneasy? 'The stock certificates are in a safe deposit box at the bank. I'll get them for you tomorrow. But remember, Peter chose carefully. They're solid stocks that pay you decent dividends.'

'Keith wants to look them over. Before he came out here, he worked for a brokerage office. He knows all about stocks.'

'Peter says we must never buy on margin,' Elisabeth warned. 'He says it's terribly dangerous.'

'Uncle Peter's a darling,' Amy said tenderly. 'But Keith says he tends to be an old fogy about some things.'

Peter wasn't an old fogy, Elisabeth told herself in silence. He was a shrewd man. But to Amy and Keith's generation anybody over thirty-five was an old fogy. Instinct told her that Amy Winston Productions would never happen – unless Keith decreed it. She herself was now a personal manager with a client stable of one.

In the months ahead – while Amy and Keith continued to be cast as the romantic interest in the studio line-up of films – Elisabeth worried about Amy and Keith's escalating lifestyle. She suspected that none of Amy's salary went into the bank or to buy stocks these days. Keith insisted they must add a large wing to their new house, to provide space for a projection room and an indoor swimming pool. And she knew his salary was only a third of Amy's.

'Keith says fans expect us to put up a show of fancy living,' Amy said defensively when Elisabeth tried to talk to her about their soaring expenses. 'He says it's time we started entertaining.'

By late summer the new wing was finished and furnished. Amy and Keith gave a spectacular party. In the course of the evening Elisabeth gave Ellie and Chuck a tour of the house.

Chuck whistled eloquently. 'They're living like they're Mary Pickford and Douglas Fairbanks.'

'The younger Golden Couple,' Ellie drawled, but her eyes were sympathetic.

Elisabeth tried to discuss Amy and Keith's financial situation with Amy, but a wall had been erected between them.

'Mama, we're fine,' Amy insisted. 'We're both adults – we know what we're doing.'

Meaning, Elisabeth understood, she was not to ask questions or offer advice. Amy's fan mail was soaring, and Keith was convinced this was the result of the huge amount of space they were grabbing in the fan magazines. Stories about their 'palatial estate in Beverly Hills' appeared in every movie magazine. Every party was described in lavish detail.

Keith was making clumsy hints that Elisabeth was to insist on a huge increase on Amy's new contract – 'maybe a percentage of the profits'. He seethed over the length of his own contract – not to expire for another two years and providing for only three hundred dollars a week. Elisabeth strained to be polite to Keith on all occasions for Amy's sake. She sensed that he was annoyed that she continued to guide Amy's career.

'He's jealous.' Ellie was blunt. 'He sees Amy earning so much more than him. I know,' she forestalled Elisabeth's retort, 'he's yelling the studio should be paying Amy more, but he wishes *he* was the big wage earner and his little wife earning a pittance. The male attitude.'

'And he wants Amy to earn more so he can spend more,' Elisabeth interpreted.

'He kept telling Chuck at that last dinner party that he thought he and Amy should turn in their cars for twin Stutzes.'

The evening before Elisabeth was to sit down with the studio chiefs to discuss Amy's new contract, Amy dropped by the house alone. Ostensibly she was there to deliver a new bathing suit she'd promised Katie.

'Katie's asleep,' Elisabeth told her. 'I'll give it to her in the morning. She'll be thrilled.' But her eyes were questioning. She sensed Amy was here for another reason.

'You talk contracts tomorrow, right?' All at once Amy seemed self-conscious.

'Right.'

'I know this sounds crazy, but it's terribly important to me. Once you've settled on a figure, ask the studio to scramble the salaries so that most of my raise goes to Keith. You know, a new contract for him . . .' Her smile pleaded for acquiescence.

'You're sure you want to do this?' Elisabeth was uneasy. Yet if it kept Amy's marriage on an even keel, so be it.

'I'm sure.' Amy's eyes glowed with relief that this was acceptable.

'I'm asking for a major increase. The fan mail tells me it's justified, but they may try to stonewall me. Are you and Keith willing to gamble on my move if that happens?'

'Keith's willing for us to walk out if need be. He says they won't let that last for more than a few days. We make a fortune for the studio.'

'Let's take it one day at a time.' Keith was right.

Elisabeth battled over the contract in three meetings. Finally she won out – all the while inwardly furious that Amy was transferring a solid chunk of her own earnings to Keith. The studio chiefs were cynical about this arrangement but agreeable. All they cared about was that Amy was happy, grinding out pictures on a regular basis.

Early in March of the new year Chuck came to Elisabeth to report on rumors that were circulating.

'Look, you and Amy are like family. I could ignore what I hear, but that would be disloyal to you. You know those evenings when Amy is with you, working on characterization or whatever?'

'Yes?' She was ever conscious that Amy felt guilty leaving Keith alone two or three evenings each week.

'Keith's running around at some private parties that are on the wild side. I know, all new contracts have morals clauses. Everybody's conscious of Will Hays' watchful eye. But the parties go on. The whisper is that Keith always leaves early – but he's into heavy drinking.' Chuck hesitated. 'And maybe drugs.'

'You don't know that . . .' Elisabeth's heart began to pound.

'No,' Chuck acknowledged. 'Just rumors.'

'Thanks, Chuck.' Elisabeth's mind was in chaos. How did she handle this? She must deal with it – for Amy's sake. 'I do appreciate your alerting me. Though it's just a rumor.'

Elisabeth searched her mind for a way to approach Keith, to put him on warning. She mustn't jump too fast, be diplomatic yet firm. Keith must understand he was endangering both his career and Amy's. The morals clause was not to be challenged.

Amy swung into the circular driveway before their sprawling Spanish-style mansion. Dixieland jazz blared into the soft, damp night, sweet with the scent of eucalyptus. She vaguely remembered that the Fenwicks across the road had complained about the night-time noise. She'd remind Keith again to lower the volume on the phonograph.

She parked the new Stutz in the driveway, too impatient to talk to Keith to put it in the garage right now. Instead, she hurried up the path to the door in the high heels that Keith said made her legs look fabulous but which she secretly loathed. It was sweet of Dr Evans to see her so late in the evening. Keith would be thrilled when he heard the news. Wouldn't he?

As she'd expected, she found Keith stretched out on the sofa. She assumed the empty glass on the floor beside him had contained bootleg gin. Keith said Prohibition was one big joke. You could get anything you wanted in this town – probably anywhere in the country. Keith ought to stop drinking, she thought uneasily. He was always in such a foul mood in the morning.

'Keith –' He hadn't heard her come in. He was all wrapped up in his newest record.

'Hey, baby, come over here.' He moved to allow space for her on the sofa.

'Keith, I have something exciting to tell you.' She took a deep breath. Her face was luminous. 'I'm pregnant!'

Keith gaped in shock. 'The studio will kill us!'

'No,' she scolded gently. 'It fits right in with the image. The perfect young couple will become the perfect family. Keith . . .' All at once she was frightened. 'Aren't you glad?'

'We've just started a picture –' He pulled himself into a sitting position.

'I won't show for another two months – we'll finish the picture. For a while you'll make pictures without me.' She saw a faint smile lift the corners of his mouth. Did he *want* to do pictures without her? 'I'll be back at work in a few months. Keith, don't you want us to have a baby?'

'Sure I do,' he blustered. 'You just rocked me off my butt. You didn't give me a hint. Hey, honey, this calls for a drink! Can't you just see the magazine spreads? And this baby better be damned good-looking,' he joshed. 'Or we'll just give him back.'

Chapter Thirty-eight

Elisabeth was simultaneously euphoric and anxious about Amy's pregnancy. The prospect of welcoming her first grandchild filled her with joy. The family *lived*. Yet she was troubled that Amy was so young. She had been younger when Amy was born, she conceded, but she had grown up quickly in that tumultuous first year after her marriage. Katie and Hallie, too, were rapturous about a new family member.

'Maybe now Keith will settle down.' Elisabeth tried to sound hopeful in conversation with Ellie. 'If there *was* any truth to those rumors about his chasing around to wild parties.'

'The Hays office has cut down on that.'

'It's just gone underground.' But hopefully Keith was smart enough to steer clear.

'Mom's knitting like crazy for the baby. I'm crocheting,' Ellie chuckled. 'We'll be prepared even if she has quadruplets.'

'Amy's determined to work as long as possible,' a situation that disturbed Elisabeth. 'Of course, the studio is upset at having to pay her for those weeks when she won't be before the cameras – but they're already envisioning a flood of items in the gossip columns when the word gets out. Thank God for low waistlines – Amy won't show for another four or five weeks.'

At the studio Elisabeth watched Amy for signs of tiredness, commiserating with her constant sleepiness these first weeks, making sure she took afternoon naps.

While Amy napped on this April afternoon, Frank, now Amy's permanent director, sat down with Elisabeth to discuss Amy's temporary retirement.

'The cameramen have strict instructions about photographing Amy from the waist up or angles that hide that little bulge that's showing already. But I don't see us going beyond this picture,' Frank sighed. 'We can hold up the releases for a while, but at this stage in her career Amy should be seen constantly.'

'Amy wants to work,' Elisabeth reminded. 'She insists she feels fine. Why not a costume picture? That's a perfect way to hide her pregnancy.'

'Costume pictures aren't popular.' He shook his head in rejection.

'What about de Mille's *The Ten Commandments*?' she countered. 'That's doing great.'

'De Mille's picture cost a fortune! We can't get that big a budget.'

'You can do a costume picture without a million extras and expensive sets.' She delved into her mind for a subject. 'What about a picture revolving around a young American Revolutionary heroine? Not a de Mille spectacle,' she emphasized. 'A heart-warming story about this girl who was a spy for the colonists. I read about her.'

Frank lifted an eyebrow in interest. 'Write me up a couple of paragraphs on her. I'll take it up with the Chiefs.'

Frank threw himself into selling this idea. It wasn't too difficult, he admitted to Elisabeth when the approval came through. They were frantic to keep Amy before the movie-going public.

'They'll hire a top-flight screenwriter to come up fast with a script. Keith will be written in as Amy's heroic young sweetheart.'

Amy was relieved to continue working after the present film. Keith complained that his part in the new screenplay was too small.

'Hell, it's not much more than a bit part!' he told Amy indignantly.

After much theatrics – and Amy's insistence – Keith's part was enlarged. They were working against time now. Amy's costumes had to be let out almost weekly. The wardrobe mistress struggled to mask her condition. The public was not to know that Amy was pregnant until *after* the picture was released. Every studio employee was sworn to secrecy.

'This is nutty,' Amy rebelled. 'Women don't hide themselves at home anymore because they're pregnant! This is 1924!'

Late in her fifth month the picture was finished. Reluctantly Amy went into retirement. Keith was scheduled to go into another film in three weeks. The studio had tried to hire a hot new actress named Clara Bow, who'd been hopping on loan from studio to studio, but she was booked through the end of the year. When another actress was rushed in so that the studio could start filming, Keith threw tantrums on the set.

'I see the rushes, and the picture stinks,' he told Amy while he paced about their palatial bedroom.

'Let me ask Mama to work with you,' she cajoled. 'Mama's wonderful.' She felt guilty that she couldn't be there to help him.

'No!' He glared at her as though she'd joined the enemy. 'Maybe she's good with women. Not with a man.' Something akin to contempt crept into his voice.

'After this picture, tell Frank you want some time off to be with me. We'll make up for it once the baby's born.' Mama said the studio's salesman made it clear that to get one Amy Winston picture they must book four others. She could make this demand. 'Mama's reading novels like mad to find something that'll be good for us.'

'Good for you,' Keith snickered. 'She doesn't give a shit about me.' His eyes dared her to contradict him.

'You're wrong, Keith. Mama's very fond of you.' She forced herself to sound convincing. Only to herself would she admit that Mama was ever distrustful of him. 'Now stop pacing and come to bed.'

Keith's picture was taking longer than scheduled. Amy suspected this was the result of his temperamental outbreaks on the set. This wasn't a time to make trouble, she worried. She read the trade papers. Movie attendance was off, they reported. Nobody knew why. The industry was nervous.

Now in the final days of filming Keith rarely left the studio until midnight. Amy was grateful that her mother and Katie spent much time with her. Hallie was constantly sending over some tempting dish – though Pat, Amy and Keith's housekeeper considered this an affront. Pat was already warning that she expected the household to expand to include a sleep-in nurse once the baby was born.

With Pat and the maid both off on Thursdays, Amy knew her mother would arrive at the house no later than six o'clock with her dinner. Late in her seventh month now, she felt uncomfortable, restless. Mama and Ellie both warned the last two months always seemed the longest. And she was recurrently haunted by the suspicion that Keith didn't truly want the baby.

She heard a car pull up into the driveway. That would be Mama, she suspected. With the awkwardness of late pregnancy she lifted herself from her chair and headed for the door. Her mother, sister and Hallie emerged from the car, hurried to the house.

'I brang you a chicken pot pie and strawberry shortcake,' Hallie announced cheerfully. 'And I don't want you to leave a crumb, you hear?'

'We have a movie to see later,' Katie announced. 'Hallie can't wait to see it,' she teased. 'It's with Rudolph Valentino.'

Despite Hallie's urging, Amy ate only a forkful of the chicken pot pie, pushed aside the strawberry shortcake.

'I'll put it away for later,' Elisabeth said diplomatically. 'When you're hungry.'

'I feel funny,' Amy said a few minutes later while her mother and Hallie worked to set up the projector in the screening room.

Elisabeth was solicitous. 'What do you mean by "funny", darling?'

'Oooh!' Amy's eyes widened. 'I – I think that was a contraction.'

'Lotsa women go into false labor,' Hallie soothed, but Amy saw the glance that Hallie exchanged with her mother. 'It'll stop when the kid says, "I ain't ready yet – this is just a warnin'."'

'If you're not going to eat the strawberry shortcake, can I have it?' Katie asked.

'Go ahead – have it,' Amy said tersely, gearing herself for another sharp pain.

'Let's watch the picture,' Elisabeth ordered. 'Like Hallie said, lots of women have premature pains. They stop in a little while.'

Amy allowed herself to be coaxed into a comfortable armchair. Her mother propped pillows at her back. This was false labor, she told herself – she wasn't going to panic. She hadn't gone into her eighth month yet.

Twenty minutes later Amy reached out for her mother's hand.

'The pains are coming quicker!' She doubled over, breaking out into perspiration. 'I think the baby's trying to come!'

'I'll call Dr Evans.' Her mother strode towards the phone. 'We're taking you to the hospital.'

Terror gripped her. 'Am I going to lose the baby?'

'No, sugar,' Hallie soothed. 'Me, I was a seven-month baby. Mama said, "Thank you, Hallie, for savin' me two months." The baby's gonna be all right.'

Five hours later Amy gave birth to a four-pound, six-ounce girl.

'Amy, she's beautiful.' Amy saw tears of joy in her mother's eyes. 'The image of you except for the dark hair.'

'Is she going to be all right?' Fresh alarm welled in her.

'She'll be fine,' Dr Evans said briskly. 'Oh, she'll need some extra care for a while, but you won't mind that.' His smile was compassionate. 'I'll leave instructions.'

An hour later Keith arrived. Elisabeth had left word at the studio that Amy had gone into labor. Amy had insisted that he not be called away. Still, he had to know where Amy was, Elisabeth had reasoned.

'She's so little . . .' Keith stared at his tiny daughter in her mother's arms.

'Would you like to hold her?' Elisabeth asked. How could she be angry at anyone at a moment like this?

'I'd be scared – she's so little.' But he reached for one minuscule hand.

'She'll get bigger fast enough,' Hallie said. 'My two sisters kept me in hot-water bottles for almost a month. Mama didn't much care, but to my two big sisters I was their livin' doll.'

Amy was upset when Keith arranged for *Photoplay* to take exclusive pictures of her in the hospital bed with the baby.

'By giving them an exclusive we'll get terrific coverage,' Keith said effusively. 'Probably the cover.'

'She's two months early,' Amy protested. 'I don't think she ought to be exposed to people that way.'

'It's all right,' Keith soothed. 'Your mother talked to the doctor. Nobody's to get closer than ten feet.'

'Bring a yardstick.' Amy tried to be flip. She didn't want photographers here in the hospital room. This was supposed to be a very private time.

'The studio's dying to get you back before the cameras.' Keith ran the tip of his tongue across his upper lip, a sign that he was anxious. 'It won't be long, will it?'

'Three weeks,' she stipulated. 'Mama says she's found a story that'll be great for us.' Keith hadn't told her, but Mama said his just released film, without her, was doing poorly at the box offices.

'I know. Frank says they're already negotiating with Elinor Glyn to buy the rights. They're hoping to get Anita Loos to do the screenplay.' He hesitated. 'Then I can tell Frank you'll be ready to start filming in three weeks?'

'In three weeks,' Amy confirmed. 'We'll hire a trained baby nurse to take care of Ronnie.' They'd decided earlier that if she gave birth to a girl, the baby would be named Rowena Bettina Lindsay. Rowena for her great-grandmother and Bettina for her Uncle Ben. According to Jewish tradition the name must begin with the first letter of those so honored.

Yet Amy was wistful at the thought of spending so many hours at the studio each day. In truth, she yearned to be at home with her daughter. So fragile, she thought with recurrent anxiety. Everybody kept telling her the baby would thrive, but she was two months early. How could they be sure?

Elisabeth knew Amy was ambivalent about returning to work when Ronnie was still perilously small. The nurse installed in the house was efficient, warm, and somewhat awed at caring for Amy Winston's baby. But Amy felt guilty at leaving her each morning.

'Ronnie's doing well,' Elisabeth encouraged Amy. She was such a good baby, so sweet and beautiful. 'Don't expect her to gain weight by the day. Don't even look at the scale for the next two weeks. The doctor's very pleased with her.'

'I just want to be home to hold her.'

'We'll come home during the day for an hour – Frank can shoot around you.' Why not? 'And I'll insist you finish filming by six o'clock. Frank has three children, he'll understand.'

For the first few weeks – with Ronnie thriving – Keith seemed to enjoy fatherhood. He posed for photographers with his daughter in his arms. He boasted in endless interviews about how proud he was of his little family, the image that the movie industry desperately needed at this time. The marriage on 24 November of thirty-five-year-old Charlie Chaplin and pregnant sixteen-year-old Lita Grey monopolized the tabloid headlines, heaping more scandal on the movie world.

Keith joined the studio brass, plus Amy and Elisabeth, in the projection room to view the first completed film after Amy's return to work.

'I've been photographed like hell!' he yelled when the screening was over and the lights turned on again. 'What's the matter with the cameraman?'

'So in some shots you look a little puffy under the eyes,' Frank soothed. 'Only you'll see it.'

'What kind of make-up man have we got now?' Keith flared. 'Audiences expect me to look my best.'

'Cut back on the partying,' the calmer of the Chiefs told him. 'Then you won't worry about looking bleary-eyed. Anyhow, Amy is fabulous – there'll be lines at the box offices.'

Elisabeth saw Amy's shock. Neither she nor Amy had realized Keith came home late each night because of his socializing. Amy had thought Keith was working late at the studio – in part because of her leaving at six p.m. sharp each day. He'd *allowed* them to believe that, Elisabeth told herself in silent rage. And she realized, too, that Keith was seething at the inference that his appearance was not important: '*Amy is fabulous – there'll be lines at the box offices.*'

Elisabeth was grateful that Amy would have a week between pictures. The Chiefs grumbled at the delay, but rewrites on the screenplay provided this break. Amy was upset that Keith's ego had been trampled on by a careless remark. She catered to his every whim, secretly pleaded with Frank to have his part in the next film built up.

'He hasn't seen the screenplay yet,' Amy whispered to Elisabeth. 'He'll throw a fit when he reads it.'

When she was working, Amy was happy, Elisabeth thought gratefully. And she adored the baby. They all did. Katie was Ronnie's willing slave. Hallie had announced right away that she would take care of Ronnie on the nurse's day off. Something precious had come into their lives, Elisabeth told herself at sentimental intervals.

She was unnerved by Keith's temperamental fits on the set. Each time Amy looked so stricken and tried to soothe him. Only for Amy's sake did Frank tolerate these outbursts, Elisabeth understood. Keith's early potential had not been realized, would never be realized, she admitted to herself. The picture dragged on three weeks behind schedule. Frank was nervous. They were far over budget.

Late in January the new picture was finished. Keith sat in grim silence while he watched the run-through in the projection room. When the lights came up, he stalked out of the room without a word.

'Keith's so upset,' Amy whispered. 'He never did like the part.' Once there'd been electricity between them on camera. Now Keith faded into the background. Why? Elisabeth asked herself. Because he was giving nothing to the camera. He resented the tons of fan mail that arrived each day for Amy – a small amount for himself.

He resented the fact that he wasn't receiving a larger salary than Amy – and he didn't know that Amy had arranged for part of her increase to be applied to his salary. He was jealous of Amy's success.

Before Amy and Keith were to begin the next film, Frank confided to Elisabeth that the Chiefs were seething over the extra cost in bringing in the past three films with Keith.

'Either he shapes up or they'll cancel his contract. And they can do it,' Frank emphasized. 'All they have to do is invoke the morals clause.'

'What are you talking about?' Elisabeth's heart began to pound.

'I didn't want to say anything.' Frank was searching for words. 'I know Amy thinks the sun rises and sets with Keith. But he's running around behind her back. With some overheated young heiress who lives in Pasadena. Nobody wants to say anything because they love Amy, but it's no secret.'

'Put him on warning,' Elisabeth ordered, straining for calm. 'Scare him, Frank.'

Keith had a beautiful young wife and a darling little daughter. What was the matter with him? How could he do this to Amy? How could she tell Amy that Keith was having an affair?

Elisabeth struggled to deal with the situation. Frank told Keith he was on warning. From the way Keith smoldered, she understood he was scared of being dropped by the studio. But what about his affair with that girl in Pasadena? Would that stop now? She watched anxiously for some sign as they began to work on the new picture.

She was startled to discover that Katie – only ten years old but strangely wise beyond her years – had become Amy's confidante.

'Amy ought to throw that cake-eater out of the house.' In today's slang, Elisabeth interpreted, that meant Keith was a ladies' man, a lounge lizard. 'He's full of banana oil.'

'Why do you say that, Katie?'

'He told Amy he was going fishing that week between pictures,' Katie blurted out. 'But he leaves a bill right in their bedroom that says that "Mr and Mrs Keith Lindsay" were registered at some fancy hotel in Acapulco. But Amy wasn't there!'

'Did Amy confront him?' Why didn't Amy confide in *her*?

'She's scared to – he might walk out on her. I hate him!' Katie's small face was contorted with rage. 'And that's not all,' Katie resumed. 'She found a bill for a black chiffon nightgown he bought

348

at Bullock's. But he didn't give it to *her*. And he sure didn't buy it for himself!'

He left those bills around deliberately, Elisabeth suspected. Maybe, in this crazy world they lived in these days, he was pushing Amy to divorce him so he could marry that girl from Pasadena – the one Frank called the overheated young heiress.

He had a devoted, beautiful wife and a darling baby. How could he do this to them? And he knew the studio chiefs would turn green if they learned Amy and he were divorcing. The whole story would hit the tabloid headlines. It would be the Hollywood scandal of the year, Elisabeth thought in anguish. Amy's career could be destroyed.

She was Amy's mother – she ought to be able to do something to stop this catastrophe. Yet she knew she was helpless if, in truth, Keith wanted a divorce.

Chapter Thirty-nine

Elisabeth waited for Amy to confide in her, but Amy pretended everything was fine. She chatted gaily about the new cloche hats, about how short skirts were becoming. Elisabeth remembered Hallie's comment when she saw the latest lengths: 'You tell Amy to make sure she wears underpants. Boys these days are gettin' themselves some free shows!'

'Frank says he's told the studio they've got to have a fabulous wardrobe designed for me to wear in the next picture. Look at the gorgeous clothes Gloria Swanson wears. Women rush to the movies just to see her clothes.'

Katie reported that Amy was terrified that Keith would leave her. Leave Hollywood.

'Last night, Amy said, he came home smelling of *Shalimar*. You know she never wears any perfume – it makes her break out. And she found a gushy note on the floor from somebody named Cecile.' Katie seethed as she relayed this latest hurt. 'How can Keith leave town? He can't just walk out on his contract.'

'The studio would be delighted.'

Frank had hinted yesterday that not only was Keith drinking heavily but was probably into drugs. Studio heads were paralyzed by the use of drugs among their actors and actresses, despite the Hays office. The public was outraged by the stories that seeped out of Hollywood about such idols as Wallace Reid and Barbara LaMarr and Alma Rubens. Frank's words echoed in her mind now: 'Beth, you see these young people working fourteen or sixteen hours a day – sometimes more – and they're scared to death of losing all this money that's pouring into their hands each week. They want to hang on to this fairy-tale world. They look around frantically for something to help them survive. Latch on to drugs.'

Elisabeth felt a wall rising between Amy and herself that she was helpless to scale. On the surface nothing had changed between them. Amy said nothing about what was clearly devastating her. She kept up the façade that all was well between Keith and her.

Keith was just walking through his scenes, Elisabeth thought impatiently – at times sullen, arrogant. She suspected that much of his work would end up on the cutting room floor. Frank had abandoned trying to pull him into line.

Elisabeth was relieved when the final day of shooting arrived. The tension on the set these last days had been horrendous. Extra efforts were made to conceal the dark circles beneath Amy's eyes. Always slim, now she appeared fragile. Still, Elisabeth recognized, Amy's performance had been brilliant.

Elisabeth and Amy left the studio as usual at six o'clock. Keith remained to reshoot one essential scene that Frank bluntly said was awful. Now the film was to go for editing. Elisabeth knew that Keith would explode when he saw the edited movie. Frank was candid. Keith's role would be cut to shreds.

'Come in to see Ronnie for a few minutes?' Amy asked as Elisabeth parked before the house.

'How can I not do that?' Elisabeth said lovingly. 'Though just for a few minutes. Katie will be home and hungry.'

Elisabeth cuddled Ronnie for a delicious few minutes, then left. But she was anxious about what lay ahead for Amy's marriage.

Amy picked at the dinner served to her, lingered at the table over coffee. Keith would be late as usual, she warned herself. The house was wrapped in quiet. The sleep-in housekeeper off for an evening at the movies, Ronnie's nurse in her room devouring her latest batch of movie magazines. Ronnie was asleep. Read the new script, Amy ordered herself.

In the sprawling master bedroom Amy settled herself on the ivory satin chaise and began to read. Quickly she realized Keith would be furious when he read the script. Her role was spectacular, his unimportant.

What was she going to do about Keith? She felt a tightness in her throat as she recalled the trail of evidence of his philandering he'd left about the house. Yet she was afraid to question him, reproach him. His mood swings frightened her. She'd overheard a member of the crew make some whispered remark about his trying some new drug hitting Hollywood.

She tossed aside the script in a surge of distaste. What was happening to Keith and her? What was she doing wrong? He could be so sweet, so charming – and then this other side took over. One moment he adored Ronnie, the next he ignored her.

If he *was* on drugs, he needed help. She shivered, remembering how Wally Reid had been dragged off to a sanatorium, kept in a padded cell, and had died two years ago. There'd been an ugly rumor that he'd been given a final – lethal – injection of morphine. Everybody talked about how Barbara LaMarr tried every kind of drug. So far her studio managed to keep it quiet, but the movie colony knew.

Amy paced about the ornate master bedroom. She didn't like their bedroom. She didn't like this house. But she hadn't been able to tell Keith that. She wanted him to believe she liked everything he liked.

Exhausted from the long day at the studio, she prepared for bed. Only now, as she changed into one of the sheer white nightgowns Keith liked her to wear, did she allow herself to admit that it had been weeks since Keith made love to her. Who wore the black chiffon nightgown he'd bought at Bullock's?

She drifted off into troubled sleep, woke up to the sound of loud jazz ricocheting about the house. She glanced at the clock on the night table as she rose from her bed. It was past midnight. Didn't Keith realize he'd wake the baby, and the servants, with that blaring jazz record?

She hurried to the living room, where every light was ablaze.

'Keith, turn down the music before you wake the baby!' She glanced nervously towards the nursery wing.

'Oh, excuse me.' He bowed extravagantly. 'Nobody counts in this bloody house except the baby. My house!' He thumped his chest.

'Keith, please,' she pleaded. She never knew how to handle him when he was in one of these moods.

'Keith, pu-lease,' he mocked. 'Well, I'm getting out of this house. Out of this town. Tell the studio they won't see me again!' He grinned at her stare of shock. 'I'm sick of making movies! Working my butt off! I want a divorce. I need to be free!'

'You're drunk . . .' Amy was dizzy with disbelief. 'We'll work things out, Keith –'

'I'm going to Paris, spend some time on the Riviera. I hate this fucking town!'

'I'll make some coffee,' she stammered. 'We'll –'

'I'll talk to my lawyer in the morning.' She hadn't known he had a lawyer. 'He'll arrange a divorce on the grounds of desertion and mental cruelty.' He nodded in a semblance of drunken smugness, but his eyes were clear and rational. 'He'll act as your lawyer. I'll sign whatever is necessary. The party's over, Amy. I've had it with this town and with you.'

Amy watched in stunned silence while Keith sauntered towards the guest room. She heard the door slammed shut. Just like that, it was over? He hadn't been drunk, she realized now. He'd played the drunk scene because he could hide behind that for a while. He was dead sober. He was walking out of her life. Walking out on his wife and daughter.

Amy lay sleepless through the night. Twice she left her bed to tiptoe into the nursery to look in on Ronnie. How could Keith desert his baby this way? She'd wanted Ronnie to have a loving mother *and* a father. *What had she done wrong?*

With the sun just rising in the sky she abandoned efforts to sleep. She went out to the kitchen, made herself coffee. The door to the guest room was closed. Keith was asleep. If they weren't working, he liked to sleep till noon. But he'd said, 'I'll talk to my lawyer in the morning.'

Now she forced herself to return to her bedroom and prepare for the day. At the first sounds from the nursery she hurried in to Ronnie.

'She's such a happy baby,' the nurse crooned, lifting Ronnie from the crib. 'About the sweetest little one I've ever known.'

'Let me hold her while you prepare her breakfast.' Her happy little baby, who didn't know her father was walking out of her life.

Shortly before nine o'clock, when she knew Katie would be in school and Hallie off to her morning shopping, Amy went to her mother.

'Amy, I thought you'd be sleeping late this morning.' A hint of concern in her voice.

'I didn't sleep all night.' Mama knew something was wrong.

'Ronnie's all right?'

'Ronnie's fine. Keith's leaving us –' Her voice broke. 'What's

353

wrong with the women in this family? Why are we always left alone?'

'Darling, you're not alone.' Her mother led her into the living room. 'You have your family. We'll always be here for you and Ronnie.'

'What did I do to drive Keith away?' Bewilderment gave way for a moment to anger. 'I was a good wife to him!'

'You were the best, Amy. He'll never know how good you were to him.'

'Can I come home now? I hate that house! I never want to set foot in it again.'

'You'll come home,' Elisabeth soothed. 'You and Ronnie. But right now I want you to try to get some sleep. You'll lie down for a little while – and then we'll talk.'

At last, with the aid of a sedative, Amy lay huddled in slumber. Elisabeth drove to the house with Hallie, told Ronnie's nurse and the housekeeper that their services would no longer be required. There were no accommodations for sleep-in help where Amy would be living in the future. Later she'd tell the maid who came in by the day.

Neither of the two women seemed surprised, she noted. They must have heard the ugly scenes between Keith and Amy. She gave each a check for two weeks' salary, promised the best of references. The house was at their disposal for the next two weeks.

Hallie took charge of Ronnie while Elisabeth packed clothes for Amy and the baby's immediate needs. Later they'd return for Ronnie's crib and other essentials. Hallie listened with rapt attention to the nurse's instructions about Ronnie's care.

The next weeks were chaotic. Amy refused to leave the house, hovered over Ronnie. Elisabeth took charge. She explained the situation to the studio heads. 'Good riddance,' they agreed. But Frank told her the publicity department was working overtime to issue statements showing Amy as a devoted, wronged wife. With Amy in a semi-breakdown, Elisabeth agreed that the studio take her off salary until she returned to work.

Elisabeth consulted with the lawyer Keith had hired to represent Amy in the divorce. The lawyer delicately pointed out that, while Keith had signed the necessary papers, there had been no payment for his services. Elisabeth arranged for this. Now she was stunned to discover that Keith had wiped out his and Amy's bank account, and had sold her solid stocks and replaced them with fly-by-nights that Peter reported worthless. The house was in his name and a second mortgage had been taken out – unknown to Amy. His equity in the house was almost nil.

Elisabeth was grateful that Ronnie thrived. Amy was solicitous, clinging to her small daughter in almost every waking moment. The studio was anxious for her to return to work, but Amy recoiled from accepting their calls. Three months after Keith walked out, Frank came to the house to plead with her.

'Frank, I can't talk about pictures,' she told him agitatedly, and hurried from the room.

'What does her doctor say?' Frank asked.

'She won't see a doctor.' Elisabeth read the question in Frank's eyes. 'Nor a psychiatrist.' In this modern world everybody talked about Freud. Analysis was the answer to every problem. 'I've tried to convince her she needs help.' An edge of desperation crept into Elisabeth's voice. 'I'm getting nowhere.'

Frank hesitated. 'She's gaining a lot of weight. She'll need to get it off before she goes before the camera.'

Elisabeth sighed. 'I know. But all she can think about now is that Keith has left her. She blames herself.'

'Keith was a bastard. Amy's well rid of him.' Frank grunted in disgust.

'But how do I convince Amy of that?'

Frank was sympathetic – but the studio would be scouting for a replacement for Amy Winston if she didn't emerge soon from this fog that inundated her.

Elisabeth tried to remonstrate with Amy about her constant trips to the refrigerator.

'Mama, you don't understand. Food helps the pain.'

'You'll feel better if you're back at work,' Elisabeth tried yet again. 'I remember when your father died, and I –'

'I can't think about work,' Amy interrupted impatiently. 'Ronnie needs me.'

Elisabeth forced herself to weigh the situation. She had savings to see them through for months, perhaps a year, but how did she know when Amy would be herself again? Often now she thought of her grandmother. Grandma had been left with a child to support – and she'd managed this. It hadn't been easy, but they'd survived. After David died, she'd had Jerry to help her survive. When Jerry ran off to join the Canadian Air Force, she'd expected to be on her own in Hollywood, but then Amy began to work. Now she must take care of her family on her own. Like Grandma used to say, 'You do what you have to do.'

Relentlessly Elisabeth pursued the studios, from the largest to the smallest, for work. She had fine credentials as an actress. She could direct. Why would no one offer her a job?

Like a growing number of Americans, Chuck was fascinated by radio. He warned that it would soon cut in on movie attendance. Each night he and his father-in-law huddled over the expensive set they'd had made up for themselves.

'They stay up till all hours,' Ellie reported, 'trying to pick up signals from every part of the country. But the programs are so bad.'

'There's a station out in Pasadena now,' Chuck told Elisabeth. 'Get your feet wet in radio. I know, most people work for nothing. But one of these days it'll be big.'

Elisabeth was ever conscious, too, of the buzzing about the advent of 'talking pictures' sometime in the near future. Thomas Edison's early thoughts had been to combine moving pictures with voices on a phonograph. Chuck told her that researchers at Western Electric had been working on a device that could do this. And right now, rumor said, Warner Brothers – a small film company – was working with Western Electric. They'd made some musical shorts that synchronized sound with film. The system, Chuck said, was called Vita-phone.

'Picture producers have to do something,' Chuck pointed out. 'Radio's going to skim off audiences. Wait and see.'

Elisabeth became involved in a small radio group that read scenes from classical plays – no royalties to pay. 'It's a diversion,' she confided to ever sympathetic Hallie. Closer to theater than films, she thought with relish. The voice could do so much.

When the director for their radio group walked out, Elisabeth took over. There were now over 1,400 stations operating across the country – including stations in department stores – though rarely were performers paid. When a Poverty Row film producer heard her on a program and sought her out, she was euphoric. He offered four days' work at a minuscule sum in a movie he was preparing to produce on a shoestring.

If she did well in this part, Elisabeth reasoned, she'd have a chance to land another. Each morning for four days she left for the studio in soaring anticipation. The producers were cutting corners, of course – the shooting schedule too short to allow for a fine production – but her role was good. It could mean the beginning of a new career.

A week before Thanksgiving the movie was to have its premiere at a modest Los Angeles movie house. Elisabeth knew it would be futile to ask Amy to go to the premiere. She never ventured beyond the grounds around the house now. Nothing seemed to matter but Ronnie's wellbeing. If Ronnie sneezed, Amy was a nervous wreck. If Ronnie scraped a knee, she was distraught. Amy needed her, Elisabeth brooded, but how was she to help?

Katie and Hallie were in a festive mood when they left for the theater.

'It's a small part,' Elisabeth warned them, but in her heart she knew she'd done well. Even the other cast members had been impressed.

They took their seats as the theater darkened. Katie reached for her mother's hand. Hallie sat on the edge of her seat, waiting expectantly for the movie to begin.

'I don't come in until the middle,' Elisabeth whispered.

The three of them waited.

'In another minute –' Elisabeth squeezed Katie's hand.

But she wasn't there. The scene had been cut.

Chapter Forty

As had become a tradition, Elisabeth went with her family to the Sanchez house to celebrate New Year's Eve, Hallie carrying two pies for the occasion. She loved the warmth, the sense of family that radiated within its walls.

'How's our precious little girl?' Bella crooned, lifting Ronnie into her arms. 'I can't believe how big she's getting!'

'Hey, don't monopolize her,' Peter scolded. 'Don't you know we're going together?'

'This one's going to sleep,' Amy said after a few minutes. 'Come on, Ronnie. Upstairs.'

Elisabeth settled herself on the large, comfortable sofa beside Ellie and Chuck. Peter sat in his favorite chintz-covered armchair. Hallie disappeared with Bella into the kitchen. Katie and Ira went off in a corner to play chess. Tonight, Elisabeth vowed, she'd be cheerful. Banish the depression that threatened to overtake her.

As so often in this house, conversation focused on movie industry news.

'I keep telling Chuck – enough of this crazy business.' Peter grunted in disgust. 'Concentrate on the orange groves, help me tie up new markets. There's big money to be made.'

'I know. But right now my brain keeps telling me movies will break out into something tremendous any day,' Chuck countered. 'I want to be part of it.'

'The movies will lose out to radio.' Peter nodded with conviction. 'Radio will bring entertainment right into the house. Who needs to go chasing out to theaters, spending money, when radio's for free? You've said it yourself, Chuck.'

'Programming has to improve first,' Elisabeth said. 'I know, for a while radio audiences were excited just to hear music every night, but that's not enough. If the radio manufacturers want to sell sets, they'd better create enticing programs.' Was she wasting her time in radio? Instinct told her she wasn't. Like Chuck she was also fascinated by the prospect of 'talking pictures'. The whole entertainment world hovered on the brink of major changes.

'I have this feeling we're a breath away from "talking pictures".' Chuck startled her. It was as though he was reading her mind. 'It keeps moving closer to actuality. Remember back in 1921 when D. W. Griffith did *Dream Street*? There was some spoken dialogue in it. Then three years later Dr Lee De Forest made some sound shorts of vaudeville acts. I know, the big companies are wary of possible "talkies". Synchronization is a tricky deal. And the cost of setting up sound equipment in movie theaters across the country . . . !' He whistled eloquently. 'Take my word, it'll be some small company with a strong gambling instinct that'll launch pictures with sound. But a breakthrough is on the way – and after that, wow!'

At Amy's reappearance Bella summoned them to a festive dinner. The dining room was heady with high spirits. Yet Elisabeth was aware that Amy was here only in body. How could Amy still believe that Keith would come back to her? She'd had not one word from him since that awful night.

Early in the new year – struggling to sound casual – Elisabeth told the family they would be moving into a smaller house. She recognized Hallie's anxiety, Katie's shock. But both understood the motivation for this move. Even at this tender age Katie was a realist.

'I've found something nice quite near here.' For an instant she saw a flicker of startled comprehension in Amy's eyes. Then it was gone. Amy blocked out what she wasn't prepared to face.

'I can get a job,' Hallie said, trying to mask anxiety with a bright smile.

'You've got a job, Hallie. Managing this house. But starting next week I have a job at the studio.' Bless Frank for setting this up for her. 'I'm going to coach some of their new young actresses.' The money was small, but with careful budgeting they could manage.

Elisabeth settled into her new routine. They moved into the smaller, less expensive house. Hallie bargain-hunted, cutting down on their food costs. Amy focused on the baby. Elisabeth watched helplessly as Amy ate herself into alarming obesity. At intervals, Elisabeth knew, Katie tried to break through to her sister – to bring her back to reality, but to no avail. The studio had given up on Amy's resuming her career. There were no more stories in the movie magazines. Amy Winston might never have existed.

The months rolled past. Elisabeth was pleased when she learned that Paul had a new play on Broadway, was unhappy when it closed. 'The playwright ventured into new fields. The audiences were not happy,' a reviewer wrote. Paul had written a play around a social issue, Elisabeth interpreted. Wrong for this era. Nobody wanted to be serious.

In August the world was shocked by the death of Rudolph Valentino at a New York City hospital at the age of thirty-one. Along with millions of women throughout the country, Hallie was distraught. Elisabeth remembered how thrilled Amy and Gloria had been to see him with Pola Negri at the dinner given for her by the studio at the Alexandria Hotel in honor of her high school graduation.

'He was so young and good-looking!' Hallie sobbed inconsolably. Melodramatic rumors circulated: he had been poisoned by an abandoned lover, shot by a furious husband, succumbed to syphilis.

The official report was that Valentino had died of peritonitis after an appendix operation. When he lay in state at Campbell's Funeral Home in New York City, the streets before the home were mobbed by a hundred thousand women, fighting for a last glimpse of the Great Lover.

In October Elisabeth gave a twelfth birthday party for Katie. Tiny Ronnie, moving happily among the guests in a red velvet pinafore, captured every heart. Considering their tight budget, Elisabeth had offered Katie a modest new bicycle or a birthday party. 'A party!' she'd chosen with enthusiasm. 'If you invite ten girls, then I'll have ten presents!'

The presence of Katie and Ronnie kept her from despair, Elisabeth confided to Hallie. Katie radiated a zest for living. Ronnie was a happy, affectionate toddler who was the center of their household. And Elisabeth conceded that she derived satisfaction – though thus far no money – from her work with the shoestring radio station. Her coaching kept them in funds.

But radio was making impressive progress. Last November the radio-listening public had been galvanized by a four-hour program of music broadcast from the Grand Ballroom of the Waldorf Astoria Hotel in New York City by the new National Broadcasting Company. Now NBC was planning two networks to consist of seventy-five stations.

The new year showed sluggish signs for the movie studios. By April business in general was in a deep slump. Movie people blamed this on radio. Millions of families had radios in their homes. Many in the industry considered it a passing fancy, with no real impact on the entertainment world. All talk of possible advances in 'sound movies' dissipated. It would cost a fortune to install sound systems in the 24,000 or more movie theaters in the country. In this downturn Elisabeth was anxious about being kept on as coach at the studio. And most of all, she worried about Amy's withdrawal from life.

'She's twenty-three years old,' she lamented to Ellie. 'How much longer can this go on?'

'What about her going back to school? To college?'

'Amy won't hear of college.' Elisabeth took a deep breath, exhaled. 'I don't know how to reach her. She still has this crazy belief that one of these days Keith will show up, penitent and dying to come back to her.'

'And you still can't get her to see a psychiatrist?'

'I mention it, and she walks out of the room. But can a psychiatrist bring Keith back into her life?'

Later in the year word leaked out that Warner Brothers had signed Al Jolson to a movie contract. This evoked a lively discussion at a Friday night dinner at the Sanchez house.

'For ten years important movie producers have been trying to get Jolson to make a movie,' Chuck said with awe. 'And a small company like Warner's pulls it off.'

'Back in 1914,' Bella reminisced, 'Peter and I saw Jolson in *Dancin' Around* at the Winter Garden in New York. He was wonderful.'

'The way I hear it, Jolson will say a few lines and sing two songs,' Chuck reported. 'It'll be titled *The Jazz Singer* and advertised as a "part dialogue" movie. And Mama,' Chuck said teasingly, 'guess who else is going to be in it?'

'Tell me!' Bella glowed.

'Richard Tucker. And –' he took a dramatic pause – 'Cantor Rosenblatt.'

'Bella!' Peter searched for his wife's hand. 'This movie we have to see. Years ago,' he turned to Elisabeth, 'when we lived in Borough Park, Brooklyn, guess who was our neighbor? Cantor Josef

Rosenblatt! When he opened his mouth to practice, everybody in the neighborhood was silent. Such a voice!'

'If *The Jazz Singer* does well,' Chuck predicted, 'then every movie producer will be off to the races. It'll be a whole new world.'

Elisabeth exchanged a smile with Ellie. Chuck wrote beautiful dialogue – lost in silent movies. 'Talkies' could provide a whole new world for Chuck. About time, she thought affectionately. He had the talent. Let him have the essential ingredient of luck as well.

The enormous success of *The Jazz Singer* – which drew tremendous crowds from its opening in October – had told the movie producers and the theater owners that the time for 'talkies' had arrived. No more delays. There was consternation and terror in the hearts of Hollywood actors and actresses. How did they sound? Could they make the transition to 'talkies'? They gave radio little consideration – no money there.

The question that haunted the movie industry was how to cope with this new dimension. How much sound – dialogue – should be in the new films? Should they be like stage productions? What to do with stars whose voices didn't match their screen personalities?

Elisabeth launched a feverish campaign for a movie role. She was what the studios needed. She could act. She had a voice proven on stage and on radio. Why was she constantly rejected?

'I wish we had a part for you,' Frank told her self-consciously. 'But you're past the young leading lady age. You're too young and beautiful for character roles.'

'Frank, I'm forty-one years old!'

'You look barely thirty,' he pointed out. He cleared his throat. She saw a familiar glint in his eye – the glint that told her the Chiefs had something to suggest. 'I can line up a new job for you – as voice coach. It'll pay better than what you're doing now.'

'What will it pay?' A voice coach was an urgent requirement with studios going into sound.

Elisabeth settled down to rigorous bargaining with Frank. So it wasn't acting money. She was in no position to be fussy. For the next two days, with Frank as go-between, she battled with the Chiefs. The final offer was higher than she'd dared to anticipate. With that coming in each week they could manage comfortably. Maybe she could even put a few dollars into the bank. She would be the studio voice coach. Instinct told her this was a job that could last for years.

Elisabeth was upset when Amy fabricated an excuse not to go to the family Hanukkah party at the Sanchez house.

'I just know I have a cold coming on. You all take Ronnie – she'll love it.'

The others were settled in the car for the drive to the Sanchezes when Ronnie announced she had to go to the bathroom.

'I'll take her.' With a good-humored smile Hallie scooped up Ronnie and left the car.

'Mama, we have to talk,' Katie began when they were alone, then paused.

Elisabeth tensed. 'About what, Katie?'

'About Amy. She's having trouble telling you. I mean – it's awful expensive –'

'What's expensive?'

'Analysis.' Katie took a deep breath. 'She thinks she ought to go into analysis.'

'We'll manage.' Elisabeth's throat tightened. 'But what brought this on?' Amy confided in Katie. Not in her mother.

'I kind of pushed her.' Katie's smile was wry. 'I told her she had to do something about her craziness. I mean, not going anywhere except to the Sanchezes. Eating herself into a blimp. I asked her – "How's Ronnie going to feel when she's in school and you won't go to school events? Suppose her teacher asks her to be class mother and you won't do it? How'll Ronnie feel?"'

'Katie, you're wonderful!' Tears blurring her vision, Elisabeth reached to draw Katie into her arms. 'We'll manage her analysis. Whatever it costs, we'll handle it.'

She could take private students on the side. The studio didn't own all her time. Please, God, let this be a breakthrough for Amy. Let Amy reclaim her life.

Chapter Forty-one

The hysteria that wracked the movie world in 1928 was providing a financial bonanza for Elisabeth. Nothing like the kind of money Amy had been earning, she conceded, but she was able to pay their bills, to put money in the bank each week. Sometimes she felt guilty that she felt such satisfaction in this.

Knowing she could provide a needed service – and using this as leverage – she stipulated that she would be at the studio only at specified hours each day. This would permit her to take on private students, of which there was no shortage in this critical period. Though she winced when she'd heard the fees commanded by analysts, she was determined to provide this for Amy.

'It won't help overnight,' Ellie cautioned. 'People say it can take years.'

'As long as Amy's helped,' Elisabeth said, 'that's all that counts.' Some might declare that money couldn't buy happiness, but often it paved the way.

'These days everybody considers themselves an amateur analyst.' Ellie raised her eyebrows in distaste. 'And they're sure the world revolves around sex.' A glint of laughter in her eyes now. 'Of course, without it there'd be no world.'

'Amy seems to like this Dr Hartman.' Frank had helped her choose Amy's analyst. Hartman's patients included several major stars. 'She doesn't say anything about her sessions, and I wouldn't dare ask. But each time she comes home from her appointment with him, she seems a little more serene. At least for a while.'

'At what you're paying, she should.'

'He'd like her to come in three times a week.' Elisabeth sighed. She was struggling to pay for two sessions a week.

'Sure.' Ellie's face was eloquent. 'He's got his eyes on a new Hispano-Suiza.'

Elisabeth labored to revise the speech patterns of her anxious students, most of them stars of silent films. A few who persisted would survive, she predicted to Ellie. Many would fall into reluctant retirement.

'Don't cry over them,' Ellie chided. 'They've got fortunes stashed away from the Golden Years.'

The year was speeding past, Elisabeth mourned. For the past two months Amy had been seeing Dr Hartman three times a week, but was she making progress? She still left the house only for her sessions with Dr Hartman and for their frequent Friday evening dinners at the Sanchez house. She was still obsessive about Ronnie's wellbeing. And in her heart, Elisabeth knew, she still chastised herself for the failure of her marriage.

It was agonizing to realize that Amy was perfect for talking pictures. She was young, beautiful, talented. Her speaking voice – her diction – lovely. All she had to do to climb up the ladder again was to lose weight. But Amy wanted no part of a career now.

Last night she'd been stunned by a remark Amy dropped into a conversation about the new Joan Crawford movie: 'I only wanted to do movies because it was an escape from life. I thought if I worked hard and we had money, we'd stop moving around. We'd stay in one place.'

How had Amy concocted that nonsense about not liking to make movies? Was that what therapy made her believe? She'd pleaded to be allowed to work at the studio. She'd adored it.

What was it Ellie said? 'Audiences give Amy a love she sops up like a sponge.' The camera had been her lover. Until she married, and lost, Keith.

It had been a rough year for the studio heads, Elisabeth acknowledged as the days moved inexorably into 1929. Many held high-salaried contracts with stars who might not make the crossover into talking pictures. They battled with mechanical problems of sound and the new equipment involved. New, improved systems were being devised, but – like in the old days with the Edison patents – they had difficulty getting around the patents held this time by Western Electric. Sound stages had to be built. New stars had to be groomed. But the transition must be made. Talking pictures were the future.

Elisabeth began to be troubled by a strange hostility she felt in

Amy. At first reticent about her sessions with Dr Hartman, now Amy began to verbalize her thoughts.

'Dr Hartman says I have to recover from my terrible childhood,' Amy said one evening when they sat alone in the living room. Elisabeth on the point of dozing from exhaustion. But Amy's words thrust her into startled wakefulness.

'What about your "terrible childhood"?' Elisabeth made it appear a perplexed enquiry.

'Mama, you know!' Amy was impatient. 'The way I was dragged from pillar to post, never knowing what was going to happen to me next.'

'Amy, I did what was necessary.' Elisabeth reeled from this accusation. 'Each move was a matter of survival.'

'I know that.' Amy was straining to be polite. 'And I forgive you.' *Amy forgave her?* 'But it was dreadful for a tiny child to be left alone all day with a stranger – that woman in the boarding house in New York. Each day I wondered if you'd truly come back to me as you said.'

Elisabeth gritted her teeth to keep from blurting out the reminder that Amy had shown no signs of alarm at being left with Mrs O'Brien. And what alternative had she had? Just listen and say nothing. If this was going to bring Amy back to herself, then she must accept being the villainess.

Elisabeth became alerted to Amy's varying moods when she returned from her sessions with Dr Hartman. On some occasions, she seemed more relaxed. On others she exuded a silent reproach. But always Elisabeth was conscious that she was being evaluated as a mother – and found lacking.

Between Monday, 21 October and Tuesday, 29 October – now being called Black Tuesday – millions of American families felt the calamitous crash of the American stock market. On 24 October stocks had plunged so badly that eleven well-known Wall Streeters committed suicide. By 29 October stockholders were frantically selling solid stocks to raise money to stay afloat. Elisabeth remembered with pain how proud Peter had been that he'd invested wisely for Amy. No buying on margin – which he'd dismissed as a disease afflicting the country.

So many nights Elisabeth lay sleepless, blaming herself for the loss of Amy's fortune. But how could she have refused to turn over Amy's bank account and stocks? Amy was a grown – married – woman then.

Was Dr Hartman right? Had she been an inadequate mother?

The Stock Crash hit hard in Hollywood. Rumors were that Cecil B. de Mille had personally lost a million dollars. Paramount was on the verge of bankruptcy. Several small companies had been wiped out. All were facing financial problems. Stars such as John Gilbert who'd earned $10,000 a week last year but who'd bought 'on margin' faced devastating losses.

In June of 1930 Elisabeth was unnerved to find her income slashed. The studio was retrenching. Stage actors, with their perfect diction, had begun to flow into Hollywood. Stars with voice problems were being dropped.

'Amy, I'm sorry,' Elisabeth apologized after much inner debate. But what choice did she have? 'You'll have to cut Dr Hartman's visits down to once a week.' Even that would be difficult, she warned herself.

Amy was dismayed. 'He might not keep me on.'

'I'm sure a lot of his patients are cutting back,' Elisabeth soothed. Hallie – bless her loving heart – had insisted that she didn't need her salary, reluctantly accepted a small allowance. 'Everybody is cutting back.'

'I'll try to make him understand.' But Amy was shaken.

'He'll understand,' Elisabeth said drily.

By the end of the year Elisabeth was brushed by panic. The studio continued to cut back. She sensed that at any time she would be removed from the payroll. It wasn't just Hollywood that was suffering, she realized. The whole country was suffering. What was being labeled a depression was threatening to spread to Europe.

She told herself it was absurd, but she was drawn into spending as much time as possible with her radio group. She'd quickly realized that the station was delighted to give her as much freedom as she wished as long as there was no money involved. She could choose the scenes she wished to do – from classic plays that she relished directing and performing. These hours at the studio were an oasis of cherished pleasure in the midst of a frightening world.

The group fluctuated as members became involved in personal

financial crises. She tried futilely to involve Amy. Radio was going to be so important in the very near future. Movie audiences were shrinking, but radio cost people nothing.

'Let's face it, Beth – the country's in terrible shape,' Ellie reminded in one of their late-night phone calls. 'You know how passionate Chuck is about "talkies", but right now he's working full time in the groves and grateful that Pop's able to keep going.'

'I wish he'd consider trying to write for radio. Right now movies are on hold, but radio has a big future ahead of it.'

'It's great if you're writing for *Amos 'n' Andy*,' Ellie flipped. 'But that's not Chuck's *schtick*. And he can't sing like Rudy Vallee. Why aren't there any dramatic shows?'

Now stage performers – facing a strong slowdown in play production – swarmed to the West. Movie producers struggled to build a new star system with actors and actresses who could handle the spoken word. Late in February Elisabeth was given one week's notice by the studio. Coaching was to be discontinued. She'd managed to save some money in the days before Amy began her sessions with Dr Hartman. But how long would that last?

She came from her last day at the studio and her list of private students had by now evaporated – with the compelling knowledge that she must provide for four lives in addition to her own. Like millions of Americans, she lived in terror of tomorrow.

Was it time to move on? Back to New York? The growing entertainment medium was radio. Most network programs originated from there. Advertisers were buying time on evening shows because night-time radio sold products. But why was daytime radio so dull? Nothing truly entertaining was broadcast during daytime hours when millions of women were at home during the day. Wouldn't they enjoy programming that would make the hours of house cleaning and cooking less of a bore?

It was absurd to feel guilty about enjoying the work at the radio station, Elisabeth thought impatiently as she prepared to leave the station this afternoon. She wasn't depriving the family of anything. And some day this experience might prove useful.

'You have a wonderful voice for radio.' Ted Mitchell, a newcomer to the group, fell into step beside her. An ingratiating young man who'd volunteered to play background piano music for their weekly program. He played fairly well, wrote poetry, in emergencies could fill in as an actor. But no local radio producer offered to pay for that, she thought grimly.

'Thank you, Ted.'

'You've been doing this quite a while, haven't you?' he asked with candid admiration. 'You know the whole scene. Acting, directing, producing.'

'Almost five years.' Her brief escapes from reality.

'Wow! You've learned all the angles.' A wistful glint in his eyes. 'I'm trying to convince my father to buy me a small radio station back in New York.' He chuckled at her air of astonishment. 'My old man's loaded. He manufactures men's shirts.' Ted mentioned a long-established line. 'He wants to see me involved in something away from this town.'

Elisabeth smiled faintly. 'He's read too many newspaper stories about the wild life out here?'

'That's it. And he's given up on the weird idea of my coming into the shirt business, settling down out there in Pittsburgh and getting married.' He hesitated, not sure how to proceed. 'I'm not interested in women except as talent to present on radio.' His eyes were candid as they met hers. He wanted her to understand this wasn't a romantic pitch.

'Starting up a radio station sounds like an enormous assignment.'

'But this is the time, Beth.' He exuded enthusiasm. 'My father can afford to lose $25,000.'

Elisabeth flinched. *How many families would that feed and house for a year?*

'Not that I expect to lose it – I did my homework. I know I can set up a small local station with that kind of money.'

'Do you know enough to handle it?' she asked as they headed down the flight of stairs to the street, an outlandish idea charging across her mind.

'I don't, but *you* do.' He voiced her thought. 'Let me set up a dinner meeting with my father. He's here in town for two weeks on some business deal. You can help me sell this – if he thinks I have somebody sharp and responsible to come in as general manager.'

'We could talk about it.' Excitement spiraled in her.

Elisabeth said nothing at home about this sudden development. As general manager of the station, she'd be paid a fair salary, she pinpointed. Not a large salary because the station would be just beginning to operate, but a living salary.

She met with Ted's father, and recognized that he was impressed with her. He haggled over figures, wanted a breakdown – which Elisabeth offered to supply – but she knew Ted would get his radio station. Grandma would say: 'You see? God provides.' She returned home with a feeling of moving into another world.

Arriving at the house she sensed that Hallie was impatient to talk to her.

'Hallie, what's bothering you?' For a moment they were alone. Katie wasn't home yet from school. Amy was reading to Ronnie on the deck.

'Well, you know I never did trust banks,' Hallie reminded her self-consciously. Long ago Elisabeth had tried to convince Hallie to open a savings account. 'But I'm getting a big lump under my mattress, and I thought I'd just give this to you . . .' Hallie reached behind a sofa pillow and produced a thick wad of five-dollar bills.

Tears filled Elisabeth's eyes. 'I may just need to borrow that for a while – to see us through to my new job. I haven't told you or the girls yet. We may be moving to New York City.' Hallie's eyes widened, first in shock, then in joyous anticipation. 'Don't say anything yet to anybody – not even to Amy or Katie. The deal isn't entirely set, but I may have a job running a small – *very* small – radio station in New York.'

The next six weeks were chaotic. Ted's father was coming through with the necessary funds, but he sometimes overwhelmed them with advice. Ted prepared to leave for the city. Without waiting for his father's approval he'd applied to the Federal Radio Commission for a broadcasting license. He expected it to come through straight away, and Elisabeth was immediately put on salary.

Now she told Amy and Katie about their prospective move. Katie was delighted – this was an exciting adventure. Amy was startled, upset.

'I don't want to leave here! I thought you'd always be here for me.' Terror mixed with reproach in Amy's voice.

'I will be,' Elisabeth said gently. 'Only it must be in New York. I'll have a job there. Amy, we have to go where I can earn a living for us.'

Two days later she saw Ted off at the Pasadena railroad station.

She was guaranteed a year's work, she reminded herself. She wouldn't think beyond that.

'Look, Beth, expect us to lose money the first year.' Ted was philosophical. 'We can handle that. We're not trying to be a network, just a small local station offering daytime programming that will appeal to women. That's the way to hook advertisers – and make a profit in time.'

Elisabeth was aware that Paul was living in New York. Even in such a large city they might just run into each other, the way people in related fields often did. Dear God, it would be wonderful to see him – even for just a brief encounter.

But Paul hadn't come to her. Katie would be seventeen in October. Paul's son was two years older and must be in college now. Paul could have come to her, Elisabeth tormented herself.

As the time to leave approached, Elisabeth was conscious of how much she would miss Ellie and Chuck and Ellie's parents. Ellie worried about her parents' health – both were showing signs of the advancing years. Chuck was taking on much of the responsibility of running the groves.

'I know Chuck's grateful for the financial security,' Ellie confided. 'In times like these it's such a relief to know we have that. But he frets because he has no time to write. He can't even consider writing for pictures – or trying to get a grip on radio writing. But times won't always be like this.' She struggled for an air of optimism. 'President Hoover has to do something to make conditions improve.'

Elisabeth was relieved when Ted phoned to say he'd found a sublet for himself and another for her in the same building – on the Upper West Side.

'For a three-bedroom apartment, it's a great deal,' he assured her.

The rent was higher than she'd anticipated, but they would manage, she resolved. Already Katie was talking about getting a weekend job – if something was miraculously available.

Flinching at the cost but reasoning it was less expensive than buying new furniture and house equipment, Elisabeth arranged for shipment to their new apartment. She sold the car – far past its good years – for a pittance. But then, who had cash these days?

Ted had rented space for the station in a low-rent neighborhood, he reported in a phone call two days later.

'We should have our license any day. Keep thinking women's

programs,' he ordered exuberantly. 'That's going to be the next big move in radio.'

Ellie and her mother drove Elisabeth and the family to the railroad station – all of them squeezed into Ellie's 1927 Ford. Elisabeth was beset by conflicting emotions. Was she making a terrible mistake to drag the family across the country again? Yet what was there for them here in Hollywood? As in so many traumatic moments in her life, Grandma's voice echoed in her mind. 'When times are bad, you dig inside for the strength to see them through. Tell yourself, "Tomorrow will be better."'

Chapter Forty-two

The trip east was less arduous than Elisabeth feared, though they traveled cheaply out of respect for their limited funds. Amy and Katie took turns reading to or playing games with Ronnie. When effervescent, ever curious Ronnie became restless, Hallie would take her by the hand and lead her off for 'visitin'' in other cars.

Elisabeth sensed that Amy had left Dr Hartman behind with less reluctance than anticipated. Yet at intervals Amy talked about her 'painful childhood' – as though, Elisabeth thought defensively, this was responsible for the failure of her marriage.

Others had what they felt were terrible childhoods – but they let go. Hallie had risen above a childhood that included physical and mental abuse, rape by her stepfather. Elisabeth had felt a lack in her own childhood – but she hadn't allowed it to destroy her.

Ted met them at Grand Central Station – where Elisabeth was assaulted by a flood of memories. He took them by taxi to the six-story building just off West End Avenue in the West Eighties where they were to live. He was on the second floor. Their apartment was on the sixth.

'We never lived so high up!' Katie was enthralled.

Hallie staked a claim to the smallest bedroom – little more than a closet – behind the kitchen. Amy and Ronnie would have the largest, Elisabeth and Katie the other. The furniture had preceded them by a day, and Ted had directed the placement. In every critical time, Elisabeth thought with gratitude, someone came into her life to help. Ted was a warm, sweet friend as well as her employer.

Ted insisted that she take three days to see her family settled in. The most important objective was to register Katie and Ronnie in their respective schools.

Hallie was awed by the accessibility of groceries. 'My goodness, I can just go around the corner and buy milk and vegetables and meat an' everything! I don't hafta drive everywhere!' Terrified at first of driving, Hallie had become an expert.

Now Ted and Elisabeth focused on the business of setting up the 500-watt station. They studied the daytime programming on other stations – none of it attention-grabbing. Programs that dealt with such subjects as gardening, food, tooth care. Night-time programming consisted of music.

It would be months, Elisabeth conceded, before they were in a position to broadcast anything radical. Meanwhile, she became producer/director/actress. In addition to handling all technical aspects of running the station, Ted concentrated on trying to interest local advertisers in what they had to offer. They were a staff of two doing the work of six.

'Don't be too arty,' Ted cautioned Elisabeth. 'Think in terms of the ordinary listener who loves *Amos 'n' Andy*.' He chuckled. 'Yeah, I know. We're a tiny station, we don't have a budget for their kind of salaries.'

Elisabeth made contact with a local drama school, held auditions, set up a night-time program that featured readings from classic plays in public domain – free of any royalty payments. She directed. The drama students were happy to perform. At Ted's insistence she played the leading roles. But for daytime programming she still sought a new format.

Eager to be knowledgeable about what was being broadcast, Elisabeth contrived to listen to a new NBC program called *Lum and Abner*, a summer replacement for a variety show, *Gene and Glenn*. On NBC's Blue Network she listened to *Clara, Lu and Em*. She reported on these successes to Ted.

'They'll draw audiences,' she said. 'But there's something else needed to entice women to turn on their radios and listen while they're cleaning, washing clothes, ironing, cooking. I have this tingling that tells me there's something about to burst upon the scene that'll make daytime radio an important part of the industry.'

She was relieved that Katie and Ronnie were fitting in so well with their new lives. Katie immediately made friends. Ronnie had what Amy called her 'park friends'. At intervals Hallie took Ronnie and frequent playmates to the Museum of Natural History and to the zoo.

Aware that they were living in an expensive city and on a strict budget, Hallie shopped for food bargains, devised pleasing meals at limited costs. With school out for the summer Amy spent much time on Riverside Drive with Ronnie, though Elisabeth surmised that she was reticent with other mothers she encountered. Katie tried with a wealth of determination to find a summer job. Nothing was available in these economic conditions. Now she spent time each day as Elisabeth's 'assistant'.

It was impossible to live in Manhattan and not realize the desperate lives suffered by so many, Elisabeth thought. They were *lucky*, though their lifestyle had skidded far downward. Newspapers reported that the American economy was at a standstill – people starving. Destitute men lived in improvised shanty towns along nearby Riverside Drive and were spilling now into Central Park. New York City – the richest in the nation – was providing $2.39 a week as relief for whole families. And there were many sections, Elisabeth thought in pain, where there were no relief agencies.

In September Katie entered her senior year at high school. Her grades were always excellent, Elisabeth reminded herself. No doubt in her mind that Katie would be accepted at Hunter College – where tuition was free for those girls who met their admission standards. This daughter would earn the college education she herself had been denied.

Aware that Elisabeth relished reading *Variety*, Ted decreed it was an expense required by the studio. He vowed to show his father that he could succeed at business despite these terrible times, spent eighteen hours a day either in the actual studio operation or on sales calls. He insisted that on most evenings Elisabeth leave in time for dinner with her family, though he knew that even at home her mind churned with studio business.

On this late September evening, while Katie focused on homework and Amy ordered a protesting Ronnie to bed, Elisabeth sat down with the new *Variety* for what Hallie called her 'little resting time'. She accepted another cup of tea from Hallie and began to read, ever drawn to theater news, though the family budget prohibited attendance at the dwindling number of plays being offered. All at once her heart began to pound. Her eyes clung to the page. 'Paul Coleman's new play is in rehearsal . . .'

Another comedy, she noted. In these trying times he wouldn't dare risk something not considered commercial. Too many theaters were dark, too many producers stripped of their finances by the stock crash. Paul would like Ted, she thought.

It pleased her that Ted loved theater. At any possible opportunity he was at a Broadway play – 'Top balcony seats most of the time,' he admitted. His father had financed the station with the stipulation Ted's salary be modest. Occasionally his mother secretly sent small checks.

On a balmy autumn morning Ted rushed into the station with the news that somebody must be brought in to relieve him next evening.

'I got lucky!' he crowed. 'Tickets for the Katherine Cornell play. You know, *The Barretts of Wimpole Street*.' A smash hit.

'I'll cover for you,' she offered. She was scheduled to leave at 7.30. She'd stay until their ten o'clock sign-off time.

'No way,' he effervesced. 'I've got two tickets. In the orchestra. Through my old man's connections,' he conceded. 'You're coming with me. Ask Katie to take over.'

Elisabeth stared at him in disbelief. 'We can't leave her in charge – she's a kid.'

'She's a bright kid. And tonight's just music. She knows how to handle it. She worked here all summer. Beth, it's only for two hours.'

'I'll ask her,' she said uneasily.

'You'll tell her,' Ted corrected. 'You're the mother.'

With a rare sense of festivity Elisabeth left the station with Ted to head for Times Square. Katie was thrilled at being in charge, she thought tenderly. Katie had her feet on the ground, bless her. How had she done so well with one child and been an inadequate mother to the other?

Clinging to Ted's arm as they pushed their way through the theater-going hordes – despite the Depression, some people still led normal lives – Elisabeth remembered her first sight of Times Square. She'd been so young, so fascinated at being here. Both she and Jerry so full of dreams.

'The play's at the Empire,' Ted said, 'but we're early. Let's walk around a bit. God, this beats Pittsburgh!'

As they walked in and out of the side streets to the left and the right of Broadway, Ted regaled her with inside stories about theater.

'Did I tell you what happened with *The Barretts of Wimpole Street* when it opened at the Hanna Theater in Cleveland?'

'No.' It was strange and wonderful to be here – for a little while feeling carefree. 'What happened?'

'The stagehands' union ordered them to cut fifteen minutes from the performance. Stagehands are only allowed to work for three hours – the play ran fifteen minutes over.'

'That didn't make the playwright happy –'

All at once Elisabeth stopped dead – her eyes frozen to the display before the theater at their left.

'Beth?' Ted lifted an eyebrow in enquiry.

'I was just reading the sign there,' she stammered. This was the theater where Paul's play was to open in four nights.

Ted checked his watch. 'We'd better start back. I hate rushing into the theater at the very last moment. I like to sit there and soak up the atmosphere for a while.'

The play was marvelous, Elisabeth agreed with Ted later while they headed uptown on the IRT; Cornell was marvelous. But her brain was saturated with the knowledge that Paul's play opened four nights from now.

He could have come to her, she tormented herself yet again. Tommy was grown now. Paul didn't have to dance to Doris's music in order to see his son. He'd forgotten what they'd shared. It had been just an incident in his busy life. What a stupid romantic she'd been, harboring the wistful hope that one day there might be a time for Paul and her.

Berating herself for childish behavior Elisabeth sought out newspaper ads for Paul's new play, scanned the gossip columns for tidbits. Her heart pounding, she read a brief newspaper interview, where Paul obviously charmed the interviewer but refused to discuss his personal life. '"The play's the thing," says playwright Paul Coleman. "I'm just its midwife."'

On the opening night of Paul's play she was tense, so nervous Hallie predicted she was coming down with a cold. The next morning she left the apartment forty minutes earlier than usual in her impatience to see what the *Times* critic had to say about the play. She bought the newspaper at her usual Broadway corner, turned anxiously to the theater section to read the review right there. It was fine. Why did she feel so relieved, so pleased? Paul meant nothing in her life.

Three evenings later – knowing it was absurd of her – she left the northbound IRT at Times Square rather than remain aboard until the West 86th Street station. She walked with pounding heart to the theater where Paul's play was appearing. Reviews would be posted outside the theater. Provided they were favorable.

She paused before the display, needing to know that the critics had given the play good reviews.

'Beth?' An incredulous, familiar voice intruded. 'Beth, it *is* you!'

She spun about to Paul, his face luminous as he gazed down at her.

'The same beautiful features,' he said softly.

'I read about the play . . .' Her voice was unsteady, her heart pounding. The years had been good to him – a touch of grey in his hair now, an aura of distinction that added to his quiet good looks. 'You received great reviews.'

'It's not the play I wanted to write.' His smile was wry.

'I know that,' she whispered.

'Only you would know.' His eyes clung to her face, as though to reassure himself that she was truly here. 'We can't just stand here this way.' He reached for her arm. She trembled at his touch. 'There's a coffee shop just down the street.'

'All right.' This was absurd. She was forty-five years old. She and Paul had been apart for fourteen years! How could she feel this way?

'I lost track of you,' he scolded. 'I could find no Amy Winston movies.' All at once he was alarmed. 'Amy's all right?'

'She married Keith Lindsay. They were divorced. She – she refused to do any more movies.'

His eyes caressed her in the old familiar way. 'I even resorted to reading movie magazines, hoping for some lead to where you were.'

'We've been in New York about six months.' He could have written Chuck. Chuck would have told him. Tommy was grown – Doris couldn't hold his son over him anymore. But he hadn't come to her. 'I was offered a job managing a small radio station here in New York. Conditions are ghastly in Hollywood –'

'Here –' He led her to the door of a small coffee shop that appeared uncrowded. They walked to a booth at the rear.

'How's Tommy?' She strained to be casual.

He closed his eyes for an instant, as though in pain. 'Tommy is why I keep writing shitty plays. Why I couldn't go back to Hollywood to find you. He always seemed so happy, so bright. But even before he was to start his first year of college, we knew something wasn't right. We didn't think it could happen to somebody so young. Beth, he's schizophrenic. Doris keeps running with him from doctor to doctor. Nothing seems to help. He's terrified of going into a sanitarium.'

'Oh Paul . . .' All this time she'd been silently furious at him – and he was in such pain.

'But you're here now.' It was a reverent whisper. 'Beth, I have to see you. I can't let you out of my life again.' His eyes pleaded with her.

'Yes,' she agreed after a moment. Paul needed her. She needed him. Nobody would be hurt. 'Oh, I've missed you so.'

Chapter Forty-three

Again, Elisabeth battled with guilt that she could feel such joy at being with Paul when she knew the agony that gripped most of his waking hours. But for a little while she could ease the horrendous burden of Tommy's illness. Ostensibly Paul shared a lavish apartment in the East 70s with Doris and Tommy. In truth, much of his time was spent in a modest one-bedroom in a brownstone off Riverside Drive in the West 80s – a few blocks from her own apartment.

Doris still insisted the world must believe she and Paul were the ideal married couple – and no one must know that Tommy had been diagnosed as schizophrenic. Paul admitted he wasn't sure Doris accepted the diagnosis.

For once, Elisabeth thought in a whimsical moment, fate had smiled upon her. Her working hours had been shortened. Ted's father had intervened in the station operation despite his original vow to remain on the sidelines.

'You're trying to do too much too fast,' he'd blasted them on a business trip to New York. 'Cut back on your broadcasting hours.'

For a little while each day she could be with Paul. He talked to her about Tommy, about his frustrations at being pigeonholed in his writing. What he scathingly called his 'mindless comedies' – but mainly he talked about Tommy and the nightmare his life had become.

'We couldn't believe what was happening to Tommy. *He* couldn't believe it. His first couple of months at college were fine. Then there was a bad period when he'd wake up in his dorm room and scream endlessly. We brought him home, took him to doctors. Sometimes he's so happy, he's sure he's all right. Then the craziness starts again. Last month he didn't eat or sleep for eight days and nights – he could have died.'

Now there was a live-in male nurse. Paul covered for him on his hours off.

'We're terrified he'll try to kill himself, not even knowing he's doing this. And lately he's hearing voices, seeing visions that leave him terribly shaken.'

'There's so much research going on,' Elisabeth comforted on this gray late December morning when she was able to siphon off an hour to be with him. 'Someone will come up with medication that'll control the situation.'

They sat on the living-room sofa and sipped black coffee that seemed to be Paul's constant companion.

He seemed to be pondering on her prediction. 'I pray somebody working in a lab somewhere will come up with a cure – or at least with a medication to control the condition.' Paul put aside his half-empty coffee cup and studied her face. 'How did I survive the years without you?'

'We're together now. For a little while each day we can shut out the rest of the world. I'm grateful.'

'I bring you my pain,' he apologized.

'I want to help. I wish I knew of some miraculous cure.'

'You do help.' He reached for her hand. 'Part of you is with me every waking moment of the day. And on lucky nights,' he joshed, 'I dream of you.'

'Happy dreams?' She picked up his shift in mood, allowed him to draw her to her feet. Knowing their destination.

'Dreams the Hays Office would never allow.'

'Something by Cecil B. de Mille?' She recalled his daring bathroom scenes with Gloria Swanson.

'Even de Mille wouldn't dare put my dreams on a movie screen.'

Arm in arm they walked into the small bedroom. The drapes were always closed, as though anticipating their passionate encounters. They paused beside the bed and, eyes making love, began to undress. Unexpectedly Elisabeth chuckled. Paul lifted an eyebrow, half-questioning, half-reproaching.

'I'm thinking how silly Hollywood is. They truly believe that love and passion stop at twenty-five.'

'Some things improve with the years,' he drawled, drawing her into his arms. 'And we're a prime example.'

* * *

Conditions in 1932 continued on a devastating path. Few believed that Hoover could be re-elected. In the past year newspapers informed the country that there had been over 5,000 bank failures. Unemployment continued to soar, was expected to reach close to twenty-five per cent by the end of the year. Salaries – for those with jobs – were down sixty per cent. It was estimated that twenty-eight percent of the population had no income whatsoever.

Schools were closing down in some areas. Elisabeth was shaken by the report that 300,000 children in New York City were not in school because the City had no funds to provide for them, and that of those in school twenty percent suffered from malnutrition. Each night she thanked God that Katie and Ronnie were not among them. So far, she thought gratefully, she was managing to provide for her family. But fear surged through her – along with compassion – each time she saw a pile of furniture on a sidewalk and knew a family was being evicted.

Elisabeth was ever aware of the instability of the radio station. She studied the programming being offered by the networks and the larger local stations. Of course, they couldn't compete with the likes of Kate Smith, Fats Waller, the Boswell Sisters or Morton Downey. Like many listeners she felt a personal pull towards *The Goldbergs*, a family held together by the mother. Their audience was enormous. If that formula worked so well at night, why couldn't it be equally effective as daytime radio? If strong enough, daytime radio could capture the housewife audience. That could mean strong sales for advertisers of household products. She knew that frantic efforts were being made to harness that audience.

She wrote to Chuck to urge him to write a daytime serial she and Ted could try to sell. It wasn't what he'd like to write, she conceded, but it could make a lot of money if handled well. But after a long, impatient wait, she received a letter from Ellie.

I know I've been remiss in writing, but this has been an awful time. How can I tell you without delivering a terrible shock? Pop died five weeks ago. Mom succumbed three weeks later. We miss them so much. We're both working seventeen hours a day – Ira as well – to keep the groves from going under in these terrible conditions. I should have written immediately – please forgive me.

Elisabeth and the family grieved for Bella and Peter Sanchez. They'd been so close for so many years.

'They was good people,' Hallie mourned. 'I'm glad we had them for a while.'

Every pollster in the country predicted a Democratic landslide in the coming presidential election. In February Al Smith announced he'd seek the Democratic nomination. On 7 April radio audiences heard the voice of another would-be candidate on national radio: Franklin D. Roosevelt, governor of New York.

'Smith won't win,' Paul predicted. 'The country isn't ready for a Catholic president. But I like the New York governor.'

'All of a sudden I realized that Amy has never voted.' Shock rippled through Elisabeth. 'We fought so hard for the vote – and women are just throwing it away!' But Katie was already demanding why she must wait until she was twenty-one to vote. 'Why can't we vote at eighteen?'

As Ted had predicted, they were losing money each month at the station. But he stubbornly insisted 'the tide will turn our way'. Paul was upset when his play closed in early May. Of the sixty-eight legitimate theaters in New York, less than a third had a play running, though Paul was quick to point out that Eugene O'Neill's *Mourning Becomes Electra* had played to full houses – 'even the six-dollar seats'.

'It's going to be rough without those royalties coming in,' he admitted to Elisabeth. 'Tommy's medical bills are horrendous.'

But in the coming months Tommy seemed to be pulling out of the bad scenes. He was lucid, sure he was at last in control of his life. The nurse was discharged.

'If Tommy is over this horror,' Paul told Elisabeth with fragile hope, 'then I can insist on a divorce.'

But how could they be married? Elisabeth was shaken by this possibility. Her first responsibility was to her family, surely Paul must understand that. Yet at the same time she prayed that Paul would be free.

But by autumn Tommy's condition had deteriorated to a new low. It became necessary to hire around-the-clock male nurses. Doris became hysterical at suggestions Tommy should be institutionalized.

'The prospect turns me sick,' Paul confessed to Elisabeth. 'In lucid moments Tommy's terrified of just that.'

'It might be the best way to treat him,' Elisabeth said gently.

'Neither Doris nor Tommy can see that,' Paul sighed. 'It's two against one.'

In June, in honor of Katie's high school graduation Hallie baked a cake. 'Chocolate inside and out,' Katie decreed. Elisabeth was unhappy that Amy refused to attend the graduation exercises, provided some weak excuse. Seven-year-old Ronnie was enthralled at being allowed to be in the audience along with her grandmother and Hallie. After hearing the story about the Chicago schoolteachers who were being paid in 'script' – to be redeemed when the Depression was over – and who hitchhiked to work so that half a million children wouldn't be out on the streets, Katie vowed she'd be a schoolteacher. The ambition of many Hunter students. Elisabeth was touched and pleased.

After all the festivities – and with every crumb of Hallie's cake consumed except for a generous slice, and Ronnie sound asleep – Elisabeth sat down with a final cup of tea to read Katie's college brochure. Hallie had gone downstairs with the last piece of cake, designated for an elderly neighbor who was a night owl. Exhausted from the evening's event, Katie had gone to bed.

'You'll have a daughter in college,' Amy said with grim humor. 'Sorry I couldn't oblige.'

'You could still.' Elisabeth strived to sound casual.

Amy stared in disbelief. 'You're still trying to rule my life!'

'Amy, what are you talking about?' Amy was upset because of all the fuss made over Katie today, Elisabeth thought guiltily. 'When have I tried to rule your life?' Was that what Katie thought of her?

'Always!' Amy lashed back. 'Nothing I ever did was right. You always had to correct everything I did in every movie I ever made. Nothing I could do on my own was ever right!'

'I always tried to help you.' Elisabeth felt as though she were on a merry-go-round that refused to stop. 'I was your coach – I wanted you to do your very best.'

'I was your little puppet! That's what they all thought at the studio. You never let me be *me*!' She spun around and stalked from the room.

Was that Dr Hartman talking? *Damn him.*

Shortly before election day – with Roosevelt the Democratic candidate and anticipated winner – radio executives became aware that a potent new formula for daytime radio had burst upon the scene. A new show, *Betty and Bob* – presented on NBC – was drawing listeners in startling numbers. Elisabeth and Ted listened to half a dozen episodes, dissected the content, then launched a campaign to find material with the same ingredients. They were euphoric when they encountered a writer eager to work with them without benefit of immediate pay. Janet Adams was a housewife with a working husband.

'He's a Federal customs inspector,' Janet told them. 'That's like a trust fund.'

Janet was not entirely happy with the caliber of acting talent willing to work 'for a chance to be heard', even on a shoestring station.

'You've got Beth,' Ted cajoled. 'She'll carry the show.'

With alternate coaxing and praising – and extravagant predictions of a future financial bonanza – Ted persuaded Janet to come up with scripts for a dozen episodes. He and Elisabeth would be providing basic plotting. Their efforts were directed towards introducing the series to their meager audience. Hallie was enlisted as critic for the first episode. She was intrigued.

'Hallie's our Crossley rating,' Ted declared with satisfaction as he sat with Elisabeth in the studio after the others had gone – though not before being briefed on Hallie's reaction.

'I'm not sure,' Elisabeth confessed. 'It seems on the unrealistic side to me.'

'Nobody wants realism these days. We're on the right track. You're not a housewife – you don't understand.'

'You are?' She shifted to a lighter mood.

'I can see what's happening. There's this ad man named Frank Hummert and a woman named Anne Ashenhurst that he's tied up with – they've got a writer named Andrews trying to turn out daytime radio geared to housewives. And I hear there's a teacher named Irna Phillips doing the same experimenting. Beth, we're playing in the right league.'

When Elisabeth came home on the evening of 3 March, she was greeted by Hallie with the triumphant news that she had been among the depositors at the Grand Central branch of Bowery Savings Bank who'd managed to withdraw their savings. Banks across the nation were in chaos. Bank holidays had been declared by governors in seventeen states and more were about to join them.

'You were always telling me not to hide my money under the mattress,' Hallie said with a winsome smile, 'and when you pestered me to take back what I'd given you, I took your advice at last and put it in the bank. But then I been reading the newspapers and I knowed somethin' awful was about to happen.' She took a deep, blissful breath. 'But I got my money out – and I think maybe it goes back under the mattress. Exceptin' if you be needin' it.'

'I'll keep that in mind,' Elisabeth said gently.

On the following morning New Yorkers woke up to the knowledge that the thirty-second President of the United States was to be inaugurated in Washington D.C. They learned, also, that Governor Lehman had joined other governors in declaring the day a bank holiday.

In Washington D.C. – on this raw, sleet-ridden morning – over 100,000 people gathered before the Capitol. Millions of others huddled before their radios. At noon – hatless and coatless despite the weather – Franklin D. Roosevelt was inaugurated. Along with millions of Americans – in farmhouses and urban apartments, in hobo jungles and flophouses, in factories and sweatshops – Elisabeth thrilled to the new president's statement that 'the only thing we have to fear is fear itself'. Hope had sprung alive in the hearts of a nation.

Elisabeth and Ted launched their series. Ted began to fight desperately for a sponsor. He and Elisabeth knew that Janet would not keep grinding out scripts without regular checks. But it was May before he reeled in the first prospective sponsor.

'The man's nuts, of course.' Ted was glum. 'He's talking about a one-week sponsorship. What kind of results can he expect in a week?'

'We'll make sure he sees results.' Elisabeth's mind shot into high gear. 'I'll have Ellie write from California, ask her to round up other people who'll send in fan letters. Talk to your mother out in Pittsburgh – have her engineer a fast response. They'll write that they love the show and want to hear more.'

'Beth, we're not a network show. Nobody hears us outside of our local area.'

Elisabeth hesitated only a moment. 'Then we'll have local people write in. Hallie will handle that.' Hallie created friends wherever she went: in the grocery store, the bakery, the church she visited every Sunday.

Elisabeth worried, too, that their amateur talent was not up to what was required if they were to snare advertisers, yet she knew their bankroll was growing slim. They couldn't afford salaries – even money for Janet – until they had contracts with sponsors.

'Work with these kids,' Ted exhorted. 'We need bodies there at the microphones.' There had been near-crises in the past when a needed body didn't show up. Twice Ted had to fill in – 'Hey I'm no actor. I write poetry, do a bit of painting!' – and on three occasions they drafted Katie, self-conscious but determined to be helpful.

Ted gave the cast – in truth, in a revolving door situation – an eloquent description of the opportunity that lay ahead when the sponsor made the one-week try-out official. Elisabeth was pleased with the enthusiasm he evoked. The first two days went off with only minor problems. Then on the third day a young would-be actress popped in – to save a five-cent telephone call – to report that she couldn't do today's show. She had an interview for a job at Macy's.

'I'm sorry, I have to be there.'

Elisabeth knew it was futile to plead with her. Even to land an interview for a job was an accomplishment, though she wished the girl had given more warning. They couldn't cut out her part – no way. Her mind in chaos, she hurried into the small studio where Ted was already setting out the morning's scripts. She briefed him on this new crisis.

'Call Amy,' he ordered. He'd been at the apartment for dinner several times in the past month. He'd met Amy, knew her background. 'I can't play an eighteen-year-old girl no matter how hard I try.'

'Amy won't do it.' Elisabeth searched her mind for a replacement. Katie was at college. The two women who might be available were older character women.

'What do you mean – Amy won't do it?' Ted was indignant. 'She's your daughter – you support her. Tell her to get her butt down her pronto.' He checked the clock. 'If she leaves right away, she'll be here in time to look over the script before we start rehearsal. Call her!'

Elisabeth called home. Amy answered.

'Amy, we have a serious problem.' Amy knew about the trial sponsorship. 'I need you to come to the station right now to fill in for a girl who's walked out on us –'

'I can't do that!' Amy's voice was shrill.

'It's urgent, Amy.' Elisabeth was conscious of a tic in one eyelid. Her throat felt constricted. 'We could lose our sponsor. We –'

'No!' Amy broke in. 'I can't do it!'

'You'll do it, Amy.' Anger soared in Elisabeth. 'Get yourself right down here and –'

'I have to pick up Ronnie at school.' Panic in Amy's voice.

'Ronnie comes home alone now.' Darling, independent little Ronnie. 'Amy, you can't let me down! I've always been there for you. Now you be there for me!'

Twenty-five minutes later Amy walked into the station's reception room.

'There's nothing to memorize,' Elisabeth reminded, handing Amy a script. 'You just have to read Veronica.' Elisabeth managed a synthetic calm.

'I'll probably sound awful.' But Amy was turning the pages in search of Veronica's first speech.

'You'll sound fine.' Elisabeth warned herself to be light on direction when they began rehearsal, Amy's earlier accusation etched on her brain. 'The rest of the cast will be here in ten minutes. Sit down and read the script.'

'Break down the part for me,' Amy said after a moment. It was as though – for the moment – the past few years had never happened.

In minutes the others arrived. An aura of excitement permeated the small studio. Everyone was aware of the potential of their performances. Elisabeth intercepted a glint of recognition when she introduced Amy. It was eight years since Amy had appeared in a movie, but they recognized the still lovely, young face, distorted only a bit by the added seventy pounds.

At the beginning of the program their announcer made a brief statement that this morning the role of Veronica would be played by Amy Winston. How many in the audience, Elisabeth asked herself, would remember the young silent screen star? This was the first time Amy's voice would be heard by the public. Fleetingly Elisabeth envisioned a revived film career – Amy's voice was perfect for talkies – but then the vision evaporated. Amy would have to reduce drastically before she could face a camera.

Amy gave a performance that elicited an admiring reaction from the others. Between the two of them they'd carried off this episode with distinction, Elisabeth told herself in relief. Two more episodes and their sponsor must make a decision. Would he continue the series – or drop it?

For a fragment of time Elisabeth and Ted were jubilant. By the end of the week fan mail was arriving – not solely that mandated by the station. Their anticipated sponsor conceded the response was great. Then why was he looking so unhappy?

'You've got something good going.' He took a deep breath, exhaled. 'But I'm in a rough situation. Business is bad. Creditors have been breathing down my neck. My accountant tells me that I can't take on any more expenses. Not one red cent.' He paused. Suddenly he looked gray. 'I may have to go into bankruptcy. Twenty-seven years of slaving away at the business – and now I could lose everything.'

Chapter Forty-four

In the face of their sole sponsor's defection Elisabeth and Ted sat down to dissect their own financial situation. They couldn't hold on much longer. Elisabeth suggested a drastic, painful cut in their salaries.

'We'll manage somehow,' she insisted defiantly.

'I'll give up my flat,' Ted declared. Unexpectedly he smiled. 'That won't be too bad. Mark's been dying for me to move in with him.' Ted and Mark had met seven months ago at a party in Greenwich Village. Mark was a struggling artist – 'loads of talent', Ted said. His parents provided him with a small stipend 'to keep him from embarrassing them back home'.

'Your father will be livid.' Ted's father closed his eyes to Ted's preferred lifestyle but would balk at his sharing an apartment with Mark.

'He won't have to know. I'll tell him and my mother I'm having trouble getting my mail at home – they're to write me at the station.'

'We must keep the series going somehow.' Elisabeth was somber. 'And we have to keep Janet writing.' It was futile to try again to bring in Chuck – even if he could write this material. Ellie wrote that she and Chuck, along with Ira, were working seventeen hours a day to keep the business afloat.

'There are two worlds today,' Ellie wrote. 'Those with jobs and those without. I look around, and I'm terrified we won't make it. Though Chuck believes President Roosevelt is on the right track. I see neighbors here on relief, and my heart cries for them. They feel so humiliated, so ashamed to have to take. I don't want that to happen to us.'

With Elisabeth's already modest salary cut Hallie walked from store to store, searching for bargains. Amy seemed – at last – to understand their perilous financial status. Falteringly she offered to help at the station.

The weeks blended into months. Conditions showed no improvement. In a money-starved society – though Ted pointed out bitterly that there were those like his father who continued not to suffer from the Depression – radio became the major entertainment. Movies offered diversion for those who could afford the ten-cent admission.

Elisabeth cherished the hours she could contrive to spend with Paul, ever fearful that their meetings might be discovered. Lately Paul was tied down more than in the past to the apartment where he and Doris struggled to care for Tommy.

'It's so frustrating,' Paul told Elisabeth on this stormy January evening after they'd arrived at his apartment drenched to their skins, and had both changed into ancient bathrobes. 'For a week – sometimes two – Tommy's all right – happy, sure he's got this thing licked. And then it starts again.' Paul closed his eyes for a moment as though to wash away reality. 'This new doctor keeps insisting we put him into a sanitarium for a while. He's developed some new treatment program. Doris is against it, but I think we ought to give it a try.'

'You're right, Paul.' Hope was a precious commodity.

'It'll be wildly expensive, but my agent told me this morning that he might be able to line up some work for me in Hollywood. Perhaps a one-picture deal. On the strength of the last play.' He frowned in distaste. 'I hate the Hollywood scene – and I'll miss you terribly.'

'I'll miss you. But it won't be for long.' She managed a shaky smile. Hollywood was not a pleasant place these days, beset by a rash of tragedies. Clara Bow and Buster Keaton were in private sanitariums, their careers – their lives – desolate shells. Handsome Milton Sills had driven his limousine over Dead Man's Cove on Sunset Boulevard. Alma Rubens and Barbara LaMarr – both drug addicts – were dead as a result of their habits. Jeanne Eagles – who briefly electrified movie audiences – died of a deliberate overdose of heroin. All of them so young.

'I've got this awful writer's block.' Paul broke into her introspection. 'I've told you, I can't get moving on another play. If I'm in Hollywood and Tommy remains at home, as Doris insists, we'll have to hire round-the-clock nurses again. He has phenomenal strength when he goes into one of those bad periods. I told my agent that if the money's good, I'll go out there.'

Three weeks later Paul left for Hollywood. He had signed a six-month contract that would pay him amazingly well. Elisabeth saw him off on the Twentieth Century Limited.

'I'll write you care of the station,' he told her. Both of them conscious of the need to keep their relationship secret. 'We can't deny ourselves that. I'll give you my address as soon as I'm settled.'

'Take care of yourself.' One final embrace and he must board the train. 'I'll miss you every minute of every day,' Elisabeth whispered.

'A time will come when we won't have to play these silly games,' he promised. 'Remember, I'll love you always.'

Elisabeth and Ted sought feverishly for programs that would draw listeners. They began an amateur contest, scheduled musical events using talent willing to work for carfare.

'I've been trying to locate this young singer I heard the other day,' Ted told Elisabeth. 'You know, willing to work for nothing, hoping for a break. But damn, I can't get a lead. His name's Sinatra. Frank Sinatra. I tell you, the kid's got a future.'

And then Janet decided she'd had enough. As far as she could see, the series was going nowhere.

'Janet, this is close to what's hitting the networks and is getting sponsored,' Elisabeth emphasized. 'Look at what's happening with *Just Plain Bill*, *The Romance of Helen Trent*, *Ma Perkins* –'

'My husband says I've wasted enough time. This is the last script, Beth. You know,' Janet tried for a flippant note. 'My master's voice.'

Elisabeth frowned in annoyance. She recoiled from the universal acceptance of the man being 'the master of the house'.

Mark, Ted's friend, came to their rescue. He brought in an aggressive, ambitious woman named Caroline Webb.

'She wants to write like Eugene O'Neill,' he confided before bringing her to meet with Elisabeth and Ted. 'But she'll settle for anything that gets performed.'

Elisabeth sat down with Caroline, explained the formula. 'It's fifteen minutes long. And each episode ends with a question – what happens next to the heroine? It's ordinary people fighting to survive. Plenty of storm and stress. Maybe the critics don't like them, but housewives love them. Listen to the network daytime shows – you'll understand what I'm saying. Don't turn up your nose at them,' Elisabeth warned. 'It's not art, but it's what women want. It's what sponsors are buying.' Magic words to Caroline, who yearned for a penthouse on Central Park South and a white Rolls Royce. And hope soared in Elisabeth and Ted when they realized Caroline had a real knack for writing for housewives.

Ted persuaded his mother to come across with a 'small loan': 'Your father mustn't know.' It was now or never, Elisabeth and Ted realized. They knew they could never compete with night-time network radio, which offered such hugely successful programs as Jack Benny, George Burns and Gracie Allen, Major Bowes, Fred Allen. But they *could* – miraculously – hope to match the sponsored daytime programs being provided by the likes of Frank Hummert, now married to Anne Ashenhurst.

By the time Paul returned from Hollywood, Elisabeth sensed the tide was turning for Ted and her. But her concern on this first meeting with Paul was for him.

'You look so tired.' Elisabeth searched his face anxiously.

'I'm writing such shit, Beth. I know – there are some good films coming out of Hollywood. But I'm supposed to write comedies. Frivolous material to make people forget how rotten their everyday lives are.'

'That's a service, Paul.' But she understood his feelings. She looked back with nostalgia on the years in Melbourne and the year in London when she'd acted in fine plays.

'You're not exactly enthralled with what you're doing.' Tenderly he read her mind.

'I'm grateful to have it. I'm realistic.'

'How's the financial situation?' He knew they lived on the edge of a precipice.

'I have a sense of a breakthrough,' she said after a moment. Was it bad luck, the way Hallie fearfully warned, to talk about it? Not to Paul. 'Ted's going after a major sponsor, who's considering a try-out on a local station. If he likes the show, he may take it network.'

'Where would that leave you and the station?'

'Ted and I have developed the show – it belongs to us. And if that happened, Ted would try to sell the station and pay back his father. We wouldn't need it with a show on network radio.'

'Is there that kind of money in daytime programming?' Paul seemed amazed.

'A lot of money.'

'I feel like a whore.' Paul chuckled. 'I told you what they paid me out there on the coast. Though I don't think I endeared myself.' His smile was wry. 'I have a tendency to speak my mind. But at any rate I came back with a substantial cushion. And now that I'm home we can cut down on the nurses for Tommy. He's still on a seesaw, seeming to be making progress one month – then a relapse the next. Even in lucid intervals he's in such anxiety about what lays ahead. He and Doris are both fighting against his going into a sanitarium.'

'Write a play that pleases *you*,' Elisabeth urged. That would provide him with some relief, she thought. Intervals of escape.

'I have an idea floating about in my mind.'

'Then develop it, Paul. Give yourself a break.'

'I just might do that.' He reached to pull her close. They had a fierce hunger to satisfy.

Perspiring on this sultry late August evening, Katie waited for her close friend and classmate Olivia to arrive at their meeting place in front of the Automat. Summer in the city was miserably hot. On rough days – when she felt extravagant – she'd go into an air-conditioned movie just to cool off. Some nights she and Olivia splurged on a bus ride up Riverside Drive, sitting on the upper deck.

Amy hated the summers, she thought with compassion. The summers meant infantile paralysis epidemics, and Amy was terrified for Ronnie. They all were. They conspired between them to keep Ronnie away from other children for these two bad months. Of course, it hit grown-ups, too. A girl in her class nearly died of it last summer. Now she was in a leg-brace and out of school.

Her eyes lighted as she spied Olivia hurtling towards her at her usual breakneck speed.

'You don't walk fast in this weather,' Katie scolded.

'Let's go in and have a beef pot pie and coffee, then head for Columbus Circle.' Olivia led her into the Automat. This was their special Saturday night treat during the summer.

With nickels in hand they collected beef pies from the proper cubicles, then, one at a time, went to the coffee urn.

'Thank God, school's opening in a few days.' Olivia uttered a mock sigh. 'My mother will stop whining, "Why can't you find a summer job?"'

Katie shrugged. 'Who can find a job these days?'

'Was your mother upset when you told her you were switching majors?' Olivia asked when they'd settled themselves at a table.

'Mom's not that way. Maybe she was disappointed – she has this enormous respect for teachers. But I said I want to be a journalist, like Martha Gellhorn or Dorothy Thompson. She accepts that.'

'Let's eat and get up to Columbus Circle.' Olivia's eyes glowed. 'It's exciting to wander around in the crowd and listen to all the speakers.' Many of them young men, an admitted attraction. And it was free.

'It's good experience if we're going to be journalists.' She and Olivia had been friends since their freshman year. Olivia complained about being stuck in an all-girls' school: 'How are we supposed to meet fellas?'

They ate with relish, hurried out of the Automat and up Broadway to Columbus Circle. Already speakers were hawking their causes atop soapboxes while the curious gathered around one or another.

'Katie, let's go over there,' Olivia whispered. 'Wow, he's cute! He looks a lot like Paul Muni.'

The two girls left the orator who was bewailing the plight of unions to join the cluster of people – mostly young like themselves – around the eloquent young man who was speaking about the Young Communist League.

'There's a branch at Hunter,' Katie remembered. Not that she or Olivia were involved.

'And at City College,' Olivia pointed out. 'He's a student there, I'll bet.'

They hung around and listened to him talk. His name was Morty Kleinman. At regular intervals his eyes met Katie's.

'He's going to try to pick you up,' Olivia whispered. 'Maybe he's got a friend.'

He gestured to somebody in the crowd to come to relieve him, headed for Katie and Olivia.

'You two go to Hunter?' he guessed.

'How do you know that?' Katie was curious. Olivia was right. He *was* cute, kind of dynamic.

'Well, I figured you're not at City College – where I go.'

'Not unless they passed a rule to admit girls.' She wasn't intrigued by the Young Communist League, but she felt drawn to Morty Kleinman.

'It's hot as hell. Why don't we go cool off in the park?'

'Why not?' Olivia accepted for them, but her eyes were straying.

'Hey, Charlie!' Morty called, and beckoned to someone in the crowd. 'Charlie goes to City, too. He's sharp. A born leader.'

'For the Young Communist League?' Katie was wary.

'The Student League for Industrial Democracy – SLID.' He grinned. 'You wouldn't know about that. It's a student movement for peace.'

'I'm for peace. My father died in the war.' She had no memory of her father, but Amy loved him as her stepfather. Mom said he'd died a hero, fighting for freedom.

'My father was too old to go, but an uncle was killed. This movement started at Columbia and Berkeley, but we plebeian students,' he drawled, 'climbed aboard, too. We want to have every male college student pledge that if Congress declares war, we won't serve. We're against compulsory ROTC, against Fascism. We mean to fight for student rights and academic freedom. We –'

'Get off the soapbox.' Charlie sauntered over to join them. 'It's time to play.' He was introduced to the two girls, quickly recognized that Morty had established his rights to pursue Katie. Good-humoredly Charlie focused on Olivia. 'OK, let's go cool off in the park.'

Morty was three years older than the two girls. He'd dropped out of college, played the hobo scene for two years, returned to live with his parents on the Lower East Side and re-enrolled in college.

'For seven months I lived in New Orleans,' he reminisced, 'alternating between lousy jobs and the soup kitchen. Great town, New Orleans. O. Henry called it one of the three romantic cities in this country.'

'What about San Francisco?' Katie challenged. Mom thought it was a wonderful city – before the big earthquake. 'What about New York?'

He looked at her. 'They're the other two.'

Later Charlie walked Olivia to her subway. Morty walked with Katie all the way up to her apartment, talking freely about himself. He was determined to earn a college degree.

'It's important to have a marketable skill.' His grin was lopsided.

'Of course, if the current climate continues, we'll move out into a society that doesn't want us.'

He was working at three part-time, low-paying jobs for the summer, hoped to hang on to two of them during the school year.

'I'm damn lucky to have them. But I have to give something at home. My folks are fighting against going on "relief". I think that would kill them. My old man was a big wheel in the union a few years ago. But what good are unions today?'

'I don't know much about them.' Katie was candid. 'Only that they're very weak now.'

'Look, what are you doing tomorrow?' Morty's smile was electric. 'What do you say we grab a subway and head out for Brighton?'

'Sounds good to me.' Katie was intrigued by Morty Kleinman. He wasn't just a college kid. He'd spent two years on the rails. He'd seen a lot, learned a lot. 'Let's go early before the crowds descend.'

Katie and Morty met at every opportunity, though this was limited by school demands and Morty's part-time jobs. She was entranced by his colorful tales of life on the rails, by his eloquence when he spoke about the dire state of the nation. And the first time he kissed her good night, she knew she was in love with him. Still, she ignored the passionate question she read in his eyes each time they met.

Olivia was frank. 'So I'm sleeping with Charlie. Whose business is it but ours?' She grimaced. 'Of course, Mom would kill me if she knew. But I'm a grown-up – it's my decision to make.'

Katie knew that in Morty and Charlie's circle, 'free love' was acceptable. Not in her circle, she reminded herself. But there was no way she and Morty could get married now. They had two years of college ahead of them plus graduate school. She refused regularly even to go up to his room. He lived in a hall bedroom in a brownstone on West 70th Street, just off Broadway, far more comfortable for the amorous embraces Katie permitted than the dark foyer or the elevator in her apartment house. They'd abandoned covert sections of Central Park since the onset of dropping temperatures.

On a bitterly cold December Saturday afternoon when twilight closed in on the city and the sky threatened to unleash a barrage of snow, Morty persuaded her to go to his room.

'We've got to stop this coy craziness of yours,' he reproached. 'I want to make love to you. I'm tired of all these stop signals.'

Panic brushed her. Morty meant to drop their relationship if she wouldn't sleep with him. She wanted to – he didn't know how badly she wanted to!

'Well?' He stopped dead on the sidewalk, waited for her response.

'All right,' she whispered. Like Olivia said, it was nobody's business but theirs.

They climbed three flights of dark stairs to his three-dollar-a-week bedroom at the end of the hall. Katie was trembling as he fumbled with the lock.

'I'll make us tea,' he promised, arm at her waist as he led her into the tiny bedroom, furnished in 'rooming-house maple'. Narrow, with one window, a wash basin jutting out into the room near the window.

'You pull a kitchenette out of the wall?' She tried to be flip. Her heart was pounding.

'A hot-plate in the closet.' He grinned. 'If you're a good kid, I'll make us spaghetti for dinner.'

'What about before dinner?'

'Oh, baby, dessert comes first.'

She closed her eyes as his arms pulled her close. For a few moments they swayed together – then both were urgent in their demands for more.

Chapter Forty-five

When Elisabeth and Ted were about to concede defeat – though Caroline doggedly wrote ahead – the would-be sponsor came through. He was buying time for a three-month period beginning the first of the year. Like Elisabeth and Ted, Caroline was elated.

'There's this fellow who lives next to me,' she reported. 'He's a publicist – at the moment he's an unemployed publicist.' Her grimace was eloquent. 'I think I can persuade him to do some work for us now that we have a sponsor, even though it's just local. You know, with the promise of paid assignments if the program's picked up after the trial period.'

Elisabeth gathered he didn't just live next door to Caroline. He shared her bed.

Before the first program was broadcast, their unpaid publicist had planted items in several newspaper columns. 'All right, so he can't get daytime radio into Winchell's column. People are reading about us!'

Despite the long hours devoted to station business, Elisabeth found time to worry about Katie's first involvement with a boy. Her conversation always seemed to include some mention of Morty Kleinman. Elisabeth had met him briefly. He seemed bright, serious-minded, polite. Very much concerned about the future of the country, Katie told her with pride.

They weren't serious, Elisabeth comforted herself. At their age it was natural to be attracted to the opposite sex. Both had their education to complete. Katie had decided just these last months that she didn't want to teach. She wanted to be a journalist. That meant two years of graduate study. Elisabeth blocked from her mind the cost this would entail.

At last Paul had convinced both Doris and Tommy that Tommy should be committed to a sanitarium for treatment. Right after the first of the year, Tommy would enter a sanitarium just outside of Boston. Doris would stay in a hotel there for the duration.

'You know how hotel costs have skidded downward,' Paul told Elisabeth. Mildly defensive – though they both knew Doris would opt for the easiest way of life. Now he tried for humor. 'I hear that at the Ritz or the Pierre here in New York you can get a room as low as six dollars a night. Guests must be blessing the Depression.'

'Most guests at the Ritz or the Pierre don't know there *is* a Depression.' She voiced the dreaded subject now. 'When do you have to leave for the coast?' He was practically commuting, she thought tiredly. But the deal his agent had just set up for him would pay for Tommy's care in that posh sanitarium where he would be for a minimum of six months.

'The day after New Year's. I'll see Tommy and Doris settled in Boston, then take off. God, I hate these long separations, Beth –'

'I suppose the new play goes on hold?' Her eyes were wistful.

'I still haven't gotten past the first act.' He took a deep breath, exhaled. 'My head's always in a jumble these days.'

'Everything comes in cycles.' One of Grandma's pet theories. 'Now you'll see the happy cycle.'

Her words to Paul seemed to be prophetic for Ted and herself, Elisabeth thought in the coming few weeks. Under her direction Caroline was coming in with material that she sensed was *right*. Though most of their talent was barely above amateur status, she and Amy were able to carry the show. Fan mail was coming in regularly.

At the end of the three months the sponsor announced he was buying the package.

'But I want to move it to network radio.'

'No sweat,' Ted assured him. 'Elisabeth and I own both the station and the package – but each company operates separately.'

Ted was euphoric, immediately putting the station up for sale. It was a matter of ego, he admitted, to be able to repay his father. His cut on the radio package would support Mark and him in Paris, he told Elisabeth in soaring optimism.

'Sure, I know many Americans are coming back home. But Paris is bursting with exciting people – artists, writers, composers – refugees running from Hitler's Germany and from Spain. Everything is cheap once you know where to look.'

'Suppose the series flops? Suppose he doesn't renew?' Where would she be then, with the station gone?

'Honey, it'll go on for years,' he predicted. 'And even if it doesn't, both you and Amy have your feet steeped in daytime radio. You know the scene. You'll pick up acting jobs with no problem.'

The first hint of spring was in the air, Amy realized as she hurried from the radio station to the apartment. She'd come to love the changes of season that New York provided, in such contrast to the Southern California climate. She glanced at a clock in a store window. Good. She'd be home well before Ronnie arrived home from school.

Hallie teased her about her obsession to be there when Ronnie walked into the apartment. Maybe Ronnie wouldn't be upset, but she remembered all those years ago in New York. She'd been so frightened when Mama went off in the morning that she'd never return.

Reaching for her key she could smell the tempting aromas of bread baking in the oven. Cinnamon and raisin, she identified walking into the foyer. Each day Hallie popped a small bread that was 'almost cake' into the oven so that the three of them could have what she called their 'afternoon tea'. It was Hallie's way of saying, 'Times may be tough, but we can live nicely.'

Within minutes Ronnie was home. The three of them gathered around the kitchen table for their 'tea' – though for Ronnie this was a cup of hot chocolate, Hallie's response to Ronnie's refusal to drink plain milk.

'You oughta be glad you can have milk,' Hallie reproached futilely. 'Lot's of little kids would be glad for it.'

She hated that Ronnie had to be aware of people scavenging in garbage cans, standing in breadlines, being evicted from apartments – but how could she protect Ronnie from seeing the world as it was?

'Do you have a lot of homework for tonight?' Hallie's usual question.

'Yeah.' Ronnie sighed. 'We have to do this composition on what our mothers do while we're at school. Hallie, can I have another piece of cinnamon bread?'

Was Ronnie going to tell her class that her mother was an actress on radio? Amy wondered. She hated it. She always felt as though the others were looking at her in disgust that she was so fat. But the audience couldn't see, she comforted herself. She hated having to go to the station five days a week, to have to be so close to other people. She never knew what to say to them. They were all so sure of themselves.

She felt guilty each time she acknowledged to herself the parade of candy bars she consumed so ravenously – always outside the apartment. Only Hallie knew of the nocturnal trips to the bread box for chunks of her wonderful bread. She kept vowing to go on a strict diet, but it never happened.

'Mama, can I tell them you used to be a movie star?' Ronnie asked as they settled themselves in the living room.

'No!' Amy was startled by the sharpness of her rejection. 'That was a long time ago.' Ronnie couldn't remember – that was Mama and Hallie talking.

'What should I say?' Ronnie frowned in contemplation. 'Donna's mother is a nurse. Celia's mother is a bookkeeper. You know, I think it's exciting to say my mother's a radio actress.'

'All right,' Amy capitulated. 'You can say that.'

Now she was being paid a weekly salary. Mama wouldn't let her contribute to the house expenses: 'Put it in the bank for Ronnie's college.' Thank God, bank accounts were now safe.

Tonight she found it difficult to sleep. She left the bedroom on tiptoe lest in her restlessness she awaken Ronnie. This composition Ronnie talked about disturbed her. *She was doing nothing with her life*. Ronnie said a classmate's mother was a nurse, another a bookkeeper. All at once she was conscious of an aching need to have Ronnie be proud of her.

Sitting in the kitchen with a cup of tea and a chunk of Hallie's perfect apple strudel, Amy arrived at a decision. Her heart was pounding. Tomorrow she'd talk about this with Mama.

It was to be a year of unexpected happenings, Elisabeth told herself when Amy came to her and – her voice unsteady but her eyes determined – said she wanted to go to college now.

'If I can get into Hunter,' she conceded. She understood there was no money for a private college.

'You'll take the exam and you'll pass it. Katie will help you. We'll find a tutor. Amy, you'll go to college.' What she'd longed for but never expected to happen was happening.

'I want to be a social worker.' Her eyes seemed to plead for approval. 'I want to do something useful with my life. Like my father.' Though she had only the vaguest memory of him, she had been brought up on stories of his dedication to humanity. That was her heritage, Elisabeth had told herself with pride.

'Then so be it.' Tears stung Elisabeth's eyes. Her baby was taking hold of her life at last.

'I'll go over to the Admissions office at Hunter and look into the test deal.' Amy seemed relieved at her approval. 'And if I can't make it into Hunter this first try, then I'll take the test again. I'll go for my masters in social work.' Amy had given this deep thought, Elisabeth realized. 'Maybe – if I work hard – I'll win a scholarship to the Columbia School of Social Work.'

Things were going well for Amy. Elisabeth knew how conscientious Amy could be – she would earn her masters.

But Katie was unhappy Morty was taking off a term at City College to go down to New Orleans.

'He's setting up some student group down there.' Katie was trying to accept Morty's defection from classes. 'He's so upset about rumors that Huey Long is planning to run for president on a third party. The man's a Fascist!'

'Huey Long has too many enemies to get anywhere,' Elisabeth soothed. She caught herself on the point of quoting Paul. Only Ellie knew about her relationship with Paul, and she had sworn not to admit this even to Chuck. 'I know Long has people down in Louisiana on his side. As governor he did a lot of good things – but then he went totally corrupt. The dictator of Louisiana,' Elisabeth said scornfully.

'I'm scared Morty will open his big mouth in the wrong places.'

Elisabeth's mind darted back through the years to David's fight in Melbourne on behalf of non-whites who were being persecuted.

'Maybe I ought to go down there to be with him –'

Elisabeth's face was drained of color. 'You finish your education!' Katie was serious about this boy.

Early in the summer Ted began negotiations to sell the station. Their series was going well. Soon Elisabeth would be handling the program on her own. At painful intervals she was unnerved by the responsibility. If the program didn't stay on the air, she'd be job-hunting.

'Beth, you're the sharpest businesswoman I've ever met. Even my father says that,' Ted encouraged. 'You'll hold this package together and expand it.'

'We'll need office space somewhere once the station is sold,' Elisabeth plotted. 'Something cheap. And I'd like to bring in another writer, so Caroline and I can start to build another series.' They could afford it, she reasoned. The Hammerts were expanding like mad. 'I'll do the rough plotting. Caroline can work out the details, then hand it over to another writer to do the dialogue.' An assembly-line deal.

'The best thing that ever happened to me was meeting you,' Ted said with relish. 'Just keep my share of the profits coming to me in Paris. Life will be good for Mark and me.' His face softened. 'I'm just a would-be entrepreneur – but Mark has real talent. I respect that.'

Late in June Paul wrote that he'd signed an extension on his studio contract. But he would be in New York for a week in August after a few days in Boston. Was this all she and Paul were ever to have? Elisabeth asked herself in despairing moments. But each had obligations. Neither would walk away from those obligations.

As always, summers in New York brought terror to parents because it was then that infantile paralysis struck. This year Hallie – with devious wisdom and an enlarged household budget – was contriving to have Ronnie and two of her best friends spend much time in the apartment. This would be a card-playing summer, she'd decreed – with Ronnie luncheon hostess each day.

Ronnie was ever a delight to Elisabeth, a constant reminder of Grandma. Even small mannerisms were the same, she marveled lovingly. Ronnie was the center of their household – at moments spoiled outrageously.

Now Ronnie was enthralled that her mother, accepted at Hunter, would soon be spending her evenings poring over school books. 'Mom, that's keen!'

For the summer Katie was working for Winston Productions, as the new company had been named. Amy was part of the radio cast, to be written out once classes began.

Despite her heavy work schedule Elisabeth plotted to spend time each day with Paul during his brief stay in the city.

'I wish we could be together all night,' Paul said wistfully as Elisabeth lay in his arms this first evening.

'I wish so, too.' What would happen if she said to the family, 'I won't be home tonight?' Yet she knew she couldn't bring herself to say this. There was nothing *wrong* in her being with Paul this way. His marriage had been non-existent since Tommy was a small boy. Only circumstances kept Paul entrapped. 'But I'm grateful for now.'

'I feel better about Tommy than in a long time. *He* feels the doctors are helping him – and that's what is so important.'

Paul talked with distaste about his work in Hollywood, the lust for big profits.

'Sure, there're some decent movies coming out these days. Von Sternberg is doing *Crime and Punishment*. I hear *Little Man, What Now?* is solid. But mostly the studios are turning out brassy musicals.'

'What about your play?'

Paul sighed. 'On the back burner. But enough talk for now –'

'Paul, is it obscene that we can be so passionate at our age?' But her face was luminous as she lifted her mouth to his.

'It's a gift.'

Too soon she was at Grand Central yet again to see Paul off. He hoped to be home again by the first of the new year. She would cherish that thought.

Late in August Elisabeth and Amy saw Ted and Mark off on the elegant liner *Ile de France*. 'Spectacular yet comfortable,' Ted told them. 'Take my mother's word for that.'

'The bar in the lounge is the largest afloat,' Mark contributed.

The final moments before she and Amy must go ashore were poignantly sweet to Elisabeth. She always seemed to be saying good-bye to someone close – yet she should be happy for Ted. He would love living in Paris, where he and Mark would be accepted for what they were: two charming, talented, witty Americans. Yet Ted's departure would leave a void in her life.

'You'll come to visit us in Paris one of these days,' Ted said ebulliently. 'Keep the programs going. Our lives are in your hands,' he added dramatically.

*   *   *

For the first time – on Thanksgiving – Katie brought Morty home for dinner. Elisabeth didn't want to see Katie romantically involved so young, yet she had to admit the family liked Morty. He brought a kind of pleasant excitement to the dinner table, catered to each of them in turn. Knowing Elisabeth's background in theater, he told them about encountering Ethel Barrymore in New Orleans.

'The great lady of the American stage,' he confided, 'was drunk as a lord.'

Morty talked in a more somber note about Hitler's vicious Nuremberg laws that were causing such consternation among Jews – and all right-thinking people – around the world.

'Why don't other countries do something to stop him?' Ronnie demanded with the typical passion of an eleven-year-old. 'He's a bad man!'

'Nobody wants to start another war,' Katie told her. 'But some noisy condemnation might help.'

'Thank God for Mayor LaGuardia,' Elisabeth said softly. 'He's not afraid to condemn.'

Marty was blunt about feeling no regret for the assassination of Huey Long in September.

'The man was a damned Fascist!'

Immediately after the midafternoon dinner, Amy excused herself.

'Mom has to study for a test,' Ronnie told Morty. 'She's at Hunter, too. Like Katie.'

Slowly Elisabeth's confidence in the progress of the radio series was growing. This wasn't what she'd hoped to do with her life – but the money was fine and the security growing more positive. If their first sponsor should withdraw, there was another avid to pick up the series. She had her two daughters in college, her granddaughter indoctrinated with the importance of education. She should be happy.

Paul arrived in New York on New Year's Day 1936 – after spending four days in Boston. Elisabeth met him at Grand Central, accompanied him to his apartment. His exhilaration at Tommy's apparent improvement was foiled by the knowledge that he was on what he bluntly called the studio's 'shit list'.

'I open my big mouth too often.' His smile was rueful. 'I've been uptight about Tommy's taking two steps forward, then regressing a step. Still, the doctors feel they see daylight ahead. But I'll have to look around to raise funds to pay the bills.'

'What about writing for radio?' That could keep Paul in New York.

'What about it?' Paul jeered. 'I can't write for Jack Benny or Burns and Allen. I'd never be able to do the daytime radio *schtick*. And I'm too rich,' he said playfully, 'to find work with the WPA theater project.'

'What about the play?' But she knew the answer to that. When did he have time to write for himself out in Hollywood?

'I'll have my agent try for some magazine articles – you know, the freelance writer scene. But let's don't think about that now. I feel so good, just being here with you.'

'You'll feel even better soon . . .' She knew Paul loved it when she was slightly naughty.

'Beth,' he asked huskily, 'when will there be a time for *us*?'

Not just these brief reunions, Elisabeth understood. A *normal* life. It filled her with pain that her family couldn't know this love she felt for Paul.

Late in April Paul met her for dinner at a quiet restaurant near her office with the news he'd snared a magazine assignment.

'It's not Hollywood money,' he conceded, 'but it'll handle my bills as long as I stay with it.' He paused. 'I'm offered a job as foreign correspondent.' He named a prestigious national weekly.

'Where will you be based?'

'Spain.' He surprised her with this admission. 'I'm to leave next week for Madrid.'

'Isn't there supposed to be fighting there?' Alarm spiraled in Elisabeth as she recalled items in the newspapers. 'Something about the recent elections . . . ?'

'Certain army leaders want to overthrow the Republic.' Paul was somber. 'The League of Nations is trying to stay out of it. But let's face it. This is one more Fascist move in Europe. We've got Hitler in Germany, Mussolini in Italy – and now fighting to overthrow Abyssinia. The march of Fascism has to be stopped.'

'But the Popular Front won the election!' This was the alliance of Republicans, Socialists, and some Communists. 'Spain's a democracy.'

'But they have the army, the Church, and the large landowners against them. It could become ugly.'

407

'Paul, it's a dangerous assignment!'

'Beth, I have to accept. I need the money.' He paused. 'And perhaps in some tiny way I can help in the fight to stop the spread of Fascism. The future of civilization is at stake. The madmen must be stopped.'

Chapter Forty-six

Elisabeth waited impatiently for a letter from Paul. Meanwhile, she read with fear the reports on the troubles in Spain. Strikes were taking place throughout the country. Street fighting broke out in many towns and cities. Gunmen in cars toured the streets. Revenge killings abounded.

At last a letter arrived. Paul was staying at the Florida Hotel in Madrid, 'courtesy of the expense account'. He played down personal danger, talked about the arrival of other correspondents who sensed – as he did – that this was about to become a civil war. Elisabeth fought insomnia night after night. Paul should not be in Spain.

On the happy side Elisabeth looked forward to Katie's graduation at Hunter. Katie was ecstatic at the prospect of attending Columbia's School of Journalism as a day student in the fall – made possible by the success of Winston Productions. As Hallie said, 'Lots of folks are havin' bad times – but there's them that ain't.'

Morty was at the apartment with noticeable regularity these days – which Elisabeth attributed to Hallie's tasty meals more than a need to share in family conversation. He uttered pessimistic remarks at steady intervals about being part of the 'locked-out generation'. This evening – while Morty dug appreciatively into Hallie's pot roast – Katie reminded him that unemployment had been cut in half, though it was still painfully high.

'Maybe I can get a job running an elevator at Macy's once I have a degree. I hear that's a requisite.' Morty paused for a sardonic smile. Elisabeth gathered his approval of the New Deal had hit bottom in this past year.

'I can vote this November,' Katie gloated, determined to redirect the table talk. This was a household strongly behind FDR, though the Gallop report said the Republicans had a fifty–fifty chance of winning. 'My first presidential election.'

The family attended Katie's graduation en masse. Tears blurred the view for Elisabeth. Her younger daughter was about to receive her college degree – and God willing, Amy would follow suit in three years. What had been denied her would not be denied her daughters or her granddaughter.

Katie would work in her mother's office for the summer. Jobs were still hard to find. Morty had acquired some low-paying job that was taking him around the country. Elisabeth felt a simmering unease about Morty's politics. Did that job have something to do with the Young Communist League? The possibility was unsettling. But, of course, nobody took Communists seriously.

On 18 July civil war erupted in Spain. Elisabeth prayed that Paul would come home, but reality broke through wishful thinking. Paul was in Spain to report on the war many had anticipated. Fascism was on the march in Europe. Voices were raised in outrage. The forces that threatened to overthrow Republican Spain must be stopped.

In August, in a cafeteria on Broadway in the 70s, Katie sat and listened to Morty express his fury over the fighting in Spain. At a nearby table three other young people were involved in a similar diatribe. Democracy was at stake if Fascism continued its insidious spread. The fighting in Spain could lead to another world war. But the United States, Great Britain and France opted for non-intervention. Earlier in the month the French border had been closed.

'Katie, the world can't let the Republic go down the drain!' A vein throbbed in Morty's forehead. 'Maybe other countries won't come to the aid of Spain, but the young of the world will take action.'

Katie was frightened when Morty was unreachable for five days. Had he taken off for Spain on his own? Did he think he was another Don Quixote? On the sixth day he called her at the office.

'Where the hell have you been?' Relief made her sharp.

'I've been dragged into a dozen conferences – about the situation in Spain.'

'You might have called me!'

'All I could think about was, what can we do to help? I'm sorry, baby.'

'And what came out of all these conferences?'

'I'm not running off to fight in Spain,' he soothed. 'At least, not yet. The important deal at this point is to raise money. For guns, for medical supplies. I'm on a committee. Look, stop worrying. If you don't see me for a couple of weeks, I'm all right.' She heard garbled voices in the background. 'Katie, I gotta run. I'll be in touch, I promise.'

Ten days later Morty called at the office.

'Meet me at the cafeteria,' he said tersely. 'Now.'

'I can't just yet.' She looked at the clock. 'In about half an hour.'

'Be there, Katie. This is important!'

'All right, Morty.' What was he up to now?

Within twenty minutes Katie was striding into the cafeteria, already filling up with early diners. She spied Morty at their favorite table at the rear and hurried towards him.

'Missed you baby.' He reached for her hand.

'You know where to find me.' Her eyes reproachful.

'I'll get us coffee.' He rose to his feet and headed for the serving counter.

When he returned with the coffee, he began, 'We're getting word from Spain that what the Republicans need most at the moment are medical supplies. We've got money that has to be taken to Paris and handed over to the committee there. But it has to be by somebody who won't be suspected of working for the Popular Front.'

'But why?'

'We were warned that Americans caught fighting Franco will lose their passports. We have to avoid that.' He paused, his eyes seemed to weigh her.

'You're going,' she guessed.

He shook his head impatiently. 'Are you nuts? I'm a marked man. This has to be entirely innocent. A pair of tourists. You and Olivia.'

She gaped in shock. 'Morty, classes start in two and a half weeks!'

'You'll be back before school opens. I've got a pair of tickets, tourist class for the *Ile de France*. No problems getting reservations when money's so tight for most people. You leave in four days. I'll help you get passports in that time. We have contacts. You're two college graduates celebrating getting your degrees.'

'Morty, I don't know . . .' Mom would be furious. Olivia's mother would be furious.

'Damn it, Katie, this is urgent!' His eyes dared her to refuse. 'People's lives depend on it!'

Katie dreaded the encounter with her mother – even while her mind sought for arguments to buttress her plotted efforts. She told herself defensively that her father would have understood. He'd run off to fight beside the Canadians in the World War and died in the cause of freedom. Mama would be anxious for her safety, but Mama knew she was a grown woman now – it was her decision to make.

'You are going to do *what*?' Elisabeth gaped in disbelief when Katie had outlined her plans.

'It's something Olivia and I have to do. The money is going for medical supplies. We won't be going to Spain,' Katie soothed. 'Just to Paris. A contact will pick up the money there.'

'It's illegal!' Yet she remembered Paul's presence in Madrid. His words ricocheted in her mind: '. . . perhaps in some tiny way I can help in the fight to stop the spread of Fascism. The future of civilization is at stake. The madmen must be stopped.'

Elisabeth had read with horror about the atrocities being committed by the Nationalists, as they called themselves, under Franco's command. All over Spain whole garrisons were revolting. Franco set up a Fascist government in Burgos. Civilians were being killed, prisoners massacred. Paul wrote – thus far without censorship – that in Republican territory peasants and workers were ravaging villages and towns. Franco and the army were not alone in committing atrocities.

'You're going to Paris,' Elisabeth emphasized. 'Promise you don't set foot on Spanish territory.'

'Olivia and I are a pair of tourists going to spend a week in Paris,' Katie reiterated. 'We're booked into a small hotel on the Left Bank. We'll spend time with Ted and Mark. It'll look perfectly normal. But we're delivering $50,000 to buy medical supplies for the Loyalists.'

Elisabeth knew about the special girdles stuffed with hundred-dollar bills that each girl would wear, more sewn into their heavily lined bathrobes. And she knew, too, that she wouldn't draw an easy breath until Katie and Olivia were back in New York.

Katie and Olivia sailed on schedule. Both were dazzled by the splendor of the *Ile de France*, yet at the same time ever conscious of their mission. They were friendly to shipmates, but – as Morty had warned – avoided close contacts. Olivia's mother, unaware of the purpose of their trip, had been convinced that it was a graduation gift for Katie. 'But Katie wouldn't have any fun alone, so I joined the party.'

Katie admitted to relief when they left the ship, boarded the boat train for Paris.

'We'll have a chance to test our French,' Katie said exuberantly when they left the Gare St-Lazare to travel to their hotel by taxi.

The hotel was a small, sleazy structure on a narrow, winding street. The furniture spare and showing signs of age. The girls dismissed this. So they weren't staying at the Ritz. This was not a pleasure trip, though both were determined to make their week here eventful.

As promised, a note had been left for them. A visitor would arrive at eight p.m. They were fearful of leaving the hotel until they had delivered their booty. Suppressing giggles – checking to make sure the door was locked – they removed the store of hundred-dollar bills from their hiding places and shoved them into the briefcase brought along for this purpose.

At exactly eight o'clock their visitor arrived, displayed the agreed identification. He was a young Englishman – probably no more than twenty, they guessed – who explained that at midnight he would be leaving Paris to travel south and sneak across the border into Spain.

'You've done well,' he approved, with covert glances at Katie's legs. 'I hope we'll meet again soon.'

'Is it bad there?' Katie asked sympathetically.

'It's hell . . .' For a moment he seemed twenty years older. 'But we'll win, comrades. The world will be a better place!'

'Comrades?' Katie lifted an eyebrow in surprise when she and Olivia were alone. That reeked uncomfortably of some of Morty's Young Communist League friends.

'Just a figure of speech,' Olivia dismissed this breezily. 'Let's go somewhere to eat. I'm starving. And call your friends.' A cable had advised Ted of their imminent arrival.

Ted and Mark picked them up at their hotel, took them out to dinner, regaled them with stories about the delights of the Left Bank.

'We'll show you the town,' Ted promised, 'not just the tourist spots.' For a moment he was wistful. 'A lot of Americans have gone home. Paris isn't what it used to be.'

Still, Katie and Olivia were enthralled at seeing the 'tourist sights': Notre-Dame, the Arc de Triomphe, the Eiffel Tower, the Champs-Élysées. They took a carriage ride through the Bois de Boulogne and sipped Pernod liqueurs at the Ritz Bar. At Sylvia Beach's Shakespeare

& Company Katie bought a copy of a novel by André Gide for her mother.

'I hear the store's having financial problems,' Mark said sympathetically. 'It's become a Paris landmark, that shouldn't happen. But Gide, the stories say, is rounding up some people to help the store stay afloat. A lot of people can't afford to buy books these days.'

One evening they dined with Ted and Mark in their 'apartment-cum-studio' – and with unexpected shyness Mark showed his latest paintings. Ted reveled in Mark's talent. It was clear Mark wasn't just a dilettante. Katie and Olivia were impressed.

On their last day in Paris the two girls shopped at Galeries Lafayette for presents to take back home. In the evening they dined with Ted and Mark at what Ted called their big splurge of the year. Dinner at Maxim's. Only now did Katie tell the two men the real reason for their trip to Paris.

'Oh God, Katie!' Ted grimaced in disgust. 'Don't you know the Loyalists are being manipulated by Russia? This isn't a war for the people of Spain – it's war between Russia on one side and Germany and Italy on the other. Wake up, kiddos!'

Katie and Olivia exchanged startled glances.

'Franco's fighting to make Spain a dictatorship. Everybody knows that!' Katie's eyes were reproachful.

'Sure. And Russia is fighting to make it a Communist state. You won't read that in American newspapers. You'll just read about the urgency to crush the rise of Fascism before it takes over the world. But we've heard Russian diplomats – drunk as any capitalist – boast about the help they're preparing to send to Spain. Thousands of soldiers, tons of guns and ammunition. They're organizing volunteers from all over Europe, Canada and the United States to go to fight in Spain. Not to stop Fascism but to promote Communism.'

En route home, Katie and Olivia searched their minds for the truth. Ted and Mark must be wrong. Morty said that people – many of them brilliant, famous, from all over the world – would be flocking to Spain to help the Loyalists drive out Fascism.

Katie ignored the sultry heat in her impatience to arrive at the cafeteria. Morty would be there waiting for her. She needed to hear him say Ted and Mark were wrong about the fighting in Spain. She tugged at the back of her lilac cotton dress that clung wetly between her shoulder blades. It would be comfortable in the air-conditioned cafeteria, she remembered with relief.

Inside the cafeteria she spied Morty at their regular table. He had his face buried in a copy of the *New York Post*.

'Hi . . .' Her voice was breathy from exertion.

'Sit down, baby. I'll get us iced tea.' He rose with a reassuring smile and charged across the floor to the serving counter.

She sat at the edge of her chair. On the phone Morty told her he knew their mission had been accomplished. He'd been at work when she called – the conversation had had to be brief.

'How did you like Paris?' He grinned, deposited the two tall, frosty glasses on the table.

'We were upset by what my mother's friends told us.'

'Upset about what?' He seemed amused.

'Ted and Mark told us that Russia is preparing to ship troops and guns into Spain.'

'The Popular Front needs all the help they can get!'

'My mother's friends in Paris said this wasn't a war to save the world from Fascism. They –'

'Hey, what kind of shit did they throw at you?' Morty broke in. 'Is Russia fighting to save the Republic for the Spanish people – or to back up the Communists there?'

'Be realistic, Katie.' He grunted in annoyance. 'The workers and the peasants in Spain have had a terrible time. The Republic wasn't helping them. Russia will make the elected government understand that the workers and the peasants must have their fair share. They –'

'Morty, are you telling me that Russia means for the government to go as far left as Communism?'

'It has to be that way.' All at once Morty abandoned pretense. 'The poor in Spain won't get their share unless Franco is beaten and the Communists take over the government.'

'So it's what Ted said. Russia is fighting against Germany and Italy. Communism against Fascism.'

'Katie, stop getting so hot under the collar. You know how rotten it's been in Spain except for the lucky few. It's time to push the clock ahead and –'

'Answer me, Morty! Are you taking your orders from Russia?'

'I'm taking my orders from the Young Communist League,' he shot back. 'I never lied about being a member!'

415

'I thought that was just some silly college organization. You said you were fighting against Fascism!'

'Damn it, I am!' A vein hammered at his temple.

'But not for democracy! For Communism!'

'Get off the soapbox, Katie!'

'I hate Fascism – but I want no part of Communism!' Her eyes glittered with contempt.

'What's democracy done for this country?' He kept his voice low now because the tables around them were becoming occupied. 'Communism can lift us out of this rotten depression. Allow ordinary people to lead decent lives. A lot of people in this country believe that with me.'

'I never really knew you at all, Morty.'

'Knock it off, Katie. Stop being a naïve little idiot.'

'Thank God, you sent me to Paris. I might have gone on believing you were ready to go to Spain to fight Franco because you were so dedicated to democratic principles.' People at the next table were beginning to stare, but she didn't care. She rose to her feet, reached for her purse. 'Goodbye, Morty,' she said scathingly. 'I never want to see you again!'

Chapter Forty-seven

Elisabeth listened with compassion while Katie poured out her tale of disenchantment with Morty.

'I feel like such a jerk, Mom!'

'Too trusting, Katie – but not a jerk.'

'I hate men.' Katie grunted in disgust.

'Not that, either. There're despicable men and despicable women.' In frustrated moments Elisabeth placed Doris in that category. 'But, darling, never condemn the whole human race for the ugliness you see in some. Your father and Amy's father were fine, decent men.'

'I thought the Young Communist League was just some college years rebellion – I didn't think Morty really swallowed their line. All the people who're talking about going off to fight beside the Loyalists, don't they understand what they're doing?'

'You didn't until Ted and Mark talked to you about it. These young men and women who're gathering together to fight with the Loyalists believe with all their hearts that they're doing what is right. They're taking a stand against Hitler and Mussolini and now Franco. They're desperate to stop Fascism. They don't want to see another world war.'

'How long do you think the fighting will last?'

'Who can say?' Elisabeth wished Paul would come home. She read about the atrocities and was afraid for him. Just this morning she'd read that within the next six weeks the first International Brigade, organized by French writer André Malraux, was expected to arrive in Spain. Those fine young men – being deluded by the Commies. She forced herself to continue. 'President Roosevelt means to keep this country neutral. Most people agree with him.'

'I feel so sorry for the Spanish people,' Katie said softly. 'They voted for Democracy. They're pawns in the hands of Communist and Fascist leaders.'

Elisabeth knew Katie was hurting, was grateful that she was so involved with school, with less time to remember. Katie never talked about Morty, yet at unwary moments she wore an air of painful loss.

In the months ahead Katie, like Elisabeth, devoured all news from Spain. On 17 October the first of the International Brigades – from Europe – arrived in Spain. Soviet supply ships docked at Barcelona. Nationalist planes that had been bombing Madrid soon found opposition in the skies. Russia accused Germany and Italy of blatantly violating their non-intervention pact. For a while there was hope that the fighting would soon stop.

Paul had warned Elisabeth that his letters would not get through. He wrote when someone was leaving Spain and could mail his letters with some prospect of their reaching their destination. He wasn't happy with the reporting, nor with the censoring of his own articles.

The new year rolled in. On 20 January FDR was inaugurated for a second presidential term. Economic conditions seemed little better than when he'd begun his first term, but by spring an upturn was taking place. Industrial output increased. The unions were regaining strength. Unemployment was dropping though the statistics were still far from healthy. There was a feeling that the country was pulling out of the crisis.

Life had evolved a holding pattern, Elisabeth thought. Amy and Katie were totally immersed in school. Ronnie intrigued with the image of Katie as a journalist. 'I'm going to be a journalist, too,' she vowed. Elisabeth found solace in work. Ever amazed at the success she was enjoying. This was not what she had envisioned as her life's work, but the daytime series on radio were financially rewarding beyond her expectations. She focused now on producing and directing. Only when a crisis arose did she take on an acting role.

The war in Spain raged on. Reading between the lines of Paul's occasional letters, she gathered he was disillusioned with what had seemed such an idealistic crusade. He complained, in letters mailed to her outside of Spain, about censorship. He was frank. He remained on the job because the checks were supporting Tommy's medical care.

In August the US economy took a disastrous tumble. Almost overnight production suffered the worst drop in American history. But Elisabeth's income soared as she added new series to her roster. This was a bumper year for daytime radio, beginning with Irna Phillips' new *The Guiding Light*. Elisabeth was holding her own with such newcomers as *Our Gal Sunday*, *Lorenzo Jones*, and *The Road to Life*.

Battling guilt at this extravagance when so many were hurting, Elisabeth moved the family into a large apartment on West End Avenue, with five bedrooms – one for each – and a maid's room that she commandeered as her home office. To the family this was a slice of heaven.

'Our whole house back home coulda fit into my bedroom here,' Hallie chortled.

Elisabeth was working twelve to fourteen hours a day, but still there were nights when she lay sleepless, worrying about Paul in Madrid; distressed that Amy continued to do nothing about her shocking weight gain; fearful that Katie still hurt from the break with Morty. Better now than later, Elisabeth consoled herself. As at anguished moments in the past, she could not discard her pain that Amy regarded her as a bad mother.

'Honey, knock it off,' Ellie wrote in reply to a recent letter in which she blamed herself for Amy's unhappiness. 'Amy's quoting what that damn Dr Hartman dredged up. With therapists the mother is always to blame.'

Early in the new year, 1938, a shocking number of Americans were near starvation. Roosevelt, who had earlier been advised to balance the budget, sent a big-spending program to Congress – and it was passed by both houses. The economy began to improve.

In Spain the chaos continued. Germany and Italy sent troops, tanks, planes and artillery to General Franco. The Russians did the same for the Loyalists and sent hundreds of technical advisors as well. By now the International Brigade boasted such outspoken liberals as George Orwell, Ernest Hemingway and Paul Robeson. Then on Friday, 11 March, Americans turned on their radios and learned that Hitler's army had marched into Austria.

In the next few days radio broadcasts were interrupted repeatedly with bulletins about Hitler's progress. On Sunday evening at eight o'clock a CBS announcer came on to the air to announce that the scheduled program would not be heard. Instead, listeners would hear a special half-hour report on the reactions from European capitals to Hitler's invasion and annexation of Austria.

Gathered around the living-room radio with her family, Elisabeth was impressed by this first international news roundup.

'Wow!' Katie was enthralled by the reporting. 'It's almost like being there!'

The following night the same format was offered. Elisabeth was especially drawn to the reporting of a young American in Vienna, named Edward Murrow. And she was frightened for the Jews that remained in Austria. She was frightened for the world. Where would Hitler stop?

Seven weeks later Elisabeth received a letter from Paul that had been mailed from London. She closed her office door, impatiently ripped open the envelope.

My dearest –

By the time you read this I'll be in Bougy Villars – a small village near Geneva, Switzerland. Tommy and Doris are en route to join me. Doris learned of a doctor at a tiny sanitarium close by that's doing exciting research on schizophrenia. Their results have been amazing. I've rented a house through someone here with contacts in Switzerland. The worst part is that I won't be able to receive mail from you, but I'll try hard to write as often as I can. More about Spain later. I must devote myself now to my personal crusade. To help Tommy emerge from this nightmare that has consumed his life so long. I worry about how he would survive if something happened to me –

So again, they'd face separation. Through tear-blurred eyes Elisabeth read the remainder of Paul's letter. But at least, she consoled herself, he was away from the dangers of Spain. Maybe in that village near Geneva he would have the time to work on a new play. How wonderful if he could return from Switzerland with Tommy's health restored and with a new play to offer Broadway producers.

Paul inspected the clock on the living-room wall of the small, white stucco house he'd rented for six months with an option to renew if this should be necessary. He'd leave in ten minutes for the railroad station. After the horror of Madrid the quiet here was awesome. He stood at the window and gazed at the view that seemed destined to calm the most tense of residents.

The house sat on a grapevine-covered mountainside that over-looked beautiful Lake Geneva and faced Mont Blanc – today shrouded in clumps of fog. Elisabeth would love being here, he thought with a surge of tenderness. The magnificent view would be lost on Doris. She would complain that the kitchen was too small, the furniture too worn, the mattresses not to her liking.

But this doctor was achieving dramatic results in treating schizo-phrenic patients. The average treatment time was six months to a year, with patients given selected weekends at home with their families. The medication had not yet been approved in the United States, but it was receiving high praise in Europe. Paul had never felt so optimistic, so hopeful. When Tommy's life began again, then so would his.

On schedule he left the house for the drive to the large, drab Geneva railroad station. He was pleased with the four-year-old Mer-cedes he had been able to buy here. He felt secure in the knowledge that their funds, transferred to a Geneva bank, were more than sufficient to see them through the year Tommy's treatment might require. He was eager to see Tommy, though he knew his son would be under heavy sedation so that the male nurse who traveled with him and Doris would encounter no problems. The nurse would remain at the house overnight, then head for home.

Meeting the train – on time, as Swiss trains always were – Paul waited eagerly for Tommy to disembark. Each time they were apart for a long time he found it difficult to look at his handsome son and accept the fact of his illness. Tommy had been a supreme accomplish-ment of his life, the one that gave him the most happiness.

All at once passengers were disembarking. The atmosphere was electric. There was Tommy – appearing sleepy, as though he'd been partying the night away. His nurse was a tall, strapping young man who kept a hand at Tommy's elbow as though to steady him. Doris rushed forward after issuing a series of commands about her luggage in shaky French.

'Paul, I'm exhausted from all this traveling! You know how terri-fied I am of ships.' She held up her cheek for a kiss, calculated to infer that they were a devoted couple. 'I hope this house is not too awful.'

All the way home to Bougy Villars Doris rattled on about pre-sumed slights by her 'women friends' back in New York.

'How many bedrooms?' she demanded suspiciously as Paul turned into the uphill driveway to the house. 'It looks so small.'

'It's as big as the apartment back in New York.'

'How many bedrooms?' Doris repeated, her voice accusing now.

'Three.' Why did he always get this terrible tension between his shoulder blades after five minutes in Doris's company?

'Where will we put up guests?' He felt her simmering rage.

'We're not here to put up guests, Doris. We're here to be near Tommy, to be able to see him regularly.'

'But with our having a house in Switzerland my friends will expect to stop off to see us the next time they're in Europe.'

'Then they'll just have to understand.' Paul comforted himself with the knowledge that Tommy was too sedated to know his parents were quarreling again. That had always upset him – when he'd been well.

Paul steeled himself to face a grueling six months – or a year if Tommy's doctor so decreed. He'd turn his bedroom into a workplace. Dig into the play that had been floating around in his mind all those months in Spain. Work had always been his escape. It would be again.

Elisabeth was moved to tears of joy when Katie was graduated from the Columbia School of Journalism with a master's degree, though this was a rough time for Katie to find a place for herself in the newspaper world. Meanwhile, she worked in the office of Winston Productions.

Elisabeth enjoyed Katie's enthusiasm for radio news. Though this was not her field of operation, she, too, saw radio reaching new heights with news broadcasting. And like Katie, she was fascinated by the newscasts of Ed Murrow with his 'Hello, America. This is London calling.'

'What about a woman newscaster?' Katie demanded. 'Why isn't Martha Gellhorn broadcasting from Spain?'

'They probably don't have facilities for broadcasting from Spain. But don't you worry, Katie. One of these days women will be broadcasting the news.' For women it was always an uphill battle.

Elisabeth was intrigued by the developments in the new field of television, though Katie warned that this could kill her daytime radio market.

'I'm not worried,' Elisabeth insisted. In truth, she devoured everything that was written about the subject. 'The transition will be simple, the way talking pictures evolved from silents.'

'Mom, that wasn't easy. Look at all the stars who fell by the wayside.' Katie knew about John Gilbert, Conrad Nagel, Charles Farrell, Ramon Novarro – and the others. She knew that Louise Brooks had fallen from stardom to a job in Macy's, that Mae Murray – once Princess Mdivani via marriage – had been arrested for vagrancy on charges of sleeping on a bench in Central Park.

'Some will make the transition,' Elisabeth amended. Amy could have made it beautifully if she'd lost eighty pounds – but Amy's heart was in social work now.

The entire household, including news-conscious Ronnie, clung to the radio in late September when Hitler met in Munich with Great Britain's Prime Minister, Neville Chamberlain, French Premier Edouard Daladier, and Mussolini to discuss the fate of the Sudetenland, part of Czechoslovakia. Czechoslovakia had no say in the matter. In an effort to avoid war the other countries agreed to Nazi Germany's annexing the Sudetenland. Hitler vowed this would be his final demand for land.

It was during the Munich crisis that for the first time American radio supplied news on a twenty-four-hour basis. The American audience was hungry for foreign news. They learned that in London gas masks were being distributed – yet American life continued as normal. But the happenings around the world made insomniacs of Americans who couldn't accept the national wish of isolationism.

Katie chased after possible newspaper and magazine assignments that would take her to Spain or Austria or Czechoslovakia.

'Why can't I connect with something?' she wailed. 'So much is happening! I want to be part of it!'

Elisabeth was secretly grateful that Katie's efforts to secure international journalistic assignments were futile. She suspected, too, that Katie still chafed from the break with Morty. Not that she was in love with him any longer – but furious with herself for being misled. Neither Katie nor Amy had any social life, Elisabeth worried. Amy was engrossed in earning her degree, Katie vowing to pursue her career.

Elisabeth was exhilarated by the aura of hope in Paul's most recent letter:

I know we'll have to be here for at least another six months, but we see slow but steady improvement. Tommy spends alternate weekends at the house with us. He admits now that he had considered suicide at regular intervals, but that's gone from his agenda. He just wants to get well and resume his life again. And you and I can make plans for our lives.

Would there ever be a time when they could be together without these painful separations? Would Amy and Katie accept him in their lives? He would be a wonderful stepfather and stepgrandfather, Elisabeth thought tenderly.

Katie proved an efficient assistant to Elisabeth at Winston Productions, but Elisabeth knew she was frustrated by her inability to find a job in her chosen field. Now, in her off hours she was trying to write and sell magazine articles. Her friend Olivia had acquired a job in a law office through 'family connections'. Olivia admitted she hated her job. Katie was impatient with Olivia's yearning to 'find a cute boy and get married'. Amy was straining for high grades that would help her land a scholarship to Columbia's School of Social Work when she graduated from Hunter in June.

'Mom, Amy's such a jerk,' Katie told Elisabeth in frustration. 'She's breaking her back to come up with top grades, but she won't let me help her. I've been through these courses – I could save her time.'

'Let her be,' Elisabeth soothed. Amy had to prove to herself that she could manage on her own.

On 28 March 1939 Franco marched in triumph into Madrid. The bloody civil war was over. Over a million people had died. Much of Spain lay in ruins. And when the Abraham Lincoln Brigaders returned home, the FBI confiscated their passports. They were considered a security risk. They'd flocked to Spain with such idealism – to stop Fascism before it could take over the world. Paul, too, had felt that way. Later he'd become disillusioned.

In June Elisabeth again had the pleasure of seeing a daughter awarded a college degree. If she accomplished nothing more in her life, she confided to Hallie in exhilaration, she was proud of this. Grandma would have been so happy to know her great-granddaughters were educated women.

Amy spent the summer in an intensive reading program. So insecure, Elisabeth fretted, yet so determined. She yearned to give Amy confidence in herself, to make her understand that as a child actress – and later – she had provided pleasure to millions of moviegoers.

Elisabeth was tense from worry about the situation in Europe in the final days of August. Just yesterday Germany and the Soviet Union had signed a non-aggression pact. Dictatorships joining hands. Tonight – long after the others in the apartment were asleep – she clung to the radio, the volume muted, listening to accounts from Washington, London, Paris. Everywhere there was fear that Hitler would advance on Poland despite the efforts of England and France to prevent this.

She was grateful for the letter she'd just received from Paul. In fifteen days he – along with Tommy and Doris – would be leaving Switzerland and heading for New York.

Beth, I can't believe it's finally happening! On this new medication Tommy can live a normal life. Once he's settled in a job and in his own apartment, I'm demanding Doris divorce me.

Thank God, Paul was coming home. How wonderful it would be to see him! Of course, it would be a while before he was a free man. Somehow, in that time, she must find a way to make Amy and Katie understand that Paul would not be an intrusion. His presence would enrich their lives.

Now Elisabeth made a sudden decision to take the family out of the hot, steamy city for the approaching Labor Day weekend. The office could run without her for four days. They'd leave Friday morning, return to the city on Tuesday morning.

She'd been offered the use of an oceanfront house at Southampton by an executive at the network, but had left the invitation hanging. Call her now.

'Darling, I'm leaving Thursday for California on business or I'd be there for sure, but the house and the cars are yours,' her would-be hostess said blithely. 'Send someone over to pick up the keys. I'll jot down a memo about how to get there, which restaurants you'll enjoy.'

Elisabeth looked forward to the brief holiday. She was shaken when on Thursday – the day before they were to leave for South-ampton – word came through that women and children were being evacuated from London. Thank God, Paul was coming home.

By ten a.m. on Friday Elisabeth and her brood were aboard a Long Island Railroad train en route to Southampton. The atmosphere was festive. This was a respite from worrying about what was hap-pening in Europe. All over the country, those who could afford it were running off for this holiday weekend. The New York news-papers were predicting record crowds at Coney Island, Brighton and the Rockaways.

The house was a masterpiece that sat just beyond the dunes, the sound of the ocean crashing against the shore an exquisite symphony. Oh, it was lovely, Elisabeth thought. Ronnie and Hallie bubbled with enthusiasm. Amy was preoccupied with thoughts about gradu-ate school, with classes scheduled to begin immediately after the holiday. Like Elisabeth herself, Katie was concerned about the threat of war.

Late in the evening – as always searching for news – Elisabeth and Katie were galvanized by the words of the newscaster. The Nazis had invaded Poland – without declaring war. Far into the night they listened. The British and French were demanding that Hitler's troops pull out of Poland. Instead the Nazis were forging ahead. Warsaw was being bombed.

It was happening all over again, Elisabeth agonized. Franco's vic-tory in Spain had been but a prelude to another world war.

Chapter Forty-eight

In their mountainside house near Bougy Villars Paul hovered before the radio and listened to the accounts of Hitler's invasion of Poland. Somber and shaken, Tommy sat on the edge of a chair he'd pulled up beside his father. Doris returned to the living room with another of her endless cups of tea.

'Are we going to listen to this all night? That's all we've done for the past three days. Thank heaven we're getting out of this boring village!'

'Doris, be quiet!' Paul increased the volume of the radio. 'Great Britain and France have declared war! Don't you understand what that means?'

'We heard a few minutes ago that the SS *Athenia* was sunk by a German submarine,' Tommy said. 'Thirty Americans died.'

'Oh my God!' Doris was ashen. 'We can't sail! The Atlantic must be infested with German submarines!'

'We can fly out of Marseilles or Lisbon,' Paul pointed out. 'We'll –'

'Fly?' Doris screeched in shock. 'You'll never get me to set foot on an airplane!'

'Doris, the *Yankee Clipper* has been flying to New York via Marseilles and Lisbon for a year now. It's safe.'

'I won't set foot on an airplane!' Her eyes defied him. For the moment Paul had forgotten Doris's aversion to traveling except by train. 'We could be killed!'

'We could go by train to Le Havre,' Paul tried again, 'book passage on a ship that's headed across the Atlantic –'

'Are you crazy? Didn't Tommy just say that the *Athenia* was sunk? Thirty Americans died!'

'We can sit it out here,' Tommy said appeasingly, gazing from his mother to his father. 'How long can the fighting last?'

'At this point we have no idea.' People all over Europe must be trying to leave via Marseilles or Lisbon. What was the chance of their being able to get reservations? And this bickering wasn't good for Tommy. The doctor said they should avoid traumatic situations for the next year. 'We'll have to play it by ear. One thing we can be sure – the fighting will never spread to Switzerland. This has been neutral territory for over a hundred years.'

'Thank God, all our money is in a Geneva bank. We'll be all right here.' But a twitch in Doris's left eyelid betrayed her inner anxiety.

Prompted by Katie, Elisabeth bought a shortwave radio. This allowed Americans to hear – every thirty seconds – the first strains of a Chopin polonaise, an indication that Radio Warsaw was still in operation, though the rest of Poland had fallen. But early on the morning of 17 September Russian troops invaded from the opposite side to partition the country with Germany and Warsaw fell. Resuming broadcast, Radio Warsaw belted out 'Deutschland über Alles'. In October Russian troops occupied Latvia, Estonia, and Lithuania. The next month they moved into Finland.

In a fireside chat back on 3 September FDR had said, 'This nation will remain a neutral nation, but I cannot ask that every American remain neutral in thought as well.' Anti-war groups were vociferous in their demands that the United States remain out of the war. Ellie wrote to Elisabeth that she worried that Ira would be drafted. 'I'm scared to death we'll be dragged into the war and Ira will have to fight.'

Elisabeth constantly reminded herself that Paul was safe in Switzerland. She was angry that, for no reason she could understand, the NBC and Mutual networks stopped reporting news from Europe for a while. Practical Hallie suspected this was because broadcasting from Europe 'cost a lot of money'. But CBS continued its coverage, for which Elisabeth was grateful.

In the midst of all that was happening, Elisabeth asked herself how could that lunatic Senator Wheeler start up insisting on a probe of Hollywood. And he had other Senators backing him up. According to them, Hollywood was plotting to drag the US into the war. From the first day the investigation was aimed at condemning Jewish producers. Elisabeth was incensed that the news media gave the investigation such wide coverage.

'But *Life* said this is the funniest political circus of the year,' Katie pointed out.

Elisabeth was ever conscious that the British lived with gas masks at hand, were evacuating many of their children – some to Canada and the United States. She remembered her growing up years in London and was fearful for the country. She sighed with relief when somehow, Paul contrived to get a letter through to her: 'I don't know when I'll be able to write again – but we're safe from the fighting here. It's frustrating the way fate cancelled our plans to return to New York – but, Beth, a time will come for us.'

Normally Elisabeth read and re-read Paul's letters, then destroyed them lest they go astray. But she couldn't bring herself to destroy this one. How could she know when she'd hear from him again?

With war in Europe the economy in the United States was on an upswing. Factories were receiving huge orders for armaments and military uniforms. Liberty ships were transporting millions of tons of food. 'No problem gettin' flour or canned goods anymore,' said Hallie. 'I guess folks has finally figured we got plenty to eat here in this country.'

Again, Elisabeth had a sense that her life was on hold. Amy was involved in graduate school. Katie had sold a short story to an obscure magazine – 'So they paid me just ten dollars. It's a start!' Elisabeth was not surprised that Ted and Mark had chosen to remain in Paris – though most Americans had raced home.

'Let's be honest, Beth,' Ted wrote. 'It's a matter of time before the Germans invade France. We want to be here to do whatever little we can to stop them. France has been good to us.'

An avid follower of war news, Katie complained – and Ronnie vigorously agreed – that many Americans didn't seem to understand that war was being fought in Europe, 'except for the way they all rushed to the grocery stores to pile up food the first two or three months after Poland was invaded. Don't they know that people are dying because of the war?'

'Even though we're separated by two oceans, that doesn't mean we can't be drawn into the war,' added Ronnie. 'But all the girls at school talk about is who's cuter – Clark Gable in *Gone with the Wind* or Errol Flynn in *The Adventures of Robin Hood*.'

But by late spring of 1940 the war in Europe was eroding American isolationism. In April Nazi troops occupied Denmark and Norway.

A month later Holland, Belgium and Luxembourg fell. With the surrender of Belgium, 400,000 British and French soldiers, trapped around Dunkirk on the Channel coast, had to be rescued by every-thing the British could put into the water – from destroyers to small craft in the hands of civilians. In June the Nazis occupied Paris. Elisabeth was frightened for Ted and Mark. The war had become personal.

What was happening with Paul in Switzerland? Everybody was convinced tiny Switzerland would be untouched. But how could they know?

The atmosphere in the small mountainside house near Bougy Villars reeked of tension much of the time. This would not be a short-term war, Paul forced himself to admit. For many waking hours he was able to hide away from reality in his improvised office, where he worked long hours at the new play. Doris buried herself in her collection of Kathleen Norris novels, reading and rereading, sulky because new American romances were not available. Tommy had become a voracious reader. This situation was bad for him, Paul fretted. Soon it would be a year since they'd expected to leave for home.

Provide for a long haul – that was the road to survival. Saying nothing to Doris or Tommy, Paul began to build a new frame-work for their existence. In Geneva he tracked down a job for him-self as teacher of English three days a week. He searched until he found a college in the area that would accept Tommy. This would be a road to sanity for the three of them. Doris would relish having the house to herself for swatches of time, so she'd be less difficult. And Tommy would be less restless, less fearful of losing his grip on reality.

'What do you mean, you took a job?' Doris was astounded, sus-picious when he told her. Tommy looked hopeful.

'We don't know how long we'll have to stay here. Our funds are not inexhaustible. When this ghastly war is over, we'll need money to take us back home. And, Tommy –' he turned to his son – 'I've arranged for you to resume college studies when the school year begins. This doesn't have to be a wasted period.'

'Dad, I'm almost twenty-eight . . .' Tommy seemed ambivalent.

'You won't be the first to attend college late.' He was matter-of-fact. 'You'll start with a light course load. Your French is adequate. It's become fluent in these past two years. You'll do fine.'

'Would it apply to a degree back home?' There was a glint of anticipation in Tommy's eyes now.

'I'm sure it will. You'll have to go for an interview next week, but there'll be no problem. It's back to the books for you, old boy.'

In September Amy entered her second year of graduate school. As always in the first days of a new school year she was agonizingly conscious of being older than her classmates. This year the situation was exacerbated by the fact that the professor of the class she was to attend was around her own age, or possibly a few years younger. He was good-looking and charming, with the female students quickly forming a Kevin Conway fan club. He must be aware of this, Amy thought, though he gave no sign that he did.

He was a fine teacher, she acknowledged. He was bright, had a sense of humor, and he was compassionate. His attitude towards her was the same as towards the other students. He didn't treat her as a misfit. She wished the girls in the class wouldn't gush over him the way they did. They weren't sixteen-year-olds drooling over Robert Taylor. They were one school year from becoming professional social workers.

It unnerved her when she realized that she looked forward to Kevin Conway's classes. It was because he was sweet, so concerned about drawing her into active participation. He felt sorry for her, she taunted herself, yet she basked in his attentions. Sometimes in class it seemed as though he was talking to her alone. There was a special rapport between them, she reasoned, because they were about the same age.

'I'll bet you like Gershwin and Cole Porter,' he said playfully, falling into step beside her one day after a class.

'I think they're wonderful.'

'What about the ocean?' he pursued.

'I lived in California when I was younger,' she told him. 'I had a long-time love affair with the Pacific.'

'Mr Conway!' Two girl students managed to draw him away. 'You have to settle a dispute for us!'

He shot Amy a helpless glance and diverted his attention to the two girls.

431

A few days later a classmate sidled up beside Amy in the hall as they emerged from Kevin Conway's class.

'Amy, Conway's got a thing for you,' she drawled. Her eyes telegraphed her astonishment. Why would a gorgeous young professor single out Amy when he had half a dozen very pretty girls panting for his attention – slim young girls?

'He's looking for protection from you young vampires,' Amy said, striving to appear amused.

That was it. She was protection. He knew he couldn't afford to become involved with a female student. The university would frown on that. And he knew he'd never become involved with *her*. Yet she was conscious of unfamiliar stirrings within her that had been long denied. How absurd for her to harbor romantic feelings about Kevin Conway.

Elisabeth gloried in the knowledge that in June Amy would have her master's, be on her way to a new career. Yet she worried that Amy shut herself off from any socializing that didn't revolve around the family. Her two daughters regarded men as creatures who had no role in their lives. She yearned to erase the bitterness that scarred their hearts and souls – but felt helpless to do this. At sixteen Ronnie had just discovered 'boys'.

Standing at a curb waiting for a taxi after an eleven-hour day at the office – and taxis were becoming hard to find these days – Elisabeth remembered the sweet tableau this morning before she left for the office and Ronnie for school. Ronnie had been reading to Hallie, so serious and sad, from Alice Duer Miller's *The White Cliffs*. For herself the poetry held a special poignance. She could never totally push aside her British birth.

She kept a radio on her desk at the office, lest she miss one painful news item. On one September night alone 1,500 Nazi planes dropped 4,400,000 pounds of high explosives on London. It was the worst disaster to hit London since the Great Fire. Dear God, she dreaded the prospect of American boys dying in the war – but how much longer could the United States refrain from intervening?

Elisabeth and Katie were engaged in a continuing debate about the future of television. She couldn't believe radio was in danger of becoming obsolete. Look at the way daytime radio was expanding – and thank God for this. Always careful about money, she rejoiced in the way her savings were growing. The daytime serials were in such demand. In the past three years, she estimated, another sixty programs had hit the airwaves. Between ten a.m. and six p.m. there was an endless array of serials. All of them dedicated to the premise that happiness is in the family.

Arriving home, she was touched that yet again the girls had insisted Hallie hold up dinner. Hallie had instructions to serve dinner no later than seven o'clock which allowed study time for Amy and Ronnie.

'They said they wasn't gonna eat until you sat down at the table, too,' Hallie effervesced. 'So sit yo'self down and lemme serve.'

Over dinner, Elisabeth knew Katie would bring up the latest she'd heard about television. Ever since seeing television at the World's Fair last year, Katie had been after her to buy a DuMont television set for the apartment. It was such a tiny picture! And there was so little to see. But she knew she'd probably cave in and buy a set.

'Mom, *when* are you going to buy a television set?' Katie asked accusingly, yet with special verve tonight.

'When I can see you on the set,' Elisabeth joshed.

'What about a play I wrote?' Katie's lovely face was luminous.

'You wrote a play?' Ronnie bubbled.

'I sold a fifteen-minute script to that television station up in Schenectady.' Katie was striving for nonchalance.

'Katie, how wonderful!'

'When can we see it?' Hallie was awed.

'When they show it.' Katie shrugged. 'Sometime next month. That is, if we have a set.' Her smile, aimed at her mother, was impish.

'We'll have a set,' Elisabeth promised.

'I'm not about to leave my job,' Katie giggled. 'They paid me ten bucks for the play.'

'Can I tell the kids at school?' Ronnie asked. 'Wow, they won't believe me!'

'They'll believe you.' Elisabeth's smile was wry. Ronnie had forgotten that once her mother had been one of the most promising young movie stars in the country. The kids might not believe it, but their parents would remember Amy Winston.

Katie was restless. Why was it so hard to get a job as a reporter in this city? She knew she could land a job on a small-town newspaper

– but New York was where so much was happening. She wanted to be *here*. Finally, just before Christmas, she nailed down a newspaper job.

'I'm going to work for a new newspaper in town,' she reported at dinner that night. She turned to her mother. 'I told them I had to give you two weeks' notice. Of course, it's not exactly as a reporter,' she conceded. 'I'll be a typist in the business office. But I'll be on the inside. When an opening comes up, zingo. I'll campaign for it.'

'I'm going to work on our school paper next term,' Ronnie announced. Ever eager to follow in Katie's footsteps, Elisabeth thought tenderly. 'I figured it would be good experience.'

'Great.' Katie nodded in approval. 'I'll wait a while, then ask if I can do a television column once a week. Well, people do have television sets, and they'll want to know what they can see.'

In the coming months Katie tried to push her way into the reporting end of the newspaper. They talked about possibly allowing her to do some college graduation coverage at the end of the school year.

'I'm so frustrated,' she confessed to her mother. 'A war is going on in most of the rest of the world. Not just soldiers but thousands of civilians are dying in the air raids! I want to write about it!'

'Darling, I'm grateful that you're here.' Elisabeth reached for Katie's hand.

'I feel so useless.' Katie squinted in thought. 'I'm going to take the civil service tests. If all I can do in a newspaper office is type, then let me do it for the government. Maybe in some little way I'll be helping the war effort.'

In June Amy received her master's degree from the Columbia School of Social Work. Oddly, it seemed to her that Amy regretted the end of school. Was she afraid of having to go out and face the job market? But almost immediately Amy reported that she had a job with a private philanthropic agency.

'One of my instructors set it up for me,' she confided. 'His sister works in the field, and they had an opening in her office.'

'I knew you'd have no trouble. Not with your grades.'

That same month – to the astonishment of most of the world – Nazi troops launched a massive three-pronged invasion of Russia. By mid-July, with Russian defenses crumbling, it seemed likely that all of Russia would fall. Americans clung to their radios for news, ever fearful that this country, too, would be drawn into the war.

In late August, having taken civil service exams, Katie was notified that an opening was available for her.

'In New York?' her mother asked hopefully.

'Yeah.' Katie sighed. 'I was hoping for Washington D.C. That's where all the action is these days.'

Paul knew while he made breakfast for himself and Tommy that Doris would be in a foul mood today. The days when she didn't emerge from her bedroom and languidly ask, 'Is coffee up?' meant she was fuming once again about their 'house arrest' situation.

'There's time for another cup of coffee,' Paul told Tommy. It was incredible the way Tommy was finding himself at returning to school. He was eager to learn, enjoying casual relationships with classmates. 'I think when I drop you off at school I'll drive over to Ferney.'

'Is it safe?' Tommy was anxious. Ferney was four miles from Geneva – but in France.

'It's fine. There's no German presence this close to the border. My class today doesn't start till early afternoon. I've been hankering for a long time to see Ferney.' He smiled at Tommy's questioning grunt. 'That was where Voltaire spent his last years.'

He dropped off Tommy at his school and headed for the border. He was careful about the mileage he put on the car. Thank God for the fine mechanic he had found in Rolle, for new cars were not to be had. He knew he'd have no trouble at Customs: he was an American citizen, a teacher at a prestigious Geneva school.

About a mile past the Customs barrier Paul became aware of a car following him. No, he was being paranoid, he reproached himself. Why would anyone tail him? But a few minutes later, when he slowed, the ancient Citroën pulled up beside him. The driver leaned towards him, the car window open.

'Please,' the man at the wheel addressed Paul in accented English, 'it is important that I talk with you. There's a turnoff just ahead. Please take it. I'll follow.'

Paul hesitated, but the desperation in the other man's eyes won out. He watched for the turn-off, swung onto a narrow dirt road in a deserted area that once had been a farm.

He stepped out of the car and waited for the other driver to join him.

435

'We know you are an American. We have friends at the school where you teach, but they must be nameless,' he added quickly, 'for everyone's sake. I am Jean Simon. We – a group of French not in sympathy with our Vichy government – are working to remove Jewish children from France before they can be apprehended by the Nazis.'

'How can I help?' Paul was puzzled, yet felt himself caught up in Simon's sense of urgency.

'I have two little ones in the trunk of my car. Two days ago their parents were taken by Nazi troops, their only crime that they are Jews. The children were at school. One of our group was able to spirit them away, bring them here. It isn't safe for them in France.' His eyes pleaded for help.

'They're to cross the border in the trunk of my car,' Paul interpreted.

'Drive them to a farmhouse near Rolle. That's all you have to do. We will take care of them once they are across the border.'

The air was suddenly electric. Spain had been a terrible mistake, Paul told himself. This was not.

'There will be other children,' Paul guessed.

'Until this awful war is over.'

'How will I know when to come here?' His mind was charging ahead. 'Won't they become suspicious at Customs?'

'You are a coin collector. You have just heard about a numismatic shop in Ferney. Once a week you will come over to see what new has arrived. The owner will give you instructions.' Simon seemed achingly relieved. 'Bless you for helping us.'

'How could I not help?' Paul forced a smile. 'Bring me the children.'

Like his cohort he scanned the area, fearful that they were being watched. No one in sight. The other man hurried to his car, opened the trunk, helped out a little girl about five, a little boy perhaps two years older. The little girl reached for her brother's hand. Both bewildered, terrified. What will happen to their parents? Paul asked himself in anguish. But he knew the answer. How many more children like these two must be rescued?

This was something that must be done. All over Europe, he suspected, there would be ordinary men and women like himself who would reach out to help at this time when madmen sought to rule the world. He knew his fate if he were caught. But how could he not be part of the chain to help these innocent children to remain alive?

Chapter Forty-nine

Katie and Olivia sat at what they'd come to call 'their table' at the cafeteria on Broadway in the 80s. It had become a habit for them to meet for a late lunch on Sundays. The early December day was cold, depressingly gray. They lingered over their coffee and debated about going to a neighbourhood movie or traveling downtown to the Apollo to see a foreign film.

'I'm so bored with my job,' Olivia sighed. 'Maybe Mom's right. Maybe I should think about teaching.'

'I'm bored, too,' Katie admitted. 'I thought, Wow, I'm working for the Navy. It's like being part of the war effort. Except, of course, we're not in the war.'

'You don't want us to be in the war.' Olivia gaped in reproach. 'I don't want to see my brothers fighting in Europe!'

'I don't know. Maybe I should quit and go back to work for Mom. But that's boring, too.'

'What about writing for her programs?' Olivia giggled. 'You've got an inside track.'

'I couldn't write that stuff even if I wanted to. But I'm not exactly setting the world on fire.'

'You've had three plays on that television station up in Schenectady. Boy, was my mother impressed! Even if we don't have a television.' She whistled eloquently. 'Not at those prices.'

'I want to be over in Europe reporting on the war.'

'And dodging bullets?'

'Why are there so few women correspondents over there? I read somewhere that General Montgomery – you know, the British general – refused to have any women correspondents with the British forces. Isn't that outrageous?'

'At least you've got all those good-looking navy lieutenants around you. The lawyers in my office are grandfathers. They like to pat my ass, but there's no future with them.'

'Olivia, when will you realize the world doesn't revolve around men?'

'Without them there'd be no future world.' She giggled. 'I worry about the future, Katie. It's my civic duty.'

'I don't believe it!' a man behind the serving counter bellowed, his voice ricocheting about the cafeteria. Heads turned in his direction. 'You're kidding. It's some crazy joke!'

'No!' Another man turned around to face those at the tables. 'The word just came through! Pearl Harbor's been bombed. The Japs made an early morning attack! Half the fleet's been disabled!'

'Let's go to my place!' Was this some sick joke – or was it true? Katie reached for her purse, pushed back her chair. 'We can listen to the shortwave radio!'

From the faces of those they passed on the street Katie and Olivia knew the man in the cafeteria had not been some sick comic. The American fleet had been attacked and was in shambles.

'We're in the war,' Katie said grimly while they hurried across Broadway. 'Even the isolationists can't deny that.'

At Katie's office there was a demand for more help. Civil Service lists were insufficient to fill the need. In April Katie was able to bring Olivia into her office. She herself was promoted to supervisor. Every bit of correspondence that came through – the sea of cables that had to be copied, filed away – held special portent. This was not just a naval office. This was Naval Intelligence.

As the months passed, Katie felt that – though hardly the work she yearned to do – her job was a small contribution to the war effort. Olivia mourned that she'd never get married, the way the draft was 'sucking up all the cute guys'.

'I feel so old,' she told Katie while they waited impatiently in the small restaurant across from their office building for hamburgers and coffee to be brought to their tiny table. A half-hour lunch period went fast. 'I mean, Ronnie's at Hunter already!'

'At twenty-seven we're not exactly old maids.'

'Sssh.' Olivia glanced about nervously. 'I thought when I came to work at the navy, I'd meet all these gorgeous young j.g.s. Where are they?'

'Out fighting a war. The young ones.' Katie shifted slightly on her banquette seat to allow the heavy-set woman beside her to leave. Immediately her place was taken by a rangy young man who reminded Katie of Gary Cooper. The waitress frowned when he indicated he was holding the opposite chair for a friend.

'Run down with me to Klein's tonight?' Olivia asked Katie. 'Another cousin is getting married. I need a long dress for the wedding. Why spend a lot of money for something I'll wear twice?'

'The navy's really snapping up the best-looking gals.' The man at the next table beamed an ingratiating smile in their direction.

Katie and Olivia exchanged a swift, warning glance, allowed themselves a polite acknowledgment.

'Lawyers like me should have such luck. My secretary looks like Frankenstein's twin sister. An identical twin.'

A waitress came and took his order. He leaned back, stifled a yawn.

'I just got back from Washington. Didn't get more than three hours' sleep a night the whole week I was down there. On a big case for a defense plant.' He held up a hand to someone who'd just entered the restaurant. 'Over here, Joe.'

Not until they were out in the street did Katie and Olivia discuss the encounter.

'He doesn't work for the navy,' Olivia said. 'I know, we're taking up a lot of floors now, we can't know everybody. But he isn't in uniform.'

'I think we ought to report that little incident.' Katie was grim. 'He was fishing.'

'Do we want to get mixed up in something like espionage?' Olivia seemed simultaneously fearful and intrigued.

'We do.'

Back in their office Katie and Olivia approached their lieutenant, reported what had happened.

'Probably just a big-mouth out to pick up girls. I mean, it must be fairly common knowledge that this building houses naval business.' He frowned in thought. 'Still, I'd like you to talk about it to someone in a better position to judge.'

Katie was impressed by the crisp questioning of the officer to whom they were sent. He asked if they would be willing to pursue this further, warning that there was an element of risk. Olivia looked scared.

'Of course,' Katie replied for both. 'What would you like us to do?'

They were sworn not to discuss the situation with anyone – not even close family. They were to lunch again at the restaurant, allow themselves to be picked up.

'It may be that this man has no designs other than to pick up one or the other of you. But let's give him every chance to identify himself. You'll be under the eyes of a team set up for this purpose. We don't mean to expose you to danger if it's at all avoidable.'

The following day Katie and Olivia went to lunch at their usual place, headed for their usual table – oddly available when they arrived.

'They've got half the place staked out,' Katie said under her breath. 'Look happy, Olivia.'

As they sat down, the couple at the next table left. Moments later the Gary Cooper type sauntered into the restaurant, surveyed the scene, and headed for the table he'd occupied yesterday – just this moment being vacated. Every move choreographed by the navy, Katie suspected. She offered a faint smile of recognition as he sat down.

'You discovered what I discovered,' he said, grinning. 'They make the best hamburger downtown right here.'

'There's Howard,' Olivia said according to plan, and waved to a quietly handsome young man in a beat-up suede jacket. They'd met him earlier, had been briefed on how to bring him into the picture. 'Come over here –'

The Gary Cooper type was annoyed, Katie observed, but masked this in a second. She surmised he'd had other plans.

The two girls talked to Howard, a cue for the stranger to introduce himself. In moments they were a festive quartet. The deal was to lead 'Chris' – the Gary Cooper type – into suggesting a double date. He took the bait. The four were to go out that evening to the Roosevelt Grill for dinner, then down to a club in Greenwich Village that Howard said was terrific.

'Tomorrow's Saturday,' Olivia suddenly realized. 'We have to work.'

Katie kicked her under the table. 'We'll call in sick.'

Self-conscious about lying, Katie told her mother she and Olivia were going to the movies and that she'd be late back.

According to plot Katie and Olivia were to feed Chris facts that would lead to his unmasking – if, indeed, he was a spy. Katie was grateful for Howard's presence. Beneath his casual exterior she found an intensity that was appealing. Not like Morty, she pinpointed while they drove in a cab to the Village club. Morty was always on a soapbox.

Dinner was uneventful – disappointing, Katie thought. Chris bragged about 'the big defense plant' he was representing down in Washington.

'But I can't complain,' he said cheerfully. 'I'm billing a lot of hours. But the government can sure be a pain in the butt.'

Howard pretended to be sympathetic. 'Hey, I'm an accountant. I've had my run-ins with the government.'

To the music of Guy Lombardo Katie danced with Chris and Olivia with Howard. Then they switched partners.

'I'd better warn you,' Howard said, his smile wry, 'I'm not much of a dancer.'

'Neither am I.' But he was all right, Katie decided a moment later. She liked the way he held her. She liked him. Chris – as he called himself – had held her too tight when they were dancing. His gaze kept wandering down the front of her dress. 'Are you getting anything from that creep?'

'It's too early. We'll go to this club in the Village. Don't have more than one drink.' He reminded her of earlier instructions. 'Pretend you're getting high. Feed him the information, the way we planned. If he's what we suspect, we'll know by two a.m.'

'The party will break up early.'

'He'll be panting to get away to report what you've let slip. *If* he's into spying.'

'Will you call and let me know?'

'At that hour?' He chuckled. 'Your family might not appreciate that. I'll get word to you at the office tomorrow.'

'Yeah, Mom would be nervous.'

'My mother is terrified of any call after ten o'clock at night. When my father got home from fighting in Europe in the First World War, he sat in a cafeteria till six a.m. because he didn't want to scare the daylights out of my mother. And for an Irishman that was tough.'

'My father died fighting with the Canadian Air Force. I was a baby – I don't have even the faintest memory of him.'

'My mother said that was the worst year of her life. She always found excuses when her parents tried to drag her to Friday night services at the synagogue, but in the ten months Dad was overseas, she was there every Friday night, praying he'd make it home. If he hadn't been in the army reserve, he wouldn't have been drafted. You know – a married man with two children.'

They left the restaurant and headed by taxi for the downtown club. Their conversation was convivial. Howard was devoted to Woody Guthrie and Josh White. Chris was into jazz.

'Any time give me Albert Ammons or Pete Johnson and I'm happy. And don't forget the king – Meade "Lux" Lewis.'

In the small, dark, smoke-filled club Katie gave a remarkable performance of feeling her first drink. Heady with success as Chris deviously led her down the path to providing what he believed to be top-secret information. As plotted, Howard – the 'accountant' – focused on Olivia. Then all at once, Chris remembered a late business call to Washington.

'Damn, I don't have the number with me – I'll have to beat it home.'

Katie pretended regret, gave him a phony phone number. He'd made it clear he meant to continue seeing her. He left in a rush, suggesting that Howard 'put the girls into a cab'.

'You'll let us know what happens?' Katie asked Howard.

'You'll know,' he promised, and hesitated. 'Perhaps it'll be wiser if I call you at home tomorrow evening.'

'Sure.' Katie gave him her home phone number.

But Howard didn't wait to call her at home. He was standing in front of the office building when Katie and Olivia arrived for work the following morning.

'You gals did good.' He seemed exhausted but pleased. Had he been to sleep at all last night? 'We caught the bastard along with five others. Congratulations.'

'Wow!' Olivia was impressed. 'But thank God, it's over. I was scared to death every minute.'

'Can I call you, anyway?' Howard asked Katie. 'My schedule is insane, but maybe we could have dinner and catch a play some night?'

'I'd like that,' Katie told him. 'Whenever it fits into your schedule.'

*　　*　　*

Paul gazed warily at the sky as he drove away from the school. Could there be snow this early in October? He dreaded driving over the mountain roads to the house in bad weather. But he'd received word to go to the shop in Ferney as soon as possible. He'd have no trouble crossing the border. That part was a snap.

Early on he'd started up a friendly relationship with the Customs guards. He'd established himself as an avid coin collector. They rarely bothered to ask for his passport, though he carried it with him always. They thought it amusing but foolhardy that an American teacher in Geneva would pursue coins in Nazi-occupied France. Of course, Switzerland was surrounded by the Allies' enemies – Germany, Austria and Italy, as well as occupied France – but the Swiss considered themselves forever neutral.

How many children had he hidden in the trunk of this beat-up car? He'd stopped counting. But on each return trip he was conscious of the pounding of his heart as he approached Customs. Ever aware that there could be a time when some cagey guard would say, 'Open the trunk.' His French was good, his German shaky. But in either language those three words could be disastrous.

He was startled to find the shop closed. What had happened? Instinct told him to hurry back across the border as quickly as he could manage. No. First drive to their customary pick-up spot, he decided after a moment's indecision. Had Monsieur Bardot, his contact on these trips, been taken in by the Nazis?

He spied a car in the secluded section where he customarily made his pick-ups. But it was a *different* car from usual. Few traveled in this area. He drove past, managing a swift glance at the man behind the wheel. Casually dressed yet with the bearing of a German officer.

He passed the car, stopped and backed up. 'Excuse me,' he began in his decent French. 'I seem to have made a wrong turn. Could you point me to the main road?'

By the time he returned to the house – after picking up Tommy at his college – snow was beginning to fall. He was fearful for Monsieur Bardot. But he suspected he would be contacted again, with a new role to play. As long as there were children who must be brought out of Nazi-occupied France, then he would be available to play chauffeur.

Was Monsieur Bardot in Nazi hands?

Chapter Fifty

Elisabeth was delighted that Amy had become close friends with a woman at the agency. Laura was the sister of Kevin Conway, who had recommended Amy for the job at the agency. She was a year older than Amy. Laura was able to coax Amy into going to a movie or a play or museum at regular intervals. With so many men in uniform it was common to see pairs of women strolling about Times Square or in Greenwich Village on weekends – seeking diversion to relieve the tensions brought on by the times.

When Passover arrived, Elisabeth was surprised but pleased when Amy suggested having Laura over for dinner on the first night.

'Her parents are down in Florida visiting cousins. Laura will be all alone.'

'Amy, you don't need a reason to invite a friend over for dinner. Laura's always welcome here.'

'We don't have a real *seder*,' Elisabeth explained to Laura Conway when she arrived at the house with Amy at the end of the working day. 'But Hallie's learned to prepare a dinner in keeping with tradition.'

'I hear Hallie's the family treasure. And thanks for having me.' Laura Conway was not a pretty woman but she radiated a compelling charm. 'This is the second Passover when we've been a family divided. Last year Kevin, my brother, was at camp out in Texas. This year he's in North Africa and our parents are in Florida.'

'It's a time when many families are divided.' Elisabeth's tone was sympathetic.

She was surprised that Laura's brother was young enough to be in military service. Somehow, she'd thought he was considerably her senior. Amy had talked about his being such a dedicated teacher, such a compassionate man – and she'd envisioned a professor in his fifties, in a tweed jacket and nursing a pipe.

Over dinner – pausing at intervals to compliment Hallie on her chicken soup and matzo balls, her *tzimmis* – Laura talked with deep affection about her brother.

'Kevin enlisted right after Pearl Harbor. He was almost thirty-five, but the draft's taking men up to thirty-six. He's a first lieutenant now. He can't say where he is, of course, but when he wrote that he was getting a deep tan, we knew he was in North Africa.'

Elisabeth had thought that Katie might invite the young navy lieutenant she was seeing occasionally. She'd mentioned that his parents lived in a suburb of Chicago, so he'd hardly be going home. He'd picked Katie up only once at the apartment. Usually they met outside. He'd seemed a charming young man. But then he might have felt self-conscious, being the only man at the dinner table.

The conversation dwelled briefly on the war, then Laura talked about a case she was handling – without mentioning names because that was a breach of confidence.

'Before he enlisted, Kevin spent hours trying to convince this boy that it was important for him to stay in school. It wasn't his job, it was mine, but Kevin's so devoted to teaching that he'd help out that way.'

Elisabeth's gaze moved from Laura to Amy. The tender glow in Amy's eyes sent waves of shock through her. Her mind charged back through the years. She remembered that same glow in Amy's eyes when people talked about Keith. *Amy was in love with Kevin Conway.* All at once Elisabeth understood Amy's naked anxiety about the progress of the war in North Africa. Kevin was there. She was concerned about the war on all fronts – but at any mention of the North African campaign Amy dropped whatever she was doing to listen with total attention.

That last year at Hunter Amy had talked often about 'Mr Conway' – her favorite of all her professors, but with her total lack of self-confidence Amy would never think that he might be interested in her as a woman. She'd reveled in knowing he considered her worthy of special attention in class. He was sending a message – but Amy wasn't receiving.

'Kevin told my boss she couldn't afford not to hire Amy.' Laura punctuated Elisabeth's introspection. 'He said Amy was everything a social worker should be.'

*　　*　　*

Hurrying from the subway on this late October afternoon, Katie enjoyed the spill of sunlight on Times Square. She was glad that daylight savings was in effect all the year for the duration of the war. She was relieved, too, to be back on the daytime schedule after a run on the four p.m. to midnight shift. The swing shift made it difficult to merge her hours with Howie's always upside-down schedule. She'd heard from him last night – he was coming in from Washington D.C. where he seemed to be spending much time these days.

She hadn't seen Howie in three weeks. It seemed for ever. She knew never to question him regarding his current assignment or his whereabouts. She longed to become involved again in one of his missions, but that wasn't happening. She understood that had been a one-shot deal.

She was meeting Howie at Roth's, their favorite restaurant in the area. There was pleasing privacy there, the lighting muted, the food excellent. And it was in the heart of Times Square, close to the first-run movie houses and the theaters.

They'd kissed passionately in the protective darkness of isolated balcony seats at the Paramount and the Capital, and in blissfully empty elevators at her apartment building. But his eyes asked questions to which she ached to respond. There just never seemed to be the time or place. She recoiled from their going to a hotel – even if that were possible. In these times hotel rooms were difficult to come by.

Faintly breathless with anticipation, noting the earlier sunshine had given way to drab grayness, she waited outside the restaurant. Her eyes searched the rush-hour crowd for sight of Howie. There he was! Her smile was luminous as she watched him push his way towards her, handsome in his navy blues.

'Hi –' He reached to pull her close for a moment, then with an arm at her waist prodded her towards the restaurant's entrance.

Over dinner he told her that the apartment he shared with two other navy officers was his alone for the next five days.

'Craig and Larry are off on assignments.' He paused, his eyes seeming to be intent on memorizing her face. 'I'm shipping out in about five days. Out of the country –'

'Oh, Howie . . .' Her heart began to pound. How could she have expected him to remain here for the duration?

'There's time for us to get married,' he managed to lopsidedly smile, 'if you're so inclined.'

'I'm so inclined,' she whispered.

'Let's skip dessert,' he said and chuckled. 'I've got a special dessert in mind.'

Suddenly it was urgent that they make love. What had happened to so many other couples was about to happen to them: a separation that would put an ocean between them, for how long nobody knew.

They left the restaurant, searched for a taxi – their numbers ever dwindling. At last, in the comfort of a northbound taxi, Howie reached to pull her in his arms. So what can the driver see in the dark? Katie asked herself defiantly.

Hand in hand they left the taxi and hurried into the lobby of the small apartment house on Central Park West. Grateful for an unoccupied elevator, they swayed together while the elevator made a slow trip to the sixth floor. Inside the apartment Howie swept her into his arms and carried her into the tiny bedroom that was his.

'This is our wedding night,' he murmured. 'So it's a little premature.'

'These next four days have to make up for the time we'll miss ahead.'

'They'll be spectacular, Katie. I promise.'

Please God, keep Howie safe. Let him come home soon.

Elisabeth arranged exquisite long-stemmed white and red roses at the makeshift *chuppah*. Their scent lent a romantic atmosphere to the living room. Convivial sounds ricocheted about the apartment. Katie had been so sweet. 'Mom, I never wanted a big wedding at the Plaza or the Hampshire House. Just the immediate family and right here in the apartment.' It was too late for Howie's family and his married sister to come from the suburb of Chicago, but they were delighted that he was to be married. Katie had talked by phone with his parents and sister.

'And, Mom, I'm not pregnant,' Katie had solemnly assured her.

Then Howie arrived and moments later the rabbi. Katie and Howie wanted a religious ceremony. The war had made so many conscious of their Jewishness, Elisabeth thought tenderly.

'Mom, you organized everything so fast,' Howie told her, reaching for a warm embrace.

448

'I'm a businesswoman. I know how to organize.' She'd sent them to their family doctor for their blood tests, checked on the hours the Marriage License Bureau was open, arranged for the rabbi. And Hallie had been cooking for the past two days for the wedding dinner.

Watching the ceremony Elisabeth prayed that Howie would come home safely. She thought about Kevin, whom Amy loved, and prayed for him, too. And Paul had been constantly in her thoughts these past four days. She kept telling herself he was safe in Switzerland. But oh, how she wished for some word from him.

Again, New Year's Eve was a quiet time in Elisabeth's household. Ronnie had talked about joining a group of school friends for the Times Square celebration, then decided against this.

'We went last year and it was weird,' she recalled as the family sat down to dinner. 'And it wasn't just because of the brown-out. There was a hollowness to the laughter. Almost an air of hysteria. I mean, how could we celebrate the new year with so many American boys fighting a war? So many dying.'

'Talking like the reporter for *Our World*,' Katie joshed. Shortly before Christmas Ronnie had acquired a part-time job on a new weekly.

'The job is fine,' Elisabeth said with reservations, 'but remember you still have almost two years at Hunter – and then graduate school.'

'This is great experience,' Ronnie chided. 'Get with it, Grandma.'

'Is there anything on television tonight?' Hallie was fascinated by the medium.

'Hallie, you know the networks have been off the air since right after Pearl Harbor. Of course there's still DuMont, the local television station.'

Katie's face lighted up. 'Next month I have a play on, remember?' Despite her forty-eight-hour-a-week job and the steady flow of letters to Howie, she salvaged time to focus on television plays, though admitting her real ambition was to write for a major newspaper.

'I think it's a matter of time before daytime radio serials find a place in television.' Elisabeth held up a hand at Katie's air of skepticism. 'I've heard all the warnings: "Women can listen to radio and do their housework at the same time. But will they stop whatever they're doing to sit down and watch television?" And I know – sets are terribly expensive now.' She considered their own a business investment – and one they could now easily afford.

'Once this bloody war is over, I'll bet the price of sets zooms down fast. That's when we'll see a flood of new sets in American living rooms, and a rash of new programs. Night-time shows,' Katie ribbed her mother.

Elisabeth refused to be baited. 'Women's daytime television series will be as popular as the radio serials. Maybe even more.'

At disturbing intervals Elisabeth was aware that she was a success in a business that provided her with no personal satisfaction. And often she was filled with guilt because she was so prosperous at a time when so many in Europe led such deprived lives. The money she earned was impressive. But even now she remembered the towering pleasure of live theater performances, of feeling the cherished reactions of live audiences. She was building security for the family. That should be sufficient satisfaction.

In February Elisabeth's thoughts often dwelled on the fate of 'the German cousins'. Had they, somehow, managed to survive the Nazi onslaught? Were they endangered by the five days of relentless bombing of German aircraft industries early this month? There were rumors that soon there would be a major Allied invasion of Europe. Americans waited impatiently for this to happen.

On 7 June 1944 the world learned of a massive invasion of almost 3,000,000 men on the previous day. The Allies had 5,000 large ships, 4,000 smaller landing craft, plus 1,000 aircraft to facilitate this movement. At noon Eastern Standard Time *The Romance of Helen Trent* was interrupted by an announcer. Ed Murrow made a brief report of the invasion. Throughout the day and far into the night Americans clung to their radios. But six days after D-Day, the first of Hitler's secret weapons – the pilotless V-1 buzz bombs – hit London.

In Italy Allied troops pushed forward. The Italians declared Rome an 'open city' – it would not be defended. The Allies moved onward, their next important destination was Florence. By the end of July the Allies were preparing to capture this city. Americans felt that the war could not continue much longer. Peace seemed close.

August was a steamy month in New York City. People flocked to the movies, to air-conditioned cafeterias and restaurants. Fans whirred through the nights like a somber symphony in apartments and houses throughout the five boroughs. Laura reported that her mother was upset at the lack of mail from Kevin.

'So much is happening in Europe right now,' Amy consoled, yet she was anxious that Laura's family hear from Kevin.

On a Friday morning in late August Amy was uneasy when Laura didn't appear at the office. She always called if she couldn't come in. Throughout the morning Amy's eyes clung to the wall clock at regular intervals. At 11.30 she decided to phone the Conways' apartment. Laura answered.

'Laura, we're all worried about you,' Amy began.

'Amy, can you come to the apartment?' Laura's voice sounded drained.

'Of course . . .' Amy's heart began to pound.

'We were just notified by the War Department. Amy –' her voice was an agonized whisper, 'Kevin has been listed as "Missing in Action".'

Shaken – dazed – Amy explained Laura's absence and was given leave to go to her. Amidst tokens of sympathy for Laura and her family, encouragement that Kevin would surface in time, she hurried from the office and sought a taxi. What was it with her family that every man who was loved seemed doomed? Katie's father, her father. Why had this happened to Kevin?

At the Conway apartment Amy forced herself to take charge. She cooked for the stricken family, called the War Department to plead for more information. Belatedly she remembered to phone her mother. If she didn't arrive for dinner, Mom would be worried.

She called her mother at the office. Mom was always the last to leave.

'Hello.' Her mother – crisp yet friendly – picked up on her private line.

'Mom, I won't be home for dinner. I won't be home tonight.' She struggled to keep her voice even. 'Laura had terrible news. Kevin's reported as "Missing in Action".'

'Oh, Amy . . .'

'I have to stay with Laura and her family tonight. Explain to the others –'

'Yes, darling. But "missing in action" can be a temporary status. It happens, Amy. Kevin will be found,' she said encouragingly. 'We'll all pray for him. Tell Laura and her family.'

In her office at Winston Productions Elisabeth sat motionless. Her mind careened back to the awful day when David was murdered. She'd felt her life was over. And then there'd been the telegram from the War Department, telling her that Jerry had been killed in action. She knew the pain Amy was feeling. Her eyes closed in anguish.

Poor Amy. My poor darling baby . . .

Chapter Fifty-one

In September London was hit by the first of the dangerous V-2 bombs. They arrived with no warning – in devastating silence, their launch pads two hundred miles away somewhere in Holland. Germany was being bombed by American planes by day and British planes by night. The fighting in the Pacific was furious, with the Allies attacking island after island in a painful race to Japan. On 25 October the Japanese, desperate to stop the Allied advance, began to strike with kamikazes – suicide planes. Over and over again Elisabeth thanked God that Paul was in neutral Switzerland.

She was unnerved at the way Amy was steadily losing weight, her clothes too large. Laura dragged her to Altman's to shop for replacements: 'Amy, choose younger things. Stop dressing like an old lady.' Now there were younger fashions in her size.

Elisabeth was ever conscious of Amy's pain, but what could she do to alleviate it? Amy shared her anguish with no one. Not even Laura knew.

By December Amy was forced yet again to buy new clothes. She'd lost over fifty pounds.

'Mom, you look gorgeous!' Ronnie bubbled when Laura insisted Amy model an especially attractive outfit. 'I'm so glad you decided to go for a skinny look!' She giggled. 'Of course, you're not exactly skinny yet – but you're close.'

Elisabeth forced back words of reproach. Ronnie had swallowed Amy's fabricated story of 'being tired of looking like a circus tent'. It was wonderful that Amy was losing the hated pounds she'd gained, but at what a cost!

Katie was blunt. 'You ought to see a doctor, Amy. You're losing too much too fast.' Elisabeth knew Katie was close to panic. Her mind was dreaming up horrible explanations for Amy's weight loss.

At dinner with the family Laura had let it slip that their boss, too, was concerned about the state of Amy's health.

Each day that passed with no word of Kevin's reappearance reinforced Amy's fears. For her parents' sake, Laura pretended optimism, reported infrequent stories of men who had been 'missing in action' for months being found – 'and in good health'.

Elisabeth comprehended the depth of Amy's pain. After all these years of being convinced she could never love again, it had happened – and she had done nothing to bring that new love to fruition.

With the arrival of 1945 most Americans were convinced the end of the war was in sight. Katie longed to see Howie safely home. Amy clung to a shred of hope, along with Laura, that Kevin was still alive. In January FDR was inaugurated for an unprecedented fourth term. But on 12 April the nation was stunned to hear that he had died of a cerebral hemorrhage. The nation was in mourning.

On 30 April Hitler and Eva Braun committed suicide. On 2 May Berlin fell. Later that day Nazi forces in Italy surrendered. On 7 May the Nazi general Alfred Jodl surrendered to General Eisenhower – signing unconditional surrender documents in Rheims, France. President Truman declared the following day as V-E Day. The war in Europe was over.

In cities and towns across the country – and in every Allied nation – people rejoiced that the killing was over. They sang, danced. Strangers embraced. On Wall Street tickertape was tossed from windows, littering the street below. Times Square erupted in celebration as people poured from offices and shops.

Sitting at her desk in her office, with Katie hovering near, Elisabeth tried to absorb what was taking place. The fighting in *Europe* was over. American troops would come home. But wouldn't they then head for the Pacific?

'In months – maybe weeks – the war will be over everywhere!' Katie read her mother's thoughts. But her eyes exuded relief and joy and anticipation. 'Howie'll be home! We'll start to live again!'

There was no word of Kevin. Elisabeth cried inside for Amy. For Amy there was happiness that the war in Europe was over. But what of Kevin? The War Department continued to list him as 'missing in action'. The uncertainty was bitter – for Kevin's parents, his sister. For Amy.

*   *   *

In the mountainside house in Bougy Villars Paul hovered before the radio along with Doris and Tommy. At last it was over. Their 'house arrest' here was over.

'We can go home!' Doris was jubilant. She turned to Tommy. 'You'll register for two or three courses. Then you'll be eligible to take the teachers' exams for New York state!'

'It'll be a while before we can go home,' Paul warned. 'We –'

'Why will it be a while?' Doris interrupted, her eyes defiant.

'There'll be no ships available for months. Millions of troops will have to be transported across the Atlantic first. Then the thousands of GI brides and their babies. After they're all home, people like us will be given passage.'

'That's outrageous! Months?' She turned from Paul to Tommy.

'There are just so many ships –'

'Doris, be logical. How many army personnel can each ship carry? If they're crammed to the gills – and they will be – each will be lucky to carry fifteen thousand –'

'Oh, it's going to be impossible! Paul, contact the American Embassy. We've been imprisoned here for years. Don't we have rights, too?'

'I'll put in a petition, but don't expect miracles. We haven't been fighting a war.'

Weeks passed without any indication when civilians would be able to acquire passage across the Atlantic. School closed, and Paul lost his hours of escape to Geneva. The atmosphere in the Bougy Villars house was horrendous. Doris was ever at fever pitch, damning everyone for their predicament. Paul worried about the effect of this on Tommy. He was shaken when Tommy showed signs of irritability, and then discovered that he was not taking his medication on the rigid schedule that kept him in remission.

'Tommy, you mustn't ever let that happen!' he exhorted. 'We'll be out of here soon. You can lead a normal life if you stay with your medication.'

'I'm sorry, Dad . . .'

Paul understood. Living in this house with his mother was becoming a hazardous situation.

'Tommy –' he sought for the right words – 'until we can go home, I think it would be good if you saw Dr Edwards again.'

'Yeah.' His eyes were disconsolate. 'Will you set it up for me?'

Knowing it was futile, Paul drove into Geneva the next morning to check again with the revitalized travel agency they had favored before the war. The earliest date projected by the agency for travel across the Atlantic was in February or March of the following year.

'Monsieur,' the woman was apologetic, 'so many soldiers must be transported home first. But if you'd like a trip to Paris or London?'

Paul left in low spirits. It was important for Tommy's sake that they get back to New York. And he was conscious, too, that their funds – healthy when they'd first arrived in Switzerland – had been seriously depleted. He'd send the new play to his agent, Bill Madison. He'd had the final draft typed up several weeks ago. Have Bill start looking for a producer.

He stopped in a café for lunch, a welcome respite from the ugly atmosphere at the house. Most of Europe was facing desperate shortages, but here he could have a decent lunch. Dawdling over coffee, he heard the lively conversation of a pair of businessmen at a nearby table. All at once he realized that the international telephone service was now available on a personal basis – a rare situation during the war years.

He could phone Elisabeth in New York. Not from home, of course. At the school. Go there now, make arrangements. Oh God, how wonderful it would be to hear her voice again!

At the school – in the privacy of the headmaster's office – he waited with surging impatience for his call to be put through. Was Elisabeth still at the old business number? Was everything the same between them despite the painful years of silence?

'Hello?' The connection clear and sweet.

'Beth –' He was dizzy with excitement. 'How great to hear your voice!'

'Paul?' Disbelief merged swiftly into joyousness. 'Paul, where are you?'

'In Geneva. It'll be months before we can get passage home. But I discovered it was possible to make personal phone calls again.'

'You're all right?' He sensed her joy at hearing from him – and her anxiety.

'I'm fine. And we've seen a near-miraculous improvement in Tommy's health. On this new medication he can function normally. He's been in college. God, there's so much to tell you. It's still not the time to write. But now that the phone service is available, I'll call you regularly. How have you been?'

'Surviving.' A touch of wry laughter in her voice now. 'Your letters were cherished, I was frustrated that I couldn't write in return. But all that's over now. You'll be coming home.'

'With Tommy back to normal I'll insist that Doris divorce me. It's long past due.'

'I'll be here, Paul.'

'I love you, Beth.'

'I love you, too.' Again, laughter in her voice. 'Would anybody believe that we could feel this way at our ages?'

'You know what Browning said – "Grow old along with me!/The best is yet to be." Or something like that.'

Reluctantly Elisabeth ended the conversation. The call must be costing Paul a fortune. But he'd call again and again before he came home. Their lives were touching again. Tears filled her eyes, blurred her vision. But tears of relief, joy, anticipation.

She hadn't talked about the family – that would come later. Now it seemed so strange to her that her daughters and her granddaughter had read Paul's pieces from Spain, but they had no awareness that this was the man most important in her own life. He and Katie and Ronnie could talk journalism, she thought tenderly.

She'd been so happy at attending Ronnie's graduation from Hunter last week – and upset when it seemed for a while that Ronnie would reject a degree in journalism. Amy, Katie and herself had pounced on Ronnie. Life would wait. Go to school now.

On 26 July the United States – along with Britain and China – demanded that the Japanese surrender. The Japanese rejected this. Early on the morning of 6 August an American B-29 dropped an atomic bomb over Hiroshima.

The whole world was rocked as the news seeped through. Elisabeth listened, white-faced and trembling, to a newscast about the power of the bomb. It was possible, the newscaster reported, that the atom bomb – the equivalent of thousands of tons of TNT – could obliterate whole cities on contact. It was science fiction becoming reality.

Figures began to pour in. It was estimated that as many as 200,000 had been killed or injured. Many thousands suffered indescribable thermal burns. Elisabeth felt sick as she listened to the reports. Yet she understood that President Truman had realized the huge toll of American lives that an American invasion of Japan would cost. He presumed the Japanese government would now accept surrender terms.

Still, Japan refused the offered surrender terms. Three days later another atomic bomb was dropped on Nagasaki. On 10 August the Japanese government agreed to accept the Allied terms of surrender – provided the Emperor agreed on the conditions. On 2 September the final surrender documents were signed. World War II was over.

Katie received word from Howie that he expected to come home in about ten days: 'I'm hitching a ride on a plane bringing home a bunch of correspondents.' Now her already frantic search for an apartment grew even more frenzied. A few days later she came home to make a triumphant announcement. She'd signed a lease on a one-bedroom apartment off Riverside Drive at 88th Street – in a brownstone that had seen better days.

'But it has possibilities,' Katie said exuberantly.

'How did you find it?' Ronnie was awed. 'People are going crazy trying to rent apartments! I know,' she pinpointed before Katie could reply. 'You offered more "key money".'

Katie sighed. 'What other way is there now? I "bought the furniture". And don't ask me what I paid because it was outrageous. But Howie will come home to his own apartment. It's worth it.'

Katie's job was winding down. For now she'd return to Winston Productions until she and Howie took up their lives again. They were plotting to write a book based on Howie's wartime experiences, both excited about the potential of this. After that, Katie said, they wanted to become involved with news reporting on television.

'Look, television is going to take off like crazy now that the war is over. Howie and I want to be part of it – as correspondents.'

Elisabeth knew this was a rough time for Amy. But at least, she tried to comfort herself, Amy loved her work. Slim and beautiful now, Amy wanted no part of the entertainment field. So be it, Elisabeth thought. Amy was doing what most people yearned to do with their lives. She was working in a field that gave her tremendous satisfaction. But other soldiers were coming home – and Kevin was still missing.

Soon, Elisabeth warned herself to accept, Katie would be gone from the apartment. Ronnie was dropping hints about how she'd love to move into a place near the Columbia campus with a friend who was also going on to graduate school.

'She bit off more than she could chew,' Ronnie reported. 'She needs a roommate to share the rent.'

All right, Elisabeth told herself, she'd put up the allowance for this, once Amy approved. But act fast before Ronnie's friend found someone else.

Elisabeth wouldn't allow herself to plan ahead for her own life. It would be months before Paul came home. How long before he could persuade Doris to divorce him? She forced herself to be realistic. Would Doris ever agree to a divorce?

Howie came home. Katie was ecstatic. A week later Ronnie, bubbling over with gratitude, moved into her friend's apartment.

'I'll be home regularly,' Ronnie promised, hugging her grandmother and mother in turn. 'How can I do without Hallie's cooking?' She kissed Hallie in a burst of exuberance.

How empty the apartment seemed without Katie and Ronnie, Elisabeth thought in the following weeks. But that was part of life. They wouldn't stop loving one another because they were living apart. Any more than she had ever stopped loving Paul all these years.

For the first night of Hanukkah, in December, the family gathered together. Amy invited Laura to join them. Laura was almost like family. Elisabeth gazed about the dining-room table with pleasure. Her mind darted back through the years to the house in Lexham Gardens – with three generations at the dining table. They were three generations here.

Hallie had surpassed even herself at this dinner. Gefilte fish, her roast chicken – which the family declared could not be matched – potato *latkes*, carrots glazed in honey, and for dessert Hallie's incomparable hamantashen, which Katie and Ronnie insisted were too wonderful to be served only at Purim.

'You didn't learn to make this down South,' Howie teased Hallie.

'From my friend in the South Bronx,' Hallie said with an elfin grin. 'She cooks for a family in our building. She taught me.'

They lingered at the table, graced with the brass candelabra that Elisabeth told the others was a replica of the one that she remembered from her childhood. The single candle marking the first night – plus

459

the *shamus* candle – had burned low. And once again she asked herself if she would ever know what happened to her mother in Germany.

'I know I shouldn't do it,' Howie said and groaned. 'But I can't resist this hamantashen.'

The ring of the phone in the living room was a jarring note.

'I'll get it.' Elisabeth rose to her feet. Amy and Ronnie had gone to the kitchen for coffee refills.

She hurried into the living room, picked up the phone.

'Hello?'

'Beth, may I speak to Laura?' Elisabeth was conscious of tension in Mrs Conway's voice. 'I'm sorry to break in at dinner time this way –'

'I'll get Laura –' She forestalled herself from saying 'Happy Hanukkah'. What had upset Laura's mother? Her throat tightened in alarm as she hurried into the dining room. She knew Laura's father was in fragile health. 'Laura, it's your mother –'

'Oh . . .' Laura stumbled to her feet, darted anxiously from the room.

'Oh my God!' Moments later Laura's shaken voice filtered into the dining room.

Amy stood frozen at the dining room entrance. Ronnie hastily set down the cups she carried, took those from her mother. Everyone about the table listened to the monosyllabic responses from Laura at the receiver. Laura put down the phone, seemed to be fighting for composure. She walked back into the dining room.

'That was Mom. She just had a telephone call from Washington, D.C. The War Department. Kevin's been found.' Instinctively Elisabeth's eyes swung to Amy. Her face was luminous. *Kevin was alive.* 'He's in an army hospital unit in Rome. There's no word about his condition.'

Chapter Fifty-two

Amy faced each day with eager hope that more information would come through about Kevin. He was *alive*. She wouldn't allow herself to consider what his condition was. Laura's mood swung from high to low and back again.

'If he'd just write. Or maybe call us –'

'Laura, it's such a little while since he was found.' Amy tried for optimism in the moments when Laura's mood sagged. 'It's routine for him to be admitted to a hospital for evaluation.' Somewhere she had read this.

'Gail won't be in today.' Laura remembered to alert Amy. 'One of us will have to take over her caseload if she's out more than a day or two.'

'Is she sick, or is it her little girl?' For the last six months Gail had cut back on her frequent absences.

'Her eight-year-old is in the hospital for an emergency appendectomy. Most times Gail manages to come in – I mean, if her kid has a cold or a sore throat. Last year she was put on warning: show up or be fired. Her husband walked out four years ago so she can't afford to lose her job.'

'But it's rough on her little girl.' Amy's mind darted back through the years to the times when she was tiny and her mother dashed off early each morning, leaving her with a woman she scarcely knew. She'd been so scared.

'Gail calls her almost every hour if she's home from school with a cold or temperature or something. What else can she do?'

Amy stared at Laura. All at once fresh insight flooded her. Mom hadn't wanted to leave her. She'd had no recourse. Mom was always out there fighting for survival. Why hadn't *she* understood?

'Amy, are you OK?' Laura was solicitous. 'You look so strange.'

'I'm fine.' Amy managed a smile. 'I was just thinking how rough life must be sometimes for Gail.' Rough for Mom – but she'd refused to understand.

Each day Amy arrived at the office with poignant hope that Laura would come in to say they'd heard from Kevin. But the new year was approaching with no word. Amy tried not to dwell on morbid explanations. She knew that Laura and her parents shared these painful conjectures.

An insomniac for years, Amy awoke before six o'clock on the last day of December. There would be an office party today. The work day would be cut short. There'd be a family gathering at the apartment. Katie and Howie would be over. Ronnie was coming, along with her roommate. It would be a quiet New Year's Eve, though there'd be the usual madness at Times Square.

Heat rose into the radiators, sending a cozy warmth into her bedroom. She'd stay in bed a while longer. Nobody was stirring yet. Then the morning silence was shattered by the shrillness of the phone. Probably a wrong number at this hour – but Amy threw off the blankets and hurried into the living room to pick up the phone before it awoke the others.

'Hello?'

'Amy, I know it's awfully early, but I had to call you!' A breathless excitement in Laura's voice. 'Kevin called from Rome! He's fine – and he'll be home in seven or eight days.'

'Oh Laura, thank God –'

'He said he'd been wounded and, somehow, missed by the medics. There'd been a rough battle, with many casualties. He was taken in by an old couple in a nearby farmhouse. They took care of him, nursed him back to health – but he was suffering from amnesia. He remembered nothing until just a few weeks ago. Something happened – he didn't get around to saying what. But he knew who he was. He rushed to get in touch with army authorities. They wanted to check him out medically before sending him home. He asked about you, Amy . . .' An odd, reflective quality in her voice now.

'He remembered me?'

'He said he carried a photograph of you in his jacket pocket, cut from your yearbook. He said he used to take it out every night before he went to sleep and gaze at it. He wondered if you were his girlfriend back home – or his wife.'

'Laura, I never thought he'd remember me. When you told me he was missing, it was as though part of me had died.' Tears blurred her vision.

'I think,' Laura said softly, 'that you and Kevin have a lot of catching up to do.'

Reading newspaper accounts of the efforts to bring the troops home – and sympathizing with thousands of GIs who bemoaned the slow demobilization – Elisabeth realized that Paul would be lucky to be home by April. She was aware, too, that he would encounter difficulty in persuading Doris to divorce him. But he would be coming home. They would find time to be together.

Many Americans had worried that with so many men – and women – leaving military service, the country would be beset by unemployment. Perhaps a return of the Depression. But that wasn't happening. Women who'd worked hard through the years were leaving their jobs to become housewives, to begin families. Many GIs were returning to college under the GI Bill. Some, with government loans and money saved, were opening up small businesses. But inflation was unnerving, the housing situation desperate. She worried about Paul's finding an apartment when he arrived in New York.

She was disturbed by one trend that kept popping up. Of course, the *Chicago Herald Tribune*'s declaration back in 1907 that nickelodeons appealed to 'the lowest passions of childhood ... wholly vicious, they should be censored and suppressed' was long dismissed. In 1920 the International Reform Bureau wanted to 'rescue the motion pictures from the hands of the Devil and 500 un-Christian Jews'. In 1934 there was Mrs Dilling, who published *The Red Network*. Writer Gilbert Seldes labeled it a 'witch hunt'.

In September of 1941 Senator Wheeler of Idaho – along with a clique of like-minded senators – instigated a preliminary investigation of Hollywood filmmakers. *Life* called it 'the funniest political circus of the year'. Then just a few months ago Senator John Rankin told the House Un-American Activities Committee that he knew of a Hollywood group out to overthrow the government, and that he had cohorts on their trail. Was this an indication of more such rabble-rousing?

Her greatest joy was watching Amy and Kevin together. They would be married in early June. Kevin was completely recovered except for a slight limp that would cause him no difficulty. He was already teaching again. Amy was forty-two but – God willing – hoped to give Kevin a son or daughter. It was as though her life was just beginning, Elisabeth thought with gratitude.

In the mountainside house in Bougy Villars the horrible tension had just been relieved. Paul, Doris, and Tommy were scheduled to take a train to Le Havre tomorrow morning. The next day they would board a ship to take them to New York. Doris would not be happy when she saw their accommodations, Paul suspected, but this was not a time to be fussy. The great ocean liners were still in the process of being refurbished after years of serving as troop ships.

'I don't know why you couldn't have written to some real estate agents in New York to line up an apartment for us,' Doris complained. 'I hate to think what our furniture is like after being in storage all these years.'

'Doris, I've told you, there's a terrible housing crunch in New York. We'll have to look around – see what we can do. We may be lucky just to find a furnished sublet at first.'

'I'll hate a sublet. We've been putting up with this awful place far too long. If it's too bad in New York, I'll fly down to Bermuda for a few weeks. Until you locate something habitable.'

'That's not in our budget, Doris.' He'd explained that, too.

'I suppose I should go home for a couple of weeks to see my sisters. While you're lining up some hovel for us to live in.'

He had not yet approached Doris about a divorce. Let that wait until they were in New York and Tommy settled in. Nothing must occur to set Tommy back in his recovery. But whatever it took to buy a divorce – alimony for ever – he would agree. He paused at his bedroom window to gaze at distant, snow-capped Mont Blanc, the one thing he would miss back in New York.

'Paul, the mail hasn't arrived yet,' Doris complained. 'The man is coming later every day!'

'The road is bad this morning. And he rides a bike.'

It amazed him that Doris was suddenly in steady correspondence with her two sisters back in South Carolina. Perhaps learning about the death of her father and mother during the years they were in Switzerland softened her. She'd been estranged from all of them for years. They'd exchanged New Year's cards once a year – 'to show we're civilized,' Doris said.

464

'Are you sure you've packed everything?' Doris probed.

'I'm all packed except for traveling clothes.'

'You're certain Tommy will be able to get his medication in New York?'

'He'll get it.' Plus he was traveling with six months' supply.

'And I don't understand why you haven't heard from Bill Madison,' Doris grunted in disgust.

'He knows we're heading home. And he's not going to find a producer in a few days.'

'He's had your new play for weeks.' She hadn't read it. She'd never read his work.

'Let him be, Doris.' On the last play they'd waited almost eighteen months before a contract was signed. He felt a flicker of apprehension. Maybe he'd talk to Bill about tracking down some radio work, or television.

He suspected that, with the war over, television sets were pouring off the assembly lines. The postwar economy was in great shape, and advertising agencies would be grabbing at television as a powerful way to sell products. He didn't want to go out to Hollywood again. He meant to stay in New York. Television would be the new scene. Surely he could adapt to the television medium. Hell, it was closer to theater than radio.

Paul felt a surge of excitement at beginning their trip home. They were emerging from exile. Doris complained about all the shortcomings of the trip, but Tommy shared with him the pleasure of the Atlantic crossing. When they reached New York they stood on the deck together and watched the Statue of Liberty come into view.

'Now I know how all the generations of immigrants felt when they saw Miss Liberty,' Paul said reverently. 'And with the war over, this country has emerged as the greatest power in the world.'

Elisabeth was constantly aware that Paul was arriving home. She waited for that precious phone call that told her he was here. Since that first call, Paul had phoned her each week. It had been poignantly sweet to hear his voice, to know that nothing had changed between them.

On a Sunday afternoon – when normally she would be home but had come in to clear up some data – the office phone rang. Before she lifted the receiver she knew the caller was Paul.

'Hi . . .' Her voice breathless with anticipation.

'You knew it was me,' Paul said gently and chuckled. 'I can't be grammatically correct at a moment like this.'

'Who else would phone me at the office on a Sunday afternoon? This is the number I knew you'd call.'

'I'm calling from the Plaza lobby. We docked about three hours ago. Can we meet somewhere?'

'Here at the office?' Her heart was pounding. 'There's no one here –'

'I'll be there in ten minutes.'

'Hurry,' she ordered. 'I'll be waiting.'

Though she knew he couldn't be here instantly, she rushed from her office, down the hall to the reception area. To be there when he emerged from the elevator and walked to the door.

Soon she heard the elevator chugging to a stop. She flung the door wide. He was striding towards her. They might have seen each other just a week ago, she thought. He'd changed barely at all. A sprinkling of gray in his hair now.

'Oh Beth!' He reached to pull her into his arms. 'Beautiful as ever . . .'

'You're needing glasses.' A lilt in her voice.

'No. Just you.'

'Let's go inside.' Nothing had changed for them. 'I want you all to myself.'

She led him by the hand to her private office, closed the door behind them. 'I feel like twenty, welcoming my lover back from the wars.'

'Sssh,' he ordered. 'Enough of talk . . .'

'Paul, I have to admit I'm not having much luck with the play.' Bill Madison fumbled with the letter opener on his desk, a sure sign to Paul that he was upset. 'It's not your usual style.'

'I know. But this is the way I really want to go.'

'The feeling is that the subject matter just won't sell. I mean, the Spanish Civil War when we've just emerged from World War II?'

'What do you suggest?' No sense playing games.

'I suggest you file it away for a few years. Have you given any thought to a screen-writing assignment?' Madison's face brightened. 'I could –'

466

'I don't want to leave New York. I want to take roots right here. Bill, I've been in virtual exile for the last few years. First in Spain, then Switzerland.' He hesitated. 'What about radio? *Lux Radio Theater?*'

'I'll look into it. But it's not like films – the market is limited.'

'Bill, I don't want to go to Hollywood.' A vein pounded at his temple.

'You mentioned you'd needed real money –'

'See what you can line up for me in radio.' God, did he need real money. 'Look into the television situation –'

'The market is limited,' Madison stressed again, 'but I'll try to set up some luncheons. Be prepared to discuss two or three plot lines. You'd do a hell of a lot better in Hollywood.'

'That's out.'

'OK . . .' But Bill Madison wasn't happy.

Paul left his agent's office and walked out of the building into a sunlit mid-May afternoon. In the four weeks that he'd been back in the city he'd enjoyed just being able to walk about familiar streets. They were lucky, Bill had told him, to find a six-month sublet.

Doris bitched constantly about its inadequacies. She had taken over the master bedroom. He shared the smaller bedroom with Tommy. In this rotten housing situation people doubled up. Tommy should have a place of his own, but with their shrinking finances he'd have to wait. If Doris would stay out of Saks and Bergdorf's, they could survive for a year.

He flinched at the prospect of spending a whole year with Doris. Yet last night had been a breakthrough. Ever since they arrived, he'd been dropping subtle hints to her that with Tommy getting his life together – working in a bookstore for now, until the opening of college in September – this might be the time for them to go their separate ways.

Last night, when she'd carried on yet again about how she hated the apartment, he came right out and suggested she go out to Nevada for a divorce. 'That'll get you out of the apartment for six weeks.' The inference being that he'd move out and leave the apartment to her. Hopefully Tommy would have a small place of his own by then.

He'd braced himself for fireworks. Instead, Doris stared at him with that icy glare of hers and stated her terms.

'I'll require a healthy settlement, of course. And alimony. When you can handle that, let's see a lawyer.'

Damn! How was he going to come up with that any time soon?

Chapter Fifty-three

Ronnie hurried from her last class. She was to have an early dinner with Katie and Howie. They were trying to decide on a group wedding present for her mother and Kevin. She felt a flicker of guilt as she envisioned Grandma living alone in that big apartment with just Hallie.

At the apartment the three settled down to dinner immediately because Ronnie had an evening interview with the subject of an article she'd been commissioned to write.

'How do you work in this madhouse?' She stared about in amusement at the pile-up of books scattered about the small living room and encroaching even into the dining area.

'Katie's a slavedriver. Everything has to be double-checked.' Howie pretended to duck as Katie lifted a fist in mock rage.

'How's the book coming?' Ronnie asked.

'It's coming.' Katie exchanged a confident glance with Howie. 'Howie wants me to stop working even part time so we can focus on finishing it by the end of the year.'

Ronnie hesitated for a moment. 'Grandma's going to throw a fit – but I don't want to go back to school next year.' A defiant glint in her eyes. Mom understood. 'I want to get out in the field full time.'

'You'll have your degree in another year.' Katie was shocked.

'I love working on the magazine. They're offering me a full-time job. If I turn them down, I could lose out altogether. And they're on the verge of snaring a big investor. That means a major expansion.'

'You're not yet twenty-two years old – you can wait a year.' Katie turned appealingly to Howie.

'A degree could take you into something more important.'

'Bullshit. I want to follow up with the magazine. It's going places. I want to go with it. '

'Don't tell your grandmother till after the wedding,' Howie advised. 'Don't spoil that for her.'

'I'm working on my editor to send me to Germany on an assignment. It'll take a lot of working on him,' Ronnie added because Katie flinched. 'But sometime in the fall I'd like to go to Berlin.'

'You don't speak German!'

Ronnie grinned. 'I do now. A little. I've been taking a crash course the last six months. Everybody's writing about the concentration camps – and I know how important that is. But I'd like to do a story about the average German family. They weren't all Nazis, you know.'

'Mom won't like that either,' Katie predicted. 'Remember, we have family over there – or had.'

'I know how Grandma tried to track down her mother when you all were over in London that year. I know about "the German cousins". But that's no reason for me not to go to Germany to try to write what could be a great story.'

Katie sighed, turned to Howie. 'This one wants a Pulitzer Prize before she's twenty-five.'

'OK, enough of this,' Ronnie said briskly. 'What do we buy as a group present for Mom and Kevin?'

Amy and Kevin's wedding was a small family affair, like that of Katie and Howie. This time Howie's parents were present as well as Kevin's. Hallie had overruled Elisabeth's suggestion that the wedding dinner be catered.

'I cook the weddin' dinner for all my kids,' she vowed. 'I'll just start two days ahead.'

For Elisabeth it was a poignant occasion. She remembered Amy's marriage to Keith – which Amy had yearned to be a small, private affair. She and Amy were both furious that photographers and reporters were staked out in front of the house even while Amy dressed.

But that era was long past. It was as though Amy had been reborn. Kevin and Amy would never be rich in the ordinary sense – but they were rich in their love and in working in fields that gave them such satisfaction.

Tears filled Elisabeth's eyes as the rabbi spoke the words that made Kevin and Amy husband and wife. At long last her firstborn was at peace with herself.

*　　*　　*

Elisabeth was grateful for the hours she and Paul were able to be together – yet ever fearful that her family would discover this liaison. In the eyes of the world Paul was still a married man. They met in out-of-the-way restaurants, made love in the privacy of her office when the staff was away. On this sweltering August Sunday evening they left her office for dinner at a Lower Second Avenue restaurant – far off the track from family members.

'I think a Nobel prize should be given to the man who invented air-conditioning,' Elisabeth said as they reveled in the comfort of the restaurant.

'I wish we could go away for a few days. Just the two of us.' Paul's eyes made love to her.

'I wish that, too.' They were so close to that. Doris had made it clear. The day Paul would sign over what she considered a suitable settlement, she'd take a train out to Reno.

'I've laid the cornerstone.' His smile was wry. 'I've got one network radio play under my belt. Bill's still trying to sell me on Hollywood.' He paused. 'I'm going to tell him if he can set up a one-picture deal, I'll take it. Provided they pay me a bundle. I might just persuade Doris to take a cluster of post-dated checks on the strength of a chunk of cash upfront.'

'You'll hate going out there again. I'll hate not seeing you for three months.' Would these separations never end?

'Perhaps you could contrive a business reason for coming out for a week?' His smile was a whimsical plea.

'I will!'

The office could run without her for that long. She could be out there to persuade some fading star to consider the lead in the new 'soap' she was packaging. Oh, it would be good to spend a whole week with Paul. Not to have to look over their shoulders each time they were together. And it'd be a chance to see Ellie and Chuck and Ira.

Five weeks later – while Paul waited impatiently for word on a pending movie deal – his agent summoned him to a meeting.

'He's probably lined up something,' Paul told Elisabeth in a call from a phone booth downstairs from Madison's office. 'I'll phone as soon as I can.'

The reception room was empty. He was ushered immediately into Bill Madison's lush private office, a symbol of his long-time success.

'You're looking great,' Bill said with a show of high spirits. 'I have a lunch date with the radio people for tomorrow.' Paul sensed a covert apprehension in his agent.

'Bill, what's up?' He was too impatient for this dalliance.

'I've been huddling with people on the Coast. I can't figure out what's happening. When we first talked, three producers were hot to hire you. All of a sudden all three have pulled back. Did you have any problems the last time you were out there?'

'I haven't been in Hollywood for years,' he reminded Madison. 'I had the usual skirmishes. Nothing serious.' He felt a sudden chill. Hollywood had seemed his road to freedom. 'What's this all about?'

Madison seemed to be weighing his explanation. 'I may be off the wall – but this could have something to do with HUAC. You know, the House Un-American Activities Committee.' Paul stared in bewilderment. 'Hell, you know they've been sniping at Hollywood for years. Now they're getting nastier.'

'What's that got to do with me?'

'All kinds of crazy rumors are floating around. Everybody's scared of being called a Communist.'

'I'm not a Communist.'

'I know that, and you know that.' Madison forced himself to meet Paul's gaze. 'But you spent two years in Madrid during the Spanish Civil War.'

'I was there as foreign correspondent.' Paul struggled for calm. 'I don't get it.'

'You were concerned for the peasants and –'

'This is a barrel of crap!' Paul broke in. 'You read the play. It shows that I was disillusioned with both the Fascists and the Communists. Sure, I felt sorry for the Spanish peasants! What decent human being wouldn't have, seeing what they were going through?'

'I'll try some other companies,' Bill soothed. 'But I don't know if the response will be any different.'

'All right, see if you can line up more radio deals,' Paul said after a moment. But that wasn't the kind of money he needed to get Doris out of his life.

Elisabeth was pleased when Ronnie dropped by the apartment for dinner, and grateful that she, along with Amy and Katie, always called first. For the past few weeks – because Paul was so troubled

472

that assignments were not coming in – she'd taken to inviting him for dinner once or twice a week. They could spend a quiet evening together without worrying about being seen. Doris's demands would take an upswing if she knew about them.

She was conscious of Hallie's avid curiosity, her delight each time Paul was at the apartment. Hallie was an incurable romantic. Still, Hallie knew not to mention Paul's presence to the others in the family.

'Hallie, Ronnie's coming for dinner,' Elisabeth reported. 'She called me at the office.'

'Then I gotta make my apple cobbler with the rum sauce she likes so much,' Hallie decided. 'We got plenty of apples and a bottle of rum.'

'If I didn't know you better, I'd suspect you of taking a nip every now and then.'

From the moment Ronnie arrived, Elisabeth sensed she had something special to report. But she'd do that in her own time. Not until they were reveling in Hallie's dessert – topped tonight by a smidgen of whipped cream – did Ronnie spring her surprise.

'Grandma, don't be upset,' Ronnie warned and took a deep breath. 'I've persuaded the magazine to send me to Berlin to do a story on an ordinary German family. I'll be there three weeks –'

'Now you want to go to Germany?' All at once Elisabeth's mind charged back through the years to her last summer with 'the German cousins' in Berlin. What had happened to them? What had happened to Mama? 'Ronnie, the situation there is horrible.' Her voice was strident. 'Conditions are awful all over Europe. People are suffering unbelievable shortages.'

'I can handle that.' Ronnie switched on her always potent charm. 'I'll be there for just three weeks. But I think there's a great story to write about. Katie and Howie agree with me.'

Elisabeth sighed. 'You're stubborn. Like all the women in this family.' She'd been upset when Ronnie refused to go back to Columbia for her second year at the School of Journalism. But she'd understood what was driving Ronnie. 'When will you be leaving?'

'The first of November. I have my passport – that's no problem.' Ronnie had been planning this for weeks.

'When you're in Berlin,' Elisabeth said softly, 'would you look in the phone book to see if any of the cousins might be listed? I'll give you the names I remember. If you talk to anyone, explain that you're the great-great-granddaughter of Rae Kahn, who was Rae Wassermann before she was married.'

'Sure, Grandma.' Ronnie's expression told Elisabeth this session had gone easier than she'd anticipated.

Ronnie arrived at Orly Airport in the afternoon, exhausted from the flight, yet exhilarated by the knowledge that she was in Europe.

She would have liked to linger in Paris for two or three days but reminded herself that the magazine was providing for only three weeks in Europe. She'd need every minute of that time for her Berlin interviews. Late tonight a second flight would deposit her in Berlin. But she'd remember to call Ted and Mark between flights, as Grandma asked.

She hadn't expected to feel qualms about traveling to Berlin. But once settled in her seat on the Berlin-bound plane she was assaulted by memories of the horrifying newsreels that showed victims of the concentration camps, by newspaper accounts, and especially by the voice of Ed Murrow, reporting on radio about what he'd seen at Buchenwald. '*I pray you to believe what I've said about Buchenwald. I've reported what I saw and heard, but only part of it. For most of it I have no words . . .*'

She'd been warned about shortages, not only in Germany but all over Europe. She'd packed soap, toilet tissue, a few chocolate bars, her warmest pajamas and robe because heating fuel was rationed. Inflation was wild, she'd been told, black marketeers rampant.

She acquired a taxi to take her to her small hotel – accommodations arranged by the office – remembering to bargain on the fee. En route she became aware of the devastation wrought by Allied bombers, still in evidence despite the passage of over a year. She was startled to see that street signs were all in Russian. Professional offices and shops had notices in English and Russian. Everywhere there were movie houses and cafés.

Her hotel was right off the Kurfürstendamm, her room small but neat. And cold. Though the night was bitter, not a whisper of heat rose in the single radiator. Not at this hour. She'd go to bed, toss her coat atop the threadbare blankets.

She fell asleep in minutes. She'd slept little on the long flight. She awoke seven hours later with an instant realization of the task ahead.

She'd planned her routine, knew exactly how she was to proceed. She had a letter from her publisher to a relief organization that would direct her to the area where she meant to interview families.

Shivering in the dank morning cold she prepared for the day, grateful that she had brought her warmest clothes. A hotel clerk directed her to a nearby café where she had a surprisingly decent breakfast. Now she waited in line for thirty-five minutes for a bus to take her to the office of the relief organization.

Her contact at the office, a German woman who spoke fluent English, was efficient and eager to help. The woman was grateful, Ronnie suspected, to see an American who was prepared to write with compassion about the problems of ordinary Germany families.

'Not every family will be willing to speak with you,' the woman warned. 'They've been through rough times. But I've prepared a list of prospects, along with directions on how to reach them.'

The first three days only two families were willing to be interviewed. These two were nostalgic for earlier times. Now just to survive was a battle. Relief efforts were slight because of lack of funds.

'If you have money, you can buy almost anything on the black market – but the prices!' A middle-aged mother of three rolled her eyes in horror. 'It's $50 for a pound of coffee, $120 for a pound of butter . . .'

'Do you smoke?' her husband, long unemployed, asked hopefully.

'No, I'm sorry . . .'

The following morning she stuffed two candy bars into her purse. It wasn't that she meant to bribe prospective interviewees, she told herself guiltily. But the eyes that stared back at her radiated suffering. She needed to have them trust her enough to speak freely. *Were* they former Nazis? Or just unfortunate people caught up in Hitler's frenzy, helpless to stop the slaughter?

She was startled to discover her first family of the day was Jewish. She realized this when the woman – in her late thirties, widowed and a mother of two – reached for a photograph of her late husband and the telltale concentration camp tattoo on her arm was revealed.

'My husband died in Buchenwald,' the woman explained. 'My two daughters and I survived. How, I don't know . . .' She spread her hands in a gesture that said she didn't really care that they had.

Two little girls, aged four and six, clung to their mother. They seemed fascinated by Ronnie. Her shaky German, she surmised.

'Would it be all right if I give the girls a candy bar?' Ronnie felt a tightening in her throat. How thin the three of them were, even now – a year and a half since V-E Day.

The woman's face lightened. 'It would be a little bit of heaven for them,' she whispered.

Ronnie reached into her purse, impulsively brought out both chocolate bars, handed them to the mother.

'Wait, *Liebchens*,' she said and hurried off to respond to a knock at the door.

She pulled the door wide. A young man with rumpled dark hair and pleasant features walked into the room. Ronnie tried to follow the rapid-fire conversation between the other two adults. Now the young man turned accusingly to Ronnie.

'Why do you bother these people? Haven't they been through enough?' His English was perfect, though his accent was German.

'I'm on assignment by an American magazine.' Why was she stammering this way? She was doing nothing wrong. The woman was breaking one chocolate bar in two, handed one part to each of the little girls. The other bar would be for later. 'Americans are concerned about ordinary people in the aftermath of the war.' He grunted in disbelief. 'Just a few weeks ago – on Yom Kippur eve – President Truman called for Great Britain to allow 100,000 Jewish refugees to emigrate to Palestine. As an American and a Jew I applaud him for that. Most Americans did.'

'You're Jewish?' He seemed surprised.

'Yes.'

'Let us go somewhere and talk.' He was brusque, but his voice softened when he turned to the other woman. In German – which Ronnie managed to understand – he told her that everything was all right. He would be back later.

Her companion introduced himself. He was Erich Waters. He'd been at boarding school and college in Switzerland during the war years.

'There's a café three blocks from here where we can get a halfway decent cup of coffee. These day's it's never crowded. We can talk there.'

They walked in silence to the café. It was obvious that the owner knew Erich Waters, held him in deep respect. They were brought coffee that wasn't watered down.

'This is the first Jewish family you've interviewed?' he asked when they were alone.

'Yes. Is there something wrong about that?' Her eyes were defiant.

'Most Jews are in detention camps. Lisl and her daughters are the rare lucky ones. But that's a long story for another time. I'll take you to one of the camps. Write about that when you go back to the United States.' His voice was harsh, his eyes pained. This is a man who cares about people, she thought.

'I will,' she said softly.

'There are camps here in Germany and others in Cyprus. Worse,' he said with contempt, 'than the camps where Americans held German prisoners during the war.'

She listened, sipped her coffee without tasting, while he told her about the efforts of Palestinian Jews to bring these displaced persons to their own country.

'The British only allow 1,500 a month – when there are hundreds of thousands waiting. The Royal Navy, the Royal Air Force, thousands of British soldiers patrol the coast, but still we manage to bring illegal ships ashore.' By 'we', she understood, he meant the Haganah, the unofficial Jewish defense group. 'It grows harder each month.' He paused, his eyes searching hers. 'There's a yacht we're aching to buy. It's at anchor at Hamburg. The owners won't sell to us. They're afraid they'll be accused of aiding illegal immigration. They're British, in Hamburg to set up some manufacturing venture. But a rich American heiress could persuade them to sell. And in the dark of the night,' he whispered, 'we can stow away hundreds of displaced persons, and make a run for the coast of Palestine.'

'I'm not a rich American heiress.'

'You could play the part with some coaching.' He paused. 'Think what a terrific story you'd have for your magazine.'

'I'll try it,' she said instantly. 'But not because I'll have a terrific story for my magazine.'

Chapter Fifty-four

Erich took Ronnie to meet a majestic older woman in a mansion at the edge of Berlin, an area untouched by British or American bombs or Russian shells. Not Jewish, he explained, but *sympatico*. Multilingual Frau Mueller would plot their approach. She herself was suspect, but a young American heiress was acceptable.

'Tomorrow we go shopping for your wardrobe,' she told Ronnie. 'You must look the role. With a mass of luggage you'll move into the Hotel Adlon. It's where an American heiress would choose to stay. I'll have luncheon with you there, meet you one afternoon for tea. I'll spread the word that you're Doris Duke's cousin. That you're restless, interested in buying a yacht to cruise the Greek Isles. The word will reach Hamburg. Without a doubt you'll be approached with an offer of a yacht. You'll be undecided at first, then with typical American "spontaneity" you agree to buy. You'll pay with traveler's cheques.'

'My mother or grandmother should be playing this,' Ronnie told the other two with a flippant air. But her eyes were serious. 'They were both actresses.'

'It's a game,' Frau Mueller said. 'You'll play it well.'

Ronnie absorbed detailed coaching by Frau Mueller – whispered to have been in earlier years the mistress of German royalty. It was clear that Frau Mueller had vast sums of money at her disposal, a situation best left unquestioned, Erich warned. She chartered a private plane to fly herself and Ronnie to Paris to shop. In remarkably untouched Paris, they stayed at the Ritz. The family will never believe this. The following morning they returned to Berlin. Ronnie was registered at the Hotel Adlon, where fashionable Berliners gathered for luncheon or afternoon tea.

In the midst of such want she was uncomfortable in luxury surroundings, yet the cause was worthy. No way could she have refused this role. She was ever conscious of the displaced persons who must be smuggled into Palestine. Why was the British government so against this?

Ronnie had expected to be part of this scene for three or four days, but Frau Mueller was determined not to rush: 'We can't afford a mistake.' Now Erich joined them for dinner each evening, well-dressed, wearing an ultra-expensive wristwatch. He was to appear to be her lover.

According to plan, Erich lingered with her in the Adlon dining room evening after evening. At intervals he held her hand, gazed amorously into her eyes. But their conversations were always decorous. Yet Ronnie felt an involuntary closeness to Erich as he talked about himself. He was only a year older than she, but he'd gone through such upheavals in his life. Lying awake in bed – too tense to fall asleep immediately – she replayed in her mind the conversations of each night.

'Right after Kristallnacht my parents shipped me off to boarding school in Switzerland. They opened a bank account for me. My father knew it was the time to leave Germany, but my grandmother was too frail to travel. My mother wouldn't leave her and, of course, my father wouldn't leave my mother. I had no word of them after 1941. No word from aunts and uncles, cousins. They all waited too long to try to leave. It was as though they'd all been swept off the earth.'

Another night he talked about his father's ambitions for him.

'My father wanted me to be a physicist. I never told him I was determined to be a photographer. I think I decided on Kristallnacht. Because photographs of what happened that night could say more than a whole book. In my last letter from him and my mother he said if the war was over by the time I had my degree, I should go to the United States. Be a pioneer. I think that he knew we'd never be together again.'

Just tonight he had told her about Lisl, the woman she'd interviewed.

'After the war was over in Europe, I returned to Berlin. I searched everywhere for my parents, for the aunts and uncles and cousins. Then I met Lisl. She told me my mother and father had died in Buchenwald, like her husband. My grandmother had collapsed of a heart attack and died the day my father and mother were taken away. I was able to get Lisl and the children out of the DP camp. My own funds were just enough to see me through the university, but I try to help them when I can.'

She had great respect for Erich's talents as a photographer. The magazine would be pleased with the photographs he was supplying for her story – not quite the story they had expected.

'Photography is a good cover for me,' he confided. 'I can go to a lot of places with my cameras without arousing suspicions.'

But Ronnie was growing uneasy with the passage of time. She was scheduled to leave Berlin in one week. Then the following morning Frau Mueller phoned.

'We're meeting two Englishmen for lunch today. They're interested in selling a yacht.' Even on the phone Frau Mueller kept up the pretense. 'Darling, I think it's exactly what you want.' She chuckled. 'And there'll be a substantial commission for me in the sale. But you understand that.'

'Of course.' But that commission, Erich had told her, was to go back into their fund.

As scheduled, Ronnie and Frau Mueller met with the two Englishmen for lunch in the Adlon dining room. Ronnie pretended to be doubtful when they showed her photographs of the yacht.

'I do so want to see the Greek Isles,' Ronnie conceded casually. 'Even this time of year it should be lovely there. But this yacht seems rather spartan.'

Now the two Englishmen became lyrical about their property, coaxed her to go to Hamburg to board it. She agreed, traveled to Hamburg with Erich and Frau Mueller. She was appalled at the condition of the city, where over sixty percent of the houses had been destroyed. Most trees had been cut down last winter to provide fuel. But she admired the yacht, bargained on price, as coached by Erich.

She'd thought her part in the negotiations was over when the sale was consummated – feeling almost wistful that she wouldn't be seeing Erich again. But Erich explained that she would be needed another few days, for window dressing.

'You have to go to Hamburg to collect your yacht,' Erich pointed out. 'I'll go with you. And Frau Mueller will chaperone,' he drawled. 'Bring your luggage. You'll fly home from Hamburg. Don't worry,' he forestalled her protests. 'Frau Mueller will handle the change of reservations.'

On the appointed day they took a train to Hamburg. Erich played the attentive lover, Frau Mueller the diplomatic chaperone. Ronnie was astonished to discover the yacht's crew consisted of Americans.

'We have American friends,' Erich said. 'And don't try to go below. Every inch of space down there is occupied.' He chuckled at her bewildered stare. 'In the middle of the night – for the past three nights – we've been stowing our "cargo".'

She was unnerved when Erich explained they were to sail from Hamburg at dusk, with herself and Frau Mueller aboard. 'You'll leave the ship with Frau Mueller when we're a mile at sea. You'll spend the night at a hotel in Hamburg, fly out the next day.'

'I'm not a great swimmer . . .' She tried for levity.

'The boat that'll pick you up is absolutely safe.' All at once there was a reflective glow in his eyes. 'But you know, I'll miss you.'

'I'll miss you, too.' She paused. Then the electric moment passed. 'Will you write to me from Palestine and let me know if everything worked out?'

'I'll write you,' he promised.

Elisabeth listened to Ronnie's tale of her adventures in Berlin with pride. She'd tried to teach her daughters and granddaughter a sense of responsibility – and each in her own way had proved a good student.

Ronnie would for ever cherish her part in helping in an urgent cause. Erich Waters had written to say their mission was successful. Ronnie was so excited that the magazine was, indeed, publishing his photographs and interested in further photographs from Palestine.

'Wasn't this better than going back to school?' Ronnie challenged. 'Once the article is published, I'll have a leg up career-wise.'

'The magazine is happy, I gather.'

'They're ecstatic.' Ronnie glanced at her watch. 'I'd better take off. I have to be at the radio station at eight a.m. tomorrow. Be sure you listen to me being interviewed.'

'I'll be listening. Oh, Katie says your magazine should look into a possible television interview as well. Television sets are being sold like mad, I hear.'

Hallie appeared in the doorway. 'You ain't leavin' without taking a package with you. You know you love my rugelach.'

'Hallie, if I get fat, it's your fault!'

Then Ronnie was off, and the apartment seemed empty again.

'I'll bring you a cup of tea,' Hallie told Elisabeth. 'It's that time of night.'

Why was she so restless tonight? Not just tonight – she'd been restless for years. She worked hard. Ronnie said she'd never known anybody who worked as hard. Perhaps, she thought, in a flash of clairvoyance, because she saw nothing ahead for her beyond her continuing, unsatisfying success. Her financial situation had improved beyond her wildest expectations. With her bank accounts, her blue-chip stocks, she'd never have to worry financially – and Amy and Katie and Ronnie would never need to worry. This should be enough.

Yet there was this void in her life. Was it time for her to turn her life around? Sell the business, or delegate much of the work? For a while she thought Ted and Mark would return after the war, that Ted would be ready to take over the business – but their hearts belonged to Paris.

Let her learn from them. Start her life anew. Paul was convinced it was a matter of time before he'd be free. They could be together for the rest of their years. She could return to her other first love. Theater. But that was a wild fantasy!

I'm sixty years old, what roles would there be in theater for me now? Bit parts if I'm lucky. But to create even a small part – to bring it to life with every nuance the writer intended would be so exhilarating! Or to direct a play. What pleasure that could give me!

It would be enough to be with Paul for the rest of their years. A rebirth. She glanced at the clock. If he could get away from the apartment, Paul would call to see if he had an 'all-clear'. He knew not to come up without calling first. Nor could he phone from his apartment, sublet now for another six months. Why was he having such trouble finding an assignment? They'd both always taken it for granted that as a last resort he could write a screenplay. But that wasn't happening.

She loved his new play. Bill Madison refused to offer it to any more producers. It *wasn't* controversial. It told of the disillusionment of American volunteers with both the Loyalists and the Fascists. It was an ode to democracy. She was so touched when Paul said he'd written the feminine lead with her in mind. 'I saw you in every scene.

I know, you're a big radio producer now, but in my mind I saw you playing Katarina.'

Paul had been home almost nine months – and still he was tied to that apartment with Doris. She wasn't going to budge on the divorce until she saw a bundle of money. And Paul, poor darling, kept walking into dead ends. His sole happiness was that Tommy was remaining in school to earn a masters in engineering.

She had some pull in radio circles. Could she help Paul land an assignment? He was a fine writer – people in radio and movies knew that.

The following morning, feeling guilty at doing this without first consulting Paul, she phoned a top-level producer who owed her a favor.

'Paul Coleman?' her big-wheel colleague said with an air of unease. 'He's a friend of yours?'

'For many years.'

'Beth, tell the guy to stop spinning his wheels. He's not going to sell in this town or in Hollywood.'

'Why?' She was astounded.

'You know how uptight people in this business are about possible Communist infiltration.' He was clearly uncomfortable. 'I don't have to tell you about the House Un-American Activities Committee.'

'What has that got to do with Paul? He's not a Communist!'

'He did that whole batch of articles from Madrid during the Spanish Civil War. Sympathetic articles.'

'Sympathetic towards the Americans in the Abraham Lincoln Brigade. That doesn't make him a Communist –'

'We're moving into a weird period. I tell you, Beth, the guy won't find work in the entertainment field.'

This was unreal, Elisabeth thought. Should she repeat this to Paul? Oh God, it would crush him. Maybe it was just what Bill Madison had told Paul. Hollywood was planning to make fewer films in the coming year. And how many dramatic shows were being presented on radio? Paul had been away from the scene for several years. He needed to prove himself all over again. Yet she couldn't shake from her mind the words she'd just heard: 'He's not going to sell in this town or in Hollywood.'

Not until ten days past New Year's could Elisabeth bring herself to tell Paul what she'd been told about the climate in radio and films. He'd come to the apartment for dinner, and now they prepared to listen to *Mr and Mrs North*. Paul hoped to sell a script for the series.

'I can't believe it!' But he was apprehensive. 'I'm going to see Bill. Ask him outright if I'm on some blacklist.'

'Maybe you'd better.' It wasn't just the settlement for Doris that was at stake. She knew that Paul would soon run out of funds. She knew, too, that he would balk at accepting help from her.

In the morning Paul went to Bill Madison's office, arriving only moments after the office opened.

'I haven't heard from you in weeks,' Paul began.

'That's because I've had nothing to report.' But Bill's eyes avoided meeting his.

'I've heard a weird rumor,' Paul began.

'You mean this vendetta against the movie and radio people?' Bill seemed relieved to have this out in the open. 'We've been together a long time, Paul. You're my friend – not just a client.' He was fiddling with the telltale letter opener again. 'All kinds of rumors are afloat. And they're more than rumors. HUAC is out for blood. The whole thing will break out into the open at any time. The word is that a lot of producers, actors, directors, writers, are Commies. Look, I know in most cases it's not true,' he forestalled a rejection by Paul, 'but the country's in a strange stage. It's going to get worse before it gets better.'

'You're telling me I'm through as a writer?' Paul's head was reeling.

Bill hesitated. 'I can probably line up some work for you if you write under a pseudonym. But the money will be way less than normal. Maybe fifteen – twenty percent of your usual fees.'

Paul sat motionless, struggling to deal with this. What else could he do to earn a living except write? 'All right, Bill. See what you can line up for me.'

He returned to the apartment. Doris was sprawled on the sofa and reading one of her endless women's magazines. As succinctly as possible he filled her in on the situation. The magazine she had been reading fell from her fingers. Her face drained of color.

'How can they do this to you?' Her voice was shrill.

'It's happening. This Red scare. And it's gaining terrible momentum.'

'You were stupid to go to Spain!' she shrieked.

'We needed the money.' She'd been happy enough to spend it. 'And I wasn't there as a Communist supporter.'

'You may be dragged before the House Un-American Activities Committee! Exposed before the whole world!'

'Meanwhile, Bill thinks he can get some work for me under a pseudonym. The money will be a fraction of what I'm usually paid. We can't afford this apartment when the lease runs out. We'll have to learn to economize. We –'

'Do you think I'll stay with you and face the kind of disgrace that's lying ahead?' She rose to her feet, her color high. 'I've given you the best years of my life – but no more, Paul. I won't share your shame! I'm going to Reno. I won't bear your name a day longer than I have to!'

'I'll provide what alimony I can afford,' he said tiredly.

'You do that,' she said with menacing calm. 'I'm going back home to live with my sisters. That big old house belongs to the three of us now.' A malicious glint in her eyes. 'Plus we share a sizeable inheritance. But you owe me.'

'Have your lawyer contact me.'

Doris was leaving him. He'd be free – in a world that had slapped a devastating label on him.

'I'll leave for Reno in the morning. I'll –' She stopped dead. Neither of them had realized that Tommy had come into the apartment. He stood there, dazed, disbelieving. 'Tommy, you're welcome to come down to visit me any time you like. You're still my son.' She swung about and stalked to her bedroom.

'You and Mother are getting a divorce?'

'It's been coming a long time,' Paul said gently. This wasn't good for Tommy. He should have been prepared.

'I knew for a long time – most of my life – that you had a strange kind of marriage. I never remember your sharing a room. But then I had problems of my own . . .'

'Tommy, you and I will get along just fine.' How much had he heard? 'We'll have to budget for a while, but you can continue at school. This is a temporary climate in the country. You know about HUAC?' Tommy nodded. 'Some on the committee are convinced that Hollywood – and radio – are hotbeds of Communism. Rumors are flying that there'll be some ugly investigations.'

'And Mother's pulling out before any of it could brush off on her.'

'That's about it.'

'That's why she ran everywhere with me,' Tommy said. 'She couldn't bear having the world believe she had a schizophrenic son. She had to prove I was all right.' Paul saw the tic in his right eyelid. The inevitable signal that he was distraught.

'Tommy, you and I can handle this. We'll do just fine on our own. I can still write. It'll just have to be under a pseudonym.' He searched Tommy's face. This was the kind of upheaval the doctors had cautioned against. But Tommy was in school – he had a new security.

Tommy would be all right.

Chapter Fifty-five

Elisabeth tried to comfort Paul in his anxiety about Tommy's mental state.

'He'll be all right. He has *you*. He knows you'll always be there for him.'

Even with Doris in Reno – a divorce imminent – she understood that their own plans must wait. Paul was terrified that Tommy would regress. He watched to make sure Tommy stayed on his medication. He talked about his work, to show Tommy that life was going on without Doris.

'We don't have to hide anymore from your girls,' Paul reminded. 'I'm practically a free man.'

'I want you to get to know them. Come to dinner Friday. They'll all be here. Bring Tommy.'

Paul hesitated. 'I don't think Tommy is ready for more changes in his life. Let's give him a little breathing space.' He managed a tender smile. 'But I'll be there.'

Elisabeth pointedly asked the others to arrive on Friday evening at fifteen minutes earlier than she'd suggested to Paul. The apartment radiated a convivial atmosphere as Amy and Kevin and Katie and Howie arrived almost simultaneously. Ronnie trailed in moments later. Only Hallie knew that Paul, too, was coming for dinner.

Striving to appear casual, Elisabeth mentioned that a long-time friend who was back in New York was coming for dinner.

'He's had several plays on Broadway and has written screenplays – though he prefers the theater.' She was conscious of five pairs of eyes focused on her with avid interest. It was the first time she had ever invited a man unknown to them to dinner. 'His name is Paul Coleman.'

'He did that terrific series of articles on the Spanish Civil War,' Katie pounced. 'Where did you meet him, Mom?'

'Oh, long ago. He was a director then, at a time when I was in New York and acting in those "quickies" for the nickelodeons. Later we ran into each other in Hollywood.'

She'd answered their barrage of questions by the time the doorbell rang again. 'I'll get it.'

Right away she knew they all liked Paul. He was warm, unassuming, interested in what they each had to say. He and Katie launched into colorful reminiscences about the Spanish Civil War. It was an instant bond between them. With Kevin he talked about his teaching experiences in Geneva.

All at once a fresh anxiety leaped into Elisabeth's mind. If this craziness about the HUAC kept escalating, Katie, too, could be in trouble. Katie and Howie plotted to team up as correspondents once the book was finished. If Katie's small bit on behalf of the Loyalists ever came out – or her relationship with Morty – she, too, would find radio and television closed to her. Just this last week she'd learned – belatedly, it appeared – that both NBC and CBS, as well as some individual radio stations, dropped 'left-leaning' correspondents because of pressure from sponsors.

Then Hallie was summoning them all to the table. Elisabeth intercepted a bright-eyed exchange between Katie and Howie because it was obvious that Hallie knew Paul. Why was she being self-conscious? She wanted her family to know Paul. That was why he was here tonight. And they liked him, she told herself with relief.

Paul waited for an elevator in the lobby of his apartment house with a sense of wellbeing. Though Beth's daughters and granddaughter – and the husbands – didn't know about him, he felt he knew the three women. He'd heard so much about them at those intervals when he and Beth were in the same locale. He remembered seeing Amy – probably no more than ten or twelve – at some Hollywood charity affair.

An elevator came to a purring stop at his floor. A couple emerged. He strolled inside. Tommy would probably be home by now. He worked Friday evenings and Saturdays at the bookstore. At their door he heard the radio blaring out a jukebox favorite. He frowned, reached for his key. Why was Tommy playing the radio loud?

He entered the foyer and stopped dead. The disorder in the living room sent warning signals across his brain. Pillows were tossed on the floor, the coffee table upended, two lamps smashed on the rug. Had there been an intruder? But instinct told him otherwise.

'Tommy?' Warily at first, then louder. 'Tommy!'

He saw Tommy crouched on the floor in his bedroom. Mumbling to himself. Hallucinating. Unaware of his father's presence. What he had been fearful of happening had occurred. While anguish spiraled in him, Paul searched in his wallet for the card of the psychiatrist in New York he was to call if Tommy should suffer a relapse. Despite the hour – because this was an emergency – he reached for the phone.

Elisabeth insisted that Paul come to dinner most evenings. She knew he was distraught about Tommy's relapse. He spent long hours each day at the typewriter, trying to clear his mind enough to allow him to work. Bill Madison had lined up two radio assignments for him at, as he'd warned, shockingly low fees.

'I wrote Doris that Tommy's back in hospital. She said if he wished to talk to her, she'd be willing. She also complained that she wasn't receiving alimony payments.'

'She doesn't need alimony payments!' Elisabeth's eyes glistened with rage. 'She admitted she had a hefty inheritance.'

'My ex-wife never has enough money,' Paul said bitterly.

'She should contribute to Tommy's hospital care.' Her voice softened. She knew Paul was unnerved by the weekly bills presented by the fancy sanitarium where Tommy was being treated. 'But let me help, Paul. I've done well these past few years –'

'Beth, I can't do that.'

'I've been doing a lot of thinking these past weeks. About us – about me. I can set the business up so that it requires much less of my time. I've always been so slow to delegate responsibility, but that's all wrong.' She was talking with compulsive haste now. It was time that she and Paul had a life. 'Your divorce is final next week. I want us to be married. I –'

'Beth, you know how much I want that. But I can't drag you down with my troubles.'

'We'll work together to bring Tommy out of this,' she said passionately. 'And to hell with those creeps who're afraid to present your play. We'll do it ourselves. Not on Broadway, but at some theater down in the Village. And if you still want me, I'll play Katarina. And direct,' she added. 'I know I can do that.' She was breathless, waiting for Paul to emerge from his aura of disbelief.

'This is fantasy land,' he warned. But she saw excitement taking root in him.

'We can make it real!'

'Tommy's so upset in his lucid periods. He's terrified of being transferred to a state institution. He feels Dr Weinstein can really help him.'

'He'll remain there until he can come home again. To us. Let him know that.'

'Beth, you'd be wonderful as Katarina.' He reached for her hand. 'I wrote that part for you. And yes, I'm sure you can direct. But you know it's a huge gamble.'

'It's our gamble. Nobody can tell us what to do. And the cost of doing a play downtown is minuscule compared to Broadway. Paul, it's a chance for both of us to turn our lives around. We've waited so long. Let's not wait any longer.'

'Have you any idea how much I love you? My "woman for all seasons",' he said tenderly.

'Have you any idea how much I love you?' The huge void in her life was about to evaporate. 'If there was champagne in this house, I'd pop a cork right now.'

'Beth, you said Hallie went out to the movies with a friend. When do you suppose she'll be home?'

'Not for a long time.' Her smile was dazzling. 'After the movie they'll go to Tip Toe Inn for hot chocolate.'

'Then there's time for us?'

'Oh yes. I guarantee that.' But she left the sofa to go into the foyer to drop the chain into place.

'Did I ever tell you that you're a very sexy lady?'

'At my age?' she chided.

'Beth, you'll be sexy at seventy-five.'

Elisabeth awoke in the morning with the knowledge that much work lay ahead. She'd call a staff meeting, schedule promotions. Her life would no longer revolve around the office. She lay in bed for an additional few moments. It wouldn't come as an entire surprise to the girls to hear that she and Paul would be married.

She frowned at the intrusion of the doorbell, glanced at the clock. It was just seconds past eight.

'I'm comin', I'm comin',' Hallie called as she charged to the door.

Moments later Hallie walked into her bedroom with a box from a florist shop.

'Somebody's feelin' real romantic.' She grinned, waiting while Elisabeth opened the box, gazed in pleasure at the red roses that lay there.

'Oh, they're lovely.'

'It's Valentine's day.' Hallie flashed an impish smile.

'Right, Hallie.' Their eyes met in silent conversation. 'Put them in water, please. It's been for ever since anybody sent me flowers.' Except business people buttering her up.

A few blocks uptown Ronnie, too, had an unexpected caller at her apartment door just as she was preparing to leave for the magazine office.

'Who is it?'

'Cablegram, miss.' A cheery voice, no doubt hoping for a huge tip.

Who was sending her a cable? But even before she ripped open the envelope she knew the sender was Erich Waters. Each week since her return from Germany she'd received a letter, presumably to report on the follow-up of their mission. It had been a tight call, but the yacht crew had found a strip of beach unpatrolled by the Royal Navy or Royal soldiers. 'Everybody waded to shore in safety,' Erich had written. He had more photographs if she wished to do a follow-up story. She realized this offer was an effort not to lose touch with her.

With a surge of excitement she read the cable:

HAPPY VALENTINE'S DAY STOP BRITISH GOVERN-MENT TODAY REFERRED PALESTINE PROBLEM TO UNITED NATIONS STOP BIG STORY STOP TAKE NEXT FLIGHT TO TEL AVIV STOP CABLE TRAVEL SCHEDULE STOP WILL MEET.'

The signature: 'Erich Waters.'

Ronnie rushed to the office, pausing en route to pick up a copy of the morning's *Times*. It was true! The British government had

491

turned the matter over to the United Nations. Oh yes, Erich was right. This would be a terrific story.

'What makes you think this is such an urgent story?' her editor stalled, yet she saw a glint in his eyes that said he was interested. 'The old boy won't OK another big expense account.'

'The whole world will be watching.' Ronnie struggled to conceal her impatience. 'Every news magazine in the country will send correspondents there.' She hesitated. 'I'll pay for my own passage . . .'

She left the office in triumph. How soon could she leave? Her passport was in order. Check with the airlines about passage. And call Mom and tell her that she'd be leaving at any moment if a flight was scheduled.

'I'm sorry, Ronnie,' the secretary in her mother's office said. 'Amy's out in the field. There's no way to reach her until the end of the day.'

Ronnie tried to reach Kevin.

'He's between classes. We'll leave a message that you called.'

Call Grandma. She dialed the private line. Moments later Elisabeth's voice came to her.

'Grandma, you'll have to tell Mom for me if I don't get through to her before my flight leaves.' Ronnie strived to sound matter of fact. 'I'm going to Tel Aviv on a story. I just heard – the British turned over the Palestine question to the United Nations.'

'I'm not surprised.' She heard relief in her grandmother's voice. 'Even Churchill advised it six months ago. I suppose they got tired of supporting 100,000 soldiers there. But what do you mean, you're leaving for Tel Aviv?'

On the long flight – with changes of planes that kept her anxious about arriving on schedule – Ronnie told herself she was racing to Tel Aviv for a story. Erich Waters was a great contact. With his gift for photography they made a terrific team. But she remembered those electric moments when something more potent in their relationship had shone through. It wasn't just the drama of the situation, there was something else. How could she feel this way about a man she'd known such a short while?

She breathed a deep sigh of relief when her connecting flight at last set down at the Tel Aviv airport. Almost immediately she spied Erich waiting for her just beyond Customs.

'I like a woman who knows how to respond to a crisis.' He reached for her portable typewriter, hesitated, leaned forward to kiss her lightly on the cheek. A brotherly kiss, she mocked herself while her heart began to pound. 'I've got a mess of negatives hanging in my darkroom already.'

'Tell me what the response has been here,' she prompted while he guided her through the crowds to the outside.

'For Jews this offers great hope – and great fear. Most feel that the United Nations will be sympathetic. And if they are,' Erich's face tightened, 'then we can expect all kinds of terrorism from the Arabs. A delegation of Arabs met with Bevin in London. They warned they'd accept no form of partition or any immigration.'

'If the United Nations agrees to a Jewish state, then there'll be war?'

'You can count on that.' Erich was grim.

'I don't want to think about it.' Ronnie shivered. A small Jewish state against a hostile Middle East?

'We don't have to bother with a bus,' he explained when they walked outdoors. 'I've borrowed a heap from a friend who's away from town for the usual reason.' Shepherding illegal immigrants from the horrific DP camps into Palestine, she interpreted. 'I'll drive us home.' He chuckled at the wariness she exuded now. 'My friend is allowing you the use of his flat. It's on the floor above mine. It'll be convenient for both of us.'

She hadn't expected the beauty of Tel Aviv. 'Everything's so white. So modern!' They drove on wide tree-lined avenues flanked by super-modern apartment houses in a quietness she found surprising.

'It's siesta time.' He read her thoughts. 'Later this area will be crawling with activity.'

The house where Erich lived was less impressive than those they'd passed on the boulevards. Erich filled her in on the photographs he'd taken thus far as they made their way into the building, climbed the stairs to his friend's fourth-floor flat where she was to stay.

'You're probably starving.' He grinned compassionately. 'Unpack your gear later. Come down to my flat, and I'll feed you my special brand of falafel in a pitta, and hummus on crackers. My friend Len – this is his flat – complains about my coffee. But that's because he likes only espresso.'

'I'm starving,' she admitted. 'I'll love your coffee.'

Erich's flat, a replica of Len's, was in total disarray. His closet-sized bedroom had become a darkroom. He slept on a cot in the tiny living room, where makeshift bookcases held the books he'd collected in his years in Switzerland. Camera equipment lay scattered about on tables.

'Look at these pictures.' He showed her to a threadbare club chair, dumped a pile of just developed pictures into her lap. 'While we eat, I'll give you a breakdown on them.'

Ronnie studied each photograph with care. In her mind – without having seen much of Tel Aviv in this critical period – she was already framing words to tell her story. In the Pullman-style kitchen Erich hummed as he went about preparing their meal.

'Are these more photos?' Ronnie gazed curiously at a thick scrap-book that lay on a shelf. She was sure that someone other than Erich had been so solicitous as to provide a black velvet jacket for it that showed signs of age.

Erich stood still, silent at the folded-out doors of the kitchenette.

'That's the family jewel,' he said after a moment. 'It made its way from one branch of the family to the other. I'm the only one left now except for a distant cousin somewhere. My father managed to have it brought to me in Zurich by a book salesman calling on the university library, just before I lost contact with my parents.' His eyes reflected his pain. 'By then the others were all gone. They dis-appeared off the face of the earth. To the camps, I realized later. There's this scrapbook and a box of letters. My father could be very sentimental. He thought that one day some publisher might make a book of the photos and letters.'

'May I look at the scrapbook?' Ronnie asked, and was instantly sorry. 'But maybe that would be an intrusion –'

'No.' His eyes probed hers.

She shouldn't have come down here, she thought, shaken by the message she read there. A message that echoed her own feelings.

'Here . . .' He reached for the scrapbook, brought it to her. 'It goes back to the turn of the century and comes up to World War I.' He sighed. 'I don't know why the hell I keep carrying it around with me. I guess it's my last real touch with my father and mother.'

Ronnie opened the scrapbook, stared at the first page of photo-graphs. All at once she was ice cold. The photos of a girl – probably younger than she – were strangely familiar. They could have been

494

photos of *her*. She leaned forward to read the tiny scrawl beneath the first: 'Elisabeth, in Melbourne.'

Her eyes moved over other photos on the first page in dizzying disbelief. 'Amy, at six months.' 'Amy at one year, with Elisabeth.'

'Erich, these photographs . . .' Her voice sounded harsh to her own ears. Could this be just a coincidence? 'Who are they? What are their names?'

'I'm not sure.' He paused, startled by her air of shock. 'My mother was a Kahn before she married.'

Ronnie heard her grandmother's voice, just before she went to Berlin: 'Tell them you're Rae Kahn's great-great-granddaughter.'

'My name was originally Wassermann – my father arranged for it to be changed legally in Zurich. He wanted it Anglicized. I think he believed there was a branch of the family somewhere in the United States. It was a story handed down through the years among the cousins.' He was perplexed by her reaction. 'There were a lot of cousins.'

'The letters,' Ronnie said urgently. 'May I see the letters?'

'They're here.' He reached for a silver casket engraved with a pastoral scene. He waited, puzzled.

Before she opened the box, Ronnie was sure that she would see her grandmother's familiar scrawl. She lifted the lid, gazed with a sense of awe at the writing.

'Ronnie, what is it?'

'These photos, the letters. My grandmother was thrown out of the family by her father back in 1902 when she married my grandfather. She never saw any of them again – not her parents, her grandmother, nor her two brothers. She remembered visiting cousins in Berlin, but was never able to track them down. When she was in London after the First World War, she had ads run in Berlin newspapers, but nobody replied. These are the letters she wrote to her grandmother, whom she adored: Rae Kahn. There was never a response, but she's always clung to the hope that her grandmother received those letters, the photographs of herself and of my mother and my aunt . . .'

'This means we're related?' Erich seemed stunned.

'Distant cousins,' Ronnie pinpointed. 'Erich, it would be the most wonderful gift in the world to my grandmother to know that *her* grandmother received and cherished these letters and photographs.

495

Would you –' She stopped short, startled by a sharp knock at the door.

With a sudden wariness Erich crossed to respond. 'Who is it?

'Len. Open up!'

Erich pulled the door wide. Len charged into the room, slammed the door shut behind him.

'Erich, you have to get out of Palestine! We've received secret information. In the morning you're to be arrested by the British. And you can't use my car, they'll recognize it, hold you on some pretext until the papers come through in the morning.' With only a fleeting glance at Ronnie, he continued, 'I'll be back in an hour to drive you to Haifa.' A momentary grin lighted his face. 'In a British lorry.'

Ronnie turned to Erich. 'I'll go with you. If anybody questions us, we're an American foreign correspondent and her photographer.'

'Ronnie, no –'

'Yes!' Len pounced. 'That'll give you a fighting chance if anybody's suspicious.'

'Be here in half an hour,' Erich urged. 'I can pack in ten minutes.'

Chapter Fifty-six

Her eyes mirroring alarm, Amy clutched at the cup of tea that Hallie had just placed in her hands.

'I'm so worried, Mom. I called the magazine to find out where Ronnie would be staying. They told me they didn't know. She'd left in such a rush there was no time to make reservations. She's off somewhere in Palestine, but we don't know where.'

'Amy, she's all right.' She must show confidence, Elisabeth ordered herself. 'Ronnie's got her feet on the ground.'

'Mom, she's so impulsive –'

'This is a bad time in Palestine,' Kevin conceded, 'but Ronnie has friends there. That photographer she talked about. She said Palestine's his port of operations.'

'It's so awful not to be able to contact her if we want to.' Amy gazed from her mother to Kevin. 'Should we try to have the State Department track her down?'

'No, Amy. She's over there to do a story. We mustn't interfere. This is a crucial time for Jews in Palestine.' There were 700,000 Jews – against the whole Arab world. 'And she's only been there for hours. It's a very long flight, with several connections to be made. We'll hear from her,' Elisabeth said with conviction. 'Give her time.'

In less than half an hour Len was back at Erich's flat. Erich and Ronnie had eaten, not knowing when they'd eat again. They'd brought down Ronnie's luggage. Erich had tossed two changes of clothes and his stash of photos of Tel Aviv at the time of the British proclamation into a duffel bag.

'The lorry's at the back of the building. Let's go out that way.' Len looked about the room. 'This is all you're taking?'

'We need to travel light.' Erich had a pair of cameras hanging about his neck, his duffel bag. Ronnie had her valise plus typewriter.

'The scrapbook and the letters, Erich.' Even at this crucial moment Ronnie knew that Grandma's treasures must not be left behind. 'Take them with us.'

'Yeah.' Erich brought them down from their resting place, opened up his duffel bag, shoved the scrapbook and the casket inside.

'All right,' Len ordered. 'Let's get this show on the road. Oh –' He stopped short, reached into a pocket of his jacket. 'You'll need cash –' He handed over a roll of bills. 'Erich, you've done your share in this bloody fight. Don't come back until it's safe.' When the United Nations had designated part of Palestine as a homeland for the Jews.

Ronnie and Erich settled themselves within the protective covering of the lorry. Len – now in British uniform – took his place behind the wheel. They knew that despite the British resolution the streets would still be patrolled by British soldiers. Len plotted a route that would have fewer patrols than on the main road between Tel Aviv and Haifa, though the journey would be longer than normal.

'Erich, don't go back to Berlin,' Ronnie pressed as the lorry moved through the night. 'Come to New York with me. You have a valid passport?' she asked in sudden alarm.

'A Swiss passport.'

'You're a good photographer – you'll find work in New York. I don't know what the rules are for you to remain permanently, but I'm sure my grandmother would sponsor you if that's the route.'

An unanticipated glint of laughter lit his eyes. 'I could stay if I marry an American citizen . . .'

'Don't push it,' she flipped. For a moment her heart sang. But they were cousins. 'We'll work something out.' He mustn't go back. To the Arabs as well as the British, he was a wanted man.

The trip to Haifa was uneventful. Len sat whistling at the wheel as they were stopped at one point by British soldiers. Then he was waved on. No problems, Ronnie thought with relief. They were on their way home.

Elisabeth hurried into the apartment, grateful for the cozy warmth on this biting cold late afternoon.

'The office called,' Hallie reported, ambling into the living room. 'I said you'd get back to them as soon as you came in.'

'I should have called from outside.' She felt a fleeting touch of guilt. No. They ought to be able to handle whatever came up without her. She picked up the phone, settled into a chair.

'I'll bring you coffee. But nothing else,' Hallie warned. 'I don't want you spoilin' your appetite. I got one of my drunken pot roasts on the stove.' Meaning, one of her gourmet roasts with burgundy.

As Elisabeth expected, the office questions were ones they could handle on their own. The staff just lacked confidence because she'd always been available.

While she was sipping her coffee the phone rang again. It was Amy.

'Mom, I'm so *relieved*. I just got in from work. There's a cable from Ronnie – from Athens.' A question in her voice.

'What's she doing in Greece?' Cyprus she could understand – that's where the British were dumping DPs they caught trying to get into Palestine.

'She's on her way home already. I suppose she changed planes in Athens.' Any hesitated a moment. 'She asked me if you'd be willing to put up a friend for a few days, until he can find a place to live.'

'That young photographer?'

'She didn't say. Probably. Will you go along with that?'

'Of course, he can stay here, with all the empty bedrooms I have!' Thank God, Ronnie wasn't remaining over there. Nobody knew what would happen in Palestine with the British walking out.

'Oh, she said to tell you she had a grand surprise for you.'

'I know,' Elisabeth chuckled. 'She wanted to be sure I'll take in her friend.'

They spoke a few moments longer, then Kevin arrived home.

'Mom, I'll talk to you later. I want to tell Kevin about the cable.'

Paul appeared for dinner thirty minutes later. He was in high spirits.

'Did you look at the playhouse?' Elisabeth asked, hanging away his coat in the foyer closet. 'Do you think the stage is large enough?'

'It's great. I was impressed.'

'Then I'll call in the morning and tell the owner he has a deal.' Her face was incandescent. She'd walked into the tiny playhouse and felt that, at last, she'd come home.

'Beth, you're sure you want to go through with this?' But she sensed his own excitement. This was what they had both wanted for most of their lives.

499

'How can you ask me that?' She shook her head in mock reproach. 'I can't wait for us to start casting. I can't wait to be in rehearsal. I can't wait to see your play come alive. I feel reborn!'

Over dinner they talked about Tommy's progress.

'I think just knowing that he can stay here until he feels he's ready to leave is speeding his recovery,' Paul said. 'The doctors are very pleased.'

'I expect I'll be having a houseguest for at least a week.' She told him about Ronnie's cable. 'But that doesn't mean Hallie and I won't be expecting you for dinner every night.' She squinted reflectively. 'I wonder what Ronnie meant – she says she has a grand surprise for me. Paul, you don't suppose she's married this photographer? They barely know each other!'

'Beth, I fell in love with you the first day we met.'

'It took me a few days . . .' Even then she'd known that Paul would be the great love of her life. 'Anyhow, I'll be a nervous wreck until she gets home.'

'Ya'll get to the table,' Hallie sang out. 'My pot roast don't wait for nobody.'

Ronnie and Erich's flight landed at Idlewild shortly past eight p.m. Once they had passed through Customs, Ronnie went to a pay telephone to call her grandmother.

'We're at Idlewild. Please would you call Mom and Katie and ask them to come to the apartment? I want us all to be together tonight. I –'

'Ronnie, it'll be so late by the time you get here.'

'Humor me, Grandma. Tell them to be at the house in about an hour. Oh, I'm taking it for granted you'll put up Erich for three or four days?'

'Darling, yes . . .' She hesitated. 'Paul's here. Is that –'

'No problem,' Ronnie broke in. 'He's almost like family.' She turned from the phone for a moment. 'I've got to run. Erich's got a cab for us.'

'See you soon!'

Elisabeth put down the phone for a moment. What was so important that Amy and Katie must be here, too – and Kevin and Howie? Had she married this photographer in Palestine?

'You look anxious.' Paul was solicitous.

'Why is Ronnie insisting that the whole family be here?' She reached for the phone again. 'I have to call Amy and Katie and tell them to come over.'

'I'll take off,' Paul said when she'd made the two calls.

'No, Ronnie says it's fine for you to be here.' They'd got the message about Paul and her, she thought gratefully. 'Ronnie says you're almost like family.

'I can't wait to make it official.'

'June,' she reminded. 'It's my last chance to be a June bride. I'd better tell Hallie the others are coming over. She won't be happy unless she's got a cake or pie warming in the oven.'

'Better make it two. There'll be nine of us with Hallie.'

She hurried down the hall to Hallie's bedroom. She heard the sound of Hallie's little radio behind the closed door. Hallie never missed listening to *Mr and Mrs North*.

'Hallie,' she called gaily. 'Company's coming.'

Within minutes Hallie was in the kitchen making brownies: 'Ronnie loves brownies.' Tantalizing aromas of fresh coffee began to drift through the apartment. Paul was trying to divert Elisabeth's attention from worrisome conjectures by delving into discussion about their coming production in the small downtown playhouse.

Twenty minutes later Amy and Kevin were in the apartment. Amy wore that soft glow of early pregnancy. Just this morning she had called to say that she was sure now that she was pregnant. 'Mom, it's a small miracle.' It was time to tell Ronnie and the others.

Katie and Howie arrived right after Amy and Kevin.

'What is so important that we had to come rushing over at this hour?' Katie demanded.

'She's bringing that photographer she met in Berlin with her.' Amy's eyes were anxious. 'You know how impulsive Ronnie can be.'

'Maybe she's trying to get him a job on the magazine,' Howie surmised. 'It's expanding like crazy.'

'It's a long way to come for a job,' Kevin said, chuckling.

'I got fresh coffee coming up.' Hallie bustled in from the kitchen. 'But the brownies aren't ready to come out of the oven yet.'

They sat down with cups of fragrant coffee. The conversation was lively, focused on the coming situation in Palestine.

'Even if the United Nations devise a plan to give the Jews their own state, there's going to be a hell of a lot of trouble before it happens.' Howie was somber. 'The Arabs want it all.'

The doorbell rang. Silence fell over the living room – an air of expectancy radiating from everyone. Her face alight, Elisabeth hurried to the foyer, opened the door.

'Grandma, Hallie's baking,' Ronnie effervesced, depositing her valise and typewriter on the foyer floor. 'It better be brownies.' She pulled the young man with her into the foyer. He seemed slightly overwhelmed, Elisabeth thought. He carried a duffel bag and with engaging awkwardness set it down beside Ronnie's valise.

'Everybody, this is Erich Waters.'

Ronnie took him by the hand, drew him into the living room. She introduced each of the others in turn. Elisabeth intercepted the loaded glances she exchanged with Erich. He went back and retrieved the duffel bag.

'Erich and I said we wouldn't just dump this on you all at once,' she began, and Elisabeth tensed. 'But you all know me – I've got no patience.'

Erich was opening the duffel bag. He pulled out a battered carton. Ronnie took it from him.

'I told you Erich grew up in Berlin and went to school in Switzerland. That his family died in the Nazi camps. But his father sent him these before he died. Grandma, they're for you.' She reached into the carton to bring out first a velvet-covered scrapbook, took it to her grandmother.

'I knew Erich's father?' Bewildered, Elisabeth took the scrapbook in her hands.

'We don't know,' Ronnie said. 'You may have met long ago when you visited the "German cousins" in Berlin. You said there were many cousins . . .'

Elisabeth lowered her eyes to this gift Ronnie had brought her from Palestine. Her mouth felt suddenly dry, her throat tight. This was just a scrapbook. Why did she feel so strange? Her mind darted back through the years to that last summer in Berlin. As though it were yesterday she visualized the cluster of cousins gathered about the old piano in the Victorian living room.

'Grandma, open it,' Ronnie urged.

Elisabeth managed a shaky smile. 'Yes . . .'

The others seemed to sense that this was a momentous occasion.

Slowly she lifted the black velvet cover that showed signs of the passage of many years. Her eyes focused on the array of photographs pasted across the page. Her heart began to pound. Amy as a baby. Amy and herself. A photograph of David holding Amy in his arms. *The ones she'd sent Grandma.*

Her face luminous, she turned the pages. Grandma saved all the photographs she had sent through the years. Grandma had cherished them.

'There's more.' Ronnie took a silver casket from the carton, held it out to her grandmother. She turned apologetically to Erich. 'I couldn't wait.'

Elisabeth closed the scrapbook. Dizzy at the miracle that was happening, she took the silver casket, lifted the lid. *Her letters. Grandma had saved all her letters.*

'They were passed down among the cousins,' Erich explained, 'the American branch of the family.' His voice was husky. 'I'm all that remains of the German cousins – but the American cousin has kept the family very much alive.'

'I knew always – even though she didn't dare write because that would have been in defiance of my father's wishes – that Grandma loved me.' Tears blurred Elisabeth's vision. 'Mama loved Papa, but she loved me, too. Why else would she have preserved the only contact she could ever have with me?'

'You were a legend in the family,' Erich told her. 'I grew up hearing about the cousin who'd been an actress in Melbourne, had appeared in American movies.'

'That was a long time ago.' But right now it seemed like yesterday.

'I'm proud to be part of the family.' Yet Elisabeth saw pain in his eyes as they turned to rest on Ronnie.

She pondered a moment. Was she mistaking what she felt between Ronnie and Erich? 'A distant part of the family – but very welcomed. I'd say fifth or sixth cousins when it comes down to your generation and Ronnie's.' She paused. 'Did you know that Eleanor and Franklin Roosevelt were fifth cousins?'

She saw the spontaneous joy shared between Ronnie and Erich. Did the others understand, as she and Ronnie and Erich understood? It was all right for fifth cousins to be in love. To marry. As Eleanor and Franklin Roosevelt had done.

Now her eyes sought Paul's. Perhaps he – more than anybody else

– realized what these gifts from Palestine meant to her. She felt a wonderful release. Her father believed she had disgraced the family. Grandma and Mama had not shared that belief.

One of Grandma's favorite quotations tickertaped across her mind: 'When times are bad, you dig inside for the strength to see them through. Tell yourself, "Tomorrow will be better."'

Tomorrow was here – and it was wonderful.